An Introduction to Language

Sixth Edition

Victoria Fromkin
University of California, Los Angeles

Robert Rodman
North Carolina State University, Raleigh

Harcourt Brace College Publishers

Fort Worth Philadelphia San Diego New York Orlando Austin San Antonio
Toronto Montreal London Sydney Tokyo

Publisher:	Christopher P. Klein
Executive Editor:	Michael Rosenberg
Product Manager:	Ilse Wolfe West
Developmental Editor:	Tia Black
Project Editor:	Matt Ball
Art Director:	David Day
Production Manager:	Melinda Esco and Linda McMillan

Cover Image: "Conversation Piece," bronze sculpture by Hanna Damasio

ISBN: 0-03-018682-X
Library of Congress Catalog Card Number: 97-72207

Address for orders:
Harcourt Brace College Publishers
6277 Sea Harbor Drive
Orlando, FL 32887-6777
1-800-782-4479

Address for editorial correspondence:
Harcourt Brace College Publishers
301 Commerce Street, Suite 3700
Fort Worth, TX 76102

Web site address:
http://www.hbcollege.com

Printed in the United States of America

0 1 2 3 4 5 6 039 9 8 7

To Disa and Zachary
and
To the memory of Shelby

About the Authors

Victoria Fromkin received her bachelor's degree from the University of California, Berkeley, in economics in 1944 and her M.A. and Ph.D. in Linguistics at the University of California, Los Angeles (UCLA) in 1963 and 1965, respectively. She has been a member of the faculty of the UCLA Department of Linguistics since 1966, and served as its Chair from 1972 to 1976. From 1979 to 1989 she served as the UCLA Graduate Dean and Vice Chancellor of Graduate Programs. She has been a visiting professor at the University of Stockholm, Cambridge, and Oxford. Dr. Fromkin served as president of the Linguistic Society of America in 1985, president of the Association of Graduate Schools in 1988, and Chair of the Board of Governors of the Academy of Aphasia. She received the UCLA Distinguished Teaching Award and the Professional Achievement Award, and serves as the U.S. Delegate and a member of the Executive Committee of the International Permanent Committee of Linguists (CIPL). She is an elected Fellow of the American Academy of Arts and Sciences, the American Association for the Advancement of Science, the New York Academy of Science, the American Psychological Society, and the Acoustical Society of America and in 1996 was elected to membership in the National Academy of Sciences. She has published over one hundred books, monographs, and papers on topics concerned with phonetics, phonology, tone languages, African languages, speech errors, processing models, aphasia, and the brain/mind/language interface, all research areas in which she has worked.

Robert Rodman received his bachelor's degree from UCLA in mathematics in 1961, a Masters degree in mathematics in 1965, a Masters degree in linguistics in 1971, and his Ph.D. in linguistics in 1973. He has been on the faculties of the University of California at Santa Cruz, the University of North Carolina at Chapel Hill, Kyoto Industrial College, and North Carolina State University, where he is currently an Associate Professor of Computer Science and Industrial Engineering. Dr. Rodman has published papers in the areas of linguistics, computer science, and industrial engineering. His current areas of interest are in computer speech processing, and in particular in 'lip synching'—animating a face to speech; 'voice recognition'—computer identification of persons by voice alone; and in computer-telephone interfaces. Dr. Rodman resides in Raleigh, North Carolina, with his wife, Helen, and their two dogs.

Preface

An Introduction to Language has been highly successful at introducing linguistics, the study of human language, both to linguistics majors and majors in diverse fields. This is a book students enjoy and understand and a book professors find effective and thorough.

As a discipline, linguistics continues to make important contributions not only to the field of education but also to other fields including sociology, psychology, law, medicine, technology, and communication. For this reason, *An Introduction to Language,* sixth edition, includes new material that will strengthen its appeal to a wider audience. Material has been added to the sixth edition that reflects new developments in linguistics and related fields. Much of this information will enable students to gain insight and understanding about linguistic issues and debates appearing in the national media and will help professors and students stay current with important linguistic research.

New material has been added in many chapters and sections. The second chapter, "The Neurobiology of Language," includes new findings on brain research and the production of language. Highly detailed illustrations of MRI and PET scans of the brain are also included. In addition, this chapter highlights some of the new results and tremendous progress in the study of neurobiology over the last few years.

Chapters 3 through 7, in Part Two, "Grammatical Aspects of Language," have been substantially revised. These chapters now have a greater emphasis on linguistic data and less on formalisms used in different theories covered in more advanced courses. Also, important "how-to" sections on morphological and phonological analysis have been added. These sections will help students work the more difficult problems and exercises in these chapters.

Part Three, "The Psychology of Language," reflects the rapid changes that have occurred in our understanding of the psychological basis of language. Chapter 8 covers language acquisition of spoken and sign language by hearing and deaf infants, respectively. A separate section traces the entire sixty-year history of attempts to teach human language to primates. Many of the exaggerated claims on this topic are placed in scientific perspective.

Chapter 9 includes new results on psycholinguistic studies of language processing. Chapter 10, in Part 4, "Language in Society," includes new material on language variation and the study of ethnic minority and social dialects. Attitudes toward language and how they reflect the views and mores of society are included in an expanded section of this chapter. The scientific basis for discussing such topics as Ebonics, African-American dialects of English, is established. Another section on language and sexism reflects a growing concern with this topic.

Chapter 11 on language change includes new examples that apply the comparative method. The sixth edition also takes a new distributed approach to sign languages more in line with the fact that sign languages are now accepted as fully bona fide human languages. Thus, instead of presenting sign language as an isolated section, sign language is discussed in each of the sections dealing with the grammatical aspects of language.

A revised glossary of technical terms can be found in the appendix. The glossary has been expanded and improved.

The order of presentation of Chapters 3–7 is somewhat nontraditional, as it was in previous editions. Our combined experience of fifty years of teaching supported by recommendations of colleagues throughout the world have convinced us that it is easier for the novice to approach the structural aspects of language by first looking at morphology, syntax, and semantics, and then proceeding to phonetics and phonology, which many students find daunting. The book is structured so that individual instructors can present material in the traditional order of phonetics, phonology, morphology, syntax, and semantics (Chapters 6, 7, 3, 4, 5), if they wish.

As in previous editions, the primary concern has been with basic ideas rather than detailed expositions. This book assumes no previous knowledge on the part of the reader. A list of references at the end of each chapter is included to accommodate any reader who wishes to pursue the subject in more depth. Each chapter concludes with a summary and exercises to enhance the student's interest in and comprehension of the textual material.

We are deeply grateful to the individuals too numerous to mention who have sent us suggestions, corrections, criticisms, cartoons, language data, and exercises, all of which we have tried to incorporate in this new edition. We owe special thanks to Jon Hareide Aarbakke, Susan Ballance, Paul Baltes, Merry Bullock, Lyle Campbell, Richard S. Cervin, Don Churma, Billy Clark, Charles J. Coker, Roy Dace, J. Day, David Deterding, Anthony Diller, Gregoire Dunant, M. Therese Gallegos, Mary Ghaleb, Lila R. Gleitman, Mark Hansell, Nina Hyams, Olaf Jäkel, Yan Jiang, Irina Kalika, Rachel Lagunoff, Yonata Levy, Monica Macaulay, Peggy MacEachern, Marcyliena Morgan, Pamela Munro, JaeHo Myung, Jihwan Myeong, Almerinda Ojeda, Gunter Radden, Willem J. de Reuse, Otto Santa Ana, Dawn L. Sievers, Gabriella Solomon, B. Stefanow, Ean Taylor, Larry Trask, Rudolf Weiss, John C. White, Howard Williams, and Mary Wu. Many of these individuals responded to specific queries sent by electronic mail through the Linguistic List network, and we thank the network editors Anthony Aristar and Helen Dry. We are especially grateful to Drs. Antonio and Hanna Damasio of the University of Iowa Medical School for information on their brain studies and the MRI and PET illustrations, and to Hanna Damasio for the photographs of her sculpture "Conversation Piece," which appears on the front and back covers and inside the book.

In addition we would like to thank the following reviewers for their helpful recommendations: William Benware, University of California, Davis; Curtiss Bobbitt, University of Great Falls; Robin Brown, University of Minnesota; M. Therese Gallegos, University of Texas, Brownsville; James Ney, Arizona State University; Kenneth Miner, University of Kansas; Mehmet Yavas, Florida Intenational University; and Valdis Zeps, University of Wisconsin.

We also want to thank the editorial and production team at Harcourt Brace: Tia Black, developmental editor; and particularly Matt Ball, project editor, for all his help in producing this sixth edition; Melinda Esco and Linda McMillan, production managers; David Day, designer; and Shirley Webster, permissions editor. We are particularly grateful to our acquisitions editor, Michael Rosenberg, for his insight and continued support.

The responsibility for errors in fact or judgment is, of course, ours alone. We continue to be indebted to the instructors who have used the earlier editions and to their students, without whom there would be no sixth edition.

Vicki Fromkin
Robert Rodman

Contents

Preface ix

Part 1
The Nature of Human Language

Chapter 1
What Is Language?

Linguistic Knowledge 4
 Knowledge of the
  Sound System 4
 Knowledge of Words 5
  Arbitrary Relation of Form
   and Meaning 5
 The Creativity of Linguistic
  Knowledge 9
 Knowledge of Sentences and
  Nonsentences 11
Linguistic Knowledge
 and Performance 12
What Is Grammar? 14
 Descriptive Grammars 14
 Prescriptive Grammars...................15
 Teaching Grammars 17
Language Universals 18
 Sign Language: Evidence for
  Language Universals 20
 American Sign
  Language (ASL) 21
Animal "Languages" 22
 "Talking" Parrots 23
 The Birds and the Bees 24
What We Know about Language 26
Summary 27
 References for Further Reading 28
Exercises 29

Chapter 2
Brain and Language

The Human Brain 34
 The Modularity of the Brain 35
  Evidence from Childhood
   Brain Lesions..........................38
  Split Brains 40
  More Experimental Evidence 42
 More Evidence for Modularity........43
  Aphasia 44
  Distinct Categories of
   Conceptual Knowledge 48
The Autonomy of Language 49
 Asymmetry of Abilities...................49
  Laura 49
  Christopher...............................50
 Genetic Evidence for
  Language Autonomy.................51
The Evolution of Language 51
 In the Beginning:
  The Origin of Language..............51
  God's Gift to Mankind?.............53
  The First Language 53
  Human Invention or the
   Cries of Nature? 54
 The Development of Language
  in the Species..........................55
Summary 56
 References for Further Reading 58
Exercises 58

Part 2
Grammatical Aspects of Language

Chapter 3
Morphology:
The Words of Language

Dictionaries	65
Classes of Words	67
Lexical Content Words	67
Function Words.............................	67
Morphemes: The Minimal Units	
of Meaning	68
Bound and Free Morphemes..........	70
Prefixes and Suffixes	71
Infixes	72
Circumfixes	73
Huckles and Ceives	73
Rules of Word Formation	75
Lexical Gaps	76
Derivational Morphology...............	76
"Pullet Surprises".........................	80
Sign Language Morphology	81
Word Coinage	82
Compounds	83
Meaning of Compounds	85
Universality of Compounding	86
Acronyms	86
Back-Formations	87
Abbreviations	88
Words from Names	88
Blends..	89
Grammatical Morphemes	89
Inflectional Morphemes	90
Exceptions and Suppletions	92
Morphology and Syntax	93
Morphological Analysis:	
Identifying Morphemes	95
Summary	96
References for Further Reading......	98
Exercises	98

Chapter 4
Syntax:
The Sentence Patterns
of Language

Grammatical or Ungrammatical?	106
What Grammaticality	
Is Based On.............................	107
What Grammaticality	
Is Not Based On	108
What Else Do You Know	
about Syntax?	109
Sentence Structure	111
Syntactic Categories	112
Phrase Structure Trees.................	114
More Phrase Structure Trees	116
The Infinitude of Language	118
Phrase Structure Rules	120
Growing Trees: The	
Relationship between	
Phrase Structure Rules and	
Phrase Structure Trees	122
Trees That Won't Grow	126
Rules in Other Languages	128
More Phrase Structure Rules	129
The Lexicon	133
Subcategorization.......................	134
More Lexical Differences	135
Sentence Relatedness	136
Transformational Rules.................	137
Long-Distance Relationships	143
"Wh-" Sentences..........................	144
More about Sentence Structure	145
Sign Language Syntax	147
Summary	148
References for	
Further Reading	148
Exercises	149

Chapter 5
The Meanings of Language

Lexical Semantics (Word Meanings)   **158**
Semantic Properties 159
Evidence for Semantic
Properties..........................160
Semantic Properties
and the Lexicon 161
More Semantic Relationships ..162
-nyms...................................162
Homonyms and Polysemy 163
Synonyms 165
Antonyms 166
Formation of Antonyms 167
Hyponyms...............................168
Metonyms 168
Retronyms...............................168
Proper Names 168
Phrase and Sentence Meaning   **171**
Phrasal Meaning 172
Noun-Centered Meaning 172
Sense and Reference 174
Verb-Centered Meaning 175
Thematic Roles 175
Thematic Roles in Other
Languages 177
The Theta-Criterion 178
Sentential Meaning 178
The "Truth" of Sentences 178
Paraphrase 179
Entailment 180
Contradiction 180
When Semantics and
Syntax Meet 181
Words versus Phrases 181
When Passives Do Not Work 182
Pronouns and
Coreferentiality....................183
When Rules Are Broken   **184**
Anomaly: No Sense and
Nonsense 184
Metaphor 187
Idioms.....................................188

Pragmatics   **190**
Linguistic Context: Discourse........191
Pronouns 191
Anaphora..........................192
Missing Parts 193
The Articles *The* and *A* 194
Situational Context 195
Maxims of Conversation 195
Speech Acts 197
Presuppositions 198
Deixis 199
Summary   **201**
References for Further Reading....203
Exercises   **204**

Chapter 6
Phonetics:
The Sounds of Language

Sound Segments   **213**
Identity of Speech Sounds 215
Spelling and Speech   **216**
The Phonetic Alphabet 218
Articulatory Phonetics   **221**
Airstream Mechanisms.................222
Consonants 223
Places of Articulation 223
Bilabials: [p] [b] [m] 223
Labiodentals: [f] [v] 224
Interdentals: [θ] [ð]...............224
Alveolars:
[t] [d] [n] [s] [z] [l] [r] 224
Palatals: [ʃ]/[š] [ʒ]/[ž] [č] [ǰ] ..224
Velars: [k] [g] [ŋ] 224
Uvulars: [R] [q] [G]................224
Glottal: [ʔ] [h] 224
Manners of Articulation 225
Voiced and
Voiceless Sounds 225
Aspirated and
Unaspirated Sounds....226
Nasal and Oral Sounds 228
Stops: [p] [b] [m] [t] [d]
[n] [k] [g] [ŋ] [č] [ǰ] [ʔ] 229

Fricatives: [s] [z] [f] [v]
[θ] [ð] [š] [ž]...................230
Affricates 231
Liquids: [l] [r] 232
Glides: [j] [w] 232
Phonetic Symbols for American
English Consonants..............233
Vowels 234
Tongue Position 235
Lip Rounding 236
Diphthongs.............................236
Nasalization of Vowels 237
Tense and Lax Vowels 238
Dialect Differences 238
Major Classes.............................239
Noncontinuants and
Continuants 239
Obstruents and Sonorants 239
Consonants and Vowels 239
Labials: [p] [b] [m] [f] [v] 239
Coronals: [d] [t] [n] [s]
[z] [š] [ž] [č] [ǰ]...............239
Anterior 240
Sibilants: [s] [z] [š] [ž] [č] [ǰ] ..240
Syllabic Sounds........................240
Prosodic Suprasegmental
Features 240
Tone and Intonation 240
Diacritics   242
Phonetic Symbols and
Spelling Correspondences   243
Sign-Language Primes   245
Summary   247
References for
Further Reading 248
Exercises   248

Chapter 7
Phonology:
The Sound Patterns
of Language

Phonemes: The Phonological
Units of Language   254
Sounds That Contrast 254
Minimal Pairs...........................255
Free Variation 257
Minimal Pairs in ASL 258
Phonemes, Phones,
and Allophones 259
Complementary Distribution 261
Distinctive Features   262
Feature Values...........................262
Predictability of Redundant
(Nondistinctive) Features 264
Unpredictability of Phonemic
Features 266
More on Redundancies 267
Syllable Structure 269
Sequential Constraints   269
Lexical Gaps 271
Natural Classes   271
Feature Specifications for
American English Consonants
and Vowels.............................273
More on Prosodic Phonology   274
Intonation...............................274
Word Stress.............................276
Sentence and Phrase Stress 278
The Rules of Phonology   279
Assimilation Rules 280
Feature Changing Rules 283
Dissimilation Rules 284
Feature Addition Rules 284
Segment Deletion and
Addition Rules 285
Movement (Metathesis) Rules 287
From One to Many and
from Many to One 288
The Function of
Phonological Rules 291
Slips of the Tongue: Evidence
for Phonological Rules 292
The Pronunciation of Morphemes   293
Morphophonemics 295
More Sequential Constraints........297
Phonological Analysis:
Discovering Phonemes   300
Summary   303
References for
Further Reading 305
Exercises   306

Part 3
The Psychology of Language

Chapter 8
Language Acquisition

Stages in Language Acquisition   **318**
The First Sounds 319
Babbling 320
First Words 321
The Two-Word Stage 324
From Telegraph to Infinity 325
Theories of Child
   Language Acquisition   **328**
Do Children Learn
   by Imitation?............................328
Do Children Learn
   by Reinforcement? 329
Do Children Learn Language
   by Analogy? 330
Children Form Rules and
   Construct a Grammar 331
Errors or Rules? 333
The Acquisition
   of Phonology 333
Acquisition of Morphology 334
The Acquisition of Syntax 336
Learning the Meaning
   of Words..................................337
The Biological Foundations of Language
   Acquisition   **339**
The "Innateness Hypothesis" 339
The "Critical-Age Hypothesis" 342
The Acquisition of Bird Songs ..344
The Acquisition of ASL 345
Learning a Second (or Third or . . .)
   Language   **346**
Theories of Second-Language
   Acquisition 348
Second-Language Teaching
   Methods...................................349
Can Chimps Learn Human Language?   **350**
Gua 351

Viki 351
Washoe...351
Sarah 351
Learning Yerkish 352
Koko..352
Nim Chimpsky 353
Clever Hans............................354
Kanzi 355
Summary   **355**
References for Further Reading....357
Exercises   **358**

Chapter 9
Language Processing:
Humans and Computer

The Human Mind at Work:
   Human Language Processing   **361**
Comprehension 363
The Speech Signal 363
Speech Perception and
   Comprehension 365
Comprehension Models and
   Experimental Studies 367
Lexical Access and Word
   Recognition 367
Syntactic Processing 369
Speech Production 370
Planning Units 370
Lexical Selection......................371
Application and
   Misapplication of Rules........372
Nonlinguistic Influences 373
Silicon at Work: Computer
   Processing of Human Language   **373**
Machine Translation 374
Text Processing 375
Computers That Talk and Listen....376
Talking Machines (Speech
   Synthesis)..............................377

Knowing What to Say 379
Machines for Understanding
    Speech................................381
    Speech Recognition 382
    Speech Understanding........383
    Parsing 383

Semantic Processing........386
Pragmatic Processing 387
Computer Models of Grammars   388
Summary   389
    References for Further Reading....391
Exercises   392

Part 4
Language in Society

Chapter 10
Language in Society

Dialects   399
    Regional Dialects...........................400
    Accents..401
Dialects of English   402
    Phonological Differences..............403
    Lexical Differences 404
    Dialect Atlases...............................404
    Syntactic Differences....................406
The "Standard"   407
    Language Purists 408
    Banned Languages 409
    The Revival of Languages..............411
African American English (AAE)   412
    Phonology of African American
        English 413
    R-Deletion...................................413
    L-Deletion...................................413
    Consonant Cluster
        Simplification 413
    Neutralization of [i] and [ɛ]
        before Nasals 414
    /ɔj/ → /ɔ/ 414
    Loss of Interdental
        Fricatives 414
    Syntactic Differences between
        AAE and SAE 414
    Double Negatives 414

Deletion of the Verb "Be" 415
    Habitual "Be" 415
History of African American
    English 416
Latino (Hispanic) English   417
    Chicano English (ChE) 419
    Phonological Variables
        of ChE...............................419
    Syntactic Variables in ChE 420
Lingua Francas   420
Pidgins and Creoles   421
    Pidgins 422
    Creoles 425
Styles, Slang, and Jargon   425
    Styles 425
    Slang...............................426
    Jargon and Argot 427
Taboo or Not Taboo?   428
    Euphemisms 432
    Racial and National Epithets 433
Language, Sex, and Gender   434
    Marked and Unmarked Forms 435
    The Generic "He" 437
    Language and Gender 438
**Secret Languages and
    Language Games   439**
Summary   440
    References for
        Further Reading 442
Exercises   443

Chapter 11
Language Change:
The Syllables of Time

The Regularity of Sound Change   450
  Sound Correspondences 451
  Ancestral Protolanguages 451
Phonological Change   452
  Phonological Rules 453
  The Great Vowel Shift 454
Morphological Change   456
Syntactic Change   457
Lexical Change   459
  Borrowings 459
  History and
    Borrowed Words 460
  New Words 462
  Loss of Words 462
  Semantic Change 463
    Broadening...........................463
    Narrowing............................463
    Meaning Shifts 463
Reconstructing "Dead" Languages   464
  The Nineteenth-Century
    Comparativists 464
    Cognates 465
  Comparative Reconstruction........467
  Historical Evidence 470
Extinct and Endangered Languages   472
The Genetic Classification
  of Languages   473
  Languages of the World 476
Types of Languages   478

Why Do Languages Change?   480
Summary   482
  References for
    Further Reading 483
Exercises   483

Chapter 12
Writing:
The ABCs of Language

The History of Writing   492
  Pictograms and Ideograms 493
  Cuneiform Writing 495
  The Rebus Principle.....................497
  From Hieroglyphs
    to the Alphabet 498
Modern Writing Systems   499
  Word Writing..............................499
  Syllabic Writing 500
  Consonantal Alphabet
    Writing 502
  Alphabetic Writing 502
Reading, Writing, and Speech   505
  Reading.....................................507
  Spelling.....................................507
  Spelling Pronunciations...............511
Summary   512
  References for
    Further Reading 513
Exercises   513

Glossary   519
Index   541

An Introduction to Language

Sixth Edition

PART 1

The Nature of Human Language

Reflecting on Noam Chomsky's ideas on the innateness of the fundamentals of grammar in the human mind, I saw that any innate features of the language capacity must be a set of biological structures, selected in the course of the evolution of the human brain.

S. E. Luria, *A Slot Machine, A Broken Test Tube, An Autobiography*

The nervous systems of all animals have a number of basic functions in common, most notably the control of movement and the analysis of sensation. What distinguishes the human brain is the variety of more specialized activities it is capable of learning. The preeminent example is language.

Norman Geschwind, 1979

Chapter 1
What Is Language?

When we study human language, we are approaching what some might call the "human essence," the distinctive qualities of mind that are, so far as we know, unique to man.

Noam Chomsky, *Language and Mind*

By permission of Johnny Hart and Creators Syndicate, Inc.

Whatever else people do when they come together—whether they play, fight, make love, or make automobiles—they talk. We live in a world of language. We talk to our friends, our associates, our wives and husbands, our lovers, our teachers, our parents and in-laws. We talk to bus drivers and total strangers. We talk face-to-face and over the telephone, and everyone responds with more talk. Television and radio further swell this torrent of words. Hardly a moment of our waking lives is free from words, and even in our dreams we talk and are talked to. We also talk when there is no one to answer. Some of us talk aloud in our sleep. We talk to our pets and sometimes to ourselves.

The possession of language, perhaps more than any other attribute, distinguishes humans from other animals. To understand our humanity one must understand the nature of language that makes us human. According to the philosophy expressed in the myths and religions of many peoples, it is language that is the source of human life and power. To some people of Africa, a newborn child is a *kuntu*, a "thing," not yet a *muntu*, a "person." Only by the act of learning does the child become a human being. Thus, according to this tradition, we all become "human" because we all know at least one language. But what does it mean to "know" a language?

LINGUISTIC KNOWLEDGE

When you know a language, you can speak and be understood by others who know that language. This means you have the capacity to produce sounds that signify certain meanings and to understand or interpret the sounds produced by others. We are referring to normal-hearing individuals. Deaf persons produce and understand sign languages just as hearing persons produce and understand spoken languages. The languages of the deaf communities throughout the world are, except for their modality of expression, equivalent to spoken languages.

Everyone knows a language. Five-year-old children are almost as proficient at speaking and understanding as are their parents. Yet the ability to carry out the simplest conversation requires profound knowledge that most speakers are unaware of. This is as true of speakers of Japanese as of English, of Armenian as of Navajo. A speaker of English can produce a sentence having two relative clauses without knowing what a relative clause is, like

> My goddaughter who was born in Sweden and who now lives in Iowa is named Disa, after a Viking queen.

In a parallel fashion, a child can walk without understanding or being able to explain the principles of balance and support, or the neurophysiological control mechanisms that permit one to do so. The fact that we may know something unconsciously is not unique to language.

What, then, do speakers of English or Quechua or French or Mohawk or Arabic know?

Knowledge of the Sound System

B.C. By Johnny Hart

By permission of Johnny Hart and Creators Syndicate, Inc.

Knowing a language means knowing what sounds (or signs[1]) are in that language and what sounds are not. This unconscious knowledge is revealed by the way speakers of

---

[1] The sign languages of the deaf will be discussed throughout the book. As stated, they are essentially the same as spoken languages, except that they use gestures instead of sounds. A reference to 'language' then, unless speech sounds or spoken languages are specifically mentioned, includes both spoken and signed languages.

one language pronounce words from another language. If you speak only English, for example, you may substitute an English sound for a non-English sound when pronouncing "foreign" words. Most English speakers pronounce the name Bach with a final *k* sound because the sound represented by the letters *ch* in German is not an English sound. If you pronounce it as the Germans do, you are using a sound outside the English sound system. French people speaking English often pronounce words like *this* and *that* as if they were spelled *zis* and *zat.* The English sound represented by the initial letters *th* is not part of the French sound system, and the French mispronunciation reveals the speakers' unconscious knowledge of this fact.

Knowing the sound system of a language includes more than knowing the inventory of sounds. It includes knowing which sounds may start a word, end a word, and follow each other. The name of a former president of Ghana was *Nkrumah,* pronounced with an initial sound identical to the sound ending the English word *sing* (for most Americans). While this is an English sound, no word in English begins with the *ng* sound. Most speakers of English mispronounce this name (by Ghanaian standards) by inserting a short vowel before or after the *ng* sound. Children who learn English recognize this fact about our language, just as Ghanaian children learn that words in their language may begin with the *ng* sound.

We will learn more about sound systems in Chapters 6 and 7.

Knowledge of Words

Knowing the sounds and sound patterns in our language constitutes only one part of our linguistic knowledge. In addition, knowing a language is knowing that certain sound sequences signify certain concepts or **meanings.** Speakers of English know what *boy* means and that it means something different from *toy* or *girl* or *pterodactyl.* When you know a language you know words in that language, that is, the sound units that are related to specific meanings.

Arbitrary Relation of Form and Meaning

> The minute I set eyes on an animal I know what it is. I don't have to reflect a moment; the right name comes out instantly. I seem to know just by the shape of the creature and the way it acts what animal it is. When the dodo came along he [Adam] thought it was a wildcat. But I saved him. I just spoke up in a quite natural way and said "Well, I do declare if there isn't the dodo!"
>
> Mark Twain, *Eve's Diary*

If you do not know a language, the words (and sentences) will be mainly incomprehensible, because the relationship between speech sounds and the meanings they represent in the languages of the world is, for the most part, an **arbitrary** one. You have to learn (when you are acquiring the language) that the sounds represented by the letters *house*

(in the written form of the language) signify the concept ; if you know French,

this same meaning is represented by *maison;* if you know Twi, it is represented by

ɔdaŋ; if you know Russian, by *dom;* if you know Spanish, by *casa.* Similarly, the is represented by *hand* in English, *main* in French, *nsa* in Twi, and *ruka* in Russian.

The following are words in some different languages. How many of them can you understand?

    a. kyinii
    b. doakam
    c. odun
    d. asa
    e. toowq
    f. bolna
    g. wartawan
    h. inaminatu
    i. yawwa

Speakers of the languages from which these words are taken know that they have the following meanings:

    a. a large parasol (in a Ghanaian language, Twi)
    b. living creature (in a Native American language, Papago)
    c. wood (in Turkish)
    d. morning (in Japanese)
    e. is seeing (in a California Indian language, Luiseño)
    f. to speak (in a Pakistani language, Urdu); aching (in Russian)
    g. reporter (in Indonesian)
    h. teacher (in a Venezuelan Indian language, Warao)
    i. right on! (in a Nigerian language, Hausa)

These examples show that the sounds of words are only given meaning by the language in which they occur, despite what Eve says in Mark Twain's satire *Eve's Diary*. A pterodactyl could have been called *ron, blick,* or *kerplunkity.*

As Shakespeare has Juliet say:

> What's in a name? That which we call a rose
> By any other name would smell as sweet.

This arbitrary relationship between the **form** (sounds) and **meaning** (concept) of a word in spoken language is also true of the sign languages used by the deaf. If you see someone using a sign language you do not know, it is doubtful that you will understand the message from the signs alone. A person who knows Chinese Sign Language would find it difficult to understand American Sign, and vice versa.

Signs that may have originally been **mimetic** (similar to miming) or **iconic** (with a nonarbitrary relationship between form and meaning) change historically as do words, and the iconicity is lost. These signs become **conventional,** so knowing the shape or movement of the hands does not reveal the meaning of the gestures in sign languages.

FIGURE 1-1   Arbitrary relation between gestures and meanings of the signs for *father* and *suspect* in ASL and CSL.[2]

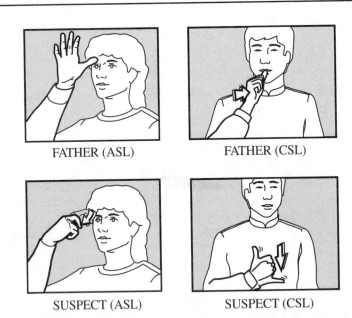

FATHER (ASL)   FATHER (CSL)

SUSPECT (ASL)   SUSPECT (CSL)

There is some **sound symbolism** in language—that is, words whose pronunciation suggests the meaning. A few words in most languages are **onomatopoeic**—the sounds of the words supposedly imitate the sounds of nature. Even here, the sounds differ from one language to another, reflecting the particular sound system of the language. In English we say *cockadoodledoo* to represent the rooster's crow, but in Russian they say *kukuriku*.

Sometimes particular sound sequences seem to relate to a particular concept. In English many words beginning with *gl* relate to sight, such as *glare, glint, gleam, glitter, glossy, glaze, glance, glimmer, glimpse,* and *glisten*. However, such words are a very small part of any language, and *gl* may have nothing to do with "sight" in another language, or even in other words in English, such as *gladiator, glucose, glory, glycerine, globe,* and so on.

English speakers know the *gl* words that relate to sight and those that do not; they know the onomatopoeic words and all the words in the basic vocabulary of the language. There are no speakers of English who know all 450,000 words listed in *Webster's Third New International Dictionary;* but even if there were and that were all they

---

[2] From *What the Hands Reveal about the Brain* by Howard Poizner, Edward S. Klima, Ursula Bellugi. 1987. Cambridge, MA: MIT Press.

knew, they would not know English. Imagine trying to learn a foreign language by buying a dictionary and memorizing words. No matter how many words you learned, you would not be able to form the simplest phrases or sentences in the language or understand a native speaker. No one speaks in isolated words. (Of course, you could search in your traveler's dictionary for individual words to find out how to say something like "car—gas—where?" After many tries, a native might understand this question and then point in the direction of a gas station. If you were answered with a sentence, however, you probably would not understand what was said or be able to look it up, because you would not know where one word ended and another began.) Chapter 5 will further explore word meanings.

The Creativity of Linguistic Knowledge

By permission of Johnny Hart and Creators Syndicate, Inc.

Knowledge of a language enables you to combine words to form phrases, and phrases to form sentences. You cannot buy a dictionary of any language with all its sentences, because no dictionary can list all the possible sentences. Knowing a language means being able to produce new sentences never spoken before and to understand sentences never heard before. The linguist Noam Chomsky refers to this ability as part of the **creative aspect** of language use. Not every speaker of a language can create great literature, but you, and all persons who know a language, can and do create new sentences when you speak and understand new sentences created by others.

This creative ability is due to the fact that language use is not limited to stimulus-response behavior. It's true that if someone steps on our toes we will automatically respond with a scream or gasp or grunt, but these sounds are really not part of language; they are involuntary reactions to stimuli. After we automatically cry out, we can say "That was some clumsy act, you big oaf" or "Thank you very much for stepping on my toe because I was afraid I had elephantiasis and now that I can feel it hurt I know it isn't so," or any one of an infinite number of sentences, because the particular sentence we produce is not controlled by any stimulus.

Even some involuntary cries like *ouch* are constrained by our own language system, as are the filled pauses that are sprinkled through conversational speech—*er* or *uh* or *you know* in English. They contain only the sounds found in the language. French speakers, for example, often fill their pauses with the vowel sound that starts with their word for egg—*oeuf*—a sound that does not occur in English. Knowing a language includes knowing what sentences are appropriate in various situations. Saying "Hamburger costs $2.00 a pound" after someone has just stepped on your toe would hardly be an appropriate response, although it would be possible.

Consider the following sentence: "Daniel Boone decided to become a pioneer because he dreamed of pigeon-toed giraffes and cross-eyed elephants dancing in pink skirts and green berets on the wind-swept plains of the Midwest." You may not believe the sentence; you may question its logic; but you can understand it, although you probably never heard or read it before now.

Knowledge of a language, then, makes it possible to understand and produce new sentences. If you counted the number of sentences in this book that you have seen or heard before, the number would be small. Next time you write an essay or a letter, see how many of your sentences are new. Few sentences are stored in your brain, to be pulled out to fit some situation or matched with some sentence that you hear. Novel sentences never spoken or heard before cannot be stored in your memory.

Simple memorization of all the possible sentences in a language is impossible in principle. If for every sentence in the language a longer sentence can be formed, then there is no limit to the length of any sentence and therefore no limit to the number of sentences. In English you can say:

This is the house.

or

This is the house that Jack built.

or

This is the malt that lay in the house that Jack built.

or

This is the dog that chased the cat that killed the rat that ate the malt that lay in the house that Jack built.

And you need not stop there. How long, then, is the longest sentence? A speaker of English can say:

The old man came.

or

The old, old, old, old, old man came.

How many "olds" are too many? Seven? Twenty-three?

It is true that the longer these sentences become, the less likely we would be to hear or to say them. A sentence with 276 occurrences of "old" would be highly unlikely in either speech or writing, even to describe Methuselah; but such a sentence is theoretically possible. If you know English, you have the knowledge to add any number of adjectives as modifiers to a noun.

All human languages permit their speakers to form indefinitely long sentences; "creativity" is a universal property of human language.

To memorize and store an infinite set of sentences would require an infinite storage capacity. However, the brain is finite, and even if it were not, we could not store novel sentences.

Knowledge of Sentences and Nonsentences

When you learn a language you must learn something finite—your vocabulary is finite (however large it may be)—and that can be stored. If sentences in a language were formed by putting one word after another in any order, then language could simply be a set of words. You can see that words are not enough by examining the following strings of words:

(1) a. John kissed the little old lady who owned the shaggy dog.
    b. Who owned the shaggy dog John kissed the little old lady.
    c. John is difficult to love.
    d. It is difficult to love John.
    e. John is anxious to go.
    f. It is anxious to go John.
    g. John, who was a student, flunked his exams.
    h. Exams his flunked student a was who John.

If you were asked to put a star or asterisk before the examples that seemed "funny" or "no good" to you, which ones would you star? Our "intuitive" knowledge about what is or is not an allowable sentence in English convinces us to star b, f, and h. Which ones did you star?

Would you agree with the following judgments?

(2) a. What he did was climb a tree.
    b. *What he thought was want a sports car.[3]
    c. Drink your beer and go home!
    d. *What are drinking and go home?
    e. I expect them to arrive a week from next Thursday.
    f. *I expect a week from next Thursday to arrive them.
    g. Linus lost his security blanket.
    h. *Lost Linus security blanket his.

If you find the starred sentences unacceptable as we do, you see that every string of words does not constitute a well-formed sentence in a language. Knowledge of a language determines which strings of words are and which are not sentences. Therefore, in addition to knowing the words of the language, linguistic knowledge includes **rules** for forming sentences and making the kinds of judgments you made about the examples in (1) and (2). These rules must be finite in length and finite in number so that they can be stored in our finite brains; yet they must permit us to form and understand an infinite set of new sentences, as we discussed earlier. They are not rules determined by a judge or a legislature or even rules taught in a grammar class. They are unconscious constraints on sentence formation that children discover about the language.

A language, then, consists of all the sounds, words, and possible sentences. When you know a language, you know the sounds, the words, and the rules for their combination.

---

[3] The asterisk is used before examples that speakers, for any reason, find unacceptable. This notation will be used throughout the book.

LINGUISTIC KNOWLEDGE AND PERFORMANCE

"What's one and one and one and one and one and one and one and one and one and one?" "I don't know," said Alice. "I lost count." "She can't do Addition," the Red Queen interrupted.

Lewis Carroll, *Through the Looking-Glass*

The Born Loser reprinted by permission of NEA, Inc.

Speakers' linguistic knowledge permits them to form longer and longer sentences by joining sentences and phrases together or adding modifiers to a noun. Whether you stop at three, five, or eighteen adjectives, it is impossible to limit the number you could add if desired. Very long sentences are theoretically possible, but they are highly improbable. Evidently there is a difference between having the knowledge necessary to produce sentences of a language and applying this knowledge. It is a difference between what you know, which is your linguistic **competence,** and how you use this knowledge in actual speech production and comprehension, which is your linguistic **performance.**

Speakers of all languages—spoken and signed—have the knowledge to understand or produce sentences of any length. When they attempt to use that knowledge, though—when they perform linguistically—there are physiological and psychological reasons that limit the number of adjectives, adverbs, clauses, and so on. They may run out of breath, their audience may leave, they may lose track of what they have said, and of course, no one lives forever.

When we speak we usually wish to convey some message. (Although it seems that some of us occasionally like to talk just to hear our own voices.) At some stage in the act of producing speech we must organize our thoughts into strings of words. Sometimes the message gets garbled. We may stammer, or pause, or produce **slips of the tongue.** We may even sound like Tarzan in the cartoon by Gary Larson, who illustrates the difference between linguistic knowledge and the way we use that knowledge in performance.

THE FAR SIDE copyright 1991, 1987, and 1986, Universal Press Syndicate. Reprinted with permission. All rights reserved.

For the most part, linguistic knowledge is not conscious knowledge. The linguistic system—the sounds, structures, meanings, words, and rules for putting them all together—is learned subconsciously with no awareness that rules are being learned. Just as we may be unconscious of the rules that allow us to stand or walk, to crawl on all fours if we choose, to jump or catch a baseball, or to ride a bicycle, our unconscious ability to speak and understand and to make judgments about sentences reveals our knowledge of the rules of our language. This knowledge represents a complex cognitive system. The nature of this system is what this book is all about.

WHAT IS GRAMMAR?

> We use the term "grammar" with a systematic ambiguity. On the one hand, the term refers to the explicit theory constructed by the linguist and proposed as a description of the speaker's competence. On the other hand, it refers to this competence itself.
>
> N. Chomsky and M. Halle, *The Sound Pattern of English*

Descriptive Grammars

The sounds and sound patterns, the basic units of meaning, such as words, and the rules to combine them to form new sentences constitute the **grammar** of a language. The grammar, then, is what we know; it represents our linguistic competence. To understand the nature of language we must understand the nature of this internalized, unconscious set of rules, which is part of every grammar of every language.

Every human being who speaks a language knows its grammar. When linguists wish to describe a language, they attempt to describe the grammar of the language that exists in the minds of its speakers. There may be some differences among speakers' knowledge, but there must be shared knowledge, because it is this grammar that makes it possible to communicate through language. To the extent that the linguist's description is a true model of the speakers' linguistic capacity, it will be a successful description of the grammar and of the language itself. Such a model is called a **descriptive grammar.** It does not tell you how you should speak; it describes your basic linguistic knowledge. It explains how it is possible for you to speak and understand, and it tells what you know about the sounds, words, phrases, and sentences of your language.

We have used the word *grammar* in two ways: the first in reference to the **mental grammar** speakers have in their brains; the second as the model or description of this internalized grammar. Almost two thousand years ago the Greek grammarian Dionysius Thrax defined grammar as that which permits us either to speak a language or to speak about a language. From now on we will not differentiate these two meanings, because the linguist's descriptive grammar is an attempt at a formal statement (or theory) of the speakers' grammar.

When we say in later chapters that there is a rule in the grammar—such as "Every sentence has a noun phrase subject and a verb phrase predicate"—we posit the rule in both the mental grammar and the descriptive model of it, the linguist's grammar. When we say that a sentence is **grammatical,** we mean that it conforms to the rules of both grammars; conversely, an **ungrammatical** (starred, unacceptable) sentence deviates in some way from these rules. If, however, we posit a rule for English that does not agree with your intuitions as a speaker, then the grammar we are describing differs in some way from the mental grammar that represents your linguistic competence; that is, your language is not the one described. No language or variety of a language (called a **dialect**) is superior to any other in a linguistic sense. Every grammar is equally complex and logical and capable of producing an infinite set of sentences to express any thought. If something can be expressed in one language or one dialect, it can be expressed in any other language or dialect. It might involve different means and different words, but it can be expressed.

No grammar, therefore no language, is either superior or inferior to any other. Languages of technologically undeveloped cultures are not primitive or ill formed in any way.

Prescriptive Grammars

It is a rule up with which we should not put.

Winston Churchill

I don't want to talk grammar. I want to talk like a lady.

G. B. Shaw, *Pygmalion*

"So, then . . . Would that be 'us the people' or
'we the people?'"

© by Chronicle Features.

The views expressed in the section above are not those of all grammarians now or in the past. From ancient times until the present, "purists" have believed that language change is corruption and that there are certain "correct" forms that all educated people should use in speaking and writing. The Greek Alexandrians in the first century, the Arabic scholars at Basra in the eighth century, and numerous English grammarians of the eighteenth and nineteenth centuries held this view. They wished to prescribe rather than describe the rules of grammar, which gave rise to the writing of **prescriptive grammars.**

With the rise of capitalism, a new middle class emerged who wanted their children to speak the dialect of the "upper" classes. This desire led to the publication of many prescriptive grammars. In 1762 an influential grammar, *A Short Introduction to English Grammar with Critical Notes,* was written by Bishop Robert Lowth. Lowth, influenced by Latin grammar and by personal preference, prescribed a number of new rules for English. Before the publication of his grammar, practically everyone—upper-class, middle-class, and lower-class speakers of English—said *I don't have none, You was wrong about that,* and *Mathilda is fatter than me.* Lowth, however, decided that "two negatives make a positive" and therefore one should say *I don't have any;* that even when *you* is singular it should be followed by the plural *were;* and that *I* not *me, he* not *him, they* not *them,* and so forth should follow *than* in comparative constructions. Many of these prescriptive rules were based on Latin grammar, which had already given way to different rules in the languages that developed from Latin. Because Lowth was influential and because the rising new class wanted to speak "properly," many of these new rules were legislated into English grammar, at least for the **prestige dialect.**

The view that dialects that regularly use double negatives are inferior cannot be justified if one looks at the standard dialects of other languages in the world. Romance languages, for example, utilize double negatives, as the following examples from French and Italian show:

French: Je ne veux parler avec personne.
          I not want speak with no-one.
Italian: Non voglio parlare con nessuno.
          not I-want   speak with no-one.
English translation: "I don't want to speak with anyone."

Grammars such as Lowth's are different from the descriptive grammars we have been discussing. Their goal is not to describe the rules people know, but to tell them what rules they should know.

In 1908, a grammarian, Thomas R. Lounsbury, wrote: "There seems to have been in every period in the past, as there is now, a distinct apprehension in the minds of very many worthy persons that the English tongue is always in the condition approaching collapse and that arduous efforts must be put forth persistently to save it from destruction."

Today our bookstores are filled with books by language "purists" attempting to do just that. Edwin Newman, for example, in his books *Strictly Speaking* and *A Civil Tongue,* rails against those who use the word *hopefully* to mean "I hope," as in "Hopefully, it will not rain tomorrow," instead of using it "properly" to mean "with hope." What Newman fails to recognize is that language changes in the course of time and words change meaning, and the meaning of *hopefully* has been broadened for most English speakers to include both usages. Other "saviors" of the English language blame television, the schools, and even the National Council of Teachers of English for failing to preserve the standard language, and they mount attacks against those college and university professors who suggest that African American English (AAE)[4] and other

---

[4] AAE is also called African American Vernacular English (AAVE), Ebonics, and Black English (BE). This is a dialect spoken by some but by no means all African Americans.

dialects are viable, living, complete languages. Although not mentioned by name, the authors of this textbook would clearly be among those who would be criticized by these new prescriptivists.

There is even a literary organization dedicated to the proper use of the English language, called the Unicorn Society of Lake Superior State College, which issues an annual "dishonor list" of words and phrases of which they do not approve, including the word "medication," which they say "We can no longer afford. It's too expensive. We've got to get back to the cheaper 'medicine.' "[5] At least these guardians of the English language have a sense of humor; but they as well as the other prescriptivists are bound to fail. Language is vigorous and dynamic and constantly changing. All languages and dialects are expressive, complete, and logical, as much so as they were 200 or 2000 years ago. If sentences are muddled, it is not because of the language but because of the speakers. Prescriptivists should be more concerned about the thinking of the speakers than about the language they use. Hopefully this book will convince you of this.

Linguists object to prescriptivism for a number of reasons. The views are elitist, in that they assume that the linguistic grammars and usages of a particular group in society (usually the more affluent and those with political power) are the only correct ones. Prescriptivists, for the most part, seem to have little knowledge of the history of the language and less about the nature of language. They seem to be unaware of the fact that all dialects are rule governed and that what is grammatical in one language may be ungrammatical in another (equally prestigious) language.

The **standard** dialect may indeed be a better dialect for someone wishing to obtain a particular job or achieve a position of social prestige. But linguistically it is not a better form of the language.

Teaching Grammars

By permission of Johnny Hart and Creators Syndicate, Inc.

The descriptive grammar of a language attempts to describe everything speakers know about their language. It is different from a **teaching grammar,** which is used to learn another language or dialect. Teaching grammars are those we use in school to fulfill

---

[5] *Los Angeles Times,* Jan. 2, 1978, Part 1, p. 21.

language requirements. They can be helpful to those who do not speak the standard or prestige dialect but find it would be advantageous socially and economically to do so. Teaching grammars state explicitly the rules of the language, list the words and their pronunciations, and aid in learning a new language or dialect.

It is often difficult for adults to learn a second language without being instructed, even when living for an extended period in a country where the language is spoken. Teaching grammars assume that the student already knows one language and compares the grammar of the target language with the grammar of the native language. The meaning of a word is given by providing a **gloss**—the parallel word in the student's native language, such as *maison,* "house" in French. It is assumed that the student knows the meaning of the gloss "house," and so the meaning of the word *maison.*

Sounds of the target language that do not occur in the native language are often described by reference to known sounds. Thus the student might be aided in producing the French sound u in the word *tu* by instructions such as "Round your lips while producing the vowel sound in *tea.*"

The rules on how to put words together to form the grammatical sentences also refer to the learners' knowledge of their native language. Thus the teaching grammar *Learn Zulu* by Sibusiso Nyembezi states that "The difference between singular and plural is not at the end of the word but at the beginning of it," and warns that "Zulu does not have the indefinite and definite articles 'a' and 'the.' " Such statements assume students know the rules of their own grammar, in this case English. Although such grammars might be considered prescriptive in the sense that they attempt to teach the student what is or is not a grammatical construction in the new language, their aim is different from grammars that attempt to change the rules or usage of a language already learned.

This book is not primarily concerned with either prescriptive or teaching grammars. The matter, however, is considered in a later chapter in the discussion of standard and nonstandard dialects.

LANGUAGE UNIVERSALS

In a grammar there are parts that pertain to all languages; these components form what is called the general grammar. In addition to these general (universal) parts, there are those that belong only to one particular language; and these constitute the particular grammars of each language.

Du Marsais, c. 1750

The way we are using the word *grammar* differs in another way from its most common meaning. In our sense, the grammar includes everything speakers know about their language—the sound system, called **phonology;** the system of meanings, called **semantics;** the rules of word formation, called **morphology;** and the rules of sentence formation, called **syntax.** It also, of course, includes the vocabulary of words—the dictionary or **lexicon.** Many people think of the grammar of a language as referring solely to the syntactic rules. This latter sense is what students usually mean when they talk about their class in "English grammar."

Our aim is more in keeping with that stated in 1784 by the grammarian John Fell in *Essay towards an English Grammar:* "It is certainly the business of a grammarian to find out, and not to make, the laws of a language." This business is just what the linguist attempts—to find out the laws of a language, and the laws that pertain to all languages. Those laws that pertain to all human languages, representing the universal properties of language, constitute a **universal grammar.**

About 1630, the German philosopher Alsted first used the term *general grammar* as distinct from *special grammar.* He believed that the function of a general grammar was to reveal those features "which relate to the method and etiology of grammatical concepts. They are common to all languages." Pointing out that "general grammar is the pattern 'norma' of every particular grammar whatsoever," he implored "eminent linguists to employ their insight in this matter."[6]

Three and a half centuries before Alsted, the scholar Robert Kilwardby held that linguists should be concerned with discovering the nature of language in general. So concerned was Kilwardby with universal grammar that he excluded considerations of the characteristics of particular languages, which he believed to be as "irrelevant to a science of grammar as the material of the measuring rod or the physical characteristics of objects were to geometry."[7] Kilwardby was perhaps too much of a universalist; the particular properties of individual languages are relevant to the discovery of language universals, and they are of interest for their own sake.

Someone attempting to study Latin, Greek, French, or Swahili as a second language may assert, in frustration, that those ancient scholars were so hidden in their ivory towers that they confused reality with idle speculation; yet the more we investigate this question, the more evidence accumulates to support Chomsky's view that there is a universal grammar that is part of the human biologically endowed language faculty. It may be thought of "as a system of principles which characterizes the class of possible grammars by specifying how particular grammars are organized (what are the components and their relations), how the different rules of these components are constructed, how they interact, and so on."[8]

To discover the nature of this Universal Grammar whose principles characterize all human languages is a major aim of **linguistic theory.** The linguist's goal is to discover the "laws of human language" as the physicist's goal is to discover the "laws of the physical universe." The complexity of language, a product of the human brain, undoubtedly means this goal will never be fully achieved. But all scientific theories are incomplete; new hypotheses are proposed to account for more data. Theories are continually changing as new discoveries are made. Just as Newtonian physics was enlarged by Einstein's theories of relativity, so the linguistic theory of Universal Grammar develops, and new discoveries shed new light on what human language is.

---

[6] V. Salmon. 1969. "Review of *Cartesian Linguistics* by N. Chomsky," *Journal of Linguistics* 5: 165–187.

[7] Ibid.

[8] Noam Chomsky. 1979. *Language and Responsibility* (based on conversations with Misou Ronat), New York: Pantheon, p. 180.

Sign Languages: Evidence for Language Universals

> It is not the want of organs that [prevents animals from making] . . . known
> their thoughts . . . for it is evident that magpies and parrots are able to utter
> words just like ourselves, and yet they cannot speak as we do, that is, so as
> to give evidence that they think of what they say. On the other hand, men
> who, being born deaf and mute . . . are destitute of the organs which serve
> the others for talking, are in the habit of themselves inventing certain signs
> by which they make themselves understood.
>
> René Descartes, *Discourse on Method*

The sign languages of the deaf provide some of the best evidence to support the notion that humans are born with the ability to acquire language, and that these languages are governed by the same universal properties.

Deaf children, who are unable to hear the sounds of spoken language, do not acquire spoken languages as hearing children do. However, deaf children of deaf parents who are exposed to sign language learn sign language in stages parallel to language acquisition by hearing children learning oral languages. As we noted earlier, these sign languages are human languages that do not utilize sounds to express meanings. Instead, sign languages are visual-gestural systems that use hand and body gestures as the forms used to represent words. Sign languages are fully developed languages, and those who know sign language are capable of creating and comprehending unlimited numbers of new sentences, just like speakers of spoken languages.

Current research on sign languages has been crucial in the attempt to understand the biological underpinnings of human language acquisition and use. Some understanding of sign languages is therefore essential.

About one in a thousand babies is born deaf or with a severe hearing deficiency. One major effect is the difficulty the deaf have in learning a spoken language. It is nearly impossible for those unable to hear language to learn to speak naturally. Normal speech depends to a great extent on constant auditory feedback. Hence a deaf child will not learn to speak without extensive training in special schools or programs designed especially for the deaf.

Although deaf persons can be taught to speak a language intelligibly, they can never understand speech as well as a hearing person. Seventy-five percent of the words spoken cannot be read on the lips with any degree of accuracy. The ability of many deaf individuals to comprehend spoken language is therefore remarkable; they combine lip reading with knowledge of the structure of language and the semantic redundancies.

If, however, human language is universal in the sense that all members of the human species have the ability to learn a language, it is not surprising that nonspoken languages have developed as a substitute for spoken languages among nonhearing individuals. The more we learn about the human linguistic ability, the more it is clear that language acquisition and use are not dependent on the ability to produce and hear sounds, but on a much more abstract cognitive ability, biologically determined, that accounts for the similarities between spoken and sign languages.

American Sign Language (ASL)

The major language used by the deaf in the United States is **American Sign Language** (or **AMESLAN** or **ASL**). ASL is an independent, fully developed language that historically is an outgrowth of the sign language used in France and brought to the United States in 1817 by the great educator Thomas Hopkins Gallaudet. Gallaudet was hired to establish a school for the deaf, and after studying the language and methods used in the Paris school founded by the Abbé de l'Épée in 1775, he returned to the United States with Laurent Clerc, a young deaf instructor, establishing the basis for ASL.

The grammar of ASL, like that of all human languages, has its own grammar which includes everything speakers know about their language—the system of gestures equivalent to the phonology of spoken languages,[9] the morphological, syntactic, and semantic systems, and a mental lexicon of signs.

The other sign language used in the United States is called **Signed English** (or **Siglish**). Essentially, it consists in the replacement of each spoken English word (and grammatical elements such as the *s* ending for plurals or the *ed* ending for past tense) by a sign. The syntax and semantics of Signed English are thus approximately the same as those of ordinary English. The result is unnatural in that it is similar to speaking French by translating every English word or ending into its French counterpart: Problems result because there are not always corresponding forms in the two languages.

If there is no sign in ASL, signers utilize another mechanism, the system of finger spelling. This method is also used to add new proper nouns or technical vocabulary. Sign interpreters of spoken English often finger spell such words. A manual alphabet consisting of various finger configurations, hand positions, and movements gives visible symbols for the alphabet and ampersand.

Signs, however, are produced differently than are finger-spelled words. "The sign DECIDE cannot be analyzed as a sequence of distinct, separable configurations of the hand. Like all other lexical signs in ASL, but unlike the individual finger-spelled letters in D-E-C-I-D-E taken separately, the ASL sign DECIDE does have an essential movement but the hand shape occurs simultaneously with the movement. In appearance, the sign is a continuous whole."[10] This sign is shown in Figure 1-2.

An accomplished signer can sign at a normal rate, even when there is a lot of finger spelling. Television stations sometimes have programs that are interpreted in sign for the deaf in a corner of the TV screen. If you have ever seen such a program, you will have seen how well the interpreter kept pace with the spoken sentences.

Language arts are not lost to the deaf. Poetry is composed in sign language, and stage plays such as Sheridan's *The Critic* have been translated into sign language and acted by the National Theatre of the Deaf (NTD). Sign Language was so highly thought of by the anthropologist Margaret Mead that, in an article discussing the possibilities of a universal second language, she suggests using some of the basic ideas that sign languages incorporate.

---

[9] The term *phonology*, which was first used to describe the sound systems of language, has been extended to include the gestural systems of sign languages.

[10] Klima and Bellugi, *The Signs of Language,* pp. 38 and 62.

FIGURE 1.2   The ASL sign DECIDE: (a) and (c) show transitions from the sign; (b) illustrates the single downward movement of the sign.

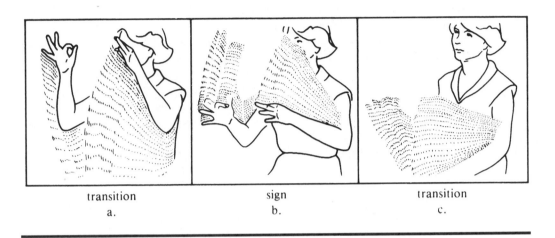

transition	sign	transition
a.	b.	c.

ANIMAL "LANGUAGES"

No matter how eloquently a dog may bark, he cannot tell you that his parents were poor but honest.

Bertrand Russell

Whether language is the exclusive property of the human species is an interesting question. The idea of talking animals probably is as old and as widespread among human societies as language is itself. No culture lacks a legend in which some animal plays a speaking role. All over West Africa, children listen to folktales in which a "spider-man" is the hero. "Coyote" is a favorite figure in many Native American tales, and there is hardly an animal who does not figure in Aesop's famous fables. Hugh Lofting's fictional Doctor Doolittle's major accomplishment was his ability to communicate with animals.

If language is viewed only as a system of communication, then many species communicate. Humans also use systems other than their language to relate to each other and to send "messages." The question is whether the kinds of grammars that represent linguistic knowledge acquired by children with no external instruction, and which are used creatively rather than as responses to internal or external stimuli, are unique to the human animal.

"Talking" Parrots

Copyright © 1991 by Chronicle Features.

Most humans who acquire language utilize speech sounds to express meanings, but such sounds are not a necessary aspect of language, as evidenced by the sign languages of the deaf. The use of speech sounds is therefore not a basic part of what we have been calling language. The chirping of birds, the squeaking of dolphins, and the dancing of bees may potentially represent systems similar to human languages. If animal communication systems are not like human language, it will not be due to a lack of speech.

Conversely, when animals vocally imitate human utterances, it does not mean they possess language. Language is a system that relates sounds (or gestures) to meanings. "Talking" birds such as parrots and mynah birds are capable of faithfully reproducing words and phrases of human language that they have heard; but when a parrot says "Polly wants a cracker," she may really want a ham sandwich or a drink of water or nothing at all. A bird that has learned to say "hello" or "good-bye" is as likely to use one as the other, regardless of whether people are arriving or departing. The bird's utterances carry no meaning. They are speaking neither English nor their own language when they sound like us.

Talking birds do not dissect the sounds of their imitations into discrete units. Polly and Molly do not rhyme for a parrot. They are as different as *hello* and *good-bye* (or as similar). One property of all human languages (which will be discussed further in Chapter 6) is the discreteness of the speech or gestural units, which are ordered and reordered, combined and split apart. Generally, a parrot says what it is taught, or what it hears, and no more. If Polly learns "Polly wants a cracker" and "Polly wants a dough-nut" and also learns to imitate the single words *whiskey* and *bagel*, she will not sponta-neously produce, as children do, "Polly wants whiskey" or "Polly wants a bagel" or "Polly wants whiskey and a bagel." If she learns *cat* and *cats* and *dog* and *dogs* and then learns the word *parrot,* she will be unable to form the plural *parrots* as children do by the age of three; nor can a parrot form an unlimited set of utterances from a finite set of units nor understand utterances never heard before. Recent reports of an African gray parrot named Alex studied by Dr. Irene M. Pepperberg of the University of Arizona sug-gest that new methods of training may result in more learning than was previously believed possible. When the trainer uses words in context, Alex seems to relate some sounds with their meanings. This is more than simply imitation, but it is not in any way similar to the way children acquire the complexities of the grammar of any language. It is more like a dog learning to associate certain sounds with meanings, such as *heel, sit, fetch,* etc. Alex's ability may go somewhat beyond that. However, the ability to produce sounds similar to those used in human language even if meanings are related to these sounds cannot be equated with the ability to acquire the complex grammar of a human language.

The Birds and the Bees

> The birds and animals are all friendly to each other, and there are no dis-putes about anything. They all talk, and they all talk to me, but it must be a foreign language for I cannot make out a word they say.
>
> Mark Twain, *Eve's Diary*

Most animals possess some kind of "signaling" communication system. Among the spi-ders there is a complex system for courtship. The male spider, before he approaches his lady love, goes through an elaborate series of gestures to inform her that he is indeed a spider and not a crumb or a fly to be eaten. These gestures are invariant. One never finds a creative spider changing or adding to the particular courtship ritual of his species.

A similar kind of gesture language is found among the fiddler crabs. There are forty different varieties, and each variety uses its own particular claw-waving movement to signal to another member of its "clan." The timing, movement, and posture of the body never change from one time to another or from one crab to another within the particu-lar variety. Whatever the signal means, it is fixed. Only one meaning can be conveyed. There is not an infinite set of fiddler crab sentences.

The imitative sounds of talking birds have little in common with human language, but the calls and songs of many species of birds do have a communicative function, and they resemble human languages in that there may be "dialects" within the same species. **Bird calls** (consisting of one or more short notes) convey messages associated with the immediate environment, such as danger, feeding, nesting, flocking, and so on. **Bird songs** (more complex patterns of notes) are used to stake out territory and to attract mates. There is no evidence of any internal structure to these songs, nor can they be segmented into independently meaningful parts as words of human language can be. In a study of the territorial song of the European robin,[11] it was discovered that the rival robins paid attention only to the alternation between high-pitched and low-pitched notes, and which came first did not matter. The message varies only to the extent of how strongly the robin feels about his possession and to what extent he is prepared to defend it and start a family in that territory. The different alternations therefore express intensity and nothing more. The robin is creative in his ability to sing the same thing in many different ways, but not creative in his ability to use the same units of the system to express many different messages with different meanings.

Despite certain superficial similarities to human language, bird calls and songs are fundamentally different kinds of communicative systems. The number of messages that can be conveyed is finite, and messages are stimulus controlled.

This distinction is also true of the system of communication used by honeybees. For a long time it has been believed that a forager bee is able to return to the hive and tell other bees where a source of food is located. It does so by forming a dance on a wall of the hive that reveals the location and quality of the food source. For one species of Italian honeybee, the dancing behavior may assume one of three possible patterns: round (which indicates locations near the hive, within twenty feet or so), sickle (which indicates locations at twenty- to sixty-feet distance from the hive), and tail-wagging (for distances that exceed sixty feet). The number of repetitions per minute of the basic pattern in the tail-wagging dance indicates the precise distance; the slower the repetition rate, the longer the distance.

The bees' dance is an effective system of communication for bees. It is capable, in principle, of infinitely many different messages, like human language; but unlike human language, the system is confined to a single subject—distance from the hive. The inflexibility was shown by an experimenter who forced a bee to walk to the food source. When the bee returned to the hive, it indicated a distance twenty-five times farther away than the food source actually was. The bee had no way of communicating the special circumstances in its message. This absence of creativity makes the bees' dance qualitatively different from human language.[12]

In the seventeenth century, the philosopher and mathematician René Descartes pointed out that the communication systems of animals are qualitatively different from the language used by humans:

> It is a very remarkable fact that there are none so depraved and stupid, without even excepting idiots, that they cannot arrange different words together, forming of them a statement by which they make known their thoughts; while, on the other hand, there is no other animal, however perfect and fortunately circumstanced it may be, which can do the same.[13]

---

[11] R. G. Busnel and J. Bremond. 1962. "Recherche du Support de l'Information dans le Signal Acoustique de Défense Territoriale du Rougegorge," *C. R. Acad. Sci. Paris* 254: 2236–2238.

[12] K. Von Frisch. *The Dance Language and Orientation of the Bees,* translated by L. E. Chadwick, Cambridge, MA: Belknap Press of Harvard University Press, 1967.

[13] René Descartes. 1967. "Discourse on Method," *The Philosophical Works of Descartes,* Vol. I, trans. by E. S. Haldane and G. R. Ross, Cambridge, England: Cambridge University Press, p. 116.

Descartes goes on to state that one of the major differences between humans and animals is that human use of language is not just a response to external, or even internal, emotional stimuli, as are the sounds and gestures of animals. He warns against confusing human use of language with "natural movements which betray passions and may be . . . manifested by animals."

To hold that animals communicate by systems qualitatively different from human language systems is not to claim human superiority. Humans are not inferior to the one-celled amoeba because they cannot reproduce by splitting in two; they are just different sexually. They are not inferior to hunting dogs, whose sense of smell is far better than human animals. All the studies of animal communication systems, including those of chimpanzees (discussed in Chapter 8), provide evidence for Descartes' distinction between other animal communication systems and the linguistic creative ability possessed by the human animal.

WHAT WE KNOW ABOUT LANGUAGE

There are many things we do not yet know about the nature of human languages, their structures and use. The science of linguistics is concerned with these questions. The investigations of linguists throughout history and the analysis of spoken languages date back at least to 1600 B.C. in Mesopotamia. We have learned a great deal since that time. A number of facts pertaining to all languages can be stated.

1. Wherever humans exist, language exists.
2. There are no "primitive" languages—all languages are equally complex and equally capable of expressing any idea in the universe. The vocabulary of any language can be expanded to include new words for new concepts.
3. All languages change through time.
4. The relationships between the sounds and meanings of spoken languages and between the gestures and meanings of sign languages are for the most part arbitrary.
5. All human languages utilize a finite set of discrete sounds (or gestures) that are combined to form meaningful elements or words, which themselves form an infinite set of possible sentences.
6. All grammars contain rules for the formation of words and sentences of a similar kind.
7. Every spoken language includes discrete sound segments, like p, n, or a, that can all be defined by a finite set of sound properties or features. Every spoken language has a class of vowels and a class of consonants.
8. Similar grammatical categories (for example, noun, verb) are found in all languages.
9. There are semantic universals, such as "male" or "female," "animate" or "human," found in every language in the world.
10. Every language has a way of referring to past time, negating, forming questions, issuing commands, and so on.

11. Speakers of all languages are capable of producing and comprehending an infinite set of sentences. Syntactic universals reveal that every language has a way of forming sentences such as:

Linguistics is an interesting subject.

I know that linguistics is an interesting subject.

You know that I know that linguistics is an interesting subject.

Cecelia knows that you know that I know that linguistics is an interesting subject.

Is it a fact that Cecelia knows that you know that I know that linguistics is an interesting subject?

12. Any normal child, born anywhere in the world, of any racial, geographical, social, or economic heritage, is capable of learning any language to which he or she is exposed. The differences we find among languages cannot be due to biological reasons.

It seems that Alsted and Du Marsais (and we could add many other universalists from all ages) were not spinning idle thoughts. We all speak human language.

SUMMARY

We are all intimately familiar with at least one language, our own. Yet few of us ever stop to consider what we know when we know a language. There is no book that contains the English or Russian or Zulu language. The words of a language can be listed in a dictionary, but not all the sentences can be; and a language consists of these sentences as well as words. Speakers use a finite set of rules to produce and understand an infinite set of possible sentences.

These rules comprise the **grammar** of a language, which is learned when you acquire the language and includes the sound system (the **phonology**), the structure of words (the **morphology**) how words may be combined into phrases and sentences (the **syntax**), the ways in which sounds and meanings are related (the **semantics**), and the words or **lexicon.** The sounds and meanings of these words are related in an **arbitrary** fashion. If you had never heard the word *syntax* you would not, by its sounds, know what it meant. The gestures used by deaf signers are also arbitrarily related to their meanings. Language, then, is a system that relates sounds (or hand and body gestures) with meanings; when you know a language you know this system.

This knowledge (linguistic **competence**) is different from behavior (linguistic **performance**). If you woke up one morning and decided to stop talking (as the Trappist monks did after they took a vow of silence), you would still have knowledge of your language. This ability or competence underlies linguistic behavior. If you do not know the language, you cannot speak it; but if you know the language, you may choose not to speak.

Grammars are of different kinds. The **descriptive grammar** of a language represents the unconscious linguistic knowledge or capacity of its speakers. Such a grammar is a model of the **mental grammar** every speaker of the language knows. It does not teach the rules of the language; it describes the rules that are already known. A grammar that attempts to legislate what your grammar should be is called a **prescriptive grammar.** It prescribes; it does not describe, except incidentally. **Teaching grammars** are written to help people learn a foreign language or a dialect of their own language.

The more linguists investigate the thousands of languages of the world and describe the ways in which they differ from each other, the more they discover that these differences are limited. There are linguistic universals that pertain to all parts of grammars, the ways in which these parts are related and the forms of rules. These principles comprise **Universal Grammar,** which forms the basis of the specific grammars of all possible human languages.

If language is defined merely as a system of communication, then language is not unique to humans. There are, however, certain characteristics of human language not found in the communication systems of any other species. A basic property of human language is its **creative aspect**—a speaker's ability to combine the basic linguistic units to form an infinite set of "well-formed" grammatical sentences, most of which are novel, never before produced or heard.

The fact that deaf children learn **sign language** shows that the ability to hear or produce sounds is not a necessary prerequisite for language learning. All the sign languages in the world, which differ like spoken languages do, are visual-gestural systems that are as fully developed and as structurally complex as spoken languages. The major sign language used in the United States is **American Sign Language** (also referred to as **Ameslan** or **ASL**).

We thus see that the ability to hear or produce sounds is not a necessary condition for the acquisition of language; nor is the ability to imitate the sounds of human language a sufficient basis for learning language. "Talking" birds imitate sounds but can neither segment these sounds into smaller units, nor understand what they are imitating, nor produce new utterances to convey their thoughts.

Birds, bees, crabs, spiders, and most other creatures communicate in some way, but the information imparted is severely limited and stimulus-bound, confined to a small set of messages. The system of language represented by intricate mental grammars, which are not stimulus-bound and which generate infinite messages, is unique to the human species.

Because of linguistic research throughout history, we have learned much about Universal Grammar, the properties shared by all languages.

References for Further Reading

Bolinger, Dwight. 1980. *Language—The Loaded Weapon: The Use and Abuse of Language Today.* London: Longman.

Chomsky, Noam. 1986. *Knowledge of Language: Its Nature, Origin, and Use.* New York and London: Praeger.

Chomsky, Noam. 1975. *Reflections on Language.* New York: Pantheon Books.

Chomsky, Noam. 1972. *Language and Mind.* Enlarged ed. New York: Harcourt Brace Jovanovich.

Crystal, David. 1984. *Who Cares about Usage?* New York: Penguin.

Gould, J. L., and C. G. Gould. 1983. "Can a Bee Behave Intelligently?" *New Scientist* 98: 84–87.

Hall, Robert A. 1950. *Leave Your Language Alone.* Ithaca, NY: Linguistica.

Jackendoff, Ray. 1994. *Patterns in the Mind: Language and Human Nature.* New York: Basic Books.

Klima, Edward S., and Ursula Bellugi. 1979. *The Signs of Language.* Cambridge, MA: Harvard University Press.

Lane, Harlan. 1984. *When the Mind Hears: A History of the Deaf.* New York: Random House.

Milroy, James, and Lesley Milroy. 1985. *Authority in Language: Investigating Language Prescription and Standardisation.* London: Routledge & Kegan Paul.

Newmeyer, Frederick J. 1983. *Grammatical Theory: Its Limits and Possibilities.* Chicago, IL: University of Chicago Press.

Nunberg, Geoffrey. 1983. "The Decline of Grammar." *Atlantic Monthly,* December.

Pinker, Steven. 1994. *The Language Instinct.* New York: William Morrow and Co., Inc.

Safire, William. 1980. *On Age.* New York: Avon Books.

Sebeok, T. A., ed. 1977. *How Animals Communicate.* Bloomington, IN: Indiana University Press.

Shopen, Timothy, and Joseph M. Williams, eds. 1980. *Standards and Dialects in English.* Rowley, MA: Newbury House.

Sternberg, Martin L. A. 1987. *American Sign Language Dictionary.* New York: Harper & Row.

Stokoe, William. 1960. *Sign Language Structure: An Outline of the Visual Communication System of the American Deaf.* Silver Springs, MD: Linstok Press.

Von Frisch, K. 1967. *The Dance Language and Orientation of Bees,* trans. by L. E. Chadwick. Cambridge, MA: Belknap Press of Harvard University Press.

EXERCISES

1. An English speaker's knowledge includes the sound sequences of the language. When new products are put on the market, the manufacturers have to think up new names for them that conform to the allowable sound patterns. Suppose you were hired by a manufacturer of soap products to name five new products. What names might you come up with? List them.

   We are interested not in the spelling of the words but in how they are pronounced. Therefore, describe in any way you can how the words you list should be pronounced. Suppose, for example, you named one detergent *Blick.* You could describe the sounds in any of the following ways:

   bl as in *blood,*
   i as in *pit,*
   ck as in *stick*

   bli as in *bliss,*
   ck as in *tick*

   b as in *boy,*
   lick as in *lick*

2. Consider the following sentences. Put a star (*) after those that do not seem to conform to the rules of your grammar, that are ungrammatical for you. State, if you can, why you think the sentence is ungrammatical.

   a. Robin forced the sheriff go.

   b. Napoleon forced Josephine to go.

   c. The Devil made Faust go.

   d. He passed by a large sum of money.

   e. He came by a large sum of money.

   f. He came a large sum of money by.

   g. Did in a corner little Jack Horner sit?

   h. Elizabeth is resembled by Charles.

   i. Nancy is eager to please.

   j. It is easy to frighten Emily.

   k. It is eager to love a kitten.

   l. That birds can fly amazes.

   m. The fact that you are late to class is surprising.

   n. Has the nurse slept the baby yet?

   o. I was surprised for you to get married.

   p. I wonder who and Mary went swimming.

   q. Myself bit John.

   r. What did Alice eat the toadstool with?

   s. What did Alice eat the toadstool and?

3. It was pointed out in this chapter that a small set of words in languages may be onomatopoeic; that is, their sounds "imitate" what they refer to. *Ding-dong, tick-tock, bang, zing, swish,* and *plop* are such words in English. Construct a list of ten new words. Test them on at least five friends to see if they are truly nonarbitrary as to sound and meaning.

4. Although sounds and meanings of most words in all languages are arbitrarily related, there are some communication systems in which the "signs" unambiguously reveal their "meaning."

   a. Describe (or draw) five different signs that directly show what they mean. Example: a road sign indicating an S curve.

   b. Describe any other communication system that, like language, consists of arbitrary symbols. Example: traffic signals, where red means stop and green means go.

5. Consider these two statements: I learned a new word today. I learned a new sentence today. Do you think the two statements are equally probable, and if not, why not?

6. What do the barking of dogs, the meowing of cats, and the singing of birds have in common with human language? What are some of the basic differences?

7. A wolf is able to express subtle gradations of emotion by different positions of the ears, the lips, and the tail. There are eleven postures of the tail that express such emotions as self-confidence, confident threat, lack of tension, uncertain threat, depression, defensiveness, active submission, and complete submission. This system seems to be complex. Suppose there were a thousand different emotions that the wolf could express in this way. Would you then say a wolf had a language similar to a human's? If not, why not?

8. Suppose you taught a dog to *heel, sit up, beg, roll over, play dead, stay, jump,* and *bark* on command, using the italicized words as cues. Would you be teaching it language? Why or why not?

9. State some rule of grammar that you have learned is the correct way to say something, but that you do not generally use in speaking. For example, you may have heard that *It's me* is incorrect and that the correct form is *It's I.* Nevertheless you always use *me* in such sentences; your friends do also, and in fact, *It's I* sounds odd to you.

   Write a short essay presenting arguments against someone who tells you that you are wrong. Discuss how this disagreement demonstrates the difference between descriptive and prescriptive grammars.

Chapter 2
Brain and Language

The functional asymmetry of the human brain is unequivocal, and so is its anatomical asymmetry. The structural differences between the left and the right hemispheres are visible not only under the microscope but to the naked eye. The most striking asymmetries occur in language-related cortices. It is tempting to assume that such anatomical differences are an index of the neurobiological underpinnings of language.

Antonio and Hanna Damasio, University of Iowa, School of Medicine, Department of Neurology

[The brain is] the messenger of the understanding [and the organ whereby] in an especial manner we acquire wisdom and knowledge.

Hippocratic Treatise on the Sacred Disease, c. 377 B.C.E.

The attempts to understand the complexities of human cognitive abilities and especially the acquisition and use of language are as old and as continuous as history. Three long-standing problems of science include: the nature of the brain, the nature of human language, and the relationship between the two. The view that the brain is the source of human language and cognition goes back over 2000 years. Assyrian and Babylonian cuneiform tablets mention disorders of intelligence that may develop "when man's brain holds fire." Egyptian doctors in 1700 B.C.E. noted in their papyrus records that "the breath of an outside god" had entered their patients who became "silent in sadness." The philosophers of ancient Greece also speculated about the brain/mind relationship but neither Plato nor Aristotle recognized the brain's crucial function in cognition or language. Aristotle's wisdom failed him when he suggested that the brain is a cold sponge whose function is to cool the blood. But others writing in the same period showed greater insight, as shown by the Hippocratic treatises dealing with epilepsy quoted above.

A major approach in the study of the brain/mind relationship has been through an investigation of language. Research on the brain in humans and nonhuman primates, anatomically, psychologically, and behaviorally, is, for similar reasons, helping to answer the questions concerning the neurological basis for language. The study concerned with the biological and neural foundations of language is called **neurolinguistics.**

THE HUMAN BRAIN

"Rabbit's clever," said Pooh thoughtfully.
"Yes," said Piglet, "Rabbit's clever."
"And he has Brain."
"Yes," said Piglet, "Rabbit has Brain."
There was a long silence.
"I suppose," said Pooh, "that that's why he never understands anything."

A. A. Milne, *The House at Pooh Corner*[1]

We have learned a great deal about the brain—the most complicated organ of the body—in the last two millennia. It lies under the skull and consists of approximately ten billion nerve cells (neurons) and billions of fibers that interconnect them. The neurons or gray matter form the **cortex,** the surface of the brain, under which is the white matter, which consists primarily of connecting fibers. The cortex is the decision-making organ of the body. It receives messages from all the sensory organs, and it initiates all voluntary actions. It is "the seat of all which is exclusively human in the mind" and the storehouse of "memory." Somewhere in this gray matter the grammar that represents our knowledge of language resides.

FIGURE 2-1   3-D reconstruction of the normal living human brain. The images were obtained from magnetic resonance data using the Brainvox technique. Left panel = view from the top. Right panel = view from the front following virtual coronal section at the level of the dashed line. (Courtesy Hanna Damasio)

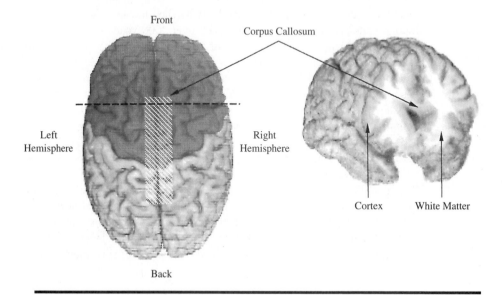

Front

Corpus Callosum

Left
Hemisphere

Right
Hemisphere

Cortex   White Matter

Back

[1] A. A. Milne. 1928. *House at Pooh Corner,* New York: E. P. Dutton.

The brain is divided into two parts (called **cerebral hemispheres**), one on the right and one on the left. These hemispheres are connected like conjoined twins right down the middle, by the **corpus callosum.** This "freeway" between the two brain halves consists of two million fibers connecting the cells of the left and right hemispheres, as shown in Figure 2-1.

In general, the left hemisphere controls the movements of the right side of the body, and the right hemisphere the movements of the left side. If you point with your right hand, it is the left hemisphere which has "directed" your action. This is referred to as **contralateral** brain function.

The Modularity of the Brain

PEANUTS reprinted by permission of UFS, Inc.

It only takes one hemisphere to have a mind.

A. W. Wigan, 1844

Since the middle of the nineteenth century, there has been a basic assumption that it is possible to find a direct relation between language and the brain, and a continuous effort to discover direct centers where language capacities (competence and performance) may be localized.

In the early part of the nineteenth century Franz Joseph Gall put forth theories of **localization,** that is, that different human abilities and behaviors were traceable to specific parts of the brain. Some of Gall's views are amusing when looked at from our present state of knowledge. For example, he suggested that the frontal lobes of the brain were the locations of language because when he was young he had noticed that the most articulate and intelligent of his fellow students had protruding eyes, which he believed reflected overdeveloped brain material. He also put forth a pseudoscientific theory called "organology" that later came to be known as **phrenology,** the practice of determining personality traits, intellectual capacities and other matters by examination of the "bumps" on the skull. A disciple of Gall's, Johann Spurzheim, introduced phrenology to America, constructing elaborate maps and skull models such as the one shown in Figure 2-2, in which language is located directly under the eye.

FIGURE 2-2   Phrenology skull model.

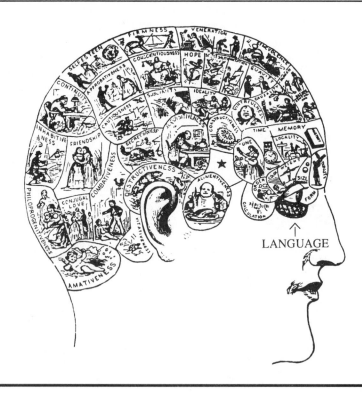

LANGUAGE

Although phrenology has long been discarded as a scientific theory—except for a few remaining adherents like a current writer who refers to herself as "a practicing witch"—Gall's view that the brain is not a uniform mass and that linguistic capacities are functions of localized brain areas has been upheld. Gall was in fact a pioneer and a courageous scientist in arguing against the prevailing view that the brain was an unstructured organ. He instead argued in favor of **modularity,** with the brain divided into distinct anatomical faculties (referred to as cortical organs) that were directly responsible for specific cognitive functions, including language.

Language was the first distinct cognitive module to be supported by scientific evidence. In 1861, Paul Broca specifically related language to the left side of the brain. At a scientific meeting in Paris, he stated that we speak with the left hemisphere on the basis of his finding that damage to the front part of the left hemisphere (now called **Broca's area**) resulted in loss of speech, whereas damage to the right side did not.[2] He

---

[2] Broca, though a major figure in the history of neuroscience, held extremely racist and sexist views based on incorrect measurements of the brains of men and women and different races. His false view correlating brain size with intelligence is thoroughly demolished by Stephen Jay Gould (1981) in *The Mismeasure of Man,* New York: W. W. Norton.

determined this by autopsy investigations after the death of patients with language deficits following brain injury. Language, then, is said to be **lateralized,** the term used to refer to any cognitive functions which are primarily localized to one side of the brain or the other.

Today, patients with such damage or lesions in Broca's area are said to have **Broca's aphasia. Aphasia** is the neurological term used to refer to language disorders that follow brain lesions caused by a stroke, a tumor, a gunshot wound, other traumas, or an infection. The speech output of many Broca's aphasia patients is characterized by labored speech, word-finding pauses, loss of "function" words, and quite often, disturbed word order. Auditory comprehension for colloquial conversation gives the impression of being generally good although controlled testing reveals considerable impairments when comprehension depends on the syntactic structure, that is, how words are combined into phrases and sentences.

Thousands of years before Broca, the relation between the left hemisphere and language was intuitively recognized. In the 135th Psalm, there is an implicit recognition of the role of the left brain in speech (although contralateral brain function was of course not understood) in the verse that states: "If I will forget thee, Jerusalem, let my right hand die—let my tongue stick to the roof of my mouth."

The Hippocratic physicians, mentioned above, also reported that loss of speech often occurred simultaneously with paralysis of the right side of the body. But it was Broca whose name is most closely associated with the left lateralization of language.

In 1874, thirteen years after Broca's Paris paper, Carl Wernicke presented a paper that described also on the basis of autopsy studies another variety of aphasia shown by patients with lesions in the back portion of the left hemisphere. Unlike Broca's patients, Wernicke's spoke fluently with good intonation and pronunciation, but with numerous instances of lexical errors (word substitutions) often producing **jargon** and **nonsense words.** They also had difficulty in comprehending speech.

The area of the brain that, when damaged, seems to lead to these symptoms is now, not surprisingly, known as **Wernicke's area,** and the patients are said to suffer from **Wernicke's aphasia.** The view of the left side of the brain, as constructed by the neurologist Hanna Damasio, in Figure 2-3, shows Broca's and Wernicke's areas of the brain.

We no longer have to depend on surgical investigations of the brain or wait until patients die to determine where their brain lesions are. New technologies such as MRI

FIGURE 2-3   Lateral (external) view of the left hemisphere of the human brain, showing the position of Broca and Wernicke regions—two key areas of the cortex related to language processing.

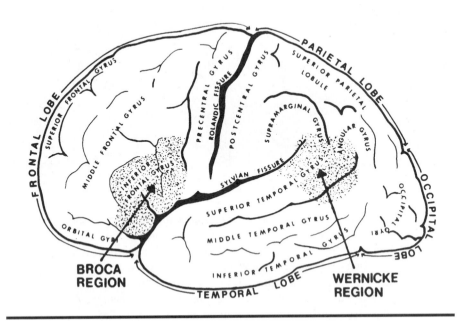

(an acronym for *Magnetic Resonance Imaging*) makes it possible to see where the sites of lesions are in the living brain. In addition, the new technique called PET (*Positron Emission Tomography*) has revolutionized the study of the brain, making it possible to detect changes in brain activities and relate these changes to focal brain damage and cognitive tasks. PET permits experimenters to look into a living normal brain and see what areas are affected when different stimuli are involved, since degrees of metabolic activity can be viewed and one can see what areas of the brain are more active than others dependent on the function being carried out. MRI and PET studies reaffirm the lateralization of language.

Figures 2-4 and 2-5 show the MRI scans of the brains of a Broca's aphasic and a Wernicke's aphasic patient. The black areas show the sites of the lesions. Each diagram represent a brain "slice."

There is now a consensus that the so-called higher mental functions are greatly lateralized. Research shows that though the nervous system is generally symmetrical— what exists on the left exists on the right and vice versa—the two sides of the brain form an exception.

Evidence from Childhood Brain Lesions

Children who have suffered prenatal, perinatal, or childhood brain lesions provide additional evidence that language is lateralized and that the brain is differentiated in regard to language and nonlanguage abilities.

FIGURE 2-4[3]   3-D reconstruction of the brain of a living patient with Broca's aphasia. Note area of damage in left frontal region (dark gray), which was caused by a stroke. (Courtesy Hanna Damasio)

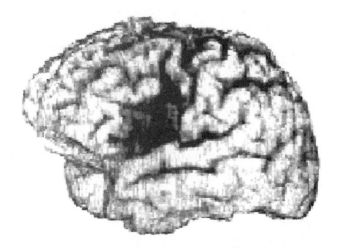

FIGURE 2-5[4]   3-D reconstruction of the brain of a living patient with Wernicke's aphasia. Note area of damage in left posterior temporal and lower parietal region (dark gray), which was caused by a stroke. (Courtesy Hanna Damasio)

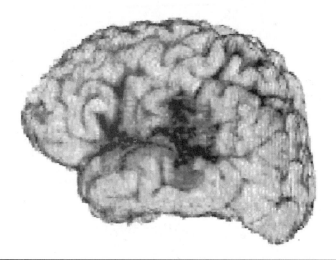

[3] Hanna and Antonio R. Damasio. 1989. *Lesion Analysis in Neuropsychology,* New York: Oxford University Press, p. 53.
[4] Ibid., p. 107.

Studies of **hemiplegic** children, those with acquired unilateral lesions of the brain who retain both hemispheres (one normal and one diseased), show differential cognitive abilities. Those with left damaged hemispheres show deficiency in language acquisition and performance with the greatest impairments in their syntactic ability, whereas children with right hemisphere lesions acquire language as do normal children.

There have also been studies of children with one hemisphere removed (called **hemidecorticates**) either within the first year of life or later in childhood. Although the IQ scores and cognitive skills proved to be equivalent no matter which hemisphere was removed, children whose left hemisphere was removed outperformed those with right hemisphere removal in visual and spatial abilities. In language, the right hemidecorticates (those with removal of the right hemisphere) surpassed the left hemidecorticates. Both hemispheres appear to be equivalent in the ability to acquire the meaning and referential structure of common words, but the ability to acquire the complex syntactic rules for sentence formation was impaired in left but not right hemidecorticates.

It appears that even from birth the human brain is lateralized to the left for language since language usually does not develop normally in children with early left hemisphere brain lesions.

Split Brains

"ROGER DOESN'T USE THE LEFT SIDE OF THE BRAIN OR THE RIGHT SIDE. HE JUST USES THE MIDDLE."

© S. Harris.

Aphasia studies and those of early childhood brain lesions provide good evidence that language is primarily processed in the left hemisphere. Other evidence is provided by mature patients who have one of the hemispheres removed. If the right hemisphere is cut out, language remains intact, although other cognitive losses may result. Because language is such an important aspect of our daily life, surgical removal of the left hemisphere is only performed in dire cases of malignant brain tumor.

Split-brain patients also provide evidence for language lateralization and for understanding brain functions. In recent years it was found that persons suffering from serious epilepsy could be treated by cutting the corpus callosum, the membrane connecting the two hemispheres, illustrated in Figure 2-1. When this pathway is split there is no communication between the "two brains."

The psychologist Michael Gazzaniga states:

> With [the corpus callosum] intact, the two halves of the body have no secrets from one another. With it sectioned, the two halves become two different conscious mental spheres, each with its own experience base and control system for behavioral operations. . . . Unbelievable as this may seem, this is the flavor of a long series of experimental studies first carried out in the cat and monkey.[5]

When the brain is split surgically, certain information from the left side of the body is received only by the right side of the brain and vice versa (because of the crisscross contralateral phenomenon discussed above). For example, suppose a monkey is trained to respond with its hands to a certain visual stimulus, such as a flashing light. If the brain is split after the training period, and the stimulus is shown only to the left visual field (the right brain), the monkey will perform only with the left hand, and vice versa. Many such experiments have been done on animals. They all show the independence of the two sides of the brain.

Persons with split brains have been tested by psychologists, showing that, like the monkey brain, the two human hemispheres are distinct. However, these tests showed that messages sent to the two sides of the brain result in different responses, depending on which hemisphere receives the message. As noted earlier, sensory information is received in the contralateral, opposite, side of the brain from the side of the body from which it is sent. In a split-brain patient, the information in the right hemisphere cannot get access to the left hemisphere. If an apple is put in the left hand of a split-brain human whose vision is cut off, the person can use it appropriately but cannot name it. The right brain senses the apple and distinguishes it from other objects, but the information cannot be relayed to the left brain for linguistic naming. By contrast, if a banana is placed in the right hand, the subject is immediately able to name it as well as to describe it.

Various experiments of this sort have been performed, all providing information on the different capabilities of the "two brains." The right brain does better than the left in pattern-matching tasks, in recognizing faces, and in spatial orientation. The left hemisphere is superior for language, for rhythmic perception, for temporal-order judgments, and for mathematical thinking. According to Gazzaniga, "the right hemisphere as well as the left hemisphere can emote and while the left can tell you why, the right cannot."

---

[5] Michael Gazzaniga. 1970. *The Bisected Brain,* New York: Appleton-Century-Crofts.

Studies of human split-brain patients have shown that when the interhemispheric visual connections are severed, visual information from the right and left visual fields becomes confined to the left and right hemispheres respectively. Because of the crucial endowment of the left hemisphere for language, written material delivered to the right hemisphere cannot be read if the brain is split, because the information cannot be transferred to the left hemisphere.

An image or picture that is flashed to the right visual field of a split-brain patient (and is therefore processed by the left hemisphere) can be named. However, when the picture is flashed in the left visual field and lands in the right hemisphere, it cannot be named.

More Experimental Evidence

Since Broca's proposal that "we speak with the left hemisphere," evidence to support the left lateralization of language continues to grow. All the early research involved brain-damaged patients. As mentioned earlier, in the last few decades new technologies like PET and MRI and also *functional MRI or f* MRI permit us to explore the specialized capabilities of the two hemispheres in normal individuals, as well as brain-damaged patients. Another experimental technique that has been used with normal subjects, called **dichotic listening,** uses auditory signals. Subjects hear two different sound signals simultaneously through earphones. For example, a subject may hear *boy* in one ear and *girl* in the other, or *crocodile* in one ear and *alligator* in the other; or the subject may hear a horn tooting in one ear and rushing water in the other. When asked to state what they heard in each ear, subjects are more frequently correct in reporting linguistic stimuli (words, nonsense syllables, and so on) delivered directly to the right ear but are more frequently correct in reporting nonverbal stimuli (musical chords, environmental sounds, and so on) delivered to the left ear. That is, if subjects hear *boy* in the right ear and *girl* in the left ear, they are more likely to report the word heard in the right ear correctly. If they hear coughing in the right ear and laughing in the left, they are more apt to report the laughing stimulus correctly. The same acoustic signal may be processed in one hemisphere or the other depending on whether the subjects perceive it as part of their language system or not. Thai speakers show a right ear advantage (left hemisphere) in distinguishing between syllables that contrast in tone (pitch contours); Thai is a tone language in which such syllables pronounced with different pitch are words with different meanings. English subjects do not show the right ear advantage when they hear the same stimuli, because English is not a tone language.

Both hemispheres receive signals from both ears, but the contralateral stimuli compete successfully with the "same side" **ipsilateral** stimuli (right to right and left to left), either because they are received earlier, or because they are not weakened by having to cross the corpus callosum. The fact that the left hemisphere has an edge in linguistic processing and the right hemisphere is better at nonverbal material determines the accuracy with which subjects report on what they have heard.

These experiments are important not only because they show that language is lateralized but also because they show that the left hemisphere is not superior for processing all sounds, but only for those that are linguistic in nature. That is, the left side of the brain is specialized for language, not sounds.

Other experimental techniques are also being used to map the brain and to investigate the independence of different aspects of language and the extent of the independence of language from other cognitive systems. Even before the spectacular new technologies were introduced in the 1970s, researchers were taping electrodes to different areas of the skull and investigating the electrical activity of the brain. In such experiments the electrical signals emitted from the brain in response to different kinds of stimuli (called **event related brain potentials** or **ERPs**) are measured. For example, electrical differences may result when the subject hears speech sounds and nonspeech sounds. One study showed electrical potential differences in timing and area of response when subjects heard sentences that were meaningless, such as

*The man admired Don's headache of the landscape.[6]

as opposed to meaningful sentences like:

The man admired Don's sketch of the landscape.

These experiments show that neuronal activity in different locations varies with different stimuli and different tasks.

The results of these studies, using different techniques and diverse subjects, both normal and brain damaged, are converging to provide the information we seek on the relationship between the brain and various language and nonlanguage cognitive systems.

More Evidence for Modularity

> . . . the human mind is not an unstructured entity but consists of components which can be distinguished by their functional properties.
>
> Neil Smith and Ianthi-Maria Tsimpli. 1995. *The Mind of a Savant.* Oxford: Blackwell's.

Although neurolinguistics is still in its infancy, our understanding has progressed a great deal since a day in September 1848, when a foreman of a road construction gang named Phineas Gage became a famous figure in medical history. He achieved his "immortality" when a four-foot-long iron rod was blown through his head. Despite the gaping tunnel in his brain, Gage maintained the ability to speak and understand and retained whatever intellectual abilities he had prior to the injury, although he suffered major changes in his personality (he became "cranky" and "inconsiderate"), in his sexual behavior, and in his ability to control his emotions or make plans. Both Gage and science benefited from this explosion. Phineas gained monetarily by becoming a one-man touring circus; he traveled all over the country charging money to those curious enough to see him and the iron rod. Nevertheless, he died penniless twelve years after the accident. Science benefited because brain researchers were stimulated to learn why his intelligence remained intact.

No autopsy was performed when Gage died in 1861 (the year Broca delivered his seminal paper). Dr. John Harlowe, the doctor first called after Gage's accident,

---

[6] The asterisk, *, shows that there is something unacceptable about the sentence as discussed in Chapter 1.

convinced Gage's sister that his body should be exhumed and his skull preserved for science. This was done and the skull and the iron bar have been kept in the Harvard Medical School since that time. Dr. Harlowe did indeed contribute to scientific knowledge in this way. Approximately one hundred and thirty years after the exhumation, Dr. Hanna Damasio, a neurologist at the University of Iowa School of Medicine, using the most advanced neuro-imaging techniques and a computer program called Brainvox was able to reconstruct Gage's brain showing the area through which the bar had traveled and the hole it had left. She was able to show unequivocally that the damage was neither to the motor area nor the language areas of the brain, but to that section called the prefrontal cortices.[7] Furthermore, Dr. Antonio Damasio and his colleagues have further shown that patients with damage to this area show the same kind of personality changes as did Gage.[8]

That damage to some parts of the brain results in language loss whereas damage to other parts of the brain shows intact language with other kinds of deficits supports Gall's view of a structured brain with separate faculties.

Aphasia

In the discussion above, we saw that aphasia has been an important area of research in the attempts to understand the relation between brain and language. The interest in aphasia did not start with Broca. In the New Testament, St. Luke reports that Zacharias could not speak but could write, showing the early recognition of the autonomy of different aspects of linguistic knowledge. And in 30 B.C.E. the Roman writer Valerius Maximus describes an Athenian who was unable to remember his "letters" after being hit in the head with a stone. Pliny, who lived from 23 to 79 C.E., also refers to this same Athenian, noting that "with the stroke of a stone, he fell presently to forget his letters only, and could read no more; otherwise his memory served him well enough."

Numerous clinical descriptions of patients with language deficits and preserved nonlinguistic cognitive systems were published from the fifteenth to the eighteenth century. Johanne Gesner in 1770 did not attribute these language difficulties to either general intellectual deficits or loss of memory in general but instead to a specific impairment to language memory, stating: "Just as some verbal powers can become weakened without injury to others, memory also can be specifically impaired to a greater or lesser degree with respect to only certain classes of ideas."

Other reports describe patients suffering from acquired dyslexia (loss of ability to read) who nevertheless preserved their ability to write, and patients who could write to dictation but could not read back what they had written.

Carl Linnaeus in 1745 published a case study of a man suffering from **jargon aphasia,** who spoke "as it were a foreign language, having his own names for all words." An important observation regarding word substitution errors was made by Ryklof Michel von Goens in 1789 in his reference to a patient whom he described as follows: "After an illness, she was suddenly afflicted with a forgetting, or, rather, an incapacity or

[7] H. Damasio, T. Grabowski, R. Frank, A. M. Galaburda, and A. R. Damasio. 1994. "The Return of Phineas Gage: The Skull of a Famous Patient Yields Clues about the Brain," *Science* 264: 1102–05.

[8] Antonio R. Damasio. 1994. *Descartes' Error: Emotion, Reason, and the Human Brain,* New York: Avon Books.

confusion of speech. . . . If she desired a chair, she would ask for a table. . . . Sometimes she herself perceived that she misnamed objects; at other times, she was annoyed when a *fan*, which she had asked for, was brought to her, instead of the *bonnet*, which she thought she had requested."

The description of this and other similarly afflicted patients reveals that they substituted words that were semantically or phonologically similar to the intended ones, producing errors similar to normal word substitution errors or to those produced by the patient who called Ronald Reagan "John Wayne."

Other kinds of linguistic breakdown were also described in detail. In 1770 Johann Gesner discussed bilingual asymmetry in which, for example, an abbot retained his ability following brain damage to read Latin but not German.

Such detailed historical descriptions of language loss following brain damage, together with the controlled scientific studies of aphasia that have been conducted in the last fifty years, provide unequivocal evidence that language is predominantly and most frequently a left-hemisphere function. In the great majority of cases, lesions to the left hemisphere result in aphasia but injuries to the right do not (although such lesions result in perceptual difficulties, defects in pattern recognition, and other cognitive deficits). If both hemispheres were equally involved with language this should not be the case.[9]

The language impairments suffered by aphasics are not due to any general cognitive or intellectual impairments. Nor are they due to loss of motor or sensory controls of the nerves and muscles of the speech organs or hearing apparatus. Aphasics can produce sounds and hear sounds. Whatever loss they suffer has to do only with the production or comprehension of language (or specific parts of the grammar).

This is dramatically shown by the fact that deaf signers with damage to the left hemisphere show aphasia for sign language similar to the language breakdown in hearing aphasics. Bellugi and her colleagues at the Salk Institute have found that deaf patients with lesions in Broca's area show language deficits similar to those found in hearing patients—severe dysfluent, agrammatic sign production.[10] While deaf aphasic patients show marked sign language deficits, they have no difficulty in processing nonlinguistic visual spatial relationships, just as hearing aphasics have no problem with processing nonlinguistic auditory stimuli. Thus, the left hemisphere is not lateralized for hearing or speech, but for language.

As shown by the different symptoms of Broca's and Wernicke's aphasias, many aphasics do not show total language loss. Rather, different aspects of language are impaired. Broca's aphasics are often referred to as **agrammatic** because of their particular problems with syntax—putting words together to form phrases and clauses and sentences—as the following sample of the speech of an agrammatic patient with damage to Broca's area illustrates. The patient was asked what brought him back to the hospital and answered:

> Yes—ah—Monday ah—Dad—and Dad—ah—Hospital—and ah—
> Wednesday—Wednesday—nine o'clock and ah Thursday—ten o'clock ah

---

[9] For some people—about a third of all left-handers—there is still lateralization, yet it is the right side that is specialized for language. In other words, the special functions are switched, but asymmetry still exists.

[10] H. Poizner, E. Klima, and U. Bellugi. 1987. *What the Hands Reveal about the Brain,* Cambridge, MA: MIT Press.

doctors—two—two—ah doctors and—ah—teeth—yah. And a doctor—ah girl—and gums, and I.[11]

As this patient illustrates, agrammatic aphasics produce ungrammatical utterances, frequently omitting function words like *a* or *the* or *was* and parts of words like the past tense suffix *-ed*. They also have difficulty in interpreting sentences correctly when comprehension depends on syntactic structure. Thus, they have a problem with determining "who did what to whom" in sentences such as:

(a) The cat was chased by the dog

where either the subject or the object of the sentence can logically be doing the chasing since in real life cats and dogs can chase each other. But they have less difficulty with

(b) The car was chased by the dog

where the meaning of the sentence is provided by nonlinguistic knowledge. They know that cars do not under normal circumstances chase dogs and so use that knowledge to interpret the sentence, whereas in the first sentence the interpretation depends on knowledge of the English passive construction. Normal speakers will have no difficulty because they use their knowledge of syntax—of the fact that a *by* phrase shows a passive construction in which the subject of the sentence is acted upon by the noun following the *by*.

Wernicke's aphasics, on the other hand, produce fluent, but often unintelligible speech, have serious comprehension problems and difficulty in lexical selection. One patient replied to a question about his health with:

I felt worse because I can no longer keep in mind from the mind of the minds to keep me from mind and up to the ear which can be to find among ourselves.

Some aphasics have difficulty in naming objects that are presented to them, which shows a lexical defect. Others produce semantically meaningless jargon such as the patient who described a fork as "a need for a schedule"; another, when asked about his poor vision said "My wires don't hire right." While some of these aphasics substitute words that bear no semantic relationship to the correct word, such as calling a chair an engine, others substitute words which, like normal speech errors, are related semantically, substituting for example, *table* for *chair* or *boy* for *girl*.

Another kind of aphasia called **jargon aphasia** results in the substitution of one sound for another. Patients with Wernicke's aphasia often produce such jargon. Thus *table* might be pronounced as *sable*. An extreme variety of phonemic jargon results in the production of nonsense forms—nonoccurring but possible words. One patient, a physician prior to his aphasia, when asked if he was a doctor, replied:

Me? Yes sir. I'm a male demaploze on my own. I still know my tubaboys what for I have that's gone hell and some of them go.

---

[11] Harold Goodglass. 1973. "Studies on the Grammar of Aphasics," in *Psycholinguistics and Aphasia,* Goodglass and S. Blumstein, eds., Baltimore, MD: John Hopkins University Press.

The kinds of language impairments found in aphasics provide information on the nature of the grammar. If we find that damage to different parts of the brain leads to impairment of different components of the grammar, this is good evidence to support the models proposed by linguistics.

Patients that produce long strings of jargon that sound like well-formed grammatical language but that are uninterpretable show that knowledge of the sound sequences by which we represent words in our mental dictionaries can be disassociated from their meanings. That is, we may look at a picture, know what it is, but be unable to produce the string of sounds that relates to the concept.

The substitution of semantically related words provides evidence as to the organization of our mental dictionaries. The aphasics' errors are similar to word substitution errors of normals in that the substituted words are not just randomly selected but are similar to the intended words either in their sounds or in their meanings. Some of the most interesting examples of such substitutions are produced by aphasic patients who become dyslexic after brain damage. They are called **acquired dyslexics** because prior to the brain lesion they were normal readers (unlike developmental dyslexics who have difficulty learning to read). One group of these patients, when reading aloud words printed on cards, produced the kinds of substitutions shown in the following examples.[12]

Stimulus	Response 1	Response 2
act	*play*	*play*
applaud	*laugh*	*cheers*
example	*answer*	*sum*
heal	*pain*	*medicine*
south	*west*	*east*

Note that these patients did not always substitute the same words in two different testing periods. In fact, at times they would read the correct word, showing that the problem was in performance (accessing the correct form in the lexicon) not in competence, since they could sometimes get to the right word and produce it.

The substitution of phonologically similar words, such as *pool* for *tool* or *crucial* for *crucible,* also provides information on the organization of the lexicon. Words in the lexicon seem to be connected to other words by both phonology and semantics. Words are not simply represented in one list, but in a network of connections.

The difference between word classes that constitute different parts of speech is revealed in aphasia cases by the omission of function words[13] in the speech of Broca's aphasics and in some cases of acquired dyslexia. Patient G. R., who produced the semantically similar word substitutions cited above, was unable to read these function words at all; when presented with words like *which* or *would,* he just said, "No" or "I hate those little words"; but he can read, though with many semantic mistakes, as shown in the following reading errors.

---

[12] Patient G. R., as reported in F. Newcombe and J. Marshall. 1984. "Varieties of Acquired Dyslexia: A Linguistic Approach," *Seminars in Neurology* 4, no. 2: 181–195.

[13] Function words and word endings like the *s* that forms plurals or the *ed* that forms past tense are called grammatical morphemes and will be discussed in Chapter 3.

Stimulus	Response	Stimulus	Response
witch	*witch*	which	*no!*
bean	*soup*	been	*no!*
hour	*time*	our	*no!*
eye	*eyes*	I	*no!*
hymn	*bible*	him	*no!*
wood	*wood*	would	*no!*

These errors suggest that the mental dictionary in our brains is divided into parts, one consisting of major content words and the other of grammatical words. Furthermore, it suggests that these two classes of words are processed in different areas or by different neural mechanisms, further supporting the view that the brain is structured in a complex fashion. One can think of the grammar as a mental module in the brain with submodular parts.

Most of us have experienced word-finding difficulties in speaking if not in reading, as Alice did when she said:

> "And now, who am I? I will remember, if I can. I'm determined to do it!" But being determined didn't help her much, and all she could say, after a great deal of puzzling, was "L, I know it begins with L."

This **"tip-of-the-tongue"** (**TOT** as it is often referred to) phenomenon is not uncommon. But if you never can find the word you want, you can imagine how serious a problem aphasics have. Aphasics with such problems are said to suffer from **anomia.**

Distinct Categories of Conceptual Knowledge

Dramatic evidence for a differentiated and structured brain is provided by studies of both normal individuals and patients with lesions in other than Broca's and Wernicke's areas. Some patients have difficulty naming individuals (unique persons); others have problems with naming animals, and still others cannot name tools. The patients in each group have brain lesions in separate and distinct regions of the left temporal lobe. Through use of MRI techniques the exact shape and location of the brain lesions of these patients were located. No overlap in the lesion sites in the three groups was found. In a follow-up study of normal subjects in a PET word-retrieval experiment, the experimenters at the University of Iowa found differential activation when asked to name persons, animals, or tools of just those sites damaged in the lesion patients.[14] Further evidence for the separation of cognitive systems is provided by the neurological and behavioral findings that following brain damage some patients lose the ability to recognize sounds or colors or familiar faces while retaining all other perceptual abilities. A patient may not be able to recognize his wife when she walks in the room until she starts to talk; then he will know who she is.

---

[14] H. Damasio, T. J. Grabowski., D. Tranel, R. D. Hichwa, and A. R. Damasio. 1996. "A Neural Basis for Lexical Retrieval," *Nature* 380 (11, April): 499–505.

THE AUTONOMY OF LANGUAGE

In addition to brain-damaged individuals who had acquired and lost language, there are cases of children (without brain lesions) who have difficulties in acquiring language or are much slower than the average child. These children show no other cognitive deficits; they are not autistic or retarded and have no perceptual problems. They are said to be suffering from a **Specific Language Impairment (SLI).** It is only their linguistic ability that is affected.

As children with SLI show, language may be impaired with general intelligence intact. But can language develop normally with general intelligence impaired? If such individuals can be found, it argues strongly for the view that language does not derive from some general cognitive ability. The question as to whether the language faculty from birth is domain specific—is in our genes—or whether it is derivative of more general intelligence is a controversial question receiving much attention and debate among linguists, psychologists, and neuropsychologists. There is a growing body of evidence to support the view that the human animal is biologically equipped from birth with an autonomous language faculty that itself is highly specific and that does not derive from the human general intellectual ability.

Asymmetry of Abilities

The psychological literature documents numerous cases of intellectually handicapped individuals who, despite their disabilities in certain spheres, show remarkable talents in others. The classic cases include individuals who are superb musicians or artists or draftsmen but lack the simple abilities required to take care of themselves. These people were traditionally known as "idiot savants" but now, fortunately, are generally referred to simply as **savants.** Some of the most famous savants are human calculators who can perform complex arithmetic processes at phenomenal speed, or calendrical calculators who can tell you almost instantaneously on which day of the week falls any date in the last or next century.

Until recently, most of the savants have been reported to be linguistically handicapped. They may be good mimics who can repeat speech like parrots but show meager creative language ability.

While such cases strongly argue for domain specific abilities and suggest that certain talents do not require general intelligence, they do not decisively respond to the suggestion that language is one ability that is derivative of general cognitive abilities.

The more recent literature is now reporting on cases of language savants who have acquired the highly complex grammar of their language (as well as other languages in some cases) without parallel nonlinguistic abilities of equal complexity.

Laura

Jeni Yamada[15] has studied one severely retarded young woman, named Laura, with a nonverbal IQ of 41–44. Laura lacks almost all number concepts including basic

---

[15] Jeni E. Yamada. 1990. *Laura: A Case for the Modularity of Language,* Cambridge, MA: Bradford Books, MIT Press.

counting principles, can draw only at a preschool level, and has an auditory memory span limited to three units. Yet, when at the age of sixteen she was asked to name some fruits, she responded with *pears*, *apples*, and *pomegranates*, and in this same period produced syntactically complex sentences like *He was saying that I lost my battery powered watch that I loved; I just loved that watch* or *Last year at school when I first went there, three tickets were gave out by a police last year.*

Laura cannot add 2 + 2. She is not sure of when "last year" is or whether it is before or after "last week" or "an hour ago," nor does she know how many tickets were "gave out" nor whether three is larger or smaller than two. Although Laura produces sentences with multiple embeddings; can conjoin verb phrases, produce passives, inflect verbs for number and person to agree with the grammatical subject; and forms past tenses when the time adverbial structurally refers to a previous time, she can neither read nor write nor tell time. She does not know who the president of the United States is or what country she lives in or even her own age. Her drawings of humans resemble potatoes with stick arms and legs. Yet, in a sentence imitation task she both detected and corrected surface syntactic and morphological errors.

Laura is but one of many examples of children who display well-developed phonological, morphological, and syntactic linguistic abilities; seemingly less-developed lexical, semantic, or referential aspects of language; and severe deficits in nonlinguistic cognitive development.

In addition, any notion that linguistic ability results simply from communicative abilities or develops to serve communication functions is also negated by studies of children with fully developed structural linguistic knowledge but with almost a total absence of pragmatic or communicative skills. The ability to communicate in a social setting seems to depend on different cognitive skills than the acquisition of language.

Christopher

Another dramatic case of a linguistic savant named Christopher[16] has been reported. Christopher has a nonverbal IQ between 60 and 70 and is institutionalized because he is unable to take care of himself. Christopher finds the tasks of buttoning a shirt, cutting his fingernails, or vacuuming the carpet too difficult. According to the detailed investigation of Christopher, his "linguistic competence in his first language is as rich and as sophisticated as that of any native speaker." Furthermore, when given written texts in some fifteen to twenty languages, he translates them immediately into English. The languages include Germanic languages like Danish, Dutch, and German; Romance languages like French, Italian, Portuguese, and Spanish; as well as Polish, Finnish, Greek, Hindi, Turkish, and Welsh. He learned them either from speakers who used the languages in his presence or from grammar books. The investigators of this interesting man conclude that his linguistic ability is independent of his general conceptual or intellectual ability.

---

[16] Neil Smith and Ianthi-Maria Tsimpli. 1995. *The Mind of a Savant: Language Learning and Modularity,* Oxford, England: Blackwell's.

Such cases argue against the view that linguistic ability derives from general intelligence, since in these cases language develops against a background of deficits in nonlinguistic intellectual abilities.

Genetic Evidence for Language Autonomy

Studies of genetic disorders also reveal that one cognitive domain can develop normally simultaneous with abnormal development in other domains. Children with Turner's syndrome (a chromosomal anomaly) reveal normal or advanced language simultaneous with serious nonlinguistic cognitive deficits. Similarly, the studies of the language development in children with Williams syndrome reveal a unique behavioral profile in which there appears to be a selective preservation of linguistic functions in the face of severe general cognitive deficits.

Thus evidence from aphasia, Specific Language Impairments, and other genetic disorders, along with the asymmetry of abilities as revealed in linguistic savants, supports the view of the language faculty as an autonomous, genetically determined, independent, brain (mind) module.

THE EVOLUTION OF LANGUAGE

As the voice was used more and more, the vocal organs would have been strengthened and perfected through the principle of the inherited effects of use; and this would have reacted on the power of speech. But the relation between the continued use of language and the development of the brain has no doubt been far more important. The mental powers in some early progenitor of man must have been more highly developed than in any existing ape, before even the most imperfect form of speech could have come into use.

Charles Darwin, *The Descent of Man*

If the human brain is structured and wired for the acquisition and use of language, how (and when) did this development occur? Two scholarly societies, the American Anthropological Association and the New York Academy of Sciences, held forums in 1974 and 1976 to review research on this question. It is not a new question, and seems to have arisen with the origin of the species.

In the Beginning: The Origin of Language

Nothing, no doubt, would be more interesting than to know from historical documents the exact process by which the first man began to lisp his first words, and thus to be rid for ever of all the theories on the origin of speech.

M. Muller, 1871

Drawing by Leo Cullum; © 1995 The New Yorker Magazine, Inc.

All religions and mythologies contain stories of language origin. Philosophers through the ages have argued the question. Scholarly works have been written on the subject. Prizes have been awarded for the "best answer" to this eternally perplexing problem. Theories of divine origin, evolutionary development, and language as a human invention have all been suggested.

The difficulties inherent in answering this question are immense. Anthropologists think that the species has existed for at least one million years, and perhaps for as long as five or six million years. But the earliest deciphered written records are barely six thousand years old, dating from the writings of the Sumerians of 4000 B.C.E. These records appear so late in the history of the development of language that they provide no clue to its origin.

For these reasons, scholars in the latter part of the nineteenth century, who were only interested in "hard science," ridiculed, ignored, and even banned discussions of language origin. In 1886, the Linguistic Society of Paris passed a resolution "outlawing" any papers concerned with this subject.

Despite the difficulty of finding scientific evidence, speculations on language origin have provided valuable insights into the nature and development of language, which prompted the learned scholar Otto Jespersen to state that "linguistic science cannot refrain forever from asking about the whence (and about the whither) of linguistic evolution." A brief look at some of these speculative notions will reveal this.

God's Gift to Mankind?

And out of the ground the Lord God formed every beast of the field, and every fowl of the air, and brought them unto Adam to see what he would call them; and whatsoever Adam called every living creature, that was the name thereof.

Genesis 2:19

According to Judeo-Christian beliefs, God gave Adam the power to name all things. Similar beliefs are found throughout the world. According to the Egyptians, the creator of speech was the god Thoth. Babylonians believed the language giver was the god Nabu, and the Hindus attributed our unique language ability to a female god; Brahma was the creator of the universe, but language was given to us by his wife, Sarasvati.

Belief in the divine origin of language is closely intertwined with the magical properties that have been associated with language and the spoken word. Children in all cultures utter "magic" words like *abracadabra* to ward off evil or bring good luck. Despite the childish jingle "Sticks and stones may break my bones, but names will never hurt me," name-calling is insulting, cause for legal punishment, and feared. In some cultures, when certain words are used, one is required to counter them by "knocking on wood."

In many religions only special languages may be used in prayers and rituals. The Hindu priests of the fifth century B.C.E. believed that the original pronunciations of Vedic Sanskrit had to be used. This led to important linguistic study, since their language had already changed greatly since the hymns of the Vedas had been written. The first linguist known to us is Panini, who, in the fourth century B.C.E., wrote a detailed grammar of Sanskrit in which the phonological rules revealed the earlier pronunciation for use in religious worship.

While myths and customs and superstitions do not tell us very much about language origin, they do tell us about the importance ascribed to language.

There is no way to prove or disprove the divine origin of language, just as one cannot argue scientifically for or against the existence of God.

The First Language

Imagine the Lord talking French! Aside from a few odd words in Hebrew, I took it completely for granted that God had never spoken anything but the most dignified English.

Clarence Day, *Life with Father*

Among the proponents of the divine origin theory a great interest arose in the language used by God, Adam, and Eve. For millennia, "scientific" experiments have reportedly been devised to verify particular theories of the first language. In the fifth century B.C.E. the Greek historian Herodotus reported that the Egyptian pharaoh Psammetichus (664–610 B.C.E.) sought to determine the most primitive "natural" language by experimental methods. The monarch was said to have placed two infants in an isolated mountain hut, to be cared for by a mute servant. The Pharaoh believed that without any linguistic input the children would develop their own language and would thus reveal the original tongue of man. Patiently the Egyptian waited for the children to become old enough to talk. According to the story, the first word uttered was *bekos,* the word for "bread" in Phrygian, the language spoken in a province of Phrygia in the northwest corner of what is now modern Turkey. This ancient language, which has long since died out, was thought, on the basis of this "experiment," to be the original language.

History is replete with other proposals. In the thirteenth century, the Holy Roman Emperor Frederick II of Hohenstaufen was said to have carried out a similar test, but the children died before they uttered a single word. James IV of Scotland (1473–1513), however, supposedly succeeded in replicating the experiment with the surprising results, according to legend, that the Scottish children "spak very guid Ebrew," providing "scientific evidence" that Hebrew was the language used in the Garden of Eden.

But J. G. Becanus in the sixteenth century argued that German must have been the primeval language, since God would have used the most perfect language. In 1830 the lexicographer Noah Webster asserted that the "proto-language" must have been Chaldee (Aramaic), the language spoken in Jerusalem during the time of Jesus. In 1887, Joseph Elkins maintained that "there is no other language which can be more reasonably assumed to be the speech first used in the world's gray morning than can Chinese."

The belief that all languages originated from a single source—the **monogenetic theory of language origin**—is not only found in the Tower of Babel story in Genesis, but also in a similar legend of the Toltecs, early inhabitants of Mexico, and in the myths of other peoples as well.

We are no further along today in discovering the original language (or languages) than was Psammetichus, given the obscurities of prehistory.

Human Invention or the Cries of Nature?

> Language was born in the courting days of mankind; the first utterances of speech I fancy to myself like something between the nightly love lyrics of puss upon the tiles and the melodious love songs of the nightingale.
>
> Otto Jespersen, *Language, Its Nature, Development and Origin*

The Greeks speculated about everything in the universe, including language. The earliest surviving linguistic treatise that deals with the origin and nature of language is Plato's *Cratylus.* A commonly held view among the classical Greeks, expressed by Socrates in this dialogue, was that at some ancient time there was a "legislator" who gave the correct, natural name to everything, and that words echoed the essence of their meanings.

Despite all the contrary evidence, the idea that the earliest form of language was imitative, or echoic, was proposed up to the twentieth century. Called the bow-wow theory, it claimed that a dog would be designated by the word *bow-wow* because of the sounds of his bark.

A parallel view states that language at first consisted of emotional ejaculations of pain, fear, surprise, pleasure, anger, and so on. This proposal that the earliest manifestations of language were "cries of nature" was proposed by Jean Jacques Rousseau in the middle of the eighteenth century.

Another hypothesis suggests that language arose out of the rhythmical grunts of men working together. A more charming view was suggested by Jespersen, who proposed that language derived from song as an expressive rather than a communicative need, with love being the greatest stimulus for language development.

Just as with the beliefs in a divine origin of language, these proposals are untestable.

The Development of Language in the Species

There is much interest today among biologists as well as linguists in the relationship between the development of language and the evolutionary development of the human species. There are those who view language ability as a difference in degree between humans and other primates—a continuity view—and those who see the onset of language ability as a qualitative leap—the discontinuity view. There are those on both sides of the "discontinuity" view who believe that language is species-specific.

In trying to understand the development of language, scholars past and present have debated the role played by the vocal tract and the ear. For example, it has been suggested that speech could not have developed in nonhuman primates because their vocal tracts were anatomically incapable of producing a large enough inventory of speech sounds. According to this hypothesis, the development of language is linked to the evolutionary development of the speech production and perception apparatus. This, of course, would be accompanied by changes in the brain and the nervous system toward greater complexity. Such a view implies that the languages of our human ancestors of millions of years ago may have been syntactically and phonologically simpler than any language known to us today. The notion "simpler," however, is left undefined. One suggestion is that this primeval language had a smaller inventory of sounds.

One evolutionary step must have resulted in the development of a vocal tract capable of producing the wide variety of sounds utilized by human language, as well as the mechanism for perceiving and distinguishing them. That this step is insufficient to explain the origin of language is evidenced by the existence of mynah birds and parrots, which have the ability to imitate human speech, but not the ability to acquire language.

More importantly, we know from the study of humans who are born deaf and learn sign languages that are used around them that the ability to hear speech sounds is not a necessary condition for the acquisition and use of language. In addition, the lateralization evidence from brain-damaged deaf signers discussed above shows that the brain is neurologically equipped to learn language rather than speech.

The ability to produce and hear a wide variety of sounds therefore appears to be neither necessary nor sufficient for the development of language in the human species.

A major step in the development of language most probably relates to evolutionary changes in the brain. One view of this is expressed by the MIT linguist Noam Chomsky:

> It could be that when the brain reached a certain level of complexity it simply automatically had certain properties because that's what happens when you pack 10^{10} neurons into something the size of a basketball.[17]

This is similar to the view expressed by the Harvard biologist Stephen Jay Gould:

---

[17] N. Chomsky. 1994. Video. The Human Language Series. Program Three. By Gene Searchinger.

The Darwinist model would say that language, like other complex organic systems, evolved step by step, each step being an adaptive solution. Yet language is such an integrated "all or none" system, it is hard to imagine it evolving that way. Perhaps the brain grew in size and became capable of all kinds of things which were not part of the original properties.[18]

Stephen Pinker, however, supports a more Darwinian natural selection development of what he calls "the language instinct":

All the evidence suggests that it is the precise wiring of the brain's microcircuity that makes language happen, not gross size, shape, or neuron packing.[19]

More research is clearly needed in the attempt to resolve this controversy. Another thing that is not yet clear is what role, if any, hemispheric lateralization played in language evolution. Lateralization certainly makes greater specialization possible. Research conducted with birds and monkeys, however, shows that lateralization is not unique to the human brain. Thus, while it may constitute a necessary step in the evolution of language, it is not a sufficient one.

While we do not yet have definitive answers to the origin of language in the brain of the human species, the search for these answers goes on and provides new insights into the nature of language and the nature of the human brain.

SUMMARY

The attempt to understand what makes human language acquisition and use possible has led to research on the brain-mind-language relationship. **Neurolinguistics** studies the brain mechanisms and anatomical structures underlying language representation and use.

The brain is the most complicated organ of the body, controlling motor and sensory activities and thought processes. Research conducted for over a century reveals that different parts of the brain control different body functions. The nerve cells that form the surface of the brain are called the **cortex,** which serves as the intellectual decision maker, receiving messages from the sensory organs and initiating all voluntary actions. The brain of all higher animals is divided into two parts called the **cerebral hemispheres,** which are connected by the **corpus callosum,** a pathway that permits the left and right hemispheres to communicate with each other.

Although each hemisphere appears to be a mirror image of the other, the left hemisphere controls the right hand, leg, visual field, and so on, and the right brain controls the left side of the body, which is referred to as **contralateral** control of functions. Despite the general symmetry of the human body, there is much evidence that the brain is asymmetric; the left and right hemispheres are specialized for different functions.

Evidence from **aphasia**—language dysfunction as a result of brain injuries—and from surgical removal of parts of the brain, electrical stimulation studies, emission

---

[18] S. J. Gould. 1994. Video. The Human Language Series. Program Three. By Gene Searchinger.

[19] S. Pinker. 1995. *The Language Instinct,* New York: Morrow.

tomography results, dichotic listening, and experiments measuring brain electrical activity show a lack of symmetry of function of the two hemispheres. These results are further supported by studies of split-brain patients, who, for medical reasons, have had the corpus callosum severed. In the past, the studies of the brain and language depended on surgery or autopsy. Today, new technologies such as **MRI (Magnetic Resonance Imaging)** and **PET (Positron Emission Tomography)** makes it possible to see the sites of lesions in the living brain to detect changes in brain activities and to relate these changes to focal brain damage and cognitive tasks.

For normal right-handers and many left-handers, the left side of the brain is specialized for language. This **lateralization** of functions is genetically and neurologically conditioned. Lateralization refers to any cognitive functions that are primarily localized to one side of the brain or the other.

In addition to aphasia, other evidence supports the lateralization of language. Children with early brain lesions in the left hemisphere resulting in the surgical removal of parts or the whole of the left brain show specific linguistic deficits with other cognitive abilities remaining intact. If the right brain is damaged, however, language is not disordered but other cognitive disorders may result.

Aphasia studies show impairment of different parts of the grammar. Patients with **Broca's aphasia** exhibit impaired syntax and speech problems, whereas **Wernicke's aphasia** patients are fluent speakers who produce semantically empty utterances and have difficulty in comprehension. **Anomia** is a form of aphasia in which the patient has word-finding difficulties. **Jargon aphasia** patients may substitute words unrelated semantically to their intended messages; others produce phonemic substitution errors, sometimes resulting in nonsense forms, making their utterances uninterpretable.

The **modularity** of the language faculty—its independence from other cognitive systems with which it interacts—is supported by brain-damage studies and by children with **Specific Language Impairments (SLI)** who are normal in all other regards. The ability to acquire language seems to be genetically determined, as shown by the cases of linguistic **savants**—individuals who are fluent in language and deficient in general intelligence. Given such individuals, linguistic ability does not seem to be derived from some general cognitive ability but specific to language.

An important question is how language developed in the course of evolution of the human brain. The origin of language in the species has been a topic for much speculation throughout history.

The idea that language was God's gift to humanity is found in religions throughout the world. The continuing belief in the miraculous powers of language is tied to this notion. The assumption of the divine origin of language stimulated interest in discovering the first primeval language. There are legendary experiments in which children were isolated in the belief that their first words would reveal the original language.

Opposing views suggest that language is a human invention. The Greeks believed that an ancient "legislator" gave the true names to all things. Others have suggested that language developed from "cries of nature," early gestures, onomatopoeic words, or even from songs to express love.

There is currently research being conducted by linguists, evolutionary biologists, and neurologists concerning the evolution of language. Some scholars suggest that language and the human animal arose simultaneously, and that from the start the human animal was genetically equipped to learn language. Studies of the evolutionary development of the brain provide some evidence for physiological and anatomic preconditions for language development.

References for Further Reading

Caplan, D. 1987. *Neurolinguistics and Linguistic Aphasiology.* Cambridge, England: Cambridge University Press.

Coltheart, M., K. Patterson, and J. C. Marshall, eds. 1980. *Deep Dyslexia.* London, England: Routledge & Kegan Paul.

Damasio, H. 1981. "Cerebral Localization of the Aphasias," in *Acquired Aphasia,* M. Taylor Sarno, ed., New York: Academic Press, pp. 27–65.

Gardner, H. 1978. "What We Know (and Don't Know) about the Two Halves of the Brain." *Harvard Magazine* 80: 24–27.

Gazzaniga, M. S. 1970. *The Bisected Brain.* New York: Appleton-Century-Crofts.

Geschwind, N. 1979. "Specializations of the Human Brain." *Scientific American* 206 (September): 180–199.

Grodzinsky, Y. 1990. *Theoretical Perspectives on Language Deficits.* Cambridge, MA: A Bradford Book, MIT Press.

Lenneberg, Eric H. 1967. *Biological Foundations of Language.* New York: Wiley.

Lesser, R. 1978. *Linguistic Investigation of Aphasia.* New York: Elsevier.

Lieberman, Philip. 1984. *The Biology and Evolution of Language.* Cambridge, MA: Harvard University Press.

Newcombe, F., and J. C. Marshall. 1972. "World Retrieval in Aphasia." *International Journal of Mental Health* 1:38–45.

Patterson, K. E., J. C. Marshall, and M. Coltheart, eds. 1986. *Surface Dyslexia.* Hillsdale, NJ: Erlbaum.

Pinker, Steven. 1995. *The Language Instinct.* New York: Morrow.

Poizner, Howard, Edward S. Klima, and Ursula Bellugi. 1987. *What the Hands Reveal about the Brain.* Cambridge, MA: MIT Press.

Searchinger, Gene. 1994. *The Human Language Series: 1, 2, 3.* New York: Equinox Film/Ways of Knowing, Inc.

Segalowitz, S. 1983. *Two Sides of the Brain.* Englewood Cliffs, NJ: Prentice Hall.

Springer, S. P., and G. Deutsch. 1981. *Left Brain, Right Brain.* San Francisco, CA: W. H. Freeman.

Stam, J. 1976. *Inquiries into the Origin of Language: The Fate of a Question.* New York: Harper & Row.

Yamada, J. 1990. *Laura: A Case for the Modularity of Language.* Cambridge, MA: A Bradford Book, MIT Press.

EXERCISES

1. The Nobel Prize laureate Roger Sperry has argued that split brain patients have two minds:

   Everything we have seen so far indicates that the surgery has left these people with two separate minds, that is, two separate spheres of consciousness. What is experienced in the right hemisphere seems to lie entirely outside the realm of experience of the left hemisphere.

   Another Nobel Prize winner in physiology, Sir John Eccles, disagrees. He does not think the right hemisphere can think; he distinguishes between "mere consciousness," which animals possess as well as humans, and language, thought, and other purely human cognitive abilities. In fact, according to him, the human aspect of human nature is all in the left hemisphere.

Write a short essay discussing these two opposing points of view, stating your own opinion on how to define "the mind."

2. A. Some aphasic patients, when asked to read a list of words, substitute other words for those printed. In many cases there are similarities between the printed words and the substituted words. The data given below are from actual aphasic patients. In each case state what the two words have in common and how they differ:

	Printed Word	Word Spoken by Aphasic
a.	liberty	freedom
	canary	parrot
	abroad	overseas
	large	long
	short	small
	tall	long
b.	decide	decision
	conceal	concealment
	portray	portrait
	bathe	bath
	speak	discussion
	remember	memory

B. What do the words in groups a and b reveal about how words are likely to be stored in the brain?

3. The following are some sentences spoken by aphasic patients, collected and analyzed by Dr. Harry Whitaker. In each case state how the sentence deviates from normal nonaphasic language.

a. There is under a horse a new sidesaddle.

b. In girls we see many happy days.

c. I'll challenge a new bike.

d. I surprise no new glamour.

e. Is there three chairs in this room?

f. Mike and Peter is happy.

g. Bill and John likes hot dogs.

h. Proliferate is a complete time about a word that is correct.

i. Went came in better than it did before.

4. The investigation of individuals with brain damage has been a major source of information as to the neural basis of language and other cognitive systems. One might suggest that this is like trying to understand how an automobile engine works by looking at a damaged engine. Is this a good analogy? If so, why? If not, why not? In your answer discuss how a damaged system can or cannot provide information about the normal system.

5. What are the arguments and evidence that have been put forth to support the notion that there are two separate parts of the brain?

6. Discuss the statement by A. W. Wigan that "It only takes one hemisphere to have a mind."

7. In this chapter, dichotic listening tests in which subjects hear different kinds of stimuli in each ear were discussed. These tests showed that though there were fewer errors made in reporting linguistic stimuli such as the syllables *pa, ta, ka* when heard through an earphone on the right ear; other nonlinguistic sounds such as a police car siren were processed with fewer mistakes if heard by the left ear. This is due to the contralateral control of the brain. There is also a technique which permits visual stimuli to be received either by the right visual field (going directly to the left hemisphere) or the left visual field (going directly to the right hemisphere). (The eye is divided in this way.) What might some visual stimuli be that could be used in an experiment to further test the lateralization of language?

PART 2

Grammatical Aspects of Language

The theory of grammar is concerned with the question: What is the nature of a person's knowledge of his language, the knowledge that enables him to make use of language in the normal, creative fashion? A person who knows a language has mastered a system of rules that assigns sound and meaning in a definite way for an infinite class of possible sentences.

N. Chomsky, *Language and Mind*

Chapter 3

Morphology: The Words of Language

A word is dead
When it is said,
Some say.
I say it just
Begins to live
That day.

Emily Dickinson, "A Word"

Every speaker of every language knows tens of thousands of words. *Webster's Third International Dictionary of the English Language* has over 450,000 entries. Most speakers don't know all these words. It is estimated that the average high school graduate knows about 60,000 words. The college graduate must then know many more words, including many in this book that readers will be learning for the first time. It has been estimated that a child of six knows as many as 13,000 words. If she produces her first word at the age of two, then she has learned 3,250 words a year, an average of 9 new words a day.

Words are an important part of linguistic knowledge and constitute a component of our mental grammars. But one can learn thousands of words in a language and still not know the language. Anyone who has tried to make himself understood in a foreign country by simply using a dictionary knows this to be true. On the other hand, without words we would be unable to convey our thoughts through language.

What is a word? What do you know when you know a word? Suppose you hear someone say *morpheme* and haven't the slightest idea what it means, and you don't know what the "smallest unit of linguistic meaning" is called. Then you don't know the word *morpheme*. A particular string of sounds must be united with a meaning and a meaning must be united with specific sounds in order for the sounds or the meaning to be a word in our mental dictionaries. Once you learn both the sounds and their related meaning, you know the word. It becomes an entry in your mental **lexicon** (the Greek word for *dictionary*).

Someone who doesn't know English would not know where one word begins or ends in an utterance like *Thecatsatonthemat*. We separate written words by spaces but in the spoken language there are no pauses between most words. Without knowledge of the language, one can't tell how many words are in an utterance. A speaker of English has no difficulty in segmenting the stream of sounds into six individual words: *the, cat, sat, on, the,* and *mat.* Similarly, a speaker of the American Indian language Potawatomi knows that *kwapmuknanuk* (which means "they see us") is just one word.

The lack of pauses between words in speech has provided humorists and songwriters with much material. During World War II, the chorus of one of the Top Ten tunes sung by Bing Crosby and Bob Hope used this fact about speech to amuse us:

Mairzy doats and dozy doats	(Mares eat oats and does eat oats,
And liddle lamzy divey,	And little lambs eat ivy,
A kiddley-divey too,	A kid'll eat ivy too,
Wouldn't you?	Wouldn't you?)

The fact that the same sounds can be interpreted differently, even between languages, gave birth to an entertaining book. The title, *Mots D'Heures: Gousses, Rames,*[1] was derived from the fact that *Mother Goose Rhymes,* spoken in English, sounds to a French speaker like the French words meaning "Words of the Hours: Root and Branch." The first rhyme in French starts:

Un petit d'un petit
S'étonne aux Halles.

When interpreted as if it were English it would sound like:

Humpty, dumpty
Sat on a wall.

This shows that in a particular language, the form (sounds or pronunciation) and the meaning of a word are like two sides of a coin. *Un petit d'un petit* in French means "a little one of a little one" but in English the sounds represent the name *Humpty Dumpty.*

Similarly, in English, the sounds of the letters *bear* and *bare* represent four **homonyms** (also called **homophones**), different words with the same sounds, as shown in the sentences:

She can't bear (tolerate) children.
She can't bear (give birth to) children.
Bruin bear is the mascot of UCLA.
He stood there—bare and beautiful.

Couch and *sofa,* though they have the same meaning, are two words because they are represented by two different strings of sounds.

Sometimes we think we know a word even though we don't know what it means. In an introductory linguistic class, all 397 students had heard the word *antidisestablishmentarianism* and believed it to be the longest word in the English language. Yet, many

---

[1] Luis d'Antin Van Rooten, ed. and annotator. 1993. *Mots D'Heures: Gousses, Rames. The d'Antin Manuscrip,* London: Grafton.

of these same students were unsure of its meaning. According to the way we have defined what it means to "know a word"—pairing a string of sounds with a particular meaning—such individuals do not really know this word.

Information about the longest or shortest word in the language is not part of linguistic knowledge of a language, but general conceptual knowledge **about** a language. Children do not learn such facts the way they learn the sound/meaning correspondences of the words **of** their language. Both children and adults have to be told that *antidisestablishmentarianism* is the longest word in English or discover it through an analysis of a dictionary. Actually, should they wish to research this question they would find that the longest word in *Webster's Seventh International Dictionary* is *pneumonoultramicroscopicsilicovolcanoconiosis,* a disease of the lungs. As we shall see in Chapter 8, children don't have to conduct such research; they learn words like *elephant, disappear, mother,* and all the other words they know without being taught them explicitly or looking them up in a dictionary.

Since each word is a sound-meaning unit, each word stored in our mental dictionaries must be listed with its unique phonological representation, which determines its pronunciation, and with its meaning. For literate speakers, the spelling or **orthography** of most of the words we know is also in our lexicons.

Each word listed in your mental lexicon includes other information as well, such as whether it is a noun, a pronoun, a verb, an adjective, an adverb, a preposition, a conjunction. That is, it must specify its **grammatical category,** or **syntactic class.** You may not consciously know that a form like *love* is listed as both a verb and a noun, but a speaker has such knowledge, as shown by the phrases *I love you* and *You are the love of my life.* If such information is not in the mental lexicon, we would not know how to form grammatical sentences, nor be able to distinguish grammatical from ungrammatical sentences. The classes of words, the syntactic categories—such as nouns, verbs, adjectives, and so on—and the semantic properties of words, which represent their meanings, will be discussed in later chapters.

DICTIONARIES

Dictionary, n. A malevolent literary device for cramping the growth of a language and making it hard and inelastic.

Ambrose Bierce, *The Devil's Dictionary*

By permission of Johnny Hart and Creators Syndicate, Inc.

The dictionaries that one buys in a bookstore contain some of the information found in our mental dictionaries. The first dictionary to be printed in England was the Latin-English *Promptuorium parvulorum* in 1499; another Latin-English dictionary by Sir Thomas Elyot was published in 1538. Noah Webster, who lived from 1758 until 1843, published *An American Dictionary of the English Language* in two volumes in 1828. It included seventy thousand entries.

One of the best efforts at lexicography (defined as "the editing or making of a dictionary" in *Webster's Third New Dictionary of the English Language: Unabridged*) was the *Dictionary of the English Language* by Dr. Samuel Johnson, published in 1755 in two volumes.

The aim of most early lexicographers, whom Dr. Johnson called "harmless drudges," was to "prescribe" rather than "describe" the words of a language, to be, as in the stated aim of one Webster's dictionaries, the "supreme authority" of the "correct" pronunciation and meaning of a word. It is to Johnson's credit that in his Preface he stated he could not construct the language but could only "register the language."

All dictionaries, from *The Oxford English Dictionary* (often referred to as the *OED* and called the greatest lexicographic work ever produced), to the more commonly used collegiate dictionaries, provide the following information about each word: (1) spelling, (2) the "standard" pronunciation, (3) definitions to represent the word's one or more meanings, and (4) parts of speech, e.g., noun, verb, preposition. Other information may be included such as the etymology or history of the word, whether the word is nonstandard (such as *ain't*) or slang, vulgar, or obsolete. Many dictionaries provide quotations from published literature to illustrate the given definitions, as was first done by Johnson.

In recent years, perhaps due to the increasing specialization in science and the arts or the growing fragmentation of the populace, we see the proliferation of hundreds of specialty and subspecialty dictionaries. A reference librarian at UCLA's Engineering and Mathematical Sciences Library estimates that her library has more than six hundred such books.

Dictionaries of slang and jargon have been around for many years, as have multilingual dictionaries, but in addition to these, the shelves of bookstores and libraries are now filled with dictionaries written specifically for biologists, engineers, agriculturists, economists, artists, architects, printers, gays and lesbians, transvestites, athletes, tennis players, and almost any group that has its own set of words to describe what they think and what they do. Our own mental dictionaries probably only include a small set of the entries in all of these dictionaries, but each word is in someone's lexicon.

CLASSES OF WORDS

Lexical Content Words

In English, nouns, verbs, adjectives, and adverbs make up the largest part of the vocabulary. They are the **content** words of a language, which are sometimes called the **open class** words because we can and regularly do add new words to these classes. A new verb, *download,* which means to transfer information from one computer system to another, entered English with the computer revolution. New adverbs like *weatherwise* and *saleswise* have been added in recent years, as well as adjectives like *biodegradable.*

Function Words

Conjunction junction, what's your function?

Song on the children's TV program *Schoolhouse Rock*

Other syntactic categories include **grammatical words** or **function words**. Conjunctions, like *and* and *or,* prepositions, like *in* and *of,* the articles *the* and *a/an,* part of the class of **determiners** (see Chapter 4), and pronouns have been referred to as being **closed class** words.

It is difficult to think of new conjunctions or prepositions or pronouns that have recently entered the language. The small set of personal pronouns such as *I, me, mine, he, she,* and so on, are part of this class. With the growth of the feminist movement, some proposals have been made for adding a new neutral singular pronoun that would be neither masculine nor feminine and that could be used as the general, or **generic,** form. If such a pronoun existed it might have prevented the department chairperson in a large university from making the incongruous statement: "We will hire the best person for the job regardless of his sex." The UCLA psychologist Donald MacKay has suggested that we use "e," pronounced like the letter name, for this pronoun with various alternative forms; others point out that *they* and *their* are already being used as neutral third person singular forms, as in "Anyone can do it if they try hard enough" or "Everyone can do their best." The use of the various forms of *they* is reported to be Standard British English used on the BBC (British Broadcasting System) with *anyone* and *everyone* now considered either singular or plural, similar to such words as *committee* or *government*.

These classes of content and function words appear to have psychological and neurological validity. As discussed earlier, some brain-damaged patients have greater difficulty in using, understanding, or reading function words than content words. Some are unable to read function words like *in* or *which* but can read the lexical content words *inn* and *witch.* Other patients do just the opposite. The two classes of words also seem to function differently in **slips of the tongue** produced by normal individuals. For example, a speaker may inadvertently switch words producing "the journal of the editor" instead of "the editor of the journal," but the switching or exchanging of function words has not been observed. The important feature of these two classes is their function rather than their degree of "openness." An **open class** in one language may be **closed** in another. In Akan, the major language spoken in Ghana, for example, there are only a handful of adjectives; most English adjectives are in the verb class in Akan. Instead of saying *"The sun is bright today,"* an Akan speaker will say *"The sun brightens today."*

MORPHEMES:
THE MINIMAL UNITS OF MEANING

"They gave it me," Humpty Dumpty continued, "for an un-birthday present."

"I beg your pardon?" Alice said with a puzzled air.

"I'm not offended," said Humpty Dumpty.

"I mean, what is an un-birthday present?"

"A present given when it isn't your birthday, of course."

Lewis Carroll, *Through the Looking-Glass*

Reprinted with special permission of United Feature Syndicate, Inc.

In the cartoon above, Luanne is as aware as Humpty Dumpty that the prefix *un-* means "not," as further shown in the following pairs of words:

A	B
desirable	undesirable
likely	unlikely
inspired	uninspired
happy	unhappy
developed	undeveloped
sophisticated	unsophisticated

Webster's Third New International Dictionary lists about 2700 adjectives beginning with *un.*

If the most elemental units of meaning, the basic linguistic signs, are assumed to be the words of a language, it would be a coincidence that *un* has the same meaning in all the column B words. But this is no coincidence. The words *undesirable, unlikely, uninspired, unhappy,* and the others in column B consist of at least two meaningful units: *un + desirable, un + likely,* and so on.

Just as *un* occurs with the same meaning in the words above, so does *phon* in the following words. (You may not know the meaning of some of them but you will when you finish this book.)

phone	phonology	phoneme
phonetic	phonologist	phonemic
phonetics	phonological	allophone
phonetician	telephone	euphonious
phonic	telephonic	symphony

Phon is a minimal form in that it can't be divided into more elemental structures. *Ph* doesn't mean anything; *pho,* though it may be pronounced like *foe,* has no relation in meaning to it; and *on* is not the preposition spelled *o-n.* In all the words on the list *phon* has the identical meaning, "pertaining to sound."

The internal structure of words is rule-governed. *Uneaten, unadmired,* and *ungrammatical* are words in English, but **eatenun, *admiredun,* and **grammaticalun* (to mean "not eaten," "not admired," "not grammatical") are not, because we do not form a negative meaning of a word by **suffixing** *un* (that is, by adding it to the end of the word), but by **prefixing** it (that is, by adding it to the beginning).

When Samuel Goldwyn, the pioneer moviemaker, announced: "In two words: im-possible" he was reflecting the common view that words are the basic meaningful elements in a language. We have seen that this cannot be so, since some words are formed by combining a number of distinct units of meaning. The traditional term for the most elemental unit of grammatical form is **morpheme.** The word is derived from the Greek word *morphe,* meaning "form." Linguistically speaking, then, Goldwyn should have said: "In two morphemes: im-possible."

The study of the internal structure of words, and of the rules by which words are formed, is called **morphology.** This word itself consists of two morphemes, *morph + ology.* The morphemic suffix *-ology* means "science of" or "branch of knowledge concerning." Thus, the meaning of *morphology* is "the science of word forms."

Knowing a language implies knowing its morphology. Like most linguistic knowledge, this is generally unconscious knowledge.

A single word may be composed of one or more morphemes:

one morpheme	boy
	desire
two morphemes	boy + ish
	desire + able
three morphemes	boy + ish + ness
	desire + able + ity
four morphemes	gentle + man + li + ness
	un + desire + able + ity
more than four	un + gentle + man + li + ness
	anti + dis + establish + ment + ari + an + ism[2]

A morpheme may be represented by a single sound, such as the morpheme *a* meaning "without" as in *amoral* or *asexual,* or by a single syllable, such as *child* and *ish* in *child + ish.* A morpheme may also consist of more than one syllable: by two syllables, as in *aardvark, lady, water;* or by three syllables, as in *Hackensack* or *crocodile;* or by four or more syllables, as in *salamander.*

A morpheme—the minimal linguistic sign—is thus a grammatical unit in which there is an arbitrary union of a sound and a meaning that cannot be further analyzed. This may be too simple a definition, but it will serve our purposes for now. Every word in every language is composed of one or more morphemes.

Bound and Free Morphemes

6-3
© 1991 Bil Keane, Inc.
Dist. by Cowles Synd. Inc.

"Mommy said to behave, so I'm bein' as hayve as I can."

Reprinted with special permission of King Features Syndicate.

---

[2] Some speakers have even more morphemes in this word than are shown.

Prefixes and Suffixes

Some morphemes like *boy, desire, gentle,* and *man* constitute words by themselves. Other morphemes like *-ish, -ness, -ly, dis-, trans-,* and *un-* are never words but always parts of words. Thus, *un-* is like *pre- (prefix, predetermine, prejudge, prearrange)* and *bi- (bipolar, bisexual, bivalve);* it occurs only before other morphemes. Such morphemes are called **prefixes.**

Prefixing is very widespread in the languages of the world. In Isthmus Zapotec, for example, the plural morpheme *ka-* is a prefix:

zigi	"chin"	kazigi	"chins"
zike	"shoulder"	kazike	"shoulders"
diaga	"ear"	kadiaga	"ears"

Other morphemes occur only as **suffixes,** following other morphemes. English examples of suffix morphemes are *-er* (as in *singer, performer, reader,* and *beautifier*), *-ist* (in *typist, copyist, pianist, novelist, collaborationist,* and *linguist*) and *-ly* (as in *manly, sickly, spectacularly,* and *friendly*), to mention only a few.

These prefix and suffix morphemes are **bound** morphemes because they cannot occur unattached, as distinct from **free** morphemes like *man, sick, spectacle, friend,* and so on. Of course in speaking we seldom use even free morphemes alone. We combine all morphemes into larger units—phrases and sentences.

Morphemes are the minimal linguistic signs in all languages. In Turkish, if you add *-ak* to a verb, you derive a noun, as in:

dur	"to stop"	dur + ak	"stopping place"
bat	"to sink"	bat + ak	"sinking place" or "marsh/swamp"

In English, in order to express reciprocal action we use the phrase *each other,* as in *understand each other, love each other.* In Turkish a morpheme is added to the verb:

anla	"understand"	anla + s	"understand each other"
sev	"love"	sev + is	"love each other"

The reciprocal suffix in these examples is pronounced as *s* after a vowel and as *is* after a consonant. This is similar to the process in English in which we use *a* as the indefinite article morpheme before a noun beginning with a consonant, as in *a dog,* and *an* before a noun beginning with a vowel, as in *an apple.* We will discuss the various pronunciations of morphemes in Chapter 7.

In Piro, an Arawakan language spoken in Peru, a single morpheme, *kaka,* can be added to a verb to express the meaning "cause to":

cokoruha	"to harpoon"	cokoruha + kaka	"cause to harpoon"
salwa	"to visit"	salwa + kaka	"cause to visit"

In Karuk, a Native American language spoken in the Pacific Northwest, the locative adverbial meaning "in," "on," or "at" is formed by adding *-ak* to a noun:

ikrivaam	"house"	ikrivaamak	"in a house"

It is accidental that both Turkish and Karuk have a suffix -*ak.* Despite the similarity in form, the two meanings are different. Similarly, the reciprocal suffix -*s* in Turkish is similar in form to the English plural -*s.* Also in Karuk, the suffix -*ara* has the same meaning as the English -*y,* that is, "characterized by":

> aptiik   "branch"   aptikara   "branchy"

These examples illustrate again the arbitrary nature of the linguistic sign.

In Russian the suffix -*shchik* (pronounced like the beginning of the word *she* followed by *chick*) added to a noun is similar in meaning to the English suffix -*er* in words like *reader, teacher,* or *rider,* which when added to a verb means "one who —" The Russian suffix, however, is added to nouns, not verbs, as shown in the following examples.

Russian		**Russian**	
atom	"atom"	atomshchik	"atom-warmonger"
baraban	"drum"	barabanshchik	"drummer"
kalambur	"pun"	kalamburshchik	"punner"
beton	"concrete"	betonshchik	"concrete worker"
lom	"scrap"	lomshchik	"salvage collector"

The examples given above from different languages also illustrate free morphemes like *boy* in English: *dur* in Turkish, *salwa* in Piro, and *lom* in Russian.

Infixes

Some languages also have **infixes,** morphemes that are inserted into other morphemes. Bontoc, a language spoken in the Philippines, is such a language, as is illustrated by the following:

Nouns/Adjectives		**Verbs**	
fikas	"strong"	fumikas	"to be strong"
kilad	"red"	kumilad	"to be red"
fusul	"enemy"	fumusul	"to be an enemy"

In this language the infix -*um*- is inserted after the first consonant of the noun or adjective. Thus, a speaker of Bontoc who learns that *pusi* means "poor," would understand the meaning of *pumusi,* "to be poor," on hearing the word for the first time. Just as an English speaker who learns the verb *sneet* would know that *sneeter* is one who sneets, a Bontoc speaker who knows that *ngumitad* means "to be dark" would know that the adjective "dark" must be *ngitad.*

English has a very limited set of infixes. English infixing was a subject of the *Linguist List*, a discussion group on the Internet, in November of 1993, and again in July of 1996. The interest in these infixes in English may be due to the fact that one can only infix obscenities as full words that are inserted in another word, usually into adjectives or adverbs. The most common infix in America is the word *fuckin* and all the euphemisms for it, such as *friggin, freakin, flippin,* or *fuggin* as in *abso-fuggin-lutely* or *Kalama + flippin + zoo.* In Britain, a common infix is *bloody,* an obscene term in British English, and its euphemisms, such as *bloomin.* In the movie and stage musical

My Fair Lady, abso + *bloomin* + *lutely* occurs in one of the songs sung by Eliza Doolittle.

Circumfixes

Some languages have **circumfixes,** morphemes that are attached to a root or stem morpheme both initially and finally. These are sometimes called **discontinuous morphemes.** In Chickasaw, a Muskogean language spoken in Oklahoma, the negative is formed by using both a prefix *ik-* and the suffix *-o.* The final vowel of the affirmative is deleted before the negative suffix is added. Examples of this circumfixing are:

Affirmative		Negative	
chokma	"he is good"	ik + chokm + o	"he isn't good"
lakna	"it is yellow"	ik + lakn + o	"it isn't yellow"
palli	"it is hot"	ik + pall + o	"it isn't hot"
tiwwi	"he opens (it)"	ik + tiww + o	"he doesn't open (it)"

An example of a more familiar circumfixing language is German. The past participle of regular verbs is formed by adding the prefix *ge-* and the suffix *-t* to the verb root. This circumfix added to the verb root *lieb* "love" produces *geliebt,* "loved" (or "beloved," when used as an adjective).

Huckles and Ceives

> It had been a rough day, so when I walked into the party I was very chalant, despite my efforts to appear gruntled and consolate. I was furling my wieldy umbrella . . . when I saw her. . . . She was a descript person. . . . Her hair was kempt, her clothing shevelled, and she moved in a gainly way.
>
> "How I Met my Wife," by Jack Winter. *The New Yorker,* July 25, 1994.

A morpheme was defined as the basic element of meaning, a phonological form that is arbitrarily united with a particular meaning and that cannot be analyzed into simpler elements. This definition has presented problems for linguistic analysis for many years, although it holds for most of the morphemes in a language. Consider words like *cranberry, huckleberry,* and *boysenberry.* The *berry* part is no problem, but *huckle* and *boysen* occur only with *berry,* as did *cran* until *cranapple* juice came on the market, and other morphologically complex words using *cran-* followed. The *boysen-* part of *boysenberry* was named for a man named Boysen who developed it as a hybrid from the blackberry and raspberry. But few people are aware of this and it is a bound stem morpheme that only occurs in this word. *Lukewarm* is another word with two stem morphemes, with *luke* occurring only in this word, because it is not the same morpheme as the name *Luke.*

Bound forms like *huckle-, boysen-,* and *luke-* require a redefinition of the concept of morpheme. Some morphemes have no meaning in isolation but acquire meaning only in combination with other specific morphemes. Thus the morpheme *huckle,* when joined with *berry,* has the meaning of a special kind of berry that is small, round, and purplish blue; *luke* when combined with *warm* has the meaning "sort of" or "somewhat," and so on.

Just as there are some morphemes that occur only in a single word (combined with another morpheme), there are other morphemes that occur in many words, but seem to lack a constant meaning from one word to another. What is the meaning of *-ceive* in *receive, perceive, conceive,* and *deceive,* or the *-mit* in *remit, permit, commit, submit, transmit,* and *admit?* The meaning of such morphemes depends on the entire word in which they occur, on their morphological context.

Reprinted with special permission of King Features Syndicate.

There are other words that seem to be composed of prefix + root morphemes in which the roots like *cran-* or *-ceive* never occur alone, but always with a specific prefix. Thus we find *inept,* but no **ept, inane,* but no **ane, incest,* but no **cest, inert* but no **ert, disgusted,* but no **gusted.*

Similarly, the stems of *upholster, downhearted,* and *outlandish* do not occur by themselves: **holster* and **hearted* (with these meanings), and **landish* (except as the maiden name of V. A. Fromkin) are not free morphemes. In addition, *downholster, uphearted,* and *inlandish,* their "opposites," are not found in any English lexicon.

To complicate things a little further, there are words like *strawberry* in which the *straw* has no relationship to any other kind of *straw; gooseberry,* which is unrelated to *goose;* and *blackberry,* which may be blue or red. While some of these words may have historical origins, there is no present meaningful connection. The *Oxford English Dictionary* entry for the word *strawberry* states that

> The reason for the name has been variously conjectured. One explanation refers the first element to Straw . . . a particle of straw or chaff, a mote describing the appearance of the achenes scattered over the surface of the strawberry.

That may be true of the word's origin, but today, the *straw-* in *strawberry* is not the same morpheme as that found in *strawlike* or *straw-colored.*

The meaning of a morpheme must be constant. The morpheme *-er* means "one who does" in words like *singer, painter, lover,* and *worker,* but the same sounds represent the comparative morpheme, meaning "more," in *nicer, prettier,* and *taller.* Thus, two different morphemes may be pronounced identically. The identical form represents two morphemes because of the different meanings. The same sounds may occur in another word and not represent any separate morpheme. The final syllable in *butcher, er,* is not a separate morpheme, since a butcher is not one who butches. (In an earlier form of English the word *butcher* was *bucker,* "one who dresses bucks." The *-er* in this word was then a separate morpheme.) Similarly, in *water* the *-er* is not a distinct morpheme ending; *butcher* and *water* are single morphemes, or **monomorphemic** words. This follows from the concept of the morpheme as a sound-meaning unit.

Nonaffix lexical content morphemes that cannot be analyzed into smaller parts, such as *system, boy,* or *cran,* are called **root** morphemes. When a root morpheme is combined with affix morphemes it forms a **stem.** Other affixes can be added to a stem to form a more complex stem, as shown in the following:

root	Chomsky	*(proper) noun*
stem	Chomsky + ite	*noun + suffix*
word	Chomsky + ite + s	*noun + suffix + suffix*
root	believe	*verb*
stem	believe + able	*verb + suffix*
word	un + believe + able	*prefix + verb + suffix*
root	system	*noun*
stem	system + atic	*noun + suffix*
stem	un + system + atic	*prefix + noun + suffix*
stem	un + system + atic + al	*prefix + noun + suffix + suffix*
word	un + system + atic + al + ly	*prefix + noun + suffix + suffix + suffix*

As one adds each additional affix to a stem, a new stem and a new word is formed.

All morphemes are bound or free. Affixes (prefixes, suffixes, and infixes) are bound morphemes. Root morphemes can be bound or free, as illustrated by the following:

	Free	Bound
Root	dog, cat, aardvark, corduroy, run, bottle, hot, separate, phone, museum, school . . . (and 1000s more)	huckle(berry), (dis)gruntle, (un)couth, (non)chalance, (per)ceive, (in)ept, (re)mit, (in)cest, (homo)geneous . . . (and less than a hundred more)
Affix		(friend)ship, (lead)ership, re(do), homo(geneous), hetero(geneous), trans-(sex)ual, (sad)ly, (tall)ish, a(moral), (and many others)

(Note that there are some morpheme types not listed in this chart, such as *the* or *and* or the *-ing* in *going.*)

RULES OF WORD FORMATION

"I never heard of 'Uglification,' " Alice ventured to say. "What is it?" The Gryphon lifted up both its paws in surprise. "Never heard of uglifying!" it exclaimed. "You know what to beautify is, I suppose?" "Yes," said Alice doubtfully: "it means—to make—anything—prettier." "Well, then," the Gryphon went on, "if you don't know what to uglify is, you are a simpleton."

Lewis Carroll, *Alice in Wonderland*

When the Mock Turtle listed the different branches of Arithmetic for Alice as "Ambition, Distraction, Uglification, and Derision," Alice was very confused. She wasn't really a simpleton, since *uglification* was not a common word in English until Lewis Carroll used it. There are many ways in which words enter a language. Some of these are discussed in Chapter 11, on language change.

Lexical Gaps

Speakers of a language may know tens of thousands of words. Dictionaries, as we noted, include hundreds of thousands of words, all of which are known by some speakers of the language. But no dictionary can list all **possible words** since it is possible to add to the vocabulary of a language in many ways. There are always gaps in the lexicon—words that are not in the dictionary but that can be added. Some of the gaps are due to the fact that a permissible sound sequence has no meaning attached to it (like *blick,* or *slarm,* or *krobe*). Note that the sequence of sounds must be in keeping with the constraints of the language. **bnick* is not a "gap" because no word in English can begin with a *bn.* We will discuss such constraints in Chapter 7.

Other gaps are due to the fact that possible combinations of morphemes have not been made (like *ugly + ify* or *linguistic + ism*). Morphemes can be combined in this way because there are **morphological rules** in every language that determine how morphemes combine to form new words.

The Mock Turtle added *-ify* to the adjective *ugly* and formed a verb. Many verbs in English have been formed in this way: *purify, amplify, simplify, falsify.* The suffix *-ify* conjoined with nouns also forms verbs: *objectify, glorify, personify.* Notice that the Mock Turtle went even further; he added the suffix *-cation* to *uglify* and formed a noun, *uglification,* as in *glorification, simplification, falsification,* and *purification.*

Derivational Morphology

Bound morphemes like *-ify* and *-ation* are called **derivational morphemes.** When they are added to root morphemes or stems a word is derived. This method of word formation reflects the wonderful creativity of language.

Suppose you hear someone say: "He likes to be nussed." You might ask "Is he really nussable?" even if you don't know what the verb *nuss* means. Children do this all the time. This means we must have a list of the derivational morphemes in our mental dictionaries as well as the rules that determine how they are to be added to roots or stems to form new stems or words. We saw above that morphemes occur in a fixed order, as *un + loved* but not **loved + un.* In addition, the order in which each new morpheme is affixed in a complex word is significant. A word is not a simple sequence of morphemes but has a **hierarchical structure.** Consider the word *unsystematically,* composed of five morphemes. As shown in the example above, the root is *system,* a noun, to which we added *atic,* an adjectival suffix, and then added the prefix *un-,* which is added to adjectives to form the new adjective stem (or word) *unsystematic.* If we had added the prefix *un* first, we would have derived a nonword **unsystem* since *un* cannot be added to nouns.

The hierarchical structure of this word can be diagrammed as follows:

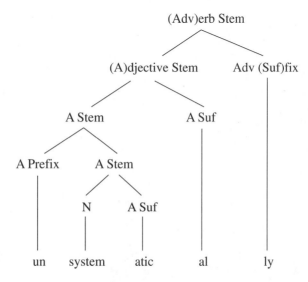

This diagram shows that the entire word—*unsystematically*—is an adverb stem which is composed of an adjective stem—*unsystematical* plus *-ly,* an adverbial derivational suffix. The adjective stem itself is composed of an adjective stem *unsystematic,* which is composed of an adjectival prefix *un-* and another adjective stem *systematic* (composed of the noun *system* and the adjective suffix *-atic* plus the adjective suffix *al*).

If this seems very complicated, it is. Morphological rules of word formation are complex. Yet every speaker of English knows them and uses them to form new words like *uglify* or *squishable* or *linguisticism,* and to understand words not heard before, like the first time one hears the word *Chomskian.* We also unconsciously use these rules in rejecting some forms as being impossible as words in English, such as **nationism.*

As the examples show, a derived word may add additional meaning to the original word (such as the negative meaning of words prefixed by *un-*) and may be in a different grammatical class than the underived word. When a verb is suffixed with *-able,* the result is an adjective, as in *desire + able* or *adore + able.* Or, when the suffix *-en* is added to an adjective, a verb is derived, as in *dark + en*. One may form a noun from an adjective, as in *sweet + ie*. Other examples are:

Noun to Adjective	Verb to Noun	Adjective to Adverb	Noun to Verb	Adjective to Noun	Verb to Adjective
boy + ish	acquitt + al	exact + ly	moral + ize	tall + ness	read + able
virtu + ous	clear + ance	quiet + ly	vaccin + ate	specific + ity	creat + ive
Elizabeth + an	accus + ation		brand + ish	glori + ous	migrat + ory
pictur + esque	confer + ence		haste + n		
affection + ate	sing + er				
health + ful	conform + ist				
alcohol + ic	predict + ion				
life + like	free + dom				

Not all derivational morphemes cause a change in grammatical class.

Noun to Noun	Verb to Verb	Adjective to Adjective
friend + ship	un + do	pink + ish
human + ity	re + cover	in + flammable

Many prefixes fall into this category:

a + moral	mono + theism
auto + biography	re + print
ex + wife	semi + annual
super + human	sub + minimal

There are also suffixes of this type:

vicar + age	New Jersey + ite
old + ish	fadd + ist
Paul + ine	music + ian
America + n	pun + ster

When new words enter the lexicon by the application of morphological rules, it is often the case that other complex forms will not. For example, when *Commun + ist* entered the language, words such as *Commun + ite* (as in *Trotsky + ite*) or *Commun + ian* (as in *grammar + ian*) are often not used. There may however exist alternative forms: for example, *Chomskyan* and *Chomskyist* and perhaps even *Chomskyite* (all meaning "follower of Chomsky's views of linguistics"). *Linguist* and *linguistician* are both used, but the possible word *linguite* is not. The redundancy of such alternative forms, all of which conform to the regular rules of word formation, may explain some of the accidental gaps in the lexicon. This further shows that the actual words in the language constitute only a subset of the possible words.

There are many other derivational morphemes in English and other languages, such as the suffixes meaning "diminutive," as in the words *pig + let* and *sap + ling*.

Some of the morphological rules are **productive**, meaning that they can be used freely to form new words from the list of free and bound morphemes. The suffix *-able* appears to be a morpheme that can be conjoined with any verb to derive an adjective with the meaning of the verb and the meaning of *-able*, which is something like "able to be" as in *accept + able, blam(e) + able, pass + able, change + able, breath + able, adapt + able,* and so on. The meaning of *-able* has also been given as "fit for doing" or "fit for being done."

Such a rule might be stated as:

(1) VERB + able → ADJ "able to be VERB-ed"
e.g. accept + able = "able to be accepted"

The productivity of this rule is illustrated by the fact that we find *-able* in such morphologically complex words as *un + speakabl(e) + y* and *un + come + at + able.*

We have already noted that there is a morpheme in English meaning "not" that has the form *un-* and that, when combined with adjectives like *afraid, fit, free, smooth, American,* and *British,* forms the **antonyms,** or negatives, of these adjectives; for example, *unafraid, unfit, un-American,* and so on.

We can also add the prefix *un-* to derived words that have been formed by morphological rules:

un + believe + able
un + accept + able
un + talk + about + able
un + keep + off + able
un + speak + able

The rule that forms these words may be stated as:

(2) un + ADJECTIVE = "not-ADJECTIVE"

This seems to account for all the examples cited. Yet we find *happy* and *unhappy, cowardly* and *uncowardly,* but not *sad* and **unsad* or *brave* and **unbrave.* The starred forms that follow may be merely **accidental gaps** in the lexicon. If someone refers to a person as being **unsad* we would know that the person referred to was "not sad," and an **unbrave* person would not be brave. But, as the linguist Sandra Thompson[3] points out, it may be the case that the "un-Rule" is not as productive for adjectives composed of just one morpheme as for adjectives that are themselves derived from verbs.

The rule seems to be freely applicable to an adjectival form derived from a verb, as in *unenlightened, unsimplified, uncharacterized, unauthorized, undistinguished,* and so on.

It is true, however, that one cannot always know the meaning of the words derived from free and derivational morphemes from the morphemes themselves.

---

[3] S. A. Thompson. 1975. "On the Issue of Productivity in the Lexikon," *Kritikon Litterarum* 4: 332–349.

Thompson has also pointed out that the *un-* forms of the following have unpredictable meanings:

unloosen	"loosen, let loose"
unrip	"rip, undo by ripping"
undo	"reverse doing"
untread	"go back through in the same steps"
unearth	"dig up"
unfrock	"deprive (a cleric) of ecclesiastic rank"
unnerve	"fluster"

Although the words above must be listed in our mental lexicons since their meanings cannot be determined by knowing the meanings of their parts, morphological rules must also be in the grammar, revealing the relation between words and providing the means for forming new words. Morphological rules may be more or less productive. The rule that adds an *-er* to verbs in English to produce a noun meaning "one who performs an action (once or habitually)" appears to be a very productive morphological rule; most English verbs accept this suffix: *lover, hunter, predictor* (notice that *-or* and *-er* have the same pronunciation), *examiner, exam-taker, analyzer,* and so forth. Now consider the following:

sincerity	from	*sincere*
warmth	from	*warm*
moisten	from	*moist*

The suffix *-ity* is found in many other words in English, like *chastity, scarcity,* and *curiosity;* and *-th* occurs in *health, wealth, depth, width,* and *growth.* We find *-en* in *sadden, ripen, redden, weaken, deepen.* Still, the phrase **The fiercity of the lion* sounds somewhat strange, as does the sentence **I'm going to thinnen the sauce.* Someone may use the word *coolth,* but, as Thompson points out, when such words as *fiercity, thinnen, fullen,* or *coolth* are used, usually it is either an error or an attempt at humor. It is possible that in such cases a morphological rule that was once productive (as shown by the existence of related pairs like *scarce/scarcity*) is no longer so. Our knowledge of the related pairs, however, may permit us to use these examples in forming new words, by analogy with the existing lexical items.

"Pullet Surprises"

DRABBLE reprinted by permission of UFS, Inc.

That speakers of a language know the morphemes of that language and the rules for word formation is shown as much by the errors made as by the nondeviant forms produced. Morphemes combine to form words. These words form our internal dictionaries. No speaker of a language knows all the words. Given our knowledge of the morphemes of the language and the morphological rules, we may guess the meaning of a word we do not know. Sometimes we guess wrong.

Amsel Greene collected errors made by her students in vocabulary-building classes and published them in a book called *Pullet Surprises.*[4] The title is taken from a sentence written by one of her high school students: "In 1957 Eugene O' Neill won a Pullet Surprise." What is most interesting about these errors is how much they reveal about the students' knowledge of English morphology. Consider the creativity of these students in the following examples:

Word	Student's Definition
deciduous	"able to make up one's mind"
longevity	"being very tall"
fortuitous	"well protected"
gubernatorial	"to do with peanuts"
bibliography	"holy geography"
adamant	"pertaining to original sin"
diatribe	"food for the whole clan"
polyglot	"more than one glot"
gullible	"to do with sea birds"
homogeneous	"devoted to home life"

The student who used the word *indefatigable* in the sentence

She tried many reducing diets, but remained indefatigable

clearly shows morphological knowledge: *in,* meaning "not" as in *ineffective; de* meaning "off" as in *decapitate; fat,* as in "fat"; *able,* as in *able;* and combined meaning, "not able to take the fat off."

SIGN LANGUAGE MORPHOLOGY

Sign languages are rich in morphology. Like spoken languages, they have root and affix morphemes, free and bound morphemes, lexical and grammatical morphemes, derivational and inflectional morphemes, and morphological rules for their combination to form signed words.

Figure 3-1 illustrates the derivational process in ASL equivalent to the formation of the nouns *comparison* and *measuring* from the verbs *compare* and *measure* in English. Everything about the root morpheme remains the same except for the movement of the hands.

---

[4] Amsel Greene. 1969. *Pullet Surprises,* Glenview, IL: Scott, Foresman & Co.

FIGURE 3-1   Derivationally related sign in ASL.[5]

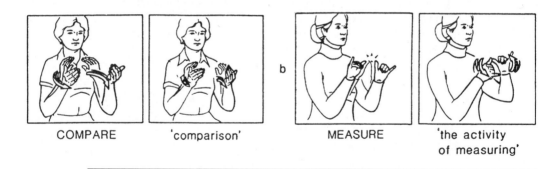

COMPARE   'comparison'   MEASURE   'the activity
                                                           of measuring'

Copyright © 1987 Massachusetts Institute of Technology. Reproduced by permission of MIT Press.

Inflection of sign roots also occurs in ASL and all other sign languages, which characteristically modify the movement of the hands and the spatial contours of the area near the body in which the signs are articulated.

WORD COINAGE

PEANUTS reprinted by permission of UFS, Inc.

We have seen that new words may be added to the vocabulary of a language by derivational processes. New words may also enter a language in a variety of other ways. Some are created outright to fit some purpose. Madison Avenue has added many new words to English, such as *Kodak, nylon, Orlon,* and *Dacron.* Specific brand names such as *Xerox, Kleenex, Jell-O, Frigidaire, Brillo,* and *Vaseline* are now sometimes used as the generic name for different brands of these types of products. Notice that some of these

---

[5] Howard Poizner, Edward S. Klima, and Ursula Bellugi. 1987. *What the Hands Reveal about the Brain,* Cambridge, MA: MIT Press.

words were created from existing words: *Kleenex* from the word *clean* and *Jell-O* from *gel,* for example.

In computer speech processing the new words *cepstrum* and *cepstral* were purposely formed by reordering the letters of *spectrum* and *spectral.* Speakers do not agree on the pronunciation of these two words. Some say "sepstrum" with an *s*-sound, since the *c* precedes an *e.* Others say "kepstrum" since the *c* is pronounced as a *k* in the source word *spectrum.* Greek roots borrowed into English have also provided a means for coining new words. *Thermos* "hot" plus *metron* "measure" give us *thermometer.* From *akros* "topmost" and *phobia* "fear" we get *acrophobia,* "dread of heights." An ingenious cartoonist, Robert Osborn, has "invented" some phobias, to each of which he gives an appropriate name:[6]

logizomechanophobia	"fear of reckoning machines" from Greek *logizomai* "to reckon or compute" + *mekhane* "device" + *phobia*
ellipsosyllabophobia	"fear of words with a missing syllable" from Greek *elleipsis* "a falling short" + *syllabē* "syllable" + *phobia*
pornophobia	*"fear of prostitutes"* from Greek *porne* "harlot" + *phobia*

Latin, like Greek, has also provided prefixes and suffixes that are used productively with both native and nonnative roots. The prefix *ex-* comes from Latin:

ex-husband   ex-wife   ex–sister-in-law

The suffix *-able/-ible* that was discussed above is also Latin, borrowed via French, and can be attached to almost any English verb, as we noted above, and as further illustrated in:

writable   readable   answerable   movable

Compounds

> . . . the Houynhnms have no Word in their Language to express any thing that is evil, except what they borrow from the Deformities or ill Qualities of the Yahoos. Thus they denote the Folly of a Servant, an Omission of a Child, a Stone that cuts their feet, a Continuance of foul or unseasonable Weather, and the like, by adding to each the Epithet of Yahoo. For instance, Hnhm Yahoo, Whnaholm Yahoo, Ynlhmnawihlma Yahoo, and an ill contrived House, Ynholmhnmrohlnw Yahoo.
>
> Jonathan Swift, *Gulliver's Travels*

---

[6] *An Osborn Festival of Phobias.* Copyright © 1971 by Robert Osborn. Text copyright © 1971 by Eve Wengler. Reprinted by permission of Liveright Publishers, New York.

PEANUTS reprinted by permission of UFS, Inc.

New words may be formed by combining words together to form **compound** words. There is almost no limit on the kinds of combinations that occur in English, as the following list of compounds shows:

	Adjective	Noun	Verb
Adjective	bittersweet	poorhouse	highborn
Noun	headstrong	rainbow	spoonfeed
Verb	carryall	pickpocket	sleepwalk

Frigidaire is a compound formed by combining the adjective *frigid* with the noun *air.*
When the two words are in the same grammatical category, the compound will be in this category: noun + noun—*girlfriend, fighter-bomber, paper clip, elevator-operator, landlord, mailman;* adjective + adjective—*icy-cold, red-hot,* and *worldly-wise.* In many cases, when the two words fall into different categories, the class of the second or final word will be the grammatical category of the compound: noun + adjective—*headstrong, watertight, lifelong;* verb + noun—*pickpocket, pinchpenny, daredevil, sawbones.* On the other hand, compounds formed with a preposition are in the category of the nonprepositional part of the compound; *overtake, hanger-on, undertake, sundown, afterbirth, downfall, uplift.*

Though two-word compounds are the most common in English, it would be difficult to state an upper limit: Consider *three-time loser, four-dimensional space-time, sergeant-at-arms, mother-of-pearl, man about town, master of ceremonies,* and *daughter-in-law.*

Spelling does not tell us what sequence of words constitutes a compound; whether a compound is spelled with a space between the two words, with a hyphen, or with no separation at all is idiosyncratic, as shown, for example, in *blackbird, gold-tail,* and *smoke screen.*

Meaning of Compounds

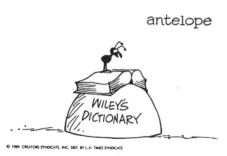

By permission of Johnny Hart and Creators Syndicate, Inc.

The meaning of a compound is not always the sum of the meanings of its parts; a *black-board* may be green or white. Everyone who wears a red coat is not a *Redcoat.* The difference between the sentences *She has a red coat in her closet* and *She has a Redcoat in her closet* could be highly significant under certain circumstances.

Other compounds show that, underlying the juxtaposition of words, different grammatical relations are expressed. A *boathouse* is a house for boats, but a *cathouse* is not a house for cats. (It is slang for a house of prostitution or whorehouse.) A *jumping bean* is a bean that jumps, a *falling star* is a star that falls, and a *magnifying glass* is a glass that magnifies; but a *looking glass* is not a glass that looks, nor is an *eating apple* an apple that eats, and *laughing gas* does not laugh.

In all these examples, the meaning of each compound includes at least to some extent the meanings of the individual parts. However, there are other compounds that do not seem to relate to the meanings of the individual parts at all. A *jack-in-a-box* is a tropical tree, and a *turncoat* is a traitor. A *highbrow* does not necessarily have a high brow, nor does a *bigwig* have a big wig, nor does an *egghead* have an egg-shaped head.

As we pointed out earlier in the discussion of the prefix *un-,* the meaning of many compounds must be learned as if they were individual simple words. Some of the meanings may be figured out, but not all. If you had never heard the word *hunchback,* it might be possible to infer the meaning; but if you had never heard the word *flatfoot,* it is doubtful you would know it means "detective" or "policeman," even though the origin of the word, once you know the meaning, can be figured out.

Therefore, the words as well as the morphemes and the morphological rules must be part of our mental grammars. Dr. Seuss uses the rules of compounding when he explains that "when tweetle beetles battle with paddles in a puddle, they call it a *tweetle beetle puddle paddle battle.*"[7]

The pronunciation of compounds differs from the way we pronounce the sequence of two words forming a noun phrase. In a compound, the first word is usually stressed

---

[7] Dr. Seuss. 1965. *Fox in Sox,* New York: Random House, p. 51.

(pronounced somewhat louder and higher in pitch) and in a noun phrase the second word is stressed. Thus we stress *Red* in *redcoat* but *coat* in *red coat*.

Universality of Compounding

Other languages have rules for conjoining words to form compounds, as seen by French *cure-dent*, "toothpick"; German *Panzerkraftwagen*, "armored car"; Russian *cetyrexetaznyi*, "four-storied"; Spanish *tocadiscos*, "record player." In the Native American language Papago the word meaning "thing" is *haʔichu*, and it combines with *doakam*, "living creatures," to form the compound *haʔichu doakam*, "animal life."

In Twi, by combining the word meaning "son"or "child," *ɔba*, with the word meaning "chief," *ɔhene*, one derives the compound *ɔheneba*, meaning "prince." By adding the word "house," *ofi*, to *ɔhene*, the word meaning "palace," *ahemfi*, is derived. The other changes that occur in the Twi compounds are due to phonological and morphological rules in the language.

In Thai, the word "cat" is *mɛɛw*, the word for "watch" (in the sense of "to watch over") is *fâw*, and the word for "house" is *bâan*. The word for "watch cat" (like a watchdog) is the compound *mɛɛwfâwbâan*—literally, "catwatchhouse."

Compounding is a common and frequent process for enlarging the vocabulary of all languages.

Acronyms

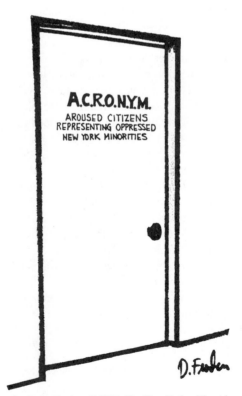

Drawing by D. Fradon. © 1974. The New Yorker Magazine, Inc.

Acronyms are words derived from the initials of several words. Such words are pronounced as the spelling indicates: NASA from *N*ational *A*eronautics and *S*pace *A*gency, UNESCO from *U*nited *N*ational *E*ducational, *S*cientific, and *C*ultural *O*rganization, and UNICEF from *U*nited *N*ations *I*nternational *C*hildren's *E*mergency *F*und. *Radar* from "*ra*dio *d*etecting *a*nd *r*anging," *laser* from "*l*ight *a*mplification by *s*timulated *e*mission of *r*adiation," and *scuba* from "*s*elf-contained *u*nderwater *b*reathing *a*pparatus," show the creative efforts of word coiners, as does *snafu,* which was coined by soldiers in World War II and is rendered in polite circles as "situation normal, all fouled up." A new acronym that has recently been added to the English language and that is sadly used very frequently these days is AIDS, from the initials of *A*cquired *I*mmune *D*eficiency *S*yndrome. When the string of letters is not easily pronounced as a word, the acronym is produced by sounding out each letter, as in NFL for *N*ational *F*ootball *L*eague or UCLA (*U*niversity of *C*alifornia, *L*os *A*ngeles), which may also be pronounced as if it were spelled *youcla.*

Acronyms are being added to the vocabulary daily with the proliferation of computers and widespread use of the Internet, including MORF (*male or female?*), FAQ (*frequently asked questions*), WYSIWYG (*what you see is what you get*) and POP (*post office protocol*) among many more.

Back-Formations

Copyright © by Mell Lazarus.

Ignorance sometimes can be creative. A new word may enter the language because of an incorrect morphological analysis. For example, *peddle* was derived from *peddler* on the mistaken assumption that the *er* was the "agentive" suffix. Such words are called **back-formations.** The verbs *hawk, stoke, swindle,* and *edit* all came into the language as back-formations—of *hawker, stoker, swindler,* and *editor. Pea* was derived from a singular word, *pease,* by speakers who thought *pease* was a plural. Language purists sometimes rail against back-formations and cite *enthuse* (from *enthusiasm*) as an example of language corruption; but language is not corrupt (although the speakers who use it may be), and many words have entered the language this way.

Some word coinage, similar to the kind of wrong morphemic analysis that produces back-formations, is deliberate. The word *bikini* is from the Bikini atoll of the Marshall Islands. Because the first syllable *bi-* in other words, like *bipolar,* means "two," some clever person called a topless bathing suit a *monokini.* Historically, a number of new words have entered the English lexicon in this way. Based on analogy with such pairs as *act/action, exempt/exemption, revise/revision,* new words *resurrect, preempt,* and *televise* were formed from the existing words *resurrection, preemption,* and *television.*

Abbreviations

Abbreviations of longer words or phrases also may become "lexicalized": *Nark* for *narcotics agent; tec* (or *dick*) for *detective; telly,* the British word for *television, prof* for *professor, piano* for *pianoforte,* and *gym* for *gymnasium* are only a few examples of such "short forms" that are now used as whole words. Other examples are *ad, bike, math, gas, phone, bus,* and *van* (for *advertisement, bicycle, mathematics, gasoline, telephone, omnibus,* and *vanguard* respectively). This process is sometimes called **clipping.**

Words from Names

The creativity of word coinage (or vocabulary addition) is also revealed by the number of **eponyms** in the English vocabulary, words that derive from proper names of individuals or places.

Willard R. Espy[8] has compiled a book of fifteen hundred such words. They include common and widely used terminology:

sandwich	Named for the fourth Earl of Sandwich, who put his food between two slices of bread so that he could eat while he gambled.
robot	After the mechanical creatures in the Czech writer Karel Capek's play *R.U.R.,* the initials standing for "Rossum's Universal Robots."
gargantuan	Named for Gargantua, the creature with a huge appetite created by Rabelais.
jumbo	After an elephant brought to the United States by P. T. Barnum. ("Jumbo olives" need not be as big as an elephant, however.)

Espy admits to ignorance of the Susan, an unknown servant, from whom we derived the compound *lazy susan,* or the Betty or Charlotte or Chuck from whom we got *brown betty, charlotte russe,* or *chuck wagon.* He does point out that *denim* was named for the material used for overalls and carpeting, which originally was imported "de Nêmes" ("from Nîmes") in France, and *argyle* from the kind of socks worn by the chiefs of Argyll of the Campbell clan in Scotland.

---

[8] W. R. Espy. 1978. *O Thou Improper, Thou Uncommon Noun: An Etymology of Words That Once Were Names,* New York: Clarkson N. Potter.

Blends

By permission of Johnny Hart and Creators Syndicate, Inc.

Two words may be combined to produce **blends.** Blends are similar to compounds but parts of the words that are combined are deleted and so they are "less than" compounds. *Smog,* from *smoke + fog; motel,* from *motor + hotel;* and *urinalysis,* from *urine + analysis* are examples of blends that have attained full lexical status in English. The word *cranapple* may be a blend of *cranberry + apple. Broasted,* from *broiled + roasted,* is a blend that has limited acceptance in the language, as does Lewis Carroll's *chortle,* from *chuckle + snort.* Carroll is famous for both the coining and the blending of words. In *Through the Looking-Glass* he describes the "meanings" of the made-up words in "Jabberwocky" as follows:

> . . . "Brillig" means four o' clock in the afternoon—the time when you begin broiling things for dinner. . . . "Slithy"means "lithe and slimy.". . . You see it's like a portmanteau—there are two meanings packed up into one word. . . . "Toves" are something like badgers—they're something like lizards—and they're something like corkscrews . . . also they make their nests under sun-dials—also they live on cheese. . . . To "gyre" is to go round and round like a gyroscope. To "gimble" is to make holes like a gimlet. And "the wabe" is the grass-plot round a sun-dial. . . . It's called "wabe" . . . because it goes a long way before it and a long way behind it. . . . "Mimsy" is "flimsy and miserable" (there's another pormanteau . . . for you).

Carroll's "portmanteaus" are what we have called blends, and such words can become part of the regular lexicon. Blending is even done by children; Elijah Peregrine, the grandson of a friend of one of the authors, when less than three years old formed the word *crocogator* by blending *crocodile* and *alligator.*

GRAMMATICAL MORPHEMES

". . . and even . . . the patriotic archbishop of Canterbury found it advisable—"

"Found what?" said the Duck.

"Found it," the Mouse replied rather crossly; "of course you know what 'it' means."

> "I know what 'it' means well enough, when I find a thing," said the Duck; "it's generally a frog or a worm. The question is, what did the archbishop find?"
>
> Lewis Carroll, *Alice's Adventures in Wonderland*

Morphological rules for combining morphemes into words differ from the syntactic rules of a language that determine how words are combined to form sentences. There is, however, an interesting relationship between morphology and syntax. In the discussion of derivational morphology, we saw that certain aspects of morphology have syntactic implications in that nouns can be derived from verbs, verbs from adjectives, adjectives from nouns, and so on. There are other ways in which morphology is dependent on syntax.

When we combine words to form sentences, these sentences are combinations of morphemes, but some of these morphemes, similar to *-ceive* or *-mit,* which were shown to derive a meaning only when combined with other morphemes in a word, derive a meaning only when combined with other morphemes in a sentence. For example, what is the meaning of *it* in the sentence ***It's*** *hot in July,* or in *The Archbishop found **it** advisable*? What is the meaning of *to* in *He wanted her **to** go*? *To* has a grammatical meaning as an infinitive marker, and it is also a morpheme required by the syntactic, sentence-formation rules of the language. Similarly for *have* in *Cows **have** walked here,* which is a grammatical marker for the present perfect; and for the different forms of *be* in both *The baby **is** crying* and *The baby's diaper **was** changed,* which function, respectively, as a progressive marker and as a passive voice marker.

Inflectional Morphemes

"LOOKS LIKE WE SPEND MOST OF OUR TIME INGING... YOU KNOW, LIKE SLEEPING, EATING, RUNNING, CLIMBING..."

DENNIS THE MENACE® used by permission of Hank Ketcham and © by North America Syndicate.

Many languages, including English to some extent, contain bound morphemes that are for the most part purely grammatical markers, representing such concepts as tense, number, gender, case, and so forth.

Such bound grammatical morphemes are called **inflectional morphemes** (or, less technically, inflectional endings); they never change the syntactic category of the words or morphemes to which they are attached. They are always attached to complete words. Consider the forms of the verb in the following sentences:

(a) I sail the ocean blue.
(b) He sails the ocean blue.
(c) John sailed the ocean blue.
(d) John has sailed the ocean blue.
(e) John is sailing the ocean blue.

In sentence (b) the *s* at the end of the verb is an agreement marker; it signifies that the subject of the verb is third person, is singular, and that the verb is in the present tense. It doesn't add any lexical meaning. The *-ed* and *-ing* endings are morphemes required by the syntactic rules of the language to signal tense or aspect.

English is no longer a highly inflected language. But we do have other inflectional endings such as the plural suffix, which is attached to certain singular nouns, as in *boy/boys* and *cat/cats*. At the present stage of English history, there are a total of eight bound inflectional affixes:

English Inflectional Morphemes		**Examples**
-s	third person singular present	She wait-**s** at home.
-ed	past tense	She wait-**ed** at home.
-ing	progressive	She is eat-**ing** the donut.
-en	past participle	Mary has eat-**en** the donuts.
-s	plural	She ate the donut-**s**.
-'s	possessive	Disa**'s** hair is short.
-er	comparative	Disa has short-**er** hair than Karin.
-est	superlative	Disa has the short-**est** hair.

Inflectional morphemes in English typically follow derivational morphemes. Thus, to the derivationally complex word *un + like + ly + hood* one can add a plural ending to form *un + like + ly + hood + s* but not **unlikeslyhood*. However, with compounds such as those previously discussed, the situation is complicated. Thus, for many speakers, the plural of *mother-in-law* is *mothers-in-law* whereas the possessive form is *mother-in-law's*.

Some languages are highly inflected. Finnish nouns, for example, have many different inflectional endings, as shown in the following example (don't be concerned if you don't know what all the specific case endings mean)[9]:

---

[9] Examples are from L. Campbell. 1977. "Generative Phonology vs. Finnish Phonology: Retrospect and Prospect," *Texas Linguistic Forum* 5: 21–58.

(sg. = singular; pl. = plural)

mantere	nominative sg.
mantereen	genitive (possessive) sg.
manteretta	partitive sg.
mantereena	essive sg.
mantereeseen	illative sg.
mantereita	partitive pl.
mantereisiin	illative pl.
mantereiden	genitive pl.

Students often ask for definitions of derivational morphemes as opposed to inflectional morphemes. There is no easy answer; probably the simplest is to say that derivational morphemes are bound morphemes that are not inflectional. Inflectional morphemes signal grammatical relations and are required by the syntactic sentence formation rules. Derivational morphemes, when affixed to roots and stems, change the grammatical word class and/or the basic meaning of the word, which may then be inflected as to number (singular or plural), tense (present, past, future), and so on.

Exceptions and Suppletions

PEANUTS reprinted by permission of UFS, Inc.

The regular rule that forms plurals from singular nouns does not apply to words like *child/children, man/men, sheep/sheep, criterion/criteria.* These words are exceptions to the English inflectional rule of plural formation. Similarly, verbs like *sing/sang* or *bring/brought* are exceptions to the regular past tense rule in English.

When, as children, we are learning the language, that is, acquiring (or constructing) the grammar, we have to learn specifically that the plural of *man* is *men* and that the past of *go* is *went.* For this reason we often hear children say *mans* and *goed;* they first learn the regular rules, and until they learn the exceptions to these rules, they apply them generally to all the nouns and verbs. These children's errors, in fact, show that the regular rules exist.

Some of the irregular forms must be listed separately in our mental lexicons, as **suppletive** forms. That is, one cannot use the regular rules of inflectional morphology to add affixes to words that are exceptions like *bring/brought,* but must replace the noninflected form with another word. It is possible that for regular words, only the singular forms are listed since we can use the inflectional rules to form plurals. But this can't be so with exceptions.

When a new word enters the language it is the regular inflectional rules that apply. The plural of *Bic* is *Bics,* not **Bicken.*

The past tense of the verb *hit,* as in the sentence *Yesterday John hit the roof,* and the plural of the noun *sheep,* as in *The sheep are in the meadow,* show that some morphemes seem to have no phonological shape at all. We know that *hit* in the above sentence is *hit + past* because of the time adverb *yesterday,* and we know that *sheep* is the phonetic form of *sheep + plural* because of the plural verb form *are.* Thousands of years ago the Hindu grammarians suggested that some morphemes have a **zero-form;** that is, they have no phonological representation. In our view, however, because we would like to hold to the definition of a morpheme as a constant sound-meaning form, we will suggest that the morpheme *hit* is marked as both present and past in the lexicon, and the morpheme *sheep* is marked as both singular and plural.

Morphology and Syntax

> "Curiouser and curiouser!" cried Alice (she was so much surprised, that for the moment she quite forgot how to speak good English).
>
> Lewis Carroll, *Alice's Adventures in Wonderland*

Some grammatical relations can be expressed either inflectionally (morphologically) or syntactically (as part of the sentence structure). We can see this in the following sentences:

England's queen is Elizabeth II.	The Queen of England is Elizabeth II.
He loves books.	He is a lover of books.
The planes which fly are red.	The flying planes are red.
He is hungrier than she.	He is more hungry than she.

Some of you may form the comparative of *beastly* only by adding *-er. Beastlier* is often used interchangeably with *more beastly.* There are speakers who say either. We know the rule that determines when either form of the comparative can be used or when just one can be used, as pointed out by Lewis Carroll in the quotation above.

What one language signals with inflectional affixes, another does with word order and another with **function words.** For example, in English, the sentence *Maxim defends Victor* means something different from *Victor defends Maxim.* The word order is very important. In Russian, all the following sentences mean "Maxim defends Victor": (The letter č is pronounced like the *ch* in the word *cheese;* the *j* is pronounced like the *y* in *yet.*)

> Maksim zaščiščajet Viktora.
> Maksim Viktora zaščiščajet.
> Viktora Maksim zaščiščajet.
> Viktora zaščiščajet Maksim.

The inflectional suffix *-a* added to the name *Viktor* to derive *Viktora* shows that Victor, not Maksim, is defended.

In English, to convey the future meaning of a verb we must use a function word *will,* as in *John will come Monday.* In French, the verb is inflected for future tense. Notice the difference between "John is coming Monday," *Jean **vient** lundi,* and "John will come Monday," *Jean **viendra** lundi.* Similarly, where English uses the grammatical markers *have* and *be,* mentioned above, other languages use affixing to achieve the same meaning, as illustrated with Indonesian:

dokter mem + eriksa saja	"The doctor examines me."
saja dip + eriksa oleh dokter	"I was examined by the doctor."

In discussing derivational and compounding morphology, we noted that knowing the meaning of the distinct morphemes may not always reveal the meaning of the morphologically complex word. This problem is not true of inflectional morphology. If we know the meaning of the word *linguist,* we also know the meaning of the plural form *linguists;* if we know the meaning of the verb *analyze,* we know the meaning of *analyzed* and *analyzes* and *analyzing.* This reveals another difference between derivational and inflectional morphology.

Figure 3-2 shows the way one may classify English morphemes.

FIGURE 3-2

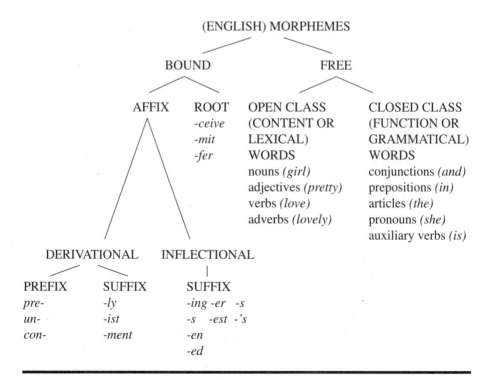

The mental grammar of the language that is internalized by the language learner includes a lexicon listing all the morphemes and the derived words of the language. The morphological rules of the grammar permit speakers to use and understand the morphemes and words in forming and understanding sentences, and in forming and understanding new words.

MORPHOLOGICAL ANALYSIS: IDENTIFYING MORPHEMES

Speakers of a language can easily learn how to analyze a word of their language into its component morphemes, since their mental grammars include a mental lexicon of morphemes and the morphological rules for their combination. But suppose you didn't know English and were a linguist from the planet Mars wishing to analyze the language. How would you find out what the morphemes of English were? How would you determine whether a word in that language had one or two or more morphemes?

The first thing to do would be to ask native speakers how they would say various words. (It would of course help if the speakers knew Martian so you could ask your questions in Martian. If not, you would have to do quite a bit of miming and gesturing and acting.) Suppose then, you collected the following sets or *paradigms* of forms:

ADJECTIVE	MEANING	
ugly	"very unattractive"	
uglier	"more ugly"	
ugliest	"most ugly"	
pretty	"nice looking"	
prettier	"more nice looking"	
prettiest	"most nice looking"	
tall	"large in height"	
taller	"more tall"	
tallest	"most tall"	etc.

To determine what the morphemes are in such a list, the first thing a field linguist would do is to see if there are any forms that mean the same thing in different words, that is, to look for **recurring** forms. We find them: *ugly* occurs in *ugly, uglier, ugliest,* all three of which words include the meaning "very unattractive." We also find that *er* occurs in *prettier* and *taller* adding the meaning "more" to the adjectives to which it is attached. Similarly, *est* adds the meaning "most." Furthermore, by asking additional questions of our English speaker we find that *er* and *est* do not occur in isolation with the meanings of "more" and "most." We can therefore conclude that the following morphemes occur in English:

ugly	root morpheme
pretty	root morpheme
tall	root morpheme
er	bound morpheme "comparative"
est	bound morpheme "superlative"

As we proceed further we find there are other words that end with *-er—singer, lover, bomber, writer, teacher* and many more words in which the *-er* ending does not mean "comparative" but, when attached to a verb, changes it to a noun who "verbs," i.e., *sings, loves, bombs, writes, teaches.* So we conclude that this is a different morpheme even though it is pronounced the same as the comparative. We go on and find words like *number, somber, umber, butter, member* and many others in which the *er* has no separate meaning at all—a somber is not one who sombs and a member does not memb—and therefore these words must be monomorphemic.

Once you have fully described the morphology of English, you might want to go on to describe another language. A language called Paku was written by one of the authors of this book (Fromkin) for a television series called *Land of the Lost,* originally shown on NBC in 1974 and 1975. This was a language used by the monkey people called Pakuni. Suppose you found yourself in this strange land and attempted to find out what the morphemes of Paku were. Again, you would collect your data from a native Paku speaker and proceed as the Martian did with English. Consider the following data from Paku:

me	"I"	meni	"we"
ye	"you (singular)"	yeni	"you (plural)"
we	"he"	weni	"they (masculine)"
wa	"she"	wani	"they (feminine)"
abuma	"girl"	abumani	"girls"
adusa	"boy"	adusani	"boys"
abu	"child"	abuni	"children"
Paku	"one Paku"	Pakuni	"more than one Paku"

By examining these words you find that all the plural forms end in *-ni* and the singular forms do not. You therefore conclude that *-ni* is a separate morpheme meaning "plural" which is attached as a suffix to a noun.

While these are rather simple examples of how one proceeds to conduct a morphological analysis, the principles remain the same and you are on the road to becoming a morphologist.

SUMMARY

Knowing a language means knowing the words of that language. When you know a word you know both its **form** (sound) and its **meaning;** these are inseparable parts of the linguistic **sign.** The relationship between the form and meaning is **arbitrary**. That is, by hearing the sounds (form) you cannot know the meaning of those sounds without having learned it previously.

Each word is stored in your mental **lexicon** with information on its pronunciation (phonological representation), its meaning (semantic properties), and its syntactic class or category specification. For literate speakers, its spelling or **orthography** will also be given.

In spoken language, words are not separated by pauses (or spaces as in written language). One must know the language in order to segment the stream of speech into separate words.

Words are not the most elemental sound-meaning units; some words are structurally complex. The most elemental grammatical units in a language are **morphemes.** A morpheme is the minimal unit of linguistic meaning or grammatical function. Thus, *moralizers* is an English word composed of four morphemes: *moral + ize + er + s.*

The study of word formation and the internal structure of words is called **morphology.** Part of one's linguistic competence includes knowledge of the language's morphology—the morphemes, words, their pronunciation, their meanings, and how they are combined. Morphemes combine according to the morphological rules of the language. A word consists of one or more morphemes. Lexical content morphemes that cannot be analyzed into smaller parts are called **root** morphemes. When a root morpheme is combined with affix morphemes it forms a **stem**. Other affixes can be added to a stem to form a more complex stem.

Some morphemes are **bound** in that they must be joined to other morphemes, are always parts of words and never words by themselves. Other morphemes are **free** in that they need not be attached to other morphemes; *free, king, serf,* and *bore* are free morphemes; *-dom,* as in *freedom, kingdom, serfdom,* and *boredom* is a bound morpheme. **Affixes,** that is **prefixes, suffixes, infixes,** and **circumfixes,** are bound morphemes. Prefixes occur before, suffixes after, infixes in the middle of, and circumfixes around stems.

Some morphemes, like *huckle* in *huckleberry* and *-ceive* in *perceive* or *receive,* have constant phonological form but meanings determined only by the words in which they occur. They are thus also bound morphemes.

Lexical content or **root** morphemes constitute the major word classes—nouns, verbs, adjectives, adverbs. These are **open class** items because their classes are easily added to.

Morphemes may be **derivational** or **inflectional.** Derivational **morphological rules** are rules of word formation. Derivational morphemes, when added to a root or stem, may change the syntactic word class and/or the meaning of the word; for example, adding *-ish* to the noun *boy* derives an adjective, and prefixing *un-* to *pleasant* changes the meaning by adding a negative element. Inflectional morphemes are determined by the rules of syntax. They are added to complete words, whether simple **monomorphemic** words or complex **polymorphemic** words (i.e., words with more than one morpheme). Inflectional morphemes never change the syntactic category of the word.

Some grammatical morphemes or **function words,** together with the bound inflectional morphemes, constitute a **closed class;** they are inserted into sentences according to the syntactic structure. The past tense morpheme, often written as *ed,* is added as a suffix to a verb, and the future tense morpheme *will,* is inserted in a sentence according to the syntactic rules of English.

The grammars of sign languages also include a morphological component consisting of root, derivational, and inflectional sign morphemes, and the rules for their combination.

Grammars also include ways of increasing the vocabulary, of adding new words and morphemes to the lexicon. Words can be **coined** outright, limited only by the coiner's imagination and the phonetic constraints of English word formation. **Compounds** are also a source of new words. Morphological rules combine two or more words to form complex combinations like *lamb chop, deep-sea diver,* and *laptop,* a new word spawned by the computer industry. Frequently, the meaning of compounds cannot be predicted from the meanings of their individual morphemes.

Acronyms are words derived from the initials of several words—like AWOL, which came into the language as the initials for "*a*way *without *l*eave." **Blends** are similar to compounds but usually combine shortened forms of two or more morphemes or words. *Brunch,* a late morning meal, is a blend of *breakfast* and *lunch.* **Eponyms** (words taken from proper names such as *john* for "toilet" or "prostitute's customer"), **back-formations,** and **abbreviations** also add to the given stock of words.

While the particular morphemes and the particular morphological rules are language-dependent, the same general processes occur in all languages.

References for Further Reading

Anderson, Stephen R. 1992. *A-Morphous Morphology.* Cambridge, England: Cambridge University Press.

Aronoff, Mark. 1976. *Word Formation in Generative Grammar.* Cambridge, MA: MIT Press.

Bauer, Laurie. 1983. *English Word-formation.* Cambridge, England: Cambridge University Press.

Hammond, Michael, and Michael Noonan, eds. 1988. *Theoretical Morphology: Approaches in Modern Linguistics.* San Diego: Academic Press, Inc.

Jensen, John T. 1990. *Morphology: Word Structure in Generative Grammar.* Amsterdam/Philadelphia: John Benjamins Publishing.

Marchand, Hans. 1969. *The Categories and Types of Present-Day English Word-Formation,* 2nd ed. Munich: C. H. Beck'sche Verlagsbuchhandlung.

Matthews, P. H. 1976. *Morphology: An Introduction to the Theory of Word Structure.* Cambridge, England: Cambridge University Press.

Scalise, Sergio. 1984. *Generative Morphology.* Dordrecht, Holland/Cinnaminson, U.S.A: Foris Publications.

Spencer, Andrew. 1991. *Morphological Theory: An Introduction to Word Structure in Generative Grammar.* London: Basil Blackwell.

EXERCISES

1. Here is how to estimate the number of words in your mental lexicon. Consult any standard dictionary.

   (1) Count the number of entries on a typical page. They are usually bold-faced. _____

   (2) Multiply the number of words per page by the number of pages in the dictionary. _____

   (3) Pick four pages in the dictionary at random, say, pages 50, 75, 125, 303. Count the number of words on these pages. _____

   (4) How many of these words do you know? _____

   (5) What percentage of the total words on the four pages do you know? _____

   (6) Multiply the words in the dictionary by the percent you arrived at in (5). You know approximately _____ English words.

2. Divide the following words by placing a + between their separate morphemes. (Some of the words may be *monomorphemic* and therefore indivisible.)

   Example: replaces   re + place + s

   a. retroactive
   b. befriended
   c. televise
   d. margin
   e. endearment
   f. psychology
   g. unpalatable
   h. holiday
   i. grandmother
   j. morphemic
   k. mistreatment
   l. disactivation
   m. saltpeter
   n. airsickness

3. Match each expression under A with the one statement under B that characterizes it.

A	**B**
a. noisy crow	1. compound noun
b. eat crow	2. root morpheme plus derivational prefix
c. scarecrow	3. phrase consisting of adjective plus noun
d. the crow	4. root morpheme plus inflectional affix
e. crowlike	5. root morpheme plus derivational suffix
f. crows	6. grammatical morpheme followed by lexical morpheme
	7. idiom

4. Write the one proper description from the list under B for the italicized part of each word in A.

A	**B**
a. terroriz*ed*	(1) free root
b. un*civil*ized	(2) bound root
c. terror*ize*	(3) inflectional suffix
d. *luke*warm	(4) derivational suffix
e. *im*possible	(5) inflectional prefix
	(6) derivational prefix
	(7) inflectional infix
	(8) derivational infix

5. A. Consider the following nouns in Zulu and proceed to look for the recurring forms. Note that the ordering of morphemes is not identical across languages. Thus, what is a prefix in one language may be a suffix or an infix in another.

umfazi	"married woman"	abafazi	"married women"
umfani	"boy"	abafani	"boys"
umzali	"parent"	abazali	"parents"
umfundisi	"teacher"	abafundisi	"teachers"
umbazi	"carver"	ababazi	"carvers"
umlimi	"farmer"	abalimi	"farmers"
umdlali	"player"	abadlali	"players"
umfundi	"reader"	abafundi	"readers"

a. What is the morpheme meaning "singular" in Zulu?

b. What is the morpheme meaning "plural" in Zulu?

c. List the Zulu stems and their meanings to which the singular and plural morphemes are attached.

B. The following Zulu verbs are derived from noun stems by adding a verbal suffix.

fundisa	"to teach"	funda	"to read"
lima	"to cultivate"	baza	"to carve"

d. Compare these to the words in section A that are related in meaning, e.g., *umfundisi* "teacher," *abafundisi* "teachers," *fundisa* "to teach." What is the derivational suffix morpheme that specifies the category verb?

e. What is the nominal suffix morpheme (that is, the suffix that forms nouns)?

f. State the morphological noun formation rule in Zulu.

g. What is the stem morpheme meaning "read"?

h. What is the stem morpheme meaning "carve"?

6. Examine the following words from Michoacan Aztec.

nokali	"my house"	mopelo	"your dog"
nokalimes	"my houses"	mopelomes	"your dogs"
mokali	"your house"	ipelo	"his dog"
ikali	"his house"	nokwahmili	"my cornfield"
kalimes	"houses"	mokwahmili	"your cornfield"
		ikwahmili	"his cornfield"

a. The morpheme meaning "house" is:

(1) kal   (2) kali   (3) kalim   (4) ikal   (5) ka

b. The morpheme meaning "cornfields" is:

(1) kwahmilimes (2) nokwahmilimes (3) nokwahmili (4) kwahmili
(5) ikwahmilimes

c. The word meaning "his dogs" is:

(1) pelos (2) ipelomes (3) ipelos (4) mopelo (5) pelomes

d. If the word meaning "friend" in this language is **mahkwa,** then the word meaning "my friends" is:

(1) momahkwa (2) imahkwas (3) momahkwames
(4) momahkwaes (5) nomahkwames

e. The word meaning "dog" in this language is:

(1) pelo (2) perro (3) peli (4) pel (5) mopel

7. The following infinitive and past participle verb forms are found in Dutch.

Root	Infinitive	Past Participle	
wandel	wandelen	gewandeld	"walk"
duw	duwen	geduwd	"push"
zag	zagen	gezegd	"saw"
stofzuig	stofzuigen	gestofzuigd	"vacuum-clean"

With reference to the morphological processes of prefixing, suffixing, infixing, and circumfixing discussed in this chapter and the specific morphemes involved:

a. State the morphological rule for forming an infinitive in Dutch.

b. State the morphological rule for forming the Dutch past participle form.

8. Below are some sentences in Swahili:

mtoto	amefika	"The child has arrived."
mtoto	anafika	"The child is arriving."
mtoto	atafika	"The child will arrive."
watoto	wamefika	"The children have arrived."
watoto	wanafika	"The children are arriving."
watoto	watafika	"The children will arrive."
mtu	amelala	"The man has slept."
mtu	analala	"The man is sleeping."
mtu	atalala	"The man will sleep."
watu	wamelala	"The men have slept."
watu	wanalala	"The men are sleeping."
watu	watalala	"The men will sleep."
kisu	kimeanguka	"The knife has fallen."
kisu	kinaanguka	"The knife is falling."
kisu	kitaanguka	"The knife will fall."

visu	vimeanguka	"The knives have fallen."
visu	vinaanguka	"The knives are falling."
visu	vitaanguka	"The knives will fall."
kikapu	kimeanguka	"The basket has fallen."
kikapu	kinaanguka	"The basket is falling."
kikapu	kitaanguka	"The basket will fall."
vikapu	vimeanguka	"The baskets have fallen."
vikapu	vinaanguka	"The baskets are falling."
vikapu	vitaanguka	"The baskets will fall."

One of the characteristic features of Swahili (and Bantu languages in general) is the existence of noun classes. There are specific singular and plural prefixes that occur with the nouns in each class. These prefixes are also used for purposes of agreement between the subject-noun and the verb. In the sentences given, two of these classes are included (there are many more in the language).

a. Identify all the morphemes you can detect, and give their meanings.

> Example: -toto "child"
> *m-* noun prefix attached to singular nouns of Class I
> *a-* prefix attached to verbs when the subject is a
> singular noun of Class I

Be sure to look for the other noun and verb markers, including tense markers.

b. How is the verb constructed? That is, what kinds of morphemes are strung together and in what order?

c. How would you say in Swahili:

(1) The child is falling.

(2) The baskets have arrived.

(3) The man will fall.

9. One morphological process not discussed in this chapter is called **reduplication**—the formation of new words through the repetition of part or all of a word—which occurs in a number of languages. The following examples from Samoan exemplify this kind of morphological rule.

manao	"he wishes"	mananao	"they wish"
matua	"he is old"	matutua	"they are old"
malosi	"he is strong"	malolosi	"they are strong"
punou	"he bends"	punonou	"they bend"
atamaki	"he is wise"	atamamaki	"they are wise"
savali	"he travels"	pepese	"they sing"
laga	"he weaves"		

a. What is the Samoan for:

(1) they weave

(2) they travel

(3) he sings

b. Formulate a general statement (a morphological rule) that states how to form the plural verb form from the singular verb form.

10. Below are listed some words followed by incorrect definitions. (All these errors are taken from Amsel Greene's *Pullet Surprises*.)

Word	Student Definition
stalemate	"husband or wife no longer interested"
effusive	"able to be merged"
tenet	"a group of ten singers"
dermatology	"a study of derms"
ingenious	"not very smart"
finesse	"a female fish"

For each of these incorrect definitions, give some possible reasons why the students made the guesses they did. Where you can exemplify by reference to other words or morphemes, giving their meanings, do so.

11. Dal Yoo[10] expresses the belief that abbreviations and acronyms occur in the United States more than in any other country. He refers, for example, to the acronyms generated in the 1991 Gulf war, by both pro- and antiwar demonstrations such as SMASH "*S*tudents *M*obilized *A*gainst *S*addam *H*ussein" and SCUD "*S*adly *C*onfused *U*npatriotic *D*emonstrators." He also refers to a neon sign on a downtown high-rise building in Philadelphia reading PSFS for "*P*hiladelphia *S*avings *F*und *S*ociety," which was referred to by a local tour guide as meaning, instead, "*P*hiladelphia *S*mells *F*unny *S*ometimes." Dr. Yoo is a medical doctor who writes: "When I have no idea what the patient has, I apply my favorite of all the abbreviations, GOK syndrome '*G*od *O*nly *K*nows.'" Such acronyms show how innovative our linguistic ability is.

a. List ten acronyms currently in use in English. Do not use the ones given in the text.

b. Invent ten new acronyms (listing the words as well as the initials).

12. There are many asymmetries in English in which a root morpheme combined with a prefix constitutes a word but without the prefix is a nonword. A number of these are given in this chapter.

---

[10] Dal Yoo. 1991. "The World of Abbreviations and Acronyms," *Verbatim: The Language Quarterly* (Summer): 4–5.

A. Below are a list of such nonword roots. Add a prefix to each root to form an existing English word.

Words	**Nonwords**
_____	*descript
_____	*cognito
_____	*beknownst
_____	*peccable
_____	*promptu
_____	*plussed
_____	*dominatable
_____	*nomer

B. There are many more such multimorphemic words for which the root morphemes do not constitute words by themselves. See how many you can think of.

13. We have seen that the meaning of compounds is often not revealed by the meaning of its composite words. Crossword puzzles and riddles often make use of this by providing the meaning of two parts of a compound and asking for the resulting word. For example, infielder = diminutive + cease. Read this as asking for a word which means "infielder" by combining a word which means "diminutive" with a word which means "cease." The answer is *shortstop*. See if you can figure out the following:

a. sci-fi TV series = headliner + journey

b. campaign = farm building + tempest

c. at-home wear = dip + court attire

d. kind of pen = formal dance + sharp end

e. conservative = correct + part of an airplane

Chapter 4
Syntax:
The Sentence Patterns
of Language

To grammar even kings bow.

J. B. Molière, *Les femmes savantes,* II, 1672

"*I don't sing because I am happy. I am
happy because I sing.*"

Knowing a language includes the ability to construct phrases and sentences out of morphemes and words. The part of the grammar that represents a speaker's knowledge of these structures and their formation is called **syntax.** The aim of this chapter is to show you what syntactic structure is and what the rules that determine syntactic structure are like. Most of the examples will be from the syntax of English, but the principles that account for syntactic structures are universal.

Part of what we mean by *structure* is word order. As suggested by the above cartoon, the meaning of a sentence depends to a great extent on the order in which words occur in a sentence. Thus,

> Athens defeated Sparta

does not have the same meaning as

> Sparta defeated Athens.

Sometimes, however, a change of word order has no effect on meaning.

> The Chief Justice swore in the new President.
> The Chief Justice swore the new President in.

The grammars of all languages include **rules of syntax** that reflect speakers' knowledge of these facts.

GRAMMATICAL OR UNGRAMMATICAL?

Reprinted with special permission of King Features Syndicate.

The syntactic rules of a grammar also account for the fact that even though the following sequence is made up of meaningful words, it has no meaning.

> Chief swore president the Justice the in new

In English and in every language, every sentence is a sequence of words, but not every sequence of words is a sentence. Sequences of words that conform to the rules of syntax are said to be **well formed** or **grammatical** and those that violate the syntactic rules are therefore **ill formed** or **ungrammatical.**

What Grammaticality Is Based On

In Chapter 1 you were asked to indicate strings of words as grammatical or ungrammatical according to your linguistic intuitions. Here is another list of word sequences. Disregarding the sentence meanings, use *your* knowledge of English and place an asterisk in front of the ones that strike you as peculiar or funny in some way.

 (a) The boy found the ball
 (b) The boy found quickly
 (c) The boy found in the house
 (d) The boy found the ball in the house
 (e) Disa slept the baby
 (f) Disa slept soundly
 (g) Zack believes Robert to be a gentleman
 (h) Zack believes to be a gentleman
 (i) Zack tries Robert to be a gentleman
 (j) Zack tries to be a gentleman
 (k) Zack wants to be a gentleman
 (l) Zack wants Robert to be a gentleman
 (m) Jack and Jill ran up the hill
 (n) Jack and Jill ran up the bill
 (o) Jack and Jill ran the hill up
 (p) Jack and Jill ran the bill up
 (q) Up the hill ran Jack and Jill
 (r) Up the bill ran Jack and Jill

We predict that speakers of English will "star" **b, c, e, h, i, o, r.** If we are right, this shows that grammaticality judgments are not idiosyncratic or capricious but are determined by rules that are shared by the speakers of a language.

The syntactic rules that account for the ability to make these judgments include, in addition to rules of word order, other constraints. For example:

- The rules specify that *found* must be followed directly by an expression like the *ball* but not by *quickly* or *in the house* as illustrated in **a–d.**
- The verb *sleep* patterns differently than *find* in that it may be followed solely by a word like *soundly* but not by other kinds of phrases such as *the baby* as shown in **e** and **f.**
- Examples **g–l** show that *believe* and *try* function in opposite fashion while *want* exhibits yet a third pattern.
- Finally, the word order rules that constrain phrases such as *run up the hill* differ from those concerning *run up the bill* as seen in **m–r.**

Sentences are not random strings of words. Some strings of words that we can interpret are not sentences. For example, we can understand (o) above even though we recognize it as ungrammatical. We can fix it up to make it grammatical. To be a sentence, words must conform to specific patterns determined by the syntactic rules of the language.

What Grammaticality Is Not Based On

> *Colorless green ideas sleep furiously.* This is a very interesting sentence, because it shows that syntax can be separated from semantics—that form can be separated from meaning. The sentence doesn't seem to mean anything coherent, but it sounds like an English sentence.
>
> Howard Lasknik, *The Human Language: Program One*

Grammaticality is not based on what is taught in school but on the rules constructed unconsciously as children. Children acquire most of the syntactic rules of their language even before learning to read. (This is discussed at greater length in Chapter 8.)

The ability to make grammaticality judgments does not depend on having heard the sentence before. You may never have heard or read the sentence

Enormous crickets in pink socks danced at the prom

but your syntactic knowledge tells you that it is grammatical.

Grammaticality judgments do not depend on whether the sentence is meaningful or not, as shown by the following sentences:

Colorless green ideas sleep furiously.
A verb crumpled the milk.

Although these sentences do not make much sense, they are syntactically well formed. They sound "funny," but they differ in their "funniness" from the following strings of words:

*Furiously sleep ideas green colorless.
*Milk the crumpled verb a.

You may understand ungrammatical sequences even though you know they are not well formed. To most English speakers

*The boy quickly in the house the ball found

is interpretable although these same speakers know that the word order is irregular. On the other hand, grammatical sentences may be uninterpretable if they include nonsense strings, that is, words with no agreed-on meaning, as shown by the first two lines of "Jabberwocky" by Lewis Carroll:

*'Twas brillig, and the slithy toves
Did gyre and gimble in the wabe;*

Such nonsense poetry is amusing because the sentences comply with syntactic rules and sound like good English. Ungrammatical strings of nonsense words are not entertaining:

*Toves slithy the and brillig 'twas
wabe the in gimble and gyre did.*

Nor does grammaticality depend on the truth of sentences—if it did, lying would be impossible—nor on whether real objects are being discussed, nor on whether something is possible. Untrue sentences can be grammatical, sentences discussing unicorns can be grammatical, and sentences referring to pregnant fathers can be grammatical.

Unconscious knowledge of the syntactic rules of grammar permits speakers to make grammaticality judgments.

WHAT ELSE DO YOU KNOW ABOUT SYNTAX?

Reprinted with special permission of North America Syndicate.

Syntactic knowledge goes beyond being able to decide which strings are grammatical and which are not. It accounts for the double meaning, or **ambiguity**, of expressions like the one illustrated in the cartoon above. The humor of the cartoon depends on the ambiguity of the phrase *synthetic buffalo hides,* which can mean "buffalo hides that are synthetic," or "hides of synthetic buffalo."

This example illustrates that within a phrase, certain words are grouped together. Sentences have structure as well as word order. The words in the phrase *synthetic buffalo hides* can be grouped in two ways. When we group like this:

>   synthetic (buffalo hides)

we get the first meaning. When we group like this:

>   (synthetic buffalo) hides

we get the second meaning.

The rules of syntax allow both these groupings, which is why the expression is ambiguous. The two structures may also be illustrated by the following diagrams:

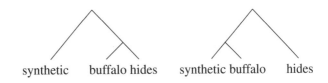

Many sentences exhibit such ambiguities, often leading to humorous results. Consider the following two sentences, which appeared in classified ads:

> For sale: an antique desk suitable for lady with thick legs and large drawers.

> We will oil your sewing machine and adjust tension in your home for $10.00.

In the first ad, the humorous reading comes from the grouping . . . *(for lady with thick legs and large drawers)* as opposed to the intended . . . *(for lady) (with thick legs and large drawers)* where the legs and drawers belong to the desk. The second case is similar.

Because these ambiguities are a result of different structures, they are instances of **structural ambiguity.**

Contrast these sentences with

> This will make you smart.

The two interpretations of this sentence are due to the two meanings of *smart*— "clever" or "burning sensation." Such lexical or word-meaning ambiguities, as opposed to structural ambiguities, will be discussed further in Chapter 5.

Syntactic knowledge also enables us to determine the **grammatical relations** in a sentence, such as **subject** and **direct object,** and how they are to be understood. Consider the following sentences:

(1) Mary hired Bill.
(2) Bill hired Mary.
(3) Bill was hired by Mary.

In (1) *Mary* is the subject and is understood to be the employer that did the hiring. *Bill* is the direct object and is understood to be the employee. In (2) *Bill* is the subject and *Mary* is the direct object, and as we would expect, the meaning changes so that we understand Bill to be Mary's employer. In (3) the grammatical relationships are the same as in (2), but we understand it to have the same meaning as (1), despite the structural differences between (1) and (3).

Syntactic rules reveal the grammatical relations between the words of a sentence and tell us when structural differences result in meaning differences and when they do not. We see that grammatical relations like subject and direct object do not always tell us 'who does what to whom' since in (1) and (2) the grammatical subject is the "who" but in (3) the subject is the "whom." These **thematic roles,** as opposed to grammatical relations, will be discussed in the next chapter.

The syntactic rules permit speakers to produce and understand an unlimited number of sentences never produced or heard before, the creative aspect of language use.

Thus, the syntactic rules in a grammar must at least account for:

1. the grammaticality of sentences
2. word order
3. structural ambiguity

4. grammatical relations
5. whether different structures have differing meanings or the same meaning
6. the creative aspect of language

A major goal of linguistics is to show clearly and explicitly how syntactic rules account for this knowledge. A theory of grammar must provide a complete characterization of what speakers implicitly know about their language.

SENTENCE STRUCTURE

I really do not know that anything has ever been more exciting than diagramming sentences.

Gertrude Stein

Syntactic rules determine the order of words in a sentence, and how the words are grouped. The words in the sentence

The child found the puppy

may be grouped into *(the child)* and *(found the puppy),* corresponding to the subject and predicate of the sentence. A further division gives *(the child) ((found)(the puppy)),* and finally the individual words: *((the)(child)) ((found)((the) (puppy))).* It is easier to see the parts and subparts of the sentence in a **tree diagram:**

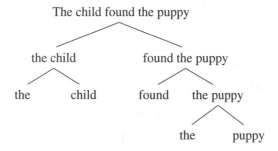

The "tree" is upside down with its "root" being the entire sentence, *The child found the puppy,* and its "leaves" being the individual words, *the, child, found, the, puppy.* The tree conveys the same information as the nested parentheses, but more perspicuously. The groupings and subgroupings reflect the **hierarchical structure** of the tree.

The tree diagram shows among other things that the phrase *found the puppy* is naturally divided into two branches, the two groups, *found* and *the puppy.* A different division, say *found the* and *puppy,* is unnatural in the sense that speakers of English would not use *found the* by itself or as an answer to the question "What did you find?" An answer might be *the puppy* but not *found the.* In fact, *found the* cannot be an answer to any question. A word like *found* never occurs in a single group followed only by *the.*

Other sentences with the same meaning as the original sentence can be formed; for example:

It was the puppy the child found
The puppy was found by the child

and in all such arrangements *the puppy* remains intact. *Found the* does not remain intact, nor can the sentence be changed by moving *found the* around. All these facts show that *the puppy* is a natural structure whereas *found the* is not.

Only one tree representation consistent with an English speaker's syntactic knowledge can be drawn for the sentence *The child found the puppy*. But the phrase *synthetic buffalo hides* has two such trees, one for each of its two meanings:

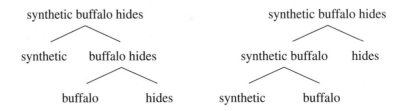

Every sentence has one or more corresponding **constituent structures** composed of hierarchically arranged parts called **constituents**. These may be graphically depicted as tree structures. Each tree corresponds to one of the possible meanings. Structural ambiguity can be explicitly accounted for by multiple tree structures.

Syntactic Categories

" I MISS THE GOOD OLD DAYS WHEN ALL WE HAD TO WORRY ABOUT WAS NOUNS AND VERBS."

Copyright © by S. Harris.

Each of the groupings in the tree diagram of *The child found the puppy* is a member of a large family of similar expressions. For example, *the child* belongs to a family that includes *the police officer, your neighbor, this yellow cat, he,* and countless others. Each member of this family can be substituted for *the child* without affecting the grammaticality of the sentence, although the meanings of course would change.

> A police officer found the puppy.
> Your neighbor found the puppy.
> This yellow cat found the puppy.
> He found the puppy.

A family of expressions that can substitute for one another without loss of grammaticality is called a **syntactic category.**

The child, a police officer, and so on belong to the syntactic category **Noun Phrase (NP),** one of several syntactic categories in English and every other language in the world. Noun Phrases may function as the subject or as various objects in a sentence, and only Noun Phrases may do so. NPs always contain some form of a noun (common nouns like *boy,* proper nouns like *John,* or pronouns like *he*). Since *he* is a single word, you may question our calling it a phrase, but technically a syntactic phrase can consist of one or more words. In fact an NP can even include a verbal complex as shown by:

Romeo who was a Montague loved *Juliet who was a Capulet.*

The NP subject of this sentence is *Romeo who was a Montague* and the object, also an NP, is *Juliet who was a Capulet.*

Part of the syntactic component of a grammar is the specification of the syntactic categories in the language, since this constitutes part of speakers' knowledge. That is, speakers of English know that items **a, b, e, f, g** and **i** in (2) are Noun Phrases even if they have never heard the term before.

(2) (a) a bird
(b) the red banjo
(c) have a nice day
(d) with a balloon
(e) the woman who was laughing
(f) it
(g) John
(h) went
(i) that the earth is round

You can test this claim by inserting each expression into the context "Who discovered _____ ?" and "_____ was seen by everyone."

Only those sentences in which NPs are inserted are grammatical, because only NPs can function as subjects and objects.

There are other syntactic categories. The expression *found the puppy* is a **Verb Phrase (VP).** Verb Phrases always contain a Verb (V), which may be followed by other categories, such as a Noun Phrase or Prepositional Phrase (PP). This shows that one syntactic category may contain other syntactic categories. In (3), the Verb Phrases are those that can complete the sentence "The child _____ ."

(3) (a) saw a clown
     (b) a bird
     (c) slept
     (d) smart
     (e) is smart
     (f) found the cake
     (g) found the cake in the cupboard
     (h) realized that the earth was round

Inserting **a, c, e, f, g** and **h** will produce grammatical sentences whereas the insertion of **b** or **d** would result in an ungrammatical string. Thus, **a, c, e, f, g** and **h** are Verb Phrases.

Other syntactic categories are **Sentence (S), Determiner (Det), Adjective (Adj), Noun (N), Pronoun (Pro), Preposition (P), Prepositional Phrase (PP), Adverb (Adv), Auxiliary Verb (Aux),** and **Verb (V).** Some of these syntactic categories have traditionally been called "parts of speech." All languages have such syntactic categories; in fact, categories such as Noun, Verb, Pronoun, and Noun Phrase are universally found in the grammars of all human languages. Speakers know the syntactic categories of their language, even if they do not know the technical terms.

Phrase Structure Trees

> Who climbs the Grammar-Tree distinctly knows
> Where Noun and Verb and Participle grows.
>
> John Dryden, *"The Sixth Satyr of Juvenal"*

The fact that *The child found the puppy* belongs to the syntactic category of Sentence, that *the child* and *the puppy* are Noun Phrases, that *found the puppy* is a Verb Phrase, and so on, can be illustrated in a tree diagram by supplying the name of the syntactic category of each word grouping. These names are often referred to as **syntactic labels.**

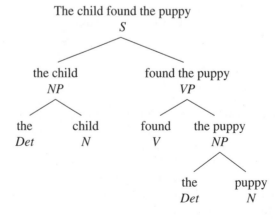

A tree diagram with syntactic category information provided is called a **phrase structure tree.** (It is also sometimes referred to as a **constituent structure tree.**) This tree shows that a sentence is both a linear string of words and a hierarchical structure with phrases nested in phrases.

Three aspects of speakers' syntactic knowledge of sentence structure are disclosed in phrase structure trees:

1. the linear order of the words in the sentence,
2. the groupings of words into particular syntactic categories,
3. the hierarchical structure of the syntactic categories (e.g. a Sentence is composed of a Noun Phrase followed by a Verb Phrase, a Verb Phrase is composed of a Verb that may be followed by a Noun Phrase, and so on).

Every sentence of English and of every human language can be represented by a phrase structure tree that explicitly reveals these properties. These trees represent the linguistic properties that are part of speakers' mental grammars.

The phrase structure tree above is correct, but it is redundant. The word *child* is repeated three times in the tree, *puppy* is repeated four times, and so on. We can streamline the tree by writing the words only once at the bottom of the diagram. Only the syntactic categories to which the words belong need to remain at the higher levels.

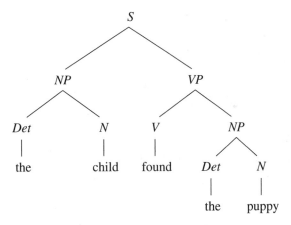

No information is lost in this simplified version. The syntactic category of each individual word appears immediately above that word. In this way *the* is shown to be a Determiner,[1] *child* a Noun, and so on. The lowest categories in the tree, those immediately

---

[1] The category *Determiner* includes the Articles *the* and *a* as well as a number of other expressions such as *these, every, five, my, your cousin Mabel's,* etc.

above the words, are called **lexical categories.** In Chapter 3 we discussed the fact that the syntactic category of each word is listed in our mental dictionaries. We now see how this information functions in the syntax of the language. We have not given a definition of these categories. All traditional definitions fail. In the sentence *Seeing is believing, seeing* and *believing* are nouns but are neither "persons, places, nor things." The grammar of the language and the syntactic rules define these categories.

The larger syntactic categories, such as Verb Phrase (VP), are identified as consisting of all the syntactic categories and words below that point or **node** in the tree. The VP in the above phrase structure tree consists of syntactic category nodes V and NP, and the words *found, the,* and *puppy,* which is consistent with our observation that *found the puppy* is a VP. Since *the puppy* can be traced up the tree to the node NP, this constituent is a Noun Phrase.

The phrase structure tree also states implicitly what combinations of words are not syntactic categories. For example, since there is no node above the words *found* and *the* that connects them, the two words do not constitute a syntactic category, as discussed earlier.

The phrase structure tree also shows that some syntactic categories are composed of other syntactic categories. The Sentence *The child found the puppy* consists of a Noun Phrase, *the child,* and a Verb Phrase, *found the puppy.* The Verb Phrase consists of the Verb *found* and the Noun Phrase *the puppy.* The Determiner *the* and the Noun *puppy* together constitute a Noun Phrase, but individually neither is an NP.

A syntactic category includes all the categories beneath it in the tree. For example, the S in the tree above is composed of an NP followed by a VP. An S is also a Det followed by an N followed by a V followed by a Det followed by an N. The "all" is important; an S is not Det N V Det; that would omit the final N, which is a part of the S (that is, *the boy found the* is not a Sentence). Every higher node is said to **dominate** all the nodes below it.

More Phrase Structure Trees

> The structure of every sentence is a lesson in logic.
>
> John Stuart Mill, *Inaugural address at St. Andres*

Every language contains sentences of varying phrase structure. The phrase structure tree below differs from the previous tree not only in the words that terminate it but also in its syntactic categories and structure.

This tree shows that a Verb Phrase may also consist of a Verb followed by a Noun Phrase followed by a Prepositional Phrase (PP). A Prepositional Phrase is shown to consist of a Preposition (P) followed by a Noun Phrase. This tree also illustrates that Noun Phrases may occur in three different structural positions representing three different grammatical relations: immediately below the S as the **subject,** immediately below the VP as the **direct object,** and immediately below the PP as a **prepositional object.**

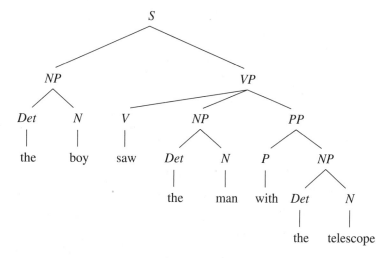

Just as tree structures reveal ambiguities in phrases like *synthetic buffalo hides,* they also account for sentence ambiguities like *The boy saw the man with the telescope.* One meaning of this sentence—"the boy used a telescope to see the man"—is revealed by the phrase structure tree above. The key element is the position of the PP directly under the VP, where it has an adverbial function and modifies the Verb *saw.*

In its other meaning, "the boy saw a man who had a telescope," the PP *with the telescope* is positioned directly under the NP direct object, where it modifies the Noun *man.* Two different interpretations are possible because the rules of syntax permit different structuring of the same linear order of words, as revealed by the two phrase structure trees.

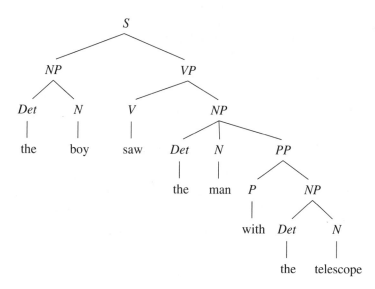

The Infinitude of Language

> So, naturalists observe, a flea
> Hath smaller fleas that on him prey;
> And these have smaller fleas still to bite 'em,
> And so proceed ad infinitum.
>
> Jonathan Swift, "On Poetry, A Rhapsody"

PEANUTS reprinted by permission of UFS, Inc.

There is no longest sentence in any language, because speakers can lengthen any sentence by various means, such as adding an adjective or, as in Snoopy's sentence, adding clauses. Even children know how to produce and understand very long sentences, and know how to make them even longer, as illustrated by the children's rhyme about the house that Jack built.

> *This is the farmer sowing the corn,*
> *that kept the cock that crowed in the morn,*
> *that waked the priest all shaven and shorn,*
> *that married the man all tattered and torn,*
> *that kissed the maiden all forlorn,*
> *that milked the cow with the crumpled horn,*
> *that tossed the dog,*
> *that worried the cat,*
> *that killed the rat,*
> *that ate the malt,*
> *that lay in the house that Jack built.*

This rhyme begins with *This is the house that Jack built,* continues by lengthening it to *This is the malt that lay in the house that Jack built,* and so on.

You can add any of the following to the beginning of the rhyme and still have a grammatical longer sentence:

> I think that . . .
> What is the name of the unicorn that noticed that . . .
> Ask someone if . . .
> Do you know whether . . .

This limitless aspect of language is also reflected in phrase structure trees. We have seen that an NP may appear immediately under a PP, which PP may occur immediately under a higher NP, as in *the man with the telescope.* The complex (but comprehensible) Noun Phrase *the girl with the feather on the ribbon on the brim,* as shown in the phrase structure tree below, illustrates that one can repeat the number of NPs under PPs under NPs without a limit.

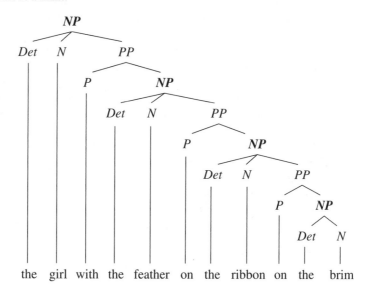

This phrase structure tree for the Noun Phrase illustrates that any syntactic category may be represented by a phrase structure tree, that is, be the topmost node. It also illustrates the repetition of the NP within PP within NP and so on.

The NP diagrammed above, though cumbersome, violates no rules of syntax and is a grammatical Noun Phrase. Moreover, it can be made even longer by expanding the final NP—*the brim*—by adding another PP—*of her hat*—to derive the longer phrase—*the girl with the feather on the ribbon on the brim of her hat.*

The repetition of categories within categories is common in all languages. It allows speakers to use the same syntactic categories several times, with several different functions, in the same sentence. Our brain capacity is finite, able to store only a finite number of categories and rules for their combination. Yet, with these finite means, an infinite set of sentences can be represented.

This linguistic property also illustrates the difference between competence and performance discussed in Chapter 1. All speakers of English have as part of their linguistic competence—their mental grammars—the ability to put NPs in PPs in NPs ad infinitum. But as the structures grow longer and longer they become increasingly difficult to produce and understand. This could be due to short-term memory limitations, muscular fatigue, breathlessness, or any number of performance factors.

Thus while such rules give a speaker access to infinitely many sentences, no speaker utters or hears an infinite number in a lifetime; nor is any sentence of infinite length, although in principle there is no upper limit on sentence length. This property of grammars also accounts for the creative aspect of language use, since it permits speakers to produce and understand sentences never spoken before.

PHRASE STRUCTURE RULES

> Everyone who is master of the language he speaks . . . may form new . . .
> phrases, provided they coincide with the genius of the language.
>
> Michaelis, *Dissertation* (1769)

A phrase structure tree is a formal device for representing speaker knowledge. When we speak we are not aware that we are producing sentences with such structures, but controlled experiments show that we use them in speech production and comprehension, as we'll see in Chapter 9. We don't use the tree structure diagrams per se, but we are unconsciously aware of the structures on which these trees are based.

When we look at other phrase structure tree representations of English, we see certain patterns emerging. In ordinary sentences, the S is always subdivided into NP VP. NPs generally contain Nouns; VPs always contain Verbs; PPs consist of a Preposition followed by a Noun Phrase.

Of all logically possible tree structures, few actually occur, just as all word combinations do not constitute grammatical phrases or sentences. For example, a nonoccurring tree structure in English is:

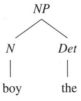

Both grammatical and ungrammatical trees must be accounted for in the grammar. Again, some kind of formal notation is required, preferably one that reveals speakers' knowledge precisely and concisely. To do this, linguists write grammars that include **phrase structure rules** that specify the constituency of syntactic categories in the language.

For example, in English a Noun Phrase (NP) can be a Determiner (Det) followed by a Noun (N). Thus one of the several allowable NP subtrees looks like this:

The phrase structure rule that makes this explicit can be stated as:

NP → Det N

This rule conveys two facts:

A Noun Phrase can be a Determiner followed by a Noun.
A Determiner followed by a Noun is a Noun Phrase.

The left side of the arrow is the category whose components are defined on the right side. The right side of the arrow also shows the linear order of these components. Phrase structure rules make explicit speakers' knowledge of the order of words and the grouping of words into syntactic categories.

The phrase structure trees of the previous section show that the following phrase structure rules are part of the grammar of English.

(a) VP → V NP
(b) VP → V NP PP

Rule (**a**) states that a Verb Phrase can be a Verb followed by a Noun Phrase. Rule (**b**) states that a Verb Phrase can also be a Verb followed by a Noun Phrase followed by a Prepositional Phrase. These rules are general statements, which do not refer to any specific Verb Phrase, Verb, Noun Phrase, or Prepositional Phrase.

Rules (**a**) and (**b**) can be summed up in one statement: A Verb Phrase may be a Verb followed by a Noun Phrase, which may or may not be followed by a Prepositional Phrase. By putting parentheses around the optional element, we can abbreviate rules (**a**) and (**b**) with a single rule:

VP → V NP (PP)

In fact the NP is also optional, as shown in the following trees:

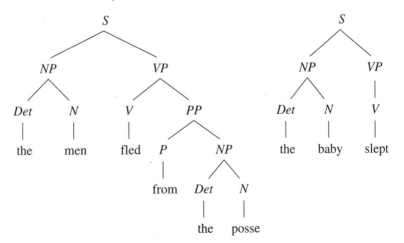

In the first case we have a Verb Phrase consisting of a Verb plus a Prepositional Phrase, corresponding to the rule VP → V PP. In the second case, the Verb Phrase consists of a

Verb alone, corresponding to the rule VP → V. All the facts about the Verb Phrase we have seen so far are revealed in the single rule:

VP → V (NP) (PP)

This rule states that a Verb Phrase may consist of a Verb followed optionally by a Noun Phrase and/or a Prepositional Phrase.

Other rules of English are:

S → NP VP
PP → P NP

Growing Trees: The Relationship between Phrase Structure Rules and Phrase Structure Trees

I think that I shall never see
A poem lovely as a tree

Joyce Kilmer, *"Trees"*

Phrase structure trees may not be as lovely to look at as the trees Kilmer was thinking of, but if a poem is written in grammatical English, its phrases and sentences can be represented by trees, and those trees can be specified by phrase structure rules.

The rules that we have discussed, repeated here, define some of the phrase structure trees of English.

S → NP VP
NP → Det N
VP → V (NP) (PP)
PP → P NP

There are several possible ways of viewing phrase structure rules. They can be regarded as tests that trees must pass to be grammatical. Each syntactic category mentioned in the tree is examined to see if the syntactic categories immediately beneath it agree with the phrase structure rules. If we were examining an NP in a tree, it would pass the test if the categories beneath it were Det and N, in that order, and fail the test otherwise, insofar as our (incomplete) set of phrase structure rules is concerned. (Obviously, in a more adequate grammar of English, NPs would be specified to include many more structures.)

The rules may also be viewed as a way to construct phrase structure trees that conform to the syntactic structures of the language. This is by no means suggestive of how speakers actually produce sentences. It is just another way of representing their knowledge, and it applies equally to speakers and listeners.

Conventions on generating trees have been developed. *Generating* as used here simply means "specifying." One convention is that the root of the tree, the S, occurs at the top instead of the bottom. Another convention specifies how the rules are to be applied:

First, find a rule with an S on the left side of the arrow, and put the categories on the right side below the S, as shown here:

Once started, continue by matching any syntactic category at the bottom of the partially constructed tree to a category on the left side of a rule, and expanding the tree with the categories on the right side. Proceed in this manner until only categories remain that never appear on the left-hand side of any rule, like Det, N, and so on.

We may expand the tree started above by applying the NP rule to produce:

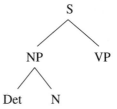

The categories at the bottom are Det, N, and VP, but only VP occurs to the left of an arrow in the set of rules. The VP rule is actually four rules abbreviated by parentheses. They are:

> VP → V
> VP → V NP
> VP → V PP
> VP → V NP PP

Any one of them may be chosen to apply next; the order in which the rules appear in the grammar is irrelevant. (Indeed, we might equally have begun by expanding the VP rather than the NP.) Suppose VP → V PP is chosen to apply. Then the tree has grown to look like this:

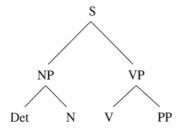

Convention dictates that we continue in this way until none of the categories at the bottom of the tree appear on the left-hand side of any rule. Thus the PP must be expanded into a P and an NP, and that NP expanded into a Det and an N. We can use a rule as many times as it can apply. In this tree, the NP rule was used twice. After we have applied all the rules that can apply, the tree looks like this:

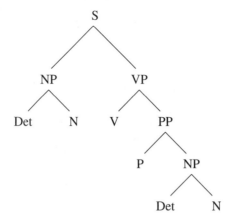

By following these conventions, only trees specified by the phrase structure rules can be generated. By implication, any tree not so specified will be ungrammatical. Whether we choose to use the rules to generate only well-formed trees, or use the rules to test the grammaticality of all possible trees, is immaterial. Both methods achieve the goal of revealing syntactic knowledge. Most books on language use the rules to generate trees.

The categories that occur to the left of the arrow in a phrase structure rule are called **phrasal categories;** categories that never occur on the left side of any rule are **lexical categories.** Phrase structure trees always have lexical categories at the bottom since the rules must apply until no phrasal categories remain. The lexical categories are traditionally called "the parts of speech," and include Determiners, Nouns, Verbs, Prepositions, and so on.

The previous tree structure corresponds to a very large number of sentences because each lexical category may contain many words, all listed and marked as to category in the lexicon. This is particularly true of the major, open class categories discussed in Chapter 3, such as Noun or Verb. This tree structure corresponds to the following sentences and millions more.

The boat sailed up the river.
A girl laughed at the monkey.
The sheepdog rolled in the mud.
The lions roared in the jungle.

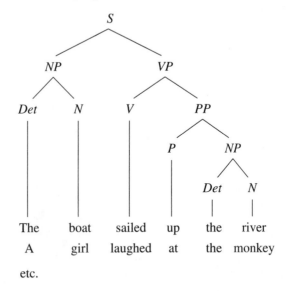

etc.

At any point during the growth of a tree, any rule may be used providing its left side category occurs somewhere at the bottom of the tree. At the point where we chose the rule VP → V PP, we could equally well have chosen VP → V or VP → V NP PP. This would have resulted in a different tree that, when the lexical categories were filled, would have been the structure for such sentences as:

The boys left (VP → V)
The wind swept the kite into the sky. (VP → V NP PP)

Since there are an infinite number of possible sentences in every language, there are limitless numbers of trees, but only a finite set of phrase structure rules that specify the trees allowed by the grammar of the language.

Trees That Won't Grow

THE FAR SIDE copyright 1991, 1987 and 1986 UNIVERSAL PRESS SYNDICATE.
Reprinted with permission. All rights reserved.

Just as speakers know which structures and strings of words are permitted by the syntax of their language, they know which are not. Such knowledge is specified implicitly by the phrase structure rules.

Since the rule S → NP VP is the only S rule in our (simplified) grammar of English, the following word sequences and their corresponding structures do not constitute English sentences.

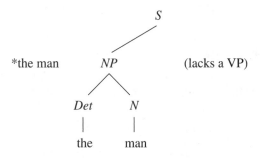

*the man   NP   (lacks a VP)

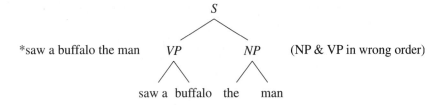

*saw a buffalo   (lacks an NP)   VP

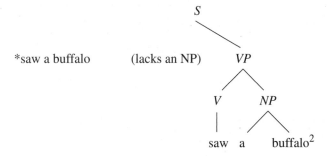

*saw a buffalo the man   VP   NP   (NP & VP in wrong order)

Similarly, *boy the*

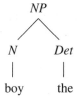

---

[2] Nonpertinent parts of the tree are sometimes omitted, in this case the Det and N of the NP, *a buffalo*.

cannot be an NP in English because no NP rule of English syntax specifies that a Determiner can follow a Noun.

Rules in Other Languages

> Whenever the literary German dives into a sentence, that is the last you are going to see of him till he emerges on the other side of the Atlantic with his Verb in his mouth.
>
> Mark Twain, *A Connecticut Yankee in King Arthur's Court*

Other languages have different phrase structure rules, hence different tree structures. In Swedish the Determiner may follow the Noun in some NPs, for example, in *mannen* "the man" (*mann* "man" + *en* "the"). The ungrammatical tree of English is a grammatical tree structure in Swedish:

There are languages that have "postpositions" that function like prepositions of English but come after the Noun Phrase instead of preceding it. In Japanese *Tokyo kara* means "from Tokyo." The following tree, which does not occur in English, is found in Japanese:

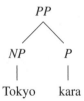

The grammar of Japanese contains the phrase structure rule

PP → NP P

but not the rule

PP → P NP

Such differences between these languages and English are reflected in the phrase structure rules of the respective grammars.

In English the Verb is always the first member of the Verb Phrase, as can be seen from the VP rule. In German, however, the Verb may occur in the final position of the Verb Phrase in some circumstances. German contains sentences such as

Ich glaube dass Tristan Isolde liebt

which, if translated word for word, would be "I believe that Tristan Isolde loves," meaning "I believe that Tristan loves Isolde."

Despite these differences in detail, all grammars of all languages have the type of rule we are calling a phrase structure rule, which characterizes the structure of phrases, sentences, and syntactic categories of the language.

More Phrase Structure Rules

By permission of Johnny Hart and Creators Syndicate, Inc.

There are many sentences of English whose structure is not accounted for by the phrase structure rules given so far, including:

    (a) Pretty girls whispered softly.
    (b) The man with the hat smiled.
    (c) The teacher believes that the student knows the answer.

Sentence (a) may be represented by this phrase structure tree:

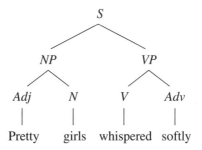

From this example we see that a Determiner is optional in the NP. Moreover, two new lexical categories appear: Adjective (Adj) and Adverb (Adv), both optional. All this suggests modifications to both the NP rule and the VP rules:

$$\text{NP} \rightarrow \text{(Det) (Adj) N}^3$$
$$\text{VP} \rightarrow \text{V (NP) (PP) (Adv)}$$

The addition of an optional Adverb to the VP rule allows for four more sentence types:

The wind blew softly.
The wind swept through the trees noisily.
The wind rattled the windows violently.
The wind forced the boat into the water suddenly.

The NP in sentence (b), *the man with the hat,* is similar to *the man with the telescope* seen earlier, and has the following structure:

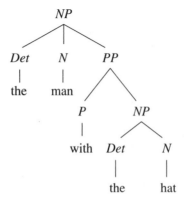

All but the final NP in the example *the girl with the feather on the ribbon on the brim of her hat* also has this structure.

The NP rule can be modified once more to include the option of a Prepositional Phrase:

$$\text{NP} \rightarrow \text{(Det) (Adj) N (PP)}$$

Sentence (c) contains another sentence within itself. The inside sentence, *the student knows the answer,* is **embedded** in the larger sentence *the teacher believes that the*

---

[3] As pointed out earlier, any number of adjectives may be strung together. For simplicity our rules will allow only one adjective and would need to be changed to fully account for English speakers' knowledge.

student knows the answer. What should the phrase structure of this sentence be? Before we attempt to answer this question, we should look at some other data.

> That the student knows the answer is believed by the teacher.
> That the student knows the answer disturbed the teacher.

In both cases the expression *that the student knows the answer* patterns like a Noun Phrase. Compare

> The child is believed by the teacher.
> The child disturbed the teacher.

These examples suggest that by putting the word *that* in front of a sentence, it will function like an NP. The phrase structure tree for (c), then, is:

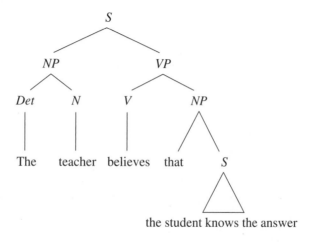

We omit the internal structure of the embedded sentence because it's not relevant. Another NP phrase structure rule is suggested:

NP → *that* S

This rule is different than previous rules in that it contains a word (*that*) rather than a category. In the next section we'll see how words are put into phrase structure trees in general. This rule is a special case.

We now see how the ability all speakers have to embed sentences within sentences, as illustrated by the cartoon at the beginning of this section, is captured. Here is an illustrative phrase structure tree:

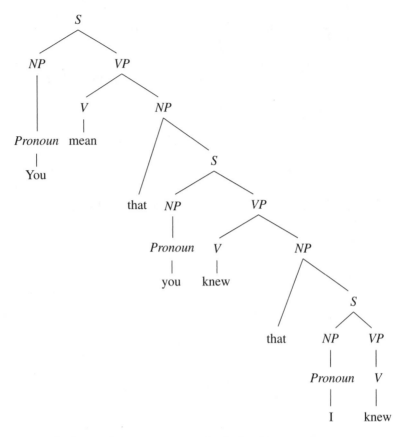

We need one final NP rule to account completely for this structure.

NP → Pronoun

Here are the phrase structure rules we have discussed so far. These are all the phrase structure rules we will present in this chapter.

1. S → NP VP
2. NP → (Det) (Adj) N (PP)
3. NP → *that* S
4. NP → Pronoun
5. VP → V (NP) (PP) (Adv)
6. PP → P NP

A complete grammar of English would have many more such rules. However, even this mini-grammar can specify an infinite number of possible sentences due to the fact that several categories (S, NP, VP) appear on both the left and right sides of several rules. Thus the rules explain our observations that language is creative and that speakers with their finite memories can still produce and understand an infinite set of sentences.

There are still many sentence types of English not encompassed by these rules. Only in passing have we mentioned verbal elements such as the auxiliary verbs *have* or *may* in sentences like *he may have left early.*

Nor have we explicitly accounted for the many types of Determiners besides the Articles *the* and *a* that may precede the Noun in a Noun Phrase such as *each, several, these, many of Gershwin's,* etc.

> Each boy found several eggs.
> These girls sang many of Gershwin's songs.

Rules 3 and 5 show that a whole sentence preceded by the word *that* may be embedded in a VP. In other data, different forms of sentences may be embedded in the VP. (Their source is beyond the scope of this introduction.)

> Hillary is waiting *for you to sing* (Cf. *You sing.*)
> The host regrets *the president's having left early.* (Cf. *The president has left early.*)
> The hostess wants *the president to leave early.* (Cf. *The president leaves early.*)

THE LEXICON

We next went to the School of Languages, where three Professors sat in Consultation upon improving that of their own Country.

The first Project was to shorten Discourse by cutting Polysyllables into one, and leaving out Verbs and Participles; because in Reality all things imaginable are but Nouns.

The other was a Scheme for entirely abolishing all Words whatsoever; and this was urged as a great Advantage in Point of Health as well as Brevity. For it is plain, that every Word we speak is in some degree a Diminution of our Lungs by Corrosion.

Jonathan Swift, *Gulliver's Travels*

The learned professors of languages in Laputa proposed a scheme for abolishing all words, thinking it would be more convenient if "Men [were] to carry about them such Things as were necessary to express the particular Business they are to discourse on." We doubt that this scheme could ever come to fruition, even in Laputa, not only because it would be difficult to carry around an unobservable atom or an abstract loyalty, but because our thoughts are expressed by sentences that have structure and cannot be represented by things pulled from a sack.

Speakers of any language know thousands of words. They know how to pronounce them in all contexts, they know their meaning (see Chapter 5), and they know how to combine them in Phrases or Sentences, which means that they know their syntactic category. All of this knowledge is contained in the component of the grammar called the **lexicon,** discussed in Chapter 3.

Together with the phrase structure rules, the lexicon provides the information needed for complete, well-formed phrase structure trees. The phrase structure rules account for the entire tree except for the words at the bottom. The words in the tree belong to the same syntactic categories that appear immediately above them. Through **lexical insertion,** words of the specified category are chosen from the lexicon and put into the tree. Only words that are specified as verbs in the lexicon are inserted under a node labeled *Verb,* and so on. Words such as *fish,* which belong to two or more categories, have separate entries in the lexicon, or are marked for both categories in their single listing.

Subcategorization

The lexicon contains more syntactic information than merely the lexical category of each word. If it did not, speakers of English would be unable to make the following grammaticality distinctions.

> The boy found the ball.
> *The boy found quickly.
> *The boy found in the house.
> The boy found the ball in the house.

The verb *find* is a **transitive** verb. A transitive verb must be followed by a Noun Phrase, its direct object. This additional specification is called **subcategorization** and is also included in the lexical entry of each word.

Most words in the lexicon are subcategorized for certain contexts. Subcategorization accounts for the ungrammaticality of:

> *John put the milk.
> *Disa slept the baby.

The Verb *put* occurs with both a Noun Phrase and a Prepositional Phrase, as in *John put the milk **in the refrigerator.** Sleep* is an **intransitive verb,** so it cannot be followed by an NP. This information is included as the subcategorization of each word.

Other categories besides verbs are subcategorized. For example, within the NP, if the Determiner is lacking, only a plural noun (or proper name) may be inserted; and if the Determiner is *a,* only a singular noun may be inserted. This accounts for the following:

> Puppies love warm milk.
> *Puppy loves warm milk.
> A puppy loves warm milk.
> *A puppies love warm milk.

Subcategorization within the NP affects individual nouns. *Belief* is subcategorized for both a PP or an S, as shown by the following two examples:

> the belief in freedom of speech
> the belief that freedom of speech is a basic right

The Noun *sympathy,* however, is subcategorized for a PP, but not an S:

> their sympathy for the victims
> *their sympathy that the victims are so poor

Knowledge about subcategorization may be accounted for in the lexicon as follows:

A Fragment of the lexicon	Comments
put, V, _____ NP PP	*put* is a Verb and must be followed by both an NP and a PP within the Verb Phrase
find, V, _____ NP	*find* is a Verb and must be followed by an NP within the Verb Phrase
sleep, V, _____	*sleep* is a Verb and must not be followed by any category within the Verb Phrase
belief, N, _____ (PP), _____ (S)	*belief* is a Noun and may be followed by either a PP or an S within the Noun Phrase
sympathy, N, _____ (PP)	*sympathy* is a Noun and may be followed by a PP within the Noun Phrase

Just as lexical insertion ensures that Verbs are inserted under a V node in a tree, Nouns under an N node, and so on, it also ensures that, for example, intransitive verbs such as *sleep* can only appear in trees in which the VP has no direct object. Similarly, *put* could only occur in trees where it would be followed by an NP and a PP within the Verb Phrase, and so on.

More Lexical Differences

Different words engender different syntactic behavior, and this aspect of speaker knowledge is represented in the lexicon. The verbs of English occur in a wide variety of syntactic patterns. For example, the verbs *want* and *force* appear to be similar when we consider such sentences as

> The conductor wanted the passengers to leave
> The conductor forced the passengers to leave

but they differ in another syntactic context:

> The conductor wanted to leave.
> *The conductor forced to leave

Try exhibits a third pattern differing from both *want* and *force* in that it is never followed directly by an NP:

*The conductor tried him to leave

Try is, however, similar to *want,* but not *force,* in that it can be directly followed by an infinitive (i.e., the "to" form of the verb): *The conductor tried to leave.* These differing syntactic patterns of verbs are also specified in the lexicon, thus accounting explicitly for the knowledge speakers have about these words.

The examples given show only a single verb for each pattern, but each verb cited is representative of a class of verbs. For example, *expect, need,* and *wish* pattern like *want; allow, order, persuade* pattern like *force;* and *condescend, decide,* and *manage* pattern like *try.*

Another instance of syntactically based lexical difference is found in the patterns in which *believe* and *say* appear, which are quite different than those of *want-, force-,* and *try*-class verbs:

The teachers believe Susan is outstanding.
The teachers say Susan is outstanding.
The teachers believe Susan to be outstanding.
*The teachers say Susan to be outstanding.

Both *believe* and *say* may be followed by a complete sentence. However, only *believe* can be followed by a "sentence" in which the verb occurs as an infinitive. As in the previous case, these patterns are representative of classes of verbs: *suppose* and *think* are like *believe; forget* and *insist* are like *say.*

A generalization emerges when the following examples are considered:

The teachers believe themselves to be outstanding.
*The teachers say themselves to be outstanding.

Believe-class verbs, but not *say*-class verbs, can be followed by a **reflexive pronoun,** a pronoun ending with *-self.* The differences in syntactic patterns are part of the lexical representation of these verbs.

The lexicon is a key component in the grammar, containing vast amounts of information on individual words.

SENTENCE RELATEDNESS

> Most wonderful of all are . . . [sentences], and how they make friends one
> with another.
>
> O. Henry, as modified by a syntactician

Sentences may be related in various ways. For example, they may have the same phrase structure, differing only in their words, which accounts for their differing meaning. We saw this earlier in sets of sentences such as *The boat sailed up the river, A girl laughed at the monkey,* etc.

Two sentences with different meanings may contain the same words in the same order, differing only in structure, like *the boy saw the man with the telescope.* These are cases of structural ambiguity.

Two sentences may differ in structure, possibly with small differences in grammatical morphemes, but with no difference in meaning:

The father wept silently.	The father silently wept.
The astronomer saw a quasar with a telescope.	With a telescope the astronomer saw a quasar.
Mary hired Bill.	Bill was hired by Mary.
I know that you know.	I know you know.

Two sentences may have structural differences that correspond systematically to meaning difference.

The boy is sleeping.	Is the boy sleeping?
The boy can sleep.	Can the boy sleep?
The boy will sleep.	Will the boy sleep?
El hombre está en la casa.	¿Está el hombre en la casa?
(The man is in the house.	Is the man in the house?)

The difference in the position of the verbal elements *is, can, will, está* corresponds to whether the sentence is declarative or interrogative.

Phrase structure rules account for much syntactic knowledge, but they do not account for the fact that *Mary hired Bill* has the same meaning as *Bill was hired by Mary,* but a different meaning than *Mary was hired by Bill.* Nor do they account for the systematic difference between statements and their corresponding interrogatives.

Since the grammar must account for all of a speaker's syntactic knowledge, we must look beyond phrase structure rules.

Transformational Rules

> Method consists entirely in properly ordering and arranging the things to which we should pay attention.
>
> René Descartes, *Oeuvres,* Vol. X

By permission of Johnny Hart and Creators Syndicate, Inc.

Consider the following sentences:

(a) The father wept silently.
(b) The father silently wept.

as represented in these two phrase structure trees:

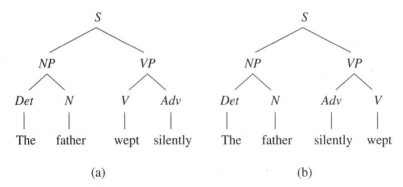

(a)　　　　　　　　　　　　　(b)

Both mean the same thing despite the position of the adverb. The phrase structure rules place the adverb at the end of the VP, thereby accounting for (a). How can (b) be accounted for? If we suggest a phrase structure rule with two optional adverbs, like this,

VP → (Adv) V (NP) (PP) (Adv)

we are faced with the unacceptable possibility of generating ungrammatical strings such as:

*The father cleverly wept bitterly.

A solution to this problem is to allow the phrase structure rules to generate the adverb in VP final position, and have another formal device, called a **transformational rule,** move the adverb in front of the verb, thus deriving the structure that represents (b) from the structure that represents (a).

The basic sentences of the language, whose phrase structure trees are called **deep structures,** are specified by the phrase structure rules. Variants on those basic sentence structures are derived via transformations.

The structures of sentences that we actually speak—to which the rules of phonology are applied—are called **surface structures.** If no transformations apply then deep structure and surface structure are the same. If transformations apply then surface structure is the end result after all transformations have had their effect.[4]

Above, the (a) tree is the deep structure, underlying both sentences (a) and (b). The surface structure of (a) is the same as its deep structure because no transformation has been applied to it. The surface structure of (b), however, is the (b) tree because the adverb moving transformation altered its deep structure.

Much syntactic knowledge not revealed by phrase structure rules is accounted for by transformations, which alter phrase structure trees by moving, adding, or deleting elements. In particular, families of structurally related sentences are revealed by virtue of

---

[4] According to some transformational theories, certain obligatory transformations apply to all deep structures. Thus deep and surface structure are never identical. In this introductory treatment we are unable to provide such details.

having the same deep structure, with surface structure differences created by transformational rules.

A transformation similar to the one that moves adverbs, moves prepositional phrases when they occur immediately under the VP. This transformation changes the deep structure of *the astronomer saw the quasar with the telescope* into the structure corresponding to *with the telescope, the astronomer saw the quasar.*

Transformations act on structures, irrespective of the words that they contain. They are **structure dependent.** The transformational rule just described moves any PP as long as it is immediately under the VP. It would be responsible for *in the house, the puppy found the ball,* and so on.

Further proof of the structure dependency of transformations is the fact that *with a telescope, the boy saw the man* is not ambiguous. It has only the meaning "the boy used a telescope to see the man," the meaning corresponding to the phrase structure in which the PP is immediately under the VP. The structure corresponding to the other meaning "the boy saw a man who had a telescope" has its PP in the NP. The transformation does not apply to it because the structural requirements are not met.

Another transformation deletes *that* when it precedes a sentence in direct object position, but not in subject position, as illustrated by these pairs:

> I know that you know.   I know you know.
> That you know bothers me.   *You know bothers me.

This is a further demonstration that transformations are structure dependent.

Transformations also reveal speaker knowledge about the systematic relationship between statements and questions. Consider again the following:

> The boy is sleeping.
> The boy can sleep.
> The boy will sleep.

Words like *is, can,* and *will* are in a class of Auxiliary Verbs (Aux), which includes *be* and *have* as well as *may, might, would, could* and several others. They are sometimes referred to as helping verbs or auxiliary modals. They occur in such structures as this one:[5]

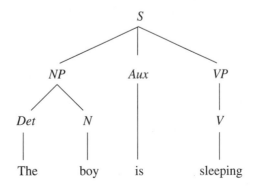

---

[5] We haven't given the S-rule for this structure, It would be S → NP Aux VP.

Now consider the interrogative sentences corresponding to the declarative ones just given:

> Is the boy sleeping?
> Can the boy sleep?
> Will the boy sleep?

The interrogatives are related to their declarative counterparts in a simple way. In the questions the Aux occurs at the beginning of the sentence rather than after the subject NP.

This relationship can be accounted for by a transformation that moves the Aux to the front of the sentence. Phrase structure rules need only generate declarative sentences as deep structures. A transformation derives the surface structure of the corresponding interrogatives.

Consider now the following declarative/interrogative sets of sentences:

> The boy who is sleeping was dreaming.
> Was the boy who is sleeping dreaming?
> *Is the boy who sleeping was dreaming?

> The boy who can sleep will dream.
> Will the boy who can sleep dream?
> *Can the boy who sleep will dream?

The ungrammatical sentences show that in forming questions it is the Auxiliary of the topmost S, that is, the one following the entire first NP, that appears at the front of the sentence, not simply the first Auxiliary in the sentence. This is illustrated in the following simplified phrase structure trees.

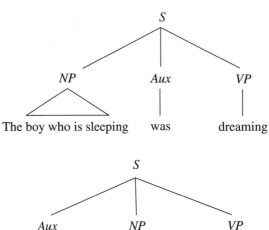

This is further evidence that syntactic categories like Noun Phrase are basic structures in language. It is also further evidence of the structure dependent nature of transformational rules. Transformations such as the one for forming questions must refer to structure, and not to the linear order of elements, in order to produce the correct results. This is not only true in English. Similar constraints and similar rules occur in other languages, as shown by the following sentences in Spanish.[6]

El hombre está en la casa.
The man is in the house.

¿Está el hombre en la casa?
Is the man in the house?

El hombre está contento.
The man is happy.

¿Está el hombre contento?
Is the man happy?

El hombre, que está contento, está en la casa.
The man, who is happy, is in the house.

¿Está el hombre, que está contento, en la casa?
Is the man, who is happy, in the house?

*¿Está el hombre, que contento, está en la casa?
Is the man, who happy, is in the house?

More than one transformation may act on a deep structure. When they do, they do so one after the other. Consider *Is the father silently weeping?* Its deep structure is *The father is weeping silently.* The adverb moving transformation produces the **underlying structure** *The father is silently weeping.* The question transformation acts on this structure to produce the surface structure *Is the father silently weeping?* This is illustrated in the following diagram:

---

[6] Examples from Chomsky (1988), *Language and Problems of Knowledge: The Managua Lectures,* Cambridge, MA: MIT Press.

Deep Structure
(from Phase Structure Rules):

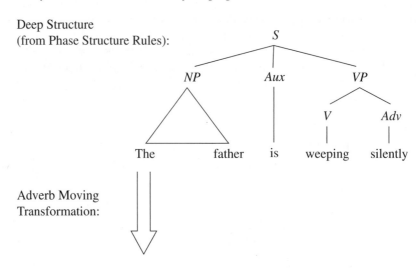

Adverb Moving
Transformation:

Intermediate Underlying
Structure:

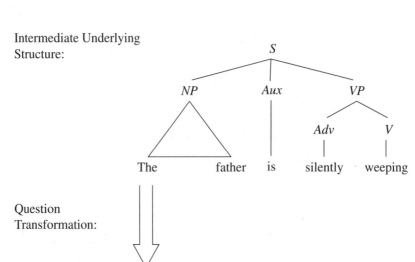

Question
Transformation:

Surface Structure:

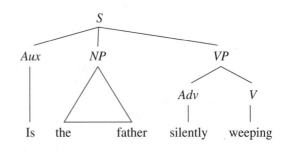

Long-Distance Relationships

Anyone who has had a girl- or boyfriend or a spouse living in another city probably cringes at the idea of long-distance relationships. But they are indispensable to the grammar of English.

Consider first the following sentences:

> The guy seems kind of cute.
> The guys seem kind of cute.

The verb has an "s" added whenever the subject is third person singular. Such a relationship is called **agreement** or **subject-verb agreement.**

Now consider these sentences:

> The guy we met at the party next door *seems* kind of cute.
> The guys we met at the party next door *seem* kind of cute.

The verb *seem* must agree with the subject, *guy* or *guys,* and that agreement takes place over a long distance. In the examples above, the distance encompassed is *we met at the party next door,* but there is no limit to how many words may intervene, as the following sentence illustrates:

> The guys (guy) we met at the party next door that lasted until three A.M. and was finally broken up by the cops who were called by the neighbors seem (seems) kind of cute.

This aspect of linguistic competence is explained by the phrase structure tree of such a sentence, which is shown below omitting much detail:

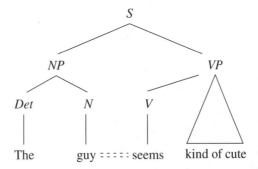

In the tree, "======" represents the intervening structure, which may, in principle, be indefinitely long and complex. But speakers of English know that agreement depends on sentence structure, not the linear order of words. Agreement is between the subject, structurally defined as the NP immediately below the S, and the main verb, structurally defined as the Verb in the VP immediately below the S. Other material can be ignored as far as the rule of agreement is concerned, although in actual performance, if the distance is too great, the speaker may forget what the head noun was.

"Wh-" Sentences

> Who's on first?
> That's right!
>
> Bud Abbott and Lou Costello

A different long-distance relationship is illustrated by the following sentences:

(a) Helen said the senator wanted to hire her aide.
(b) Helen said the senator wanted to hire who?
(c) Who did Helen say the senator wanted to hire?

Either of sentences (b) and (c) might be spoken by someone who didn't hear all of the first sentence. Note, however, that the *who* that replaced *her aide* in (b) appears at the front of (c). This is evidence for a transformation that moves the *wh-* word to the front of the sentence, similar to the transformation that moves Aux to the front in other types of questions.

Sentence (b) is the deep structure. The fact that *who* is the direct object of the verb *hire* is explicitly revealed in deep structure. In (c), despite the distance between *who* and *hire*, it is understood that *who* is the direct object. This is accounted for by the transformation together with the fact that (b) is the deep structure that underlies (c).

As in the case of agreement, the distance can be indefinitely long:

> Who did Helen say the senator wanted the congressman to try to convince the Speaker of the House to get the Vice President to hire?

Unlike the agreement situation, the nature of the intervening structure makes a difference in sentences with *wh-* words like *who, when, what,* and *which,* as shown in the following:

> Emily paid a visit to the senator that wants to hire who?
> *Who did Emily pay a visit to the senator that wants to hire?

> Miss Marple asked Sherlock whether Poirot had solved the crime.
> Who did Miss Marple ask whether Poirot had solved the crime?
> *Who did Miss Marple ask Sherlock whether had solved the crime?
> *What did Miss Marple ask Sherlock whether Poirot had solved?

> Sam Spade insulted the fat man's henchman.
> Who did Sam Spade insult?
> Whose henchman did Sam Spade insult?
> *Whose did Sam Spade insult henchman?

> Alice talked to the white rabbit in the afternoon.
> Who talked to the white rabbit in the afternoon?
> Who did Alice talk to when?
> When did Alice talk to whom?
> *Who when did Alice talk to?
> *When to whom did Alice talk?

The constraints on the formation of *wh-* questions are rather complicated, though they are part of every English speaker's competence. If this were a book on English syntax, the rules and limitations would have to be made explicit.

MORE ABOUT SENTENCE STRUCTURE

> Normal human minds are such that . . . without the help of anybody, they will produce 1000 (sentences) they never heard spoke of . . . inventing and saying such things as they never heard from their masters, nor any mouth.
>
> Huarte De San Juan, c. 1530–1592

There are many more structure-dependent relationships in language than can be discussed in an introductory text. In this section we will reexamine some familiar sentences.

Mary hired Bill.
Bill was hired by Mary.

The first of this pair is an **active** sentence; the second is **passive.** There is a systematic relationship between the structure of an active/passive pair:

(1) The subject of the passive sentence corresponds to the direct object of the active sentence.
(2) In the passive sentence a form of the verb *to be* appears in front of the main verb, which occurs in its participle form (the form that occurs after the auxiliary verb *have* as in *she has **hired** him; I have **taken** a bath*).
(3) The subject of the active sentence appears in the passive sentence in a prepositional phrase headed by the preposition *by,* or it may be omitted altogether.

Here is the phrase structure tree of (1) with the grammatical relations explicitly shown:

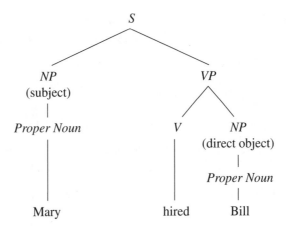

Active sentences of the form

Subject V Direct Object

have passive counterparts of the form

Direct Object *be* V-participle *by* Subject

where the *be* agrees with the direct object, which functions as the subject of the passive sentence. The following abbreviated trees illustrate the active and corresponding passive structures.

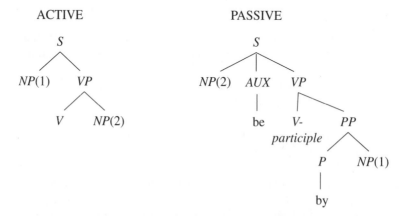

A transformation accounts for part of what English speakers know about the active-passive relationship. It applies to active sentences with the structure shown above, and transforms them into their passive structure counterparts. This shows that transformations may alter grammatical relations, change verb forms, and insert morphemes.

The active sentences are the deep structures. In deep structure the grammatical relations of subject and direct object are interpreted semantically. Since both active and passive sentences have the same deep structure, the semantic relationships are the same in both. That is why we understand Mary as the hirer and Bill as the hired in both the active and passive sentences.

This is a structure-dependent relationship, as all relationships involving transformations are. This may be seen by making up a nonsense sentence such as

The jabberwocky snicker-snacks the wabe

and observing that the passive is

The wabe is snicker-snacked by the jabberwocky.

The form of *to be* that occurs in passive sentences is an Auxiliary Verb. It follows the pattern of Aux when a passive sentence is transformed into its corresponding question:

Is the wabe snicker-snacked by the jabberwocky?

These examples also illustrate that the order in which transformations occur is significant. The passive transformation must apply first, positioning the *was* for the question transformation. They could not apply in the reverse order.

Sign Language Syntax

All languages have rules of syntax similar in kind, if not in detail, to those of English, and sign languages are no exception. A signer is as capable as an oral speaker of distinguishing *dog bites man* from *man bites dog* through the order of signing.

Many languages, including English, have a transformation that moves a direct object to the beginning of the sentence to draw particular attention to it, as in:

Many dogs my wife has rescued from the pound.

The transformation is called **topicalization** because an object to which attention is drawn generally becomes the topic of the sentence or conversation. (The deep structure underlying this sentence is *my wife has rescued many dogs from the pound.*)

In ASL a similar reordering of signs accompanied by raising the eyebrows and tilting the head upwards accomplishes the same effect. The head motion and facial expressions of a signer function as markers of the special word order, much as intonation does in English, or the attachment of prefixes or suffixes might in other languages.

There are constraints on topicalization similar to those on *wh-* preposing illustrated in a previous section. The following string is ungrammatical.

*Henchman, Sam Spade insulted the fat man's.

Compare this with the grammatical

The fat man's henchman Sam Spade insulted.

Similar constraints are found in sign languages. An attempt to sign *Henchman, Sam Spade insulted the fat man's* in ASL would result in an ungrammatical sequence of signs.

In Thai to show that an action is being done continuously, the auxiliary verb *kamlang* is inserted before the verb. Thus *kin* means "eat" and *kamlang kin* means "is eating." In English a form of *be* is inserted and the main verb changed to a gerund. In ASL the sign for a verb such as *eat* may be articulated with a sweeping, repetitive movement to achieve the same effect.

The syntax of all human languages is complex. It is not the aim of an introductory text to present the specific details of these complexities or even the arguments in support of some of the concepts we have presented in this chapter. Our aim is rather to expose the complexity of syntactic knowledge that speakers of English or any language must have.

SUMMARY

Speakers of a language recognize the grammatical sentences of their language and know how the words in a grammatical sentence must be ordered and grouped. All speakers are capable of producing and understanding an unlimited number of new sentences never before spoken or heard. They also recognize ambiguities, know when different sentences mean the same thing, and correctly perceive the grammatical relations in a sentence such as **subject** and **direct object.** This kind of knowledge is accounted for in the grammar by the **rules of syntax.**

Sentences have structure that can be represented by **phrase structure trees** containing **syntactic categories.** Such a representation reveals the linear order of words, and the constituency of each syntactic category. Syntactic categories are either **phrasal categories,** such as NP and VP, which can be decomposed into other syntactic categories, or **lexical categories,** such as Noun and Verb, which correspond to the words of the language.

A linguistic grammar is a formally stated, explicit description of the mental grammar or speaker's linguistic competence. **Phrase structure rules** characterize the basic phrase structure trees of the language, the **deep structures,** and include facts regarding syntactic constituency such as a Noun Phrase may be a Determiner followed by a Noun, but never (in English) a Noun followed by a Determiner.

In phrase structure rules a category that appears on the left side of a rule may also occur on the right side. Such rules allow the same syntactic category to appear repeatedly in a phrase structure tree, which reflects a speaker's ability to produce sentences without length limitations.

The **lexicon** represents the knowledge speakers have about the vocabulary of their language, including the syntactic category of words and what elements may co-occur together, expressed as **subcategorization** restrictions.

Transformational rules account for sentences whose surface structures are different, but have the same meaning, such as *Mary hired Bill* and *Bill was hired by Mary.* They do this by deriving multiple surface structures from a single deep structure. Much of the meaning of a sentence is interpreted from its deep structure.

Transformational rules are also used to account for the movement of Aux or *wh*-words to the beginning of interrogative sentences, and other systematic structural relationships that occur among the sentence structures of the language.

To capture the knowledge speakers have about the syntax of their language, the grammar requires, at a minimum, phrase structure rules, a lexicon richly endowed with speakers' knowledge about individual words, and a set of transformational rules describing the structure-dependent patterning that occurs throughout the language.

References for Further Reading

Akmajian, A., R. A. Demers, and R. M. Harnish. 1995. *Linguistics: An Introduction to Language and Communication,* 4th ed. Cambridge, MA: MIT Press.

Chomsky, Noam. 1957. *Syntactic Structures.* The Hague: Mouton.

Chomsky, Noam. 1965. *Aspects of the Theory of Syntax.* Cambridge, MA: MIT Press.

Chomsky, Noam. 1972. *Language and Mind,* rev. ed. New York: Harcourt Brace Jovanovich.

Chomsky, Noam. 1982. *Some Concepts and Consequences of the Theory of Government and Binding.* Cambridge, MA: MIT Press.

Gazdar, Gerald, E. Klein, G. Pullum, and I. Sag. 1985. *Generalized Phrase Structure Grammar.* Cambridge, MA: Harvard University Press.

Haegeman, Liliane. 1991. *Introduction to Government and Binding Theory.* Oxford, England: Basil Blackwell.

Horrocks, Geoffrey. 1987. *Generative Grammar.* New York: Longman Inc.

Jackendoff, R. S. 1994. *Patterns in the Mind: Language and Human Nature.* New York: Basic Books.

McCawley, James D. 1988. *The Syntactic Phenomena of English,* Vols. I, II. Chicago: University of Chicago Press.

Napoli, Donna Jo. 1993. *Syntax: Theory and Problems.* New York: Oxford University Press.

Newmeyer, Frederick J. 1981. *Linguistic Theory in America: The First Quarter Century of Transformational-Generative Grammar.* New York: Academic Press.

Pinker, Steven. 1994. *The Language Instinct.* New York: HarperPerennial.

Radford, Andrew. 1988. *Transformational Grammar.* New York: Cambridge University Press.

EXERCISES

1. Besides distinguishing grammatical from ungrammatical strings, the rules of syntax account for other kinds of linguistic knowledge, such as

    a. when a sentence is structurally ambiguous. (Cf. *The boy saw the man with a telescope.*)

    b. when two sentences of different structure mean the same thing. (Cf. *The father wept silently* and *The father silently wept.*)

    c. when two sentences of different structure and meaning are nonetheless structurally related, like declarative sentences and their corresponding interrogative form. (Cf. *The boy can sleep* and *Can the boy sleep?*)

    In each case *a* through *c,* draw on your own linguistic knowledge of English to provide an example different than the ones in the chapter, and explain why your example illustrates the point. If you know a language other than English, provide examples in that language, if possible.

2. Consider the following sentences:

    a. I hate war.

    b. You know that I hate war.

    c. He knows that you know that I hate war.

    A. Write another sentence that includes sentence *c.*

    B. What does this set of sentences reveal about the nature of language?

    C. How is this characteristic of human language related to the difference between linguistic competence and performance? (Hint: Review these concepts in Chapter 1.)

3. Paraphrase each of the following sentences in two different ways to show that you understand the ambiguity involved:

Example: Smoking grass can be nauseating.

   i.   Putting grass in a pipe and smoking it can make you sick.

   ii. Fumes from smoldering grass can make you sick.

a. Dick finally decided on the boat.

b. The professor's appointment was shocking.

c. The design has big squares and circles.

d. That sheepdog is too hairy to eat.

e. Could this be the invisible man's hair tonic?

f. The governor is a dirty street fighter.

g. I cannot recommend him too highly.

h. Terry loves his wife and so do I.

i. They said she would go yesterday.

j. No smoking section available.

4. Draw two phrase structure trees representing the two meanings of the sentence *The magician touched the child with the wand.* Be sure you indicate which meaning goes with which tree.

5. Write out the phrase structure rules that each of the following rules abbreviate. Give an example sentence illustrating each expansion.

(Hint: Do not mix the rules. That is, VP → V Det N is not one of the rule expansions of the VP rule. There are 16 rules altogether.)

   VP → V (NP) (PP) (Adv)
   NP → (Det) (Adj) N (PP)

6. In all languages, sentences can occur within sentences. For example, in exercise 2, sentence *b* contains sentence *a,* and sentence *c* contains sentence *b.* Put another way, sentence *a* is embedded in sentence *b,* and sentence *b* is embedded in sentence *c.* Sometimes embedded sentences appear slightly changed from their "normal" form, but you should be able to recognize and underline the embedded sentences in the examples below. Underline in the non-English sentences, when given, not in the translations. (The first one is done as an example):

a. Yesterday I noticed <u>my accountant repairing the toilet</u>.

b. Becky said that Jake would play the piano.

c. I deplore the fact that bats have wings.

d. That Guinevere loves Lorian is known to all my friends.

e. Who promised the teacher that Maxine wouldn't be absent?

f. It's ridiculous that he washes his own Rolls-Royce.

g. The woman likes for the waiter to bring water when she sits down.

h. The person who answers this question will win $100.

    i. The idea of Romeo marrying a 13-year-old is upsetting.

    j. I gave my hat to the nurse who helped me cut my hair.

    k. For your children to spend all your royalty payments on recreational drugs is a shame.

    l. Give this fork to the person I'm getting the pie for.

m. khăw chyâ wăa khruu maa. (Thai)

    He believe that teacher come

    He believes that the teacher is coming.

    n. Je me demande quand il partira. (French)

    I me ask when he will leave

    I wonder when he'll leave.

    o. Jan zei dat Piet dit boek niet heeft gelezen. (Dutch)

    Jan said that Piet this book not has read

    Jan said that Piet has not read this book.

7. Following the patterns of the various tree examples in the text, especially in the two sections on phrase structure rules, draw phrase structure trees for the following sentences:

    a. The puppy found the child.

    b. A frightened passenger landed the crippled airliner.

    c. The house on the hill collapsed in the wind.

    d. The ice melted.

    e. The hot sun melted the ice.

    f. A fast car with twin cams sped by the children on the grassy lane.

    g. The old tree swayed in the wind.

    h. The children put the toy in the box.

    i. The reporter realized that the senator lied.

    j. Broken ice melts in the sun.

    k. The guitar gently weeps.

    l. That the president realized that the senator lied disturbed her.

m. That the president realized that the senator lied means that she knows that he read the latest reports from congress.

8. Use the rules on page 132 to create five phrase structure trees of sentences of 6, 7, 8, 9, and 10 words in length not given in the chapter. Use your own mental lexicon to fill in the bottom of the tree.

9. We stated that the rules of syntax specify all and only the grammatical sentences of the language. Why is it important to say "only"? What would be wrong with a grammar that specified as grammatical sentences all of the truly grammatical ones plus a few that were not grammatical?

10. Here is a set of made-up phrase structure rules. The "initial" symbol is still S, and the "terminal symbols" (the ones that do not appear to the left of an arrow) are actual words:

   (i)   S → A B C
  (ii) A → *the*
 (iii) B → *children*
 (iv) C → *ran*
  (v) C → C *and* D
 (vi) D → *ran and* D
(vii) D → *ran*

   A. Give three phrase structure trees that these rules characterize.

   B. How many phrase structure trees could these rules characterize? Explain your answer.

11. Consider these data;

   i.   With a telescope, can the boy see the man?
  ii. *Can with a telescope the boy see the man?

What do these data tell you about the order of application of the transformation that moves prepositional phrases from under the VP to the front of the sentence, and the transformation that forms interrogative from declarative sentences?

12. The two sentences below contain a **verbal particle.**

   i.   He ran *up* the bill.
  ii. He ran the bill *up*.

The verbal particle *up* and the verb *run* depend on each other for the unique meaning of the phrasal verb *run up*. We know this because *run up* has a meaning different than *run in* or *look up*.

Both sentences in (i) and (ii) have the same deep structure:

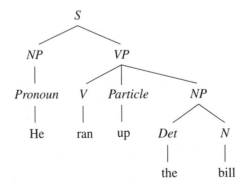

The surface structure of (ii), however, illustrates a **discontinuous dependency.** The verb is separated from its particle by the direct object NP.

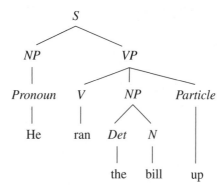

A particle movement transformation derives this surface structure from the deep structure.

A. Explain why the particle movement transformation would not derive **he ran the hill up* from the deep structure of *he ran up the hill.*

B. Most of the transformations encountered in this chapter are **optional.** Whether they apply or not, the ultimate surface structure is grammatical. This is true of the particle movement transformation in most cases, but there is one condition under which the particle movement transformation is **obligatory.** That is, failure to apply the rule will lead to ungrammatical results. What is that condition? (This exercise may require native English competency.)

13. In terms of subcategorization, explain why the following are ungrammatical.

   a. *The man located.

   b. *Jesus wept the apostles.

   c. *Robert is hopeful of his children.

   d. *Robert is fond that his children love animals.

   e. *The children laughed the man.

14. We only considered transitive verbs in the chapter, ones subcategorized in the lexicon like *find:*

   find, V, _____ NP

   There are also **ditransitive** verbs in English, ones that may be followed by two NPs, such as *give:*

   The emperor gave the vassal a castle.

   a. Think of three other ditransitive verbs in English.

    b. Give the lexical entry for one of these verbs, following the pattern of *find* above:

15. In addition to the examples given in the chapter, write down one additional verb in each of the following verb classes:

    a. *want* class:

    b. *force* class:

    c. *try* class:

    d. *believe* class:

    e. *say* class:

16. All of the *wh-* words exhibit the "long-distance" behavior illustrated with *who* in the chapter. Invent three sentences beginning with *what, which,* and *where,* in which the *wh-* word is not in its deep structure position within the sentence. Give both versions of your sentence. Here is an example with the *wh-* word *when: When could Marcy catch a flight out of here?* from *Marcy could catch a flight out of here when?*

17. There are many systematic, structure-dependent relationships among sentences, such as the one discussed in the chapter between active and passive sentences. Here is another example, based on the ditransitive verbs mentioned in exercise 14:

> The boy **wrote** the senator a letter.
> The boy **wrote** a letter to the senator.

> A philanthropist **gave** the Animal Rights movement $1,000,000.
> A philanthropist **gave** $1,000,000 to the Animal Rights movement.

    a. Describe the relationship between the first and second members of the pairs of sentences in a way similar to the way the active/passive relationship is described on page 146.

    b. State why a transformation deriving one of these structures from the other is plausible.

18. State at least three differences between English and the following languages, using just the sentence(s) given. Ignore lexical differences—that is, the different vocabulary. Here is an example:

Thai:	dèg	khon	níi	kamlang	kin.
	boy	*classifier*	this	*progressive*	eat

"This boy is eating."

	mǎaa	tua	nán	kin	khâaw.
	dog	*classifier*	that	eat	rice

"That dog ate rice."

Three differences are: (1) Thai has "classifiers." They have no English equivalent. (2) The words (Determiners, actually) "this" and "that" follow the noun in Thai, but precede the noun in English. (3) The "progressive" is expressed by a separate word in Thai. The verb does not change form. In English, the progressive is indicated by the presence of the verb *to be* and the adding of *-ing* to the verb.

a. French:

cet homme intelligent comprendra la question.
this man intelligent will understand the question
"This intelligent man will understand the question."

ces hommes intelligents comprendront les questions.
these men intelligent will understand the questions
"These intelligent men will understand the questions."

b. Japanese:

watashi	ga	sakana	o	tabete	iru.
I	*subject marker*	fish	*object marker*	eat (*ing*)	am

"I am eating fish."

c. Swahili:

mtoto alivunja kikombe.

m-	toto	a-	li-	vunja	ki-	kombe
class marker	child	he	*past*	break	*class marker*	cup

"The child broke the cup."

watoto wanavunja vikombe.

wa-	toto	wa-	na-	vunja	vi-	kombe
class marker	child	they	*present*	break	*class marker*	cup

"The children break the cups."

d. Korean:

ki sonyɔn-iee wɨyu-lɨl masi-ass-ta.

ki	sonyɔn-	iee	wɨyu-	lɨl	masi-	ass-	ta
the boy		*subject marker*	milk	*object marker*	drink	*past*	*assertion*

"The boy drank milk."

ki-nin muɔs-il mɔk-ass-ninya.

kɨ-	nɨn	muɔs-	il	mɔk-	ass-	nɨnya
he	*subject marker*	what	*object marker*	eat	*past*	*question*

"What did he eat?"

e. Tagalog:

nakita ni Pedro-ng puno na ang bus.

nakita	ni	Pedro -ng	puno	na	ang	bus.
saw	*article*	Pedro that	full	already	*topic marker*	bus

"Pedro saw that the bus was already full."

19. Transformations may delete elements. For example the surface structure of the ambiguous sentence *George wants the presidency more than Martha* may be derived from two possible deep structures:

   a.   George wants the presidency more than he wants Martha.
   b.   George wants the presidency more than Martha wants the presidency.

   A deletion transformation either deletes *he wants* from the structure of example a, or *wants the presidency* from the structure of example b. This is a case of **transformationally induced ambiguity:** two different deep structures with different semantic interpretations are transformed into a single surface structure.

   Explain the role of a deletion transformation similar to the ones just discussed in the following cartoon:

Hagar the Horrible

Reprinted with special permission of King Feature Syndicate.

Chapter 5

The Meanings of Language

Language without meaning is meaningless.

Roman Jakobson

By permission of Johnny Hart and Creators Syndicate, Inc.

For thousands of years philosophers have been pondering the **meaning** of *meaning,* yet speakers of a language can understand what is said to them and can produce strings of words that are meaningful to other speakers.

To understand language we need to know the meaning of words and the morphemes that compose them. We also must know how the meanings of words combine into phrase and sentence meanings. Finally, we must interpret the meaning of utterances in the context in which they are made.

The study of the linguistic meaning of morphemes, words, phrases, and sentences is called **semantics.** Subfields of semantics are **lexical semantics,** which is concerned with the meanings of words and the meaning relationships among words; and **phrasal** or **sentential semantics,** which is concerned with the meaning of syntactic units larger than the word. The study of how context affects meaning—for example, how the sentence *It's cold in here* comes to be interpreted as "close the windows" in certain situations—is called **pragmatics.**

LEXICAL SEMANTICS (WORD MEANINGS)

"There's glory for you!"

"I don't know what you mean by 'glory,' " Alice said.

Humpty Dumpty smiled contemptuously.

"Of course you don't—till I tell you. I meant 'there's a nice knock-down argument for you!' "

"But 'glory' doesn't mean 'a nice knock-down argument,' " Alice objected.

"When I use a word," Humpty Dumpty said, in rather a scornful tone, "it means just what I choose it to mean—neither more nor less."

"The question is," said Alice, "whether you can make words mean so many different things."

Lewis Carroll, *Through the Looking-Glass*

Learning a language includes learning the agreed-upon meanings of certain strings of sounds and learning how to combine these meaningful units into larger units that also convey meaning. We are not free to change the meanings of these words at will, for if we did we would be unable to communicate with anyone.

As we see from the above quotation, Humpty Dumpty was unwilling to accept this fact. Alice, on the other hand, is right. You cannot make words mean whatever you want them to mean. Of course, if you wish to redefine the meaning of each word as you use it, you are free to do so, but this would be an artificial and clumsy use of language, and most people would not wait around for very long to talk to you.

Fortunately there are few Humpty Dumptys. All the speakers of a language share a basic vocabulary—the sounds and meanings of morphemes and words.

Dictionaries are filled with words and their meanings. So is the head of every human being who speaks a language. You are a walking dictionary. You know the meanings of thousands of words. Your knowledge of their meanings permits you to use them to express your thoughts and to understand them when heard, even though you probably seldom stop and ask yourself: "What does *boy* mean?" or "What does *walk* mean?" The meaning of words is part of linguistic knowledge and is therefore a part of the grammar. Your mental storehouse of information about words and morphemes is what we have been calling the **lexicon.**

Semantic Properties

By permission of Johnny Hart and Creators Syndicate, Inc.

Words and morphemes have meanings. We shall talk about the meaning of words, even though words may be composed of several morphemes, as noted in Chapter 3.

Suppose someone said:

The assassin killed Thwacklehurst.

If the word *assassin* is in your mental dictionary, you know that it was some *person* who murdered some *important person* named Thwacklehurst. Your knowledge of the meaning of *assassin* tells you that it was not an animal that did the killing, and that Thwacklehurst was not a little old man who owned a tobacco shop. Knowledge of *assassin* includes knowing that the individual to whom that word refers is *human,* is a *murderer,* and is a killer of *important people.* These pieces of information, then, are some of the **semantic properties** of the word on which speakers of the language agree. The meaning of all nouns, verbs, adjectives, and adverbs—the **content words**—and even some of the **function words** such as *with* or *over* can at least partially be specified by such properties.

The same semantic property may be part of the meaning of many different words. "Female" is a semantic property that helps to define

tigress	hen	aunt	maiden
doe	mare	debutante	widow
ewe	vixen	girl	woman

The words in the last two columns are also distinguished by the semantic property "human," which is also found in

doctor   dean   professor   bachelor   parent   baby   child

The meanings of the last two of these words are also specified as "young." That is, part of the meaning of the words *baby* and *child* is that they are "human" and "young." (We will continue to indicate words by using *italics* and semantic properties by using double quotation marks.)

The meanings of words have other properties. The word *father* has the properties "male" and "adult," as do *uncle* and *bachelor;* but *father* also has the property "parent," which distinguishes it from the other two words.

Mare, in addition to "female" and "animal," must also have a property "equine." Words have general semantic properties such as "human" or "parent," as well as more specific properties that give the word its particular meaning.

The same semantic property may occur in words of different categories. "Female" is part of the meaning of the noun *mother,* of the verb *breast-feed,* and of the adjective *pregnant.* "Cause" is a verbal property of *darken, kill, uglify,* and so on.

darken	cause to become dark
kill	cause to die
uglify	cause to become ugly

Other semantic properties of verbs are shown in the following table:

Semantic Property	Verbs Having It
motion	bring, fall, plod, walk, run . . .
contact	hit, kiss, touch . . .
creation	build, imagine, make . . .
sense	see, hear, feel . . .

For the most part no two words have exactly the same meaning (but see the discussion of synonyms below). Additional semantic properties make for finer and finer distinctions in meaning. *Plod* is distinguished from *walk* by the property "slow," and *stalk* from *plod* by a property such as "purposeful."

The humor of the cartoon at the head of this section is that the verb *roll over* has a specific semantic property, something like "activity about the longest axis." The snake's attempt to roll about its shortest axis indicates trouble with semantic properties.

Evidence for Semantic Properties

Semantic properties are not directly observable. Their existence must be inferred from linguistic evidence. One source of such evidence is found in the speech errors, or "slips of the tongue," that we all produce. Consider the following unintentional word substitutions that some speakers have actually spoken.

Intended Utterance	Actual Utterance (Error)
bridge of the nose	bridge of the neck
when my gums bled	when my tongues bled
he came too late	he came too early
Mary was young	Mary was early
the lady with the dachshund	the lady with the Volkswagen
that's a horse of another color	that's a horse of another race
he has to pay her alimony	he has to pay her rent

These errors and thousands we and others have collected reveal that the incorrectly substituted words are not random substitutions but share some semantic property with the intended words. *Nose, neck, gums* and *tongues* are all "body parts" or "parts of the head." *Young, early,* and *late* are related to "time." *dachshund* and *Volkswagen* are both "German" and "small." The semantic relationships between *color* and *race* and even between *alimony* and *rent* are rather obvious.

The semantic properties that describe the linguistic meaning of a word should not be confused with other nonlinguistic properties, such as physical properties. Scientists know that water is composed of hydrogen and oxygen, but such knowledge is not part of a word's meaning. We know that water is an essential ingredient of lemonade or a bath. We need not know any of these things, though, to know what the word *water* means, and to be able to use and understand this word in a sentence.

Semantic Properties and the Lexicon

The **lexicon** is the part of the grammar that contains the knowledge speakers have about individual words and morphemes, including semantic properties. Words that share a semantic property are said to be in a semantic class, for example, the semantic class of "female" words. Semantic classes may intersect, such as the class of words with the properties "female" and "young." The words *girl* or *filly* would be members of this class.

In some cases, the presence of one semantic property can be inferred from the presence or absence of another. For example, words with the property "human" also have the property "animate," and lack the property "equine."

One way of representing semantic properties is through the use of **semantic features.** Semantic features are a formal or notational device for expressing the presence or absence of semantic properties by pluses and minuses. For example, the lexical entries for words such as *father, girl,* and *mare* would appear as follows (with other information omitted):

woman	father	girl	mare	stalk
+female	+male	+female	+female	+motion
+human	+human	+human	− human	+slow
− young	+parent	+young	− young	+purposeful
. . .	. . .	. . .	+equine	. . .
			. . .	

Intersecting classes share the same features; members of the class of words referring to human females are marked "plus" for the features *human* and *female.*

Another difference between nouns may be captured by the use of the feature [+/−count]. Consider these data:

I have two dogs.	*I have two rice(s)
He has many dogs.	*He has many rice(s)
*He has much dogs	He has much rice.

Nouns that can be enumerated—*one potato, two potatoes*—are called **count nouns.** They may also be preceded by the quantifier *many* but not by *much.* Nouns such as *rice, water, milk,* which cannot be enumerated or preceded by *many,* are called **mass nouns.** They may be distinguished in the lexicon with one feature:

dog	potato	rice	water	milk
+count	+count	−count	−count	−count

More Semantic Relationships

GARFIELD® reprinted by permission of UFS, Inc.

Our linguistic knowledge about words, their semantic properties, and the relationships among them are illustrated by the "Garfield" cartoon, which shows that "small" is a semantic property of *morsel,* but not of *glob.*

Consider the following knowledge about words that speakers of English have:

If something *swims,* it is in a liquid.
If something is *splashed,* it is a liquid.

If you say you saw a bug swimming in a container of "goop," anyone who understands English would agree that goop is surely a liquid, that is, has the semantic feature [+liquid]. Even without knowing what goop refers to, you know you can talk about pouring goop, drinking goop, or plugging a hole where goop is leaking out and forming droplets. The words pour, drink, leak, and droplet are all used with items relating to the property "liquid."

Similarly, we would know that "sawing goop in half," "melting goop," or "bending goop" are semantically ill-formed expressions because none of these activities apply sensibly to objects that are [+liquid].

In some languages, the fact that certain verbs can occur appropriately with certain nouns is reflected in the verb morphology. For example in the Native American language Navajo, there are different verb forms for objects with different semantic properties. The verbal suffix *-léh* is used with words with semantic features [+long], [+flexible], such as *rope;* whereas the verbal suffix *túh* is used for words like *spear,* which is [+long], [−flexible].

-nyms

Most wonderful of all are words, and how they . . . [relate] one with another.

O. Henry, as modified by a semantician

Words are related to one another in a variety of ways. These relationships have words to describe them that often end in the bound morpheme *-nym.*

Homonyms[1] and Polysemy

"Mine is a long and sad tale!" said the Mouse, turning to Alice and sighing.

"It is a long tail, certainly," said Alice, looking with wonder at the Mouse's tail, "but why do you call it sad?"

Lewis Carroll, *Alice's Adventures in Wonderland*

BIZARRO © by Dan Piraro. Reprinted with permission of UNIVERSAL PRESS SYNDICATE. All rights reserved.

Knowing a word means knowing both its sounds (pronunciation) and its meaning. Both are crucial in determining whether words are the same or different. If words differ in pronunciation but have the same meaning, such as *sofa* and *couch,* they are different words. Likewise, words with identical pronunciation but significantly different meanings, such as *tale* and *tail,* are also different words. Spelling is not relevant, only pronunciation. Thus, *bat* the animal and *bat* for hitting baseballs are different words because they have different meanings although they are pronounced identically.

Words like the *tale* and *tail* are called **homonyms.** Homonyms are different words that are pronounced the same, but may or may not be spelled the same. *To, too,* and *two* are homonyms despite their spelling differences.

Homonyms can create ambiguity. A word or a sentence is **ambiguous** if it can be understood or interpreted in more than one way. The sentence

---

[1] The term *homophone* is sometimes used instead of *homonym.*

I'll meet you by the bank

may mean "I'll meet you by the financial institution" or "I'll meet you by the riverside." The ambiguity is due to the two words *bank* with two different meanings. Sometimes additional context can help to disambiguate the sentence:

I'll meet you by the bank, in front of the automated teller machine.
I'll meet you by the bank. We can go skinny-dipping.

Homonyms are good candidates for humor as well as for confusion.

"How is bread made?"
"I know *that!*" Alice cried eagerly.
"You take some flour—"
"Where do you pick the flower?" the White Queen asked. "In a garden, or in the hedges?"
"Well, it isn't *picked* at all," Alice explained; "it's *ground*—"
"How many acres of ground?" said the White Queen.

The humor of this passage is due to the two sets of homonyms: *flower* and *flour* and the two meanings of *ground*. Alice means *ground* as the past tense of *grind*, whereas the White Queen is interpreting *ground* to mean "earth."

When a word has multiple meanings that are related conceptually or historically, it is said to be **polysemous** (polly-seamus). Open a dictionary of English to any page and you will find words with more than one definition, for example, *guard, music,* or *rot.* Each of these words is polysemous because each has several meanings.

Bear is polysemous, with meanings "to tolerate," "to carry," "to support" among others found in the dictionary. *Bear* is also a homonym. Homonyms generally have separate dictionary entries, often marked with superscripts "1," "2," etc. One "bear" is the polysemous verb just mentioned. The other "bear" refers to the animal. It, too, is polysemous, with other meanings such as "a falling stock market." *Bare,* which is pronounced the same as *bear,* is a third homonym.

A related concept is **homograph.** Different words are homographs if they are *spelled* identically and possibly pronounced the same. Of course if they are pronounced the same they are also homonyms. Thus *pen* the writing implement and *pen* the cage are both homographs and homonyms. *Lead* the verb and *lead* the metal are homographs but not homonyms. *Tail* and *tale* are homonyms but not homographs.

Another "-*nym*" word is used for homographs that are pronounced differently: **heteronym.** *Dove* the bird and *dove* the past tense of *dive* are heteronyms, as are *bass, bow, lead, wind,* and well over a hundred others.

We can summarize these relations among *different* words, i.e., words different in concept and historical origin:

	homonym	homograph	heteronym
Pronounced Identically	Yes	Maybe	No
Spelled Identically	Maybe	Yes	Yes

Synonyms

> Does he wear a turban, a fez or a hat?
> Does he sleep on a mattress, a bed or a mat, or a Cot,
> The Akond of Swat?
> Can he write a letter concisely clear,
> Without a speck or a smudge or smear or Blot,
> The Akond of Swat?
>
> Edward Lear, "The Akond of Swat"

There are not only words that sound the same but have different meanings; there are also words that sound different but have the same or nearly the same meaning. Such words are called **synonyms.** There are dictionaries of synonyms that contain many hundreds of entries, such as:

> apathetic/phlegmatic/passive/sluggish/indifferent
> pedigree/ancestry/genealogy/descent/lineage

A sign in the San Diego Zoo Wild Animal Park states:

> Please do not *annoy, torment, pester, plague, molest, worry, badger, harry, harass, heckle, persecute, irk, bullyrag, vex, disquiet, grate, beset, bother, tease, nettle, tantalize,* or *ruffle* the animals.

It has been said that there are no perfect synonyms—that is, no two words ever have *exactly* the same meaning. Still, the following pair of sentences have very similar meanings.

> He's sitting on the sofa. / He's sitting on the couch.

Some individuals may prefer to use *sofa* instead of *couch,* but if they know the two words, they will understand both sentences and interpret them to mean essentially the same thing. The degree of semantic similarity between words depends to a great extent on the number of semantic properties they share. *Sofa* and *couch* refer to the same type of object and share most of their semantic properties.

There are words that are neither synonyms nor near synonyms yet have many semantic properties in common. *Man* and *boy* both refer to male humans; the meaning of *boy* includes the additional semantic property of "youth," whereby it differs from the meaning of man.

A polysemous word may share one of its meanings with another word, a kind of partial synonymy. For example *mature* and *ripe* are polysemous words that are synonyms when applied to fruit, but not when applied to (smelly) animals. *Deep* and *profound* mean the same when applied to thought, but only *deep* can modify water.

Sometimes words that are ordinarily opposites can mean the same thing in certain contexts; thus a *good* scare is the same as a *bad* scare. Similarly, a word with a positive meaning in one form, such as the adjective *perfect,* when used adverbially, undergoes a "weakening" effect, so that a "perfectly good bicycle" is neither perfect nor always good. "Perfectly good" means something more like "adequate."

When synonyms occur in otherwise identical sentences, the sentences will be **paraphrases,** that is, they will have the same meaning (except possibly for minor differences in emphasis). For example:

> She forgot her handbag.
> She forgot her purse.

This use of synonyms creates **lexical paraphrase,** just as the use of homonyms creates lexical ambiguity.

Antonyms

> As a rule, man is a fool;
> When it's hot, he wants it cool;
> When it's cool, he wants it hot;
> Always wanting what is not.
>
> Anonymous

The meaning of a word may be partially defined by saying what it is *not*. *Male* means *not* female. *Dead* means not *alive*. Words that are opposite in meaning are often called **antonyms.** Ironically, the basic property of two words that are antonyms is that they share all but one semantic property. *Beautiful* and *tall* are not antonyms; *beautiful* and *ugly,* or *tall* and *short,* are. The property they do not share is present in one and absent in the other.

There are several kinds of antonymy. There are **complementary pairs:**

> alive/dead   present/absent   awake/asleep

They are complementary in that *not alive = dead* and *not dead = alive,* and so on.

There are **gradable** pairs of antonyms:

> big/small   hot/cold   fast/slow   happy/sad

The meaning of adjectives in gradable pairs is related to the object they modify. The words themselves do not provide an absolute scale. Thus we know that "a small elephant" is much bigger than "a large mouse." *Fast* is faster when applied to an airplane than to a car.

With gradable pairs, the negative of one word is not synonymous with the other. For example, someone who is *not happy* is not necessarily *sad.* It is also true of gradable antonyms that more of one is less of another. More bigness is less smallness; wider is less narrow; taller is less short.

Gradable antonyms are often found among sets of words that partition a continuum:

> *tiny – small – medium – large – huge – gargantuan*
> *euphoric – elated – happy – so-so – sad – gloomy – despondent*

Another characteristic of certain pairs of gradable antonyms is that one is **marked** and the other **unmarked.** The unmarked member is the one used in questions of degree.

We ask, ordinarily, "How *high* is the mountain?" (not "How low is it?")[2] We answer "Ten thousand feet *high*" but never "Ten thousand feet *low*," except humorously or ironically. Thus *high* is the unmarked member of *high/low.* Similarly *tall* is the unmarked member of *tall/short, fast* the unmarked member of *fast/slow,* etc.

Another kind of "opposite" involves pairs like

give/receive   buy/sell   teacher/pupil

They are called **relational opposites,** and they display symmetry in their meaning. If X *gives* Y to Z, then Z *receives* Y from X. If X is Y's *teacher,* then Y is X's *pupil.* Pairs of words ending in *-er* and *-ee* are usually relational opposites. If Mary is Bill's employ*er,* then Bill is Mary's employ*ee.*

Comparative forms of gradable pairs of adjectives often form relational pairs. Thus, if Sally is *taller* than Alfred, then Alfred is *shorter* than Sally. If a Cadillac is *more expensive* than a Ford, then a Ford is *cheaper* than a Cadillac.

If meanings of words were indissoluble wholes, there would be no way to make the interpretations we do. We know that *big* and *red* are not opposites because they have too few semantic properties in common. They are both adjectives, but *big* has a semantic property "about size," whereas *red* has a semantic property "about color." On the other hand, *buy/sell* are relational opposites because both contain the semantic property "transfer of goods or services," and they differ only in one property, "direction of transfer."

Relationships between certain semantic features can reveal knowledge about antonyms. Consider:

A word that is [+married] is [–single].
A word that is [+single] is [–married].

These show that any word that bears the semantic property "married," such as *wife,* is understood to lack the semantic property "single"; and conversely, any word that bears the semantic property "single," such as *bachelor,* will not have the property "married."

Formation of Antonyms

Reprinted by permission: Tribune Media Services.

---

[2] If the topic of conversation were "low mountains," say for the purpose of novice mountain climbing, then it might be appropriate to ask "How low is Mount Airy?" The marked/unmarked distinction is in effect if there are no contextual factors.

In English there are a number of ways to form antonyms. You can add the prefix *un-*:

likely/unlikely   able/unable   fortunate/unfortunate

or you can add *non-*:

entity/nonentity   conformist/nonconformist

or you can add *in-*:

tolerant/intolerant   discreet/indiscreet   decent/indecent

Other prefixes may also be used to form negative words morphologically: *mis-,* as in *misbehave, dis-,* as in *displease.*

Hyponyms

Speakers of English know that the words *red, white, blue,* etc. are "color" words, that is, their lexical representations have the feature [+color] indicating a class to which they all belong. Similarly *lion, tiger, leopard, lynx* have the feature [+feline]. Such sets of words are called **hyponyms.** The relationship of **hyponymy** is between the more general term such as *color* and the more specific instances of it such as *red,* etc. Thus *red* is a hyponym of *color,* and *lion* is a hyponym of *feline;* or equivalently, *color* has the hyponym *red,* and *feline* has the hyponym *lion,* and so on.

Sometimes there is no single word in the language that encompasses a set of hyponyms. Thus *clarinet, guitar, horn, marimba, piano, trumpet, violin* are hyponyms because they are "musical instruments" but there isn't a single word meaning "musical instrument" that has these words as its hyponyms.

Metonyms

A **metonym** is a word used in place of another word or expression to convey the same meaning. The use of *brass* to refer to military officers or *Moscow* to refer to the Russian government are examples of **metonymy.** *Crown* is a metonym for a monarchy and *jock* is sometimes used as a metonym for an athlete.

Retronyms

Day baseball, silent movie, surface mail, and *whole milk* are all expressions that once were redundant. In the past, all baseball games were played in daylight, all movies were silent, electronic mail didn't exist, and low-fat and skim milk were not yet conceived.

Retronym is the term reserved for these expressions. Strictly speaking, it does not apply to the individual words themselves, but the combination. Still, it's an interesting member of the "-*nym*" family of words.

Proper Names

"My name is Alice . . . "

"It's a stupid name enough!" Humpty Dumpty interrupted impatiently. "What does it mean?"

"Must a name mean something?" Alice asked doubtfully.

"Of course it must," Humpty Dumpty said with a short laugh. "My name means the shape I am—and a good handsome shape it is, too. With a name like yours, you might be any shape, almost."

Lewis Carroll, *Through the Looking-Glass*

Reprinted with special permission of North America Syndicate.

Proper names are a language's shortcuts. Imagine if we couldn't name people, places, institutions, or gods. How would you describe yourself uniquely without use of proper names? You can't say: "Eldest daughter of John and Mary Smith," obviously. How about: "The young woman who lives at 5 Oak Street?" No way! "Valedictorian of the senior class at Central High School." Sorry.

Proper names are different from most words in the language in that they refer to a specific object or entity, but usually have little meaning, or sense, beyond the power of referral.[3] That's part of the humor in Humpty Dumpty's remark about names meaning shapes.

The meaning of words like *dog* or *sincerity* impart a sense that permits you to recognize specific instances of that class of entities, or even have an abstract vision of what is meant, but you cannot pet *dog* or doubt *sincerity*. You can only pet a specific dog, Fido, or doubt a specific instance of sincerity, such as a political promise. Nothing in the world corresponds to *dog* the way *Paris* refers to the city of Paris.

Thus, proper names refer to unique (within context) objects or entities. The objects may be extant, such as those designated by

---

[3] Of course if a word with sense, such as lake, is incorporated into a proper name as in *Lake Louise,* then the proper noun has the semantic properties of *lake.* Care is needed though, since a restaurant named *Lake Louise* would not have any lake-like meaning.

Disa Karin Viktoria Lubker
Lake Michigan
The Empire State Building

or extinct, such as

Socrates
Troy

or even fictional

Sherlock Holmes
Dr. John H. Watson
Oz

Proper names are **definite,** which means they refer to a unique object insofar as the speaker and listener are concerned. If I say

Mary Smith is coming to dinner

my spouse understands Mary Smith to refer to our friend Mary Smith, and not to one of the dozens of Mary Smiths in the phone book.

Because they are inherently definite, proper names in English are not in general preceded by *the:*

*the John Smith
*the California

There are some exceptions, such as the names of rivers, ships, and erected structures:

the Mississippi
the *Queen Mary*
the Empire State Building
the Eiffel Tower
the Golden Gate Bridge

and there are special cases such as *the John Smiths* to refer to the family of John Smith. Also, for the sake of clarity or literary effect, it is possible to precede a proper name by an **article** if the resulting **noun phrase** is followed by a modifying expression such as a **prepositional phrase** or a **sentence:**

The Paris of the 1920s . . .
The New York that everyone knows and loves . . .

In some languages, such as Greek and Hungarian, articles normally occur before proper names. Thus we find in Greek: *O Spiros agapai tin Sophia,* which is literally "The Spiro loves the Sophie," where *O* is the masculine nominative form of the definite article and *tin* the feminine accusative form. This indicates that some of the restrictions we observed are particular to English, and may be due to syntactic rather than semantic rules of language.

Proper names cannot usually be pluralized, though they can be plural, like *the Great Lakes* or *the Pleiades.* There are exceptions, such as *the John Smiths* already mentioned or expressions like *the Linguistics Department has three Bobs,* meaning three people named Bob, but they are special locutions used in particular circumstances. Because proper names generally refer to unique objects, it is not surprising that they occur mainly in the singular.

For the same reason, proper names cannot in general be preceded by adjectives. Many adjectives have the semantic effect of narrowing down the field of reference, so that the noun phrase a *red house* is a more specific description than simply *a house;* but what proper names refer to is already completely narrowed down, so modification by adjectives seems peculiar. Again, as in all these cases, extenuating circumstances give rise to exceptions. Language is nothing if not flexible, and we find expressions such as *young John* used to discriminate between two people named John. We also find adjectives applied to emphasize some quality of the object referred to, such as *the wicked Borgias* or *the brilliant Professor Einstein.*

Names may be coined or drawn from the stock of names that the language provides; but once a proper name is coined, it cannot be pluralized or preceded by *the* or any adjective (except for cases like those cited above), and it will be used to refer uniquely, for these rules are among the many rules already in the grammar, and speakers know they apply to all proper names, even new ones.

PHRASE AND SENTENCE MEANING

"Then you should say what you mean," the March Hare went on.

"I do," Alice hastily replied, "at least—I mean what I say—that's the same thing, you know."

"Not the same thing a bit!" said the Hatter. "You might just as well say that 'I see what I eat' is the same thing as 'I eat what I see'!"

"You might just as well say," added the March Hare, "that 'I like what I get' is the same thing as 'I get what I like'!"

"You might just as well say," added the Dormouse . . . "that 'I breathe when I sleep' is the same thing as 'I sleep when I breathe'!"

"It is the same thing with you," said the Hatter.

Lewis Carroll, *Alice's Adventures in Wonderland*

Words and morphemes are the smallest meaningful units in language. We have been studying their meaning relationships and semantic properties as lexical semantics. For the most part, however, we communicate in phrases and sentences. The meaning of a phrase or sentence depends on both the meaning of its words and how those words are combined structurally.

Some of the semantic relationships we observed between words are also found between sentences. For example, two words may be synonyms; two sentences may be paraphrases. They may be paraphrases because they contain synonymous words, but they may also be paraphrases because of structural differences that do not affect meaning, such as

> They ran the bill up.
> They ran up the bill.

Similarly, words may be homonyms, hence ambiguous when spoken. Sentences may be ambiguous because they contain homonymous words, as in *I need to buy a pen for Shelby*, or due to their structure, as in the sentence *the boy saw the man with the telescope,* discussed in Chapter 4.

Words have antonyms; sentences can be negated. Thus the opposite of *he is alive* is both *he is dead,* using an antonym, and *he is not alive,* using negation.

Words are used for naming purposes; sentences can be used that way too. Both words and sentences can be used to refer to, or point out, objects; and both may have some further meaning beyond this referring capability, as we shall see in a later section.

The study of how word meanings combine into phrase and sentence meanings, and the meaning relationships among these larger units, is called phrasal or sentential semantics to distinguish it from lexical semantics.

Phrasal Meaning

> . . . I placed all my words with their interpretations in alphabetical order. And thus in a few days, by the help of a very faithful memory, I got some insight into their language.
>
> Jonathan Swift, *Gulliver's Travels*

Although it is widely believed that learning a language is merely learning the words of that language and what they mean—a myth apparently accepted by Gulliver—there is more to it than that, as you know by reading this book and you knew even before if you ever tried to learn a foreign language. We comprehend phrases and sentences because we know the meaning of individual words, and we know rules for combining their meanings.

Noun-Centered Meaning

We know the meanings of *red* and *balloon*. The semantic rule to interpret the combination *red balloon* adds the property "redness" to the properties of balloon. The phrase *the red balloon,* because of the presence of the definite article *the,* means "a particular instance of redness and balloonness." A semantic rule for the interpretation of *the* accounts for this.

The phrase *large balloon* would be interpreted by a different semantic rule, because part of the meaning of *large* is that it is a relative concept. *Large balloon* means *"large for a balloon."* What is large for a balloon may be small for a house and gargantuan for a cockroach; yet we correctly comprehend the meanings of *large balloon, large house,* and *large cockroach.*

The semantic rules for adjective-noun combinations are complex. *A good friend* is a kind of friend, just as a *red balloon* is a kind of a balloon. There is a merging of semantic properties. But a *false friend* is not any kind of a friend at all. The semantic properties of "friendness" are "canceled out" by the adjective "false." Thus semantic rules for noun phrases containing *good* and *false* are quite different. A third kind of rule governs adjectives like *alleged;* the meaning of *alleged murderer* is someone accused of murder, but the semantic rules in this case do not tell us whether an alleged murderer is or is not a murderer.

Exemplars of Class of Adjective (Adj)	Truth of "An Adj X is an X," (e.g., *A red ball is a ball*)
good, red, large, etc.	True
false, counterfeit, phony, etc.	False
alleged, purported, putative, etc.	Undetermined

There are many more rules involved in the semantics of noun phrases. Because noun phrases may contain prepositional phrases, semantic rules are needed for such expressions as *The house with the white fence.* We have seen how the rules account for *the house,* and *the white fence.* The semantic rules for prepositions indicate that two objects stand in a certain relationship determined by the meaning of the particular preposition. For *with,* that relationship is "accompanies" or "is part of." A preposition like *in* means a certain spatial relationship, and so on for other prepositions.

The structure of a phrase is important to its meaning. *Red brick* is a noun phrase, with the head[4] noun *brick.* Therefore *red brick* indicates a kind of brick. The head of the phrase determines its principle meaning. The expression *brick red* has the adjective *red* as its head, so the entire expression is a kind of red.

In noun compounds the final noun is generally the head, so a *dog house* is a kind of a house, namely one suitable for dogs, whereas a *house dog* is a kind of dog.

Meanings build on meanings. Noun phrase meanings are combinations of meanings of nouns, adjectives, articles, and even sentences. (The noun phrase *the man who knew too much* is a combination of *the, man,* and the sentence *he knew too much.*)[5] All these combinations make sense because the semantic rules of grammar, like rules of phonology or syntax, operate systematically and predictably to incorporate the meanings of the phrasal components into the meaning of the phrase.

Sense and Reference

It is natural . . . to think of there being connected with a sign . . . besides . . . the reference of the sign, also what I should like to call the sense of the sign. . . .

Gottlob Frege, *On Sense and Reference*

Knowing the meaning of certain noun phrases means knowing how to discover what objects the noun phrases refer to. For example in the sentence

The mason put the red brick on the wall

knowing the meaning of *the red brick* enables us to identify the object being referred to. We need only know in principle how to identify the object: A blindfolded person would also comprehend the meaning. The object "pointed to" in such a noun phrase is called its **referent,** and the noun phrase is said to have **reference.**

---

[4] The **head** of a noun phrase is the noun; the head of a verb phrase is the verb, and so on.

[5] Another semantic rule determines that *who* means the same as *the man.*

For many noun phrases there is more to meaning than just reference. For example, the noun phrases *the red brick* and *the first brick from the right* may refer to the same object, that is, may be **coreferential.** Nevertheless, we would be reluctant to say that the two expressions have the same meaning because they have the same reference. There is some additional meaning that is often termed **sense.** Thus a noun phrase may have *sense* and *reference,* which together comprise its meaning. Knowing the sense of a noun phrase allows you to identify its referent. Sometimes the term **extension** is used for *reference,* and **intension** for *sense.*

Certain proper names appear to have only reference. A name like Chris Jones may point out a certain person, its referent, but seems to have little linguistic meaning beyond that. Nonetheless, some proper names do seem to have meaning over and above their ability to refer. Humpty Dumpty suggested that his name means "a good round shape." Certainly, the name Sue has the semantic property "female," as evinced by the humor in "A Boy Named Sue," a song sung by Johnny Cash. *The Pacific Ocean* has the semantic properties of *ocean,* and even such names as *Fido, Dobbins,* and *Bossie* are associated with dogs, horses, and cows, respectively.

"There's nothing here under 'Superman'—is it possible you made the reservation under another name?"

Drawing by Maslin; © 1992 The New Yorker Magazine, Inc.

Sometimes two different proper names have the same referent, such as Superman and Clark Kent or Dr. Jekyll and Mr. Hyde. It is a hotly debated question in the philosophy of language as to whether two such expressions have the same meaning, or differ in sense.

While some proper nouns appear to have reference but no sense, other noun phrases have sense, but no reference. If not, we would be unable to understand sentences like these:

The present king of France is bald.
By the year 3000, our descendants will have left Earth.

Speakers of English can understand these sentences, even though France now has no king, and our descendants of a millennium from now do not exist.

Verb-Centered Meaning

In all languages the verb plays a central role in the meaning and structure of most sentences. In English the verb determines the number of objects and limits the semantic properties of both its subject and its objects. For example *find* requires an animate subject and is subcategorized for one object. In formal, written English, a verb is necessary to have a complete sentence.

Languages of the world, as we'll see in Chapter 11, may be classified according to whether the verb occurs initially, medially, or finally in their basic sentences.

All this is evidence for the centrality of the verb.

By permission of Johnny Hart and Creators Syndicate, Inc.

Thematic Roles   The noun phrase subject of a sentence and the constituents of the verb phrase are semantically related in various ways to the verb. The relations depend on the meaning of the particular verb. For example the NP *the boy* in *the boy found a red brick* is called the **agent** or "doer" of the action of finding. The NP *a red brick* is the **theme** and undergoes the action. (The boldfaced words are technical terms of semantic theory.) Part of the meaning of *find* is that its subject is an agent and its direct object is a theme.

The noun phrases within a verb phrase whose head is the verb *put* have the relation of theme and **goal.** In the verb phrase *put the red brick on the wall, the red brick* is the theme and *on the wall* is the goal. The entire verb phrase is interpreted to mean that the theme of *put* changes its position to the goal. *Put*'s subject is also an agent, so that in *The boy put the red brick on the wall,* "the boy" performs the action. The knowledge speakers have about *find* and *put* may be revealed in their lexical entries:

> find, V, _____ NP, (Agent, Theme)
> put, V, _____ NP PP, (Agent, Theme, Goal)

The thematic roles are contained in parentheses. The first one states that the subject is an agent. The remaining thematic roles belong to the categories for which the verb is subcategorized. The direct object of both *find* and *put* will be a theme. The prepositional phrase for which *put* subcategorizes will be a goal.

The semantic relationships that we have called *theme, agent,* and *goal* are among the **thematic roles** of the verb. Other thematic roles are **location,** where the action occurs; **source,** where the action originates; **instrument,** an object used to accomplish the action; **experiencer,** one receiving sensory input; **causative,** a natural force that brings about a change; and **possessor,** one who owns or has something. (The list is not complete.) These may be summed up:

Thematic role	Description	Example
Agent	the one who performs an action	*Joyce* ran
Theme	the one or thing that undergoes an action	Mary called *Bill*
Location	the place where an action takes place	It rains *in Spain*
Goal	the place to which an action is directed	Put the cat *on the porch*
Source	the place from which an action originates	He flew from *Iowa* to Idaho
Instrument	the means by which an action is performed	Jo cuts hair *with a razor*
Experiencer	one who perceives something	*Helen* heard Robert playing the piano
Causative	a natural force that causes a change	*The wind* damaged the roof
Possessor	one who has something	The tail of *the dog* got caught in the door

Our knowledge of verbs includes their syntactic category, how they are subcategorized, and the thematic roles that their NP subject and object(s) have, and this knowledge is explicitly represented in the lexicon.

Thematic roles are the same in sentences that are paraphrases. In both these sentences

The dog bit the stick
The stick was bitten by the dog

the dog is the agent and *the stick* is the theme.

Thematic roles may remain the same in sentences that are *not* paraphrases, as in the following instances:

The boy opened the door with the key.
The key opened the door.
The door opened.

In all three of these sentences, *the door* is the theme, the thing that gets opened. In the first two sentences, *the key,* despite its different structural positions, retains the thematic role of instrument.

The three examples illustrate the fact that English allows many different thematic roles to be the subject of the sentence (that is, the first NP under the S). These sentences had as subjects an agent *(the boy),* an instrument *(the key),* and a theme *(the door).* The sentences below illustrate other kinds of subjects.

This hotel forbids dogs.
It seems that Samson has lost his strength.

In the first example, *this hotel* has the thematic role of location. In the second, the subject *it* is semantically empty and lacks a thematic role entirely.

Thematic Roles in Other Languages

The immense value of becoming acquainted with a foreign language is that we are thereby led into a new world of tradition and thought and feeling.

Havelock Ellis, *The Task of Social Hygiene,* Chapter 10

Contrast English with German. German is much stingier about which thematic roles can be subjects. For example, in order to express the idea "this hotel forbids dogs," a German speaker would have to say:

In diesem Hotel sind Hunde verboten

literally, "in this hotel are dogs forbidden." German does not permit the thematic role of location to occur as a subject; it must be expressed as a prepositional phrase. If we translated the English sentence word for word into German, the results would be ungrammatical in German:

*Dieses Hotel verbietet Hunde.

Differences such as these between English and German show that learning a foreign language is not a matter of simple word-for-word translation. You must learn the grammar, and that includes learning the syntax and semantics and how the two interact.

In many languages thematic roles are reflected in the **case,** or **grammatical case,** of the noun. The case of a noun refers to its morphological shape, often manifested as suffixes on the noun stem. English does not have an extensive case system, but the possessive form of a noun, as in *the boy***'s** *red brick,* is called the genitive or possessive case.

In languages such as Finnish, the noun assumes a morphological shape according to its thematic role in the sentence. For example, in Finnish, *koulu* is the root meaning "school," and *-sta* is a case ending that means "directional source." Thus *koulusta* means "from the school." Similarly, *kouluun (koulu + -un)* means "to the school."

Some of the information carried by grammatical case in languages like Finnish is borne by prepositions in English. Thus *from* and *to* often indicate the thematic roles of source and goal. Instrument is marked by *with,* location by prepositions such as *on* and *in,* possessor by *of* and agent, experiencer and causative by *by* in passive sentences. The role of theme is generally unaccompanied by a preposition, as its most common syntactic function is direct object. What we are calling thematic roles in this section has sometimes been studied as *case theory.*

In German, case distinctions appear on articles as well as on nouns and adjectives. Thus in

Sie liebt den Mann

"She loves the man," the article *den* is in the accusative case. In the nominative case it would be *der.* Languages with a rich system of case are often more constraining as to which thematic roles can occur in subject position. German, as we saw above, is one such language.

The Theta-Criterion

A universal principle has been proposed called the **theta-criterion,** which states in part that a particular thematic role may occur only once in a sentence. Thus sentences like

*The boy opened the door with the key with a lock-pick

are semantically anomalous because two noun phrases bear the thematic role of instrument.

In English the thematic role of possessor is indicated two ways syntactically: either as *the boy's red hat* or as *the red hat of the boy.* However, *the boy's red hat of Bill* is semantically anomalous according to the theta-criterion because both *the boy* and *Bill* have the thematic role of possessor.

Irrespective of how we label the semantic relations that exist between verbs and noun phrases, they are part of every speaker's linguistic competence and account for much of the meaning in language.

Sentential Meaning

The meaning of sentences is built, in part, from the meaning of noun phrases and verb phrases. Adverbs may add to or qualify the meaning. *The boy found the ball yesterday* specifies a time component to the meaning of the boy's finding the ball. Adverbs such as *quickly, fortunately, often,* etc. would affect the meaning in other ways.

Like noun phrases, sentences have sense, which is usually what we are referring to when we talk about the meaning of a sentence. Some linguists would also say that certain sentences have reference, namely ones that can be true or false. Their reference, or extension, is *true* if the sentence is true, and *false* if the sentence is false.

The "Truth" of Sentences

. . . Having Occasion to talk of Lying and false Representation, it was with much Difficulty that he comprehended what I meant. . . . For he argued thus: That the Use of Speech was to make us understand one another and to receive Information of Facts; now if any one said the Thing which was not, these Ends were defeated; because I cannot properly be said to understand him. . . . And these were all the Notions he had concerning that Faculty of

> Lying, so perfectly well understood, and so universally practiced among human Creatures.
>
> Jonathan Swift, *Gulliver's Travels*

The sense of a declarative sentence permits you to know under what circumstances that sentence is true. Those "circumstances" are called the **truth conditions** of the sentence. The truth conditions of a declarative sentence are the same as the *sense* of the sentence.

In the world as we know it, the sentence

The Declaration of Independence was signed in 1776

is true, and the sentence

The Declaration of Independence was signed in 1976

is false. We know the meaning of both sentences equally well, and knowing their meaning means knowing their sense or truth conditions. We compare their truth conditions with "the real world" or historical fact, and can thus say which one is true and which one false. The truth or falsehood of these sentences is their *reference*.

You can, however, understand well-formed sentences of your language without knowing their truth value, just as you can understand the expression *the fifteenth Pope* without knowing the reference. Knowing the truth conditions is not the same as knowing the actual facts. Rather, the truth conditions—the sense—permit you to examine the world and learn the actual facts. If you did not know the linguistic meaning—if the sentence were in an unknown language—you could never determine its truth, even if you had memorized an encyclopedia. You may not know the truth of

The Mecklenburg Charter was signed in 1770

but if you know its meaning you know in principle how to discover its truth, even if you do not have the means to actually do so. For example, consider the sentence

The moon is made of green cheese.

We knew before space travel that going to the moon would test the truth of the sentence. Now consider this sentence:

Rufus believes that the Declaration of Independence was signed in 1976.

This sentence is true if some individual named Rufus does indeed believe the statement, and it is false if he does not. Those are its truth conditions. It does not matter that a subpart of the sentence is false. An entire sentence may be true even if one or more of its parts are false, and vice versa. The sense of a sentence is determined by the semantic rules which permit you to combine the subparts of a sentence and still know under what conditions the sentence is true or false.

Paraphrase

We can now give a formal definition of *paraphrase:*

Two sentences are paraphrases if they have the same truth conditions.

The following sets of sentences are paraphrases. Despite subtle differences in emphasis, they share the same truth conditions:

> The horse threw the rider.
> The rider was thrown by the horse.

> It is easy to play sonatas on this piano.
> This piano is easy to play sonatas on.
> On this piano it is easy to play sonatas.
> Sonatas are easy to play on this piano.

> Booth assassinated Lincoln.
> It was Booth who assassinated Lincoln.
> It was Lincoln who was assassinated by Booth.
> The person who assassinated Lincoln was Booth.

> The students gave money to the beggar.
> The students gave the beggar money.

Entailment

Sometimes knowing the truth of one sentence **entails** or necessarily implies the truth of another sentence. For example if you know it is true that

> Corday assassinated Marat

then you know that it is true that

> Marat is dead.

It is logically impossible for the former to be true and the latter false. Thus the sentence *Corday assassinated Marat* entails the sentence *Marat is dead.*

The sentence *The brick is red* entails *The brick is not white; Mortimer is a bachelor* entails *Mortimer is male,* and so on. These entailments are part of the semantic rules we have been discussing. Much of what we know about the world comes from knowing the entailments of true sentences.

Contradiction

Contradiction is negative entailment, that is, where the truth of one sentence necessarily implies the falseness of another sentence, for example:

> Elizabeth II is Queen of England.
> Elizabeth II is a man.

> Scott is a baby.
> Scott is an adult.

If the first sentence of each pair is true, the second is necessarily false. This relationship is called *contradiction* because the truth of one sentence contradicts the truth of the other.

When Semantics and Syntax Meet

"HE CAN SMELL BETTER THAN WE CAN, BUT HE USUALLY SMELLS WORSE."

DENNIS THE MENACE® used by permission of Hank Ketcham and
© by North America Syndicate.

Syntax is concerned with how words are combined to form phrases and sentences; semantics is concerned with what these combinations mean. The theta-criterion, discussed in a previous section, is an instance in which semantics and syntax interact. The semantic constraint that no thematic role may occur more than once has the effect of restricting the NPs and PPs that may follow the verb in a verb phrase.

Words versus Phrases

DRABBLE reprinted by permission of United Feature Syndicate, Inc.

We have seen throughout this chapter and the previous one that the same meaning may be expressed syntactically in more than one way—the phenomenon of paraphrase. The semantic property of possession may be expressed by a word in the genitive case such as *England's king,* or by an "of" construct such as *the king of England.*

A similar situation arises with certain semantic concepts such as "ability," "permission," or "obligation." These may be expressed through auxiliary verbs:

> He *can* go.
> He *may* go.
> He *must* go.

They may also be expressed phrasally, without the auxiliaries:

> He *is able* to go. / He *has the ability* to go.
> He is *permitted* to go. / He has *permission* to go.
> He is *obliged* to go. / He has an *obligation* to go.

It is often possible to substitute a phrase for a word without affecting the sense of the sentence.

> John saw Mary.
> John perceived Mary using his eyes.

> The professor lectured the class.
> The professor delivered a lecture to the class.

When Passives Do Not Work

Active-passive pairs constitute another common type of paraphrase:

> The child found the puppy.
> The puppy was found by the child.

This relationship between actives and passives is based on syntactic structure as discussed in Chapter 4. However, some active sentences do not have a well-formed passive counterpart. For example:

> John resembles Bill
> The book cost ten dollars

cannot undergo the passive transformation to give

> *Bill was resembled by John.
> *Ten dollars was cost by the book.

Semantically, when the subject of an active sentence is in a state described by the verb and direct object, there is no passive paraphrase. Since *John* is in a state of resembling Bill—John doesn't do anything—the sentence fails to passivize. This shows how the semantics of verbal relationships may affect syntactic relationships.

Passives are usually paraphrases of their active counterpart, but there are exceptions when "quantifiers,"[6]—words having to do with amounts—get involved. Consider:

> Every person in this room speaks two languages.
> Two languages are spoken by every person in this room.

These two sentence do *not* have the same truth conditions. Suppose there are three people in the room, Tom, Dick, and Harry. Tom speaks English and Russian; Dick speaks French and Italian; and Harry speaks Chinese and Thai. Then the first sentence is true. The second, however, is false because there are no two languages that everyone speaks.

Pronouns and Coreferentiality

Another example of how syntax and semantics interact has to do with **reflexive pronouns**, such as *herself* or *themselves*. The meaning of a reflexive pronoun always refers back to some antecedent. In *Jane bit herself, herself* refers to Jane. Syntactically, reflexive pronouns and their antecedents must occur within the same S in the phrase structure tree. Compare the phrase structure tree of *Jane bit herself* with that of **Jane said that herself slept:*

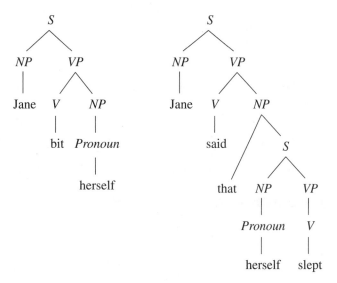

In the second tree, *Jane* is in the topmost S, but *herself* is in a different, embedded S. Syntactic and semantic rules do not allow the pronoun to be reflexive.

On the other hand, the interaction between the rules tells us that in *Jane bit her,* the pronoun *her* cannot refer to Jane; it must refer to some other person.

Sentence structure also plays a role in determining when a pronoun and a noun phrase in different clauses can be **coreferential,** that is, refer to the same object. For example in

---

[6] *Every, each, some, two, many, several, few* are some quantifiers in English.

> John believes that he is a genius

the pronoun *he* can be interpreted as John or as some person other than John. However in

> He believes that John is a genius

the coreferential interpretation is impossible. *John* and *he* cannot refer to the same person. It appears that a pronoun antecedent cannot occur to the left of its noun phrase if the two are to be coreferential. However, the rule is not that simple. In the sentence

> The fact that he is considered a genius bothers John

he and *John* can be interpreted as coreferential. A somewhat complicated semantic rule that refers to sentence structure is at work here. A precise statement of this rule goes beyond the scope of this introductory text. The point is that syntax and semantics interrelate in complex ways.

WHEN RULES ARE BROKEN

> For all a rhetorician's rules
> Teach nothing but to name his tools.
>
> Samuel Butler, Hudibras

The rules of language are not laws of nature. Only by a "miracle" can the laws of nature be broken, but the rules of language are broken every day by everybody. This lawlessness is not human perversity, but rather another way in which language is creative.

There are three kinds of rule violation that we will discuss: **anomaly,** a violation of semantic rules to create "nonsense"; **metaphor,** or nonliteral meaning; and **idioms,** in which the meaning of an expression may be unrelated to the meaning of its parts.

Anomaly: No Sense and Nonsense

> Don't tell me of a man's being able to talk sense; everyone can talk sense. Can he talk nonsense?
>
> William Pitt

If in a conversation someone said to you

> My brother is an only child

you might think that he was making a joke or that he did not know the meaning of the words he was using. You would know that the sentence was strange, or **anomalous;** yet it is certainly an English sentence. It conforms to all the grammatical rules of the language. It is strange because it represents a contradiction; the meaning of *brother* includes the fact that the individual referred to is a male human who has at least one sibling, and cannot sensibly be "an only child."

The sentence

That bachelor is pregnant

is anomalous for similar reasons; the word *bachelor* contains the semantic property "male," whereas the word "pregnant" has the semantic property "female." This clash of semantic properties make the sentence anomalous. The anomaly arises from trying to equate something that is [+male] with something that is [−male].

The semantic properties of words determine what other words they can be combined with. One sentence that is used by linguists to illustrate this fact is

Colorless green ideas sleep furiously.[7]

The sentence seems to obey all the syntactic rules of English. The subject is *colorless green ideas* and the predicate is *sleep furiously.* It has the same syntactic structure as the sentence

Dark green leaves rustle furiously

but there is obviously something wrong **semantically** with the sentence. The meaning of *colorless* includes the semantic property "without color," but it is combined with the adjective *green,* which has the property "green in color." How can something be both "without color" and "green in color"? Other such semantic violations also occur in the sentence.

Other English "sentences" make no sense at all because they include "words" that have no meaning; they are **uninterpretable.** They can only be interpreted if some meaning for each nonsense word can be dreamt up. Lewis Carroll's "Jabberwocky" is probably the most famous poem in which most of the content words have no meaning—they do not exist in the lexicon of the grammar. Still, all the sentences "sound" as if they should be or could be English sentences:

> *'Twas brillig, and the slithy toves*
> *Did gyre and gimble in the wabe;*
> *All mimsy were the borogoves,*
> *And the mome raths outgrabe.*
>
> . . .
>
> *He took his vorpal sword in hand:*
> *Long time the manxome foe he sought—*
> *So rested he by the Tumtum tree,*
> *And stood awhile in thought.*

Without knowing what *vorpal* means, you nevertheless know that

He took his vorpal sword in hand

---

[7] Noam Chomsky. 1957. *Syntactic Structures,* The Hague: Mouton.

means the same thing as

> He took his sword, which was vorpal, in hand.
> It was in his hand that he took his vorpal sword.

Knowing the language, and assuming that *vorpal* means the same thing in the three sentences (because the same sounds are used), you can decide that the sense—the truth conditions—of the three sentences are identical. In other words, you are able to decide that two things mean the same thing even though you do not know what either one means. You decide by assuming that the semantic properties of *vorpal* are the same whenever it is used.

We now see why Alice commented, when she had read "Jabberwocky":

> "It seems very pretty, but it's *rather* hard to understand!" (You see she didn't like to confess, even to herself, that she couldn't make it out at all.) "Somehow it seems to fill my head with ideas—only I don't exactly know what they are! However, *somebody* killed *something:* that's clear, at any rate—"

The semantic properties of words show up in other ways in sentence construction. For example, if the meaning of a word includes the semantic property "human" in English, we can replace it by one sort of pronoun but not another. This semantic feature determines that we call a boy *he* and a table *it,* and not vice versa.

According to Mark Twain, Eve had such knowledge in her grammar, for she writes in her diary:

> If this reptile is a man, it ain't an *it,* is it? That wouldn't be grammatical, would it? I think it would be *he.* In that case one would parse it thus: nominative *he;* dative, *him;* possessive, *his'n.*

Semantic violations in poetry may form strange but interesting aesthetic images, as in Dylan Thomas's phrase *a grief ago. Ago* is ordinarily used with words specified by some temporal semantic feature:

a week ago		*a table ago
an hour ago	but not	*a dream ago ,
a month ago		*a mother ago
a century ago		

When Thomas used the word *grief* with *ago* he was adding a durational feature to *grief* for poetic effect.

In the poetry of e. e. cummings there are phrases like

> the six subjunctive crumbs twitch.
> a man . . . wearing a round jeer for a hat.
> children building this rainman out of snow.

Though all of these phrases violate some semantic rules, we can understand them; it is the breaking of the rules that creates the imagery desired.

Anomaly occurs in many ways in language. It may involve contradictory semantic properties, nonsense words, violation of semantic rules, and so on. The fact that we are able to understand, or at least interpret, anomalous expressions, and at the same time recognize their anomalous nature, demonstrates our knowledge of the semantic system and semantic properties of the language.

Metaphor

Our doubts are traitors.

Shakespeare

Walls have ears.

Cervantes

The night has a thousand eyes and the day but one.

Frances William Bourdillon

DILBERT reprinted by permission of United Feature Syndicate, Inc.

Sometimes the breaking of semantic rules can be used to convey a particular idea. *Walls have ears* is certainly anomalous, but it can be interpreted as meaning "you can be overheard even when you think nobody is listening." In some sense the sentence is ambiguous, but the literal meaning is so unlikely that listeners stretch their imagination for another interpretation. That "stretching" is based on semantic properties that are inferred or that provide some kind of resemblance. Such nonliteral interpretations of sentences are called **metaphor.**

The literal meaning of a sentence such as

My new car is a lemon

is anomalous. You could, if driven to the wall (another metaphor), provide some literal interpretation that is plausible if given sufficient context. For example, the *new car* may be a miniature toy carved out of a piece of citrus fruit. The more common meaning, however, would be metaphorical and interpreted as referring to a newly purchased automobile that breaks down and requires constant repairs. The imagination stretching in this case may relate to the semantic property "tastes sour" that *lemon* possesses.

Metaphors are not necessarily anomalous when taken literally. The literal meaning of the sentence

Dr. Jekyll is a butcher

is that a physician named Jekyll also works as a retailer of meats or a slaughterer of animals used for food. The metaphorical meaning is that the doctor named Jekyll is harmful, possibly murderous, and apt to operate unnecessarily.

Similarly, the sentence

> John is a snake in the grass

can be interpreted literally to refer to a pet snake on the lawn named John. Metaphorically the sentence has nothing to do with a scaly, limbless reptile.

To interpret metaphors we need to understand both the literal meaning and facts about the world. To understand the metaphor

> Time is money

it is necessary to know that in our society we are often paid according to the number of hours or days worked. To recognize that the sentence

> Jack is a pussycat

has a different meaning than

> Jack is a tiger

requires knowledge that the metaphorical meaning of each sentence does not depend on the semantic property "feline." Rather, other semantic properties of these two words are referred to.

Metaphorical use of language is language creativity at its highest. Nevertheless, the basis of metaphorical use is the ordinary linguistic knowledge about words, their semantic properties, and their combining powers that all speakers possess.

Idioms

PEANUTS reprinted by permission of UFS, Inc.

Knowing a language includes knowing the morphemes, simple words, compound words, and their meanings. In addition it means knowing fixed phrases, consisting of more than one word, with meanings that cannot be inferred from the meanings of the individual words. The usual semantic rules for combining meanings do not apply. Such expressions are called **idioms.** All languages contain many idiomatic phrases, as in these English examples:

> sell down the river
> haul over the coals
> eat my hat
> let their hair down
> put his foot in his mouth
> throw her weight around
> snap out of it
> cut it out
> hit it off
> get it off
> bite your tongue
> give a piece of your mind

Idioms are similar in structure to ordinary phrases except that they tend to be frozen in form and do not readily enter into other combinations or allow the word order to change. Thus,

> (a) She put her foot in her mouth

has the same structure as

> (b) She put her bracelet in her drawer

but

> The drawer in which she put her bracelet was hers
> Her bracelet was put in her drawer

are sentences related to sentence (b).

> The mouth in which she put her foot was hers
> Her foot was put in her mouth

do not have the idiomatic sense of sentence (a).

On the other hand, the words of some idioms can be moved without affecting the idiomatic sense:

> The FBI kept tabs on radicals.
> Tabs were kept on radicals by the FBI.
> Radicals were kept tabs on by the FBI.

Idioms can break the rules on combining semantic properties. The object of *eat* must usually be something with the semantic property "edible," but in

> He ate his hat
> Eat your heart out

this restriction is violated.

Idioms often lead to humor:

> What did the doctor tell the vegetarian about his surgically implanted heart
>   valve from a pig?
> That it was okay as long as he didn't "eat his heart out."

Idioms, grammatically as well as semantically, have special characteristics. They must be entered into the lexicon or mental dictionary as single items with their meanings specified, and speakers must learn the special restrictions on their use in sentences.

Many idioms may have originated as metaphorical expressions that established themselves in the language and became frozen in their form and meaning.

PRAGMATICS

Pragmatics is concerned with the interpretation of linguistic meaning in context. Two kinds of contexts are relevant. The first is **linguistic** context—the discourse that precedes the phrase or sentence to be interpreted. Taken by itself, the sentence

> Amazingly, he already loves her

is essentially uninterpretable.[8] There are no referents for *he* and *her,* and the reason for *amazingly* is vague. But if the sentence preceding it were *John met Mary yesterday*, its interpretation would be clearer.

---

[8] The linguistic meaning is that something male and animate has arrived at a state of loving something female and animate, and the speaker finds something astonishing about it.

John met Mary yesterday
Amazingly, he already loves her

The discourse suggests the second kind of context—**situational**, or knowledge of the world. To fully interpret the sentences the listener must know the real-world referents of John and Mary. Moreover the interpretation of *amazingly* is made clear by the general belief or knowledge that a person ordinarily needs more than a day to complete the act—the completion indicated by *already*—of falling in love.

Situational context, then, includes the speaker, hearer, and any third parties present, along with their beliefs and their beliefs about what the others believe. It includes the physical environment, the subject of conversation, the time of day, and so on, ad infinitum. Almost any imaginable extralinguistic factor may, under appropriate circumstances, influence the way language is interpreted.

Pragmatics is also about language use. It tells that calling someone a *son of a bitch* is not a zoological opinion, it's an insult. It tells us that when a beggar on the street asks *do you have any spare change?* it is not a fiduciary inquiry, it's a request for money. It tells us that when a justice of the peace says, in the appropriate setting, *I now pronounce you man and wife,* an act of marrying was performed.

Because pragmatics is concerned with the interpretation and use of language in context, it may be considered part of what we call linguistic performance.

Linguistic Context: Discourse

> Put your discourse into some frame, and start not so wildly from my affair.
>
> William Shakespeare, *Hamlet*

Linguistic knowledge accounts for speakers' ability to combine phonemes into morphemes, morphemes into words, and words into sentences. Knowing a language also permits combining sentences together to express complex thoughts and ideas. These larger linguistic units are called **discourse.**

The study of discourse, or **discourse analysis,** is concerned with many aspects of linguistic performance as well as linguistic competence. Discourse analysis involves questions of style, appropriateness, cohesiveness, rhetorical force, topic/subtopic structure, differences between written and spoken discourse, and so on.

Our immediate concern is to point out a few aspects of discourse that bear on the interpretation of linguistic meaning.

Pronouns

The 911 operator, trying to get a description of the gunman, asked, "What kind of clothes does he have on?"

Mr. Morawski, thinking the question pertained to Mr. McClure, [the victim, who lay dying of a gunshot wound], answered, "He has a bloody shirt with blue jeans, purple striped shirt."

The 911 operator then gave police that description [the victim's] of a gunman.

The News and Observer, Raleigh, North Carolina, 1/21/89

Pronouns may be used in place of *noun phrases* or may be used to refer to an entity presumably known to the discourse participants. When that presumption fails, miscommunication such as the one at the head of this section may result.

Pronominalization occurs both in sentences and across the sentences of a discourse. Within a sentence, the sentence structure limits the choice of pronoun. We saw previously that a reflexive pronoun is required if both it and its antecedent are in the same S in the phrase structure tree. Likewise we saw that sentence structure also dictates whether a pronoun and noun phrase can be interpreted as coreferential.

In a discourse, prior linguistic context plays a primary role in pronoun interpretation. In the following discourse:

> It seems that the man loves the woman.
> Many people think he loves her.

the most natural interpretation of *her* is "the woman" referred to in the first sentence, whoever she happens to be. But it is also possible for *her* to refer to a different person, perhaps one indicated with a gesture. In such a case *her* would be spoken with added emphasis:

> Many people think he loves *her!*

Similar remarks apply to the reference of *he,* which is ordinarily coreferential with *the man,* but not necessarily so. Again, intonation and emphasis would provide clues.

As far as syntactic rules are concerned, pronouns are noun phrases, and may occur almost anywhere that a noun phrase may occur.[9] Semantic rules of varying complexity establish whether a pronoun and some other noun phrase in the discourse can be interpreted as coreferential. A minimum condition of coreferentiality is that the pronoun and its antecedent have the same semantic feature values for the semantic properties of number and gender.[10]

When semantic rules and contextual interpretation determine that a pronoun is coreferential with a noun phrase, we say that the pronoun is **bound** to that noun phrase antecedent. If *her* in the previous example refers to "the woman," it would be a bound pronoun. When a pronoun refers to some object not explicitly mentioned in the discourse, it is said to be **free** or **unbound.** The reference of a free pronoun must ultimately be determined by the situational context.

First and second person nonreflexive pronouns are bound to the speaker and hearer, respectively. Reflexive pronouns are always bound. They require an antecedent in the sentence.

In the preceding example, semantic rules permit *her* to be bound either to *the woman,* or to be a free pronoun, referring to some person not explicitly mentioned. The ultimate interpretation is context-dependent.

Anaphora Referring to the discourse in the previous section, it would not, strictly speaking, be ungrammatical if the discourse went this way:

---

[9] There are a few exceptions. For example, *He ran up it* sounds strange. Compare *He ran up a large bill.*

[10] An exception to this, discussed in Chapter 3, is the use of *they* in *anyone is eligible when they sign up.*

It seems that the man loves the woman.
Many people think the man loves the woman.

However, most people would find such a discourse stilted sounding. Often in discourse the use of pronouns is a stylistic decision, which is part of pragmatics.

The process of replacing a longer expression by a pronoun or another kind of "pro-form" is called **anaphora.** Here are several examples of a variety of anaphora in English:

> Jan saw *the boy with the telescope.*
> Dan also saw <u>*him*</u> (= *the boy with the telescope*).   (Pronoun)

Technically, what we call *pronouns* are "Pro-noun phrases" in that they are *anaphors* that replace entire noun phrases.

> Emily *hugged* Cassidy as <u>*did*</u> (= *hugged Cassidy*) Zachary.   (Pro-verb phrase)
> *I am sick,* <u>*which*</u> (= *I am sick* or *my being sick*) depresses me.   (Pro-sentence)

The last example shows how sentences may function as noun phrases under anaphora. The pro-form *which* is a noun phrase since it is the subject of *which depresses me.* That is one of the reasons that embedded sentences were shown in the previous chapter as immediately dominated by the node NP.

Reprinted with special permission of North America Syndicate.

Missing Parts   The process of anaphora replaces whole phrases with pro-forms. Sometimes in discourse, or even within sentences, entire phrases may be omitted and not replaced by a pro-form but still understood because of context. Such utterances taken in isolation appear to violate the rules of syntax, as in the sentence **My uncle dried,* but in the following discourse it is perfectly acceptable:

FIRST SPEAKER: My aunt washed the dishes.
SECOND SPEAKER: My uncle dried.

The second speaker is understood to mean "My uncle dried *the dishes.*" In the following example, Bill is understood to have *washed* the cherries. This illustrates a process called **gapping** by linguists.

Jill washed the grapes and Bill the cherries.

In a similar process, called "sluicing," what follows a *wh-* word in an embedded sentence is omitted, but understood.

Your ex-husband is dancing with someone, but I don't know who.
My cat ate something, and I wish I knew what.
She said she was coming over, but she didn't say when.

Missing from the end of the first sentence is *he is dancing with;* missing from the second sentence is *she ate;* and from the third sentence *she was coming over.*

The Articles *The* and *A*

PEANUTS reprinted by permission of UFS, Inc.

There are discourse rules that apply regularly, such as those that determine the occurrence of the articles *the* and *a*. The article *the* is used to indicate that the referent of a noun phrase is agreed upon by speaker and listener. If someone says

I saw the boy

it is assumed that a certain boy is being discussed. No such assumption accompanies

I saw a boy

which is more of a description of what was seen than a reference to a particular individual.

Often a discourse will begin with the use of indefinite articles, and once everyone agrees on the referen.s, definite articles start to appear. A short example illustrates this transition:

I saw *a* boy and *a* girl holding hands and kissing.
Oh, it sounds lovely.
Yes, *the* boy was quite tall and handsome, and he seemed to like *the* girl a lot.

These examples show that some rules of discourse are similar to grammatical rules in that a violation produces unacceptable results. If the final sentence of this discourse were

Yes, a boy was quite tall and handsome, and he seemed to like a girl a lot

most speakers would find it unacceptable.

Situational Context

> Depending on inflection, *ah bon* [in French] can express shock, disbelief,
> indifference, irritation, or joy.
>
> Peter Mayle, Toujours Provence

Much discourse is telegraphic in nature. Verb phrases are not specifically mentioned, entire clauses are left out, direct objects disappear, pronouns abound. Yet people still understand people, and part of the reason is that rules of grammar and rules of discourse combine with contextual knowledge to fill in missing gaps and make the discourse cohere. Much of the contextual knowledge is knowledge of who is speaking, who is listening, what objects are being discussed, and general facts about the world we live in, called **situational context.**

Often what we say is not literally what we mean. When we ask at the dinner table if someone "can pass the salt" we are not querying their ability to do so, we are requesting that they do so. If I say "you're standing on my foot" I am not making idle conversation, I am asking you to stand somewhere else. We say "it's cold in here" to mean "shut the window," or "turn up the heat," or "let's leave," or a dozen other things that depend on the real-world situation at the time of speaking.

In the following sections we will look briefly and incompletely at a few of the ways that real-world context influences and interacts with meaning, an aspect of pragmatics.

Maxims of Conversation

> Though this be madness, yet there is method in't.
>
> William Shakespeare, Hamlet

Speakers recognize when a series of sentences "hangs together" or when it is disjointed. The discourse below, which gave rise to Polonius' above remark, does not seem quite right—it is not coherent.

POLONIUS: What do you read, my lord?
HAMLET: Words, words, words.
POLONIUS: What is the matter, my lord?
HAMLET: Between who?
POLONIUS: I mean, the matter that you read, my lord.
HAMLET: Slanders, sir: for the satirical rogue says here that old men have gray beards, that their faces are wrinkled, their eyes purging thick amber and plum-tree gum, and that they have a plentiful lack of wit, together with most weak hams: all which, sir, though I most powerfully and potently believe, yet I hold it not honesty to have it thus set down; for yourself, sir, should grow old as I am, if like a crab you could go backward.[11]

---

[11] *Hamlet,* Act II, Scene ii.

Hamlet, who is feigning insanity, refuses to answer Polonius' questions "in good faith." He has violated certain conversational conventions, or **maxims of conversation.**[12] One such maxim states that a speaker's contribution to the discourse should be as informative as is required—neither more nor less, the **maxim of quantity.** Hamlet has violated this maxim in both directions. In answering "Words, words, words" to the question of what he is reading, he is providing too little information. His final remark goes to the other extreme in providing more information than required.

He also violates the **maxim of relevance** when he "misinterprets" the question about the reading matter as a matter between two individuals.

The "run on" nature of Hamlet's final remark, a violation of the **maxim of manner,** is another source of incoherence. This effect is increased in the final sentence by the somewhat bizarre choice of phrasing to compare growing younger with walking backward, a violation of the **maxim of quality,** which requires sincerity and truthfulness.

Here is a summary of the four conversational maxims, parts of the broad **Cooperative Principle.**

Name of Maxim	Description of Maxim
Quantity	Say neither more nor less than the discourse requires.
Relevance	Be relevant.
Manner	Be brief and orderly; avoid ambiguity and obscurity.
Quality	Do not lie; do not make unsupported claims.

Unless speakers (like Hamlet) are being deliberately uncooperative, they adhere to these maxims, and to other conversational principles,[13] and assume others do too. Bereft of context, if one man says (truthfully) to another *I have never slept with your wife* that would be grounds for provocation because that very topic of conversation should be unnecessary, a violation of the maxim of quantity.

Asking an able-bodied person at the dinner table *can you pass the salt?* if answered literally, would force the responder into stating the obvious, a violation of the maxim of quantity. To avoid this the person asked seeks a reason for the question, and deduces that the asker would like to have the saltshaker.

The maxim of relevance explains how saying *it's cold in here* to a person standing by an open, drafty window might be interpreted as a request to close it, else why make the remark to that particular person in the first place.[14]

Conversational conventions such as these allow the various sentence meanings to be sensibly connected into discourse meaning and integrated with context, much as rules of sentence grammar allow word meanings to be sensibly (and grammatically) connected into sentence meaning.

---

[12] These maxims were first discussed by H. Paul Grice.

[13] *Turn-taking,* knowing when it's your time to speak, is governed by conversational principles not discussed here.

[14] Because these maxims are not precisely stated, other analyses for these situations are possible. The point is that much communication relies on these maxims and similar principles.

Speech Acts

PEANUTS reprinted by permission of UFS, Inc.

You can use language to do things. You can use language to make promises, lay bets, issue warnings, christen boats, place names in nomination, offer congratulations, or swear testimony. The theory of **speech acts** describes how this is done.

By saying *I warn you that there is a sheepdog in the closet,* you not only say something, you *warn* someone. Verbs like *bet, promise, warn,* and so on are **performative verbs.** Using them in a sentence does something extra over and above the statement.

There are hundreds of performative verbs in every language. The following sentences illustrate their usage:

> I *bet* you five dollars the Yankees win.
> I *challenge* you to a match.
> I *dare* you to step over this line.
> I *fine* you $100 for possession of oregano.
> I *move* that we adjourn.
> I *nominate* Batman for mayor of Gotham City.
> I *promise* to improve.
> I *resign!*
> I *pronounce* you man and wife.

In all these sentences the speaker is the subject (that is, the sentences are in first person) who by uttering the sentence is accomplishing some additional action, such as daring, nominating, or resigning. Also, all these sentences are affirmative, declarative, and in the present tense. They are typical **performative sentences.**

An informal test to see whether a sentence contains a performative verb is to begin it with the words *I hereby. . . .* Only performative sentences sound right when begun this way. Compare *I hereby apologize to you* with the somewhat strange *I hereby know you.* The first is generally taken as an act of apologizing. In all the examples given, insertion of *hereby* would be acceptable. Snoopy in the above cartoon knows that *hereby* is used in performative sentences. The humor comes when he uses it for the nonperformative verb *despise.*

Actually, every utterance is some kind of speech act. Even when there is no explicit performative verb, as in *It is raining,* we recognize an implicit performance of *stating.* On the other hand, *Is it raining?* is a performance of *questioning,* just as *Leave!* is a performance of *ordering.* In all these instances we could use, if we chose, an actual performative verb: ***I state*** *that it is raining;* ***I ask*** *if it is raining;* ***I order*** *you to leave.*

In studying speech acts the importance of context is evident. In some situations *there is a sheepdog in the closet* is a warning, but the same sentence may be a promise or even a mere statement of fact, depending on circumstances. We call this underlying purpose—a warning, a promise, a threat, or whatever—the **illocutionary force** of a speech act.

Because the illocutionary force of a speech act depends on the context of the utterance, speech act theory is a part of pragmatics.

Presuppositions

> You mentioned your name as if I should recognize it, but beyond the obvious facts that you are a bachelor, a solicitor, a Freemason, and an asthmatic, I know nothing whatever about you.
>
> Sir Arthur Conan Doyle, "The Norwood Builder," *The Memoirs of Sherlock Holmes*

Speakers often make implicit assumptions about the real world, and the sense of an utterance may depend on those assumptions. The **presupposition(s)** of an utterance are facts whose truth is required in order that the utterance be appropriate. Consider the following sentences:

(a) Have you stopped hugging your sheepdog?
(b) Who bought the badminton set?
(c) John doesn't write poems anymore.
(d) The present King of France is bald.
(e) Would you like another beer?

Sentence (a) is inappropriate if the person addressed has never hugged their sheepdog. Thus, in sentence (a) the speaker is said to presuppose, or assume the truth of the fact that the listener has at some past time hugged their sheepdog. In (b) there is the presupposition that someone has already bought a badminton set, and in (c) it is assumed that John once wrote poetry.

We have already run across the somewhat odd (d), which we decided we could understand even though France does not currently have a king. The use of the definite article *the* usually presupposes an existing referent. When presuppositions are inconsistent with the actual state of the world, the utterance is felt to be strange unless a fictional setting is agreed upon by the participants, as in a play, for example.

Sentence (e) presupposes or implies that you have already had at least one beer. Part of the meaning of the word *another* includes this presupposition. The Mad Hatter in *Alice's Adventures in Wonderland* appears not to understand presuppositions.

> "Take some more tea," the March Hare said to Alice, very earnestly.
> "I've had nothing yet," Alice replied in an offended tone, "so I can't take more."
> "You mean you can't take *less*," said the Hatter: "It's very easy to take *more* than nothing."

The humor in this passage comes from the meaning of the word *more,* which presupposes some earlier amount.

These phenomena may also be described as **implication.** Part of the meaning of *more* implies that there has already been something. The definite article *the,* in these terms, implies the existence of the referent within the current context.

Presuppositions can be used to communicate information indirectly. If someone says *my brother is rich,* we assume that person has a brother, even though that fact is not explicitly stated. Much of the information that is exchanged in a conversation or discourse is of this kind. Often, after a conversation has ended, we will realize that some fact was imparted to us that was not specifically mentioned. That fact is often a presupposition.

The use of language in a courtroom is restricted so that presuppositions cannot influence the court or jury. The famous type of question, *Have you stopped beating your wife?,* is disallowed in court, because accepting the validity of the question means accepting its presuppositions. The question itself imparts information in a way that is difficult to cross-examine or even be consciously aware of.

Presuppositions are so much a part of natural discourse that they become second nature and we do not think of them, any more than we are directly aware of the many other rules and maxims that govern language and its use in context.

Deixis

DENNIS THE MENACE® used by permission of Hank Ketcham and © by North America Syndicate.

In all languages there are many words and expressions whose reference relies entirely on the situational context of the utterance and can only be understood in light of these circumstances. This aspect of pragmatics is called **deixis** (pronounced "dike-sis"). First and second person pronouns such as

> my   mine   you   your   yours   we   ours   us

are always deictic because their reference is entirely dependent on context. You must know who the speaker and listener are in order to interpret them.

Third person pronouns are deictic if they are *free*. If they are *bound,* their reference is known from linguistic context. One peculiar exception is the "pronoun" *it* when used in sentences such as

> *It* appears as though sheepdogs are the missing link.
> The patriotic archbishop of Canterbury found *it* advisable . . .

In these cases *it* does not function as a true pronoun by referring to some entity. Rather, it is a grammatical morpheme, a placeholder as it were, required to satisfy the English rules of syntax.

Expressions such as

> this person
> that man
> these women
> those children

are deictic, for they require situational information in order for the listener to make a referential connection and understand what is meant. The previous examples illustrate **person deixis.** They also show that the use of **demonstrative articles** like *this* and *that* is deictic.

There is also **time deixis** and **place deixis.** The following examples are all deictic expressions of time:

now	then	tomorrow
this time	that time	seven days ago
two weeks from now	last week	next April

In order to understand what specific times such expressions refer to, we need to know when the utterance was said. Clearly, *next week* has a different reference when uttered today than a month from today. If you found an undated notice announcing a "BIG SALE NEXT WEEK" you would not know whether the sale had already taken place.

Expressions of place deixis require contextual information about the place of the utterance, as shown by the following examples:

here	there	this place
that place	this ranch	those towers over there
this city	these parks	yonder mountains

The "Dennis the Menace" cartoon at the beginning of this section indicates what can happen if deictic expressions are misinterpreted.

Directional terms such as

> before/behind   left/right   front/back

are deictic insofar as you need to know which way the speaker is facing. In Japanese the verb *kuru* "come" can only be used for motion toward the place of utterance. A Japanese speaker cannot call up a friend and ask

> May I *kuru* to your house?

as you might, in English, ask "May I come to your house?" The correct verb is *iku,* "go," which indicates motion away from the place of utterance. These verbs thus have a deictic aspect to their meaning.

Deixis abounds in language use and marks one of the boundaries of semantics and pragmatics. The pronoun *I* certainly has a meaning independent of context—its semantic meaning, which is "the speaker"; but context is necessary to know who the speaker is, hence what "I" refers to.

SUMMARY

Knowing a language is knowing how to produce and understand sentences with particular meanings. The study of linguistic meaning is called **semantics. Lexical semantics** is concerned with the meanings of morphemes and words; **phrasal semantics** with phrases and sentences. The study of how context affects meaning is called **pragmatics.**

The meanings of morphemes and words are defined in part by their **semantic properties,** whose presence or absence is indicated by use of **semantic features.** Evidence for semantic properties is found in "slips of the tongue" that people make, which indicates their knowledge of these properties.

When two words have the same sounds but different meanings, they are **homonyms** (for example, *bear* and *bare*). The use of homonyms may result in **ambiguity,** which occurs when an utterance has more than one meaning. **Heteronyms** are words spelled the same but pronounced differently and having different meanings, such as *sow* the pig and *sow* meaning to scatter seeds. **Homographs** are words spelled the same, possibly pronounced the same, and having different meanings, such as *trunk* of an elephant and *trunk* for storing clothes.

When two words have the same meaning but different sounds, they are **synonyms** (for example, *sofa* and *couch*). The use of synonyms may result in **lexical paraphrase,** two sentences with the same meaning.

When a word has differing meanings that are conceptually and historically related, it is said to be **polysemous.** For example *good* means "well behaved" in *good child,* and "sound" in *good investment.* Polysemous words may be partially synonymous in that they share one or more of their meanings with other words.

Two words that are opposite in meaning are **antonyms.** Antonyms have the same semantic properties except for the one that accounts for their oppositeness. There are antonymous pairs that are **complementary** *(alive/dead),* **gradable** *(hot/cold),* and **relational opposites** *(buy/sell, employer/employee).*

Other meaning relations are also described by "-*nym*" words. **Hyponyms** are words like *red, white,* and *blue,* that share a feature indicating they all belong to the same class; **metonyms** are "substitute" words, such as *Rome* meaning "The Catholic Church"; and **retronyms** are expressions like *broadcast television* that once were redundant, but which now make necessary distinctions due to changes in the world—in this case, the advent of cable television.

Proper names are "shortcut" words used to designate particular objects uniquely, that is, they are **definite.** Proper names cannot ordinarily be preceded by an article or an adjective, or be pluralized, in English.

Languages have rules for combining the meanings of parts into the meaning of the whole. For example, *red balloon* has the semantic properties of *balloon* combined with the semantic property of *red* in an additive manner. Such combinations are not always additive. The phrase *counterfeit dollar* does not simply have the semantic properties of *dollar* plus something else.

Words, phrases, and sentences generally have **sense,** which is a part of their meaning. By knowing the sense of an expression, you can determine its **reference,** if any, namely what it points to in the world. Some meaningful expressions (for example, *the present King of France*) have sense but no reference, while others, such as proper nouns, often have reference but no sense. The sense of a declarative sentence is its **truth conditions,** that aspect of meaning that allows you to determine whether the sentence is true or false. The reference of a declarative sentence, when it has one, is its truth value, either *true* or *false.* Two sentences are **paraphrases** if they have the same truth conditions.

The meaning of a sentence is determined in part by the **thematic roles** of the noun phrases in relation to the verb. These semantic relationships indicate who, to whom, toward what, from which, with what, and so on.

In building larger meanings from smaller meanings, the semantic rules interact with the syntactic rules of the language. For example, if a noun phrase and a nonreflexive pronoun occur within the same S, semantic rules cannot interpret them to be **coreferential,** that is, having the same referent. Thus in *Mary bit her, her* refers to someone other than Mary.

Often, the truth of one sentence **entails** the truth or falseness another. If the sentence *I managed to kiss my sheepdog* is true, then the sentence *I kissed my sheepdog* is necessarily true by the semantic rules for entailment.

Sentences are **anomalous** when they deviate from certain semantic rules. *The six subjunctive crumbs twitched* and *The stone ran* are anomalous. Other sentences are **uninterpretable** because they contain **nonsense words,** such as *An orkish sluck blecked nokishly.*

Many sentences have both a literal and a nonliteral or **metaphorical** interpretation. *He's out in left field* may be a literal description of a baseball player or a metaphorical description of someone mentally deranged.

Idioms are phrases whose meaning is *not* the combination of the meanings of the individual words (for example, *put her foot in her mouth*). Idioms often violate co-occurrence restrictions of semantic properties.

The general study of how context affects linguistic interpretation is **pragmatics.** Context may be *linguistic*—what was previously spoken or written—or *knowledge of the world,* what we've called **situational context.**

Discourse consists of several sentences, including exchanges between speakers. Pragmatics is important when interpreting discourse, for example, in determining whether a pronoun in one sentence has the same referent as a noun phrase in another sentence. **Anaphora** is the general term for replacing phrases with pro-forms, including *pronouns,* which are actually *pro-noun phrases, pro-verbs,* and *pro-sentences.* Linguistic context often reveals when a missing part can be understood from something previously said, such as "will wash" in *Jan will wash grapes and Jon _____ cherries.*

Well-structured discourse follows certain rules and **maxims,** such as "be relevant," that make the discourse coherent. There are also grammatical rules that affect discourse, such as those that determine when to use the definite article *the.*

Pragmatics includes **speech acts, presuppositions,** and **deixis.** Speech act theory is the study of what an utterance does beyond just saying something. The effect of what is done is called the **illocutionary force** of the utterance. For example, use of a **performative verb** like *bequeath* may be an act of bequeathing, which may even have legal status.

Presuppositions are implicit assumptions that accompany certain utterances. *Have you stopped hugging Sue?* carries with it the presupposition that at one time you hugged Sue.

Deictic terms such as *you, there, now* require knowledge of the circumstances (the person, place, or time) of the utterance to be interpreted referentially.

References for Further Reading

Austin, J. L. 1962. *How to Do Things with Words.* Cambridge, MA: Harvard University Press.

Brown, G., and G. Yule. 1983. *Discourse Analysis.* Cambridge, England: Cambridge University Press.

Chierchia, G., and A. McConnell-Ginet. 1990. *Meaning and Grammar.* Cambridge, MA: MIT Press.

Davidson, D., and G. Harman, eds. 1972. *Semantics of Natural Languages.* Dordrecht, The Netherlands: Reidel.

Fraser, B. 1995. *An Introduction to Pragmatics.* Oxford: Blackwell.

Green, G. M. 1989. *Pragmatics and Natural Language Understanding.* Hillsdale, NJ: Lawrence Erlbaum Associates.

Grice, H. P. 1989. "Logic and Conversation." Reprinted in *Studies in the Way of Words.* Cambridge, MA: Harvard University Press.

Hawkins, J. A. 1985. *A Comparative Typology of English and German.* Austin: University of Texas Press.

Hurford, J. R., and B. Heasley. 1983. *Semantics: A Coursebook.* Cambridge, England: Cambridge University Press.

Jackendoff, R. 1983. *Semantics and Cognition.* Cambridge, MA: MIT Press.

Jackendoff, R. 1993. *Patterns in the Mind.* New York: Harper Collins.

Katz, J. 1972. *Semantic Theory.* New York: Harper & Row.

Lakoff, G. 1987. *Women, Fire, and Dangerous Things: What Categories Reveal about the Mind.* Chicago: University of Chicago Press.

Lakoff, G., and M. Johnson. 1980. *Metaphors We Live By.* Chicago: University of Chicago Press.

Larson, R., and G. Segal. 1995. *Knowledge of Meaning.* Cambridge, MA: MIT Press.

Levinson, S. C. 1983. *Pragmatics.* Cambridge, England: Cambridge University Press.

Lyons, J. 1977. *Semantics.* Cambridge, England: Cambridge University Press.

Mey, J. L. 1993. *Pragmatics: An Introduction.* Oxford, England: Blackwell.

Searle, J. R. 1969. *Speech Acts: An Essay in the Philosophy of Language.* Cambridge, England: Cambridge University Press.

Sperber, D., and D. Wilson. 1986. *Relevance: Communication and Cognition.* Oxford, England: Basil Blackwell.

EXERCISES

1. For each group of words given below, state what semantic property or properties distinguish between the classes of (a) words and (b) words. If asked, also indicate a semantic property shared by both the (a) words and the (b) words.

   Example: (a) widow, mother, sister, aunt, maid

             (b) widower, father, brother, uncle, valet

                  The (a) and (b) words are "human."

                  The (a) words are "female" and the (b) words are "male."

   A. (a) bachelor, man, son, paperboy, pope, chief

      (b) bull, rooster, drake, ram

         The (a) and (b) words are _____

         The (a) words are _____

         The (b) words are _____

   B. (a) table, stone, pencil, cup, house, ship, car

      (b) milk, alcohol, rice, soup, mud

         The (a) words are _____

         The (b) words are _____

   C. (a) book, temple, mountain, road, tractor

      (b) idea, love, charity, sincerity, bravery, fear

         The (a) words are _____

         The (b) words are _____

   D. (a) pine, elm, ash, weeping willow, sycamore

      (b) rose, dandelion, aster, tulip, daisy

         The (a) and (b) words are _____

         The (a) words are _____

         The (b) words are _____

   E. (a) book, letter, encyclopedia, novel, notebook, dictionary

      (b) typewriter, pencil, pen, crayon, quill, charcoal, chalk

         The (a) words are _____

         The (b) words are _____

   F. (a) walk, run, skip, jump, hop, swim

      (b) fly, skate, ski, ride, cycle, canoe, hang-glide

         The (a) and (b) words are _____

         The (a) words are _____

         The (b) words are _____

   G. (a) ask, tell, say, talk, converse

      (b) shout, whisper, mutter, drawl, holler

The (a) and (b) words are _____

The (a) words are _____

The (b) words are _____

H. (a) absent – present, alive – dead, asleep – awake, married – single

   (b) big – small, cold – hot, sad – happy, slow – fast

   The (a) and (b) words are _____

   The (a) words are _____

   The (b) words are _____

I. (a) alleged, counterfeit, false, putative, accused

   (b) red, large, cheerful, pretty, stupid

   (Hint: Is an alleged murderer always a murderer? Is a pretty girl always a girl?)

   The (a) words are _____

   The (b) words are _____

2. Explain the semantic ambiguity of the following sentences by providing two or more sentences that paraphrase the multiple meanings. Example: *She can't bear children* can mean either *She can't give birth to children* or *She can't tolerate children.*

   a. He waited by the bank.

   b. Is he really that kind?

   c. The proprietor of the fish store was the sole owner.

   d. The long drill was boring.

   e. When he got the clear title to the land, it was a good deed.

   f. It takes a good ruler to make a straight line.

   g. He saw that gasoline can explode.

3. The following sentences may be either lexically or structurally ambiguous, or both. Provide paraphrases showing you comprehend all the meanings.

Example:	I saw him walking by the bank.
Meaning one:	I saw him and he was walking by the river bank.
Meaning two:	I saw him and he was walking by the financial institution.
Meaning three:	I was walking by the river bank when I saw him.
Meaning four:	I was walking by the financial institution when I saw him.

   a. We laughed at the colorful ball.

   b. He was knocked over by the punch.

   c. The police were urged to stop drinking by the fifth.

   d. I said I would file it on Thursday.

   e. I cannot recommend visiting professors too highly.

   f. The license fee for pets owned by senior citizens who have not been altered is $1.50. (Actual notice)

   g. What looks better on a handsome man than a Tux? Nothing! (Attributed to Mae West)

   h. Wanted: Man to take care of cow that does not smoke or drink. (Actual notice)

   i. For Sale: Several old dresses from grandmother in beautiful condition. (Actual notice)

   j. Time flies like an arrow. (Hint: There are at least four paraphrases, but some of them require imagination.)

4. Here are a few more *retronyms:*

straight razor, one-speed bike, conventional warfare, acoustic guitar, bar soap

   A. Explain why the five examples given are retronyms.

   B. Think of five more retronyms not in the above list or previously mentioned.

   C. Think of one that is perhaps not yet widely used in the language, but which you think soon will be needed. For example, *low-definition television.*

5. It is claimed (we are not at liberty to say by whom) that there are over three hundred heteronyms in English. How many can you think of? Ten would be okay, twenty-five would be terrific, and one hundred will get your name mentioned in our Seventh Edition. Perhaps your class would like to hold a heteronym contest. We volunteer your teacher to take the winner(s) out for their favorite beverage as first prize.

6. There are other "*-nym*" words that describe semantic relations and facts about words and word classes. We mentioned *acronyms* in Chapter 3, though not in this chapter. How many more *-nym* words and their meaning can you come up with. Try for three. Five would be great. Ten is possible. (Hint: One such *-nym* word was the winning word in the 1997 National Spelling Bee.)

7. There are several kinds of antonymy. By writing a *c, g,* or *r* in column *C*, indicate whether the pairs in columns *A* and *B* are complementary, gradable, or relational opposites:

A	B	C
good	bad	
expensive	cheap	
parent	offspring	
beautiful	ugly	
false	true	
lessor	lessee	
pass	fail	

A	B	C
hot	cold	
legal	illegal	
larger	smaller	
poor	rich	
fast	slow	
asleep	awake	
husband	wife	
rude	polite	

8. For each definition below write in the first blank the word that has that meaning and in the second (and third if present) a differently spelled homonym that has a different meaning.

   For example: "A pair:" t(*wo*)   t(*oo*)   t(*o*)

   a. "Naked":   b_____   b_____
   b. "Base metal":   l_____   l_____
   c. "Worships":   p_____   p_____   p_____
   d. "Eight bits":   b_____   b_____   b_____
   e. "One of five senses":   s_____   s_____   c_____
   f. "Several couples":   p_____   p_____   p_____
   g. "Not pretty":   p_____   p_____
   h. "Purity of gold unit":   k_____   c_____
   i. "A horse's coiffure":   m_____   m_____   M_____
   j. "Sets loose":   f_____   f_____   f_____

9. Here are some proper names of restaurants found in the U.S. Can you figure out the basis for the name? (This is for fun—don't let yourself be graded.)

   a. Mustard's Last Stand
   b. Aunt Chilada's
   c. Lion on the Beach
   d. Pizza Paul and Mary
   e. Franks for the Memories
   f. Weiner Take All
   g. Dressed to Grill
   h. Deli Beloved
   i. Gone with the Wings
   j. Aunt Chovy's Pizza
   k. Polly Esther's
   l. Dewey, Cheatam & Howe
      (Hint: This is also the name of a mythical law firm.)
   m. Thai Me Up Café (truly—it's in L.A.)
   n. Romancing the Cone

10. The following sentences consist of a verb, its noun phrase subject, and various objects. Identify the thematic role of each noun phrase by writing the letter *a, t, l, i, s, g, e, c,* or *p* above the noun, standing for *agent, theme, location, instrument, source, goal, experiencer, causative,* or *possessor.*

         a   *t*   *s*   *i*

Example: *The boy took the books from the cupboard with a handcart.*

a. Mary found a ball in the house.

b. The children ran from the playground to the wading pool.

c. One of the men unlocked all the doors with a paper clip.

d. John melted the ice with a blowtorch.

e. The sun melted the ice.

f. The ice melted.

g. With a telescope, the boy saw the man.

h. The farmer loaded hay onto the truck.

i. The farmer loaded the hay with a pitchfork.

j. The hay was loaded on the truck by the farmer.

11. Some linguists and philosophers distinguish between two kinds of truthful statements: one follows from the definition or meaning of a word; the other simply happens to be true in the world as we know it. Thus, *kings are monarchs* is true because the word *king* has the semantic property "monarch" as part of its meaning; but *kings are rich* is circumstantially true. We can imagine a poor king, but a king who is not a monarch is not truly a king. Sentences like *kings are monarchs* are said to be **analytic,** true by virtue of meaning alone. Write *A* by any of the following sentences that are analytic, and *S* for "situational" by the ones that are not analytic.

a. Queens are monarchs.   _____

b. Queens are female.   _____

c. Queens are mothers.   _____

d. Dogs are four-legged.   _____

e. Dogs are animals.   _____

f. Cats are felines.   _____

g. Cats are stupid.   _____

h. George Washington is George Washington.   _____

i. George Washington was the first president.   _____

j. Uncles are male.   _____

12. The opposite of *analytic* (see previous exercise) is **contradictory.** A sentence that is false due to the meaning of its words alone is contradictory. *Kings are* *female* is an example. Write a *C* by the contradictory sentences and *S* for situational by sentences that are not contradictory.

a. My aunt is a man.

b. Witches are wicked.

c. My brother is an only child.

d. The evening star isn't the morning star.

e. The evening star isn't the evening star.

f. Babies are adults.

g. Babies can lift one ton.

h. Puppies are human.

i. My bachelor friends are all married.

j. My bachelor friends are all lonely.

13. Go on an idiom hunt. In the course of some hours in which you converse or overhear conversations, write down all the idioms that are used. If you prefer, watch the "Soaps" for an hour or two and write down the idioms. Show your parents (or whomever) this book when they find you watching TV and you claim you're doing your homework.

14. Find a complete version of "The Jabberwocky" from *Through the Looking-Glass* by Lewis Carroll. Look up all the nonsense words in a good dictionary and see how many of them are lexical items in English. Note their meaning.

15. In sports and games many expressions are "performative." By shouting *You're out*, the first base umpire performs an act. Think up a half-dozen or so similar examples and explain their use.

16. A criterion of a performance utterance is whether you can begin it with *I hereby*. Notice that if you say sentence *a* aloud it sounds like a genuine apology, but to say sentence *b* aloud sounds funny because you cannot perform an act of knowing:

a. I hereby apologize to you.

b. I hereby know you.

Test whether the following sentences are performance sentences by inserting *hereby* and seeing whether they sound right. Circle the letter of any that are performance sentences.

c. I testify that she met the agent.

d. I know that she met the agent.

e. I suppose the Yankees will win.

f. He bet her $2500 that Clinton would win.

g. I dismiss the class.

  h. I teach the class.

  i. We promise to leave early.

  j. I owe the IRS $1,000,000.

  k. I bequeath $1,000,000 to the IRS.

  l. I swore I didn't do it.

  m. I swear I didn't do it.

17. The following sentences make certain presuppositions. What are they? (The first one has been done for you.)

  a. The police ordered the minors to stop drinking.

   Presupposition: <u>The minors were drinking.</u>

  b. Please take me out to the ball game again.

   Presupposition:

  c. Valerie regretted not receiving a new T-bird for Labor Day.

   Presupposition:

  d. That her pet turtle ran away made Emily very sad.

   Presupposition:

  e. The administration forgot that the professors support the students. (Compare *The administration believes that the professors support the students,* in which there is no such presupposition.)

   Presupposition:

  f. It is strange that the United States invaded Cambodia in 1970.

   Presupposition:

  g. Isn't it strange that the United States invaded Cambodia in 1970?

   Presupposition:

h. Disa wants more popcorn.

Presupposition:

i. Why don't pigs have wings?

Presupposition:

j. Who discovered America in 1492?

Presupposition:

18. A. Consider the following "facts" and then answer the questions:

Roses are red and bralkions are too.
Booth shot Lincoln and Czolgosz, McKinley.
Casca stabbed Caesar and so did Cinna.
Frodo was exhausted as was Sam.

(a) What color are bralkions?

(b) What did Czolgosz do to McKinley?

(c) What did Cinna do to Caesar?

(d) What state was Sam in?

B. Now consider these facts and answer the questions:

Black Beauty was a stallion.
Mary is a widow.
John remembered to send Mary a birthday card.
John didn't remember to send Jane a birthday card.
Flipper is walking.
(T = true; F = false)

(e) Black Beauty was male?   T _____   F _____

(f) Mary was never married?   T _____   F _____

(g) John sent Mary a card?   T _____   F _____

(h) John sent Jane a card?   T _____   F _____

(i) Flipper has legs?   T _____   F _____

Part A illustrates your ability to interpret meanings when syntactic rules have deleted parts of the sentence; Part B illustrates your knowledge of semantic features and presupposition.

19. Circle any deictic expression in the following sentences. (Hint: Proper names and noun phrases containing *the* are *not* considered deictic expressions. Also, all sentences do not include deictic expressions.)

  a. I saw her standing there.

  b. Dogs are animals.

  c. Yesterday, all my troubles seemed so far away.

  d. The name of this rock band is "The Beatles."

  e. The Declaration of Independence was signed in 1776.

  f. The Declaration of Independence was signed last year.

  g. Copper conducts electricity.

  h. The treasure chest is to your right.

  i. These are the times that try men's souls.

  j. There is a tide in the affairs of men which taken at the flood leads on to fortune.

20. State for each pronoun in the following sentences whether it is free, bound, or either bound or free. Consider each sentence independently.

Example: John finds himself in love with her.
            himself—bound; her—free
Example: John said that he loved her.
            he—bound or free; her—free

  a. Louise said to herself in the mirror: "I'm so ugly."

  b. The fact that he considers her pretty pleases Maria.

  c. Whenever I see you, I think of her.

  d. John discovered that a picture of himself was hanging in the post office, and that fact bugged him, but it pleased her.

  e. It seems that she and he will never stop arguing with them.

  f. Persons are prohibited from picking flowers from any but their own graves. (On a sign in a cemetery.)

Chapter 6

Phonetics:
The Sounds of Language

Phonetics is concerned with describing the speech sounds that occur in the languages of the world. We want to know what these sounds are, how they fall into patterns, and how they change in different circumstances. . . . The first job of a phonetician is . . . to try to find out what people are doing when they are talking and when they are listening to speech.

Peter Ladefoged, *A Course in Phonetics*, 1982, 2nd Edition

Knowledge of a language includes knowledge of the morphemes, words, phrases, and sentences. It also includes knowing what sounds are in the language and how they may be "strung" together to form these meaningful units. Although the sounds of French or Xhosa or Quechua are uninterpretable to someone who does not speak those languages, and although there may be some sounds in one language that are not in another, the sounds of all the languages of the world together constitute a limited set of all the sounds that can be produced by the human vocal tract. This chapter will discuss these speech sounds, how they are produced, and how they may be characterized.

SOUND SEGMENTS

"Keep out! Keep out! K-E-E-P O-U-T."

HERMAN copyright 1991 by Jim Unger. Reprinted with
permission of Laughing Stock Licencing, Inc. All rights reserved.

213

The study of speech sounds is called **phonetics.** To describe speech sounds it is necessary to know what an individual sound is and how each sound differs from all others.

This is not as easy as it may seem. A speaker of English knows that there are three sounds in the word *cat,* the initial sound represented by the letter *c,* the second by *a,* and the final sound by *t.* Yet physically the word is just one continuous sound. You can **segment** the one sound into parts because you know English. The ability to analyze a word into its individual sounds does not depend on knowledge of how the word is spelled. *Not* and *knot* have three sounds even though the first sound in *knot* is represented by the two letters *kn.* The printed word *psycho* has six letters which represent only four sounds—*ps, y, ch, o.*

It is difficult if not impossible to segment the sound of someone clearing their[1] throat into a sequence of discrete units. This is because these sounds are not the sounds of any morphemes in any human language; it is not because it is a single continuous sound. You do not produce one sound, then another, then another when you say the word *cat.* You move your organs of speech continuously and produce a continuous signal.

Although the sounds we produce and hear and comprehend during speech are continuous, everyone throughout history who has attempted to analyze language has recognized that speech utterances can be segmented into individual units. According to an ancient Hindu myth, the god Indra, in response to an appeal made by the other gods, attempted for the first time to segment speech into its separate elements. After he accomplished this feat, according to the myth, the sounds could be regarded as language. Indra thus may be the first phonetician.

Speakers of English can, despite the Herman cartoon, separate *keep out* into two words because they know the language. We do not, however, pause between words even though we sometimes have that illusion. Children learning a language reveal this problem. A two-year-old child when going down stairs was told by his mother to "hold on." He replied, "I'm holding don, I'm holding don," not knowing where the break between words occurred. In the course of history, the errors in deciding where a boundary falls between two words can change the form of words. At an earlier stage of English, the word *apron* was *napron;* it was misperceived in the phrase, *a napron,* as *an apron* by so many speakers, it lost its initial *n.*

Some phrases and sentences that are clearly distinct when printed may be **ambiguous** (have two meanings) when read aloud as in the children's jingle: *I scream, you scream, we all scream for ice cream.* Read the following pairs aloud and see why we often misinterpret what we hear:

grade A	gray day
It's hard to recognize speech.	It's hard to wreck a nice beach.
The sun's rays meet.	The sons raise meat.

The lack of actual breaks between words and individual sounds often makes us think that speakers of foreign languages run their words together, not realizing that we do so also. X-ray motion pictures of someone speaking make this lack of breaks in speech

---

[1] We will use the pronouns *they, their,* and *them* as the singular or plural form when referring generally to either male or female. This is now common usage and replaces the cumbersome use of *he or she, him or her.* This is, however, not necessarily the view of all 'prescriptivist' grammarians.

very clear. One can see the tongue, jaw, and lips in continuous motion while the "individual sounds" are being produced.

Yet, if you know a language you have no difficulty segmenting the continuous sounds. In this way, speech is similar to music. A person who has not studied music cannot write the sequence of individual notes combined by a violinist into one changing continuous sound. A trained musician, however, finds it a simple task. Every human speaker, without special training, can segment a speech signal. Just as one cannot analyze a musical passage without musical knowledge, so also linguistic knowledge, which requires no special talent or instruction, is required to segment speech into pieces.

Identity of Speech Sounds

"Boy, he must think we're pretty
stupid to fall for that again."

RUBES by Leigh Rubin. By permission of Leigh Rubin
and Creators Syndicate.

It is quite amazing, given the continuity of the speech signal, that we are able to understand what words are put together to form an utterance. This ability is more surprising because no two speakers ever say the "same thing" identically. The speech signal produced when one speaker says *cat* will not be exactly the same as the signal produced by another speaker's *cat* or even the repetition of the word by the same speaker. George Bernard Shaw pointed to the impossibility of constructing any set of symbols that will specify all the minute differences between sounds in his statement:

> By infinitesimal movements of the tongue countless different vowels can
> be produced, all of them in use among speakers of English who utter the
> same vowels no oftener than they make the same fingerprints.

Yet speakers understand each other because they know the same language.

Our knowledge of a language determines when we judge physically different sounds to be the same; we know which aspects or properties of the signal are linguistically important and which are not. For example, if someone coughs in the middle of saying "How (cough) are you?" a listener will ignore the cough and interpret this simply as "How are you?" Men's voices are usually lower in overall pitch than women's; some speakers speak more slowly than others; others have a "nasal twang." Such pitch or tempo differences or personal styles of speaking are not linguistically significant.

Our linguistic knowledge, our mental grammar, makes it possible to ignore non-linguistic differences in speech. Furthermore, we are capable of making many sounds that we know intuitively are not speech sounds in our language. Many English speakers can make a clicking sound that writers sometimes represent as *tsk tsk tsk*. These sounds are not part of the English sound system. They never occur as part of the words of the utterances we produce. It is even difficult for many English speakers to combine this clicking sound with other sounds. Yet clicks are speech sounds in Xhosa, Zulu, Sotho, and Khoikhoi—languages spoken in southern Africa—just like the *k* or *t* in English. Speakers of those languages have no difficulty producing them as parts of words. *Xhosa,* the name of a language spoken in South Africa, begins with one of these clicks. Thus *tsk* is a speech sound in Xhosa but not in English. The sound represented by the letters *th* in the word *think* is a speech sound in English but not in French. The sound produced with a closed mouth when we are trying to clear a tickle in our throats is not a speech sound in any language, nor is the sound produced when we sneeze.

The science of phonetics attempts to describe all the sounds used in human language—sounds that constitute a subset of the totality of sounds that humans are capable of producing.

The way we use our linguistic knowledge to produce a meaningful utterance is complicated. It can be viewed as a chain of events starting with an idea or message in the brain or mind of the speaker and ending with a similar message in the brain of the hearer. The message is put into a form that is dictated by the language we are speaking. It must then be transmitted by nerve signals to the organs of speech articulation, which produce the different physical sounds.

Speech sounds can be described at any stage in this chain of events. The study of the physical properties of the sounds themselves is called **acoustic phonetics.** The study of the way listeners perceive these sounds is called **auditory phonetics. Articulatory phonetics**—the study of how the vocal tract produces the sounds of language—is the primary concern in this chapter.

SPELLING AND SPEECH

The one-l lama,
He's a priest.
The two-l llama,
He's a beast.

And I will bet
A silk pajama
There isn't any
Three-l lllama.

Ogden Nash[2]

Drawing by Leo Cullum © 1988 *The New Yorker Magazine,* Inc.

Alphabetic spelling represents the pronunciations of words. But frequently the sounds of the words in a language are rather unsystematically represented by **orthography**— that is, by spelling. To discuss the way different sounds are produced, it may therefore be confusing and difficult to refer to the sounds as they are spelled in English words.

Suppose all Earthlings were destroyed by some horrible catastrophe, and years later Martian astronauts exploring Earth discovered some fragments of English writing that included the following sentence:

Did h**e** bel**ie**ve that C**ae**sar could s**ee** the p**eo**ple s**ei**ze the s**ea**s?

How would a Martian phonetician decide that **e, ie, ae, ee, eo, ei,** and **ea** all represented the same sound? To add to the confusion, this sentence might crop up later:

The sill**y** am**oe**ba stole the k**e**y to the mach**i**ne.

---

[2] "The Lama" from *Verses from 1929 On* by Ogden Nash. Reprinted by permission of Curtis Brown, Ltd., London, on behalf of the Estate of Ogden Nash.

English speakers learn how to pronounce these words when learning to read and write and therefore know that *y, oe, ey,* and *i* represent the same sound as the boldface letters in the first sentence.

The Phonetic Alphabet

> The English have no respect for their language, and will not teach their children to speak it. They cannot spell it because they have nothing to spell it with but an old foreign alphabet of which only the consonants—and not all of them—have any agreed speech value.
>
> G. B. Shaw, *Preface to Pygmalion*

The discrepancy between spelling and sounds gave rise to a movement of "spelling reformers" called orthoepists. They wanted to revise the alphabet so that one letter would correspond to one sound and one sound to one letter, thus simplifying spelling. This is a **phonetic alphabet.**

By permission of Johnny Hart and Creators Syndicate, Inc.

George Bernard Shaw followed in the footsteps of three centuries of spelling reformers in England. In typical Shavian manner he pointed out that we could use the English spelling system to spell *fish* as *ghoti*—the *gh* like the sound in *enough,* the *o* like the sound in *women,* and the *ti* like the sound in *nation.* Shaw was so concerned about English spelling that he included a provision in his will for a new "Proposed English Alphabet" to be administered by a "Public Trustee" who would have the duty of seeking and publishing a more efficient alphabet. This alphabet was to have at least forty letters to enable "the said language to be written without indicating single sounds by groups of letters or by diacritical marks." After Shaw's death in 1950, 450 designs for such an alphabet were submitted from all parts of the globe. Four alphabets were judged to be equally good, and the £500 sterling prize was divided among their designers, who collaborated to produce the alphabet designated in Shaw's will. Shaw also stipulated in his will that his play *Androcles and the Lion* be published in the new alphabet, with "the original Doctor Johnson's lettering opposite the transliteration page by page and a glossary of the two alphabets." This version of the play was published in 1962.

It is easy to understand why spelling reformers believe there is a need for a phonetic alphabet. Different letters may represent a single sound:

t*o*	t*oo*	tw*o*	thr*ough*	thr*ew*	cl*ue*	sh*oe*

A single letter may represent different sounds:

d*a*me	d*a*d	f*a*ther	c*a*ll	vill*a*ge	m*a*ny

A combination of letters may represent a single sound:

*sh*oot	*ch*aracter	*Th*omas	*ph*ysics
ei*th*er	dea*l*	rou*gh*	na*ti*on
coa*t*	gla*ci*al	*th*eater	pl*ai*n

Some letters have no sound at all in certain words:

*m*nemonic	*w*hole	resi*g*n	*gh*ost
*p*terodactyl	*w*rite	ho*l*e	cor*ps*
*p*sychology	s*w*ord	de*b*t	*g*naw
bou*gh*	lam*b*	is*l*and	*k*not

Some sounds are not represented in the spelling. In many words the letter *u* represents a *y* sound followed by a *u* sound:

c*u*te	(compare: c*oo*t)
f*u*tile	(compare: r*u*le)
*u*tility	(compare: *U*zbek)

One letter may represent two sounds; the final *x* in *Xerox* represents a *k* followed by an *s.*

Whether we support or oppose spelling reform, it is clear that we cannot depend on the spelling of words to describe the sounds of English. The alphabets designed to fulfill Shaw's will were not the first phonetic alphabets. One of the earliest was produced by Robert Robinson in 1617. In Shaw's lifetime, the phonetician Henry Sweet, the prototype for Shaw's character Henry Higgins in the play *Pygmalion* or the musical play or movie *My Fair Lady,* produced a phonetic alphabet.

In 1888 the interest in the scientific description of speech sounds led the **International Phonetics Association (IPA)** to develop a phonetic alphabet that could be used to symbolize the sounds found in all languages. Since many languages use a Roman alphabet like that used in the English writing system, the IPA phonetic symbols were based on the Roman letters. These phonetic symbols have a consistent value, unlike ordinary letters that may or may not represent the same sounds in the same or different languages.

The original IPA phonetic alphabet was the primary one used all over the world by phoneticians, language teachers, speech pathologists, linguists, and anyone wishing to symbolize the "spoken word" until 1989 when, from August eighteenth to the twenty-first, approximately 120 members of the association met in Kiel, West Germany, to work on revisions. The symbols that will be used in this text are those from the revised IPA alphabet unless otherwise noted.

A phonetic alphabet should include enough symbols to represent the "crucial" linguistic differences. At the same time it should not, and cannot, include noncrucial differences, since such differences are infinitely varied.

A list of the phonetic symbols that can be used to represent speech sounds of English is given in Table 6.1. The symbols omit many details about the sounds and how they are produced in different words and in different places within words. These symbols are meant to be used by persons knowing English. These are not all the phonetic symbols needed for English sounds; when we discuss the sounds in more detail later in the chapter we will add appropriate symbols.

The symbol [ə] is called a *schwa.* It will be used in this book only to represent unstressed vowels, that is, syllables in a word that are somewhat softer and shorter than other syllables. In the word *sylLAbic,* for example, the first and last vowels are unstressed while the middle vowel is stressed—with the stressed syllable printed in capital letters. (There is great variation in the way speakers of English produce this unstressed vowel, but it is phonetically similar to the wedge symbol [ʌ] in a word like *cut,* which will be used only in stressed syllables.)

TABLE 6.1   A Phonetic Alphabet for English Pronunciation

Consonants								*Vowels*			
p	pill	t	till	k	kill	i	beet	ɪ	bit
b	bill	d	dill	g	gill	e	bait	ɛ	bet
m	mill	n	nil	ŋ	ring	u	boot	ʊ	foot
f	feel	s	seal	h	heal	o	boat	ɔ	bore
v	veal	z	zeal	l	leaf	æ	bat		
θ	thigh	č	chill	r	reef	ʌ	butt	a	pot/bar
ð	thy	ǰ	Jill	j	you	aj	bite	ə	sofa
ʃ/š	shill	ʍ	which	w	witch	ɔj	boy	aw/æw	bout
ʒ/ž	azure								

Speakers of different English dialects pronounce some words differently from those of other speakers. For example, some of you may pronounce the words *which* and *witch* identically. If you do, the initial sound of both words is symbolized by **w** in the chart. Some speakers of English pronounce *bought* and *pot* with the same vowel; others pronounce them with the vowel sounds in *bore* and *bar,* respectively. We have thus listed both words in the chart of symbols. It is difficult to include all the phonetic symbols needed to represent all English dialect differences. We are sorry if a vowel sound in your dialect is not included in the table.

Some of the symbols in Table 6.1 are those traditionally used by linguists in the United States in place of IPA symbols; others are listed below:

U.S.		IPA
š	=	ʃ
ž	=	ʒ
č	=	tʃ
ǰ	=	dʒ
ᴜ	=	ʊ

We will use [š] and [ʃ] and [ž] and [ʒ] interchangeably since students who take other classes in linguistics may be confronted with either set. We will however, use [č] and [ǰ] instead of the IPA symbols for the first and last sounds in *church* and *judge*, respectively.

Using these symbols, we can now unambiguously represent the pronunciation of words. For example, words spelled with *ou* may have different pronunciations. To distinguish between the alphabet letters and the symbols representing sounds, we can put the phonetic symbols between brackets:

Spelling	Pronunciation
though	[ðo]
thought	[θɔt]
rough	[rʌf]
bough	[baw]
through	[θru]
would	[wʊd]

Only in *rough* do the letters *gh* represent any sound; that is, the sound [f]; *ou* represents six different sounds, and *th* two different sounds. The *l* in *would,* like the *gh* in all but one of the words above, is not pronounced at all.

We will continue to use square brackets around the phonetic **transcription** when necessary to distinguish it from ordinary spelling.

ARTICULATORY PHONETICS

The principles of pronunciation are those general laws of articulation that determine the character, and fix the boundaries of every language; as in every system of speaking, however irregular, the organs must necessarily fall into some common mode of enunciation or the purpose of Providence in the gift of speech would be absolutely defeated. These laws, like every other object of philosophical inquiry, are only to be traced by an attentive observation and enumeration of particulars. . . .

John Walker (1823)[3]

The production of any speech sound (or any sound at all) involves the movement of air. Most speech sounds are produced by pushing lung air through the opening between the vocal cords—this opening is called the **glottis** and is located in the **larynx** (often referred to by the nontechnical term "voice box")—through the tube in the throat called the **pharynx,** out of the **oral cavity** through the mouth and sometimes also through the **nasal cavity** and out the nose.

FIGURE 6-1   The vocal tract.

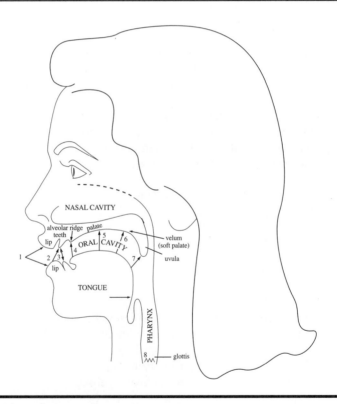

Places of articulation: 1. bilabial; 2. labiodental; 3. interdental; 4. alveolar; 5. (alveo)palatal; 6. velar; 7. uvular; 8. glottal.

---

[3] John Walker. 1823. *A Critical Pronouncing Dictionary and Expositor of the English Language,* London: A. Wilson. The 26th edition, from which this quote is taken, was published posthumously. Walker died in 1807.

What distinguishes one sound from the other? If you bang a large round drum you will get one sound; if you bang a small round drum you will get a different sound; if you bang a small oblong drum you will get still another sound. The size and shape of the air being pushed around makes a difference. This is also true in the production of speech sounds. The vocal tract through which the air passes during the production of speech is shown in Figure 6-1. When the shape of this vocal tract is changed, different sounds are produced.

Airstream Mechanisms

Sounds produced by using air from the lungs are called **pulmonic** sounds; since the air is pushed out, they are called **egressive.** The majority of sounds used in languages of the world are produced by a **pulmonic egressive** airstream mechanism. All the sounds in English are produced in this manner.

Other airstream mechanisms are used in other languages to produce sounds called **ejectives, implosives,** and **clicks.** Instead of lung air, the body of air in the mouth may be moved. When this air is sucked in instead of flowing out, **ingressive** sounds, like implosives and clicks, are produced. When the air in the mouth is pushed out, ejectives are produced; they are therefore also **egressive** sounds. Implosives and ejectives are produced by a **glottalic airstream mechanism,** while clicks are produced by a **velaric airstream mechanism.**

Ejectives are found in many American Indian and African languages as well as languages spoken in the Caucasus, a region between the Black and Caspian Seas. Implosives also occur in the languages of the American Indians and throughout Africa, India, and Pakistan. Clicks occur in the Southern Bantu languages such as Xhosa and Zulu, and in the languages spoken by the Bushmen and Khoikhoi. A detailed description of these different airstream mechanisms goes beyond the requirements of an introductory text. They are mentioned to show that sounds can be classified according to the airstream mechanism used to produce them. In the rest of this chapter we will be discussing only sounds produced by a pulmonic egressive airstream mechanism.

Consonants

The sounds of all languages fall into two major natural classes—consonants and vowels, often referred to by the cover symbols **C** and **V.** Consonantal sounds are produced with some restriction or closure in the vocal tract as the air from the lungs is pushed through the glottis out the mouth.

Places of Articulation

As stated above, different consonantal sounds result when we change the shape of the oral cavity by moving the lips and tongue, the **articulators,** and change the **place of articulation** in the oral cavity. The major consonantal place features are given below. As you read the description of each class of sounds, pronounce them and try to feel which articulators are moving and to where.

Bilabials: [p] [b] [m]   When we produce a [p], [b], or [m] we articulate by bringing both lips together. These sounds are therefore called **bilabials.**

Labiodentals: [f] [v]   We also use our lips to form **[f]** and **[v]** as in *fine* [fajn] and *vine* [vajn]. We articulate these sounds by touching the bottom lip to the upper teeth, which is why these sounds are called **labiodental,** *labio-* referring to lips and *dental* to teeth.

Interdentals: [θ] [ð]   [θ] and [ð] are both represented orthographically by the *th* in the words *thin* [θɪn], *ether* [iθər], *then* [ðɛn], and *either* [iðər]. To articulate these **interdental** ("between the teeth") sounds, one inserts the tip of the tongue between the upper and lower teeth.

Alveolars: [t] [d] [n] [s] [z] [l] [r]   **Alveolar** sounds are articulated by raising the front part of the tongue to the **alveolar ridge** (see Figure 6-1). Pronounce the words *do* [du], *new* [nu], *two* [tu], *sue* [su], *zoo* [zu]. You should feel your tongue touch or almost touch the bony tooth ridge as you produce the first sounds in these words.

To produce the **lateral [l],** the tongue is raised to the alveolar ridge with the sides of the tongue down, permitting the air to escape laterally over the sides of the tongue.

The sound **[r]** is produced in a variety of ways. Many English speakers produce [r] by curling the tip of the tongue back behind the alveolar ridge. Such sounds are also called **retroflex** sounds. In some languages, the [r] may be an alveolar **trill,** produced by the tip of the tongue vibrating against the roof of the mouth. There are other symbols which can be used for these different *r* sounds, and in a very detailed phonetic description we would include some of them. For the purposes of this book, however, we will use the symbol [r] for all the varieties produced by speakers of English.

Palatals: [ʃ]/[š] [ʒ]/[ž] [č] [j]   To produce the sounds in the middle of the words *mesher* [mɛšər] and *measure* [mɛžər], the front part of the tongue is raised to a point on the hard palate just behind the alveolar ridge. [š], the voiceless sound in *mesher* (spelled *sh*) and [ž], the voiced sound in *measure* (spelled *s*) are **palatal** sounds. (These palatal sounds are also referred to as **alveopalatals.**)

The alveopalatal region of the roof of the mouth is also the place of articulation in the production of **[č]** and **[j]**, the sounds that begin and end the words *church* and *judge*.

Velars: [k] [g] [ŋ]   Another class of sounds is produced by raising the back of the tongue to the soft palate or velum. The initial and final sounds of the words *kick* [kɪk], *gig* [gɪg], and the final sounds of the words *back* [bæk], *bag* [bæg], and *bang* [bæŋ]—[k], [g], and [ŋ]—are produced in this way and are called **velar** sounds.

Uvulars: [ʀ] [q] [ɢ]   Uvular sounds are produced by raising the back of the tongue to the uvula. The *r* in French is uvular and is symbolized by **[ʀ].** Uvular sounds are also found in other languages. Arabic for example has two uvular sounds symbolized as **[q]** and **[ɢ].**

Glottal: [ʔ] [h]   The **[h]** sound that starts words such as *house* [haws], *who* [hu], and *hair* [hɛr] is a **glottal** sound. The glottis is open; no other modification of the airstream mechanisms occurs in the mouth. The tongue and lips are usually in the position for the production of the following vowel as the airstream passes through the open glottis.

If the air is stopped completely at the glottis by tightly closed vocal cords, the sound produced is a **glottal stop.** This is the sound sometimes used instead of [t] in *button* and

Latin. It also may occur in colloquial speech at the end of words like *don't, won't,* or *can't.* In some American dialects it regularly replaces the *tt* sound in words like *bottle* or *glottal.* The glottal stop does not occur in the speech of all speakers of English. But if you say "ah-ah-ah-ah-" with one "ah" right after another and do not sustain the vowel sound, you will be producing glottal stops between the vowels. In some languages, the glottal stop functions like the stops [p] or [t] or [k] do in English. The IPA symbol for a glottal stop looks something like a question mark without the dot on the bottom **[ʔ].**

Table 6.2 summarizes the classification of the consonants of English by their place of articulation. The glottal stop is not included in this table since it is used only by some speakers in some words. The uvular sounds do not occur in English.

TABLE 6.2   Place of Articulation of English Consonants

Bilabial:	p	b	m				
Labiodental:	f	v					
Interdental:	θ	ð					
Alveolar:	t	d	n	s	z	l	r
Palatal:	ʃ	ʒ	č	ǰ			
Velar:	k	g	ŋ				
Glottal:	h						

Manners of Articulation

We have described a number of classes of consonants according to their place of articulation, yet we are still unable to distinguish the sounds in each class from each other. What distinguishes [p] from [b], or [b] from [m]? All are bilabial sounds. What is the difference between [t], [d], and [n], which are all alveolar sounds?

Speech sounds are also differentiated by the way the airstream is affected as it travels from the lungs up and out of the mouth and nose. Such features or phonetic properties have traditionally been referred to as **manners of articulation** or simply manner features.

Voiced and Voiceless Sounds   If the vocal cords are apart when the airstream is pushed from the lungs, the air is not obstructed at the glottis and it passes freely into the supraglottal cavities (the parts of the vocal tract above the glottis; see Figure 6-1). The sounds produced in this way are **voiceless** sounds: **[p], [t], [k],** and **[s]** in the English words *seep* [sip], *seat* [sit], and *seek* [sik] are voiceless sounds.

If the vocal cords are together, the airstream forces its way through and causes them to **vibrate.** Such sounds are **voiced** sounds and are illustrated by the sounds **[b], [d], [g],** and **[z]** in the words *bate* [bet], *date* [det], *gate* [get], *cob* [kab], *cod* [kad], *cog* [kag], and *daze* [dez]. If you put a finger in each ear and say the voiced "z-z-z-z-z" you can feel the vibrations of the vocal cords. If you now say the voiceless "s-s-s-s-s" you will not feel these vibrations (although you might hear a hissing sound in your mouth). When you whisper, you are making all the speech sounds voiceless.

The voiced/voiceless distinction is a very important one in English. It is this phonetic feature or property that distinguishes between word pairs like the following:

rope/robe	*fate/fade*	*rack/rag*	*wreath/wreathe*
[rop]/[rob]	[fet]/[fed]	[ræk]/[ræg]	[riθ]/[rið]

The first word of each pair ends with a voiceless sound and the second word with a voiced sound. All other aspects of the sounds of these words are identical; the position of the lips and tongue is the same in each of the paired words.

The voiced/voiceless distinction is also shown in the following pairs; the first word begins with a voiceless sound and the second with a voiced sound:

fine/vine	*seal/zeal*	*choke/joke*
[fajn]/[vajn]	[sil/zil]	[čok]/[ǰok]

The initial sounds of the first words of the following pairs are also voiceless, and for many speakers of English, the second words begin with voiced sounds. (We will discuss other differences between the initial [p] and [b] sounds below; the phonetic transcriptions of many of these words have been simplified to help the reader grasp basic concepts and may include other details that will be discussed in subsequent sections.)

peat/beat	*tote/dote*	*kale/gale*
[pit]/[bit]	[tot]/[dot]	[kel]/[gel]

Aspirated and Unaspirated Sounds

In our discussion of the voiceless bilabial stop [p], we did not distinguish the initial sound in the word *pit* from the second sound in the word *spit*. There is, however, a phonetic difference in these two voiceless stops. During the production of voiceless sounds the glottis is open and the air passes freely through the opening between the vocal cords. When a voiceless sound is followed by a voiced sound such as a vowel, the vocal cords must close in order to permit them to vibrate.

Voiceless sounds fall into two classes depending on the "timing" of the vocal cord closure. In English when we pronounce the word *pit,* there is a brief period of voicelessness immediately after the *p* sound is released. That is, after the lips come apart the vocal cords remain open for a very short time. Such sounds are called **aspirated** because an extra puff of air is produced.

When we pronounce the *p* in *spit,* however, the vocal cords start vibrating as soon as the lips are opened. Such sounds are called **unaspirated.** The *t* in *tick* and the *k* in *kin* are also aspirated voiceless stops, while the *t* in *stick* and the *k* in *skin* are unaspirated. Hold a strip of paper in front of your lips and say *pit*; a puff of air (the aspiration) will push the paper. The paper will not move when you say *spit.*

When a fully voiced [b], or any voiced stop, is produced, the vocal cords vibrate throughout the articulation. In English, voiced stops may not be fully voiced.

Figure 6-2 shows in diagrammatic form the timing of the articulators (in this case the lips) in relation to the state of the vocal cords. In the production of the voiced [b], the vocal cords are vibrating throughout the closure of the lips and continue to vibrate for the vowel production after the lips are opened. Most English speakers do not voice initial [b] to the full extent. Because we heavily aspirate an initial [p], there is no difficulty in distinguishing these two sounds. In the unaspirated *p* in *spin,* the vocal cords are open during the lip closure and come together and start vibrating as soon as the lips open. In the production of the aspirated *p* in *pin* the vocal cords remain apart for a brief period after the lip closure is released. These remarks apply to all English stops.

FIGURE 6-2   Timing of articulators and vocal-cord vibration for voiced, voiceless unaspirated, and voiceless aspirated stops.

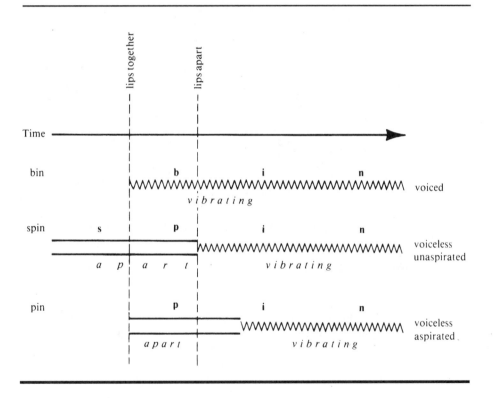

Aspirated sounds may be indicated by following the phonetic symbol with a raised **h,** as in the following examples:

pate	[pʰet]	*spate*	[spet]
tale	[tʰel]	*stale*	[stel]
kale	[kʰel]	*scale*	[skel]

Final page of the Medical Boards

Nasal and Oral Sounds   The voiced/voiceless distinction differentiates the bilabials [b] from [p]. [m] is also a bilabial and, in addition, it is voiced. What, then, distinguishes the **[m]** from the **[b]**?

[m] is a **nasal** sound. When you produce [m], air escapes not only through the mouth (when you open your lips), but also through the nose.

In Figure 6-1, the roof of the mouth is divided into the **palate** and the soft palate (or **velum**). The palate is a hard bony structure at the front of the mouth. You can feel it with your thumb. As you slide your thumb back toward the throat you will feel the velum, which is where the flesh becomes soft and is movable. Hanging down from the end of the velum is the **uvu¹a,** which you can see in a mirror if you open your mouth wide and say "aaah." When the velum is raised all the way to touch the back of the throat, the passage through the nose is cut off and air can escape only through the mouth.

Sounds produced with the velum up, blocking the air from escaping through the nose, are called **oral sounds,** since the air can only escape through the oral cavity. **[b]** is an oral sound. When the velum is lowered, air escapes through the nose as well as the mouth; sounds produced this way are called **nasal sounds. [m], [n],** and **[ŋ]** are the nasal consonants of English. All other consonant sounds are oral. The diagrams in Figure 6-3 show the position of the lips and the velum when [m], [b], and [p] are

FIGURE 6-3   Position of lips and velum for *m* (lips together, velum down) and *b*

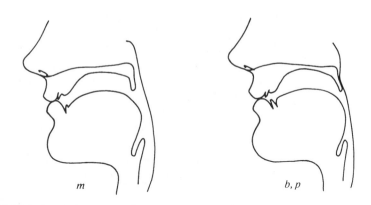

articulated. [p], like [b] and [m], is produced by stopping the airflow at the lips. It differs from both [b] and [m] by being voiceless; it differs from [m] in being oral.

The same nasal/oral difference occurs in *beet* [bit] and *meat* [mit], *dear* [dir] and *near* [nir]. The velum is raised in the production of [b] and [d], preventing the air from flowing through the nose, whereas in [m] and [n] the velum is down, letting the air go through both the nose and the mouth when the closure is released. [m], [n], and [ŋ] are therefore nasal sounds and [b], [d], and [g] are oral sounds.

These **phonetic features** or properties permit the classification of all speech sounds into four classes: voiced, voiceless, nasal, oral, in addition to the place of articulation classes discussed above. One sound may belong to more than one class, as shown in Table 6.3.

Stops: [p] [b] [m] [t] [d] [n] [k] [g] [ŋ] [č] [ǰ] [ʔ]   We are seeing finer and finer distinctions of speech sounds. **[t]** is a voiceless, alveolar, oral sound. But **[s]** is also voiceless and alveolar and oral. What distinguishes [t] from [s]?

In producing sounds, the airstream, after entering the oral cavity, may be completely stopped (as in the production of [t]), or partially obstructed (as in the articulation of [s]), or it may flow freely out of the mouth. Sounds that are **stopped completely** in the oral cavity for a brief period are, not surprisingly, called **stops.**

The final sounds in the words *top* [tap], *bomb* [bam], *dude* [dud], *dune* [dun], *root* [rut], *rack* [ræk], *rag* [ræg], *rang* [ræŋ] are stops that occur in English.

TABLE 6.3   Four Classes of Speech Sounds

	Oral	Nasal
Voiced	b d g	m n ŋ
Voiceless	p t k	*

*Nasal consonants in English are usually voiced. Both voiced and voiceless nasal sounds occur in other languages.

In the production of the nasal stops **[n], [m], [ŋ],** although the air flows freely through the nose, the airflow is blocked completely in the mouth; therefore, nasal consonants are stops.

Sounds in which there is no stoppage in the oral tract are **continuants.** All the sounds of a language are either stops or continuants (nonstops).

Nonnasal or oral stops are also called **plosives** because the air that is blocked in the mouth "explodes" when the closure is released. This explosion does not occur during the production of nasal stops because the air escapes through the nose.

[p], [b], and **[m]** are bilabial stops, with the airstream stopped at the mouth by the complete closure of the lips.

[t], [d], and **[n]** are alveolar stops; the airstream is stopped by the tongue making a complete closure at the alveolar ridge.

[k], [g], and **[ŋ]** are velar stops with the complete closure at the velum.

[č] and **[j]** are alveopalatal or palatal affricates with complete stop closure. These will be discussed below.

Although there is no stoppage of air in the oral cavity, the air is completely stopped at the glottis in the production of the glottal stop.

We have been discussing the sounds that occur in English. There are sounds, including stops, that occur in other languages but are not found in English. In Quechua, for example, a major language spoken in Bolivia and Peru, **uvular** stops occur. These are produced when the back of the tongue is raised and moved backward to form a complete closure with the uvula. The letter *q* in words in this language, as in the language name, usually represents the uvular stop phonetically symbolized as **[q].** The voiced uvular stop symbolized as **[G]** also occurs in Quechua. As noted above, glottal stops also occur in a number of languages, such as Lebanese Arabic.

Fricatives: [s] [z] [f] [v] [θ] [ð] [š] [ž]   In the production of some continuants, while the airstream is not completely stopped, it is obstructed from flowing freely. If you put your hand in front of your mouth and produce an [s], [z], [f], [v], [θ], [ð], [š], or [ž] sound, you will feel the air coming out of your mouth. The passage in the mouth through which the air must pass, however, is very narrow, causing **friction** or turbulence. Such sounds are called **fricatives.** (They are also sometimes referred to as **spirants,** from the Latin word *spirare,* "to blow.")

In the production of the labiodental fricatives **[f]** and **[v],** the friction is created at the lips, where a narrow passage permits the air to escape.

[s] and **[z]** are alveolar fricatives with the friction created at the alveolar ridge.

The palatal or alveopalatal fricatives, **[š]** and **[ž],** such as those in *mesher* [mɛšər] and *measure* [mɛžər], are produced with friction created as the air passes through the narrow opening behind the alveolar ridge. In English, the voiced palatal fricative never begins words (except in words borrowed from the French like *genre* or *gendarme* which some English speakers produce with a French pronunciation). The voiceless palatal sound begins the words *shoe* [šu] and *sure* [šur] and ends the words *rush* [rʌš] and *push* [pʊš].

In the production of the interdental fricatives **[θ]** and **[ð],** represented by *th* in *thin* and *then,* the friction occurs at the opening between the tongue and teeth.

Most dialects of modern English do not include velar fricatives, although they occurred in an earlier stage of English in such words as *right, knight, enough,* and *through,* where the *gh* occurs in the spelling. If you raise the back of the tongue as if you were about to produce a [g] or [k], but stop just short of touching the velum, you will produce a velar fricative. The *ch* ending in the German pronunciation of the composer's name *Bach* is a velar fricative. Some speakers of modern English substitute a voiceless velar fricative in words like *bucket* and a voiced velar fricative in such words as *wagon* for the velar stops that occur for other speakers in those words. [x] is the IPA symbol for the voiceless velar fricative and [ɣ] for the voiced velar fricative.

In some languages of the world, such as French, the uvular fricative [ʀ] occurs as the sound represented by *r* in French words such as *rouge* "red" or *rose* "pink." Voiced glottal fricatives, which do not occur in English, do occur in other languages, such as Czech. In Arabic pharyngeal fricatives are produced by pulling the tongue root toward the back wall of the pharynx. It is difficult to pull the tongue far enough to make a complete pharyngeal stop closure, but both voiced and voiceless pharyngeal fricatives can be produced and can be distinguished from velar fricatives.

All fricatives are continuants: Although the airstream is obstructed as it passes through the oral cavity, it is not completely stopped.

Affricates   Some sounds are produced by a stop closure followed immediately by a slow release of the closure characteristic of a fricative. These sounds are called **affricates.** The alveopalatal sounds that begin and end the words *church* and *judge* are voiceless and voiced affricates, respectively. Phonetically, an affricate may be considered a sequence of a stop plus a fricative. Thus, the *ch* in *church* is the same as the sound combination [t] + [š] as shown by observing that in fast speech *white shoes* and *why choose* may be pronounced identically. The voiceless and voiced affricates may be symbolized as [tš] (IPA [tʃ]) and [dž] (IPA [dʒ]), respectively. In the American tradition, [č], [ǰ] are the more commonly used symbols for these sounds, and are the ones used in this book.

Because the air is stopped completely during the initial articulation of an affricate, these sounds are also classified as stops.

"WHO'S MAKING ALL THOSE MISTAKES? THEY'RE *ALWAYS* PASSING THE CORRECTION PLATE."

DENNIS THE MENACE ® used by permission of
Hank Ketcham and © by North America Syndicate.

Liquids: [l] [r]   In the production of the sounds [l] and [r], there is some obstruction of the airstream in the mouth, but not enough to cause any real constriction or friction. These sounds are called **liquids.** [l] is a **lateral** liquid, as described above.

As mentioned earlier, the *r* sounds that occur in different dialects of English and different languages differ somewhat from each other. We are using the symbol [r] for this whole class of sounds. An alveolar trilled *r* occurs in many languages, such as Spanish. In addition, uvular trills occur, produced by vibrating the uvula. Some French speakers use uvular trills in the pronunciation of *r;* others use uvular fricatives. In other languages the *r* is produced by a single **tap** or a **flap** of the tongue against the alveolar ridge. In Spanish both the trilled and tapped *r* occur.

Some speakers of British English pronounce the *r* in the word *very* with a flap. It sounds like a very fast *d.* Most American speakers produce a flap instead of a [t] or [d] in words like *writer* or *rider,* or *latter* or *ladder.* The IPA symbol for the alveolar tap or flap is [ɾ]. American linguists often use the upper case [D] to represent this sound.

In English, [l] and [r] are regularly voiced. When they follow voiceless sounds, as in *please* and *price,* they may be automatically "devoiced." Many languages of the world have a voiceless *l.* Welsh is such a language; the name *Lloyd* in Welsh starts with the voiceless *l.*

Some languages may lack liquids entirely, or may have only a single one. The Cantonese dialect of Chinese has the single liquid [l]. Some English words are difficult for Cantonese speakers to pronounce, and they may substitute an [l] for an [r] when speaking English.

The reason why speakers in languages with only one liquid tend to use that sound as a substitute for the sound that does not occur in their language is because of the acoustic similarity of these sounds. This physical similarity is the reason they are grouped together in one class and why they function as a single class of sounds in certain circumstances. For example, in English, the only two consonants that occur after an initial [k], [g], [p], or [b] are the liquids [l] and [r]. Thus we have *crate* [kret], *clock* [klak], *plate,* [plet], *prate* [pret], *bleak* [blik], *break* [brek], but no word starting with [ps], [bt], [pk], and so on. (Notice that in words like *psychology* or *pterodactyl* the *p* is not pronounced. Similarly in *knight* or *knot* the *k* is not pronounced, although at an earlier stage of English it was.)

Glides: [j] [w]   The sounds [j] and [w], the initial sounds of *you* and *woo* [wu], are produced with little or no obstruction of the airstream in the mouth. When occurring in a word, they must always be either preceded or followed directly by a vowel. In articulating [j] or [w], the tongue moves rapidly in gliding fashion either toward or away from a neighboring vowel, hence the term **glide.** Glides are transition sounds that are sometimes called *semivowels.*

[j] is a **palatal** glide; the blade of the tongue is raised toward the hard palate in a position almost identical to that in producing the vowel sound [i] in the word *beat* [bit]. In pronouncing *you* [ju], the tongue moves rapidly from the [j] to the [u] vowel.

The glide **[w]** is produced by both raising the back of the tongue toward the velum and simultaneously rounding the lips. It is thus a *labio-velar* glide, or a rounded velar glide. In the dialect of English where speakers have different pronunciations for the words *which* and *witch,* the velar glide in the first word is voiceless [ʍ] (an "upside-down" w), and in the second word it is voiced [w]. The position of the tongue and the lips for [w] is similar to that for producing the vowel sound in *lute* [lut], but the [w] is a glide because the tongue moves quickly to the vowel that follows.

Phonetic Symbols for American English Consonants

The place and manner properties of speech sounds make it possible to distinguish each consonant sound from all others that occur in American English. Table 6.4 lists the consonants by their phonetic features. The rows stand for manner of articulation and the columns for place of articulation. Symbols for aspirated stops and the glottal stop are not included since this is a minimal list of symbols by which all morphemes and words can be distinguished. Thus the symbol [p] for the voiceless bilabial stop is sufficient to differentiate the word *peat* [pit] from the voiced bilabial stop symbol [b] in *beat* [bit]. If a more detailed phonetic **transcription** of these words (sometimes referred to as a **narrow** phonetic transcription) is desired, the symbol [pʰ] can be used as in [pʰit].

TABLE 6.4   Minimal Set of Phonetic Symbols for American English Consonants

	Bilabial	**Labiodental**	**Interdental**	**Alveolar**	**Palatal**	**Velar**	**Glottal**
Stop (oral)							
voiceless	p			t		k	
voiced	b			d		g	
Nasal (stop)	m			n		ŋ	
Fricative							
voiceless		f	θ	s	š		h[1]
voiced		v	ð	z	ž		
Africate							
voiceless					č		
voiced					ǰ		
Glide							
voiceless	ʍ					ʍ	h[1]
voiced	w[2]				j	w[2]	
Liquid				l r			

1. [h] is sometimes classified as a fricative because of the hissing sound produced by air or noise at the glottis. It is also sometimes classified with the glides because in many languages it combines with other sounds the way that glides do.
2. [w] is classified as both a bilabial because it is produced with both lips rounded and as a velar because the back of the tongue is raised toward the velum.

Examples of words in which these sounds (and their phonetic symbols) occur are given in Table 6.5.

TABLE 6.5   Examples of Consonants in English Words

Bilabial	Labiodental	Interdental	Alveolar	Palatal	Velar	Glottal
[p]ie [b]uy			[t]ie [d]ie		[k]ite [g]uy	
	[f]ie [v]ie	[θ]igh [ð]y	[s]igh [z]ion	me[š]er mea[ž]ure		[h]igh
				[č]ime [ǰ]iant		
[m]y			[n]igh		si[ŋ]	
			[l]ie [r]ye			
[w]hy				[j]ou		

Vowels

HIGGINS: Tired of listening to sounds?

PICKERING: Yes. It's a fearful strain. I rather fancied myself because I can pronounce twenty-four distinct vowel sounds, but your hundred and thirty beat me. I can't hear a bit of difference between most of them.

HIGGINS: Oh, that comes with practice. You hear no difference at first, but you keep on listening and presently you find they're all as different as A from B.

G. B. Shaw, *Pygmalion*

The quality of a vowel is determined by the particular configuration of the vocal tract in the production of that sound. Different parts of the tongue may be raised or lowered. The lips may be spread or pursed. The passage through which the air travels, however, is never so narrow as to obstruct the free flow of the airstream.

Vowel sounds carry pitch and loudness; you can sing vowels. They may be long or short. Vowels can "stand alone"—they can be produced without any consonants before or after them. You can say the vowels of *beat,* [bit], *bit* [bɪt], or *boot* [but] for example, without the initial [b] or the final [t].

There have been many different schemes for describing vowel sounds. They may be described by articulatory features, as in classifying consonants. Many beginning students of phonetics find this method more difficult to apply to vowel articulations than to consonant articulations. In producing a [t] you can feel your tongue touch the alveolar ridge. When you make a [p] you can feel your two lips come together, or you can watch your lips move in a mirror. Because vowels are produced without any articulators touching or even coming close together, it is often difficult to figure out just what is happening. One of the authors of this book, at the beginning of her graduate work, almost gave up the idea of becoming a linguist because she could not understand what was meant by "front," "back," "high," and "low" vowels.

These terms do have meaning, though. If you watch an X-ray movie of someone talking, you can see why vowels have traditionally been classified according to three questions:

1. How high is the tongue?
2. What part of the tongue is involved; that is, what part is raised or lowered?
3. What is the position of the lips?

Tongue Position

The three diagrams in Figure 6-4 show that the tongue in the production of the vowels in the words *he* [hi] and *who* [hu] is very high in the mouth; in [hi] it is the front part of the tongue that is raised, and in [hu] it is the back part of the tongue. (Prolong the vowels of these words and try to feel your tongue rise.)

To produce the vowel sound of *hah* [ha], the back of the tongue is lowered. (The reason a doctor examining your throat may ask you to say "ah" is that the tongue is low and easy to see over.) This vowel is therefore a low, back vowel.

The vowels [ɪ] and [ʊ] in the words *hit* [hɪt] and *put* [pʊt] are similar to those in *he* [hi] and *who* [hu] with slightly lowered tongue positions.

The vowel [æ] in *hat* [hæt] is produced with the front part of the tongue lowered, similar to the low vowel [a], but with the front rather than the back part of the tongue lowered.

The vowels [e] and [o] in *bait* [bet] and *boat* [bot] are *mid vowels,* produced by raising the tongue to a position midway between the high and low vowels discussed above. [ɛ] and [ɔ] in the words *bet* [bɛt] and *bore* [bɔr] are also mid vowels, produced with a slightly lower tongue position than [e] and [o].

To produce the vowel [ʌ] in the word *butt* [bʌt] or the **schwa** vowel [ə] which occurs in the second syllable of the words *sofa* [sofə] or *Rosa* [rozə], the tongue is neither high nor low, front nor back. These are lower mid, central vowels as shown in Figure 6-5. The vowels on the chart show the part of the tongue from front to back on the horizontal axis that is involved in the articulation of the vowel, and the height of the tongue on the vertical axis.

FIGURE 6-4   Position of the tongue in producing the vowels in *he, who,* and *hah.*

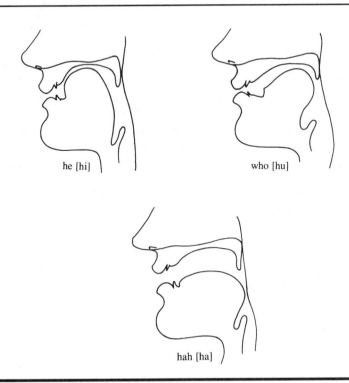

he [hi]   who [hu]

hah [ha]

Lip Rounding

Vowels also differ as to whether the lips are rounded. The vowels **[u], [ʊ], [o], [ɔ],** in *boot, put, boat,* and *bore* are **rounded vowels** produced with the lips pursed, or rounded, and the back of the tongue at decreasing heights, as shown in Figure 6-5. The low vowel **[a]** in the words *bar, bah, aha* is the only English back vowel that occurs without lip rounding. All nonback vowels in English are also unrounded.

This is not true of all languages. French and Swedish, for example, have both front and back rounded vowels. In English, a high back unrounded vowel does not occur, but in Mandarin Chinese, in Japanese, in the Cameroonian language Fe?Fe?, and in many other languages, this vowel is part of the phonetic inventory of sounds. There is a Chinese word meaning "four" with an initial [s] followed by a vowel similar to the one in *boot* but with nonrounded spread lips. This Chinese word is distinguished from the word meaning "speed" pronounced like the English word *sue* with a high back rounded vowel.

Diphthongs

Many languages, including English, have vowels called **diphthongs** that can also be described as a sequence of two sounds, vowel + glide. The vowels we have studied so far are all simple vowels called **monophthongs.** The vowel sounds in the words *bite* [bajt] and *rye* [raj] are produced with the [a] vowel sound of *father* followed by the [j] glide, resulting in **[aj].** The vowels in *bout* [bawt], *brow* [braw], and *hour* [awr] are produced by some speakers of English with a similar [a] sound followed by the glide [w], **[aw].** Some speakers of English produce this diphthong as **[æw]**, with the front low unrounded vowel instead of the back vowel. The third diphthong that occurs in English is the vowel sound in *boy* [bɔj] and *soil* [sɔjl] which is the vowel that occurs in *bore* (without the [r]) followed by the palatal glide [j], **[ɔj].**

Nasalization of Vowels

Vowels, like consonants, can be produced with a raised velum that prevents the air from escaping through the nose, or with a lowered velum that permits air to pass through the nasal passage. When the nasal passage is blocked, **oral** vowels are produced; when the nasal passage is open, **nasal** or **nasalized** vowels are produced. In English, nasal vowels occur before nasal consonants in the same syllable, and oral vowels occur before oral consonants.[4]

The words *bean, bin, bane, been, ban, boon, bun, bone, beam, bam, boom, bing, bang,* and *bong* are examples of words that contain nasalized vowels. To show the nasalization of a vowel in a phonetic transcription, a **diacritic** mark [˜] is placed over the vowel, as in *bean* [bĩn] and *bone* [bõn]. In English, these would only be necessary for a highly detailed transcription, sometimes referred to as a narrow phonetic transcription.

FIGURE 6-5   Classification of American English vowels

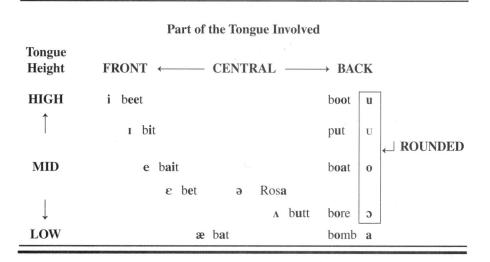

---

[4] In fast colloquial speech some speakers drop the nasal consonant when it occurs before voiceless stops such as in *hint* or *camp,* leaving just the nasal vowel, but the words originate with nasal consonants.

In languages like French, Polish, and Portuguese, nasalized vowels may occur when no nasal consonant is adjacent. In French for example, the word meaning "year" is *an* [ã] and the word for "sound" is *son* [sõ]. The *n* in the spelling is not pronounced but indicates in these words that the vowels are nasalized.

Tense and Lax Vowels

Figure 6-5 shows that the vowel **[i]** is produced with a slightly higher tongue position than **[ɪ].** This is also true for **[e]** and **[ɛ], [u]** and **[ʊ],** and **[o]** and **[ɔ].** The first vowel in each pair is often produced with greater tension of the tongue muscles than their counterparts and are often somewhat longer in duration. These vowels can be distinguished from the shorter and less tense vowels by the phonetic features **tense** and **lax** as shown in the following:

Long (Tense)		Short (Lax)	
i	beat	ɪ	bit
e	bait	ɛ	bet
u	boot	ʊ	put
o	boat	ɔ	bore

Some speakers of English may diphthongize the tense vowels slightly. For these speakers, the tense front vowels are followed by a short [j] glide [ij], [ej], and the tense back vowels by a short [w] glide [uw] and [ow]. These are sometimes written as [iʲ], [eʲ], [uʷ], and [oʷ].

In some languages there are vowels and/or consonants that differ phonetically from each other only by duration, or **length.** That is, neither height of the tongue nor tenseness distinguishes the vowel from its counterpart in pairs of words that contrast in meaning. It is customary to transcribe this difference either by doubling the symbol or by the use of a diacritic "colon" after the segment, as for example [aa] or [a:], [bb] or [b:].[5] As we noted above, the English tense vowels not only differ in length from their lax counterparts but differ qualitatively in tongue height. We are therefore using different symbols to distinguish them.

Dialect Differences

As already mentioned, but perhaps worth repeating because of the many dialects of English, the vowels in Figure 6-5 do not represent all the vowels of all dialects of English. One particular dialect spoken in England called British RP or Received Pronunciation (as the dialect spoken by the upper classes and "received" in court) has a low rounded back vowel in the word *hot* that does not occur in American English dialects and that contrasts with the unrounded low back vowel [a] in *bah*. The long tense vowels in British RP are all diphthongs. Thus the vowel in *bay* is [ej] and the vowel in *bow* is [ow], as is true for some dialects of American English. These are just a few examples of dialect diferences that occur primarily in the pronunciation of vowels.

---

[5] Long or doubled segments may be referred to as **geminate.**

Major Classes

All the classes of sounds described above combine to form larger, more general classes that are important in the patterning of sounds in the world's languages.

Noncontinuants and Continuants

As mentioned above, stop sounds are **noncontinuants.** They are produced with total obstruction of the airstream and can be distinguished from all other speech sounds, which are called **continuants,** because the stream of air flows continuously out the mouth. The nasal stops are noncontinuants.

Obstruents and Sonorants

The nonnasal stops, the fricatives, and the affricates form a major class of sounds called **obstruents.** Because the airstream cannot escape through the nose, it is either fully obstructed in its passage through the vocal tract, as in nonnasal stops and affricates, or partially obstructed in the production of fricatives.

Obstruents are distinguished from the major class of sounds called **sonorants**, sounds that are produced with relatively free airflow either through the mouth or nose that thus have greater acoustic energy than their obstruent counterparts. Nasal stops are sonorant because although the air is blocked in the mouth, it continues to resonate and move through the nose. Vowels, the liquids [l] and [r], and the glides [w] and [j] are sonorants because the air resonates without being stopped.

Fricatives are continuant obstruents because although the air is not completely stopped in its passage through the oral cavity, it is obstructed, causing the friction noted above.

Nonnasal stops and affricates are noncontinuant obstruents; there is complete blockage of the air during the production of these sounds. The closure of a stop is released abruptly as opposed to the closure of an affricate, which is released gradually, causing friction.

Consonants and Vowels

As stated above, the sounds of all the languages of the world fall into two major natural classes—consonants and vowels. Consonants include a number of subclasses: stops (including affricates and nasals), fricatives, liquids, and glides.The class of vowels include oral, nasal, front, central, back, high, mid, and low vowels.

Nasals and liquids, for the reasons given above, are sonorants; yet they resemble the obstruents in that the oral cavity is constricted during their articulation. Obstruents, liquids, and nasals form a natural class of consonantal sounds that differ phonetically from the vocalic (or nonconsonantal) class of vowels and glides.

Labials: [p] [b] [m] [f] [v]   The class of **labial** consonants includes the class of bilabial sounds—[p] [b] [m]—as well as the labiodentals—[f] and [v]. Bilabial and labial sounds are those articulated with the involvement of the lips.

Coronals: [d] [t] [n] [s] [z] [š] [ž] [č] [j]   Coronals include the alveolars—[d] [t] [n] [s] [z]—the palatals [š] [ž]—and the affricates—[č] [j]. These are sounds articulated by raising the tongue blade toward the hard palate.

Anterior: Anterior sounds are consonants produced in the front part of the mouth in front of the palato-alveolar area. They include bilabials, labiodentals, alveolars, and palatals.

Sibilants: [s] [z] [š] [ž] [č] [ǰ]   Another class of consonantal sounds is characterized by an acoustic, rather than an articulatory, property of its members. The friction created in the production of the fricatives in the words *sit* [sɪt], *zip* [zɪp], *shoe* [šu], *leisure* [ližər], and *measure* [mɛžər] and the affricates in the words *church* [čʌrč] and *judge* [ǰʌǰ] causes a "hissing" sound. These sounds are in a class of **sibilants.**

Syllabic Sounds

Traditionally it has been difficult to provide a precise definition of what constitutes a syllable, although speakers seem to be able to determine the syllabic structure of a word. From an auditory point of view, syllables have peaks of sonorance (which are also difficult to define). Every vowel constitutes a single syllable.

Liquids and nasals can be syllabic, as shown by the words *Rachel* [rečḷ], *friar* [frajr̩], *rhythm* [rɪðm̩], and *listen* [lɪsn̩]. (The diacritic under the [ḷ], [r̩] [m̩] and [n̩] show that these sounds are **syllabic.**) Placing a schwa [ə] before the syllabic liquid or nasal also shows that these are separate syllables. This is the transcription we will use.

Prosodic Suprasegmental Features

Speech sounds that are identical as to their place or manner features may differ in duration (length), pitch, or loudness. A vowel can be lengthened by prolonging it. A consonant is made long by maintaining the closure or obstruction for a longer period of time.

When we speak, we also change the **pitch** of our voice. The pitch produced depends on how fast the vocal cords vibrate; the faster they vibrate, the higher the pitch. In physical or acoustic terms, pitch is referred to as the **fundamental frequency** of the sound signal.

We are also able to change the loudness of the sounds and sound sequences. In many languages, some syllables or vowels are produced more loudly with a simultaneous change in pitch (usually higher) and longer duration than other vowels in the word or sentence. They are referred to as **stressed** or **accented** vowels or syllables. For example, the first syllable of *digest,* the noun meaning "summation of articles" or a "journal" is stressed, while in *digest,* the verb meaning "to absorb food," the second syllable receives greater stress. Stress can be marked in a number of ways: for example, by putting an accent mark over the stressed vowel.

Features like length, pitch, and the complex feature stress are used in various languages to distinguish the meaning of words and sentences. Such features are often referred to as **prosodic** or **suprasegmental** features.

Tone and Intonation

Speakers of all languages vary the pitch of their voices when they talk: The pitch produced depends on how fast the vocal cords vibrate; the faster they vibrate, the higher the pitch.

The way pitch is used linguistically differs from language to language. In English, it doesn't much matter whether you say *cat* with a high pitch or a low pitch. It will still mean "cat." But if you say [ba] with a high pitch in Nupe (a language spoken in Nigeria), it will mean "to be sour," whereas if you say [ba] with a low pitch, it will mean "to count." Languages that use the pitch of individual vowels or syllables to contrast meanings of words are called **tone** languages.

The majority of the languages in the world are tone languages. There are more than one thousand tone languages in Africa alone; many languages of Asia, such as Chinese, Thai, and Burmese, are tone languages, as are many Native American languages.

Thai is a language that has contrasting pitches or tones. The same string of segmental sounds represented by [naa] will mean different things if one says the sounds with a low pitch, a mid pitch, a high pitch, a falling pitch from high to low, or a rising pitch from low to high. Thai therefore has five linguistic tones.

[naa]	[__]	low tone	"a nickname"
[naa]	[—]	mid tone	"rice paddy"
[naa]	[⌐]	high tone	"young maternal uncle or aunt"
[naa]	[⌐\ ]	falling tone	"face"
[naa]	[⌣]	rising tone	"thick"

Diacritics are used to represent distinctive tones in the phonetic transcriptions.

[`]	L	low tone	
[¯]	M	mid tone	
[´]	H	high tone	
[^]	HL	falling tone	(High to Low)
[ˇ]	LH	rising tone	(Low to High)

We can use these diacritics placed above the vowels to represent the tonal contrasts in any language where the pitch of the vowel is important in conveying meaning as illustrated by the three contrastive tones in Nupe:

| [bá] | "be sour" | [bā] | "cut" | [bà] | "count" |
| H | | M | | L | |

Akan, sometimes called Twi, the major language of Ghana, has two tones, which are shown in these contrasting two-syllables words.

dù	à	[_ _]	"tail"	dù	á	[_ ¯]	"tree"
|	|			|	|		
L	L			L	H		

kɔ̀	tó	[_ ¯]	"go buy"	kɔ́	tɔ̀	[¯ _]	"crab"
|	|			|	|		
L	H			H	L		

In some tone languages the pitch of each tone is level; in others, the direction of the pitch (whether it glides from high to low or from low to high) is important. Tones that glide are called **contour tones;** tones that do not are called **level** or **register** tones. The contour tones of Thai are represented by using a high tone followed by a low tone for a falling glide, and a low followed by a high for a rising tone.

In a tone language, it is not the absolute pitch of the syllables that is important but the relations among the pitches of different syllables. After all, some individual speakers have high-pitched voices, others low-pitched, and others medium-pitched. In many tone languages we find a falling-off of the pitch, a continual downdrifting of the tones.

In the following sentence in Twi, the relative pitch rather than the absolute pitch is important.

"Kofi searches for a little food for his friend's child."

```
Kòfí   hwèhwé   áduàŋ   kàkrá mà   ǹ' ádàmfò   bá
| |    |  |     |  |    |  |  |    |  | |  |    |
L H    L  H     H  L    L  H  L    L  H L  L    H
```

The actual pitches of these syllables would be rather different from each other, as shown in Figure 6-5 (the higher the number, the higher the pitch):

7	fí
6	hwé á
5	Kò _____ krá
4	hwè _____ á
3	duàŋ kà _____ bá
2	mà ǹ'
1	dàmfò

The lowering of the pitch is called **downdrift.** In languages with downdrift—and many tone languages in Africa are downdrift languages—a high tone that occurs after a low tone, or a low tone after a high tone, is lower in pitch than the preceding similarly marked tone. Notice that the first high tone in the sentence is given the pitch value 7. The next high tone (which occurs after an intervening low tone) is 6; that is, it is lower in pitch than the first high tone.

This example shows that in analyzing tones, just as in analyzing segments, all the physical properties need not be considered; only essential features are important in language—in this case, whether the tone is "high" or "low" in relation to the other pitches, but not the specific pitch of that tone.

Languages that are not tone languages, such as English, are called **intonation** languages. The pitch contour of the utterance varies, but in an intonation language as opposed to a tone language, pitch is not used to distinguish words from each other.

DIACRITICS

In the sections on vowel nasalization, prosodic features, and tone we presented a number of diacritic marks that can be used to modify the basic phonetic symbols. A [˜] over the vowel was used to mark vowel nasalization, the doubling of a symbol or a [:] after the symbol to show length, an acute accent to show stress, and various accent marks to show tones.

Other diacritics provide additional ways of showing phonetic differences between speech sounds.

To differentiate a voiceless lateral liquid like the sound written *ll* in *Lloyd* as spoken in Welsh, the symbol [̥] is placed under the segmental symbol. Thus in Welsh the name is pronounced [l̥ɔjd] and in English it is pronounced [lɔjd].

Cover symbols are used when a class of sounds are referred to. A capital C is often used to represent the class of consonants, V for the class of vowels, G for glides, and L for liquids.

We can summarize these diacritics and additional symbols as follows:

C = Consonant   C: = long C
V = Vowel   V: = long V $\tilde{V}$ = nasalized V
L = Liquid   L̥ = voiceless L
G = Glide $\acute{V}$ = stressed V

Tones:

$\acute{V}$ = High $\grave{V}$ = Low $\bar{V}$ = Mid
$\check{V}$ = Rising $\hat{V}$ = Falling

PHONETIC SYMBOLS AND SPELLING CORRESPONDENCES

Table 6.6 shows the sound/spelling correspondences for American English consonants and vowels. (All possible spellings are not given; these, however, should provide enough examples to help students pair sounds and English orthography.) We have included the symbols for the voiceless aspirated stops to illustrate that what speakers usually consider as one sound may phonetically be two.

Some of these pronunciations may differ from yours, making some of the examples confusing. For example, as mentioned above, some speakers of American English pronounce the words *cot* and *caught* identically. In the dialect described here, *cot* and *caught* are pronounced differently, so *cot* is given as an example for the symbol [a]. Many speakers who pronounce *cot* and *caught* identically pronounce *car* and *core* with different vowels. If you use the vowel of *car* to say *cot* and the vowel of *core* to say *caught* you will be approximating the dialect that distinguishes the two words. There are also a number of English dialects in which an *r* sound is not pronounced unless it occurs before a vowel. Speakers of this dialect would pronounce the word *car* without the [r]. The selection of the dialect used in this book is rather arbitrary; it is in fact a mixture of a number of dialects in an attempt to provide at least the major symbols that can be used to describe dialects of American English. We are aware that this may present problems for speakers of different dialects; we apologize for this, but we have not figured out a way to solve this problem satisfactorily.

TABLE 6.6   Phonetic Symbol/English Spelling Correspondences

Consonants	
Symbol	**Examples**
p	spit tip apple ample
pʰ	pit prick plaque appear
b	bit tab brat bubble
m	mitt tam smack Emmy camp comb
t	stick pit kissed write
tʰ	tick intend pterodactyl attack
d	Dick cad drip loved ride
n	nick kin snow mnemonic gnostic pneumatic know
k	skin stick scat critique exceed
kʰ	curl kin charisma critic mechanic close
g	girl burg longer Pittsburgh
ŋ	sing think finger
f	fat philosophy flat phlogiston coffee reef cough
v	vat dove gravel
s	sip skip psychology pass pats democracy scissors fasten deceive descent
z	zip jazz razor pads kisses Xerox design lazy scissors maize
θ	thigh through wrath ether Matthew
ð	thy their weather lathe either
š	shoe mush mission nation fish glacial sure
ž	measure vision azure casual decision rouge (for those who do not pronounce this word with the final sound of *judge*)
č	choke match feature rich righteous
j	judge midget George magistrate residual
l	leaf feel call single
r	reef fear Paris singer
ǰ	you yes feud use
w	witch swim queen
ʍ	which where whale (for speakers who pronounce *which* differently than *witch*)
h	hat who whole rehash
ʔ	bottle button glottal (for some speakers)

TABLE 6.6   *continued*

Vowels	
Symbol	**Examples**
i	beet beat be receive key believe amoeba people Caesar Vaseline serene
ɪ	bit consist injury bin
e	bate bait ray great eight gauge reign they
ɛ	bet serenity says guest dead said
æ	pan act laugh comrade
u	boot lute who sewer through to too two move Lou
ʊ	put foot butcher could
ʌ	cut tough among oven does cover flood
o	coat go beau grow though toe own over
ɔ	caught stalk core saw ball awe
a	cot father palm sergeant honor hospital melodic
ə	sofa alone symphony suppose melody tedious the America
aj	bite sight by die dye Stein aisle choir liar island height sign
aw, æw	about brown doubt coward
ɔj	boy doily

The symbols given in the list are not sufficient to represent the pronunciation of words in all languages. The symbol **[x],** for example, is needed for the voiceless velar fricative in the German word *Bach,* and [ʁ]] for the French uvular fricative. English does not have rounded front vowels, but languages such as French and Swedish do. French front rounded vowels can be symbolized as follows:

[y] as in *tu* [ty] "you" (singular)	The tongue position as for [i] but the lips are rounded
[ø] as in *bleu* [blø] "blue"	The tongue position as for [e] but the lips are rounded
[œ] as in *heure* "hour"	The tongue position as in [ɛ] but the lips are rounded

SIGN-LANGUAGE PRIMES

Just as sign languages have their own morphological, syntactic, and semantic systems, they also have their equivalent of phonetics and phonology. The formal units corresponding to phonetic elements of spoken language are referred to as **primes.** The signs of the language that correspond to morphemes or words can be specified by primes of

FIGURE 6-6 ASL hand configurations (with descriptive phrases that are used to refer to them). The letters and numbers refer to the signs used for these symbols when words are finger-spelled.

/B/	/A/	/G/	/C/	/5/	/V/
[B]	[A]	[G]	[C]	[5]	[V]
flat hand	fist hand	index hand	cupped hand	spread hand	V hand

/0/	/F/	/X/	/H/	/L/	/Y/
[0]	[F]	[X]	[H]	[L]	[Y]
0 hand	pinching hand	hook hand	index-mid hand	L hand	Y hand

/8/	/K/	/I/	/R/	/W/	/3/	/E/
[8]	[K]	[I]	[R]	[W]	[3]	[E]
mid-finger hand	chopstick hand	pinkie hand	crossed-finger hand	American-3 hand	European-3 hand	nail-buff hand

three different classes: hand configuration; the motion of the hand(s) toward or away from the body; and the place of articulation, or the locus, of the sign's movement.

Figure 6-6 illustrates the hand-configuration primes.

The sign meaning "arm" can be described as a flat hand, moving to touch the upper arm. It has three prime features: flat hand, motion upward, upper arm.

SUMMARY

The science of speech sounds is called **phonetics.** It aims to provide the set of features or properties that can be used to describe and distinguish all the sounds used in human language.

When we speak, the physical sounds we produce are continuous stretches of sound, which are the physical representations of strings of discrete linguistic **segments.** Knowledge of a language permits one to segment the continuous sound into linguistic units—words, morphemes, and sounds.

The discrepancy between spelling and sounds in English and other languages motivated the development of **phonetic alphabets** in which one letter corresponds to one sound. The major phonetic alphabet in use is that of the **International Phonetic Association (IPA),** which includes modified Roman letters and **diacritics** by means of which the sounds of all human languages can be represented. To distinguish between the **orthography,** or spelling, of words and their pronunciations, **phonetic transcriptions** may be put between square brackets, as in [fənɛtɪk] for *phonetic.*

All English speech sounds are produced by the movement of lung air through the vocal tract—through the **glottis** or vocal cords, up the pharynx, through the oral cavity and out the mouth and sometimes through the nose. All human speech sounds fall into classes according to their phonetic properties or features; that is, according to how they are produced.

All speech sounds are either **consonants** or **vowels**, and all consonants are either **obstruents** or **sonorants**. Consonants are produced with some obstruction of the airstream in the **supraglottal** cavity. Consonants are distinguished according to where they are articulated in the vocal tract, their **place of articulation** including **bilabial, labiodental, alveolar, palatal, velar, uvular,** and **glottal.**

Speech sounds are also classified according to their **manner of articulation**. They may be **voiced** or **voiceless**, **oral** or **nasal;** they may be **stops, fricatives, liquids, glides,** or **vowels**. During the production of **voiced** sounds the vocal cords or glottis are together and vibrating whereas in **voiceless** sounds the glottis is open and nonvibrating. Voiceless sounds may also be **aspirated** or **unaspirated.** In the production of aspirated sounds the vocal cords remain apart for a brief time after the stop closure is released, thus producing a puff of air at the time of the release. Some classes of sounds combine to form the larger classes such as **labials, coronals, anteriors,** and **sibilants.**

Vowels form the nucleus of syllables. They differ according to the position of the tongue and lips: **high, mid,** or **low** tongue; **front** or **back** of the tongue; **rounded** or **unrounded** lips. The vowels in English may be **tense** or **lax.** Tense vowels are slightly longer in duration than lax vowels. Vowels may also be **stressed** (longer, higher in pitch, and louder) or **unstressed.**

In sign languages, instead of phonetic features there are three classes of **primes**—hand configuration, the motion of the hand(s) toward or away from the body, and the place of articulation, or the locus, of the sign's movements.

In many languages, the pitch of the vowel or syllable is linguistically significant; for example, two words may contrast in meaning if one is produced with a high pitch and another with a low pitch. Such languages are called **tone** languages as opposed to **intonation** languages in which pitch is never used to contrast words. In intonation languages, however, the rise and fall of pitch may contrast meanings of sentences. In English the statement *Mary is a teacher* will end with a fall in pitch, but as a question, *Mary is a teacher?,* the pitch will rise.

In some languages, long vowels or consonants contrast with their shorter counterparts. When they are symbolized by doubling, as in [aa] or [tt], they may be called **geminates.**

Length, pitch, and **loudness** are **prosodic** or **suprasegmental** features. Diacritics to specify such properties as **nasalization, length, stress,** or **tone** may be combined with the phonetic symbols for more detailed phonetic transcriptions.

By means of these phonetic features all speech sounds of all languages can be described.

References for Further Reading

Abercrombie, David. 1967. *Elements of General Phonetics.* Chicago: Aldine.

Catford, J. C. 1977. *Fundamental Problems in Phonetics.* Bloomington, IN: Indiana University Press.

Clark, John, and Colin Yallop. 1990. *An Introduction to Phonetics and Phonology.* Oxford, England: Blackwell.

Crystal, David. 1985. *A Dictionary of Linguistics and Phonetics.* Oxford, England: Blackwell.

International Phonetic Association. 1989. *Principles of the International Phonetics Association,* rev. ed. London: IPA.

Ladefoged, Peter. 1993. *A Course in Phonetics,* 3rd ed. Fort Worth: Harcourt Brace Jovanovich.

Ladefoged, Peter, and Ian Maddieson. 1996. *The Sounds of the World's Languages.* Oxford, England: Blackwell Publishers.

MacKay, Ian R. A. 1987. *Phonetics: The Science of Speech Production,* 2nd ed. Boston: Little Brown.

Pullum, Geoffrey K., and William A. Ladusaw. 1986. *Phonetic Symbol Guide.* Chicago: University of Chicago Press.

EXERCISES

1. Write the phonetic symbol for the *first* sound in each of the following words, according to the way you pronounce it. Example: know [n]

   Examples: ooze   [u]   psycho   [s]

   a. judge   [ ]   f. thought   [ ]
   b. Thomas   [ ]   g. contact   [ ]
   c. though   [ ]   h. phone   [ ]
   d. easy   [ ]   i. civic   [ ]
   e. pneumonia   [ ]   j. usury   [ ]

2. Write the phonetic symbol for the *last* sound in each of the following words. Example: boy [ɔj] (Dipththongs should be treated as one sound.)

a. fleece	[ ]		f. cow	[ ]
b. neigh	[ ]		g. rough	[ ]
c. long	[ ]		h. cheese	[ ]
d. health	[ ]		i. bleached	[ ]
e. watch	[ ]		j. rags	[ ]

3. Write the following words in phonetic transcription, according to your pronunciation. Examples: knot [nat], delightful [dilajtfəl] or [dəlajtfəl]. Some students may pronounce a number of words identically.

a. physics	h. Fromkin
b. merry	i. tease
c. marry	j. weather
d. Mary	j. coat
e. yellow	k. Rodman
f. sticky	l. heath
g. transcription	m. "your name"

4. Below is a phonetic transcription of one of the verses in the poem "The Walrus and the Carpenter" by Lewis Carroll. The speaker who transcribed it may not have exactly the same pronunciation as you; there are many alternate correct versions. However, there is *one* major error in each line that is an impossible pronunciation for any American English speaker. The error may consist of an extra symbol, a missing symbol, or a wrong symbol in the word. Note that the phonetic transcription that is given is a **narrow** transcription; aspiration is marked, as is the nasalization of vowels. This is to illustrate a detailed transcription. However, none of the errors involve aspiration or nasalization of vowels.

Write the word in which the error occurs in the correct phonetic transcription.

Corrected Word

a. ðə tʰãjm hæz cʌ̃m   [kʰʌ̃m]
b. ðə wɔlrəs sed
c. tʰu tʰɔlk əv mẽni θĩŋz
d. əv šuz ãnd šɪps
e. ænd silĩŋ wæx
f. əv kʰæbəgəz ænd kʰĩŋz
g. ænd waj ðə si ɪs bɔjlĩŋ hat
h. ænd wɛθər pʰɪgz hæv wĩŋz

5. The following are all English words written in phonetic transcription. Write the words using normal English orthography.

a. [hit]   _____

b. [strok]   _____

c. [fez]   _____

d. [ton]   _____

e. [boni]   _____

f. [skrim]   _____

g. [frut]   _____

h. [pričər]   _____

i. [krak]   _____

6. Write the symbol that corresponds to each of the following phonetic descriptions, then give an English word that contains this sound.

Example: voiced alveolar stop   [d] *dough*

a. voiceless bilabial unaspirated stop   [ ] _____

b. low front vowel   [ ] _____

c. lateral liquid   [ ] _____

d. velar nasal   [ ] _____

e. voiced interdental fricative   [ ] _____

f. voiceless affricate   [ ] _____

g. palatal glide   [ ] _____

h. mid lax front vowel   [ ] _____

i. high back tense vowel   [ ] _____

j. voiceless aspirated alveolar stop   [ ] _____

7. In each of the following pairs of words, the bold italicized sounds differ by one or more phonetic properties (features). Give the symbol for each of the italicized sounds, state their differences and, in addition, state what properties they have in common.

Example: ph*o*ne—ph*o*nic   The *o* in *phone* is mid, tense, round.
             The *o* in *phonic* is low, unround.
             Both are back vowels.

a. ba*th*—ba*th*e

b. redu*c*e—redu*c*tion

c. c*oo*l—c*o*ld

d. wi*f*e—wi*v*es

e. cat*s*—dog*s*

f. i*m*polite—i*n*decent

8. Write a phonetic transcription of the italicized words in the following poem entitled "English" published long ago in a British newspaper.

I take it you already ***know***
Of ***tough*** and ***bough*** and ***cough*** and ***dough?***
Some may stumble, but not ***you,***
On ***hiccough, thorough, slough*** and ***through?***
So now you are ready, perhaps,
To learn of less familiar traps?
Beware of ***heard,*** a dreadful ***word***
That looks like ***beard*** and sounds like ***bird.***
And ***dead,*** it's ***said*** like ***bed,*** not ***bead;***
For goodness' sake, don't call it ***deed!***
Watch out for ***meat*** and ***great*** and ***threat.***
(They rhyme with ***suite*** and ***straight*** and ***debt.***)
A ***moth*** is not a moth in ***mother,***
Nor ***both*** in ***bother, broth*** in ***brother.***

9. For each group of sounds listed below, state the phonetic feature or features they all share.

Example: [p] [b] [m]   Feature: labial or bilabial, stop, consonant

a. [g] [p] [t] [d] [k] [b]   _____

b. [u] [ɛ] [o] [ɔ]   _____

c. [i] [ɪ] [e] [ɛ] [æ]   _____

d. [t] [s] [š] [p] [k] [č] [f] [h]   _____

e. [v] [z] [ž] [ǰ] [n] [g] [d] [b] [l] [r] [w] [j]   _____

f. [t] [d] [s] [š] [n] [č] [ǰ]   _____

10. Write the following sentences in regular English spelling.

a. nom čamski ɪz e lɪŋgwɪst hu tičəz æt ɛm aj ti

b. fonɛtɪks ɪz ðə stʌdi əv spič sawndz

c. ɔl spokən læŋgwɪǰəz juz sawndz produst baj ðə ʌpər rɛspərətɔri sɪstəm

d. ɪn wʌn dajəlɛkt əv ɪŋlɪš kat ðə nawn ænd kɔt ðə vʌrb ar pronawnst ðə sem

e. sʌm pipəl θɪŋk fonɛtɪks ɪz vɛri ɪntərɛstɪŋ

f. vɪktɔrijə framkɪn ænd rabərt radmən ar ðə ɔθərz əv ðɪs tɛksbʊk.

11. What phonetic property or feature distinguish the sets of sounds in column A from those in Column B?

A   **B**

a. [i] [ɪ]   [u] [ʊ]   _____

b. [p] [t] [k] [s] [f]   [b] [d] [g] [z] [v]   _____

c. [p] [b] [m]   [t] [d] [n] [k] [g] [ŋ]   _____

d. [i] [ɪ] [u] [ʊ]   [e] [ɛ] [o] [ɔ] [æ] [a]   _____

e. [f] [v] [s] [z] [š] [ž]   [č] [ǰ]   _____

f. [i] [ɪ] [e] [ɛ] [æ]   [u] [ʊ] [o] [ɔ] [a]   _____

Chapter 7

Phonology: The Sound Patterns of Language

Speech is human, silence is divine, yet also brutish and dead; therefore we must learn both arts.

Thomas Carlyle (1795–1881)

Phonology is the study of telephone etiquette.

A high school student[1]

From the Arctic Circle to the Cape of Good Hope, people speak to each other. The totality of the sounds they produce constitutes the universal set of human speech sounds. The same relatively small set of phonetic properties or features characterizes all these sounds; the same classes of these sounds are utilized in all spoken languages, and the same kinds of regular patterns of speech sounds occur all over the world. Some of these sounds occur in the languages you speak and some do not. When you learn a language, you learn which sounds occur in your language and how they pattern.

Phonology is concerned with this kind of linguistic knowledge. **Phonetics** is a part of phonology and provides the means for describing speech sounds; phonology is concerned with the ways in which these speech sounds form systems and patterns in human language. Phonology, like grammar, is used in two ways—as the mental representation of linguistic knowledge and the description of this knowledge. Thus, the word *phonology* refers either to the representation of the sounds and sound patterns in a speaker's grammar, or to the study of the sound patterns in a language or in human language in general.

Phonological knowledge permits a speaker to produce sounds that form meaningful utterances, to recognize a foreign "accent," to make up new words, to add the appropriate phonetic segments to form plurals and past tenses, to produce aspirated and

---

[1] As reported in Amsel Greene. 1969. *Pullet Surprises,* Glenview, IL: Scott, Foresman & Co.

unaspirated voiceless stops in the appropriate context, to know what is or is not a sound in one's language, and to know that different phonetic strings may represent the same morpheme.

PHONEMES: THE PHONOLOGICAL UNITS OF LANGUAGE

> In the physical world the naive speaker and hearer actualize and are sensitive to sounds, but what they feel themselves to be pronouncing and hearing are "phonemes."
>
> Edward Sapir, 1933

Phonological knowledge goes beyond the ability to produce all the phonetically different sounds of a language. It includes this ability, of course. A speaker of English can produce the sound [θ] and knows that this sound occurs in English, in words like *thin* [θɪn], *ether* [iθər], and *bath* [bæθ]. English speakers may or may not be able to produce a "click" or a velar fricative, but even if they can, they know that such sounds are not part of the phonetic inventory of English. Many speakers are unable to produce such "foreign" sounds.

A speaker of English also knows that [ð], the voiced counterpart of [θ], is a sound of English, occurring in words like *either* [iðər], *then* [ðɛn], and *bathe* [beð]. French speakers similarly know that [θ] and [ð] are not part of the phonetic inventory of French and often find it difficult to pronounce words like *this* [ðɪs] and *that* [ðæt], pronouncing them as if they were spelled *zis* and *zat*.

Sounds that Contrast

Knowing the sounds (the phonetic units) of a language is only a small part of phonological knowledge.

In earlier chapters we discussed speakers' knowledge of the arbitrary sound/meaning units that comprise their vocabulary, the morphemes and words in their mental lexicons. We saw that knowing a word means knowing both its form (its sounds) and its meaning. Most of the words in a language differ both in form and meaning, sometimes by just one sound. The importance of phonology is shown by the fact that one can change one word into another simply by changing one sound.

Consider the forms and meanings of the following English words:

sip	fine	chunk
zip	vine	junk

Each word differs from the other words in both form and meaning. The difference between *sip* and *zip* is "signaled" by the fact that the initial sound of the first word is *s* [s] and the initial sound of the second word is *z* [z]. The forms of the two words—that is, their sounds—are identical except for the initial consonant sounds. [s] and [z] can therefore distinguish or **contrast** words. They are **distinctive** sounds in English. Such distinctive sounds are called **phonemes.**

We see from the contrast between *fine* and *vine* and between *chunk* and *junk* that [f], [v], [č], and [ǰ] must also be phonemes in English for the same reason—substituting a [v] for [f] or a [č] for [ǰ] produces a different word, a different form with a different meaning.

Minimal Pairs

By permission of Johnny Hart and Creators Syndicate, Inc.

The "B.C." cartoon illustrates the fact that [ɪ] and [i] in the pair *crick* and *creek* and [ʊ] and [o] in the pair *crook* and *croak* are phonemes. The substitution of one for the other makes a different word. The phonological difference between the two words in each pair is minimal because they are identical in form except for one sound segment that occurs in the same place in the string. For this reason, such pairs of words are referred to as **minimal pairs.** These four words, together with *crake,*[2] *crack,* and *crock*, constitute a **minimal set.**

All the words in the set differ by just one sound, and they all differ in meaning. The vowels that contrast these meanings are thus in the class of vowel phonemes in English.

For some speakers, *crick* and *creek* are pronounced identically, another example of regional dialect differences; but most speakers of this dialect still contrast the vowels in *beat* and *bit,* so these high front vowels are contrastive, and therefore phonemes, in their dialect.

The distinct sounds that occur in a minimal pair or a minimal set are phonemes since they contrast meanings. *Fine* and *vine*, and *chunk* and *junk* are minimal pairs in English; [f], [v], [č], and [ǰ] are phonemes in English.

Seed [sid] and *soup* [sup] are not a minimal pair because they differ in two sounds, the vowels and the final consonants. It is thus not evident as to which differences in sound make for the differences in meaning. *Bar* [bar] and *rod* [rad] do not constitute a minimal pair because although only one sound differs in the two words, the [b] occurs initially and the [d] occurs finally. However, [i] and [u] do contrast in the minimal pair *seep* [sip] and *soup* [sup], [d] and [p] contrast in *deed* [did] and *deep* [dip], and [b] and [d] contrast in the following minimal pairs:

beed	[bid]	deed	[did]
bowl	[bol]	dole	[dol]
rube	[rub]	rude	[rud]
lobe	[lob]	load	[lod]

---

[2] A crake is a short-billed bird.

Substituting a [d] for a [b] changes both the phonetic form and its meaning. [b] and [d] also contrast with [g] as in:

bill/dill/gill   rib/rid/rig

Therefore [b], [d], and [g] are all phonemes in English and *bill, dill,* and *gill* constitute a **minimal set.** We have many minimal pairs in English, which makes it relatively easy to determine what the English phonemes are. The words in the following minimal set differ only in their vowels; each vowel thus represents a distinct phoneme.

beat	[bit]	[i]	boot	[but]	[u]
bit	[bɪt]	[ɪ]	but	[bʌt]	[ʌ]
bait	[bet]	[e]	boat	[bot]	[o]
bet	[bɛt]	[ɛ]	bought	[bɔt]	[ɔ]
bat	[bæt]	[æ]	bout	[bawt]	[aw]
bite	[bajt]	[aj]	bot³	[bat]	[a]

[ʊ] and [ɔj], which are not part of the minimal set listed above, are also phonemes of English. They contrast meanings in other minimal pairs:

[ʊ]	[i]	book	[bʊk]	beak	[bik]
[ɔj]	[aj]	boy	[bɔj]	buy	[baj]

The diphthongs [ɔj], [aj], and [aw] are considered to be single vowel sounds although each includes an off-glide because, in English, they function like the monophthongal vowels, as further illustrated by the minimal set including all three diphthongs:

bile	bowel	boil
[bajl]	[bawl]	[bɔjl]

In some languages, particularly those with relatively long words of many syllables, it is not as easy to find minimal sets or even minimal pairs to illustrate the contrasting sounds, the phonemes of these languages. Even in English, which has many **monosyllabic** words (words of one syllable) and hundreds of minimal pairs, there are very few minimal pairs in which the phonemes [θ] and [ð] contrast. In a computer search, only one pair was found in which they contrast initially, one in which they contrast medially, and four with final contrasts. All four pairs in which they contrast finally are noun/verb pairs, the result of historical sound change which will be discussed in a later chapter.

[θ]	**[ð]**
thigh	**th**y
e**th**er	ei**th**er
mou**th** (noun)	mou**th** (verb)
tee**th**	tee**th**e
loa**th**	loa**th**e
wrea**th**	wrea**th**e
shea**th**	shea**th**e

---

³ A bot is the larva of a botfly.

Even if these pairs did not occur, [θ] and [ð] can be analyzed as distinct phonemes. Each contrasts with other sounds in the language, as for example *thick* [θɪk] / *sick* [sɪk] and *though* [ðo] / *dough* [do]. Note also that one cannot substitute the voiced and voiceless interdental fricatives in the words in which they do occur without producing nonsense forms; for example, if we substitute the voiced [ð] for the voiceless [θ] in *thick,* we get [ðɪk], which has no meaning, showing that the phonemes that represent its form and its meaning are inseparable. You cannot pronounce the word any way you like, substituting other sounds for the phonemes in the word.

Free Variation

Drawing by Rechter. © 1988 The New Yorker Magazine, Inc.

Some words in English are pronounced differently by different speakers. For example, some speakers pronounce the word *economics* with an initial [i] and others with an initial [ɛ]. In this word, [i] and [ɛ] are said to be in **free variation**. However, we cannot substitute [i] and [ɛ] in all words. *Did you beat the drum?* does not mean the same thing as *Did you bet the drum?* An old song of the 1930s was based on the notion of free variation:

> You say either [iðər] and I say [ajðər],
>
> You say [niðər] and I say [najðər],
>
> [iðər] [ajðər] [niðər] [najðər],
>
> let's call the whole thing off.

Minimal Pairs in ASL

There are minimal pairs in sign languages just as there are in spoken languages. Figure 7-1[4] shows minimal contrasts involving hand configuration, place of articulation, and movement.

FIGURE 7-1 Minimal contrasts illustrating major formational parameters.

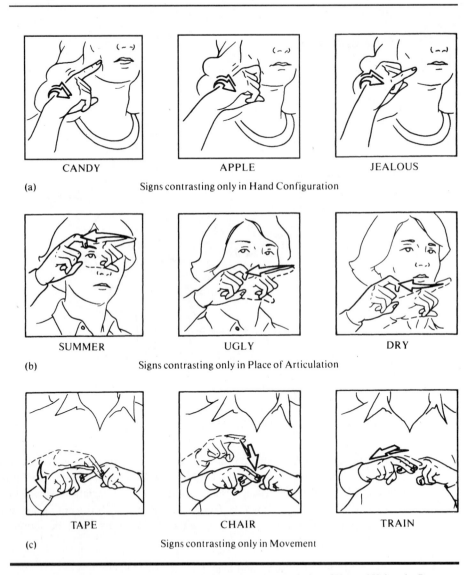

CANDY APPLE JEALOUS

(a) Signs contrasting only in Hand Configuration

SUMMER UGLY DRY

(b) Signs contrasting only in Place of Articulation

TAPE CHAIR TRAIN

(c) Signs contrasting only in Movement

---

[4] Figure 7-1 is from E. S. Klima and U. Bellugi, *The Signs of Language.* 1979. Cambridge, MA: Harvard University Press, pp. 46 and 42.

The signs meaning "candy," "apple," and "jealous" are articulated at the same place of articulation on the face, involve the same movement, but contrast minimally only in hand configuration. "Summer," "ugly," and "dry" are a minimal set contrasting only in place of articulation, and "tape," "chair," and "train" only in movement.

Phonemes, Phones, and Allophones

You may be wondering why we have included a second chapter on phonological units. The entire previous chapter discussed these sounds. But as noted earlier in discussing morphology, syntax, and semantics, linguistic knowledge is more complex than it appears to one who knows a language. Since the knowledge is unconscious, we are unaware of many of the complexities.

Phonemes are not physical sounds. They are abstract mental representations of the phonological units of a language, the units used to represent the forms of words in our mental lexicons. These phonemic representations of words, together with the phonological rules of the language, determine the phonetic units that represent their pronunciation.

If phonemes are not the actual sounds, what are they? We can illustrate the difference between a phoneme and a phonetic segment, called a **phone**, by referring to the difference between oral and nasalized vowels in English. In Chapter 6 it was noted that both oral and nasalized vowels occur **phonetically** in English. The following examples show this.

bean	[bĩn]	bead	[bid]
roam	[rõm]	robe	[rob]

Nasalized vowels occur in English syllables only before nasal consonants. If one substituted oral vowels for the nasal vowels in *bean* and *roam,* the meanings of the two words would not be changed. Try to say these words keeping your velum up until your tongue makes the stop closure of the [n] or your lips come together for the [m]. It will not be easy because in English we automatically lower the velum when producing vowels before nasals in the same syllable. Now try to pronounce *bead* and *robe* with a nasal vowel. [bĩd] would still be understood as *bead* although your pronunciation would probably be interpreted as being very nasal, which it would be. In other words, nasal and oral vowels **do not contrast**. There is just one set of vowel phonemes in English despite the fact that there are two sets of vowel phones—the set of oral vowels and the set of nasal vowels.

There is a general principle or rule in the phonology of English that tells us when nasalized vowels occur—always before nasal consonants, never before oral consonants. The oral vowels in English differ phonemically from each other whereas the differences between the oral vowels and their nasal counterparts do not. There is no principle or rule to predict when, for example, [i] occurs instead of [e] or [u] or [a] or any of the other vowel phonemes. We must learn that [i] occurs in *beat* and [e] in *bait.* We do not have to learn that the nasalized version of [i] occurs in *beam, bean, bing* ([bĩm] [bĩn] [bĩŋ]) or that the nasalized [ũ] occurs in *boom* [bũm] or *boon* [bũn]. Rather, we generalize from the occurrences of oral and nasal vowels in English, and form a mental rule that applies to [i] and [u] and all vowels that automatically nasalizes them before nasal consonants.

The rule, or general principle, that predicts when a vowel phoneme will be realized as an oral vowel phone and when the same vowel phoneme will be a nasalized phone is exemplified in Table 7.1.

TABLE 7.1   Nasal and Oral Vowels: Words and Nonwords

Words						Nonwords*		
be	[bi]	bead	[bid]	bean	[bĩn]	*[bĩ]	*[bĩd]	*[bin]
lay	[le]	lace	[les]	lame	[lẽm]	*[lẽ]	*[lẽs]	*[lem]
baa	[bæ]	bad	[bæd]	bang	[bǽŋ]	*[bǽ]	*[bǽd]	*[bæŋ]

*The asterisk shows that these are nonwords, or unacceptable forms in English.

As the words in Table 7.1 illustrate, oral vowels in English occur in final position and before nonnasal consonants; nasalized vowels occur only before nasal consonants.[5] The "nonwords" show us that nasalized vowels do not occur finally or before nonnasal consonants. Therefore oral vowels and their nasalized counterparts never contrast.

Most speakers of English are unaware that the vowels in *bead* and *bean* are different sounds. This is because speakers are aware of phonemes, not the physical sounds (phones) which they produce and hear.

Since nasalized vowels do occur phonetically but not phonemically, we can conclude that there is no one-to-one correspondence between phonetic segments and phonemes in a language. One phoneme may be realized phonetically (that is, pronounced) as more than one phone—phonetic segment. A phoneme may also be represented by only one phone.

The different phones that are the realizations of a phoneme are called the **allophones** of that phoneme. An allophone is therefore a **predictable phonetic variant** of a phoneme. In English, each vowel phoneme has both an oral and a nasalized allophone. The choice of the allophone is not random or haphazard; it is **rule-governed.** No one is explicitly taught these rules. They are learned subconsciously when the native language is acquired. Language acquisition, to a certain extent, is rule construction.

To distinguish between a phoneme and its allophones (the phonetic segments or phones that symbolize the way the phoneme is pronounced in different contexts), we will use slashes / / to enclose phonemes and continue to use square brackets [ ] for allophones or phones, e.g., [i] and [ĩ] are allophones of the phoneme /i/; [ɪ] and [ɪ̃] are allophones of the phoneme /ɪ/ etc. Thus we will represent *bead* and *bean* phonemically as /bid/ and /bin/. The rule for the distribution of oral and nasal vowels in English shows that phonetically these words will be pronounced as [bid] and [bĩn], respectively. Words are stored in our mental dictionaries in their phonemic form. We refer to these as phonemic **transcriptions.** The pronunciations of these words are given in phonetic transcriptions, between square brackets.

---

[5] More specifically, nasal vowels occur before nasal consonants that follow and are in the same syllable. For most speakers the [o] vowel in the word *roman* [ro-mə̃n] is not nasalized since it occurs before a syllable break symbolized as -, but the [ə] is because the vowel and the [n] are in the same syllable.

In Chapter 6 we mentioned another example of allophones of a single phoneme. We noted that some speakers of English substitute a glottal stop for the [t] at the end of words such as *don't* or *can't* or in the middle of words like *bottle* or *button*. The substitution of the glottal stop does not change the meanings of any words; [dõnt] and [dõnʔ] do not contrast in meaning, nor do [batəl] or [baʔəl]. [ræbəl] and [ræʔəl] do contrast, as the pronunciations of *rabble* and *rattle*, but note that [rætəl] with a [t] or [rærəl] with the flapped [ɾ] or [ræʔəl] with a glottal stop are all possible pronunciations of the word *rattle*. [t], [ɾ], and [ʔ] do not contrast; they are all allophones of the phoneme /t/.

The function of phonemes is to contrast meanings. Phonemes in themselves have no meaning, but when combined with other phonemes they constitute the forms by which meanings of words and morphemes are expressed.

Complementary Distribution

Minimal pairs illustrate that some speech sounds are contrastive in a language, and these sounds represent the set of phonemes. We also saw that some sounds are not distinct; they do not contrast meanings. [t] and [ʔ] were cited as examples of sounds that do not contrast. The substitution of one for the other does not create a minimal pair.

Oral and nasal vowels in English are also nondistinct sounds. Unlike the [t], [ʔ], and [ɾ], the allophones of /t/, the oral and nasal allophones of each vowel phoneme never occur in the same phonological context. This was illustrated in Table 7.1. They **complement** each other and are said to be in **complementary distribution.** This is further shown in Table 7.2.

TABLE 7.2   Distribution of Oral and Nasal Vowels in English Syllables

	In Final Position	Before Nasal Consonants	Before Oral Consonants
Oral vowels	Yes	No	Yes
Nasal vowels	No	Yes	No

When oral vowels occur, nasal vowels do not occur, and vice versa. It is in this sense that the phones are said to complement each other or to be in complementary distribution.

The concept of complementary distribution is illustrated by Clark Kent and Superman, who represent in different form only one person. When Clark Kent is present, Superman is not; when Superman is present, Clark Kent is not. Clark Kent and Superman are therefore in complementary distribution, just as [i] and [ĩ] are in complementary distribution. Of course, there is a difference between the "distribution" of Clark Kent and Superman and the two allophones of the phoneme /i/ since Kent and Superman can occur in the same environment (for example, talking to Lois Lane) whereas [i] and [ĩ] never occur in the same environment or under the same conditions. Kent and Superman are thus more similar to the allophones of /t/—[t] and [ʔ]—which do occur in the same environment. The important point is that the concept of two physical manifestations of a single abstract unit is true of both Clark Kent and Superman and of [i] and [ĩ].

When sounds are in complementary distribution they do not contrast with each other. The replacement of one sound for the other will not change the meaning of the word although it might not sound like typical English pronunciation. Given these facts about the patterning of sounds in a language, a phoneme can be defined as a set of phonetically similar sounds that are in complementary distribution with each other and do not contrast. A set can, of course, consist of only one member. Some phonemes are represented by only one sound, one allophone. When there is more than one allophone in the set, the phones must be **phonetically similar**, that is, share most of the same phonetic features. In English, the velar nasal [ŋ] and the glottal glide [h] are in complementary distribution; [ŋ] is not found word initially and [h] does not occur word finally. But they share very few phonetic features; [ŋ] is a voiced velar nasal stop; [h] is a voiceless glottal glide (or fricative). Therefore, they are not allophones of the same phoneme; [ŋ] and [h] are allophones of different phonemes.

We mentioned that speakers of a language perceive the different sounds of a single phoneme as being one sound. Two sounds that are not phonetically similar would not be so perceived. Furthermore, it would be difficult for children to classify such sounds together as representing one phoneme. The phonetic similarity criterion reflects the ways in which allophones function together and the kinds of generalizations that children can make in acquiring the phonological contrasts of the language.

DISTINCTIVE FEATURES

We generally are not aware of the phonetic properties or features that distinguish the phonemes of our language. Phonetics provides the means to describe these sounds, showing how they differ; phonology tells us which sounds function as phonemes to contrast the meanings of words.

In order for two phonetic forms to differ and to contrast meanings, there must be some phonetic difference between the substituted sounds. The minimal pairs *seal* [sil] and *zeal* [zil] show that [s] and [z] represent two contrasting phonemes in English. They cannot be allophones of one phoneme since one cannot replace the [s] with the [z] without changing the meaning of the word. Furthermore they are not in complementary distribution; both occur word initially before the vowel [i]. They therefore are phones which function as allophones of the phonemes /s/ and /z/. From the discussion of phonetics in Chapter 6, we know that the only difference between [s] and [z] is a voicing difference; [s] is voiceless and [z] is voiced. It is this phonetic feature that distinguishes the two words. Voicing thus plays a special role in English (and in many other languages). It also distinguishes *feel* and *veal* [f]/[v] and *cap* and *cab* [p]/[b]. When a feature distinguishes one phoneme from another, it is a **distinctive feature** (or a phonemic feature). When two words are exactly alike phonetically except for one feature, the phonetic difference is **distinctive** since this difference alone accounts for the contrast or difference in meaning.

Feature Values

One can think of voicing and voicelessness as the presence or absence of a **single feature,** voicing. Thus, a single feature can be thought of as having two values, plus (+), which signifies its presence, and minus (–), which signifies its absence. /b/ is therefore [+ voiced] and /p/ is [– voiced]. We could have called this feature "voiceless" and specified /b/ as [– voiceless] and /p/ as [+ voiceless]. We will however refer to these features by their traditional designations.

The presence or absence of nasality can similarly be designated as [+ nasal] or [– nasal] with [m] being [+ nasal] and [b] or [p] being [– nasal]. A [– nasal] sound is equivalent to an oral sound.

The phonetic and phonemic symbols are **cover symbols** for a set or bundle of distinctive features, a shorthand method of specifying the phonetic properties of the segment. Phones and phonemes are not indissoluble units; they are similar to molecules, composed of atoms—phonetic features. A more explicit transcription of /p/, /b/, and /m/ may thus be given as:

	p	b	m
Stop	+	+	+
Labial	+	+	+
Voiced	–	+	+
Nasal	–	–	+

Aspiration is not listed as a feature in the above phonemic specification of these units because it is nondistinctive and it is not necessary to include both [p] and [p^h] as phonemes. In a phonetic transcription, however, the aspiration would be specified where it occurs. This will be discussed below.

A phonetic feature is distinctive when the + value of that feature found in certain words contrasts with the – value of that feature in other words. Each phoneme must be distinguished from all other phonemes in a language by at least one feature value distinction.

Since the phonemes /b/, /d/, and /g/ contrast by virtue of their place of articulation features—labial, alveolar, and velar—these place features are also distinctive in English. Since uvular sounds do not occur in English, the place feature *uvular* is nondistinctive. The distinctive features of the voiced stops in English are shown in the following:

	b	m	d	n	g	ŋ
Stop	+	+	+	+	+	+
Voiced	+	+	+	+	+	+
Labial	+	+	–	–	–	–
Alveolar	–	–	+	+	–	–
Velar	–	–	–	–	+	+
Nasal	–	+	–	+	–	+

Each of the phonemes in the above chart differs from all the other phonemes by at least one distinctive feature.

The following minimal pairs further describe some of the distinctive features in the phonological system of English.

bat	[bæt]	mat	[mæt]	The difference between *bat* and *mat* is due only to the difference in nasality between [b] and [m]. [b] and [m] are identical in all features except for the fact that [b] is oral or [– nasal] and [m] is nasal or [+ nasal]. Therefore nasality or [± nasal]* is a distinctive feature of English consonants.
rack	[ræk]	rock	[rak]	The two words are distinguished only because [æ] is a front vowel and [a] is a back vowel. They are both low, unrounded vowels. [± back] is therefore a distinctive feature of English vowels.
see	[si]	zee	[zi]	The difference is due to the voicelessness of the [s] in contrast to the voicing of the [z]. Therefore, voicing ([± voiced]) is a distinctive feature of English consonants.

---

* The symbol ± before a feature should be read: "Plus or Minus" that feature, showing that it is a **binary-valued** feature.

Predictability of Redundant (Nondistinctive) Features

We saw above that nasality is a distinctive feature of English consonants. Given the arbitrary relationship between form and meaning, there is no way to predict that the word *mean* begins with a nasal bilabial stop [m] and that the word *bean* begins with an oral bilabial stop [b]. You learn this when you learn the words. We also saw that nasality is not a distinctive feature for English vowels; the nasality feature value of the vowels in *bean, mean, comb,* and *sing* is predictable since they occur before syllable-/word-final nasal consonants. When a feature value is predictable by rule, it is a **redundant** feature. Thus nasality is a redundant feature in English vowels, but a **nonredundant** (distinctive or phonemic) feature for English consonants.

This is not the case in all languages. In French, nasality is a distinctive feature for both vowels and consonants: *gars* pronounced [ga] "lad" contrasts with *gant* [gã], which means "glove," and *bal* [bal] "dance" contrasts with *mal* [mal] "evil/pain." In Chapter 6, other examples of French nasalized vowels are presented. Thus, French has both oral and nasal consonant phonemes and vowel phonemes; English has oral and nasal consonant phonemes, but only oral vowel phonemes.

In the Ghanaian language Akan (or Twi), like French, nasalized and oral vowels occur both phonetically and phonemically; nasalization is a distinctive feature for vowels in Akan, as the following examples illustrate:

[ka]	"bite"	[kã]	"speak"
[fi]	"come from"	[f ĩ]	"dirty"
[tu]	"pull"	[tũ]	"hole/den"
[nsa]	"hand"	[nsã]	"liquor"
[či]	"hate"	[čĩ]	"squeeze"
[pam]	"sew"	[pãm]	"confederate"

These examples show that vowel nasalization is not predictable in Akan. As shown by the last minimal pair—[pam] / [pãm]—there is no rule that nasalizes vowels before nasal consonants. Unlike English, oral and nasal vowels contrast before oral consonants, and oral and nasalized vowels (after identical initial consonants) contrast word final. The change of form—the substitution of nasalized for oral vowels, or vice versa—changes the meaning. Both oral and nasal vowel phonemes must therefore exist in Akan.

Note that two languages may have the same phonetic segments (phones) but have two different phonemic systems. Both oral and nasalized vowels exist in English and Akan phonetically; English has no nasalized vowel phonemes, but Akan does. The same phonetic segments function differently in the two languages. Nasalization of vowels in English is redundant and nondistinctive; nasalization of vowels in Akan is nonredundant and distinctive.

Another nondistinctive feature in English is aspiration. In the previous chapter we pointed out that in English both aspirated and unaspirated voiceless stops occur. The voiceless aspirated stops [pʰ] [tʰ] [kʰ] and the voiceless unaspirated stops [p] [t] [k] are in complementary distribution in English as shown in the following:

Syllable Initial before a Stressed Vowel			After a syllable Initial /s/			Nonword*		
[pʰ]	**[tʰ]**	**[kʰ]**	**[p]**	**[t]**	**[k]**			
pill	*till*	*kill*	*spill*	*still*	*skill*	[pɪl]*	[tɪl]*	[kɪl]*
[pʰɪl]	[tʰɪl]	[kʰɪl]	[spɪl]	[stɪl]	[skɪl]	[spʰɪl]*	[tʰɪl]*	[skʰɪl]*
par	*tar*	*car*	*spar*	*star*	*scar*	[par]*	[tar]*	[car]*
[pʰar]	[tʰar]	[kʰar]	[spar]	[star]	[skar]	[spʰar]*	[tʰar]*	[skʰar]*]

Where the unaspirated stops occur, the aspirated do not, and vice versa. In addition, although they do not contrast, the one set does not occur where the other set does, as shown in the nonwords. One can say *spit* with an aspirated [pʰ], as [spʰɪt], and it would be understood as *spit*, but your listeners would probably think you were spitting out your words. Given this distribution, we see that aspiration is a redundant, nondistinctive feature in English; aspiration is predictable, occurring as a feature of voiceless stops in the specified phonemic environments.

This is the reason speakers of English (if they are not analyzing the sounds as linguists or phoneticians) usually perceive the [pʰ] in *pill* and the [p] in *spill* to be the "same" sound, just as they consider the [i] and [ĩ] that represent the phoneme /i/ in *bead* and *bean* to be the "same." They do so because the difference between them, in this case the feature aspiration, is **predictable, redundant, nondistinctive,** and **nonphonemic** (all equivalent terms).

The distribution of aspirated and unaspirated voiceless stops is a fact about English phonology. There are two *p* sounds (or phones) in English, but only one /p/ phoneme. (This is also true of /t/ and /k/.)

This illustrates why we referred to the phoneme as an abstract unit. We do not utter phonemes; we produce phones, the allophones of the phonemes of the language. /p/ is a phoneme in English that is realized phonetically (pronounced) as either [p] or [pʰ]. [p] and [pʰ] are allophones of the phoneme /p/.

The notion of abstractness is not unique to phonology. We have many abstract mental concepts. The number *3* is not represented in our cognitive arithmetic system as three physical objects. It represents three anything—dogs, pencils, continents, jelly beans, linguists, phonemes, dreams, ideas. It is thus even more abstract than the phonemes of a language that are represented by specific physical objects. Children know that 3 can be three of anything; they also know that /p/ can be [p] and [p^h].

Unpredictability of Phonemic Features

We saw above that the same phones (phonetic segments) can occur in two languages but pattern differently because the phonemic system, the phonology of the languages, is different. English, French, and Akan have oral and nasal vowel phones; in English, oral and nasal vowels are allophones of one phoneme, whereas in French and Akan they represent distinct phonemes.

Aspiration of voiceless stops further illustrates the asymmetry of the phonological systems of different languages. Both aspirated and unaspirated voiceless stops occur in English and Thai (the major language spoken in Thailand), but they function differently in the two languages. Aspiration in English is not a phonemic or distinctive feature, because its presence or absence is predictable; in Thai, it is not predictable, as the following examples show:

Voiceless Unaspirated		Voiceless Aspirated	
[paa]	*forest*	[p^{h}aa]	*to split*
[tam]	*to pound*	[t^{h}am]	*to do*
[kat]	*to bite*	[k^{h}at]	*to interrupt*

The voiceless unaspirated and the voiceless aspirated stops in Thai are not in complementary distribution. They occur in the same positions in the minimal pairs above; they contrast and are therefore phonemes in Thai. In both English and Thai, the phones [p] [t] [k] [p^h] [t^h] [k^h] occur. In English they represent the phonemes /p/, /t/, and /k/; in Thai they represent the phonemes /p/, /t/, /k/, /p^h/, /t^h/, and /k^h/. Aspiration is a distinctive feature in Thai; it is a nondistinctive redundant feature in English.

The phonetic facts alone do not reveal what is distinctive or phonemic.

> **The phonetic representation of utterances shows what speakers know about the pronunciation of utterances.**
> **The phonemic representation of utterances shows what speakers know about the abstract phonological system, the patterning of sounds.**

That *pot/pat* and *spot/spat* are phonemically transcribed with an identical /p/ reveals the fact that English speakers consider the [p^h] in *pot* [p^{h}at] and the [p] in *spot* [spat] to be phonetic manifestations of the same phoneme /p/.

In learning a language a child learns which features are distinctive in that language and which are not. One phonetic feature may be distinctive for one class of sounds but predictable or nondistinctive for another class of sounds, as, for example, the feature nasality in English. Aspiration in English is predictable, nondistinctive for any class of sounds.

In Chapter 6, we pointed out that in English, the tense vowels /i/, /e/, /u/, /o/ are also higher (articulated with a higher tongue position) and longer in duration than their lax vowel counterparts /ɪ/, /ɛ/, /ʊ/, /ɔ/. The distinction between the tense and lax vowels can be shown simply by using the feature tense/lax, or [± tense]. Using this specification, the small difference in tongue height between the tense and lax vowels is nondistinctive, as is the length difference.

In other languages, long and short vowels that are identical except for length are contrastive. Thus, length can be a nonpredictable distinctive feature. Vowel length is phonemic in Danish, Finnish, Arabic, and Korean. Consider the following minimal pairs in Korean:

il	"day"	i:l	"word"
seda	"to count"	se:da	"strong"
kul	"oyster"	ku:l	"tunnel"

Vowel length is also phonemic in Japanese, as shown by the following:

biru	"building"	bi:ru	"beer"
tsuji	"a proper name"	tsu:ji	"moving one's bowels"

When teaching at a university in Japan, one of the authors of this book inadvertently pronounced Ms. Tsuji's name as Tsu:ji-san. (The *-san* is a suffix used to show respect.) The effect of this error quickly taught him to understand the phonemic nature of vowel length in Japanese.

Consonant length is also contrastive in Japanese. A consonant may be lengthened by prolonging the closure: a long *t* [t:] or [tt] can be produced by holding the tongue against the alveolar ridge twice as long as for a short *t* [t]. The following minimal pairs illustrate that length is a phonemic feature for Japanese consonants:

šite	"doing"	šitte	"knowing"
saki	"ahead"	sakki	"before"

Luganda, an African language, also contrasts long and short consonants; /kkula/ means "treasure" and /kula/ means "grow up." (In both these words the first vowel is produced with a high pitch and the second with a low pitch.)

The Italian word for "grandfather" is *nonno* /nonno/, contrasting with the word for "ninth" which is *nono* /nono/.

The phonemic contrast between long and short consonants and vowels can be symbolized by the colon, e.g., /t:/ or /a:/, or by doubling the segment, i.e., /tt/ or /aa/. Such long segments are sometimes referred to as **geminates.** Since phonemic symbols are simply cover symbols for a number of distinctive feature values, it does not matter which symbol one uses. This can be shown by specifying the features that distinguish between /nonno/ or /non:o/ and /nono/; the /nn/ or /n:/ is marked as [+ long] and the /n/ as [– long], whichever symbol is used for length.

More on Redundancies

The value of some features of a single phoneme is predictable or redundant due to the specification of the other features of that segment. That is, given the presence of certain feature values, one can predict the value of other features in that segment.

In English all front vowels are predictably nonround, and the nonlow back vowels are predictably round. Redundant features in phonemic representations need not be specified. If a vowel in English is specified as [– back] it is also redundantly, predictably [– round], and the feature value for round is absent from the representation. A "blank" would occupy its place indicating that the value of that feature is predictable by a phonological rule of the language. Similarly for vowels specified as [– back, – low], which are predictably [– round].

Similarly, in English all nasal consonant phonemes are predictably voiced. Thus voicing is nondistinctive for nasal consonants and need not be specified in marking the value of the voicing feature for this set of phonemes. Phonetically in English, the nasal phonemes may be voiceless (indicated by the small ring under the symbol) when they occur after a syllable initial /s/ as in *snoop,* which phonemically is /snup/ and phonetically may be [sn̥up]. The voicelessness is predictable from the context.

This can be accounted for at the phonemic level by the following:

Redundancy Rule: If a phoneme is [+ nasal] it is also [+ voiced].

In Burmese, however we find the following minimal pairs:

| /ma/ | [ma] | "health" | /m̥a/ | [m̥a] | "order" |
| /na/ | [na] | "pain" | /n̥a/ | [n̥a] | "nostril" |

The fact that some nasal phonemes are [+ voiced] and others [– voiced] must be specified in Burmese; the English redundancy rule does not occur in the grammar of Burmese. We can illustrate this phonological difference between English and Burmese in the following phonemic distinctive **feature matrices:**

Burmese:	**/m/**	**/m̥/**	**English:**	**/m/**
Nasal	+	+		+
Labial	+	+		+
Voicing	+	–		

Note that the value for the voicing feature is left blank for the English phoneme /m/ since the [+] value for this feature is specified by the redundancy rule given above.

As noted earlier, the value of some features in a segment is predictable because of the segments that precede or follow; the phonological context determines the value of the feature rather than the presence of other feature values in that segment. Aspiration cannot be predicted in isolation but only when a voiceless stop occurs in a word, since the presence or absence of the feature depends on where the voiceless stop occurs and what precedes or follows it. It is determined by its **phonemic environment.** Similarly, the oral or nasal quality of a vowel depends on its environment. If it is followed by a nasal consonant it is predictably [+ nasal].

For certain classes of sounds, the values of some features are universally implied for all languages. Thus, all stops—[– continuant] segments—are universally and predictably [– syllabic], regardless of their phonemic context.

Syllable Structure

Reprinted with special permission of King Feature Syndicate.

Words are composed of one or more syllables. A syllable is a phonological unit that is composed of one or more phonemes. Every syllable has a **nucleus,** usually a vowel (but may be a syllabic liquid or nasal). The nucleus may be preceded by one or more phonemes called the syllable **onset** and followed by one or more segments called the **coda.** From a very early age, children learn that certain words rhyme. In rhyming words, the nucleus and the coda of the final syllable are identical, as in the following jingle:

> Jack and **Jill**
> Went up the **hill**
> To fetch a pail of water.
> Jack fell **down**
> And broke his cr**own**
> And Jill came tumbling after.

For this reason, the nucleus + coda constitute the subsyllabic unit called a **rhyme.**

A syllable thus has a **hierarchical** structure. Using the Greek letter *sigma* σ as the symbol for the phonological unit syllable, the hierarchical structure of the monosyllabic word *splints* can be shown.

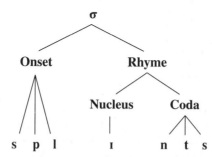

SEQUENTIAL CONSTRAINTS

Suppose you were given four cards, each of which had a different phoneme of English printed on it:

| k | | b | | l | | | ɪ | |

If you were asked to arrange these cards to form all the "possible" words that these four phonemes could form, you might order them as follows:

b	l	ɪ	k
k	l	ɪ	b
b	ɪ	l	k
k	ɪ	l	b

These arrangements are the only permissible ones for these phonemes in English. */lbkɪ/, */ɪlbk/, */bkɪl/, and */ɪlkb/ are not possible words in the language. Although /blɪk/ and /klɪb/ are not existing words (you will not find them in a dictionary), if you heard someone say:

"I just bought a beautiful new *blick*"

you might ask: "What's a 'blick'?" If you heard someone say:

"I just bought a beautiful new *bkli*"

you would probably reply, "What did you say?"

Your knowledge of English "tells" you that certain strings of phonemes are permissible and others are not. After a consonant like /b/, /g/, /k/, or /p/, another stop consonant is not permitted by the rules of the grammar. If a word begins with an /l/ or an /r/, every speaker "knows" that the next segment must be a vowel. That is why */lbɪk/ does not sound like an English word. It violates the restrictions on the sequencing of phonemes.

Other such constraints exist in English. If the initial sounds of *chill* or *Jill* begin a word, the next sound must be a vowel. /čat/ or /čon/ or /čæk/ are possible words in English, as are /jæl/ or /jot/ or /jalɪk/, but */člit/ and */jpurz/ are not. No more than three sequential consonants can occur at the beginning of a word, and these three are restricted to /s/ + /p, t, k/ + /l, r, w, y/. There are even restrictions if this condition is met. For example, /stl/ is not a permitted sequence, so *stlick* is not a possible word in English, but *strick* is.

Other languages have different sequential restrictions. In Polish *zl* is a permissible combination, as in *zloty,* a unit of currency.

The constraints on sequences of segments are called **phonotactic** constraints or simply the phonotactics of the language. If we examine the phonotactics of English we find that word phonotactics are in fact based on syllable phonotactics. That is, only the clusters that can begin a syllable can begin a word, and only a cluster that can end a syllable can end a word. Medially in a multisyllabic word, the clusters consist of a syllable final + syllable initial sequences. Words like *instruct* /ɪnstrʌkt/ with the medial cluster /nstr/ or *explicit* /ɛksplɪsɪt/ with the medial cluster /kspl/ can be divided into well-formed syllables /ɪn $ strʌkt/ and /ɛk $ splɪs $ ɪt/ (using $ to symbolize a syllable boundary). We, as speakers of English, know that "constluct" is not a possible word because the second syllable starts with a nonpermissible sequence /stl/ or /tl/.

In Asante Twi, a word may end only in a vowel or a nasal consonant. /pik/ is not a possible Twi word, because it breaks the phonotactic rules of the language, and /mba/

("not come" in Twi) is not a possible word in English for similar reasons, although it is an actual word in Twi.

All languages have constraints on the permitted sequences of phonemes, though different languages have different constraints. Just as spoken language has sequences of sounds that are not permitted in the language, so sign languages have forbidden combinations of features. They differ from one sign language to another, just as the constraints on sounds and sound sequences differ from one spoken language to another. A permissible sign in a Chinese sign language may not be a permissible sign in ASL, and vice versa. Children learn these constraints when they learn the spoken or signed language, just as they learn what the phonemes are and how they are related to phonetic segments.

Lexical Gaps

Although *bot* [bat] and *crake* [krek] are not words for some speakers, and [bʊt] (to rhyme with *put*), *creck* [krɛk], *cruke* [kruk], *cruk* [krʌk], and *crike* [krajk] are not now words in English, they are "possible words." That is, they are strings of sounds, all of which represent phonemes, in sequences that are permissible in English in that they obey the phonotactic constraints of the language. We might say that they are **nonsense words** (permissible forms with no meanings) or possible words.

Madison Avenue advertisers constantly take advantage of the fact that they can use possible but nonoccurring words for the names of new products. We would hardly expect a new product to come on the market with the name [xik], because [x] (the voiceless velar fricative) is not a phoneme in English. Nor would a new soap be called *Zhleet* [žlit], because in English, the voiced palatal fricative [ž] cannot occur initially before a liquid. Possible but nonoccurring words such as *Bic* [bɪk], before it was coined as a brand name, are **accidental gaps** in the vocabulary. An accidental gap is a form that conforms to all the phonological rules of the language but has no meaning. An actual, occurring word is a combination of both a permitted form and a meaning.

NATURAL CLASSES

Suppose you were writing a grammar of English and wished to include all the generalities that children acquire about the set of phonemes and their allophones. One way of showing what speakers of the language know about the predictable aspects of speech is to include these generalities as **phonological rules** in the phonological component of the grammar. These are not the rules that someone teaches you in school or that you must obey because someone insists on it; they are rules that are known unconsciously and that express the phonological regularities of the language.

In English phonology such rules determine the conditions under which vowels are nasalized or voiceless stops are aspirated. They are general rules, applying not to a single sound but to classes of sounds. They also apply to all the words in the vocabulary of the language, and they even apply to nonsense words that are not in the language but could enter the language (like *sint, peeg,* or *sparg,* which would be /sɪnt/, /pig/, and /sparg/ phonemically and [sĩnt], [pʰig], and [sparg] phonetically).

There are also less general rules found in all languages, and there may also be exceptions to these general rules. But what is of greater interest is that the more we examine the phonologies of the many thousands of languages of the world, the more we find that similar phonological rules apply to the same broad general classes of sounds like the ones we have mentioned—nasals, voiceless stops, alveolars, labials, and so on.

For example, many languages of the world include the rule that nasalizes vowels before nasal consonants. One need not include a list of the individual sounds to which the rule applies or the sounds that result from its application.

This rule can be stated as:

Nasalize a vowel when it is followed by a nasal consonant in the same syllable.

It will apply to all vowel phonemes when they occur in a context before any segment marked [+ nasal] in the same syllable, and will add the feature [+ nasal] to the feature matrix of the vowels.

Another rule that occurs frequently in the world's languages changes the place of articulation of nasal consonants to match the place of articulation of a following consonant. Thus, an /n/ will become an [m] before a /p/ or /b/ and will become a velar [ŋ] before a /k/ or /g/. When two segments agree in their place of articulation they are called **homorganic consonants.** This homorganic nasal rule occurs in Akan as well as English and many other languages.

Many languages have rules that refer to [+ voiced] and [– voiced] sounds. Note that the aspiration rule in English applies to the class of voiceless stops. As in the vowel nasality rule, we do not need to list the individual segments in the rule since it applies to all the voiceless stops /p/, /t/, and /k/, as well as /č/.

That we find such similar rules that apply to the same classes of sounds across languages is not surprising since such rules often have phonetic explanations and these classes of sounds are defined by phonetic features. For this reason such classes are called **natural classes** of speech sounds. **A natural class is a group of sounds that share one or more distinctive features.**

Children find it easier to learn a rule (or construct it) that applies to a natural class of sounds; they do not have to remember the individual sounds, simply the features that these sounds share.

This fact about phonological rules and natural classes illustrates why individual phonemic segments are better regarded as combinations or complexes of features than as indissoluble whole segments. If such segments are not specified as feature matrices, the similarities among /p/, /t/, and /k/ or /m/, /n/, and /ŋ/ would not be revealed. It would appear that it should be just as easy for a child to learn a rule such as

(a) **Nasalize vowels before /p/, /i/, or /z/.**

as to learn a rule such as

(b) **Nasalize vowels before /m/, /n/, or /ŋ/.**

Rule (a) has no phonetic explanation whereas rule (b) does. It is easier to lower the velum to produce a nasalized vowel in anticipation of a following nasal consonant than to prevent the velum from lowering before the consonant closure.

A natural class is a set of phonemes that can be defined by fewer features than any of its members. The class that includes the phonemes /p, t, k, b, d, g, m, n, ŋ, č, ǰ/ can be defined specifying one feature, [– continuant]. The phoneme /p/ requires three feature specifications: as does any of the other phonemes in this set.

A class of sounds that can be defined by fewer features than another class of sounds is clearly more general. Thus, the class of [– continunuant, – nasal] sounds is in some sense more natural than the class that includes all the nonnasal stops except /p/. The only way to refer to such a class is to list all the segments in that class. Try to do this with feature notation; you will see why such a class is far from natural.

This does not mean that no language has a rule that applies to a single sound or even to a class of stops excluding /p/. One does find complex rules in languages including rules that apply to an individual member of a class, but rules pertaining to natural classes occur more frequently, and an explanation is provided for this fact by reference to phonetic properties.

A phonological segment may be a member of a number of classes; for example, /s/ is a member of the class of [+ obstruent]s, [+ consonantal]s, [+ alveolar]s, [+ coronal]s, [– stop]s, [+ continuant]s, [+ sibilants]s, and so on.

The major classes discussed in Chapter 6 are all natural classes that are referred to in phonological rules of all languages. They also can be specified by + and – feature values:

[+ CONSONANTAL] = consonants
[– CONSONANTAL] = vowels

[+ SONORANT] = nasals, liquids, glides, vowels
[– SONORANT] = stops and fricatives (OBSTRUENTS)

[+ SYLLABIC] = vowels, some liquids and nasals
[– SYLLABIC] = consonants, glides, some liquids and nasals

All speech sounds can thus be specified as shown in Table 7.3.

TABLE 7.3 Feature Specification of Major Natural Classes of Sounds

	Obstruents O	Nasals N	Liquids L	Glides G	Vowels V
Features					
Consonantal	+	+	+	–	–
Sonorant	–	+	+	+	+
Syllabic	–	+/–	+/–	–	+
Nasal	–	+	–	–	+/–

Feature Specifications for American English Consonants and Vowels

Using the phonetic properties or features provided in Chapter 6 and the additional features in this chapter, we can provide feature matrices for all the phonemes in English using the + or − value for each feature. One then can easily identify the members of each class of phonemes by selecting all the segments marked + or − for a single feature. Thus, the class of high vowels, / i ɪ u ɛ / are marked [+ high] in the vowel feature chart of Table 7.4; the class of stops, /p b m t d n k g n č j/, are the phonemes marked [− continuant] on the consonant chart in Table 7.5 on the next page.

TABLE 7.4   Specification of Phonemic Features of American English Stressed Vowels

Features	i	ɪ	e	ɛ	æ	u	U	o	ɔ	a	ʌ
high	+	+	−	−	−	+	+	−	−	−	−
mid	−	−	+	+	−	−	−	+	+	−	+
low	−	−	−	−	+	−	−	−	−	+	−
back	−	−	−	−	−	+	+	+	+	+	−
central	−	−	−	−	−	−	−	−	−	−	+
rounded	−	−	−	−	−	+	+	+	+	−	−
tense	+	−	+	−	−	+	−	+	−	−	−

The feature [± mid] is not required to distinguish each vowel from every other one. The vowels marked [+ mid] are already distinguished from high and low vowels by being specified as [− high, − low]. The one stressed central vowel [ʌ] is sometimes specified as a back vowel; if this were done the feature [± front] would not be necessary. We have included the features [mid] and [central] to show more clearly the phonetic quality of the vowel phonemes.

MORE ON PROSODIC PHONOLOGY

Intonation

By permission of Johnny Hart and Creators Syndicate, Inc.

In Chapter 6, the use of pitch as a phonetic feature was discussed in reference to tone languages and intonation languages. In this chapter we have discussed the use of phonetic features to distinguish meaning. We can now see that pitch can be a phonemic feature in languages such as Chinese or Thai or Akan. Such relative pitches are referred to phonologically as contrasting **tones.** We also pointed out that there are languages that are not

TABLE 7.5 Phonemic Features of American English Consonants

Features	p	b	m	t	d	n	k	g	ŋ	f	v	θ	ð	s	z	š	ž	č	ǰ	l	r	j	w	h
Consonantal	+	+	+	+	+	+	+	+	+	+	+	+	+	+	+	+	+	+	+	+	+	−	−	−
Sonorant	−	−	+	−	−	+	−	−	+	−	−	−	−	−	−	−	−	−	−	+	+	+	+	+
Syllabic	−	−	−/+	−	−	−/+	−	−	−/+	−	−	−	−	−	−	−	−	−	−	−/+	−/+	−	−	−
Nasal	−	−	+	−	−	+	−	−	+	−	−	−	−	−	−	−	−	−	−	−	−	−	−	−
Voiced	−	+	+	−	+	+	−	+	+	−	+	−	+	−	+	−	+	−	+	+	+	+	+	−
Continuant	−	−	−	−	−	−	−	−	−	+	+	+	+	+	+	+	+	−	−	+	+	+	+	+
Labial	+	+	+	−	−	−	−	−	−	+	+	−	−	−	−	−	−	−	−	−	−	−	+	−
Alveolar	−	−	−	+	+	+	−	−	−	−	−	−	−	+	+	−	−	−	−	+	+	−	−	−
Palatal	−	−	−	−	−	−	−	−	−	−	−	−	−	−	−	+	+	+	+	−	−	+	−	−
Anterior	+	+	+	+	+	+	−	−	−	+	+	+	+	+	+	−	−	−	−	+	−	−	−	−
Velar	−	−	−	−	−	−	+	+	+	−	−	−	−	−	−	−	−	−	−	−	−	−	+	−
Coronal	−	−	−	+	+	+	−	−	−	−	−	+	+	+	+	+	+	+	+	+	+	−	−	−
Sibilant	−	−	−	−	−	−	−	−	−	−	−	−	−	+	+	+	+	+	+	−	−	−	−	−

Note: The [+ voicing] feature value is redundant for English nasals, liquids, and glides (except for /h/) and could have been left blank for this reason. The feature specifications for [± coronal], [± anterior], and [± sibilant] are also redundant. These redundant predictable feature specifications are provided simply to illustrate the segments in these natural classes. Note that we have not included the allophones [pʰ, tʰ, kʰ], since the aspiration is predictable at the beginning of syllables and these phones are not distinct phonemes in English.

tone languages, such as English. Pitch may still play an important role in these languages. It is the **pitch contour** or **intonation** of the phrase or sentence that is important.

In English, syntactic differences may be shown by different intonation contours. We say *John is going* as a statement with a falling pitch, but as a question with the pitch rising at the end of the sentence.

A sentence that is ambiguous when it is written may be unambiguous when spoken. For example:

(a) Tristram left directions for Isolde to follow.

If Tristram wanted Isolde to follow him, the sentence would be pronounced with the rise in pitch on the first syllable of *follow,* followed by a fall in pitch, as in (b).

(b) Tristram left directions for Isolde to follow.

The sentence can also mean that Tristram left a set of directions he wanted Isolde to use. If this is the intention, the highest pitch comes on the second syllable of *directions,* as in (c):

(c) Tristram left directions for Isolde to follow.

The way we have indicated pitch is of course highly oversimplified. Before the big rise in pitch the voice does not remain on the same monotone low pitch. These pitch diagrams indicate merely when there is a special change in pitch.

Thus pitch plays an important role in both tone languages and intonation languages, but in different ways.

Word Stress

By permission of Johnny Hart and Creators Syndicate, Inc.

In English and many other languages, one or more of the syllables in each content word (words other than the "little words" like *to, the, a, of,* and so on) are stressed. A stressed syllable, which can be marked by an acute accent (´) is perceived as being more prominent than unstressed syllables in the following examples:

pérvert	(noun)	as in	"My neighbor is a pervert."
pervért	(verb)	as in	"Don't pervert the idea."

| súbject | (noun) | as in | "Let's change the subject." |
| subjéct | (verb) | as in | "He'll subject us to criticism."[6] |

In some words, more than one vowel is stressed, but if so, one of these stressed vowels receives greater stress than the others. We have indicated the most highly stressed vowel by an acute accent over the vowel (we say this vowel receives the **accent,** or **primary stress,** or **main stress**); the other stressed vowels are indicated by marking a grave accent (`) over the vowels (these vowels receive secondary stress).

| rèsignátion | lìnguístics | sỳstemátic |
| fùndaméntal | ìntrodúctory | rèvolútion |

Generally, speakers of a language know which syllable receives primary stress or accent, which receives secondary stress, and which are not stressed at all; it is part of their knowledge of the language. Sometimes it is hard to distinguish between primary and secondary stress, but it is easier to distinguish between stressed and unstressed syllables.

The stress pattern of a word may differ from dialect to dialect. For example, in most varieties of American English the word *láboratòry* has two stressed syllables; in one dialect of British English it receives only one stress [ləbɔ́rətri]. Because the vowel qualities in English are closely related to whether they are stressed or not, the British vowels differ from the American vowels in this word; in fact, in the British version one vowel "drops out" completely because it is not stressed.

Just as stressed syllables in poetry reveal the metrical structure of the verse, phonological stress patterns relate to the metrical structure of a language.

There are a number of ways used to represent stress. Above we used grave and acute accent marks. We can also specify which syllable in the word is stressed by marking the syllable *s* if strongly stressed, *w* if weakly stressed, and unmarked if unstressed.

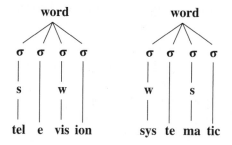

Stress is also sometimes shown by placing a *1* over the primary stressed syllable, a *2* over the syllable with secondary stress, with unstressed vowels unmarked.

| 2 | 1 | | 2 | 1 | | 1 | 2 |
| fundamental | | | introductory | | | secondary | |

---

[6] These minimal pairs show that stress is contrastive in English; it distinguishes between nouns and verbs.

Stress is a property of a syllable rather than a segment; it is a prosodic or suprasegmental feature. Tone may also be a property of a syllable rather than a single vowel; it too, then, would be a suprasegmental feature.

To produce a stressed syllable, one may change the pitch (usually by raising it), make the syllable louder, or make it longer. We often use all three of these phonetic features to stress a syllable.

Sentence and Phrase Stress

Howie Schneider

When words are combined into phrases and sentences, one of the syllables receives greater stress than all others. That is, just as there is only one primary stress in a word spoken in isolation (for example, in a list), only one of the vowels in a phrase (or sentence) receives primary stress or accent; all the other stressed vowels are "reduced" to secondary stress. A syllable that receives the main stress when the word is not in a phrase may have only secondary stress in a phrase, as is illustrated by these examples:

1 1 1 2 tight + rope → tightrope	("a rope for acrobatics")
1 1 2 1 tight + rope → tight rope	("a rope drawn taut")
1 1 1 2 hot + dog → hotdog	("frankfurter")
1 1 2 1 hot + dog → hot dog	("an overheated dog")
1 1 2 1 red + coat → Redcoat	("a British soldier")
1 1 2 1 red + coat → red coat	("a coat that is red")
1 1 1 2 white + house → White House	("the President's house")
1 1 2 1 white + house → white house	("a house painted white")

In English we place primary stress on an adjective follo'
words are combined in a compound noun (which may
words separated by a hyphen, or two separate words'
noun when the words are part of a noun phrase (NP) such.
ter 4. The differences between the pairs below are therefore p.

Compound Noun	Adjective + Noun
tightrope	tight rope
Redcoat	red coat
hotdog	hot dog
White House	white house

These minimal pairs show that stress may be predictable from the morphology and syntax. The phonology is not independent of the rest of the grammar. The stress differences between the noun and verb pairs discussed in the previous section (*subject* as noun or verb) are also predictable from the syntactic word category.

The differences in the English sentences we used to illustrate intonation contours may also be described by referring to the word on which the main stress is placed, as in the following examples:

$$\text{(a)} \quad \underline{\text{Tristram left directions for Isolde to } \overset{1}{\text{follow}}.}$$

$$\text{(b)} \quad \underline{\text{Tristram left } \overset{1}{\text{directions}} \text{ for Isolde to follow.}}$$

In sentence (a) the primary stress is on the word *follow,* and in (b) the primary stress is on *directions.*

THE RULES OF PHONOLOGY

No rule is so general which admits not some exception.

Robert Burton, *The Anatomy of Melancholy*

But that to come
Shall all be done by the rule.

Shakespeare, *Antony and Cleopatra*

Throughout this chapter we have discussed the fact that the relationship between the phonemic representations that are stored in one's mental lexicon and the phonetic representations that reflect the pronunciation of these words is **rule-governed.** The phonological rules relate the minimally specified phonemic representation of a word to the phonetic representation and are part of a speaker's knowledge of the language.

The phonemic representations are minimally specified in the mental grammar because some features or feature values are predictable. The **underspecification** reveals the redundancy of such features, a fact about the knowledge speakers have of the phonology. The grammars we write aim at revealing this knowledge; if we included these features we would fail in our goal.

The phonemic representation, then, should include only the nonpredictable distinctive features of the string of phonemes that represent the words. The phonetic representation **derived** by applying these rules includes all the linguistically relevant phonetic aspects of the sounds. It does not include all the physical properties of the sounds of an utterance, because the physical signal may vary in many ways that has little to do with the phonological system. The absolute pitch of the sound, the rate of speech, or its loudness is not linguistically significant. The phonetic transcription is therefore also an abstraction from the physical signal; it includes the nonvariant phonetic aspects of the utterances, those features that remain relatively the same from speaker to speaker and from one time to another.

Although the specific rules of phonology differ from language to language, the kinds of rules, what they do, and the natural classes they refer to are the same cross-linguistically.

Assimilation Rules

We have seen that nasalization of vowels in English is nonphonemic because it is predictable by rule. The vowel nasalization rule is an **assimilation** rule; it assimilates one segment to another by "copying" or "spreading" a feature of a sequential phoneme on to its neighboring segment, thus making the two phones more similar. Assimilation rules are, for the most part, caused by articulatory or physiological processes. There is a tendency when we speak to increase the **ease of articulation,** that is, to make it easier to move the articulators. We noted above that it is easier to lower the velum while a vowel is being pronounced before a nasal stop closure than to wait for the articulators to come together. We can state the vowel nasalization rule as:

> **Nasalize vowels and diphthongs before nasals (within the same syllable).**

This rule specifies the class of sounds affected by the rule:

> **vowels** and **diphthongs**

It states what phonetic change will occur by applying the rule:

> **Change phonemic oral vowels to phonetic nasal vowels.**

And it specifies when the rule applies, the **context** or phonemic **environment.**

> **Before nasals within the same syllable.**

All three kinds of information—**segments affected, phonemic environment, phonetic change**—must be included in the statement of a phonological rule or it will not explicitly state the regularities that constitute speakers' unconscious phonological knowledge.

Phonologists often use a shorthand notation to write rules, similar to the way scientists and mathematicians use symbols. Every physicist knows that $E = mc^2$ means "Energy equals mass times the square of the velocity of light." Children know that $2 + 2 \times 4 \div 2 = 8$ can be stated in words as "two plus two times four divided by two equals eight." We can also use such notations to state the nasalization rule as:

$$V \rightarrow [+ \text{ nasal}]/\_\_\_\_\_ [+ \text{ nasal}] (C) \$$$

Similar to the way we use "=" instead of "equals" in mathematical equations and formulas, we use an arrow " → " instead of "becomes" or "is" or "is changed to" to represent the change that the rule specifies. The segment on the left of the arrow is changed to whatever is on the right of the arrow in the specified environment. The rule applies if the nasal is the final consonant in the syllable or if it is followed by another consonant as in *dam* [dæm] and *damp* [dæmp]. The optional final consonant is thus put in parenthesis, which means that the segment may or may not be present in the environment.

What occurs on the left side of the arrow fulfills the first requirement for a rule: It specifies the class of sounds affected by the rule. What occurs on the right side of the arrow specifies the change that occurs, thus fulfilling the second requirement of a phonological rule.

To fulfill the third requirement of a rule—the phonological environment or context where the rule will apply—we can formalize the notions of "environment" or "in the environment" and the notions of "before" and "after" since it is also important to specify whether the vowels to be nasalized occur before or after a nasal. In this case the [+ nasal] segment in the context is followed by the syllable boundary symbol $ to show that the rule only applies if the nasal segment is in the same syllable. In some languages, nasalization occurs after rather than before nasal segments. We will use the following notations:

/ to mean "in the environment of "

____ is placed before or after the relevant segment(s) that determines the change.

The nasalization rule stated formally above can be read in words:

"A vowel becomes or is nasalized in the environment before a nasal segment."

Any rule written in formal notation can also be stated in words. The use of the notations is, as stated above, a shorthand way of presenting the information. It also often reveals the function of the rule more explicitly. It is easy to see in the formal statement of the rule that this is an assimilation rule since the change to [+ nasal] occurs before [+ nasal] segments.

Assimilation rules in languages reflect what phoneticians often call **coarticulation**— the spreading of phonetic features either in anticipation of sounds or the perseveration of articulatory processes. This "sloppiness" tendency may become regularized as rules of the language.

The following example illustrates how the English vowel nasalization rule applies to the phonemic representation of words and shows the assimilatory nature of the rule; that is, the change from the [– nasal] feature value of the vowel in the phonemic representation to a [+ nasal] in the phonetic representation:

	"Bob"			"bomb"		
Phonemic representation	/b	a	b/	/b	a	m/
Nasality: phonemic feature value	–	–	–	–	–	+
Apply nasal rule		NA*			↓	
Nasality: phonetic feature value	–	–	–	–	+	+
Phonetic representation	[b	a	b]	[b	ã	m]

*NA = "not applicable."

There are many other examples of assimilation rules in English and other languages. There is an optional ("**free variation**") rule in English that, particularly in fast speech, devoices the nasals and liquids in words like *snow* /sno/ [sn̥o], *slow* /slo/ [sl̥o], *smart* /smart/ [sm̥art], *probe* /prob/ [pʰr̥ob], and so on. (The devoicing of nasals was mentioned above.) The feature [– voiced] of the /s/ or /p/ carries over onto the following segment. Because voiceless nasals and liquids do not occur phonemically—do not contrast with voiced sonorants—the vocal cords need not react quickly. The devoicing will not change the meaning of the words; [slat] and [sl̥at] both mean "slot."

Vowels may also become devoiced or voiceless in a voiceless environment. In Japanese, high vowels are devoiced when preceded and followed by voiceless obstruents; in words like *sukiyaki* the /u/ becomes [u̥]. This assimilation rule can be stated as follows:

$$
\begin{bmatrix} - \text{consonantal} \\ + \text{syllabic} \end{bmatrix} \rightarrow [- \text{voiced}] / \begin{bmatrix} - \text{sonorant} \\ - \text{voiced} \end{bmatrix} \underline{\quad} \begin{bmatrix} - \text{sonorant} \\ - \text{voiced} \end{bmatrix}
$$

This rule states that any Japanese vowel (a segment that is nonconsonantal and syllabic) becomes devoiced ([– voiced]) in the environment of, or when it occurs (/) between, voiceless obstruents.[7] Notice that the dash does not occur immediately after the slash or at the end of the rule, but between the segment matrices represented as [– sonorant, – voiced].

This rule includes the three kinds of information required:

(a) the class of sounds affected: vowels ($\begin{bmatrix} - \text{consonantal} \\ + \text{syllabic} \end{bmatrix}$)

(b) the phonemic environment: between two obstruents

(c) the phonetic change: devoicing $\begin{bmatrix} - \text{consonantal} \\ + \text{syllabic} \\ + \text{voiced} \end{bmatrix}$ becomes $\begin{bmatrix} - \text{consonantal} \\ + \text{syllabic} \\ - \text{voiced} \end{bmatrix}$

The rule does not specify the class of segments to the left of the arrow as [+ voiced] because phonemically all vowels in Japanese are voiced. It therefore simply has to include the change on the right side of the arrow.

---

[7] The rule applies most often to high vowels but may apply to other vowels as well.

We can illustrate the application of this rule in Japanese as we did the vowel nasalization rule in English:

	"sukiyaki"							
Phonemic Representation	/s	u	k	i	j	a	k	i/
Voicing: phonemic feature value	−	+	−	+	+	+	−	+
Apply Devoicing rule		↓						
Voicing: phonetic feature value	−	−	−	+	+	+	−	+
Phonetic Representation	[s	ḁ	k	i	j	a	k	i]

Feature Changing Rules

The English vowel nasalization and devoicing rules and the Japanese devoicing rule change feature specifications. That is, in English the [− nasal] value of phonemic vowels is changed to [+ nasal] phonetically through a spreading process when the vowels occur before nasals. Vowels in Japanese are phonemically voiced, and the rule changes vowels that occur in the specified environment into phonetically voiceless segments.

The rules we have discussed are phonetically plausible, as are other assimilation rules, and can be explained by natural phonetic processes. This fact does not mean that all these rules have to occur in all languages. In fact, if they always occurred they would not have to be learned at all; they would apply automatically and universally, and therefore would not have to be included in the grammar of any particular language. They are not, however, universal.

There is a nasal assimilation rule in Akan that nasalizes voiced stops when they follow nasal consonants, as shown in the following example:

/ɔ bá/   [ɔbá]   "he comes"   /ɔ m̀ bá/   [ɔmmá]   "he doesn't come"
he come   *he not come*

The /b/ of the verb "come" becomes an [m] when it follows the negative /m/.

This assimilation rule also has a phonetic explanation; the velum is lowered to produce the nasal consonant and remains down during the following stop. Although it is a phonetically "natural" assimilation rule, it does not occur in the grammar of English; the word *amber,* for example, shows an [m] followed by a [b]. A child learning Akan must learn this rule, just as a child learning English learns to nasalize all vowels before nasal consonants, a rule that does not occur in the grammar of Akan.

Assimilation rules such as the ones we have discussed in English, Japanese, and Akan often have the function of changing the value of phonemic features. They are **feature-changing** or **feature-spreading** rules. Although nasality is nondistinctive for vowels in English, it is a distinctive feature for consonants, and the nasalization rule therefore changes a feature value.

The Akan rule is a feature-changing rule that shows that [m] is an allophone of /b/ as well as an allophone of /m/.

> **There is no one-to-one relationship between phonemes and their allophones.**

This fact can be illustrated in another way:

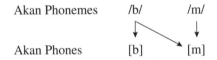

We will provide more examples of this one-to-many or many-to-one mapping between phonemes and allophones.

Dissimilation Rules

It is understandable why assimilation rules are found in so many languages. As pointed out, they permit greater ease of articulation. It might seem strange then to learn that one also finds **dissimilation** rules in languages, rules in which a segment becomes less similar to another segment rather than more similar. But such rules do exist. They also have a natural explanation, often from the point of view of the hearer rather than the speaker. That is, in listening to speech, if sounds are too similar, we may miss the contrast.

A classic example of dissimilation occurred in Latin, and the results of this process show up in modern-day English. There was a derivational suffix *-alis* in Latin that was added to nouns to form adjectives. When the suffix was added to a noun that contained the liquid /l/, the suffix was changed to *-aris,* that is, the liquid /l/ was changed to the liquid /r/. These words came into English as adjectives ending in *-al* or in its dissimilated form *-ar,* as shown in the following examples:

-al	-ar
anecdot-al	angul-ar
annu-al	annul-ar
ment-al	column-ar
pen-al	perpendicul-ar
spiritu-al	simil-ar
ven-al	vel-ar

As *columnar* illustrates, the /l/ need not be the consonant directly preceding the dissimilated segment.

Dissimilation rules are quite rare, but they do occur. The African language Kikuyu has a dissimilation rule in which a prefix added to a verb begins with a velar fricative if the verb begins with a stop but with a velar stop if the verb begins with a continuant.

Feature Addition Rules

Some phonological rules are neither assimilation nor dissimilation rules. The aspiration rule in English, which aspirates voiceless stops at the beginning of a syllable, simply adds a nondistinctive feature. As we did in the nasalization rule earlier, we can use the symbol $ to represent a syllable boundary. Generally aspiration occurs only if the following vowel is stressed. The /p/ in *pit* and *repeat* is aspirated but the /p/ in *in $ spect* or *com $ pass* is usually unaspirated (although if aspirated it will not change meaning since aspiration is nonphonemic). Using the feature [+ stress] to indicate a stressed syllable and V́ to symbolize stressed vowels, the aspiration rule may be stated:

$$\begin{bmatrix} - \text{continuant} \\ - \text{voiced} \end{bmatrix} \rightarrow [+ \text{aspirated}] \: / \: \$ \underline{\hspace{1.5cm}} \begin{bmatrix} - \text{consonatal} \\ + \text{stress} \end{bmatrix}$$

Voiceless stops ([– continuant, – voiced segments]) become (are) aspirated when they occur syllable initially before stressed vowels (/ \$ __ V́)

Aspiration is neither present nor absent in any phonemic feature matrices in English. Assimilation rules do not add new features but change phonemic feature values, whereas the aspiration rule adds a new feature not present in phonemic representations.

Remember that /p/ and /b/ (and all such symbols) are simply cover symbols that do not reveal the phonemic distinctions. In phonemic and phonetic feature matrices, these differences are made explicit, as shown in the following phonemic matrices:

	/p/	/b/	
Consonantal	+	+	
Continuant	–	–	
Labial	+	+	
Voiced	–	+	← distinctive difference

The nondistinctive feature "aspiration" is not included in these phonemic representations because aspiration is predictable.

Segment Deletion and Addition Rules

In addition to assimilation and dissimilation (feature-changing) and feature-addition rules, phonological rules can delete or add entire phonemic segments. In French, for example, as demonstrated by Sanford Schane,[8] word-final consonants are deleted when the following word begins with a consonant (oral or nasal) or a liquid, but are retained when the following word begins with a vowel or a glide, as illustrated in Table 7.6 on page 286.

Table 7.6 represents a general rule in French applying to all word-final consonants. We distinguished these five classes of sounds by the features *consonantal, sonorant, syllabic,* and *nasal.* We noted that oral and nasal consonants and liquids were specified as [+ consonantal] and vowels and glides as [– consonantal]. We can now see why such "super classes" or "cover features" are important. Using the symbol Ø to represent the "null" unit (or zero) and # as "word boundary," we can state the French rule simply as:

[+ consonantal] → Ø/_____ # # [+ consonantal]

This rule can be "translated" into words as:

---

[8] Sanford Schane. 1968. *French Phonology and Morphology,* Cambridge, MA: MIT Press.

TABLE 7.6   Distribution of Word-Final Consonants in French

Before a consonant:	/pətit tablo/	[peti tablo]	"small picture"
	/noz tablo/	[no tablo]	"our pictures"
Before a liquid:	/pətit livr/	[pəti livr]	"small book"
	/noz livr/	[no livr]	"our books"
Before a nasal:	/pətit navet/	[pəti navɛ]	"small turnip"
	/noz navets/	[no navɛ]	"our turnips"
Before a vowel:	/pətit ami/	[pətit ami]	"small friend"
	/noz amis/	[noz ami]	"our friends"
Before a glide:	/pətit wazo/	[pətit wazo]	"small bird"
	/noz wazo/	[noz wazo]	"our birds"

> **A consonantal segment (obstruent, liquid, or nasal) is deleted or becomes null (→ Ø) in the environment (/) at the end of a word (___#) which is followed by a word beginning with an obstruent or liquid or nasal (# [+ consonantal]).**

or simply as

> **Delete a consonant before a word beginning with a consonant.**

In Schane's complete analysis, many words that are pronounced with a final consonant actually have a vowel as their word-final segment in phonemic representation. The vowel prevents the rule of word-final consonant deletion from applying. The vowel itself is deleted by another, later rule. Given this rule in the grammar of French, *petit* would be phonemically /petit/. It need not be additionally represented as /peti/, because the rule determines the phonetic shape of the word.

Deletion rules also show up as optional rules in fast speech or casual speech in English. They result, for example, in the common contractions changing *he is* [hi ɪz] to *he's* [hiz] or *I will* [aj wɪl] to *I'll* [ajl]. In ordinary everyday speech most of us also delete the unstressed vowels that are shown in bold type in words like the following:

mys**t**ery   gen**e**ral   mem**o**ry   fun**e**ral   vig**o**rous   Barb**a**ra

These words in casual speech sound as if they were written:

mystry   genral   memry   funral   vigrous   Barbra

Phonological rules therefore can be either optional or obligatory.

Phonological rules may also insert consonants or vowels, which is called **epenthesis**. In some cases, epenthesis occurs to "fix up" nonpermitted sequences. In English morphemes, nasal/nonnasal consonant clusters must be homorganic, both labial, both alveolar, or both velar. We find /m/ before /p/ and /b/ as in *ample* and *amble*; /n/ before /t/ and /d/, *gentle* and *gender;* and /ŋ/ before /k/ and /g/, *ankle* and *angle*. (You may not have realized that the nasal in the last two words has a velar articulation because the spelling can obscure this fact. If you pronounce these words carefully, you will see that the back of your tongue touches the velum in the articulation of both the *n* and the *k*.) /m/ before /t, d, k, g/ does not occur morpheme internally; nor does /n/ before /p, b, k, g/ nor /ŋ/ before /p, b, t, d/. Because of this sequential constraint, many speakers pronounce the name *Fromkin* with an epenthetic [p] as if it were written *Frompkin*. She also receives letters addressed in this way.

This same process of epenthesis occurred in the history of English. The earlier form of the word *empty* had no *p*. Similarly a /d/ was inserted in the word *ganra* giving us the modern *gander*.

In the history of Spanish, many words that now start with an *e* followed by an [s] followed by another consonant came from Latin words that were not vowel initial. For example, the Spanish word *escribir,* "to write" was *scribere* in Latin (the *sc* representing /sk/), and the Spanish word for "school" *escuela* comes from the Latin word *schola* through epenthesis.

Movement (Metathesis) Rules

Phonological rules may also move phonemes from one place in the string to another. Such rules are called **metathesis** rules. They are less common, but they do exist. In some dialects of English, for example, the word *ask* is pronounced [æks], but the word *asking* is pronounced [æskɪn] or [æskɪŋ]. In these dialects, a metathesis rule "switches" the /s/ and /k/ in certain contexts. In Old English the verb was *aksian,* with the /k/ preceding the /s/. A historical metathesis rule switched these two consonants, producing *ask* in most dialects of English. Children's speech shows many cases of metathesis (which are later corrected as the child approaches the adult grammar): *aminal* [æmənəl] for *animal* and *pusketti* [pʰəskɛti] for *spaghetti* are common children's pronunciations.

In Hebrew there is a metathesis rule that reverses a pronoun-final consonant with the first consonant of the following verb if the verb starts with a sibilant. These reversals are in "reflexive" verb forms, as shown in the following examples:

Nonsibilant-Initial Verbs		Sibilant-Initial Verbs	
kabel	"to accept"	*tsadek*	"to justify"
lehit-kabel	"to be accepted"	*lehits-tadek* (not **lehit-tsadek*)	"to apologize"
pater	"to fire"	*šameš*	"to use for"
lehit-pater	"to resign"	*lehiš-tameš* (not **lehit-šameš*)	"to use"
bayeš	"to shame"	*sader*	"to arrange"
lehit-bayeš	"to be ashamed"	*lehis-tader* (not **lehit-sader*)	"to arrange oneself"

We see, then, that phonological rules have a number of different functions, among which are the following:

1. **Change feature values** (vowel nasalization rule in English).
2. **Add new features** (aspiration in English).

3. **Delete segments** (final consonant deletion in French).
4. **Add segments** (vowel insertion in Spanish).
5. **Reorder segments** (metathesis rule in Hebrew).

These rules, when applied to the phonemic representations of words and phrases, result in phonetic forms that differ from the phonemic forms. If such differences were unpredictable, we would find it difficult to explain how we can understand what we hear or how we produce utterances that represent the meanings we wish to convey. The more we look at languages, however, the more we see that many aspects of the phonetic forms of utterances that appear at first to be irregular and unpredictable are actually rule-governed. We learn, or construct, these rules when we are learning the language as children. The rules represent "patterns," or general principles.

From One to Many and from Many to One

The discussion on how phonemic representations of utterances are realized phonetically included an example from the language Akan to show that the relationship between a phoneme and its allophonic realization may be complex. The same phone may be an allophone of two or more phonemes, as [m] was shown to be an allophone of both /b/ and /m/ in Akan.

We can also illustrate this complex mapping relationship in English. Consider the vowels in the following pairs of words:

	A		**B**	
/i/	compete	[i]	competition	[ə]
/ɪ/	medicinal	[ɪ]	medicine	[ə]
/e/	maintain	[e]	maintenance	[ə]
/ɛ/	telegraph	[ɛ]	telegraphy	[ə]
/æ/	analysis	[æ]	analytic	[ə]
/a/	solid	[a]	solidity	[ə]
/o/	phone	[o]	phonetic	[ə]
/u/	Talmudic	[u]	Talmud	[ə]

In column A all the bold-faced vowels are stressed vowels with a variety of different vowel phones; in column B all the bold-faced unstressed vowels are pronounced [ə]. How can one explain the fact that the same root morphemes that occur in both words of the pairs have different pronunciations?

In the chapter on morphology we defined a morpheme as a sound/meaning unit. Changing either would make a different morpheme. It doesn't seem plausible (nor is it necessary) for speakers of English to represent these root morphemes with distinct phonemic forms if there is some general rule that relates the stressed vowels in column A to the unstressed schwa vowel [ə] in column B.

Speakers of English know (unconsciously of course) that one can derive one word from another by the addition of derivational morphemes. This is illustrated above by adding *-ition* or *-ance* to verb roots to form nouns, or *-al* and *-ic* to nouns to form adjectives. In English the syllable that is stressed depends to a great extent on the phonemic structure of the word, the number of syllables, etc. In a number of cases, the addition of derivational suffixes changes the stress pattern of the word, and the vowel which was stressed in the root morpheme becomes unstressed in the derived form. (The stress rules are rather complex and will not be detailed in this introductory text.) When a vowel is unstressed in English it is pronounced as [ə], which is a **reduced vowel.**

All the root morphemes of column A are represented phonemically by their value when stressed. A simple rule predicts that their vowels are changed to [ə] when unstressed. We can conclude then that [ə] is an allophone of all English vowel phonemes. The rule to derive the schwa can be stated simply as:

Change a vowel to a [ə] when it is unstressed.

This rule is oversimplified because when an unstressed vowel occurs as the final segment of some words, it retains its full vowel quality, as shown in words like *confetti, motto,* or *democracy.* In some dialects, all unstressed vowels, including final vowels, are reduced.

The rule that reduces unstressed vowels to schwas is another example of a rule that changes feature values.

In a phonological description of a language that we do not know, it is not always possible to determine from the phonetic transcription what the phonemic representation is. However, given the phonemic representation and the phonological rules, we can always derive the correct phonetic transcription. Of course, in our internal mental grammars this derivation is no problem, because the words are listed phonemically and we know the rules of the language.

Reprinted by permission of Creator Syndicate, Inc.

Another example will illustrate this aspect of phonology. In English, /t/ and /d/ are both phonemes, as is illustrated by the minimal pairs *tie/die* and *bat/bad.* When /t/ or /d/ occurs between a stressed and an unstressed vowel they both become a flap [D].[9] For many speakers of English, *writer* and *rider* are pronounced identically as [rajDər]; yet these speakers know that *writer* has a phonemic /t/ because of *write* /rajt/, whereas *rider* has a phonemic /d/ because of *ride* /rajd/. The "flap rule" may be stated as:

An alveolar stop becomes a voiced flap when preceded by a stressed vowel and followed by an unstressed vowel.

The application of this rule is illustrated as follows:

Phonemic Representation	write /rajt/	writer /rajt + ər/ ↓	ride /rajd/	rider /rajd + ər/ ↓
Apply Rule	NA	D	NA	D
Phonetic Representation	[rajt]	[rajDər]	ride [rajd]	ride [rajDər]

NA means "not applicable."

We are omitting other phonetic details that are also determined by phonological rules, such as the fact that in *ride* the vowel is slightly longer than in *write* because it is followed by a voiced [d], which is a phonetic rule in many languages. We are using the example only to illustrate the fact that two distinct phonemes may be realized phonetically by the same phone.

Such cases show that we cannot arrive at a phonological analysis by simply inspecting the phonetic representation of utterances. If we just looked for minimal pairs as the only evidence for phonology, we would have to conclude that [D] is a phoneme in English because it contrasts phonetically with other phonetic units: *riper* [rajpər], *rhymer* [rãjmər], *riser* [rajzər], and so forth. The fact that *write* and *ride* change their phonetic forms when suffixes are added shows that there is an intricate mapping between phonemic representations of words and phonetic pronunciations.

Notice that in the case of the "schwa rule" and the "flap rule" the allophones derived from the different phonemes by rule are different in features from all other phonemes in the language. That is, there is no /D/ phoneme, but there is a [D] phone. This was also true of aspirated voiceless stops and nasalized vowels. The set of phones is larger than the set of phonemes.

The English "flap rule" also illustrates an important phonological process called **neutralization;** the voicing contrast between /t/ and /d/ is **neutralized** in the specified environment. That is, /t/ never contrasts with /d/ in the environment between a stressed and an unstressed vowel.

---

[9] The IPA symbol for the flap is [ɾ].

Similar rules showing there is no one-to-one relation between phonemes and phones are found in other languages. In both Russian and German, when voiced obstruents occur at the end of a word or syllable, they become voiceless. Both voiced and voiceless obstruents do occur in German as phonemes, as is shown by the following minimal pair:

Tier   [ti:r]   "animal"   *dir*   [di:r]   "to you"

At the end of a word, however, only [t] occurs; the words meaning "bundle" *Bund*[10] /bʊnd/ and "colorful" *bunt* /bʊnt/ are phonetically identical and pronounced [bʊ̃nt].

The German devoicing rule, like the vowel reduction rule in English and the homorganic nasal rule, changes the specifications of features. In German, the phonemic representation of the final stop in *Bund* is /d/, specified as [+ voiced]; it is changed by rule to [– voiced] to derive the phonetic [t] in word-final position.

This rule in German further illustrates that we cannot decide what the phonemic representation of a word is, given only the phonetic form; [bʊ̃nt] can be derived from either /bʊnd/ or /bʊnt/. However, given the phonemic representations and the rules of the language, the phonetic forms are automatically derived.

The Function of Phonological Rules

The function of the phonological rules in a grammar is to provide the phonetic information necessary for the pronunciation of utterances. We may illustrate this point in the following way:

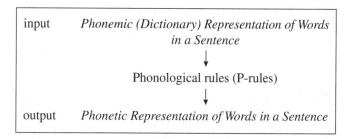

The input to the P-rules is the phonemic representation; the P-rules apply to or operate on the phonemic strings and produce as output the phonetic representation.

The application of rules in this way is called a **derivation.** We have given a number of examples of derivations that show how phonemically oral vowels become nasalized, how phonemically unaspirated voiceless stops become aspirated, how contrastive voiced and voiceless alveolar stops in English merge to become flaps, and how German voiced obstruents are devoiced. A derivation is thus an explicit way of showing both the effects of a phonological rule and the function of phonological rules (which we can abbreviate as P-rules) in a grammar.

All the examples of derivations we have so far considered show the applications of just one phonological rule. It must be the case, however, that more than one rule may apply to a word. For example, the word *tempest* is phonemically /tɛmpɛst/ (as shown

---

[10] In German, nouns are capitalized in written form.

by the pronunciation of *tempestuous* [tʰɛ̃mpʰɛsču̇əs]) but phonetically [tʰɛ̃mpəst]. Three rules apply to it: the aspiration rule, the vowel nasalization rule, and the schwa rule. We can derive the phonetic form from the phonemic representation as follows:

Underlying Phonemic Representation	/	t	ɛ	m	p	ɛ	s	t /
Aspiration Rule		tʰ						
Nasalization Rule			ɛ̃					
Schwa Rule						ə		
Surface Phonetic Representation	[	tʰ	ɛ̃	m	p	ə	s	t]

We are using phonetic symbols instead of matrices in which the feature values are changed. These derivatives are equivalent, however, as long as we understand that a phonetic symbol is a cover term representing a matrix with all distinctive features marked either + or − (unless, of course, the feature is nondistinctive, such as the nasality value for phonemic vowels in English).

Slips of the Tongue: Evidence for Phonological Rules

By permission of Johnny Hart and Creators Syndicate, Inc.

"Slips of the tongue" or "speech errors" in which we deviate in some way from the intended utterance show phonological rules in action. Some of these tongue slips are called **spoonerisms,** after William Archibald Spooner, a distinguished head of an Oxford College in the early 1900s who is reported to have referred to Queen Victoria as "That queer old dean" instead of "That dear old queen," and berated his class of students by saying, "You have hissed my mystery lecture. You have tasted the whole worm" instead of the intended "You have missed my history lecture. You have wasted the whole term." We all make speech errors, and they tell us interesting things about language and its use. Consider the following speech errors:

Intended Utterance	**Actual Utterance**
(1) gone to seed	god to seen
[gãn tə sid]	[gad tə sĩn]
(2) stick in the mud	smuck in the tid
[stɪk ˜ɪn ðə mʌd]	[smʌk ˜ɪn ðə tʰɪd]
(3) speech production	preach seduction
[spič prədʌkšə̃n]	[pʰrič sədʌkšə̃n]

In the first example, the final consonants of the first and third words were reversed. Notice that the reversal of the consonants also changed the nasality of the vowels. The vowel [ã] in the intended utterance is replaced by [a]; in the actual utterance the nasalization was lost because it no longer occurred before a nasal consonant. The vowel in the third word, which was the nonnasal [i] in the intended utterance, became [ĩ] in the error, because it was followed by /n/. The nasalization rule applied.

In the other two errors, we see the application of the aspiration rule. In the intended *stick,* the /t/ would have been realized as unaspirated because it follows the syllable initial /s/; when it was switched with the /m/ in *mud,* it was pronounced as the aspirated [tʰ], because it occurred initially. The third example also illustrates the application of the aspiration rule in performance.

THE PRONUNCIATION OF MORPHEMES

We noted that a single morpheme may have different pronunciations, that is, different phonetic forms, in different contexts. Thus *write* /rajt/ is pronounced [rajt] but is pronounced [rajDr̩] when the suffix *-er* is added.

We also saw that in French a morpheme such as /noz/ meaning "our" is pronounced [no] before words beginning with [+ consonantal] sounds and as [noz] before word-initial [– consonantal] sounds.

Furthermore, in English, **underlying** phonemic vowels "reduce" to schwa [ə] when they are unstressed. The particular phonetic forms of some morphemes are determined by regular phonological rules that refer only to the phonemic context, as is true of the alternate vowel forms of the following sets:

m[ɛ]l[ə]dy   h[a]rm[ə]ny   s[ɪ]mph[ə]ny
m[ə]l[o]dious   h[a]rm[o]nious   s[ɪ]mph[o]nious
m[ə]l[a]dic   h[a]rm[a]nic   s[ɪ]mph[a]nic

The vowel rules that determine these pronunciations are rather complicated and beyond the scope of this text. The examples are presented simply to show that the morphemes in "melody," "harmony," and "symphony" vary phonetically in these words.

Another example of a morpheme in English with different phonetic forms is the plural morpheme. In column A all the nouns end in voiced nonsibilant sounds; to form their plurals you add the voiced [z]. All the words in column B end in voiceless nonsibilant sounds, and you add a voiceless [s]. The words in C end in both voiced and voiceless sibilants, which form their plurals with the insertion of a schwa followed by [z]. This is another example of an epenthesis rule.The nouns in column D are irregular and the plural forms must be memorized.

A	B	C	D
cab	cap	bus	child
cad	cat	bush	ox
bag	back	buzz	mouse
love	cuff	garage	sheep
lathe	faith	match	criterion
cam		badge	
can			
bang			
call			
bar			
spa			
boy			

add [z]   **add [s]**   **add [əz]**

Children do not have to learn the plural rule by memorizing the individual sounds that require the [z] or [s] or [əz] plural ending, because these sounds form natural classes. A grammar that included lists of these sounds would not reveal the regularities in the language or what a speaker knows about the regular plural formation rule.

The regular plural rule does not work for a word like *child,* which in the plural is *children,* or for *ox,* which becomes *oxen,* or for *sheep,* which is unchanged phonologically in the plural. *Child, ox,* and *sheep* are exceptions to the regular rule. We learn these exceptional plurals when learning the language, often after we have constructed or discovered the regular rule, which occurs at a very early age. The late Harry Hoijer, a well-known anthropological linguist, used to play a game with his two-year-old daughter. He would say a noun and she would give him the plural form if he said the singular and the singular if she heard the plural. One day he said *ox* [aks] and she responded [ak], apparently not knowing the word and thinking that the [-s] at the end must be the plural suffix. Children also often "regularize" exceptional forms, saying *mouses* and *sheeps.*

If the grammar represented each unexceptional or regular word in both its singular and plural forms—for example, *cat* /kæt/, *cats* /kæts/; *cap* /kæp/, *caps* /kæps/; and so on—it would imply that the plurals of *cat* and *cap* were as irregular as the plurals of *child* and *ox.* Of course, they are not. If a new toy appeared on the market called a *glick* /glɪk/, a young child who wanted two of them would ask for two *glicks* /glɪks/ and not two *glicken,* even if the child had never heard the word *glicks.* The child knows the regular rule to form plurals. An experiment conducted by the linguist Jean Berko Gleason showed that very young children can apply this rule to words they never have heard previously. A grammar that describes such knowledge (the internalized mental grammar) must then include the general rule.

This rule, which determines the phonetic representation or pronunciation of the plural morpheme, is somewhat different from some of the other phonological rules we have discussed. The "aspiration rule" in English applies to a word whenever the phonological description is met; it is not the case, for example, that a /t/ is aspirated only if it is part of a particular morpheme, or only in nouns, or adjectives. The "flap rule" that changes the phonetic forms of the morphemes *write* and *ride* when a suffix is added is also completely automatic, depending solely on the phonological environment. The plural rule, however, applies only to the inflectional plural morpheme. To see that it is not purely phonological in nature, consider the following words:

race	[res]	ray	[re]	ray + pl.	[rez]	*[res]
sauce	[sɔs]	saw	[sɔ]	saw + pl.	[sɔz]	*[sɔs]
rice	[rajs]	rye	[raj]	rye + pl.	[rajz]	*[rajs]

The examples show that the [z] in the plural is not determined by the phonological context, because in an identical context an [s] occurs. It applies only to certain morphemes.

Morphophonemics

© 1981 Newspaper Enterprise Association, Inc.

The rule that determines the phonetic form of the plural morpheme is a **morphophonemic rule,** because its application is determined by both the morphology and the phonology. When a morpheme has alternate phonetic forms, these forms are called **allomorphs** by some linguists. [z], [s], and [əz] would be allomorphs of the regular plural morpheme, and determined by rule.

To show how such a rule may be applied, assume that the regular, productive, plural morpheme has the phonological form /z/, with the meaning "plural." The regular "plural rule" can be stated in two steps:

(a) **Insert a [ə] before the plural ending when a regular noun ends in a sibilant—/s/, /z/, /š/, /ž/, /č/, or /ǰ/.**

(b) **Change the voiced /z/ to voiceless [s] when it is preceded by a voiceless sound.**

If neither (a) nor (b) applies, then /z/ will be realized as [z]; no segments will be added and no features will be changed.

	bus + pl.	*butt* + pl.	*bug* + pl.
Phonemic Representation	/bʌs + z/	/bʌt + z/	/bʌg + z/
	↓		
apply rule (a)	ə	NA* ↓	NA
apply rule (b)	NA	s	NA
Phonetic Representation	[bʌsəz]	[bʌts]	[bʌgz]

*NA means "not applicable."

The plural-formation rule will derive the phonetic forms of plurals for all regular nouns (remember, this plural is /z/).

As we have formulated these rules, (a) must be applied before (b). If we applied the two parts of the rule in reverse order, we would derive incorrect phonetic forms:

Phonemic Representation	/bʌs + z/
	↓
apply rule (b)	↓ s
apply rule (a)	ə
Phonetic Representation	*[bʌsəs]

An examination of the rule for the formation of the past tense of verbs in English shows some interesting parallels with the plural formation of nouns.

A	**B**	**C**	**D**
grab	reap	state	is
hug	peak	raid	run
seethe	unearth		sing
love	huff		have
buzz	kiss		go
rouge	wish		hit
judge	pitch		
fan			
ram			
long			
kill			
care			
tie			
bow			
hoe			
add [d]	**add [t]**	**add [əd]**	

The productive regular past-tense morpheme in English is /d/, **phonemically**, but [d] (column A), [t] (column B), or [əd] (column C) **phonetically**, again depending on the final phoneme of the verb to which it is attached. D-column verbs are exceptions.

The past-tense rule in English, like the plural formation rule, must include morphological information. Notice that after a vowel or diphthong the form of the past tense is always [d], even though no phonological rule would be violated if a [t] were added, as shown by the words *tight, bout, rote.* When the word is a verb, and when the final alveolar represents the past-tense morpheme, however, it must be a voiced [d] and not a voiceless [t].

There is a plausible explanation for why a [ə] is inserted in the past tense of regular verbs ending with alveolar stops (and in nouns ending with sibilants). Because in English we do not contrast long and short consonants, it is difficult for English speakers to perceive a difference in consonantal length. If we added a [z] to *squeeze* we would get [skwizz], which would be hard for English speakers to distinguish from [skwiz]; similarly, if we added [d] to *load,* it would be [lodd] phonetically in the past and [lod] in the present, which would also be difficult to perceive.

More Sequential Constraints

Some of the sequential constraints on phonemes that were discussed previously may show up as morphophonemic rules. The English homorganic nasal constraint applies between some morphemes as well as within a morpheme. The negative prefix *in-,* which, like *un-,* means "not," has three allomorphs:

[ĭn]	before vowels:	inexcusable, inattentive, inorganic
	and alveolars:	intolerable, indefinable, insurmountable
[ĭm]	before labials:	impossible, imbalance
[ĭŋ]	before velars:	incomplete, inglorious

The pronunciation of this morpheme is often revealed by the spelling as *im-* when it is prefixed to morphemes beginning with /p/ or /b/. Because we have no letter "ŋ" in our alphabet (although it exists in alphabets used in other languages), the velar [ŋ] is written as *n* in words like *incomplete.* You may not realize that you pronounce the *n* in *inconceivable, inglorious, incongruous,* and other such words as [ŋ] because your homorganic nasal rule is as unconscious as other rules in your grammar. It is the job of linguists and phoneticians to bring such rules to consciousness or to reveal them as part of the grammar. If you say these words in normal tempo without pausing after the *in-,* you should feel the back of your tongue rise to touch the velum.

In Akan the negative morpheme also has three nasal allomorphs: [m] before /p/, [n] before /t/, and [ŋ] before /k/, as is shown in the following cases:

mɪ pɛ	"I like"	mɪ mpɛ	"I don't like"
mɪ tɪ	"I speak"	mɪ ntɪ	"I don't speak"
mɪ kɔ	"I go"	mɪ ŋkɔ	"I don't go"

We see, then, that one morpheme may have different phonetic forms or allomorphs. We have also seen that more than one morpheme may occur in the language with the same meaning but different forms—like *in-, un-,* and *not* (all meaning "not"). It is not possible to predict which of these forms will occur, so they are separate synonymous morphemes. It is only when the phonetic form is predictable by general rule that we find different phonetic forms of a single morpheme.

The nasal homorganic rule is a **feature-changing rule.** It can be stated simply as:

Change the place of articulation of a nasal consonant so that it agrees with the place feature value of a following consonant.

In other words, nasal consonants agree in place of articulation with a following consonant.

Given this rule, we can represent this *in-* negative prefix morpheme by the phonemic representation /ɪn/. Before vowels and before morphemes beginning with /t/ or /d/, the homorganic nasal rule will change nothing since the rule is not violated. The morpheme will be represented by the allomorph [ĩn](after the vowel nasalization rule applies) as, for example, in the words *indecision, interminable, inoperative.* Before a morpheme beginning with a labial consonant /b/ or /p/, the alveolar feature of /n/ will be changed by the rule to agree with the place of articulation of the labials, as in *impossible* and *impertinent.* Similarly, this feature-changing rule will assimilate the /n/ in /ɪn-/ to a velar nasal before morphemes beginning with /k/ or /g/ in words like *incoherent.*

Deriving all forms of the morpheme from /ɪn-/ is the simplest way of revealing this morphological/phonological knowledge. One could represent the morpheme as /ɪm-/ or /ɪŋ/ instead. But the rule would then have to be complicated.

> Change the place of articulation of a nasal consonant so that it agrees with the place feature value of a following consonant and change the nasal consonant to [n] before a vowel.

This will derive the correct forms of the morpheme but in a more complex fashion than is needed. Rule statements should be as simple and elegant as possible. This principle, known as *Occam's Razor*, applies not just in phonology but in all of science. In essence, the simpler the rule, the more general the explanation.

Thus, when two allophones can be derived from one phoneme, one selects as the underlying segment the allophone that makes the rules and the phonemic feature matrices as simple as possible. For example, deriving the unaspirated and aspirated voiceless stops in English from an underlying /p/ makes aspiration redundant and unnecessary as a phonemic feature value. If /pʰ/ were the phoneme, the phonemic features would be more complex.

In some cases different phonetic forms of the same morpheme may be derived by segment deletion rules, as in the following examples:

A		**B**	
sign	[sajn]	signature	[sɪgnəčər]
design	[dəzajn]	designation	[dɛzɪgnešən]
paradigm	[pʰærədajm]	paradigmatic	[pʰærədɪgmæDək]

In none of the words in column A is there a phonetic [g], but in each corresponding word in column B a [g] occurs. Our knowledge of English phonology accounts for these phonetic differences. The "[g]–no [g]" alternation is regular, and we apply it to words that we never have heard before. Suppose someone says:

"He was a salignant [səlɪgnə̃nt] man."

Even if you do not know what the word means, you might ask (perhaps to hide your ignorance):

"Why, did he salign [səlãjn] somebody?"

It is highly doubtful that a speaker of English would pronounce the verb form without the *-ant* as [səlɪgn], because the phonological rules of English would delete the /g/ when it occurred in this context. This rule might be stated as:

Delete a /g/ when it occurs before a final nasal consonant.[11]

Reprinted with special permission of North American Syndicate.

The rule is even more general, as evidenced by the pairs: *gnostic* [nostɪk] and *agnostic* [ægnastɪk] and the words *cognition, recognition, agnosia,* and others, all of which contain the same morpheme related to knowledge. It can be stated as:

Delete a /g/ when it occurs word initially before a nasal consonant or before a word-final nasal.

Given this rule, the phonemic representation of the stems in *sign/signature, design/designation, resign/resignation, repugn/repugnant, phlegm/phlegmatic, paradigm/paradigmatic, diaphragm/diaphragmatic, gnosis, agnosia, agnostic, recognition* will include a phonemic /g/ that will be deleted by the regular rule if a prefix or suffix is not added. By stating the class of sounds that follow the /g/ (nasal consonants) rather than any specific nasal consonant, the rule deletes the /g/ before both /m/ and /n/.

An alternate analysis is to represent the root morpheme *sign* as /sajn/. No /g/ would have to be deleted to derive the verb, but to derive the noun *signature* an insertion rule would be required and all the words that have a [g] in the derived words and no [g] in the roots would have to be listed. By representing the root morphemes with a phonemic /g/, the regular, automatic, nonexceptional rule of /g/ deletion stated above derives the correct forms and also reveals this phonotactic constraint in the language.

The phonological rules that delete whole segments, add segments and features, and change features also account for the various phonetic forms of some morphemes. This point can be further illustrated by the following words:

---

[11] The /g/ may be deleted under other circumstances as well, as indicated by its absence in *signing* and *signer.*

	A			**B**	
bomb	/bamb/	[bãm]	bombardier	/bambədir/	[bãmbədir]
iamb	/ajæmb/	[ajæm]	iambic	/ajæmbɪk/	[ajæmbək]
crumb	/krʌmb/	[kʰrʌm]	crumble	/krʌmbl/	[kʰrʌmbəl]

A speaker of English knows when to pronounce a /b/ and when not to. The relationship between the pronunciation of the A words and their B counterparts is regular and can be accounted for by the following rule:

Delete a word-final /b/ when it occurs after an /m/.

Notice that the underlying phonemic representation of the A and B stems is the same.

Phonemic Representation	/bamb/	/bamb + adir/	/bʌlb/
apply /b/ deletion rule	∅	NA	NA
unstressed vowel rule	NA	ə	NA
nasalization rule	ã	ã	NA
Phonetic Representation	[bãm]	[bãmbədir]	[bʌlb]

The rules that delete the segments are general phonological rules, but their application to phonemic representations results in deriving different phonetic forms of the same morpheme.

PHONOLOGICAL ANALYSIS: DISCOVERING PHONEMES

No one has to teach us, as children, how to discover the phonemes of our language. We do it unconsciously and at an early age know what they are. Before reading this book, or learning anything about phonology, you knew an *l* sound was part of the English sound system, a phoneme in English, because it contrasts words like *leaf* and *reef*. But you probably did not know that the *l* in *leaf* and the one in *feel* are two different sounds. There is only one /l/ phoneme in English, but more than one *l* phone. The /l/ that occurs before back vowels and at the end of words is produced not only as a lateral but with the back of the tongue raised toward the velum, and is therefore a *velarized l*. (Without more training in phonetics you may not hear the difference; try to sense the difference in your tongue position when you say *leaf, lint, lay, let* as opposed to *lude, load, lot, deal, dill, dell, doll.*)

The linguist from Mars, referred to in Chapter 3, who is trying to write a grammar of English, would have to decide whether the two *l* sounds observed in English words represent separate phonemes or are allophones of a single phoneme. How can this be done? How would any phonologist determine what the phonological system of a language is?

To do a phonemic analysis, the words to be analyzed must be transcribed in great phonetic detail since you don't know in advance which phonetic features are distinctive and which are not.

Consider the following Finnish words:

1. [kudot]	"failures"	5. [madon]	"of a worm"
2. [kate]	"cover"	6. [maton]	"of a rug"
3. [katot]	"roofs"	7. [ratas]	"wheel"
4. [kade]	"envious"	8. [radon]	"of a track"

Given these words, do the voiceless/voiced alveolar stops [t] and [d] represent different phonemes or are they allophones of the same phone?

Here are a few hints as to how a phonologist might proceed:

(1) Check to see if there are any minimal pairs.
(2) 2. and 4. are minimal pairs: [kate] "cover" and [kade] "envious"
    5. and 6. are minimal pairs: [madon] "of a worm" and [maton] "of a rug"
(3) [t] and [d] in Finnish thus represent the distinct phonemes /t/ and /d/.

That was an easy problem.

Now consider the data from Greek, concentrating on the following sounds, three of which do not occur in English:

[x]	voiceless velar fricative
[k]	voiceless velar stop
[c]	voiceless palatal stop
[ç]	voiceless palatal fricative

1. [kano]	"do"	9. [çeri]	"hand"
2. [xano]	"lose"	10. [kori]	"daughter"
3. [çino]	"pour"	11. [xori]	"dances"
4. [cino]	"move"	12. [xrima]	"money"
5. [kali]	"charms"	13. [krima]	"shame"
6. [xali]	"plaight"	14. [xufta]	"handful"
7. [çeli]	"eel"	15. [kufeta]	"bonbons"
8. [ceri]	"candle"	16. [oçi]	"no"

To determine the status of [x], [k], [c], and [ç], you should answer the following questions.

1. Are there are any minimal pairs in which these sounds contrast?
2. Are the sounds in complementary distribution?
3. If noncontrasting phones are found, what are the phonemes and their allophones?
4. What are the phonological rules by which the allophones can be derived?

1. By analyzing the data we find that [k] and [x] contrast in a number of minimal pairs, in for example [kano] and [xano]. [k] and [x] are therefore distinctive. [c] and [ç] also contrast in [çino] and [cino] and are therefore distinctive. But what about the velar fricative [x] and the palatal fricative [ç]? And the velar stop [k] and the palatal stop [c]?

We can find no minimal pairs that would conclusively show that these represent separate phonemes.

2. We now proceed to answer the second question: Are these phones in complementary distribution?

One way to see if sounds are in complementary distribution is to list each phone with the environment in which it is found as follows:

	before [a]	before [i]	before [e]	before [o]	before [u]	before [r]
[k]	yes	no	no	yes	yes	yes
[x]	yes	no	no	yes	yes	yes
[c]	no	yes	yes	no	no	no
[ç]	no	yes	yes	no	no	no

We see that [k] and [x] are not in complementary distribution; they both occur before back vowels. Nor are [c] and [ç] in complementary distribution. They both occur before front vowels. But the stops [k] and [c] are in complementary distribution; [k] occurs before back vowels and [r] and never before front vowels. [c] occurs only before front vowels and never before back vowels or [r]. Similarly, [x] and [ç] are in complementary distribution for the same reason. We therefore conclude that [k] and [c] are allophones of one phoneme and the fricatives [x] and [ç] are also allophones of one phoneme. The pairs of allophones also fulfill the criterion of phonetic similarity. The first two are [– anterior] stops; the second are [– anterior] fricatives.

3. Which phones should we select to represent these two phonemes? When two allophones can be derived from one phoneme, one selects as the underlying segment the allophone that makes the rules and the phonemic feature complexes as simple as possible, as we illustrated with the English unaspirated and aspirated voiceless stops.

In the case of the velar and palatal stops and fricatives in Greek, the rules appear to be equal in simplicity. In addition to the simplicity criterion, phonologists attempt to state rules that have natural phonetic explanations. Often these usually turn out to be the simplest solution. In many languages, velar sounds become palatal before front vowels. This is an assimilation rule; palatal sounds are produced toward the front of the mouth as are front vowels. Thus we select /k/ as a phoneme with the allophones [k] and [c], and /x/ as a phoneme with the allophones [x] and [ç].

4. We can now state the rule by which the palatals can be derived from the velars.

Palatalize velar consonants before front vowels.

Using feature notation we can state the rule as:

[+ velar] → [+ palatal] / ___ [– back]

Since only consonants are marked for the feature [velar] and only vowels for the feature [back], it is not necessary to include the feature [consonantal] or [syllabic] in the rule, or any other features that are not required to define the segments to which the rule applies, the change that occurs, or the segments in the environment in which the rule applies. The simplicity criterion constrains us to state the rule as simply as we can.

SUMMARY

Part of one's knowledge of a language is knowledge of the **phonology** or sound system of that language—the inventory of **phones,** the phonetic segments that occur in the language, and the ways in which they pattern. It is this patterning that determines the inventory of **phonemes**—the segments that differentiate words.

Phonetic segments are enclosed in square brackets, [ ], and phonemes between slashes, / /. When similar phones occur in **complementary distribution,** they are **allophones**—predictable phonetic variants—of phonemes. For example, in English, aspirated voiceless stops such as the initial sound in *pill* are in complementary distribution (never occur in the same phonological environment) as the unaspirated voiceless stops in words such as *spill.* Thus the aspirated [pʰ] and the unaspirated [p] are allophones of the phoneme /p/. This generalizes also to the voiceless stops /t/ and /k/. On the other hand, phones in the same environment that differentiate words, like the [b] and [m] in *boat* [bot] and *moat* [mot], represent two distinct phonemes, /b/ and /m/.

Some phones may be allophones of more than one phoneme. There is no one-to-one correspondence between the phonemes of a language and their allophones. In English, for example, stressed vowels become unstressed according to regular rules and ultimately reduce to schwa [ə], which is an allophone of each English vowel.

Phonological segments—phonemes and phones—are composed of **phonetic features** such as **voiced, nasal, labial,** and **continuant,** whose presence or absence is indicated by + or – signs. They distinguish one segment from another. When a phonetic feature causes a word contrast as **nasal** does in *boat* and *moat,* it is a **distinctive feature.** Thus, in English, the binary valued feature [± nasal] is a distinctive feature whereas [± aspiration] is not.

When two words (different forms with different meanings) are distinguished by a single phone occurring in the same position, they constitute a **minimal pair.** Some pairs, such as *boat* and *moat,* contrast by means of a single distinctive feature, in this case, [± nasal], where /b/ is [– nasal] and /m/ is [+ nasal]. Other minimal pairs may show sounds contrasting in more than one feature, for example, *dip* versus *sip,* where /d/, a voiced alveolar stop, is [+ voiced, – continuant] and /s/, a voiceless alveolar fricative, is [– voiced, + continuant]. Minimal pairs and sets also occur in sign languages: Signs may contrast by hand configuration, place of articulation, or movement.

Some sounds differ phonetically but are nonphonemic because they are in **free variation,** which means that either sound may occur in the identical environment without changing the meaning of the word. The glottal stop [ʔ] in English is in free variation with the [t] in words like *don't* or *bottle* and is therefore not a phoneme in English.

Phonetic features that are **predictable** are nondistinctive and **redundant.** The nasality of vowels in English is a redundant feature since all vowels are nasalized before nasal consonants. One can thus predict the + or – value of this feature in vowels. A feature may therefore be distinctive in one class of sounds and nondistinctive in another. Nasality is distinctive for English consonants, and nondistinctive predictable for English vowels.

Phonetic features that are **nondistinctive** in one language may be distinctive in another. Aspiration is distinctive in Thai and nondistinctive in English; both aspirated voiceless stops and unaspirated voiceless stops are phonemes in Thai.

The phonology of a language also includes constraints on the sequences of phonemes in the language, as exemplified by the fact that in English two stop consonants may not occur together at the beginning of a word; similarly, the final sound of the word *sing,* the velar nasal, never occurs word initially. These sequential constraints determine what are *possible* but nonoccurring words in a language, and what phonetic strings are "impossible" or "illegal." For example, *blick* [blɪk] is not now an English word but it could become one, whereas *kbli* [kbli] or *ngos* [ŋos] could not. These possible but nonoccurring words constitute **accidental gaps.**

Words in some languages may also be phonemically distinguished by **prosodic** or **suprasegmental** features, such as **pitch, stress,** and segment duration or **length.** Languages in which syllables or words are contrasted by pitch are called **tone** languages. **Intonation** languages may use pitch variations to distinguish meanings of phrases and sentences.

In English, words and phrases may be differentiated by **stress,** as in the contrast between the noun *pérvert* in which the first syllable is stressed, and the verb *pervért* in which the final syllable is stressed. In the compound noun *hótdog* versus the adjective + noun phrase *hot dóg,* the former is stressed on *hot,* the latter on *dog.*

Vowel **length** and consonant **length** may be phonemic features. Both are contrastive in Japanese, Finnish, Italian, and many other languages.

The relationship between the **phonemic representation** of words and sentences and the **phonetic representation** (the pronunciation of these words and sentences) is determined by **phonological rules.**

Phonological rules in a grammar apply to phonemic strings and alter them in various ways to derive their phonetic pronunciation:

1. They may be **assimilation rules** that change feature values of segments, thus spreading phonetic properties. The rule that nasalizes vowels in English before nasal consonants is such a rule.
2. They may be **dissimilation** rules that change feature values to make two phonemes in a string more dissimilar like the Latin liquid rule.
3. They may *add* **nondistinctive features** that are predictable from the context. The rule that aspirates voiceless stops at the beginning of words and syllables in English is such a rule.
4. They may *insert* segments that are not present in the phonemic string. Insertion is also called **epenthesis.** The historical rule in Spanish that inserted an [e] before word initial /s/ consonant clusters is an example of an addition or insertion rule.
5. They may *delete* phonemic segments in certain contexts. Contraction rules in English are **deletion** rules.
6. They may *transpose* or move segments in a string. These **metathesis** rules occur in many languages like Hebrew. The rule in certain American dialects that changes an /sk/ to [ks] in final position is also a metathesis rule.

Phonological rules often refer to entire classes of sounds rather than to individual sounds. These are **natural classes,** characterized by the phonetic features that pertain to all the members of a class such as voiced sounds, or, using +'s and –'s, the class specified as [+ voiced]. A natural class can be defined by fewer features than required to distinguish a member of that class. Natural classes reflect the ways in which we articulate sounds, or, in some cases, the acoustic characteristics of sounds. The occurrence of such classes, therefore, do not have to be learned in the same way as groups of sounds that are not phonetically similar. Natural classes provide explanations for the occurrence of many phonological rules.

In the writing of rules, one can use formal notations, which often reveal linguistic generalizations of phonological processes.

A morpheme may have different phonetic representations; these are determined by the **morphophonemic** and phonological rules of the language. Thus the regular plural morpheme is phonetically [z] or [s] or [əz], depending on the final phoneme of the noun to which it is attached.

There is a methodology that linguists (or students of linguistics) can use to discover the phonemes of a language, such as looking for minimal pairs and complementary distribution. The allophone of a phoneme that results in the simplest statement of the rules of distribution is selected as the underlying phoneme from which the phonetic allophones are derived. The underlying phoneme is selected from the allophone of that phoneme that results in the simplest statement of the rules of distribution, and the other allophones are derived from it via phonological rules.

The phonological and morphophonemic rules in a language show that the phonemic shape of words or phrases is not identical with their phonetic form. The phonemes are not the actual phonetic sounds, but are abstract mental constructs that are realized as sounds by the operation of rules such as those described above. No one is taught these rules, yet everyone knows them subconsciously.

References for Further Reading

Anderson, Stephen R. 1974. *The Organization of Phonology.* New York: Academic Press.

Anderson, S. R. 1985. *Phonology in the Twentieth Century: Theories of Rules and Theories of Representations.* Chicago: University of Chicago Press.

Chomsky, N., and M. Halle. 1968. *The Sound Pattern of English.* New York: Harper & Row.

Clark, John, and Colin Yallop. 1990. *An Introduction to Phonetics and Phonology.* Oxford, England: Basil Blackwell.

Clements, George N., and Samuel Jay Keyser. 1983. *CV Phonology: A Generative Theory of the Syllable.* Cambridge, MA: MIT Press.

Dell, François. 1980. *Generative Phonology.* London, England: Cambridge University Press.

Goldsmith, John A. 1990. *Autosegmental and Metrical Phonology.* Oxford, England: Basil Blackwell.

Hogg, Richard, and C. B. McCully. 1987. *Metrical Phonology: A Coursebook.* Cambridge, England: Cambridge University Press.

Hyman, Larry M. 1975. *Phonology: Theory and Analysis.* New York: Holt, Rinehart & Winston.

Kenstowicz, Michael J. 1993. *Phonology in Generative Grammar.* Oxford, England: Blackwell.

Kenstowicz, Michael, and Charles Kisseberth. 1979. *Generative Phonology: Description and Theory.* New York: Academic Press.

van der Hulst, Harry, and Norval Smith, eds. 1982. *The Structure of Phonological Representations: Part 1.* Dordrecht, Netherlands: Foris Publications.

EXERCISES

All the data in languages other than English are given in phonetic transcription without square brackets unless otherwise stated. The phonetic transcriptions of English words are given within square brackets.

1. The following sets of minimal pairs show that English /p/ and /b/ contrast in initial, medial, and final positions.

Initial	*Medial*	*Final*
pit/bit	rapid/rabid	cap/cab

   Find similar sets of minimal pairs for each pair of consonants given:

   a. /k/–/g/   _____

   b. /m/–/n/   _____

   c. /l/–/r/   _____

   d. /b/–/v/   _____

   e. /b/–/m/   _____

   f. /p/–/f/   _____

   g. /s/–/š/   _____

   h. /č/–/ǰ/   _____

   i. /s/–/z/   _____

2. A young patient at the Radcliffe Infirmary in Oxford, England, following a head injury, appears to have lost the spelling-to-pronunciation and pronunciation-to-spelling rules that most of us can use to read and write new words or nonsense strings. He also is unable to get to the phonemic representation of words in his lexicon. Consider the following examples of his reading pronunciation and his writing from dictation.

Stimulus	Reading Pronunciation	Writing from Dictation
fame	/fæmi/	FAM
café	/sæfi/	KAFA
time	/tajmi/	TIM
note	/noti/ or /nɔti/	NOT
praise	/pra-aj-si/	PRAZ
treat	/tri-æt/	TRET
goes	/go-ɛs/	GOZ
float	/flɔ-æt/	FLOT

   His reading and writing errors are not random, but rule-governed. See if you can figure out the rules he uses to relate his (spelling) orthography to his pronunciation.

3. Consider the distribution of [r] and [l] in Korean in the following words:

[ɯ] is a high back unrounded vowel. It does not affect your analysis in this problem.

rupi	"ruby"	mul	"water"
kiri	"road"	pal	"big"
saram	"person"	səul	"Seoul"
irɯmi	"name"	ilkop	"seven"
ratio	"radio"	ipalsa	"barber"

Are [r] and [l] allophones of one or two phonemes?

a. Do they occur in any minimal pairs?
b. Are they in complementary distribution?
c. In what environments does each occur?
d. If you conclude that they are allophones of one phoneme, state the rule that can derive the phonetic allophonic forms.

4. Here are some additional data from Korean:

son	"hand"	šihap	"game"
sɔm	"sack"	šilsu	"mistake"
sosəal	"novel"	šipsam	"thirteen"
sɛk	"color"	šinho	"signal"
us	"upper"	maši	"delicious"

Are [s] and [š] allophones of the same phoneme or is each an allophone of a separate phoneme?

There are no minimal pairs that will help to answer this question. Determine, instead, whether they are in complementary distribution. If they are, state their distribution. If they are not in complementary distribution, state the contrasting environment.

5. In Southern Kongo, a Bantu language spoken in Angola, the nonpalatal segments [t, s, z] are in complementary distribution with their palatal counterparts [č, š, ž], as shown in the following words:

tobola	"to bore a hole"	čina	"to cut"
tanu	"five"	čiba	"banana"
kesoka	"to be cut"	nkoši	"lion"
kasu	"emaciation"	nselele	"termite"
kunezulu	"heaven"	ažimola	"alms"
nzwetu	"our"	lolonži	"to wash house"
zevo	"then"	zenga	"to cut"
žima	"to stretch"		

a. State the distribution of each pair of segments given below. (Assume that the nonoccurrence of [t] before [e] is an **accidental gap**.)

Example: [t]—[č]: [t] occurs before the back vowels [o, a, u];
[č] occurs before [i].

[s]—[š]
[z]—[ž]

b. Using the criteria of simplicity and naturalness discussed in the chapter, state which phones should be used as the basic phoneme for each pair of nonpalatal and palatal segments in Southern Kongo.

c. Using the rules stated in the chapter as examples (phonological rules for Southern Kongo were not given), state in your own words, the **one** phonological rule that will derive all the phonetic segments from the phonemes. Do not state a separate rule for each phoneme; a general rule can be stated that will apply to all three phonemes you listed in b.

6. In some dialects of English the following words have different vowels, as is shown by the phonetic transcriptions.

A		**B**		**C**	
bite	[bʌjt]	bide	[bajd]	die	[daj]
rice	[rʌjs]	rise	[rajz]	by	[baj]
ripe	[rʌjp]	bribe	[brajb]	sigh	[saj]
wife	[wʌjf]	wives	[wajvz]	rye	[raj]
dike	[dʌjk]	dime	[dajm]	guy	[gaj]
		nine	[najn]		
		rile	[rajl]		
		dire	[dajr]		
		writhe	[rajð]		

a. How may the classes of sounds that end the words in columns A and B be characterized? That is, what feature specifies all the final segments in A and all the final segments in B?

b. How do the words in column C differ from those in columns A and B?

c. Are [ʌj] and [aj] in complementary distribution? Give your reasons.

d. If [ʌj] and [aj] are allophones of one phoneme, should they be derived from /ʌj/ or /aj/? Why?

e. Give the phonetic representations of the following words as would be spoken in the dialect described here:

life _____ lives _____ lie _____

file _____ bike _____ lice _____

f. Formulate a rule that will relate the phonemic representations to the phonetic representations of the words given above.

7. Pairs like *top* and *chop, dunk* and *junk, so* and *show* reveal that /t/ and /č/, /d/ and /ĵ/, and /s/ and /š/ are distinct phonemes in English. Although it is

difficult to find a minimal pair to distinguish /z/ and /ž/, they occur in similar if not identical environments, such as *razor* and *azure*. Consider these same pairs of nonpalatalized and palatalized consonants in the following data. (The palatal forms are optional forms that often occur in casual speech.)

Nonpalatalized		Palatalized	
[hɪt mi]	"hit me"	[hɪč ju]	"hit you"
[lid hĭm]	"lead him"	[liǰ ju]	"lead you"
[pʰæs ʌs]	"pass us"	[pʰæš ju]	"pass you"
[luz ðɛm]	"lose them"	[luž ju]	"lose you"

Formulate the rule that specifies when /t/, /d/, /s/, and /z/ become palatalized as [č], [ǰ], [š], and [ž]. Restate the rule using feature notations. Does the formal statement reveal the generalizations?

8. Here are some Japanese words in phonetic transcription. [č] is the voiceless palatal affricate that occurs in the English word *church*. [ts] is an alveolar affricate and should be taken as a *single* symbol. It is pronounced as the final sound(s) in *cats*. Japanese words (except for certain loan words) never contain the phonetic sequences *[ti] or *[tu].

tatami	"mat"	tomodači	"friend"	uči	"house"
tegami	"letter"	totemo	"very"	otoko	"male"
čiči	"father"	tsukue	"desk"	tetsudau	"help"
šita	"under"	ato	"later"	matsu	"wait"
natsu	"summer"	tsutsumu	"wrap"	čizu	"map"
kata	"person"	tatemono	"building"	te	"hand"

a. Based on these data, are [t], [č], and [ts] in complementary distribution?

b. State the distribution—first in words, then using features—of these phones.

c. Give a phonemic analysis of these data insofar as [t], [č], and [ts] are concerned. That is, identify the phonemes, and the allophones.

d. Give the phonemic representation of the phonetically transcribed Japanese words given below. Assume phonemic and phonetic representations are the same except for [t], [č], and [ts].

tatami_____	tsukue _____	tsutsumu_____
tomodači _____	tetsudau _____	čizu_____
uči _____	šita _____	kata_____
tegami _____	ato_____	koto _____
totemo _____	matsu _____	tatemono _____
otoko _____	deguši _____	te _____
hiči _____	natsu _____	tsuri _____

9. The following words are found in Paku, a language spoken by the Pakuni in the NBC television series *Land of the Lost* (a language that was created by V. Fromkin). V́ = a stressed vowel ([+ stress])

a.	ótu	"evil" (N)	h.	mpósa	"hairless"
b.	túsa	"evil" (Adj)	i.	ãmpo	"hairless one"
c.	etógo	"cactus" (sg)	j.	ãmpõni	"hairless ones"
d.	etogõni	"cactus" (pl)	k.	ãmi	"mother"
e.	Páku	"Paku" (sg)	l.	ãmĩni	"mothers"
f.	Pakũni	"Paku" (pl)	m.	áda	"father"
g.	épo	"hair"	n.	adãni	"fathers"

(1) Is stress predictable? If so, what is the rule?

(2) Is nasalization a distinctive feature for vowels? Give the reasons for your answer.

10. Consider the following English verbs. Those in column A have stress on the next-to-last syllable (called the penultimate), whereas the verbs in column B and C have their last syllable stressed.

A	**B**	**C**
astónish	collápse	afláme
éxit	exíst	uncóuth
imágine	resént	surpríse
cáncel	revólt	combíne
elícit	adópt	recáll
práctice	insíst	atóne

a. Transcribe the words under A, B, and C phonemically. (Use a schwa for the unstressed vowels even if they can be derived from different phonemic vowels. This should make it easier for you.)

e.g., *astonish* /əstanɪš/, *collapse* /kəlæps/, *aflame* /əflem/

b. Consider the phonemic structure of the stressed syllables in these verbs. What is the difference between the final syllables of the verbs in columns A and B? Formulate a rule that predicts where stress occurs in the verbs in columns A and B.

c. In the verbs in column C, stress also occurs on the final syllable. What must you add to the rule to account for this fact? (Hint: For the forms in columns A and B, the final consonants had to be considered; for the forms in column C, consider the vowels.)

11. Below are listed the phonetic transcriptions of ten "words." Some are English words, some are not words now but are possible words or nonsense words, and others are definitely "foreign" (they violate English sequential constraints).

Write the English words in regular spelling. Mark the other words "foreign" or "possible." For each word you mark as "foreign," state your reason.

	Word	Possible	"Foreign"	Reason
Example:				
[θrot]	throat			
[slig]		X		
[lsig]			X	No English word can begin with a liquid followed by an obstruent.

	Word	Possible	"Foreign"	Reason
a. [pʰril]				
b. [skrič]				
c. [know]				
d. [maj]				
e. [gnostɪk]				
f. [jũnəkɔrn]				
g. [fruit]				
h. [blaft]				
i. [ŋar]				
j. [æpəpʰlɛksi]				

12. Consider these phonetic forms of Hebrew words:

[v]–[b]		[f]–[p]	
bika	"lamented"	litef	"stroked"
mugbal	"limited"	sefer	"book"
šavar	"broke" (masc.)	sataf	"washed"
šavra	"broke" (fem.)	para	"cow"
ʔikev	"delayed"	mitpaxat	"handkerchief"
bara	"created"	haʔalpim	"the Alps"

Assume that these words and their phonetic sequences are representative of what may occur in Hebrew. In your answers below, consider classes of sounds rather than individual sounds.

a. Are [b] and [v] allophones of one phoneme? Are they in complementary distribution? In what phonetic environments do they occur? Can you formulate a phonological rule stating their distribution?

b. Does the same rule, or lack of a rule, that describes the distribution of [b] and [v] apply to [p] and [f]? If not, why not?

c. Here is a word with one phone missing. A blank appears in place of the missing sound: hid___ik.

Check the one correct statement.

(1) [b] but not [v] could occur in the empty slot.   ( )

(2) [v] but not [b] could occur in the empty slot.   ( )

(3) Either [b] or [v] could occur in the empty slot.   ( )

(4) Neither [b] nor [v] could occur in the empty slot.   ( )

d. Which one of the following statements is correct about the incomplete word ___ana?

(1) [f] but not [p] could occur in the empty slot.   ( )

(2) [p] but not [f] could occur in the empty slot.   ( )

(3) Either [p] or [f] could fill the blank.   ( )

(4) Neither [p] nor [f] could fill the blank.   ( )

e. Now consider the following possible words (in phonetic transcription):

laval   surva   labal   palar   falu   razif

If these words actually occurred in Hebrew, would they:

(1) Force you to revise the conclusions about the distribution of labial stops and fricatives you reached on the basis of the first group of words given above?   ( )

(2) Support your original conclusions?   ( )

(3) Neither support nor disprove your original conclusions?   ( )

13. In the African language Maninka, the suffix *-li* has more than one pronunciation (like the *-ed* past tense ending on English verbs, as in *reaped* [t], *robbed* [d], and *raided* [əd]). This suffix is similar to the derivational suffix *-ing,* which, when added to the verb *cook,* makes it a noun as in "Her cooking was great," or the suffix *-ion,* which also derives a verb from a noun as in *create + ion.*

Consider these data from Maninka:

bugo	"hit"	bugoli	"hitting"
dila	"repair"	dilali	"repairing"
don	"come in"	donni	"coming in"
dumu	"eat"	dumuni	"eating"
gwen	"chase"	gwenni	"chasing"

a. What are the two forms of the "ing" morpheme?

(1) _____ (2) _____

b. Can you predict which phonetic form will occur? If so, state the rule.

c. What are the "-ing" forms for the following verbs?

da   "lie down" _____   famu   "understand" _____

men   "hear"_____   sunogo   "sleep" _____

14. Consider the following phonetic data from the Bantu language Luganda. (The data have been somewhat altered to make the problem easier.) In each line, the same root or stem morpheme occurs in both columns A and B, but it has one prefix in column A, meaning "a" or "an," and another prefix in column B, meaning "little."

A		**B**	
ẽnato	"a canoe"	akaato	"little canoe"
ẽnapo	"a house"	akaapo	"little house"
ẽnobi	"an animal"	akaoobi	"little animal"
ẽmpipi	"a kidney"	akapipi	"little kidney"
ẽŋkoosa	"a feather"	akakoosa	"little feather"
ẽmmāãmmo	"a peg"	akabāãmmo	"little peg"
ẽnnõõmme	"a horn"	akagõõmme	"little horn"
ẽnnĩmiro	"a garden"	akadĩmiro	"little garden"
ẽnugẽni	"a stranger"	akatabi	"little branch"

In answering the following questions, base your answers on only these forms. Assume that all the words in the language follow the regularities shown here.

You may need to use scratch paper to work out your analysis before writing your answers in the space provided. (Hint: The phonemic representation of the morpheme meaning "little" is /aka/.)

a. Are nasal vowels in Luganda phonemic?

   Are they predictable?

b. Is the phonemic representation of the morpheme meaning "garden" /dimiro/?

c. What is the phonemic representation of the morpheme meaning "canoe"?

d. Are [p] and [b] allophones of one phoneme?

e. If /am/ represents a bound prefix morpheme in Luganda, can you conclude that [amdano] is a possible phonetic form for a word in this language starting with this prefix?

f. Is there a phonological homorganic nasal rule in Luganda?

g. If the phonetic representation of the word meaning "little boy" is [akapoobe], give the phonemic and phonetic representations for "a boy."

   Phonemic_____ Phonetic _____

h. Which of the following forms is the phonemic representation for the prefix meaning "a" or "an"?

   (1) /en/   (2) /ẽn/   (3) /ẽm/   (4) /em/   (5) /eŋ/

i. What is the **phonetic** representation of the word meaning "a branch"?

j. What is the **phonemic** representation of the word meaning "little stranger"?

k. State in general terms any phonological rules revealed by the Luganda data.

15. Here are some Japanese verb forms given in phonetic symbols rather than in the Japanese orthography. They represent two different styles (informal and formal) of present-tense verbs. Morphemes are separated by +.

Gloss	Informal	Formal
"call"	yob + u	yob + imasu
"write"	kak + u	kak + imasu
"eat"	tabe + ru	tabe + masu
"see"	mi + ru	mi + masu
"leave"	de + ru	de + masu
"go out"	dekake + ru	dekake + masu
"die"	šin + u	šin + imasu
"close"	šime + ru	šime + masu
"swindle"	kata + ru	kata + masu
"wear"	ki + ru	ki + masu
"read"	yom + u	yom + imasu
"lend"	kas + u	kaš + imasu
"wait"	mats + u	matš + imasu
"press"	os + u	oš + imasu
"apply"	ate + ru	ate + masu
"drop"	otos + u	otoš + imasu
"have"	mots + u	motš + imasu
"win"	kats + u	katš + imasu
"steal a lover"	neto + ru	neto + masu

a. List each of the Japanese verb roots in their phonemic representations.

b. Formulate the rule that accounts for the different phonetic forms of these verb roots.

c. There is more than one allomorph for the suffix designating formality and more than one for the suffix designating informality. List the allomorphs of each. Formulate the rule or rules for their distribution.

PART 3

The Psychology of Language

The field of psycholinguistics, or the psychology of language, is concerned with discovering the psychological processes that make it possible for humans to acquire and use language.

Jean Berko Gleason and Nan Bernstein Ratner,
Psycholinguistics (1993)

Chapter 8
Language Acquisition

The acquisition of language "is doubtless the greatest intellectual feat any one of us is ever required to perform."

Leonard Bloomfield, *Language* (1933)

The capacity to learn language is deeply ingrained in us as a species, just as the capacity to walk, to grasp objects, to recognize faces. We don't find any serious differences in children growing up in congested urban slums, in isolated mountain villages, or in privileged suburban villas.

Dan Slobin, *The Human Language Series.2* (1994)

Copyright © by Gail Machlin.

Every aspect of language is extremely complex; yet very young children—before the age of five—already know most of the intricate system we have been calling the grammar of a language. Before they can add 2 + 2, children are conjoining sentences, asking questions, selecting appropriate pronouns, negating sentences, forming relative clauses, and using the syntactic, phonological, morphological, and semantic rules of the grammar.

A normal human being can go through life without learning to read or write. Millions of people in the world today do. These same millions all speak and understand and can discuss as complex and abstract ideas as literate speakers can. Learning a language and learning to read and write are different. Similarly, millions of humans never learn algebra or chemistry or how to use a computer. They must be taught these skills or systems, but they do not have to be taught to walk or to talk. In fact, "We are designed to walk. . . . That we are taught to walk is impossible. And pretty much the same is true of language. Nobody's taught language. In fact you can't prevent the child from learning it."[1]

The study of the nature of human language itself has revealed a great deal about language acquisition, about what the child does and does not do when learning or acquiring a language.

1. Children do not learn a language by storing all the words and all the sentences in some giant mental dictionary. The list of words is finite, but no dictionary can hold all the sentences, which are infinite in number.
2. Children learn to construct sentences, most of which they have never produced before.
3. Children learn to understand sentences they have never heard before. They cannot do so by matching the heard utterance with some stored sentence.
4. Children must therefore construct the "rules" that permit them to use their language creatively.
5. No one teaches them these rules. Their parents are no more aware of the phonological, morphological, syntactic, and semantic rules than are the children.

Even if you remember your early years, you will not remember anyone telling you to form a sentence by adding a verb phrase to a noun phrase, or to add [s] or [z] to form plurals. Children, then, seem to act like efficient linguists equipped with a perfect theory of language, and they use this theory to construct the grammar of the language they hear.

In addition to acquiring the complex rules of the grammar (gaining linguistic competence), children also learn pragmatics, the appropriate social use of language, what certain scholars have called **communicative competence.** These rules include, for example, the greetings that are to be used, the "taboo" words, the polite forms of address, the various styles that are appropriate to different situations, and so forth.

STAGES IN LANGUAGE ACQUISITION

. . . for I was no longer a speechless infant; but a speaking boy. This I remember; and have since observed how I learned to speak. It was not that my elders taught me words . . . in any set method; but I . . . did myself . . . practice the

---

[1] N. Chomsky. 1994. In *The Human Language Series.2.* Gene Searchinger. New York: Equinox Films/Ways of Knowing, Inc.

> sounds in my memory. . . . And thus by constantly hearing words, as they occurred in various sentences . . . I thereby gave utterance to my will.
>
> St. Augustine (transl. F. J. Sheed, 1944), *Confessions* (circa 400 C.E.)

Children do not wake up one morning with a fully formed grammar in their heads or with knowledge of social and communicative intercourse. Linguistic competence develops by stages, and, it is suggested, each successive stage more closely approximates the grammar of the adult language. Observations of children in different language areas of the world reveal that the stages are similar, possibly universal. Some of the stages last for a short time; others remain longer. Some stages may overlap for a short period, though the transition between stages is often sudden.

Given the universal aspects of all human languages, signed and spoken, it is not surprising that deaf children of deaf signing parents parallel the stages of spoken language acquisition in their signing development.

The earliest studies of child language acquisition come from diaries kept by parents. More recent studies include the use of tape recordings, videotapes, and controlled experiments. Spontaneous utterances of children are recorded, and in addition various elicitation techniques have been developed so that the child's production and comprehension can be scientifically studied.

The First Sounds

> An infant crying in the night:
> An infant crying for the light:
> And with no language but a cry.
>
> Alfred Lord Tennyson, "In Memoriam H.H.S."

The stages of language acquisition can be divided into prelinguistic and linguistic stages. Most scholars agree that the earliest cries, whimpers, and cooing noises of the newborn, or neonate, cannot be considered early language. Such noises are completely stimulus controlled; they are the child's involuntary responses to hunger, discomfort, the desire to be cuddled, or the feeling of well-being. A major difference between human language and the communication systems of other species is that human language is creative, as discussed earlier, in the sense of being free from either external or internal stimuli. The child's first noises are, however, simply responses to stimuli.

During the earliest period, the noises produced by infants in all language communities sound the same.

The early view that the neonate is born with a mind that is like a blank slate is countered by the evidence showing that infants are highly sensitive to certain subtle distinctions in their environment and not to others. That is, the mind appears to be "prewired" to receive only certain kinds of information.

By using a specially designed nipple with a pressure-sensitive device that records sucking rate, it has been found that infants will increase their sucking rate when stimuli (visual or auditory) presented to them are varied, but will decrease the sucking rate when the same stimuli are presented over and over again. Experiments have shown that infants will respond to visual depth and distance distinctions, to differences between rigid versus flexible physical properties of objects, and to human faces rather than to other visual stimuli.

Similarly, newborn infants respond to phonetic contrasts found in some human languages even when these differences are not phonemic in the language spoken in the baby's home. A baby hearing a human voice over a loudspeaker saying [pa] [pa] [pa] will slowly decrease her rate of sucking; if the sound changes to [ba] or even [pʰa], the sucking rate increases dramatically. Controlled experiments show that adults find it difficult to differentiate between the allophones of one phoneme, but for infants it is a "piece of cake." Japanese infants can distinguish between [r] and [l] while their parents cannot; babies can hear the difference between aspirated and unaspirated stops even if students in an introductory linguistics course can't. Babies can discriminate between sounds that are phonemic in other languages and nonexistent in the language of their parents. For example, in Hindi, there is a phonemic contrast between a retroflex [ʈ] and the alveolar [t]. To English-speaking adults, these sound the same; to their infants, they don't.

However, babies will not respond to sound signals that never signal phonemic contrasts in any human language, such as sounds that are intermediate between say [pa] and [ba].

Furthermore, as we learned in the chapter on phonetics, a vowel that we perceive as [i] or [u] or [a] is a different physical sound when produced by a male, female, or child. Yet, babies ignore the nonlinguistic aspects of the speech signal just as we do. An [i] is an [i] is an [i] to an infant even if the physical sound is different. They do not increase their sucking rate when after hearing many [i]s spoken by a male, they then hear an [i] spoken by a female. Yet, speech communication engineers are still having difficulty programming computers to recognize these different signals as the "same."

The infants could not have learned to perceive the phonetic distinctions and ignore other nonlinguistic differences; they seem to be born with the ability to perceive just those sounds that are phonemic in some language. This partially accounts for the fact that children can learn any human language to which they are exposed. Children have the sensory and motor abilities to produce and comprehend speech, even in the period of life before language acquisition occurs.

From around six months, babies begin to lose the ability to discriminate between sounds that are not phonemic in their language. Japanese infants can no longer hear the difference between [r] and [l], which do not contrast in Japanese, whereas babies in English-speaking homes retain this perception. They have begun to learn the sounds of the language of their parents. Before that, they appear to know the sounds of human language in general.

Babbling

In the first few months, usually around the sixth month, the infant begins to **babble.** The sounds produced in this period (apart from the continuing stimulus-controlled cries and gurgles) seem to include a large variety of sounds, many of which do not occur in the language of the household.

One view suggests that it is during this period that children are learning to distinguish between the sounds of their language and the sounds that are not part of the language. During the babbling period children learn to maintain the "right" sounds and suppress the "wrong" ones. Babbling, however, does not seem to be a prerequisite for language acquisition. Infants who are unable to produce any sounds at this early stage due to physical motor problems begin to talk properly once the disability has been corrected.

It was once thought that deaf infants produced babbling sounds similar to those of normal children. This would suggest that the sounds produced do not depend on the presence of auditory input or that they are a first stage in language acquisition.

Recently, studies of vocal babbling of hearing children and manual babbling of deaf children conducted by Laura Petitto[2] and her colleagues of McGill University suggest that babbling is a specifically linguistic ability related to the kind of language input the child receives. She reports that infants from four to seven months produce a restricted set of phonetic forms, vocally, if exposed to spoken languages, and manually if exposed to signed language, drawn from the set of possible sounds and possible gestures found in spoken and signed languages.

Babbling illustrates the sensitivity of the human mind to respond to linguistic cues from a very early stage. This is dramatically demonstrated in Petitto's studies. During the babbling stage of hearing infants, the pitch, or intonation contours, produced by them begin to resemble the intonation contours of sentences spoken by adults. The semantically different intonation contours are among the first linguistic contrasts that children perceive and produce.

During this same period, the vocalizations produced by deaf babies are qualitatively different from those produced by hearing infants; they are unsystematic, nonrepetitive, and random. In parallel, the manual gestures produced by hearing babies differ greatly from those produced by deaf infants exposed to sign language. The hearing babies move their fingers and clench their fists randomly with little or no repetition of the same gestures; the deaf infants, however, use more than a dozen different hand motions repetitively, all of which are elements of American Sign Language, or the other sign languages used by deaf communities in all countries.

Petitto's view is that humans are born with a predisposition to discover the units that serve to express linguistic meanings, and that at a genetically specified stage in neural development, the infant will begin to produce these units, sounds or gestures, depending on the language input the baby receives. Thus she suggests babbling is the earliest stage in language acquisition, in opposition to the earlier view that babbling was prelinguistic and simply neuromuscular in origin.

First Words

> From this golden egg a man, Prajapati, was born. . . . A year having passed,
> he wanted to speak. He said bhur and the earth was created. He said bhuvar

---

2 L. A. Petitto and P. F. Marantette. 1991. "Babbling in the Manual Mode: Evidence for the Ontogeny of Language," *Science* 251: pp. 1493–96.

and the space of the air was created. He said suvar and the sky was created. That is why a child wants to speak after a year. . . . When Prajapati spoke for the first time, he uttered one or two syllables. That is why a child utters one or two syllables when he speaks for the first time.

Hindu Myth

Copyright © 1983, 1984 by Chronicle Features.

Sometime after one year children begin to use the same string of sounds repeatedly to mean the same thing. This is an amazing feat. How do they discover where one word begins and another one ends? They must start out like the dog Ginger in the cartoon, who hasn't the foggiest idea of what is being said. But unlike dogs, infants in a relatively short time figure it out. When they do this varies from child to child and has nothing to do with how intelligent the child is: It is reported that Einstein did not start to speak until three or four. By this time, children have learned that sounds are related to meanings, and they are producing their first words. Most children seem to go through the one word = one sentence stage. These one-word "sentences" are called **holophrastic** sentences (from *holo* "complete" or "undivided" and *phrase* "phrase" or "sentence").

One child, J. P., illustrates how much the young child has learned even before the age of two years. J. P.'s words of April 1977, at the age of sixteen months, were as follows:[3]

[ʔaw]	"not" "no" "don't"	[s:]	"aerosol spray"
[bʌʔ]/[mʌʔ]	"up"	[sʲu:]	"shoe"
[da]	"dog"	[haj]	"hi"
[iʔo]/[siʔo]	"Cheerios"	[sr]	"shirt" "sweater"
[sa]	"sock"	[sæ:]/[əsæ:]	"what's that?" "hey, look!"
[aj]/[ʌj]	"light"	[ma]	"mommy"
[baw]/[daw]	"down"	[dæ]	"daddy"

J. P.'s mother reports that before April he also had used the words [bʊ] for "book," [ki] for "kitty," and [tsi] for "tree" but seemed to have "lost" them.

What is more interesting than merely the list of J. P.'s vocabulary is the way he used these words. "Up" was originally restricted to mean "Get me up" when he was either on the floor or in his high chair, but later was used to mean "Get up!" to his mother as well. J. P. used his word for "sock" not only for socks but also for other undergarments that are put on over the feet, or through which feet are slipped through such as undershorts, which illustrates how a child may extend the meaning of a word from a particular referent to encompass a larger class.

When J. P. first began to use these words, the stimulus had to be visible; but soon, it was no longer necessary. *Dog,* for example, was first only used when pointing to a real dog but later was used for pictures of dogs in various books. A new word that entered J. P.'s vocabulary at seventeen months was *uh-oh,* which he would say after he had an accident like spilling juice, or when he deliberately poured his yogurt over the side of his high chair. His use of this word shows his developing use of language for social purposes. At this time he also added two new words meaning "no," [do:] and [no]. He used these words frequently when anyone attempted to take something from him that he wanted or tried to make him do something he did not want to do. He used this negative either imperatively (for example, "Don't do that!") or assertively (for example, "I don't want to do that"). Even in his early holophrastic stage, J. P. was using words to convey a variety of ideas, feelings, and social awareness.

According to some child-language researchers, the words in the holophrastic stage serve three major functions: They either are linked with a child's own action or desire for action (as when J. P. would say "up" to express his wish to be picked up), or are used to convey emotion (J. P.'s "no"), or serve a naming function (J. P.'s "Cheerios," "shoes," "dog," and so on).

At this stage the child uses only one word to express concepts or predications that will later be expressed by complex phrases and sentences.

Phonologically, J. P.'s first words, like the words of most children at this stage of learning English and other languages, were generally monosyllabic with a CV (consonant-vowel) form; the vowel part may be diphthongal, depending on the language being acquired. His phonemic or phonetic inventory (at this stage they are equivalent) is

---

[3] We give special thanks to John Peregrine Munro for providing us with such rich data, and to Drs. Pamela and Allen Munro, J. P.'s parents, for their painstaking efforts in recording these data.

much smaller than is found in the adult language. It was suggested by the linguist Roman Jakobson[4] that children first will acquire the sounds found in all languages of the world, no matter what language they are exposed to, and in later stages will acquire the "more difficult" sounds. For example, most languages have the sounds [p] and [s], but [θ] is a rare sound. J. P. was no exception. His phonological inventory at an early stage included the consonants [b, m, d, k], which are frequently occurring sounds in the world's languages.

Many studies have shown that children in the holophrastic stage can perceive or comprehend many more phonological contrasts than they can produce themselves. Therefore, even at this stage, it is not possible to determine the extent of the grammar of the child simply by observing speech production.

The Two-Word Stage

Even before they are two years old, children have learned a very large number of words. According to some estimates, a child will add a new word to her mental dictionary every two hours. Then, around the time of their second birthday, something new and exciting occurs. Children begin to put two words together. At first these utterances appear to be strings of two of the child's earlier holophrastic utterances, each word with its own single-pitch contour. Soon, they begin to form actual two-word sentences with clear syntactic and semantic relations. The intonation contour of the two words extends over the whole utterance rather than being separated by a pause between the two words. The following "sentences" illustrate the kinds of patterns that are found in children's utterances at this stage.[5]

allgone sock	hi Mommy
byebye boat	allgone sticky
more wet	beepbeep bang
it ball	Katherine sock
dirty sock	here pretty

During the two-word utterance stage there are no syntactic or morphological markers—that is, no inflections for number, person, tense, and so on. Pronouns are rare, although many children use *me* to refer to themselves, and some children use other pronouns as well. Bloom has noted that in noun + noun sentences such as *Mommy sock,* the two words can express a number of different grammatical relations that will later be expressed by other syntactic devices.[6] Bloom's conclusions were reached by observing the situations in which the two-word sentence was uttered. Thus, for example, *Mommy*

---

[4] R. Jakobson. 1941. *Kindersprache, Aphasie, und Allgemeine,* Uppsala, Sweden: Almqvist and Wiksell. (English translation by A. Keiler. 1968. *Child Language, Aphasia, and Phonological Universals,* The Hague: Mouton.)

[5] All the examples given in this chapter are taken from utterances produced by children actually observed by the authors or reported in the literature. The various sources are listed in the reference section at the end of the chapter.

[6] L. M. Bloom. 1972. *Language Development: Form and Function in Emerging Grammar,* Cambridge, MA: MIT Press.

sock can be used to show a subject + object relation in the situation when the mother is putting the sock on the child, or a possessive relation when the child is pointing to Mommy's sock. Two nouns can also be used to show a subject-locative relation, as in *sweater chair* to mean "The sweater is on the chair," or to show conjunction, to mean "sweater and chair."

From Telegraph to Infinity

> If we divide language development into somewhat arbitrary stages, like Syllable Babbling, Gibberish Babbling, One-Word Utterances, and Two-Word Strings, the next stage would have to be called All Hell Breaks Loose.
>
> Steven Pinker, *The Language Instinct*

There does not seem to be any three-word sentence stage. When a child starts stringing more than two words together, the utterances may be two, three, four, five words, or longer. Since the age at which children start to produce words and put words together may vary, chronological age is not a good measure of a child's language development. A child's **mean length of utterances** (MLU) rather than chronological age is thus used in the study of language development. That is, children producing utterances that average 2.3 to 3.5 morphemes in length seem to be at the same stage of grammar acquisition, even though one child may be two and another three years old.

The first childhood utterances longer than two words have a special characteristic. The function words (grammatical morphemes) such as *to, the, can, is,* and so on are missing; only the words that carry the main message—the open-class content words—occur. Children often sound as if they are reading a Western Union message, which is why such utterances are sometimes called **telegraphic speech:**[7]

Cat stand up table
What that?
He play little tune
Andrew want that
Cathy build house
No sit there

J. P.'s early sentences were similar:

Age in Months		
25 months	[danʔ ɪ ʔ tˢɪʔ]	"don't eat (the) chip"
	[bʷaʔ tat]	"(the) block (is on) top"
26 months	[mamis tu hæs]	"Mommy's two hands"
	[mo bʌs go]	"where's another bus?"
	[dædi go]	"where's Daddy?"

---

[7] Before the days of e-mail or fax machines, people would send telegrams to get a message to someone faster than by postal mail. They would be charged by the word and to save money would leave out any word that was not required for the meaning of the sentences; these would mainly be the grammatical morphemes like *the, is, are, of, for,* etc.

27 months	[ʔaj gat tu dʲus]	"I got two (glasses of) juice"
	[do bajʔ mi]	"don't bite (kiss) me"
	[kʌdər sʌni ber]	"Sonny color(ed a) bear"
28 months	[ʔaj gat pwe dɪs]	"I('m) play(ing with) this"
	[mamis tak mɛns]	"Mommy talk(ed to the) men"

Apart from lacking grammatical morphemes, these utterances appear to be sentence-like: They have hierarchical, constituent structures similar to the syntactic structures found in the sentences produced by the adult grammar.

Children's utterances are not simply words that are randomly strung together, but from a very early stage reveal their grasp of the principles of sentence formation.

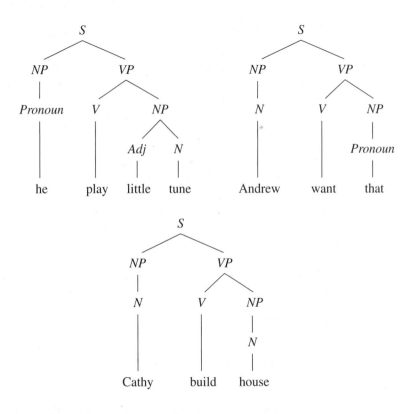

Children's utterances adhere to the word order constraints of the language they are acquiring. Children learning English do not say *Mommy men talk* for the sentence that would be *Mommy talked to the men*. In languages in which the regular word order is Subject Object Verb (SOV), such as Japanese, children do so, and do not say *Mommy talk men*.

Though utterances are described as telegraphic, the child does not deliberately leave out the noncontent words as does an adult sending a telegram. The sentences reflect the child's grammar at that particular stage of language development.

As children produce sentences that more and more closely approximate the adult grammar, they begin to use syntactic or grammatical function words and also to acquire the inflectional and derivational morphemes of the language. That these early sentences are constrained by the syntax of the language is shown by the fact that number and gender agreement in languages such as Italian, Polish, or Turkish occur in early children's utterances where this is required by the adult language. They would be unable to inflect the verb to agree with the subject Noun Phrase if they didn't know what a Noun or a Noun Phrase or a Verb was.

The UCLA linguist Nina Hyams,[8] in her study of the acquisition of Italian, reports that between the ages of 1;10 (one year, ten months) and 2;4, a number of productive inflectional processes occur in their speech. For example, in Italian, verbs must be inflected for number and person to agree with the subject. This is similar to the agreement in English for third person subjects. We say *She giggles a lot* but *They giggle a lot.* In Italian it is more complex, as the following utterances of Italian children show:

Tu legg**i** il libro	"You (2nd person singular) read the book."
Io vad**o** fuori	"I go (1st p. sg.) outside."
Dorm**e** miao dorme	"Sleeps (3rd p. sg.) cat sleeps."
Legg**iamo** il libro	"(We) read (1st p. plural) the book."

Hyams also shows that children at this very young age produce sentences in which there is gender and number agreement between the determiner ("the," "a," etc.) and the noun in a noun phrase.

E mi**a** gonna	"(It) is my (feminine singular) skirt."
Questo mi**o** bimbo	"This my (masculine singular) baby."
Guarda **ia** mela piccolin**a**	"Look at the little (fem. sg.) apple."
Guarda **il** topo piccolin**o**	"Look at the little (masc. sg.) mouse."

Grammatical morphemes enter the language of English-speaking children around the same time. Roger Brown and his associates at Harvard studied the spontaneous utterances of three children—Adam, Sarah, and Eve—over a long period of time, noting the appearance of grammatical morphemes, free and bound.[9] They found that the sequences of acquisition of the morphemes were the same for all three children, and this finding has been replicated by others. *-ing,* the ending that represents the present progressive form of the verb, as in *Me going,* was found to be among the earliest inflectional morphemes acquired. The prepositions *in* and *on* next entered the speech of the children studied, and then the regular plural ending, as in *two doggies* /tu dɔgiz/. It is interesting that the third person singular marker (as in *Johnny comes*) and the possessive morpheme (as in *Daddy's hat*), which have the same phonological shape as the plural /s/, entered the children's speech between six months and a year later, showing that acquisition of these morphemes is syntax-dependent.

Eventually all the other inflections were added, along with the syntactic rules, and finally the child's utterances sounded like those spoken by adults.

---

[8] The data included in examples were collected by M. Moneglia and E. Cresti and reported in Nina Hyams's (1986) *Language Acquisition and the Theory of Parameters,* Dordrecht, The Netherlands: Reidel Publishers.

[9] R. O. Brown. 1973. *A First Language: The Early Stages,* Cambridge, MA: Harvard University Press.

This is an incredible feat because of the complexity of the syntactic rules of all languages. Moreover, the child must figure out what these rules are from very "noisy" data. The child hears sentence fragments, false starts, speech errors, and interruptions; no one tells the child "this is a grammatical utterance and this is not." Yet, somehow the adult grammar is acquired. How does the child accomplish the task?

THEORIES OF CHILD LANGUAGE ACQUISITION

Do Children Learn by Imitation?

CHILD: *My teacher holded the baby rabbits and we patted them.*
ADULT: *Did you say your teacher held the baby rabbits?*
CHILD: *Yes.*
ADULT: *What did you say she did?*
CHILD: *She holded the baby rabbits and we patted them.*
ADULT: *Did you say she held them tightly?*
CHILD: *No, she holded them loosely.*

Courtney Cazden[10]

Reprinted by permission of Hanna-Barbera.

Various theories have been proposed to explain how children manage to acquire the adult language. Is this really a problem? Don't children just listen to what is said around them and imitate the speech they hear? Imitation is involved to some extent, of course, but the sentences produced by children show that children are not imitating adult speech. Children do not hear *Cat stand up table* or many of the utterances they produce.

---

[10] C. Cazden. 1972. *Child Language and Education,* New York: Holt, Rinehart and Winston, p. 92.

a my pencil
two foot
what the boy hit?
other one pants
Mommy get it my ladder
cowboy did fighting me

Even when children are deliberately trying to imitate what they hear, they are unable to produce sentences that cannot be generated by their grammar.

ADULT:	He's going out.	CHILD:	He go out.
ADULT:	That's an old-time train.	CHILD:	Old-time train.
ADULT:	Adam, say what I say: Where can I put them?	CHILD:	Where I can put them?

The "imitation" theory cannot account for another important phenomenon. Children who are unable to speak for neurological or physiological reasons learn the language spoken to them and understand what is said. When they overcome their speech impairment they immediately use the language for speaking.

Do Children Learn by Reinforcement?

CHILD:	Nobody don't like me.
MOTHER:	No, say "Nobody likes me."
CHILD:	Nobody don't like me.
	(dialogue repeated eight times)
MOTHER:	Now, listen carefully, say *"Nobody likes me."*
CHILD:	Oh, nobody don't likes me.

Another view of language acquisition suggests that children learn to produce correct (grammatical) sentences because they are positively reinforced when they say something right and negatively reinforced when they say something wrong. This view assumes that children are being constantly corrected for using "bad grammar" and rewarded when they use "good grammar." Brown and his colleagues[11] report from their studies that reinforcement seldom occurs, and when it does, it is usually incorrect pronunciation or incorrect reporting of facts that is corrected. They report, for example, that the ungrammatical sentence *Her curl my hair* was not corrected because Eve's mother was in fact curling her hair. However, when the syntactically correct sentence *Walt Disney comes on Tuesday* was produced, her mother corrected Eve because the program on television was shown on Wednesday. They conclude that it is "truth value rather than syntactic well-formedness that chiefly governs explicit verbal reinforcement by parents—which renders mildly paradoxical the fact that the usual product of such a training schedule is an adult whose speech is highly grammatical but not notably truthful" (p. 330).

---

[11] Brown, *A First Language.*

Even if syntactic correction occurred more often, it would not explain how or what children learn from such adult responses or how children discover and construct the correct rules.

In fact, attempts to "correct" a child's language seem to be doomed to failure. Children do not know what they are doing wrong and are unable to make corrections even when they are pointed out, as shown by the example above and the following one:

CHILD: Want other one spoon, Daddy.
FATHER: You mean, you want *the other spoon.*
CHILD: Yes, I want other one spoon, please, Daddy.
FATHER: Can you say "the other spoon"?
CHILD: Other . . . one . . . spoon.
FATHER: Say . . . "other."
CHILD: Other.
FATHER: Spoon.
CHILD: Spoon.
FATHER: Other . . . spoon.
CHILD: Other . . . spoon. Now give me other one spoon?

Such conversations between parents and children do not occur often. The above conversation was between a linguist studying child language and his child. Mothers and fathers are usually delighted that their young children are talking at all and consider every utterance a gem. The "mistakes" children make are "cute" and repeated endlessly to anyone who will listen.

Do Children Learn Language by Analogy?

It has also been suggested that children learn how to put words together to form phrases and sentences by **analogy,** by hearing a sentence and using it as a sample to form other sentences. But this doesn't work, as Lila Gleitman points out:[12]

> So suppose the child has heard the sentence "I painted a red barn." So now, by analogy, the child can say "I painted a blue barn." That's exactly the kind of theory that we want. You hear a sample and you extend it to all of the new cases by similarity. . . . In addition to "I painted a red barn" you might also hear the sentence "I painted a barn red." So it looks as if you take those last two words and switch them around in their order. . . . So now you want to extend this to the case of seeing, because you want to look at barns instead of painting them. So you have heard, "I saw a red barn." Now you try (by analogy) a . . . new sentence—"I saw a barn red." Something's gone wrong. This is an analogy, but the analogy didn't work. It's not a sentence of English.

This problem with trying to explain how children learn what is or is not a sentence in their language by analogy arises constantly.

---

[12] *The Human Language Series: Program 2.* 1994. By Gene Searchinger. New York: Equinox Films/Ways of Knowing, Inc.

Children Form Rules and Construct a Grammar

Reprinted by permission of Newspaper Enterprise Association, Inc.

The analogy theory fails along with the reinforcement theory and the imitation theory. These views cannot account for the nonrandom mistakes children make, the speed with which the basic rules of grammar are acquired, the ability to learn language **without any formal instruction,** and the regularity of the acquisition process across diverse languages and environmental circumstances.

Between the ages of five and seven, children from diverse backgrounds reach the same stage of grammar acquisition irrespective of whether their parents talk to them constantly or whether they are brought up to be seen and not heard and are seldom spoken to.

The child appears to be equipped from birth with the neural prerequisites for the acquisition and use of human language just as birds are biologically "prewired" to learn the songs of their species. And just as birds of most species cannot learn the songs of other birds, so also children can only learn languages that conform to linguistic principles, like structural dependencies and universal syntactic categories, that pertain to all human languages and that determine the class of possible languages that can be acquired by children. Thus, children born of Zulu parents raised in an English-speaking environment will learn English, and vice versa, but no children will acquire a formal language (without specific instruction) which, for example, has a rule to reverse the order of words in a sentence to form its negation. Such a rule is not in keeping with universal linguistic principles.

The different syntactic rules at any stage in acquisition govern the construction of the child's sentences at that period of development. Consider, for example, the increasing complexity of one child's negative sentences. At first the child simply added a *no* (or some negative morpheme) at the beginning or at the end of a sentence:

> no heavy
> no singing song
> no want stand head
> no Fraser drink all tea
> no the sun shining

Fraser did not hear such sentences. He used a simple way to form a negative, but it is not the way negative sentences are constructed in English. At some point he began to insert a *no* or *can't* or *don't* inside the sentence.

He no bite you
I no taste them
That no fish school
I can't catch you

The child progressed from simple rules to more complex rules, as is shown below:

		Examples
One word stage:	Single negative word	No
		allgone
First sentences:	Negative word added to beginning of sentence	No want food
		No Fraser drink all tea
Later sentences:	Negative element inserted between subject and predicate	Fraser no want some
		He no bite you
	Negative auxiliaries *don't, can't* appear	I can't catch you
	Negation "spread"—*some* becomes *no*	Fraser don't want no food.
	Negative element inserted correctly—*no* changed to *any*	I don't want any food.

All children do not show exactly the same development as the child described above, but they all show similar regular changes. One child studied by Carol Lord first differentiated affirmative from negative sentences by pitch; her negative sentences were all produced with a much higher pitch. When she began to use a negative morpheme, the pitch remained high, but then the intonation became normal as the negative syntactic markers "took over."

Similar changes in the grammar are found in the acquisition of question formation. One child first formed a question by using a "question intonation" (a rise of pitch at the end of the sentence):

Fraser water?
I ride train?
Sit chair?

At the next stage the child merely "tacked on" a question word in front of the sentence; he did not change the word order or insert *do*. This is similar to the negation stage where *no* or another negation word is put at the front of the sentence.

What he wants?
What he can ride in?
Where I should put it?
Where Ann pencil?
Why you smiling?

Such sentences are perfectly regular. They are not mistakes in the child's language; they reflect the grammar at a specific stage of development.

Errors or Rules?

> A final word about the theory of errors. Here it is that the causes are complex and multiple. . . .
>
> Henri Poincaré (1854–1912)

> Give me fruitful error any time, full of seeds, bursting with its own corrections.
>
> Vilfredo Pareto (1848–1923)

Language acquisition is a creative process. The grammar develops in stages and at each stage the child's utterances conform to the rules and regularities acquired at that stage. The mistakes (when looked at from the point of view of the adult grammar) reveal these rules. Children seem to form the simplest and most general rule they can from the language input they receive, and to be so "pleased" with their "theory" that they use the rule wherever they can.

The Acquisition of Phonology

We have seen that children appear to be neurologically prepared to perceive just those sounds that are phonemic in some language. From the earliest one-word stage they show an awareness of the phonetic features and properties that characterize natural classes of sounds. Many studies report a similar order of acquisition of classes of sounds characterized by manner of articulation; nasals are acquired first, then, glides, stops, liquids, fricatives, and affricates. Natural classes characterized by place of articulation features also appear in children's utterances according to an ordered series: labials, velars, alveolars, and palatals. It is not surprising that *mama* is an early word for many or most children.

In early language, children may not distinguish between voiced and voiceless consonants. When they first begin to contrast one set—that is, when they learn that /p/ and /b/ are distinct phonemes—they also begin to distinguish between /t/ and /d/, /s/ and /z/, and all the other contrasts between voiceless and voiced consonants. The generalizations refer, as we would expect, to natural classes of speech sounds.

A child's first words show many such substitutions, of one feature for another, or one phoneme for another. For example, the word *light* [lajt] is pronounced as *yight* [jajt] in the speech of many children, with the liquid [l] being replaced by the glide [j], and *rabbit* pronounced as *wabbit* with the liquid [r] replaced by the glide [w].

The child's errors in pronunciation are thus not random but rule-governed.

Typical phonological rules (or processes) found in early childrens' utterances include:[13]

1. Consonant cluster simplification: spoon → poon, blue → bu
2. Devoicing of final consonants: dog → dok
3. Voicing of initial consonants: truck → druck
4. Consonant articulation agreement   doggy → goggy, doddy; big → gig
   (called **consonant harmony**):

---

[13] Rules and information provided by Nina Hyams.

These rules or constraints on the child's pronunciation of words combine so that *truck* may become *guck:*

truck → **t**uck   by Rule 1—consonant cluster simplification
tuck → **d**uck   by Rule 3—voicing of initial [t]
duck → **g**uck   by Rule 4—consonant harmony

The rules are simplifications of the adult phonological representations. They are natural rules reflecting easier articulations until greater articulatory control is achieved.

It is not that the children do not hear the correct pronunciations. They do, but are unable in these early years to produce the target pronunciation. We know this from countless stories. The son of one of the authors of this textbook pronounced the word *light* as *yight* [jait] but would become very angry if someone said to him, "Oh, you want me to turn the yight on." "No no," he would reply, "not yight—yight!"

Controlled experiments also show that the child does hear the difference that he seems not able to produce. For example, a child who appears to pronounce *wing* and *ring* identically can pick out the correct picture when shown pictures of both. Furthermore, acoustic analysis of children's utterances show that what sounds to us as being the same sound in a child's pronunciation of *wing* and *ring* are physically different sounds. The differences are not perceived by the adult ear because they are nonlinguistic differences.

These phonetic/phonological pronunciations of words, which appear to be mistakes, are actually produced according to the rules at the child's stage of development.

The Acquisition of Morphology

PEANUTS reprinted by permission of UFS, Inc.

Children's errors in morphology reveal that the child has acquired the regular rules of the grammar and overgeneralizes these rules. This **overgeneralization** of constructed rules is shown when children treat irregular verbs and nouns as if they were regular. We have probably all heard children say *bringed, goed, does, singed,* or *foots, mouses, sheeps, childs.*

These mistakes tell us more about how children learn language than the correct forms they use. The child cannot be imitating; children use such forms in families where the parents never utter such "bad English." In fact, children may say *brought* or *broke* before they begin to use the incorrect forms. At the earlier stage they never use any regular past-tense forms like *kissed, walked,* or *helped.* They probably do not know that *brought* is a "past" at all. When they begin to say *played* and *hugged* and *helped* as well as *play, hug,* and *help,* they have "figured out" how to form a past tense—they have constructed the rule. At that point they form all past tenses by this rule—they overgeneralize—and they no longer say *brought* but *bring* and *bringed.* The acquisition of the rule overrides previously learned words and is unaffected by "practice" reinforcement. At a later time, children will learn that there are "exceptions" to the rule, and only then will they once more say *brought.* Children look for general patterns, for systematic occurrences.

The child's morphological rules emerge quite early. In 1958, Berko-Gleason[14] conducted a study that has now become a classic in our understanding of child language acquisition. She worked with preschool children and with children in the first, second, and third grades. She showed each child a drawing of a nonsense animal like the funny creature below and gave the "animal" a nonsense name. She would then say to the child, pointing to the picture, " This is a wug."

Then she would show the child a picture of two of the animals and say, "Now here is another one. There are two of them. There are two _____?"

The child's "task" was to give the plural form, "wugs" [wʌgz]. Another little make-believe animal was called a "bik," and when the child was shown two biks, he or she again was to say the plural form [bɪks]. Berko-Gleason found that the children applied the regular plural-formation rule to words never heard before. Because the children had never seen a "wug" or a "bik" and had not heard these "words," their ability to add a [z] when the animal's name ended with a voiced sound and an [s] when there was a final voiceless consonant showed that the children were using rules based on an understanding of natural classes of phonological segments, and not simply imitating words they had previously heard.

Children also show knowledge of the derivational rules of their language. In English, for example, we can derive verbs from nouns. From the noun *Xerox* we now xerox; from the proper noun *Watergate* we derived the verb *to watergate.* Children

---

[14] J. Berko. 1958. "The Child's Learning of English Morphology," *Word* 14: 150–177.

acquire this derivational rule early and use it very often since there are lots of gaps in their verb vocabulary (studies show that nouns are usually acquired first). Some examples are provided by Hyams:

You have to scale it.	"You have to weigh it."
I broomed it up.	"I swept it up."
He's keying the door.	"He's opening the door (with a key)."

Children's utterances reflect their internal grammars, and these grammars include derivational and inflectional rules at a very early age.

The Acquisition of Syntax

Doonesbury. Copyright 1982 & 1984, G. B. Trudeau.

Children eventually acquire all the phonological, syntactic, and semantic rules of the grammar. Not only are very young children more successful at this task than the most brilliant linguist, their grammars, at each stage, are highly similar, and deviate from the adult grammar in highly specific constrained ways.

To account for the ability of children to construct the complex syntactic rules of their grammar, it has been suggested that the child's grammar is semantically based. This view holds that the child's early language does not make reference to syntactic categories and relations (Noun, Noun Phrase, Verb, Verb Phrase, subject, object, and so on) but rather solely to semantic roles (like agent or theme). The examples of the language of Italian-speaking children of about two years old studied by Nina Hyams cited in the examples earlier, however, show that this cannot be the case: Their utterances can only be explained by reference to syntactic categories and relations.

As discussed above, Italian children at a very early age inflect the verb to agree in person and number with the subject. We repeat two of the examples here.

(a) Tu loggi il libro	"You read (2nd person singular) the book."
(b) Gira il pallone	"Turns (3rd person singular) the balloon."
	(The balloon turns.)

Subject-verb agreement cannot be semantically based, because the subject is an agent in utterance (a) but not in (b). Instead, agreement must be based on whatever noun phrase is the subject, a syntactic relationship.

Hyams upholds this position by reference to other kinds of agreement as well, such as the "modifier-noun agreement" also illustrated earlier. There is nothing intrinsically masculine or feminine about the nouns that are marked for such grammatical gender. But children produce the correct forms based on the syntactic classification of these nouns.

Children learning other languages with similar agreement rules, such as Russian, Polish, or Turkish, show this same ability to discover the structures of their language. Their grammars from an early stage reveal their knowledge of the kinds of structure dependencies mentioned in Chapter 4.

In the discussion on telegraphic speech we noted that at this stage children's utterances consist mainly of content words from the major classes of nouns, verbs, and adjectives and do not include grammatical morphemes—freestanding words or bound inflections. In the course of syntactic development these categories will develop.

It is interesting that the utterances that are produced with these categories missing are all possible in some human language. English-speaking children produce subjectless sentences like *See ball,* a grammatical sentence in Italian *vedo la palla.* Sentences without the copular verb *be* also are produced, and such sentences are common in the adult language in Russian or Hebrew. Languages like Japanese and Chinese do not have articles; Italian permits an article and a possessive pronoun in a Noun Phrase, which is not permitted in English—*Il mio libro* but **The my book.* We see that even the deviant sentences produced by children are within the range of what could be a human language; at an early stage of development, the children have not yet discovered which sentences are and are not grammatical in the language they are acquiring. This parallels the fact that in the babbling stage children produce sounds that are possible speech sounds and must learn which sounds are in and which are out of their language.

Just as human adult languages are governed by universal characteristics, we see that the child's grammar, while differing from the adult grammar in very specific ways, also follows universal principles.

Learning the Meaning of Words[15]

> Suddenly I felt a misty consciousness as of something forgotten—a thrill of returning thought; and somehow the mystery of language was revealed to me. . . . Everything had a name, and each name gave birth to a new thought.[16]
>
> Helen Keller

Most people do not see the acquisition of the meaning of words as posing a great problem. The intuitive view is that children look at an object in their sight of vision, the mother says a word, and the child connects the sounds with the particular object being

---

[15] We wish to acknowledge the contribution to this section of Lila Gleitman (1991) and her chapter "Language" in *Psychology,* 3rd ed. H. Gleitman, ed. New York: Norton.

[16] Helen Keller as quoted in J. P. Lash (1980), *Helen and Teacher: The Story of Helen Keller and Anne Sullivan Macy,* New York: Delacorte Press.

viewed. However, this is not as easy a task as one might think, as the following quote demonstrates:

> A child who observes a cat sitting on a mat also observes . . . a mat supporting a cat, a mat under a cat, a floor supporting a mat and a cat, and so on. If the adult now says "The cat is on the mat" even while pointing to the cat on the mat, how is the child to choose among these interpretations of the situation?[17]

Even if the mother simply says "cat," and the child by accident associates the word with the animal on the mat, the child may interpret *cat* as "Cat," the name of a particular animal, or of an entire species.

It is not surprising that children often overgeneralize a word's meaning. Overgeneralization is a regular process in language acquisition. For example, overgeneralization of constructed rules is shown when children treat irregular verbs and nouns as if they were regular. We have probably all heard children say *bringed, goed, does, singed* or *foots, mouses, sheeps, childs.*

They also overgeneralize the meaning of words. They may learn a word such as *papa* or *daddy* which they first use only for their own father and then extend its meaning to apply to all men. After the child has acquired her first seventy-five to one hundred words, the overgeneralized meanings become narrowed until the meanings of these words are those of the other speakers of the language. How this occurs is also not easy to explain.

The mystery surrounding the acquisition of word meanings has intrigued philosophers and psychologists as well as linguists. It has been observed that children view the world in similar fashion. They first learn basic level terms like *cat* before learning the larger class word *animal.* Various studies have also shown that if an experimenter points to an object and uses a nonsense word to a child like *blick,* saying *that's blick,* the child will interpret the word to refer to the whole object not one of its parts or attributes.

Furthermore, as children are learning the meaning of words, they are also learning the syntax of the language and the syntactic categories. Psycholinguists like Gleitman suggest that the syntax helps the child acquire meaning, pointing out that a child will interpret a word like *blicking* to be a verb if the word is used while the investigator points to an action being performed, and will interpret the word *blick* to be a noun if used in the expression *a blick* or *the blick* while looking at the same picture. For example, suppose a child is shown a picture of some funny animal jumping up and down and hears either *See the blicking* or *See the blick;* later when asked to show "blicking" the child will jump up and down, but if asked to show a blick, will point to the funny animal. Gleitman calls this process **bootstrapping;** children use their knowledge of syntax to learn whether a word is a verb and thus has a meaning referring to an action, or whether the word is a noun and thus refers to an object of some kind.

The investigation of the kinds of errors children make in forming their grammars shows that the mistakes are all in keeping with what we have called Universal Grammar, that is, the principles that constrain all grammars. Children do not construct "wild grammars"; their errors fall within the bounds of syntactic, phonological, and morphological natural linguistic processes. The regular stages and patterns shown in children's language support the notion that language acquisition is grammar construction.

---

[17] Lila R. Gleitman and Eric Wanner. 1982. *Language Acquisition: The State of the State of the Art,* Cambridge, England: Cambridge University Press, p. 10.

THE BIOLOGICAL FOUNDATIONS OF LANGUAGE ACQUISITION

Just as birds have wings, man has language.

George Henry Lewes (1817–1878)

The ability of children to form complex rules and construct grammars of the languages used around them in a relatively short time is indeed phenomenal. The similarity of the language acquisition stages across diverse peoples and languages shows that children are equipped with special abilities to know what generalizations to look for and what to ignore, and how to discover the regularities of language. Children learn language the way they learn to sit up or stand or crawl or walk. They are not taught to do these things, but all normal children begin to do so at around the same age. "Learning to walk" or "learning language" is different than "learning to read" or "learning to ride a bicycle." Many people never learn to read because they are not taught to do so, and there are large groups of people in many parts of the world that do not have any written language. However, they all have language.

The "Innateness Hypothesis"

How comes it that human beings, whose contacts with the world are brief and personal and limited, are able to know as much as they do know?

Bertrand Russell[18]

"WHAT'S THE BIG SURPRISE? ALL THE LATEST THEORIES OF LINGUISTICS SAY WE'RE BORN WITH THE INNATE CAPACITY FOR GENERATING SENTENCES."

Copyright © by S. Harris.

---

[18] Bertrand Russell. 1948. *Human Knowledge: Its Scope and Limits,* New York: Simon and Schuster.

A major question called **the logical problem of language acquisition** was posed by Chomsky when he asked: "What accounts for the ease, rapidity and uniformity of language acquisition in the face of impoverished data?"

Language acquisition seems to be easy for children. They needn't be taught the complex rules of language. But it is far from easy for a student of linguistics trying to solve a syntax problem in another language, so it can't be that the task itself is an easy one.

Acquisition is rapid; only two years from the time the child produces her first word at around the age of one until the major part of the grammar is acquired at around three. Acquisition is uniform across children and languages; children learning the thousands of languages with all their surface differences go through the same stages of phonological, morphological, and syntactic rule acquisition. Although children hear many utterances, the language that is heard is incomplete, noisy, and unstructured. The utterances include slips of the tongue, false starts, ungrammatical and incomplete sentences, and no information as to which utterances heard are well formed and which are not. Yet, children seem to learn, or mysteriously know, aspects of the grammar for which they receive no information. This is what is meant by the **impoverished data** or the **poverty of the stimulus**.

For example, children at an early age learn to form questions such as the following:

Statement	Question
Jill is going up the hill.	Is Jill going up the hill?
Jack and Jill are going up the hill.	Are Jack and Jill going up the hill?

That doesn't seem too hard a rule to learn. Move the auxiliary verb to the beginning of the sentence. But that doesn't always work.

Statement	Question
Jill who is my sister is going up the hill.	*Is Jill who __ my sister is going up the hill?
	Is Jill who is my sister ___ going up the hill?

It is not the first auxiliary verb but the auxiliary verb of the main clause which must be moved, as we saw in Chapter 4.

The rules children construct are **structure-dependent**. That is, children use syntactic rules that depend on more than their knowledge of words. They also rely on their knowledge of syntactic structures, which are not overtly marked in the sentences they hear. This is more dramatically shown in the rules for *wh-* question formation.

Statement	Question
<u>Jack</u> went up the hill.	<u>Who</u> went up the hill?
<u>Jack and Jill</u> went up the hill.	<u>Who</u> went up the hill?
Jack and <u>Jill</u> went home.	Jack and <u>who</u> went home?
Jill ate <u>bagels and lox</u>.	Jill ate <u>what</u>?
Jill ate cookies and <u>ice cream</u>.	Jill ate cookies and <u>what</u>?

To ask a question the child learns to replace the noun phrase (NP) *Jack, Jill, ice cream,* or *school,* or the coordinate NPs *Jack and Jill* or *bagels and lox* with the appropriate *wh*-question word, *who* or *what* or *where.*

It seems as if the *wh-* phrase can replace any NP subject or object. But in coordinate structures, the *wh-* word must stay in the original NP. It can't be moved, as the following sentences show.

> *Who did Jack and _____ go up the hill?
> *What did Jill eat bagels and _____?

These sentences are starred because they are ungrammatical, yet the following are acceptable:

Statement	Question
Jill ate bagels with lox.	What did Jill eat bagels with _____?
Jack went up the hill with Jill.	Who did Jack go up the hill with ____?

What accounts for the difference between the "and" questions that are ungrammatical and the "with" questions that are well formed? *Bagels and lox* is a coordinate NP, that is, two NPs conjoined with *and* (NP and NP). But *bagels with lox* is not a coordinate NP but an NP composed of an NP followed by a prepositional phrase (NP + PP), as shown by the following diagrams:

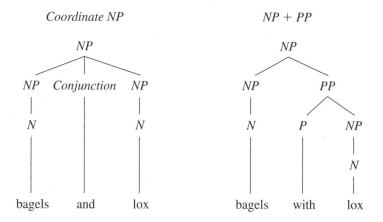

In English and all other languages that have been investigated, there seems to be a **coordinate structure constraint** that prohibits the movement of a *wh-* phrase out of a **coordinate structure.** Children make lots of mistakes in their early sentences, but, as mentioned earlier in this chapter, they do not produce sentences that could not be sentences in some human language. Children never produce sentences like the starred ones above. No one has told them these are not permitted. No one corrects them since they never utter them.

The factors mentioned above—ease and rapidity of acquisition despite impoverished input, and uniformity across children and languages—have led to the **innateness hypothesis** of child language acquisition, which posits that not only is the human species genetically prewired to acquire language, but that the kind of language is also determined. The principles referred to as Universal Grammar (or UG) determine the class of human languages that can be acquired unconsciously, without instruction, in the early years of life. This Universal Grammar underlies the specific grammars of all languages. It is what we refer to as the genetically determined language faculty of the left hemisphere of the brain.

The innateness hypothesis predicts that all languages will conform to the principles of UG. We are still far from understanding the full nature of the principles of UG. Research on more and more languages provides a way to test those principles like the coordinate structure constraint that have been posited to be part of our genetic pre-wiring. If we investigate some language in which posited UG principles are violated, we will, like scientists in every field, have to correct our theory and substitute other principles. But there seems to be little doubt that the human brain is specially equipped for acquisition of human language grammars.

The "Critical-Age Hypothesis"

It has been suggested that there is a **critical age** for language acquisition, or at least for language acquisition without special teaching and without the need for special learning. During this period, language learning proceeds easily, swiftly, and without external intervention. After this period, the acquisition of the grammar is difficult and, for some individuals, never fully achieved.

The notion of a critical age is true of many species and seems to pertain to species-specific, biologically triggered behavior. Ducklings, for example, during the period from nine to twenty-one hours after hatching, will follow the first moving object they see, whether or not it looks or waddles like a duck. Such behavior is not the result of conscious decision or external teaching or intensive practice. Its emergence unfolds on what appears in a maturationally determined order universal across the species.

In a seminal contribution to the study of the biological basis of language, Eric Lenneberg[19] first proposed that the ability to learn a native language develops within a fixed period, from birth to puberty.

There have been a number of cases of children reared in environments of extreme social isolation who constitute "experiments in nature" for testing the critical age hypothesis. Such reported cases go back at least to the eighteenth century. In 1758, Carl Linnaeus first included *Homo ferus* (wild or feral man) as a subdivision of *Homo sapiens.* According to Linnaeus, a defining characteristic of *Homo ferus* was his lack of speech or observable language of any kind. All the cases in the literature support his view.

The most dramatic cases of children raised in isolation are those described as "wild" or "feral" children, who have reportedly been reared with wild animals or have lived alone in the wilderness. In 1920 two feral children, Amala and Kamala, were found in India, supposedly having been reared with wolves. A celebrated case, documented in Francois Truffaut's film *The Wild Child,* is that of Victor, "the wild boy of Aveyron," who was found in 1798. It was ascertained that he had been left in the woods when a very young child and had somehow survived.

There are other cases of children whose isolation resulted from deliberate efforts to keep them from normal social intercourse. As recently as 1970, a child called Genie in

---

[19] Eric Lenneberg. 1967. *Biological Foundations of Language,* New York: Wiley

the scientific reports[20] was discovered; she had been confined to a small room under conditions of physical restraint, and had received only minimal human contact from the age of eighteen months until almost fourteen years. None of these children, regardless of the cause of isolation, was able to speak or knew any language at the time of reintroduction to society.

This linguistic inability could simply be because they received no linguistic input, showing that the innate neurological ability of the human brain to acquire language must be triggered by language. In the documented cases of Victor and Genie, however, it was found that they were unable to acquire language after exposure and even with deliberate and painstaking linguistic teaching.

Genie did begin to acquire some language, but while she was able to learn a large vocabulary, including colors, shapes, objects, natural categories, abstract as well as concrete terms, her syntax and morphology never fully developed. The UCLA linguist Susan Curtiss, who worked with Genie for a number of years after she was found, reports that Genie's utterances were, for the most part, "the stringing together of content words, often with rich and clear meaning but with little grammatical structure." Many of these utterances produced by Genie at the age of fifteen and older, a number of years after her emergence from isolation, are like those of children in the telegraphic stage, and like utterances of Broca's aphasia patients.

> Man motorcycle have.
> Genie full stomach.
> Genie bad cold live father house.
> Want Curtiss play piano.
> Open door key.

Genie's utterances lacked auxiliary verbs, the third person singular agreement marker, the past-tense marker, and most pronouns. She did not invert subjects and verbs to form questions. Genie started learning language after the critical age, and was never able to fully acquire the morphological and syntactic rules of English, supporting the hypothesis.

Chelsea is a woman who also supports the critical-age hypothesis. She was born deaf in Northern California, isolated from any major urban center, and wrongly diagnosed by incompetent doctors as retarded. Her devoted and caring family never believed this to be so but did not know she was deaf. When she was thirty-one, a neurologist finally correctly diagnosed her deafness and she was fitted with hearing aids. She received extensive language therapy and was able to acquire a large vocabulary but, like Genie, has not yet reached the syntactic level of even a three-year-old child.

More than 90 percent of children who are born deaf or become deaf before they have acquired language are born to hearing parents. These children have also provided information about the critical age for language acquisition. Because most of their parents do not know sign language at the time of their birth, many of these

---

[20] S. Curtiss. 1977. *Genie: A Linguistic Study of a Modern-Day "Wild Child,"* New York: Academic Press.

children receive delayed language exposure. A number of studies have investigated the acquisition of ASL among deaf signers exposed to the language at different ages. According to the University of Rochester psychologist Elissa Newport, early learners who received ASL input from birth and up to six years of age did much better in the production and comprehension of morphologically complex signs than late learners who were not exposed to ASL until after the age of twelve. There was little difference, however, in the vocabularies or the word-order constraints (which are very regular in ASL).

The case of Genie, other such isolated children, and deaf children show that children cannot fully acquire any language to which they are exposed unless they are within the critical age. Beyond the critical age the human brain appears to be unable to acquire much of syntax and inflectional morphology. In humans, then, the critical age for language acquisition does not pertain to all of language, but to specific components of the grammar.

The Acquisition of Bird Songs

THE FAR SIDE copyright 1991, 1987, and 1986 Universal Press Syndicate. Reprinted with permission. All rights reserved.

For some bird species, there is no critical age. They do not "learn" at all; the cuckoo will sing a fully developed song even if it never hears another cuckoo sing. These communicative messages are clearly innate. For other species, songs appear to be completely learned; the bullfinch, for example, will learn any song it is exposed to, even that of another species, however "unbullfinchlike" it may be. There do not appear to be any "bullfinch universals."

The chaffinch represents a different acquisition pattern. Certain calls and songs of this species will vary depending on the geographical "dialect" area that the bird inhabits. The message is the same, but the "pronunciation" or form is different. Usually a young bird will exhibit a basic version of the song shortly after hatching, and then later on will undergo further learning in acquiring its final "dialect" version of the song. Since birds from the same brood will acquire different dialects depending on the area in which they finally settle, part of the song must be learned. Since a fledgling chaffinch will sing the song of its species in a simple, degraded form, even if it has never heard it sung, some aspect of "language" is biologically determined, that is, it is innate.

The chaffinch acquires its fully developed song in several stages, just as human children appear to acquire language in several stages. Furthermore, the chaffinch brain may also be lateralized for language, as discussed in Chapter 2.

A critical age in the song-learning of chaffinches, white-crowned sparrows, zebra finches, and other species has been observed. If these birds are not exposed to the songs of their species during certain fixed periods after their birth (the period differs from species to species), song acquisition does not occur. The chaffinch is unable to learn new song elements after ten months of age. If it is isolated from other birds before attaining the full "grammar" and is then exposed again after ten months, its song will not develop further. If white crowns lose their hearing during a critical period after they have learned to sing, they produce a song that differs from other white crowns; they need to hear themselves sing to produce particular whistles and other song features. If, however, the deafness occurs after the critical period, the songs are normal.

From the point of view of human-language research, the relationship between the innate and learned aspects of bird songs is significant. Apparently the basic nature of the song of some species occurs within a critical period. Similarly, it appears that the basic nature of human language is biologically determined, whereas the details of languages that make them different from each other are learned, and that the learning must occur within a critical period.

The Acquisition of ASL

Given the universal aspects of sign and spoken languages, it is not surprising that deaf children of deaf signing parents parallel the stages of spoken language acquisition. They babble, then progress to single signs similar to the single words in the holophrastic stage and then begin to combine signs. There is also a telegraphic stage in which the grammatical signs are omitted. Grammatical or function signs appear at around the same age for deaf children as function words in spoken languages.

Bellugi and Klima[21] point out that deaf children's acquisition of the negative morphemes in American Sign Language (ASL) shows much the same pattern as in spoken

---

[21] U. Bellugi and E. S. Klima. 1976. "The Roots of Language in the Sign Talk of the Deaf," *Psychology Today* 6: 60–64.

language. _____ sed si__ ASL, with different restrictions on their use. The children acquiring ASL use ____ interchangeably in initial position of a signed sentence, like hearing children starting negative sentences with *no,* but unlike the ways in which negative signs are used in adult ASL. We see that the acquisition of ASL cannot be simple imitation any more than spoken language is acquired simply by imitation.

Hearing children of deaf parents acquire both sign language and spoken language when exposed to both, although studies have shown that the child's first signs emerge a few months before the first spoken words. It is interesting that deaf children appear to begin producing signs earlier than hearing children produce spoken words. It has been suggested that this timing may be because control of hand muscles develops earlier than the control of oral and laryngeal muscles.

Deaf children of hearing parents who are not exposed to manual sign language from birth suffer from a great handicap in acquiring language; yet language learning ability seems so strong in humans that even they begin to develop their own manual gestures to express their thoughts and desires. A study of six such children revealed that they not only developed individual signs but joined pairs and formed sentences (up to thirteen "words") with definite syntactic order and systematic constraints.

This fact, of course, should not be surprising: Sign languages are as grammatical and systematic as are spoken languages. We saw in Chapter 1 that the signs are conventional or arbitrary and not imitative. Furthermore, because all languages change in time, just as there are many different spoken languages, there are many different sign languages, all of which (spoken and sign) reveal the same linguistic universals. Deaf children often sign themselves to sleep just as hearing children talk themselves to sleep; deaf children report that they dream in sign language as French-speaking children dream in French and Hopi children dream in Hopi. Deaf children sign to their dolls and stuffed animals; slips of the hand occur similar to slips of the tongue; finger fumblers amuse signers as tongue twisters amuse speakers. We see that sign languages resemble spoken languages in all major aspects, showing that there truly are universals of language despite differences in the modality in which the language is performed. This universality is predictable because it is language that is biologically based.

LEARNING A SECOND (OR THIRD OR . . .) LANGUAGE

He that understands grammar in one language, understands it in another as far as the essential properties of Grammar are concerned. The fact that he can't speak, nor comprehend, another language is due to the diversity of words and their various forms, but these are the accidental properties of grammar.

Roger Bacon (1214–1294)

The Far Side. By Gary Larson. © 1983, 1984 Chronicle
Features, San Francisco. Reprinted with permission. All rights
reserved.

Anyone who has attempted to learn a second language in school or when visiting a foreign country knows that it is different from learning their native language. Even talented language learners require some instruction, or at least find a dictionary and teaching grammar useful. Some of us are total failures at second-language learning. We may be extremely fluent in our native language, we may get all "A's" in composition and write beautiful poetry, but still find we are unable to learn another language.

The younger you are, the easier it seems to be to learn a language. Language is unique in that no other complex system of knowledge is more easily acquired at a younger age than at an older one.

Young children who are exposed to more than one language before the age of puberty seem to acquire all the languages equally well. Many bilingual and multilingual speakers acquired their languages early in life. Sometimes one language is the first learned, but if the child is exposed to additional languages at an early age they will also be learned.

The critical age hypothesis discussed above was first proposed to explain the dramatic differences between a child's ease in learning a first language (L1) and the difficulty in learning a second language (L2) after puberty. It was believed that these differences could not be fully accounted for by the psychological, physical, and sociological factors present in second-language acquisition which could impede the learning process.

Many adults, for example, who are self-conscious about making mistakes often find learning L2 very difficult. This is not a problem for children who are unaware that they are making mistakes. The situation in which second language learning takes place will also have an influence on one's success. Many individuals attempt to learn an L2 by taking a class in high school or college. The student is exposed to the language only in a formal situation and usually for no more than a few hours a week. Even in intensive courses, the learner does not receive constant input or feedback.

On the other hand, due to the universal characteristics of human language, adults who know one language already "know" much about the underlying structure of every language. This is shown by the stages in second-language acquisition, which are similar to those in first-language acquisition. For example, Carol Chomsky[22] found that in the earliest years children learning English naively interpret sentences like *John is easy to see* as *It is easy for John to see.* French speakers learning English seem to go through a similar stage. Yet this cannot be due to any interference from French grammar, because in this sense, French is similar to English. The acquisition of grammatical morphemes (both bound and free) in learning English as a second language proceeds in similar order as in children's acquisition, no matter what the system is in the native language of the learner. However, interference from one's native phonology, morphology, and syntax can create difficulties that persist as a foreign accent in phonology and in the use of nonnative syntactic structures.

Theories of Second-Language Acquisition

"Gina is by lingal . . . that means she can say the same thing twice, but you can only understand it once."

DENNIS THE MENACE® used by permission of Hank Ketcham and by North America Syndicate.

---

[22] Carol Chomsky. 1969. *The Acquisition of Syntax in Children from Five to Ten,* Cambridge, MA: MIT Press.

There are alternative theories regarding the acquisition of L2. Stephen Krashen has proposed a distinction between acquisition—the process by which children unconsciously acquire their native language—and learning, which he defines as "conscious knowledge of a second language, knowing the rules, being aware of them, and being able to talk about them."[23]

A similar view suggests that the principles of Universal Grammar hold only during the critical period mentioned above, after which general learning mechanisms, not specific to language acquisition, operate in learning L2.

A second theory proposes that L2 is acquired on the same universal innate principles that govern L1 acquisition, which is why one finds the same stages of development even if the complete L2 grammar is not acquired due to nonlinguistic factors at work.

It is clear that children acquire their first language without explicit learning. A second language is usually learned but to some degree may also be acquired or "picked up" depending on the environmental setting and the input received by the second language learner.

More research and evidence is required before this interesting question can be resolved.

Second-Language Teaching Methods

Many approaches to foreign-language instruction have developed over the years. In one method, **grammar-translation,** the student memorizes words, inflected words, and syntactic rules and uses them to translate from English to L2 and vice versa. The **direct method** abandons memorization and translation; the native language is never used in the classroom, and the structure of the L2 language or how it differs from the native language is not discussed. The direct method attempts to stimulate learning a language as if the students found themselves in a foreign country without anyone except natives to speak to. The direct method seems to assume that adults can learn a foreign language in a way they learned their native language as children. Practically, it is difficult to duplicate the social, psychological, or physical environment of the child, or even the number of hours that the learner is exposed to the language to be learned, even if there is no critical-age factor.

An **audio-lingual** language-teaching method is based on the assumption that language is acquired mainly through imitation, repetition, and reinforcement. If this is so for second-language acquisition, it differs vastly from what we know about first-language acquisition.

Most individual methods have serious limitations: Probably a combination of many methods is required as well as motivation on the part of the student, intensive and extensive exposure, native or near-native speaking teachers who can serve as models, and instruction and instructional material that is based on linguistic analysis of all aspects of the language.

---

[23] Stephen D. Krashen. 1982. *Principles and Practice in Second Language Acquisition,* Oxford, England: Pergamon Press.

CAN CHIMPS LEARN HUMAN LANGUAGE?

> . . . It is a great baboon, but so much like man in most things . . . I do believe it already understands much English; and I am of the mind it might be taught to speak or make signs.

> Entry in Samual Pepys' *Diary,* August 1661

Reprinted courtesy Omni Magazine, 1987.

In this chapter, the discussion has centered on *human* language acquisition. Recently, much effort has been expended to determine whether nonhuman primates (chimpanzees, monkeys, gorillas, and so on) can learn human language.

In their natural habitat, primates communicate with each other in systems that include visual, auditory, olfactory, and tactile signals. Many of these signals seem to have meaning associated with the animals' immediate environment or emotional state. They can signal danger and can communicate aggressiveness and subordination. Females of some species emit a specific call indicating that they are anestrus (sexually quiescent), which inhibits attempts by males to copulate. However, the natural sounds and gestures produced by all nonhuman primates show their signals to be highly stereotyped and limited in the type and number of messages they convey. Their basic vocabularies occur primarily as emotional responses to particular situations. They have no way of expressing the anger they felt yesterday or the anticipation of tomorrow.

Despite their limited natural systems of communication, these animals have provoked an interest in whether they may have a capacity for acquiring more complex linguistic systems that are similar to human language.

Gua

In the 1930s, Winthrop and Luella Kellogg raised their infant son with an infant chimpanzee named Gua to determine whether a chimpanzee raised in a human environment and given language instruction could learn a human language. Gua understood about one hundred words at sixteen months, more words than their son at that age; but she never went beyond that. Moreover, comprehension of language involves more than understanding the meanings of isolated words. When their son could understand the difference between *I say what I mean* and *I mean what I say,* Gua could not understand either sentence.

Viki

A chimpanzee named Viki was raised by Keith and Cathy Hayes, and she too learned a number of individual words, even learning to articulate, with great difficulty, the words *mama, papa, cup,* and *up.* That was the extent of her language production.

Washoe

Psychologists Allen and Beatrice Gardner recognized that one disadvantage suffered by the primates was their physical inability to pronounce many different sounds. Without a sufficient number of phonemic contrasts, spoken human language is impossible. Many species of primates are manually dexterous, and this fact inspired the Gardners to attempt to teach American Sign Language to a chimpanzee whom they named Washoe, after the Nevada county in which they lived. Washoe was brought up in much the same way as a human child in a deaf community, constantly in the presence of people who used ASL. She was deliberately taught to sign, whereas children raised by deaf signers acquire sign language without explicit teaching, as hearing children learn spoken language.

By the time Washoe was four years old (June 1969), she had acquired eighty-five signs with such meanings as "more," "eat," "listen," "gimme," "key," "dog," "you," "me," "Washoe," and "hurry." According to the Gardners, Washoe was also able to produce sign combinations such as "baby mine," "you drink," "hug hurry," "gimme flower," and "more fruit."

Sarah

At about the same time that Washoe was growing up, psychologist David Premack attempted to teach a chimpanzee named Sarah an artificial language designed to resemble human languages in some aspects. The "words" of Sarah's "language" were differently shaped and colored plastic chips that were metal-backed. Sarah and her trainers "talked" to each other by arranging these symbols on a magnetic board. Sarah was taught to associate particular symbols with particular meanings. The form-meaning relationship of these "morphemes" or "words" was arbitrary; a small red square meant "banana," and a small blue rectangle meant "apricot," while the color red was represented by a gray chip and the color yellow by a black chip. Sarah learned a number of "nouns," "adjectives," and "verbs," symbols for abstract concepts like "same as" and "different from," "negation," and "question."

There were drawbacks to the Sarah experiment. She was not allowed to "talk" spontaneously, but only in response to her trainers. There was the possibility that her trainers unwittingly provided cues that Sarah responded to.

Learning Yerkish

BIZZARO © by Dan Piraro. Reprinted with permission of UNIVERSAL
PRESS SYNDICATE. All rights reserved.

To avoid these and other problems, Duane and Sue Rumbaugh and their associates at
the Yerkes Regional Primate Research Center began in 1973 to teach a different kind of
artificial language, called Yerkish, to three chimpanzees: Lana, Sherman, and Austin.
Instead of plastic chips, the words, called lexigrams, are geometric symbols displayed
on a computer keyboard. The computer records every button pressed; certain fixed
orders of these lexigrams constitute grammatical sentences in Yerkish. The researchers,
however, are particularly interested in the ability of primates to communicate using
functional symbols.

Koko

Another experiment aimed at teaching sign language to primates involved a gorilla
named Koko, who was taught by her trainer, Francine "Penny" Patterson. Patterson
claims that Koko has learned several hundred signs, is able to put signs together to
make sentences, and is capable of making linguistic jokes and puns, composing rhymes
such as BEAR HAIR (which is a rhyme in spoken language but not ASL), and inventing metaphors such as FINGER BRACELET for ring.

Nim Chimpsky

In a project specifically designed to test the linguistic claims that emerged from these primate experiments, another chimpanzee, named Nim Chimpsky, who was taught ASL by an experienced teacher, was studied by the psychologist H. S. Terrace and his associates.[24] Under carefully controlled experimental conditions that included thorough record-keeping and many hours of videotaping, Nim's teachers hoped to show beyond a reasonable doubt that chimpanzees had a humanlike linguistic capacity, in contradiction to the view put forth by Noam Chomsky (after whom Nim was ironically named) that human language is species-specific. In the nearly four years of study, Nim learned about 125 signs, and during the last two years Nim's teachers recorded more than 20,000 utterances including two or more signs. Nim produced his first ASL sign (DRINK) after just four months, which greatly encouraged the research team at the start of the study. Their enthusiasm soon diminished when he never seemed to go much beyond the two-word stage. Terrace concluded that "his three-sign combinations do not . . . provide new information. . . . Nim's most frequent two- and three-sign combinations [were] PLAY ME and PLAY ME NIM. Adding NIM to PLAY ME is simply redundant," writes Terrace. This kind of redundancy is illustrated by a sixteen-sign utterance of Nim's: GIVE ORANGE ME GIVE EAT ORANGE ME EAT ORANGE GIVE ME EAT ORANGE GIVE ME YOU. Other typical sentences do not sound much like the early sentences of children cited above.

> Nim eat Nim eat.
> Drink eat me Nim.
> Me Eat Me eat.
> You me banana me banana you.

Nim rarely signed spontaneously as do children when they begin to use language (spoken or sign). Only 12 percent of his utterances were spontaneous. Most of Nim's signing occurred only in response to prompting by his trainers and was related to eating, drinking, and playing; that is, it was stimulus-controlled. As much as 40 percent of his output was simply repetitions of signs made by the trainer. Children initiate conversations more and more frequently as they grow older, and their utterances repeat less and less of the adult's prior utterance. Some children hardly ever imitate in conversation. Children become increasingly more creative in their language use, but Nim showed almost no tendency toward such creativity. Furthermore, children's utterances increase in length and complexity as time progresses, finally mirroring the adult grammar, whereas Nim's language did not.

The lack of spontaneity and the excessive noncreative imitative nature of Nim's signing led to the conclusion that Nim's acquisition and use of language is qualitatively different from a child's. After examining the films of Washoe, Koko, and others, Terrace drew similar conclusions regarding the signing of the other primates.

---

[24] Collaborating with Terrace were Laura Petitto, Richard Sanders, and Thomas Bever. The results of Project Nim are reported in H. S. Terrace (1979), *Nim: A Chimpanzee Who Learned Sign Language,* New York: Knopf.

Signing chimpanzees are also unlike humans in that when several of them are together they do not sign to each other as freely as humans would under similar circumstances. There is also no evidence to date that a signing chimp (or one communicating with plastic chips or computer symbols) will teach another chimp language, or that its offspring will acquire language from the parent.

Clever Hans

Premack and the Rumbaughs, like Terrace, suggest that the sign-language studies are too uncontrolled and that the reported results were thus too anecdotal to support the view that primates are capable of acquiring a human language. They also question whether each of the others' studies, and all those attempting to teach sign language to primates, suffer from what has come to be called the Clever Hans phenomenon.

Clever Hans, a horse owned by von Osten at the turn of the century, became famous because of his apparent ability to do arithmetic, read and spell, and even solve problems of musical harmony. He answered the questions posed by his interrogators by stamping out numbers with his hoof. It turned out, not surprisingly, that Hans did not know that $2 + 2 = 4$, but he was clever enough to pick up subtle cues conveyed unconsciously by his trainer as to when he should stop tapping his foot.

Sarah, like Clever Hans, took prompts from her trainers and her environment to produce the plastic-chip sentences. In responding to the string of chips standing for

SARAH INSERT APPLE PAIL BANANA DISH

all Sarah had to figure out was to place certain fruits in certain containers, and she could decide which by merely seeing that the apple symbol was next to the pail symbol, and the banana symbol was next to the dish symbol. There is no conclusive evidence that Sarah actually grouped strings of words into constituents. There is also no indication that Sarah would understand a new compound sentence of this type; the creative ability so much a part of human language is not demonstrated by this act.

Problems also exist in Lana's acquisition of Yerkish. The Lana project was studied by Thompson and Church,[25] who were able to simulate Lana's behavior by a computer model. They concluded that the chimp's "linguistic" behavior can all be accounted for by her learning to associate lexigrams with objects, persons, or events, and to produce one of several "stock sentences" depending on situational cues (like Clever Hans).

There is another difference between the way Sarah and Lana learned whatever they learned, and the way children learn language. In the case of the chimpanzees, each new rule or sentence form was introduced in a deliberate, highly constrained way. As we noted earlier, when parents speak to children they do not confine themselves to a few words in a particular order for months, rewarding the child with a chocolate bar or a banana each time the child correctly responds to a command. Nor do they wait until the child has mastered one rule of grammar before going on to a different structure. Unless they were linguists, parents wouldn't know how to do such a thing. Young children require no special training.

---

[25] Claudia R. Thompson and Russell M. Church. 1980. "An Explanation of the Language of a Chimpanzee," *Science* 208: 313–314.

Kanzi

Research on the linguistic ability of nonhuman primates continues. Two investigators studied a different species of chimp, a male *bonobo* or *pygmy chimpanzee* named Kanzi. They used the same plastic lexigrams and computer keyboard as used with Lana. They concluded that Kanzi "has not only learned, but also invented grammatical rules that may well be as complex as these used by human two-year-old children."[26] The grammatical rule referred to was the combination of a lexigram (such as that meaning "dog") followed by a gesture meaning "go." After combining these, Kanzi would then go to an area where dogs were located to play with them. Greenfield and Savage-Rumbaugh claim that this "ordering" rule was not an imitation of his caretakers' utterances, whom they say use an opposite ordering, in which "go" was followed by "dogs."

The investigators report that Kanzi's acquisition of "grammatical skills" was much slower than that of human children, taking about three years (starting when he was five and a half years old when the study began).

Most of Kanzi's so-called sentences are fixed formulas with little if any internal structure. Kanzi has not yet exhibited linguistic knowledge of a complexity equivalent to a human three-year-old's knowledge of structure dependencies and hierarchical structure.

As often happens in science, the search for the answers to one kind of question leads to answers to other questions not originally asked. The linguistic experiments with primates have led to many advances in our understanding of primate cognitive ability. Premack has gone on to investigate other capacities of the chimp mind, such as causality; the Rumbaughs and Greenfield are continuing to study the ability of chimpanzees to use symbols. These studies also point out how remarkable it is that human children, by the age of three and four, without explicit teaching, and without overt reinforcement, create new and complex sentences never spoken and never heard before.

SUMMARY

When children learn a language, they learn the grammar of that language—the phonological, morphological, syntactic, and semantic rules—as well as the words or vocabulary. No one teaches them these rules; children just pick them up.

Before infants begin to produce words, they produce sounds, some of which will remain if they occur in the language being acquired, and others that will disappear. They do not produce sounds that never contrast meanings in any language. Deaf children exposed at birth to sign languages also produce manual babbling, showing that **babbling** is universal in first-language acquisition and is dependent on the linguistic input received.

A child does not learn the language all at once. The grammar is acquired by stages. Children's first utterances are one-word "sentences" (the **holophrastic** stage). After a few months, the two-word stage arises, in which the child puts two words together. These two-word sentences are not random combinations of words: The words have definite patterns

---

[26] The study, conducted by UCLA psychologist Patricia Marks Greenfield and Georgia State University biologist E. Sue Savage-Rumbaugh, was reported in an article in *The Chronicle of Higher Education,* 26 September 1990.

and express both grammatical and semantic relationships. Later, but still in the very early years, in what has been called the **telegraphic stage,** longer sentences appear composed primarily of content words and lacking function or grammatical morphemes. The child's early grammar lacks many of the rules of the adult grammar, but is not qualitatively different from it, and eventually it mirrors the language used in the community. Deaf children exposed to **sign language** show the same stages of language acquisition as do hearing children exposed to spoken languages.

A number of theories have been suggested to explain the acquisition process. Neither the **imitation theory,** which claims that children learn their language by imitating adult speech, nor the **reinforcement theory,** which hypothesizes that children are conditioned into speaking correctly by being negatively reinforced for errors and positively reinforced for correct usage, nor the view that children learn by **analogy,** extending one sample structure to others, is supported by observational and experimental studies. These theories can not explain the fact that children creatively form new sentences according to the rules of their language.

The ease and rapidity of children's language acquisition and the uniformity of the stages of development for all children and all languages, despite the **poverty of the stimulus** they receive, suggests that the language faculty is innate and that the infant comes to the complex task already endowed with a **Universal Grammar (UG).** UG is not a grammar like the grammar of English or Arabic but represents the principles to which all human languages conform.

A **critical-age hypothesis** has been proposed that suggests that there is a biological period during which a child may acquire its native language without overt teaching. Some songbirds also appear to have a critical period for the acquisition of their calls and songs.

The acquisition of a second or third language parallels the acquisition of one's first native language. If a second language is learned early in life, it is usually acquired with no difficulty. The difficulties encountered in attempting to learn languages after puberty may be due to the fact that they are learned after the critical age for language learning. One theory of second-language acquisition suggests that the same principles operate that account for first-language acquisition. A second view suggests that in acquiring a second language after the critical age, general learning mechanisms rather than principles specifically linguistic are used. There are a number of second-language teaching methods that have been proposed, some of them reflecting different theories of the nature of language and language acquisition. These methods, however, do not explain the apparent differences between first- and second-language acquisition.

Questions as to whether language is unique to the human species have led researchers to attempt to teach nonhuman primates systems of communication that purportedly resemble human language. Chimpanzees like Sarah and Lana have been taught to manipulate symbols to gain rewards, and other chimpanzees, like Washoe and Nim Chimpsky, have been taught a number of ASL signs. A careful examination of the utterances in ASL by these chimps show that unlike children, their language exhibits little spontaneity, is highly imitative (echoic), and reveals little syntactic structure. It has been suggested that the pygmy chimp Kanzi shows grammatical ability greater than the other chimps studied, but he still does not have the ability of even a three-year-old child.

The universality of the language acquisition process, of the stages of development, of the relatively short period in which the child constructs such a complex grammatical system without overt teaching, and the limited results of the chimpanzee experiments, suggest that the human species is innately endowed with special language acquisition abilities, that language is biologically and genetically part of the human neurological system.

All normal children everywhere learn language. This ability is not dependent on race, social class, geography, or even intelligence (within a normal range). This ability is uniquely human.

References for Further Reading

Atkinson, Martin. 1992. *Children's Syntax: An Introduction to Principles and Parameters Theory.* Oxford: Blackwell's.

Bloom, L. M. 1972. *Language Development: Form and Function in Emerging Grammar.* Cambridge, MA: MIT Press.

Bowerman, M. 1973. *Early Syntactic Development.* Cambridge, MA: MIT Press.

Brown, R. O. 1973. *A First Language: The Early Stages.* Cambridge, MA: Harvard University Press.

Celce-Murcia, M., ed. 1985. *Beyond Basics: Issues and Research in TESOL.* Rowley, MA: Newbury House.

Clark, H. H., and E. V. Clark. 1977. *Psychology and Language.* New York: Harcourt Brace Jovanovich.

de Villiers, Peter A., and Jill G. de Villiers. 1978. *Language Acquisition.* Cambridge, MA: Harvard University Press.

Ellis, R. 1985. *Understanding Second Language Acquisition.* Oxford, England: Oxford University Press.

Feldman, H., S. Goldin-Meadow, and L. Gleitman. 1978. "Beyond Herodotus: The Creation of Language by Linguistically Deprived Deaf Children." In A. Lock, ed., *Action, Symbol, and Gesture: The Emergence of Language.* New York: Academic Press, pp. 351–413.

Fischer, S. D., and P. Siple. 1990. *Theoretical Issues in Sign Language Research. Vol. 1. Linguistics.* Chicago, IL: University of Chicago Press.

Gleitman, H. 1991. *Psychology,* 3rd ed. New York: W. W. Norton, chapter 10.

Hyams, Nina. 1986. *Language Acquisition and the Theory of Parameters.* Dordrecht, The Netherlands: Reidel Publishers.

Ingram, David. 1989. *First Language Acquisition: Method, Description and Explanation.* New York: Cambridge University Press.

Klima, E. S., and U. Bellugi. 1979. *The Signs of Language.* Cambridge, MA: Harvard University Press.

Krashen, Stephen D. 1982. *Principles and Practice in Second Language Acquisition.* Oxford, England: Pergamon Press.

Landau, Barbara, and Lila R. Gleitman. 1985. *Language and Experience: Evidence from the Blind Child.* Cambridge, MA: Harvard University Press.

Premack, Ann J., and D. Premack. 1972. "Teaching Language to an Ape." *Scientific American* (October): 92–99.

Rumbaugh, D. M. 1977. *Acquisition of Linguistic Skills by a Chimpanzee.* New York: Academic Press.

Sebeok, Thomas A., and Jean Umiker-Sebeok. 1980. *Speaking of Apes: A Critical Anthology of Two-Way Communication with Man.* New York: Plenum Press.

Sebeok, Thomas A., and Robert Rosenthal, eds. 1981. *The Clever Hans Phenomenon: Communication with Horses, Whales, Apes, and People.* Annals of the New York Academy of Sciences, Vol. 364.

Terrace, Herbert S. 1979. *Nim: A Chimpanzee Who Learned Sign Language.* New York: Knopf.

Wanner, Eric, and Lila Gleitman, eds. 1982. *Language Acquisition: The State of the Art.* Cambridge, England: Cambridge University Press.

White, Lydia. 1989. *Universal Grammar and Second Language Acquisition.* Amsterdam/Philadelphia: John Benjamins.

EXERCISES

1. "Baby talk" is a term used to label the word forms that many adults use when speaking to children. Examples in English are *choo-choo* for "train" and *bow-wow* for "dog." Baby talk seems to exist in every language and culture. At least two things seem to be universal about baby talk: The words that have baby-talk forms fall into certain semantic categories (for example, food and animals), and the words are phonetically simpler than the adult forms (for example, *tummy* /tʌmi/ for "stomach" /stʌmɪk/). List all the baby-talk words you can think of in your native language; then (1) separate them into semantic categories, and (2) try to state general rules for the kinds of phonological reductions or simplifications that occur.

2. In this chapter the way a child learns negation of sentences and question formation was discussed. Can they be considered examples of a process of overgeneralization in syntax acquisition? If so, for each stage indicate *what* is being overgeneralized.

3. Find a child between two and four years old and play with the child for about thirty minutes. Keep a list of all words and/or "sentences" that are used inappropriately. Describe what the child's meanings for these words probably are. Describe the syntactic or morphological errors (including omissions). If the child is producing multiword sentences, write a grammar that could account for the data you have collected.

4. Noam Chomsky has been quoted as saying:

   It's about as likely that an ape will prove to have a language ability as that there is an island somewhere with a species of flightless birds waiting for human beings to teach them to fly.

   In the light of evidence presented in this chapter, comment on Chomsky's remark. Do you agree or disagree, or do you think the evidence is inconclusive?

5. Roger Brown and his coworkers at Harvard University (see References in this chapter) studied the language development of three children, referred to in the literature as Adam, Eve, and Sarah. The following are samples of their utterances during the "two-word stage."

see boy	push it
see sock	move it

pretty boat	mommy sleep
pretty fan	bye-bye melon
more taxi	bye-bye hot
more melon	

A. Assume that the above utterances are grammatical sentences in the children's grammars.

  (1) Write a minigrammar that would account for these sentences.

  Example: One rule might be: S → V N

  (2) Draw phrase structure trees for each utterance. Example:

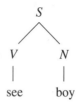

B. One observation made by Brown was that many of the sentences and phrases produced by the children were ungrammatical from the point of view of the adult grammar. The research group concluded, based on utterances such as those below, that a rule in the children's grammar for a noun phrase was:

  NP → M N (where M = any modifier)

A coat	My stool	Poor man
A celery	That knee	Little top
A Becky	More coffee	Dirty knee
A hands	More nut	That Adam
My mummy	Two tinker-toy	Big boot

  (3) Mark with an asterisk any of the above NPs that are ungrammatical in the adult grammar of English.

  (4) State the "violation" for each starred item.

  For example, if one of the utterances were *Lotsa book* you might say: "The modifier *lotsa* must be followed by a plural noun."

6. In the holophrastic (one-word) stage of child language acquisition, the child's phonological system differs in systematic ways from that in the adult grammar. The inventory of sounds and the phonemic contrasts are smaller, and there are greater constraints on phonotactic rules. (See Chapter 7 for discussion on these aspects of phonology.)

A. For each of the following words produced by a child, state what the substitution is.

> Example: spook (adult) [spuk] substitution: initial cluster [sp]
> (child) [pʰuk] reduced to single consonant; /p/
> becomes aspirated, showing that
> child has acquired aspiration rule.

(1)	don't	[dot]
(2)	skip	[kʰɪp]
(3)	shoe	[su]
(4)	that	[dæt]
(5)	play	[pʰe]
(6)	thump	[dʌp]
(7)	bath	[bæt]
(8)	chop	[tʰap]
(9)	kitty	[kɪdi]
(10)	light	[wajt]
(11)	dolly	[dawi]
(12)	grow	[go]

B. State general rules that account for the children's deviations from the adult pronunciations.

7. Children learn demonstrative words such as *this, that, these, those;* temporal terms such as *now, then, tomorrow;* and spatial terms such as *here, there, right, behind* relatively late. What do all these words have in common? Why might that factor delay their acquisition?

8. We saw in this chapter how children overgeneralize rules such as the plural rule, producing forms such as *mans* or *mouses*. What might a child learning English use instead of the adult words given:

a. children

b. went

c. better

d. best

e. brought

f. sang

g. geese

h. worst

i. knives

j. worse

Chapter 9

Language Processing: Humans and Computer

No doubt a reasonable model of language use will incorporate, as a basic component, the generative grammar that expresses the speaker-hearer's knowledge of the language; but this generative grammar does not, in itself, prescribe the character or functioning of a perceptual model or a model of speech production.

Noam Chomsky, *Aspects of a Theory of Syntax*

THE HUMAN MIND AT WORK: HUMAN LANGUAGE PROCESSING

Psycholinguistics is the area of linguistics that is concerned with linguistic performance—how we use our linguistic competence, our knowledge of language in speech (or sign) production and comprehension. The human brain is able not only to acquire and store the mental grammar, but to access that linguistic storehouse to speak and understand what is spoken.

How we process knowledge depends to a great extent on the nature of that knowledge. If, for example, language was not "open-ended," if language consisted of a finite store of fixed phrases and sentences, then speaking might simply consist of finding a sentence that expresses a thought we wish to convey with its phonological representation and producing it; comprehension could be the reverse—matching the sounds to a stored string that has been entered with its meaning. We know this is not possible because of the creativity of language. In Chapter 8, we saw that children do not learn language by imitating and storing sentences but by constructing a grammar. When we speak, we access our grammar to find the words, construct novel sentences, and produce the sounds that express the message we wish to convey. When we listen to someone speak and understand what is being said, we also access the grammar to process the utterances to assign a meaning to the sounds we hear.

Speaking and comprehending speech can be viewed as a speech chain "linking the speaker's brain with the listener's brain" as shown in Figure 9-1.

FIGURE 9-1 The Speech Chain[1]

A spoken utterance starts as a message in the brain/mind of the speaker. It is put into linguistic form and interpreted as articulation commands, emerging as an acoustic signal. The signal is processed by the ear of the listener and sent to the brain/mind, where it is interpreted.

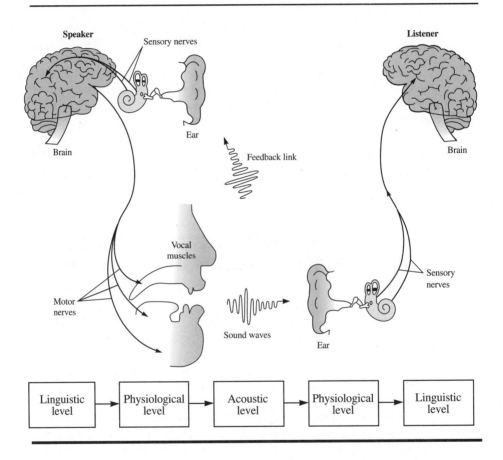

The grammar relates sounds and meanings and contains the units and rules of the language that make speech production and comprehension possible. But the grammar does not describe the psychological processes that are used in producing and understanding utterances. A theory of linguistic performance describes the relationship between the mental grammar and the psychological mechanisms by means of which this grammar is accessed to permit speech and comprehension.

[1] The figure is taken from Jean Berko Gleason and Nan Bernstein Ratner, eds. 1993. *Psycholinguistics,* Orlando, FL: Harcourt Brace, p. 273.

Comprehension

© PEANUTS reprinted by permission of United Feature Syndicate, Inc.

> "I quite agree with you," said the Duchess; "and the moral of that is—'Be what you would seem to be'—or, if you'd like it put more simply—'Never imagine yourself not to be otherwise than what it might appear to others that what you were or might have been was not otherwise than what you had been would have appeared to them to be otherwise.' "
>
> "I think I should understand that better," Alice said very politely, "if I had it written down: but I can't quite follow it as you say it."
>
> Lewis Carroll, Alice's Adventures in Wonderland

The difficulty Alice had in understanding this sentence is not surprising. What is surprising is that we usually do understand even long and complex sentences with multiply embedded relative clauses and many conjoined phrases and modifiers. Even young children can do this automatically and without conscious effort. Once in a while, of course, one stops and asks for clarification, as Christopher Robin did in listening to a story about Winnie-the-Pooh.

> Once upon a time, a very long time ago now, about last Friday, Winnie-the-Pooh lived in a forest all by himself under the name of Sanders.
> *("What does 'under the name' mean?" asked Christopher Robin.*
> *"It means he had the name over the door in gold letters, and lived under it.")*[2]

If Christopher Robin took the time to think about the meaning of the phrase *under the name of Sanders,* he may have realized that it was an ambiguous sentence. In normal conversations, nonlinguistic considerations like word frequency or what we expect to hear or what we are thinking can influence which meaning of an ambiguous sentence we come up with. One aim of psycholinguistic research is to clarify the processes by which speakers match one or more meanings to the strings of sounds they hear.

The Speech Signal

We are not conscious of the complicated processes we use to understand speech. As noted, one of the first questions concerns the problems of segmentation of the acoustic signal. To understand how this is done, some knowledge of the signal itself can be helpful.

---

[2] A. A. Milne. 1926. *Winnie the Pooh,* New York: E.P. Dutton & Co.

In Chapter 6 speech sounds were described according to the ways in which they are produced—the position of the tongue, the lips, and the velum; the state of the vocal cords; the airstream mechanisms; whether the articulators obstruct the free flow of air; and so on. All of these articulatory characteristics are reflected in the physical characteristics of the sounds produced.

Speech sounds can also be described in physical or **acoustic** terms. Physically, a sound is produced whenever there is a disturbance in the position of air molecules. The question asked by ancient philosophers as to whether a sound is produced if a tree falls in the middle of the forest with no one to hear it has been answered by the science of acoustics. Objectively, a sound is produced; subjectively, there is no sound. In fact, there are sounds we cannot hear because our ears are not sensitive to all changes in air pressure (which result from the movement of air molecules). **Acoustic phonetics** is concerned only with speech sounds, all of which can be heard by the normal human ear.

When we push air out of the lungs through the glottis, it causes the vocal cords to vibrate; this vibration in turn produces pulses of air that escape through the mouth (and sometimes also the nose). These pulses are actually small variations in the air pressure due to the wavelike motion of the air molecules.

The sounds we produce can be described in terms of how fast the variations of the air pressure occur, which determines the **fundamental frequency** of the sounds and is perceived by the hearer as **pitch.** We can also describe the magnitude or **intensity** of the variations, which determines the loudness of the sound. The quality of the speech sound is determined by the kind of vibrations, or wave form, which is determined by the shape of the vocal tract when the air is flowing through it.

An important tool in acoustic research is a computer program that decomposes the speech signal into its frequency components. When you speak into a microphone

FIGURE 9-2   A spectrogram of the words *heed, head, had,* and *who'd,* as spoken with a British accent (speaker: Peter Ladefoged, February 16, 1973).

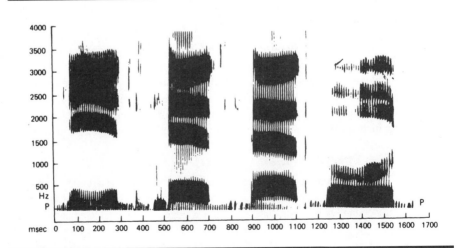

plugged into the back of the computer (or when a tape recorder is plugged in), an image of the speech signal is displayed. The patterns produced are called **spectrograms** or, more vividly, **voiceprints.** A spectrogram of the words *heed, head, had,* and *who'd* is shown in Figure 9-2.

Time in milliseconds moves horizontally from left to right; vertically, the graph represents pitch (or, more technically, frequency). Notice that for each vowel there are a number of dark bands that differ in their placement according to their pitch. They represent the strongest harmonics produced by the shape of the vocal tract and are called the **formants** of the vowels. Because the tongue is in a different position for each vowel, the formant frequencies differ for each vowel. It is the different frequencies of these formants that account for the different vowel qualities you hear. The pitch of the entire utterance (intonation contour) is shown by the voicing bar marked P on the spectrogram. When the striations are far apart, the vocal cords are vibrating slowly and the pitch is low; when the striations are close together, the vocal cords are vibrating rapidly and the pitch is high.

By studying spectrograms of all speech sounds and many different utterances, acoustic phoneticians have learned a great deal about the basic acoustic components that reflect the articulatory features of speech sounds.

Speech Perception and Comprehension

By permission of Johnny Hart and Creators Syndicate, Inc.

The comprehension of speech involves many psychological operations. One of the first questions we need to answer in trying to understand this complex process is the units that are involved. Experiments show that perceptual units occur on different levels; we can segment the speech signal into strings of phonemes, syllables, morphemes, words, and phrases.

The units we can perceive depend, as can be expected, on the language we know. Speakers of English can perceive the difference between [l] and [r] because these phones represent distinct phonemes in the language; speakers of Japanese have great difficulty in differentiating between the two because they are allophones of one phoneme in their language.

The context in which an utterance is used also helps the segmentation task. One is more likely to discern the words *night rate* than the word *nitrate* if one is talking about the cost of theater tickets or house electricity, but in a discussion of fertilizers or chemistry, perception would tend toward *nitrate.*

Although words are seldom surrounded by boundaries such as pauses, as the example above shows, words are obviously units of perception. If we hear a word in isolation, we can analyze the acoustic signal, map it onto the phonemic representation, and find its match with its meaning in the mental lexicon. When not in isolation, the perception of words is more difficult.

To see how complex speech processing is, suppose you heard someone say:

A sniggle blick is procking a slar

and were able to perceive the sounds as

/ə s n ɪ g əl b l ɪ k ɪ z p r a k ɪ ŋ ə s l a r/

You would still be unable to assign a meaning to the sounds, because the meaning of a sentence depends, at least in part, on the meanings of its words, and the only English lexical items in this string are the morphemes *a, is,* and *-ing.* The sentence lacks any English content words. (You would, however, accept it as a grammatically formed sentence in English because it conforms to the rules of English syntax.)

You can only know that the sentence has no meaning if you attempt (unconsciously or consciously) a search of your mental lexicon for the phonological strings you decide are possible words. This process is called **lexical access** and **word recognition.** Finding that there are no entries for *sniggle, blick, prock,* or *slar,* you can conclude that the sentence includes **nonsense** strings.

If instead you heard someone say *The cat chased the rat,* through a similar lexical look-up process, you would conclude that an event concerning a cat, a rat, and the activity of chasing had occurred. You could only know this by segmenting the words in the continuous speech signal, analyzing them into their phonological word units, and matching these units to similar strings stored in your lexicon, which also includes the meanings attached to these phonological representations. This still would not enable you to tell who chased whom, since this is determined by syntactic processing. Processing speech to get at the meaning of what is said requires syntactic analysis as well as knowledge of **lexical semantics.**

Stress and intonation provide some clues to syntactic structure. We know, for example, that the different meanings of the sentences *He lives in the white house* and *He lives in the White House* can be signaled by differences in their stress patterns. Such prosodic aspects of speech also help to segment the speech signal into words and phrases; syllables at the end of a phrase are longer in duration than at the beginning. Intonation contours mark boundaries of clauses. Relative loudness, pitch, and duration of syllables thus provide information in the comprehension process.

Speech comprehension is very fast and automatic. We understand an utterance as we hear it or read it. We don't wait for a pause and then say, "Hold on. I have to analyze the speech sounds, look the words up in my dictionary, and **parse** (provide a syntactic analysis of) your utterance." But how do we understand a sentence?

Comprehension involves the ability to segment the semicontinuous speech signal we hear into phonemes, morphemes, words, phrases, sentences, and even discourse.

Comprehension Models and Experimental Studies

> I have experimented and experimented until now I know that [water] never does run uphill, except in the dark. I know it does in the dark, because the pool never goes dry; which it would, of course, if the water didn't come back in the night. It is best to prove things by experiment; then you know; whereas if you depend on guessing and supposing and conjecturing, you will never get educated.
>
> Mark Twain, Eve's Diary

> In this laboratory the only one who is always right is the cat.
>
> Motto in laboratory of Arturo Rosenblueth

The psychological stages and processes that a listener goes through in comprehending the meaning of an utterance are very complex. Alternative models of speech processing have been proposed in the attempt to clarify the stages involved. Some psycholinguists suggest that speech perception and comprehension involve both **top-down** and **bottom-up processing.**

Top-down processes proceed from semantic and syntactic information to the sensory input. Using such higher level information, it is suggested that we can predict what is to follow in the signal.

Bottom-up processes move step-by-step from the incoming acoustic signal to semantic interpretation, building each part of the structure on the basis of the sensory data alone.

Evidence for at least partial top-down processing is provided in a number of experiments. For example, subjects make fewer identification errors of words when the words occur in sentences than when they are presented in isolation. This suggests that subjects are using knowledge of syntactic structures in addition to the acoustic input signal. This is true even when the stimuli are presented in the presence of noise. Subjects also do better if the words occur in grammatically meaningful sentences as opposed to grammatically anomalous sentences; identification of words in ungrammatical sentences produced the most errors. This supports the idea that subjects are not simply responding to the input word by word.

Top-down processing is also supported by the fact that when subjects hear recorded sentences in which some part of the signal is removed and a cough substituted, they "hear" the sentence without a missing phoneme, and, in fact, are unable to say which phonemic segment the cough replaced. Context plays a major role in determining what sounds the subjects replace. Thus, "[cough] eel" is heard as *wheel, heel, peel,* or *meal* depending on whether the sentence in which the distorted word occurs refers to an axle, shoe, orange, or food, respectively. We have also seen that context plays a role in word segmentation. If we heard [n a j t r e t] while checking into a motel, we would intepret it as *night rate,* whereas in a chemistry lab, we would think we heard *nitrate.* Similarly the phonetic string [w a j t š u z] would be heard as *white shoes,* rather than *why choose,* in a shoe store.

Lexical Access and Word Recognition   There has been a great deal of research by psycholinguists on *lexical access* or *word recognition,* the process by which we obtain information about the meaning of a word from our mental lexicon. A number of experimental techniques have been used in studies of lexical access.

One technique asks subjects to decide whether a string of sounds (or letters if printed stimuli are used) is or is not a word. They must respond by pressing a button if the stimulus is an actual word. In these **lexical decision** experiments, **response time** or **reaction time** measurements (often referred to as RTs) are taken. The assumption is that the longer the time it takes to respond to a particular task, the more processing is involved. Using such measurements, it has been found that lexical access depends to some extent on word **frequency**, that is, RT is faster to words that occur more frequently in speech and writing. This is evidence that comprehension performance involves both linguistic and nonlinguistic factors. Another finding is that ambiguous sentences take longer to process than unambiguous sentences. It appears that even if subjects are not aware of the multiple meanings of an ambiguous sentence, both meanings are evoked and interfere with each other. This is true of sentences that are lexically ambiguous (with words that have more than one meaning) and of sentences that are syntactically ambiguous.

Reaction time is also measured in experiments using a **priming** technique. It has been found, for example, that if subjects hear a word such as *nurse,* their response to *doctor* will be faster than to a semantically unrelated word such as *flower.* This may be due to the fact that semantically related words are located in the same part of the lexicon and once the "path" to that section has been taken, it is easier to travel that way a second time. It may also be due to the fact that other words are triggered when we look up a semantically related word.

An interesting finding in such experiments is that a lexically ambiguous word can be primed by a word referring to either meaning, even if the context of the ambiguous word disambiguates it. For example, either *harbor* or *wine* will prime the word *port* (result in faster response time) in the sentence

The ship is in port.

This suggests that in listening to speech, all the meanings represented by a phonological form will be triggered. This however argues against top-down processing, since both words are accessed even when the preceding sentence disambiguates the ambiguous word. That is, if we use information other than what is contained in the incoming signal, the sentence that was heard earlier should influence which word is accessed.

Another experimental technique, called the **naming** task, asks the subject to read aloud a printed word. (The naming task is also used in studies of aphasics, who are asked to name the object shown in a picture.) Subjects read real words faster than nonwords, and irregularly spelled words like *dough* and *enough* as fast as regularly spelled words like *doe* and *stuff,* and even faster than regularly spelled nonsense forms like *cluff.* This shows that the subjects first go to the lexicon to see if the word is there, access the phonological representation, and produce the word. They can use spelling-to-pronunciation rules if they cannot find the string of letters listed.

In naming, frequency also plays an effect. That is, frequent words are read more quickly than infrequent ones. One model of word recognition proposed by the psychologist Kenneth Forster of the University of Arizona, called the **search model,** accounts for the frequency effect by suggesting that in lexical access, the most recent words are accessed first.

Syntactic Processing

There has been more psycholinguistic research dealing with lexical access than with syntactic processing, possibly because the available experimental techniques can be more easily directed toward this question. In recent years, an increasing number of studies have concentrated on sentence processing.

One class of sentences that involves syntactic processing, as distinguished from syntactic competence, has been referred to as *garden-path sentences,* illustrated by the following:

> The horse raced past the barn fell.

Many individuals, on hearing this sentence, will judge it to be ungrammatical, yet will judge a sentence with the same syntactic structure as grammatical, such as:

> The bus driven past the school stopped.

Similarly, subjects will have no problem with:

> The horse that was raced past the barn fell.

The reason why the first sentence is called a garden-path sentence is because, as the idiom implies, we are incorrectly led to interpret the word *raced* as the main verb of the verb phrase since it immediately follows the first noun phrase. To interpret the sentence correctly we have to retrace our processing when we come to the main sentence verb *fell,* which becomes very confusing. Such backtracking seems to put a burden on short-term memory and syntactic processors and creates comprehension errors.

Such sentences highlight the distinction between syntactic competence and syntactic performance strategies.

There are a number of other techniques used experimentally in the study of speech perception and comprehension. In a **shadowing** task, subjects are asked to repeat what they hear as rapidly as possible. A few exceptionally good shadowers can follow what is being said only about a syllable behind (300 milliseconds). Most of us, however, shadow with a delay of about a second (500 to 800 milliseconds). This is still quite fast. More interesting than the speed, shadowers often correct speech errors or mispronunciations unconsciously, and even add inflectional endings if they are absent. Even when they are told the speech they are to shadow includes errors and they should repeat the errors, they are unable to do so. Lexical corrections are more likely to occur when the target word is predictable from what has been said previously. These shadowing experiments show that speech perception involves more than simply processing the incoming signal.

The ability to understand and comprehend what is said to us is a complex psychological process involving the internal grammar, motivation, frequency factors, memory, and both linguistic and nonlinguistic context.

Speech Production

U.S. ACRES reprinted by permission of UFS, Inc.

As we saw above, the speech chain starts with a speaker who, through some complicated set of neuromuscular processes, produces an acoustic signal that represents a thought, idea, or message to be conveyed to a listener, who must then decode the signal to arrive at a similar message. It is more difficult to devise experiments that provide information on how the speaker proceeds than to do so from the listener's side of the process. The best information has come from observing and analyzing spontaneous speech.

Planning Units

We might suppose that the thoughts of the speaker are simply translated into words one after the other through a semantic mapping process. Grammatical morphemes would be added as demanded by the syntactic rules of the language. The phonetic representation of each word in turn would then be mapped onto the neuromuscular commands to the articulators to produce the acoustic signal representing it.

We know, however, that this supposition is not a true picture of speech production. Although, when we speak, the sounds we produce and the words we use are linearly ordered, speech errors show that the pre-articulation stages involve units larger than the single phonemic segment or even the word, as illustrated by the above cartoon. Phrases and even whole sentences are constructed prior to the production of a single sound. Errors show that features, segments, and words can be anticipated, that is, produced earlier than intended, or reversed (as in typical spoonerisms), so the later words or phrases in which they occur must already be conceptualized. This point is illustrated in the following examples (the intended utterance to the left of the arrow, the actual utterance, including the error, to the right of the arrow).

1. The *h*iring of minority faculty. → The *f*iring of minority faculty.
   (The intended *h* is replaced by the *f* of *faculty,* which occurs later in the intended utterance.)
2. *a*d h*o*c → *o*dd h*a*ck
   (The vowels /æ/ of the first word and /a/ of the second are exchanged or reversed.)

3. *b*ig and *f*at → *p*ig and *v*at
   (The values of a single feature are switched: [+ voiced] becomes [– voiced] in *big* and [– voiced] becomes [+ voiced] in *fat*.)
4. There are many ministers in our church. → There are many churches in our minister.
   (The stem morphemes *minister* and *church* are exchanged; the grammatical plural morpheme remains in its intended place in the phrase structure.)
5. Seymour sliced the salami with a knife. → Seymour sliced a knife with the salami.
   (The entire noun phrases—article + noun—were exchanged.)

In these errors, the intonation contour (primary stressed syllables and variations in pitch) remained the same as in the intended utterances, even when the words were disordered. In the intended utterance of (5), the highest pitch would be on *knife*. In the disordered sentence the highest pitch occurred on the second syllable of *salami*. The pitch rise and increased loudness are thus determined by the syntactic structure of the sentence and are independent of the individual words. Thus syntactic structures also are units in linguistic performance.

Errors like those cited above are constrained in interesting ways. Phonological errors involving segments or features, as in (1), (2), and (3), primarily occur in content words, and not in grammatical morphemes, again showing the distinction between these lexical classes. In addition, while words and lexical morphemes may be interchanged, grammatical morphemes, free or bound inflectional affixes, may not be. As example (4) illustrates, the inflectional endings are left behind and subsequently attached, in their proper phonological form, to the moved lexical morpheme.

Such errors show that speech production involves different kinds of units—features, segments, morphemes, words, phrases, the very units that exist in the grammar. They also show that when we speak, words are structured into larger syntactic phrases that are stored in a kind of buffer memory before segments or features or words are disordered. This storage must occur prior to the articulatory stage. Thus, we do not select one word from our mental dictionary and say it, then select another word and say it. We organize an entire phrase and in many cases an entire sentence.

The constraints on which units can be exchanged or moved also suggest that grammatical morphemes are added at a stage after the lexical morphemes are selected. This provided one of the motivations for a two-lexicon grammatical model, one with lexical and derivational morphemes listed, and the other with inflectional and grammatical morphemes.

Lexical Selection

. . . Humpty Dumpty's theory, of two meanings packed into one word like a portmanteau, seems to me the right explanation for all. For instance, take the two words "fuming" and "furious." Make up your mind that you will say both words but leave it unsettled which you will say first. Now open your mouth and speak. If . . . you have that rarest of gifts, a perfectly balanced mind, you will say "frumious."

Lewis Carroll, Preface to *The Hunting of the Snark*

In Chapter 5, word substitution errors were used to illustrate the semantic properties of words. Such substitutions are seldom random; they show that in speaking, in our attempt to express our thoughts through words in the lexicon, we may make an incorrect lexical selection based on partial similarity or relatedness of meanings.

Blends, in which we produce part of one word and part of another, further illustrate the lexical selection process in speech production; we may select two or more words to express our thoughts and instead of deciding between them, produce them as "portmanteaus," as Humpty Dumpty calls them. Such blends are illustrated in the following errors:

1. splinters/blisters   →   splisters
2. edited/annotated   →   editated
3. a swinging/hip chick   →   a swip chick
4. frown/scowl   →   frowl

Application and Misapplication of Rules

> I thought . . . four rules would be enough, provided that I made a firm and constant resolution not to fail even once in the observance of them.
>
> René Descartes (1596–1650)

Spontaneous errors show that the rules of morphology and syntax, discussed in earlier chapters as part of competence, may also be applied (or misapplied) when we speak. It is hard to see this process in normal error-free speech, but when someone says *groupment* instead of *grouping, ambigual* instead of *ambiguous,* or *bloodent* instead of *bloody,* it shows that regular rules are applied to morphemes to form possible but nonexistent words.

Inflectional rules also surface. The UCLA professor who said *We swimmed in the pool* knows that the past tense of *swim* is *swam* but mistakenly applied the regular rule to an irregular form.

Morphophonemic rules also appear to be performance rules as well as rules of competence. Consider the *a/an* alternation rule in English. Errors such as *an istem* for the intended *a system* or *a burly bird* for the intended *an early bird* show that when segmental disordering changes a noun beginning with a consonant to a noun beginning with a vowel, or vice versa, the indefinite article is also changed so that it conforms to the grammatical rule.

Such utterances also reveal that in speech production, internal "editing" or monitoring attempts to prevent errors. When an error slips by the editor, such as the disordering of phonemes, the editor prevents a compounding of errors. Thus, when the /b/ of "bird" was anticipated and added to the beginning of "early" the result was not *an burly bird.* The editor applied (or reapplied) the *a/an* rule to produce *a burly bird.*

An examination of such data also tells us something about the stages in the production of an utterance. Disordering of phonemes must occur before the indefinite article is given its phonological form or the morphological rule must reapply after the initial error has occurred. An error such as *bin beg* for the intended *Big Ben* shows that phonemes are disordered before phonetic allophones are determined. That is, the intended *Big Ben* phonetically is [bɪg bɛ̃n] with an oral [ɪ] before the [g] and a nasal [ɛ̃] before the [n].

In the utterance that was produced, however, the [ĩ] is nasalized because it now occurs before the disordered [n], whereas the [ɛ̃] is oral before the disordered [g]. If the disordering occurred after the phonemes had been replaced by phonetic allophones, the result would have been the phonetic utterance [bɪn bɛ̃g].

Nonlinguistic Influences

The discussion on speech comprehension suggested that nonlinguistic factors are involved in and sometimes interfere with linguistic processing. They also affect speech production. The individual who said *He made hairlines* instead of *He made headlines* was referring to a barber. The fact that the two compound nouns both start with the same sound, are composed of two syllables, have the same stress pattern, and contain the identical second morphemes undoubtedly played a role in producing the error; but the relationship between hairlines and barbers may also have been a contributing factor.

Other errors show that thoughts unrelated structurally to the intended utterance may have an influence on what is said. One speaker said "I've never heard of classes *on April 9*" instead of the intended *on Good Friday*. Good Friday fell on April 9 that year. The two phrases are not similar phonologically or morphologically; yet the nonlinguistic association seems to have influenced what was said. A similar observation may apply to the earlier seen substitution of *firing* for *hiring* regarding minority faculty. This influence is a further example of the distinction between linguistic competence and performance.

Looking at both normal conversational data and experimentally elicited data provides the psycholinguist with evidence in the construction of models of both speech production and comprehension, the beginning and end points of the speech chain of communication.

SILICON AT WORK: COMPUTER PROCESSING OF HUMAN LANGUAGE

BIZARRO by Dan Piraro. Copyright © 1991 by Chronicle Features. Reprinted by permission.

Up until recently only human beings have had the capability to process language. Today, it is common for computers to process language. **Computational linguistics** is a subfield of linguistics and computer science that is concerned with computer processing of human language. It includes automatic machine translation of one language into another, the analysis of written texts and spoken discourse, the use of language for communication between people and computers, computer modeling of linguistic theories, and the role of human language in artificial intelligence.

Machine Translation

Egad, I think the interpreter is the hardest to be understood of the two!

R. B. Sheridan, *The Critic*

. . . There exist extremely simple sentences in English—and . . . for any other natural language—which would be uniquely . . . and unambiguously translated into any other language by anyone with a sufficient knowledge of the two languages involved, though I know of no program that would enable a machine to come up with this unique rendering. . . .

Yeshua Bar-Hillel

The first use of computers for natural language processing began in the 1940s with the attempt to develop **automatic machine translation.** During World War II, United States' scientists, without the assistance of computers, deciphered coded Japanese military communications and proved their skill in coping with difficult language problems. The idea of using deciphering techniques to translate from one language into another was expressed in a letter written to cyberneticist Norbert Wiener by Warren Weaver, a pioneer in the field of computational linguistics: "When I look at any article in Russian, I say: 'This is really written in English, but it has been coded in some strange symbols. I will now proceed to decode it.' "[3]

The aim in automatic translation is to input a written passage in the **source language** and to receive a grammatical passage of equivalent meaning in the **target language** (the output). In the early days of machine translation, it was believed that this task could be accomplished by entering into the memory of a computer a dictionary of a source language and a dictionary with the corresponding morphemes and words of a target language. The translating program attempted to match the morphemes of the input sentence with those of the target language. Unfortunately, what often happened was a process called by early machine translators "language in, garbage out."

Translation is more than word-for-word replacement. Often there is no equivalent word in the target language, and the order of words may differ, as in translating from a Subject-Verb-Object (SVO) language like English to a Subject-Object-Verb (SOV) language like Japanese. There is also difficulty in translating idioms, metaphors, jargon, and so on.

---

[3] W. N. Locke and A. D. Boothe, eds. 1955. *Machine Translation of Languages,* New York: Wiley.

These problems are dealt with by human translators because they know the grammars of the two languages and draw on general knowledge of the subject matter and the world to arrive at the intended meaning. Machine translation is often impeded by lexical and syntactic ambiguities, structural disparities between the two languages, morphological complexities, and other cross-linguistic differences. It is often difficult to get good translations even when humans do the translating, as is illustrated by some of the "garbage" printed on signs in non-English-speaking countries as "aids" to tourists:

> Utmost of chicken with smashed pot (restaurant in Greece)
> Nervous meatballs (restaurant in Bulgaria)
> The nuns harbor all diseases and have no respect for religion (Swiss nunnery hospital)
> All the water has been passed by the manager (German hotel)
> Certified midwife: entrance sideways (Jerusalem)
> The government bans the smoking of children (Turkey)

Such "translations" represent the difficulties of just finding the right words; but word choice is a minor problem in automatic translation. The syntactic problems are more complex.

The greater recognition of the role of syntax and the application of linguistic principles over the past fifty years have made it possible to use computers to translate simple texts—ones in a constrained context such as a mathematical proof—grammatically and accurately between well-studied languages such as English and Russian. More complex texts require human intervention if the translation is to be grammatical and semantically faithful. The use of computers to aid the human translator can improve efficiency by a factor of ten or more, but the day when travelers can whip out a "pocket translator," hold it up to the mouth of a native speaker, and receive a translation in their own language is as yet beyond the horizon.

Text Processing

> [The professor had written] all the words of their language in their several moods, tenses and declensions [on tiny blocks of wood, and had] emptied the whole vocabulary into his frame, and made the strictest computation of the general proportion there is in books between the numbers of particles, nouns, and verbs, and other parts of speech.
>
> Jonathan Swift, *Gulliver's Travels*

Jonathan Swift prophesied one way computers would be put to work in linguistics—in the statistical analysis of language. Computers can be programmed to reveal such properties of language as the distribution of sounds, allowable word orders, permitted combinations of morphemes, relative frequencies of words and morphemes (that is, their "general proportion"), and so on.

Such analyses can be conducted on existing texts (such as the works of Shakespeare or the Bible) or on a collection of utterances gathered from spoken or written sources, called a **corpus.** One such corpus, compiled at Brown University, consists of over one million words from fifteen sources of written American English, including passages from daily newspapers, magazines, and literary material.[4] Because this corpus is available in computer-readable form, many scholars are able to use it in their research.

A corpus of *spoken* American English, similar in size to the Brown corpus, was also collected.[5] A computer analysis of this corpus was conducted and the result was compared with the Brown corpus, which provided a contrast between written and spoken American English. Not surprisingly, the pronoun *I* occurs ten times more frequently in the spoken corpus. Profane and taboo words are, as expected, more frequent in spoken language; *shit* occurs 128 times in the spoken corpus, but only four times in the written one. All of the prepositions except *to* occur more frequently in written than in spoken English, suggesting that different syntactic structures are used in written English than in spoken English.

In the early 1990s a group of universities and companies collaborated to form the Linguistic Data Consortium (LDC), whose headquarters are at the University of Pennsylvania.[6] This group makes available vast quantities of language data, both written and spoken, from dozens of languages, both Indo- and non-Indo-European. These databases are being used extensively for research into language itself, and for testing computer language processing systems such as automatic speech recognition.

A computer can also be used to produce a **concordance** of a literary text, which gives the frequency of every word in a text and the line and page number of each occurrence. Such analyses, once carried out painstakingly over many years, were only produced for the most eminent of texts (such as the Bible). Now a concordance can be accomplished in a short time on any text that has been entered into a computer. The use of concordances on *The Federalist Papers* helped ascribe the authorship of a disputed paper to James Madison rather than to Alexander Hamilton, by comparing the concordance of the paper in question with those of known works by the two writers.

A concordance of *sounds* by computer may reveal patterns in poetry that would be nearly impossible for a human to detect. Such an analysis on the *Iliad* showed that many of the lines with an unusual number of etas (/i/) related to youth and lovemaking; the line with the most alphas (/a/) was interpreted as being an imitation of stamping feet.

Poetic and prosaic features such as assonance, alliteration, meter, and rhythm have always been studied by literary scholars. Today, computers can do the tedious mechanical work of such analyses, leaving the human more time to contemplate new ideas.

Computers That Talk and Listen

The first generations of computers had received their inputs through glorified typewriter keyboards, and had replied through high-speed printers and visual displays. Hal could do this when necessary, but most of his communication with his shipmates was by means of the spoken words. Poole and Bowman could talk to Hal as if he were a human being, and he would reply

---

[4] H. Kučera and W. N. Francis. 1967. *Computational Analysis of Present-Day American English,* Providence, RI: Brown University Press.

[5] H. Dahl. 1979. *Word Frequencies of Spoken American English,* Essex, CT: Verbatim.

[6] The Linguistic Data Consortium, 441 Williams Hall, University of Pennsylvania, Philadelphia, PA 19104-6305. E-mail: ldc@unagi.cis.upenn.edu. World Wide Web home page at URL: http://www.ldc.upenn.edu/

in the perfect idiomatic English he had learned during the fleeting weeks of his electronic childhood.

Arthur C. Clarke, 2001, A Space Odyssey

The ideal computer is multilingual; it should "speak" computer languages such as FORTRAN and Java, and human languages such as Japanese and English. For many purposes it would be helpful if we could communicate with computers as we communicate with other humans, through our native language; but the computers portrayed in films and on television as capable of speaking and understanding human language do not yet exist.

Computers are at present severely limited in their ability to comprehend and produce spoken language, and programming them to do so is one of the most difficult and challenging goals of computational linguistics. Properly programmed, a computer can "understand" language fragments with vocabularies of 100 to 1000 words in an extremely narrow context (simple syntax and a limited semantic field).[7] (The vocabulary can be larger for written language, or for language spoken with pauses between individual words.) Computers can produce synthetic speech that imitates the human voice fairly well, but humans must program them to do it and tell them what to say.

Just as human speech production and comprehension differ in the psychological mechanisms involved (although they access the same mental grammar), comprehension and production of speech by computers require entirely different programs. In some cases the attempt is to model the human processor; in others, the goal is to get the computer to speak and understand, rather than to shed light on human performance.

Computer comprehension consists of **speech recognition,** the perception of sounds and words, and **speech understanding,** the interpretation of the words recognized. Some comprehension programs bypass speech recognition by processing written text. These may be typed at a keyboard, in which case they are entered directly into the computer. Optical scanners and interpretive programs are able to convert printed text into an electronic form suitable for computers, but the process is error-prone and highly dependent on such mundane features as the quality of the paper and ink used to create the printed page originally.

Speech production consists of **language generation**—deciding what to say—and **speech synthesis,** the actual creation of speech sounds. As in attempts at computer comprehension, different research groups concentrate on one aspect or another of speech production, and with different purposes.

Talking Machines (Speech Synthesis)

Machines which, with more or less success, imitate human speech, are the most difficult to construct, so many are the agencies engaged in uttering even a single word—so many are the inflections and variations of tone and articulation, that the mechanician finds his ingenuity taxed to the utmost to imitate them.

Scientific American (January 14, 1871)

---

[7] See *Spoken Natural Language Dialog Systems* by Smith and Hipp for an excellent, detailed description of what is involved in getting a computer to understand and respond correctly to spoken input.

Early efforts toward building "talking machines" were more concerned with machines that could produce sounds that imitated human speech than with machines that could figure out what to say. In 1779, Christian Gottlieb Kratzenstein won a prize for building such a machine ("an instrument constructed like the vox humana pipes of an organ which . . . accurately express the sounds of the vowels") and for answering a question posed by the Imperial Academy of St. Petersburg: "What is the nature and character of the sounds of the vowels *a, e, i, o, u* [that make them] different from one another?" Kratzenstein constructed a set of "acoustic resonators" similar to the shapes of the mouth when these vowels are articulated and set them resonating by a vibrating reed that produced pulses of air similar to those coming from the lungs through the vibrating vocal cords.

Twelve years later, Wolfgang von Kempelen of Vienna constructed a more elaborate machine with bellows to produce a stream of air such as is produced by the lungs, and with other mechanical devices to simulate the different parts of the vocal tract. Von Kempelen's machine so impressed the young Alexander Graham Bell, who saw a replica of the machine in Edinburgh in 1850, that he, together with his brother Melville, attempted to construct a "talking head," making a cast from a human skull. They used various materials to form the velum, palate, teeth, lips, tongue, cheeks, and so on, and installed a metal larynx with vocal cords made by stretching a slotted piece of rubber. They used a keyboard control system to manipulate all the parts with an intricate set of levers. This ingenious machine produced vowel sounds and some nasal sounds and even a few short combinations of sounds.

With the advances in the acoustic theory of speech production and the technological developments in electronics, machine production of speech sounds has made great progress. We no longer have to build actual physical models of the speech-producing mechanism; we can now imitate the process by producing the physical signals electronically.

Research on speech has shown that all speech sounds can be reduced to a small number of acoustic components. One way to produce synthetic speech is to mix these important parts together in the proper proportions, depending on the speech sounds to be imitated. It is rather like following a recipe for making soup, which might read:

"Take two quarts of water, add one onion, three carrots, a potato, a teaspoon of salt, a pinch of pepper, and stir it all together."

This method of producing synthetic speech would include a "recipe" that might read:

1. Start with a tone at the same frequency as vibrating vocal cords (higher if a woman's or child's voice is being synthesized, lower for a man's).
2. Emphasize the harmonics corresponding to the formants required for a particular vowel quality.
3. Add hissing or buzzing for fricatives.
4. Add nasal resonances for any nasal sounds.
5. Temporarily cut off sound to produce stops and affricates.
6. and so on. . . .

All these "ingredients" are blended together electronically, using computers to produce highly intelligible, more or less natural-sounding speech.

Most synthetic speech still has a machinelike quality or "accent," due to small inaccuracies in simulation and because suprasegmental factors such as changing intonation and stress patterns are not yet fully understood. Still, speech synthesizers today are no harder to understand than a person speaking a slightly different dialect than one's own.

When a computer produces synthetic speech, it produces speech sounds corresponding to some input text. It must be programmed with a complex set of text-to-speech rules that translates written English into a phonetic transcription from which speech sounds are synthesized and produced. Since, in its synthesis program, the computer uses no semantic or syntactic knowledge (even if such information has been put into its memory), it will read ungrammatical and nonsensical texts in the same way as grammatical ones.

Speech synthesis has important applications. It benefits blind persons in the form of "reading machines," now commercially available. Mute patients with laryngectomies or other medical conditions that prevent normal speech can use synthesizers to express themselves. For example, Eva K. Simmons at North Carolina State University developed a communication system for an individual with so severe a form of multiple sclerosis that he could utter no sound and was totally paralyzed except for nodding his head. Using a head movement for "yes" and its absence as "no," this individual could select words displayed on a computer screen and assemble sentences expressing his thoughts, which were then "spoken" by a synthesizer.

Most of us these days hear synthesized speech when we call our bank and an "automated bank clerk" tells us our bank balance, or when a telephone information "operator" gives us a requested phone number. Most airlines offer up to the minute arrival and departure information via automatic processing using a synthetic voice. Many information services now available, such as stock prices, are automated and deliver timely information over the telephone via synthesized speech. Although some people find the speech unpleasant, and even unnerving, it makes information that is accurate and current available to millions of people over the telephone.

Knowing What to Say

Speech was given to the ordinary sort of men whereby to communicate their mind; but to wise men, whereby to conceal it.

Robert South, *Sermon* (1676)

PATIENT:	Men are all alike.
ELIZA:	In what way?
PATIENT:	They're always bugging me about something or other.
ELIZA:	Can you think of a specific example?
PATIENT:	Well, my boyfriend made me come here.
ELIZA:	Your boyfriend made you come here?
PATIENT:	He says I'm depressed much of the time.
ELIZA:	I am sorry to hear you are depressed.

Joseph Weizenbaum, *Eliza*

When a computer is "reading" a text it knows what to say, but in many applications the computer is called upon not only to speak, but to decide what to say, and to do so grammatically. This is the problem called **language generation.**

In the dialogue at the head of this section, ELIZA is a computer program designed to simulate a nondirective psychiatrist talking to a patient. ELIZA has a collection of prepared phrases stored in memory such as "In what way?" or "Tell me more" that help keep the conversation going when it doesn't "understand" the patient. When ELIZA recognizes certain syntactic patterns, however, it turns them around to make a sensible response, as when it echoes "Your boyfriend made you come here?" ELIZA was programmed with a small bit of syntactic knowledge allowing it to make grammatical utterances based on the patient's statements, but no semantic knowledge at all. If a patient says "My sniggle is untherible," ELIZA would respond with "How long has your sniggle been untherible?"

In other applications the computer is given bits of knowledge in computer-digestible form (for example, the day's baseball scores), and then programmed to state that knowledge in fluent, grammatically and semantically correct language (for example, a report of the baseball scores on the news). This program requires adherence to the rules of syntax and semantics, as well as morphology and phonetics. In some sense the machine "knows" what it is saying, because if you changed the bits of knowledge fed to it, the statement of that knowledge would change too, providing it were correctly programmed. The most sophisticated language-generation programs allow the computer to converse with a human. One such application is for repairing electronic circuits. The computer is programmed with knowledge of the circuit, and a method to enable it to understand and speak phrases and sentences within the context of the repair problem. The following dialogue was observed on one such system:[8]

COMPUTER:	This is the circuit fix-it shop. How may I help you?
TECHNICIAN:	I need to fix the RS111 circuit.
COMPUTER:	I am familiar with that circuit. The LED is supposed to be displaying alternately blinking one and seven.
TECHNICIAN:	Where is the LED?
COMPUTER:	In the middle right of the blue region is the LED.
TECHNICIAN:	No light.
COMPUTER:	What is the switch at when the LED is off?
TECHNICIAN:	The switch is down.
COMPUTER:	Put the switch up.

---

[8] The system was developed at Duke University in collaboration with North Carolina State University.

Once the computer has understood the technician's utterance, it uses rules of semantics and syntax, together with a lexicon of words and morphemes, to formulate a grammatical, sensible response, which its synthesizer program then speaks. The rules in many cases are similar to the phrase structure rules seen in Chapter 4, such as form a noun phrase from an article followed by a noun. It also has semantic rules that tells it to use *the* with the word *switch* since its "world knowledge" tells it that there is only one switch in that particular circuit.

Unlike a human, though, if the technician used unusual or complex syntax, the computer would be unable to answer because the grammar with which it is programmed is incomplete, as is any computer grammar. Similarly if the technician suddenly changed the subject and asked the computer "Who won the game last night?" or "How much is two plus two?" the computer would be stumped since both its world knowledge and linguistic knowledge are confined to the narrow realm of repairing circuits.

Machines for Understanding Speech

By permission of Johnny Hart and Creators Syndicate, Inc.

Understanding is a relative concept. We often complain that our parents or mates or children don't understand what we say, and we are probably at least partially right: 100 percent understanding is an ideal goal toward which we strive in communication, including human-computer communication.

For a machine to understand speech, it must process the speech signal into sounds, morphemes, and words, which is speech recognition, and at the same time comprehend the meaning of the words as they occur in phrases and sentences, which is speech understanding. In many machine-understanding systems these are separate stages with recognition preceding comprehension. In human language processing these two stages blend together smoothly as listeners recognize some words based on the speech signal alone, while other words have to be figured out from the meanings of words already understood.

By permission of Johnny Hart and Creators Syndicate, Inc.

Speech Recognition   Speech recognition is far more difficult than speech synthesis. It is comparable to trying to transcribe a spectrogram with only phonetic knowledge of the language spoken. As we have seen, the speech signal is not physically divided into discrete sounds. Human ability to segment the signal arises from knowledge of the grammar, which tells us how to pair certain sounds with certain meanings, what sounds or words may be omitted or squeezed together, and when two different speech signals are linguistically the same or when two similar signals are linguistically different. The difficulty of programming a computer to have and use such linguistic knowledge in recognizing speech is enormous.

There are two kinds of speech recognizers. One recognizes speech at the word level, the other at the phoneme level. A word-level recognizer keeps the acoustic patterns of its vocabulary in storage. When it receives spoken input, it matches the acoustic pattern of the input signal with all of its previously stored acoustic patterns. The best match is chosen as the word or words recognized.

A phoneme-level recognizer operates in a similar manner, pre-storing acoustic patterns of the sounds of the language and attempting to match them to incoming sound patterns. Phoneme-level recognition is more error-prone than word-level recognition because individual sounds can be confused more easily than individual words. That is, the machine is more likely to confuse the sound [b] with the sound [d] than it is to confuse the word *boy* with the word *dog;* words contain more redundant information than sounds, which helps to resolve confusions and ambiguities.

To ease the difficulties of recognition in some speech-recognizer systems, the user must insert a short pause of about one-third of a second after each word spoken. (The pause between words must exceed the pause that occurs within words during stop and affricate articulation.) This pause shifts the burden of word boundary detection to the human speaker and makes the machine recognition process more accurate, but it is inconvenient to speak in this manner and reveals that the computer is not capable of "perceiving" in the way a human perceives.

Other speech recognizers accept continuously spoken speech, providing the speaker articulates carefully and clearly. In this case the speaker may not apply certain optional rules such as vowel reduction to schwa, vowel and/or consonant deletion, consonant assimilation at word boundaries, and so on; so *did you* is pronounced [dɪd ju], not [dɪjə]. Natural, rapidly spoken continuous speech—the kind that humans usually use—is not yet machine-recognizable with a useful degree of accuracy.

Speech Understanding

> A computer understands a subset of English if it accepts input sentences which are members of this subset, and answers questions based on information contained in the input.

Daniel Bobrow

Computer comprehension of spoken language is so difficult that it is often divided into two stages: recognition and understanding. Even when recognition is successful, and a transcription of the utterance is obtained, understanding is still an exacting task. Words may have several meanings; the syntactic structure of the utterance must be ascertained; and the meaning of the entire utterance must be built up using rules of syntax and the meanings of its parts. In cases of ambiguity, contextual knowledge may be needed to arrive at the intended meaning.

Understanding also is done in stages. One stage is parsing, which is discovering the syntactic structure or structures of the utterance. Another stage is semantic processing, which combines the meanings of words, looked up in the computer's lexicon, into phrasal meanings, and so on until the entire utterance meaning is assembled. A third stage is applying contextual or world knowledge to disambiguate any utterances.

Parsing

Reprinted with special permission of North America Syndicate.

To understand a sentence you must know its syntactic structure. If you didn't know the structure of *dogs that chase cats chase birds,* you wouldn't know whether dogs or cats chase birds. Similarly, machines that understand language must also determine syntactic structure. A parser is a computer program that uses a grammar to assign a phrase structure to a string of words. Parsers may use a phrase structure grammar and lexicon similar to those discussed in Chapter 4.

For example, a parser may use a grammar containing the following rules: S → NP VP, NP → Det N, etc. Suppose the machine is asked to parse *The child found the kittens.* A top-down parser proceeds by first consulting the grammar rules and then examining the input string to see if the first word could begin an S. If the input string begins with a Det, as in the example, the search is successful, and the parser continues by looking for an N, and then a VP. If the input string happened to be *child found the kittens,* the parser would be unable to assign it a structure because it doesn't begin with a Determiner, which is required by this grammar to begin an S.

A bottom-up parser takes the opposite tack. It looks first at the input string and finds a Det (*the*) followed by an N (*child*). The rules tell it that this phrase is an NP. It would continue to process *found, the,* and *kittens* to construct a VP, and would finally combine the NP and VP to make an S.

Occasionally a parser may have to backtrack. In a sentence like *The little orange rabbit hopped,* the parser might mistakenly assume orange is a noun. Later in the parse, when the error is apparent, the parser can return to *orange* and process it as an adjective. To avoid backtracking, Mitch Marcus at M.I.T. invented the **look-ahead parser,** which is capable of scanning ahead. In the above example a look-ahead parser will find that the word following *orange* is not a verb, so that *orange* cannot be a noun and must be an adjective.

Even look-ahead parsers may have to backtrack when parsing garden-path sentences such as *The horse raced past the barn fell,* discussed earlier in this chapter. The reason for this is that the amount of structure that must be scanned ahead is too great. Even if the parser is programmed to scan far enough ahead for some examples, cases will remain where it will fail and have to backtrack. This is because the amount of structure that must be scanned ahead is, in principle, unbounded, as illustrated by *The horse with the long mane raced past the barn fell.*

In general, humans are far more capable of understanding sentences than computers. But there are some interesting cases where computers outperform humans. For example, try to figure out what the sentence *Buffalo buffalo buffalo buffalo* means. Most people have trouble determining its sentence structure, and are thus unable to understand it. A computer parser, with four simple rules and a lexicon in which *buffalo* has three entries as a noun, verb, and adjective, will easily parse this sentence as follows:

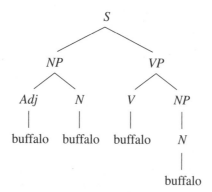

It means "Bison from the city of Buffalo deceive bison."

Regardless of details, every parser uses some kind of grammar to assign phrase structures to input strings. If a structure cannot be found, the input string is ungrammatical relative to that grammar.

A morphological parser uses rules of word formation, such as those studied in Chapters 3 and 5, to decompose words into their component morphemes. A morphological parser decomposes a word like *kittens* into *kitten + s.*

Morphological parsers also operate on morphologically complex words, such as *uncomfortably,* to decompose them into the bound morphemes *un-, -able, -ly,* and the free morpheme *comfort,* all of which have regular meanings that may be looked up in the lexicon, and rules that determine the meanings of the combinations.

As suggested, just as humans store information about words and morphemes in their mental lexicon, a machine must also store such information in a lexicon in memory or storage. Such information as syntactic category (parts of speech), pronunciation, spelling, subcategorization, plurality if irregular like *men,* tense if irregular like *found,* and elements of meaning are usually included in the computer's lexicon. Thus when a parser encounters *found,* it can use the spelling to look the word up in the lexicon, at which point the computer would know that it is a verb, that it is the past tense of *find,* and that it is transitive, among other things.

A parser may use as its grammar **transition networks** that represent the grammar as a complex of **nodes** (circles) and **arcs** (arrows). A network that is the equivalent of the phrase structure rule S → NP VP may be illustrated as:

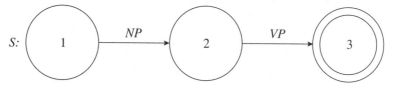

Transition Network for S → NP VP

The nodes are numbered to distinguish them; the double circle is the "final" node.

The parser would start at node 1, examine an input string of words, and if the string began with a noun phrase, "move" to node 2. (If it did not find a noun phrase, it would decide that the input string was not a sentence, unless there were other S networks in the grammar to try.) The parser would then look for a verb phrase, and if one were found the VP arc could be traversed to node 3. Because node 3 is a final node, the parser would indicate that the input string was a sentence consisting of a noun phrase and a verb phrase. The program would, of course, also have to specify what string of words constitutes an NP, VP, and so on.

Augmented transition networks (ATN) are transition networks in which each arrow not only indicates a syntactic category, but may carry other information essential to accurate parsing as well. For example, an ATN extension to the above example might carry a condition on the VP arc to ensure subject-verb agreement, as shown below:

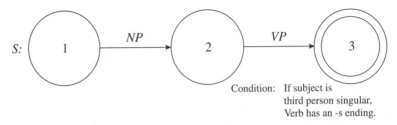

Condition: If subject is
third person singular,
Verb has an -s ending.

Augmented Transition Network for S → NP VP

Semantic Processing

Once a sentence is parsed, the machine can try to find the meaning or semantic representation. This task requires a dictionary with the meaning of each word and rules for combining meanings, as discussed in Chapter 5. The question of how to represent meaning is one that has been debated for thousands of years, and it continues to engender much research in linguistics, philosophy, psychology, cognitive science, and computer science.

One approach common to several semantic processing methods first locates the verb of the sentence—based on the sentence parse—and then identifies the thematic roles of noun phrases such as agent, theme, location, instrument, any complements, and so on.

Another approach is based on mathematical logic and represents the sentence *Zachary loves sushi* as

LOVE (ZACHARY, SUSHI)

where LOVE is a two-place predicate, or function, with arguments ZACHARY and SUSHI. Rules of semantic interpretation indicate that the reference of ZACHARY is the person named *Zachary,* the reference of SUSHI are things in the world called *sushi,* and that *Zachary* is the one loving and *sushi* is the object loved. The lexicon will indicate that *Zachary* is usually the name of a human male and *sushi* is a combination of rice with such things as raw fish, cooked egg, vegetables, and so on.

Two well-known natural-language processing systems from the 1970s used this logical approach of semantic representation. One, named SHRDLU by its developer Terry

Winograd, demonstrated a number of abilities, such as being able to interpret questions, draw inferences, learn new words, and even explain its actions. It operated within the context of a "blocks world," consisting of a table, blocks of various shapes, sizes, and colors, and a robot arm for moving the blocks. Using simple sentences, one could ask questions about the blocks and give commands to have blocks moved from one location to another.

The second system is called LUNAR, developed by William Woods. The LUNAR program was capable of answering questions phrased in simple English about the lunar rock samples brought back from the moon by the astronauts. LUNAR translated English questions into a logical representation, which it then used to query a database of information about the lunar samples.

Semantic networks are also used to represent meaning. They are similar to ATNs in appearance, consisting of nodes and arcs, but they function differently. Here is how *Zachary loves sushi* might be represented using semantic networks:

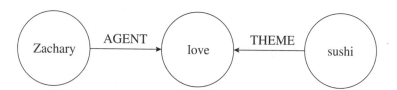

Semantic Network for *Zachary loves sushi*.

Semantic networks make thematic roles explicit, which is a crucial part of semantic interpretation.

Both logical expressions and semantic networks are convenient for machine representation of meaning because they are easily programmed and because the meanings thus represented can be used linguistically. For example, if the computer is asked "Who loves sushi?" it can search through its knowledge base for a node labeled *love,* look to see if an arc labeled THEME is connected to *sushi,* and if so, find the answer by looking for an arc labeled AGENT.

Pragmatic Processing

GARFIELD reprinted by permission of UFS, Inc.

When a sentence is structurally ambiguous, such as *He sells synthetic buffalo hides,* the parser will compute each structure. Semantic processing may eliminate some of the structures if they are anomalous, but often some ambiguity remains. For example, the structurally ambiguous sentence *John found a book on the Oregon Trail* is semantically acceptable in both its meanings. To decide which meaning is intended, situational knowledge is needed. If John is in the library researching history, the "book *about* the Oregon Trail" meaning is most likely; if John is on a two-week hike to Oregon, the "book *upon* the Oregon Trail" meaning is more plausible.

Many language processing systems have a knowledge base containing contextual and world knowledge. The semantic processing routines can refer to the knowledge base in cases of ambiguity. For example, the linguistic component of the electronic repair task system referred to earlier, will have two meanings for *The LED is in the middle of the blue region at the top.* Its knowledge base, however, disambiguates because it "knows" that the LED is in the middle of the blue region, and the blue region is at the top of the work area, rather than that the LED is in the middle, top of the blue region.

COMPUTER MODELS OF GRAMMARS

I am never content until I have constructed a . . . model of the subject I am studying. If I succeed in making one, I understand; otherwise I do not.

William Thomson (Lord Kelvin), Molecular Dynamics and the Wave Theory of Light

A theory has only the alternative of being right or wrong. A model has a third possibility: it may be right, but irrelevant.

Manfred Eigen, The Physicist's Conception of Nature

The grammars used by computers for parsing may not be the same as the grammars linguists construct for human languages, which are models of linguistic competence; nor are they similar, for the most part, to models of linguistic performance. Computers are different than people, and they achieve similar ends differently. Just as an efficient flying machine is not a replica of any bird, efficient grammars for computers do not resemble human language grammars in every detail.

Computers are often used to model physical or biological systems, which allows researchers to study those systems safely and sometimes even cheaply. For example, the performance of a new aircraft can be simulated and the test pilot informed as to safe limits in advance of actual flight.

Computers can also be programmed to model the grammar of a language. An accurate grammar—one that is a true model of a speaker's mental grammar—should be able to generate all and only the sentences of the language. Failure to generate a grammatical sentence indicates the presence of an error in the grammar, because the human mental grammar has the capacity to generate all possible grammatical sentences—an infinite set. In addition, if the grammar produces a string that speakers consider to be ungrammatical, that too indicates a defect in the grammar; although in actual speech performance we often produce ungrammatical strings—sentence fragments, slips of the tongue, word substitutions and blends, and so on—we will judge them to be ill-formed if we notice them. Our grammars cannot generate these strings.

One computer model of a grammar was developed in the 1960s by the computer scientist Joyce Friedman to test a generative grammar of English written by syntacticians at UCLA. More recently, computational linguists are developing computer programs to generate the sentences of a language and to simulate human parsing of these sentences using the rules included in various linguistic theories, such as Chomsky's government and binding theory. The computational models developed by Ed Stabler, Robert Berwick, Amy Weinberg, and Mark Johnson, among other computational linguists, show that it is possible, in principle, to use a transformational grammar, for example, in speech and comprehension, but it is still controversial whether human language processing works in this way. That is, even if we can get a computer program to produce sentences as output and to parse sentences fed into the machine as input, we still need psycholinguistic evidence that this is the way the human mind stores and processes language.

It is because linguistic competence and performance are so complex that computers are being used as a tool in the attempt to understand human language and its use. We have emphasized some of the differences between the way humans process language and the way computers process language. For example, humans appear to do speech recognition, parsing, semantic interpretation, and contextual disambiguation more or less simultaneously and smoothly while comprehending speech. Computers, on the other hand, usually have different components, loosely connected, and perform these functions individually.

One reason for this is that, typically, computers have only a single, powerful processor, capable of performing a single task at a time. Currently, computers are being designed with multiple processors, albeit less powerful ones, which are interconnected. The power of these computers lies both in the individual processors and in the connections. Such computers are capable of **parallel processing,** or carrying out several tasks simultaneously.

With a parallel architecture, computational linguists may be better able to program machine understanding in ways that blend all the stages of processing together, from speech recognition through contextual interpretation, and hence approach more closely the way humans process language.

SUMMARY

Psycholinguistics is concerned with linguistic **performance** or processing, the use of linguistic knowledge (competence) in speech production and comprehension.

Comprehension, the process of understanding an utterance, requires the ability to access the mental lexicon to match the words in the utterance we are listening to with their meanings.

Comprehension starts with the perception of the **acoustic speech signal.** The speech signal can be described in terms of the **fundamental frequency,** perceived as **pitch;** the **intensity,** perceived as loudness; and the **quality,** perceived as differences in speech sounds, such as an [i] from an [a]. The speech wave can be displayed visually as a

spectrogram, sometimes called a **voiceprint.** In a spectrogram, vowels exhibit dark bands where frequency intensity is greatest. These are called **formants** and result from the emphasis of certain *harmonics* of the fundamental frequency, as determined by the shape of the vocal tract. Each vowel has a characteristic formant pattern different from that of other vowels.

The perception of the speech signal is necessary but not sufficient for the under-standing of speech. To get the full meaning of an utterance we must **parse** the string into syntactic structures, since meaning depends on word order, constituent structure, and so on, in addition to the meaning of words. Some psycholinguists believe we uti-lize both **top-down** and **bottom-up processes** during comprehension. Top-down pro-cessing uses semantic and syntactic information in addition to the incoming acoustic signal; bottom-up processes utilize only information contained in the sensory input.

Psycholinguistic experimental studies are aimed at uncovering the units, stages, and processes involved in linguistic performance. A number of experimental techniques have proved to be very helpful. In a **lexical decision** task, subjects are asked to respond to spoken or written stimuli by pressing a button if they consider the stimulus to be a word. In **naming** tasks, subjects read from printed stimuli. The measurement of **response times, RTs,** in **naming,** and lexical decision tasks show that it takes longer to comprehend ambiguous utterances, ungrammatical compared to grammatical sen-tences, nonsense forms as opposed to real words. Reaction time is also measured in experiments using a **priming** technique, which presents a subject with a word followed by another word or a sentence. The first word primes what follows if it is semantically related. A word such as *nurse* will prime the word *doctor* such that the response to it will be faster than to a semantically unrelated word such as *flower.* Such experiments also show that all the meanings of a word are accessed despite the context of a previ-ously heard sentence that should disambiguate the meanings.

Another technique used is **shadowing,** in which subjects repeat what is being said to them as fast as possible; they often correct errors in the stimulus sentence, suggesting that they use linguistic knowledge rather than simply echoing the sounds they hear. Other experiments reveal the processes involved in accessing the mental grammar and the influence of nonlinguistic factors in comprehension.

The units and stages in speech production have been studied by analyzing sponta-neously produced speech errors. Anticipation errors, in which a sound is produced ear-lier than in the intended utterance, and **spoonerisms,** in which sounds or words are exchanged or reversed, show that we do not produce one sound or one word or even one phrase at a time. Rather, we construct and store larger units with their syntactic struc-tures specified prior to mapping these linguistic structures on to neuromuscular com-mands to the articulators. In producing speech, we select words from the mental lexicon whose meanings partially express the thoughts we wish to convey. Word substitutions and **blends** may occur, showing that words are connected to other words phonologi-cally and semantically. The production of ungrammatical utterances also shows that morphological, inflectional, and syntactic rules may be wrongly applied or fail to apply when we speak, but at the same time show that such rules are actually involved in speech production.

Computers can process language. They can be programmed to translate from a **source language** into a **target language,** and they can aid scholars analyzing a literary text or a **corpus** of linguistic data. They can also communicate with people via spoken human language.

Speech synthesis is accomplished by programming computers to imitate the human voice electronically. **Language generation** is the problem of determining what the computer should say. Sometimes canned or prepared speech is used. Other times the computer uses rules of grammar to assemble sentences from a lexicon of words and morphemes that express the intended meaning.

Speech understanding is a far more difficult task because the physical speech signal alone is insufficient for understanding a spoken message: Much linguistic knowledge is required. Machine comprehension of speech begins with **speech recognition,** which attempts to identify phonemes and words from the raw acoustic signal. To understand a string of recognized words, the machine must first **parse** the string to determine its syntactic structure. **Parsers** are computer programs that use a grammar to determine the structure of an input string. Parsers may operate top-down or bottom-up. **Look-ahead** parsers scan forward to avoid the need to backtrack. **Morphological parsers** decompose words into their component morphemes according to rules of word formation.

Once parsed, an utterance is analyzed semantically using **logical representations, semantic networks,** or other devices to represent meaning.

Computers may be programmed to model a grammar of a human language and thus rapidly and thoroughly test that grammar. Modern computer architectures include **parallel processing** machines that can be programmed to process language more as humans do in so far as carrying out many linguistic tasks simultaneously.

References for Further Reading

Allen, J. 1987. *Natural Language Understanding.* Menlo Park, CA: Benjamin/Cummings.

Barr, A., and E. A. Feigenbaum, eds. 1981. *The Handbook of Artificial Intelligence.* Los Altos, CA: I. William Kaufmann.

Berwick, R. C., and A. S. Weinberg. 1984. *The Grammatical Basis of Linguistic Performance: Language Use and Acquisition.* Cambridge, MA: MIT Press.

Carlson, Greg N., and Michael K. Tanenhaus, eds. 1989. *Linguistic Structure in Language Processing.* Dordrecht, The Netherlands: Kluwer Academic Publishers.

Caron, Jean. 1992. *An Introduction to Psycholinguistics.* Translated by Tim Pownall. Toronto, Canada: University of Toronto Press.

Carroll, D. W. 1994. *Psychology of Language.* Pacific Grove, CA: Brooks/Cole Publishing Co.

Clark, H., and E. Clark. 1977. *Psychology and Language: An Introduction to Psycholinguistics.* New York: Harcourt Brace Jovanovich.

Fodor, J. A., M. Garrett, and T. G. Bever. 1986. *The Psychology of Language.* New York: McGraw-Hill.

Foss, D., and D. Hakes. 1978. *Psycholinguistics.* Englewood Cliffs, NJ: Prentice-Hall.

Fromkin, V. A., ed. 1980. *Errors in Linguistic Performance.* New York: Academic Press.

Garman, M. 1990. *Psycholinguistics.* Cambridge: Cambridge University Press.

Garnham, A. 1985. *Psycholinguistics: Central Topics.* London and New York: Methuen.

Garrett, M. F. 1988. "Processes in Sentence Production." In F. Newmeyer, ed., *The Cambridge Linguistic Survey,* vol 3. Cambridge, England: Cambridge University Press.

Gazdar, G., and C. Mellish. 1989. *Natural Language Processing in PROLOG: An Introduction to Computational Linguistics.* Reading, MA: Addison-Wesley.

Gleason, Jean Berko, and Nan Bernstein Ratner, eds. 1993. *Psycholinguistics.* Orlando, FL: Harcourt Brace.

Hockey, S. 1980. *A Guide to Computer Applications in the Humanities.* London, England: Duckworth.

Johnson, M. 1989. "Parsing as Deduction: The Use of Knowledge in Language." *Journal of Psycholinguistic Research* 18 (1): 105–128.

Ladefoged, P. 1981. *Elements of Acoustic Phonetics,* 2d ed. Chicago, IL: University of Chicago Press.

Lea, W. A. 1980. *Trends in Speech Recognition.* Englewood Cliffs, NJ: Prentice-Hall.

Levelt, Willem J. M. 1993. *Speaking: From Intention to Articulation.* Cambridge, MA: A Bradford Book, MIT Press.

Marcus, M. P. 1980. *A Theory of Syntactic Recognition for Natural Language.* Cambridge, MA: MIT Press.

Miller, George, and Philip Johnson-Laird. 1976. *Language and Perception.* Cambridge, MA: Harvard University Press.

Osherson, D., and H. Lasnik., eds. 1990. *Language: An Invitation to Cognitive Science,* vol. 1. Cambridge, MA: MIT Press.

Slocum, J. 1985. "A Survey of Machine Translation: Its History, Current Status, and Future Prospects." *Computational Linguistics* 11 (1).

Smith, R., and R. Hipp. 1994. *Spoken Natural Language Dialog Systems.* New York: Oxford University Press.

Sowa, J., ed. 1991. *Principles of Semantic Networks.* San Mateo, CA: Morgan Kaufmann.

Stabler, E. P., Jr. 1992. *The Logical Approach to Syntax: Foundations, Specifications and Implementations of Theories of Government and Binding.* Cambridge, MA: Bradford Books, MIT Press.

Weizenbaum, J. 1976. *Computer Power and Human Reason.* San Francisco, CA: W. H. Freeman.

Winograd, T. 1972. *Understanding Natural Language.* New York: Academic Press.

Winograd, T. 1983. *Language as a Cognitive Process.* Reading, MA: Addison-Wesley.

Witten, I. H. 1986. *Making Computers Talk.* Englewood Cliffs, NJ: Prentice-Hall.

EXERCISES

1. Speech errors, commonly referred to as "slips of the tongue" or "bloopers," illustrate a difference between linguistic competence and performance since our very recognition of them as errors shows that we have knowledge of well-formed sentences. Furthermore, errors provide information about the grammar. The utterances listed below are part of the UCLA corpus of over 15,000 speech errors. Most of them were actually observed. A few are attributed to Dr. Spooner.

   (a) For each speech error, state what kind of linguistic unit or rule is involved, that is, phonological, morphological, syntactic, lexical, or semantic.

   (b) State, to the best of your ability, the nature of the error, or the mechanisms which produced it.

      (Note: The intended utterance is to the left of the arrow; the actual utterance to the right.)

      Example: ad hoc → odd hack

   (a) phonological vowel segment   (b) reversal or exchange of segments

Example: she gave it away → she gived it away

(a) inflectional morphology   (b) incorrect application of regular past-tense rule to exceptional verb

Example: When will you leave? → When you will leave?

(a) syntactic rule   (b) failure to "move the auxiliary" to form a question

(1) brake fluid → blake fruid

(2) drink is the curse of the working classes → work is the curse of the drinking classes (Spooner)

(3) we have many ministers in our church → . . . many churches in our minister

(4) untactful → distactful

(5) an eating marathon → a meeting arathon

(6) executive committee → executor committee

(7) lady with the dachshund → lady with the Volkswagen

(8) stick in the mud → smuck in the tid

(9) he broke the crystal on my watch → he broke the whistle on my crotch

(10) a phonological rule → a phonological fool

(11) pitch and stress → piss and stretch

(12) big and fat → pig and vat

(13) speech production → preach seduction

(14) he's a New Yorker → he's a New Yorkan

(15) I'd forgotten about that → I'd forgot abouten that

2. The use of spectrograms or "voiceprints" for speaker identification is based on the fact that no two speakers have exactly the same speech characteristics. List some of the differences you have noticed in the speech of several individuals. Can you think of any possible reasons why such differences exist?

3. Using a bilingual dictionary of some language you do not know, attempt to translate the following English sentences by looking up each word.

The children will eat the fish.
Send the professor a letter from your new school.
The fish will be eaten by the children.
Who is the person that is hugging that dog?
The spirit is willing, but the flesh is weak.

A. Using your own knowledge, or someone else's, give a grammatically correct translation of each sentence. What difficulties are brought to light by comparing the two translations? Mention five of them.

B. Have a person who knows the target language translate the grammatical translation back into English. What problems do you observe? Are they related to any of the difficulties you mentioned in Part A?

4. Suppose you were given a manuscript of a play and were told that it is either by Christopher Marlowe or William Shakespeare (both born in 1564). Suppose further that this work, and all of the works of Marlowe and Shakespeare, were in a computer. Describe how you would use the computer to help determine the true authorship of the mysterious play.

5. Speech synthesis is useful because it allows computers to convey information without requiring the user to be sighted. Think of five other uses for speech synthesis in our society.

6. Some advantages of speech recognition are similar to those of speech synthesis. A computer that understands speech does not require a person to use hands or eyes to convey information to the computer. Think of five other possible uses for speech recognition in our society.

7. Consider the following ambiguous sentences. Explain the ambiguity, give the most likely interpretation, and state what a computer would have to have in its knowledge base to achieve that interpretation.

> Example: A cheesecake was on the table. It was delicious and was
>   soon eaten.
> Ambiguity: "It" can refer to the cheesecake or the table.
> Likely: "It" refers to the cheesecake.
> Knowledge: Tables aren't usually eaten.

   a. John gave the boys five dollars. One of them was counterfeit.
   b. The police were asked to stop drinking in public places.
   c. John went to the bank to get some cash.
   d. He saw the Grand Canyon flying to New York.
   e. Do you know the time? (Hint: This is a pragmatic ambiguity.)
   f. Concerned with spreading violence, the president called a press conference.

8. Here is a transition network for the Noun Phrase (NP) rule given in Chapter 4:
   NP → (Det) (Adj) N (PP)

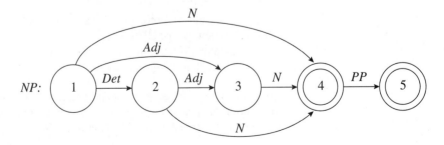

Using this as a model, draw a transition network for the Verb Phrase Rules:

VP → V (NP) (PP)

(Hint: Recall from Chapter 4 that the above rule abbreviates four rules.)

9. A. Here are some sentences along with a possible representation in predicate logic notation. Based on the examples in the text, and those in part B of this exercise, give a possible semantic network representation for each of these examples.

   (1) Birds fly. FLY (BIRDS)

   (2) The student understands the question. UNDERSTAND (THE STUDENT, THE QUESTION)

   (3) Penguins do not fly. NOT (FLY [PENGUINS])

   (4) The wind is in the willows. IN (THE WIND, THE WILLOWS)

   (5) Kathy loves her cat. LOVE (KATHY, [POSSESSIVE (KATHY, CAT)])

   B. Here are five more sentences and a possible semantic network representation for each. Give a representation of each of them using the predicate logic notation.

   (6) Seals swim swiftly.

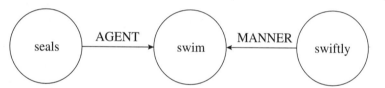

   (7) The student doesn't understand the question.

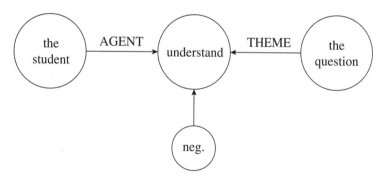

   (8) The pen is on the table.

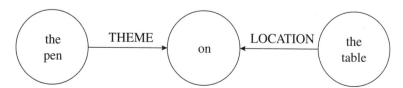

(9) My dog eats bones.

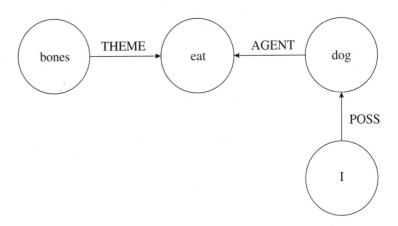

(10) Emily gives money to charity. (Hint: *Give* is a three-place predicate.)

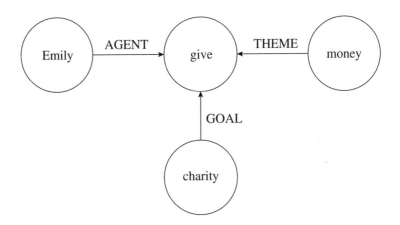

PART 4

Language in Society

Language is not an abstract construction of the learned, or of dictionary-makers, but is something arising out of the work, needs, ties, joys, affections, tastes, of long generations of humanity, and has its bases broad and low, close to the ground.

Walt Whitman

Chapter 10
Language in Society

Language is a city to the building of which every human being brought a stone.

Ralph Waldo Emerson, *Letters and Social Aims*

DIALECTS

A language is a dialect with an army and a navy.

Max Weinreich

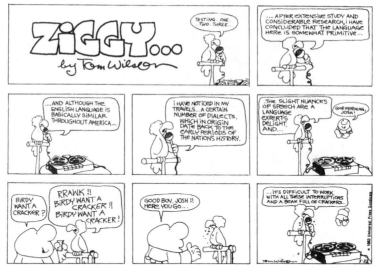

ZIGGY copyright 1983 ZIGGY & FRIENDS, INC. Distributed by Universal Press Syndicate. Reprinted with permission. All rights reserved.

All speakers of English can talk to each other and pretty much understand each other; yet no two speak exactly alike. Some differences are due to age, sex, state of health, size, personality, emotional state, and personal idiosyncrasies. That each person speaks somewhat differently from all others is shown by our ability to recognize acquaintances by hearing them talk. The unique characteristics of the language of an individual speaker are referred to as the speaker's **idiolect.** English may then be said to consist of 400,000,000 idiolects, or the number equal to the number of speakers of English (which seems to be growing every day).

399

Beyond these individual differences, the language of one group of people may show regular variations from that used by other groups of speakers of that language. When the language spoken in different geographical regions and social groups shows systematic differences, the groups are said to speak different **dialects** of the same language. The dialects of a single language may thus be defined as mutually intelligible forms of a language that differ in systematic ways from each other.

It is not always easy to decide whether the systematic differences between two speech communities reflect two dialects or two different languages. A rule-of-thumb definition can be used: When dialects become mutually unintelligible—when the speakers of one dialect group can no longer understand the speakers of another dialect group—these "dialects" become different languages. However, to define "mutually intelligible" is itself a difficult task. Danes speaking Danish and Norwegians speaking Norwegian and Swedes speaking Swedish can converse with each other; yet Danish and Norwegian and Swedish are considered separate languages because they are spoken in separate countries and because there are regular differences in their grammars. Similarly, Hindi and Urdu are mutually intelligible "languages" spoken in Pakistan and India, although the differences between them are not much greater than between the English spoken in America and Australia. On the other hand, the various languages spoken in China, such as Mandarin and Cantonese, although mutually unintelligible, have been referred to as dialects of Chinese because they are spoken within a single country and have a common writing system.

Because neither mutual intelligibility nor the existence of political boundaries is decisive, it is not surprising that a clear-cut distinction between language and dialects has evaded linguistic scholars. We shall, however, use the rule-of-thumb definition and refer to dialects of one language as mutually intelligible versions of the same basic grammar, with systematic differences between them.

Regional Dialects

> Phonetics . . . the science of speech. That's my profession. . . . (I) can spot an Irishman or a Yorkshireman by his brogue. I can place any man within six miles. I can place him within two miles in London. Sometimes within two streets.
>
> George Bernard Shaw, *Pygmalion*

Dialectal diversity develops when people are separated from each other geographically and socially. The changes that occur in the language spoken in one area or group do not necessarily spread to another. Within a single group of speakers who are in regular contact with one another, the changes are spread among the group and "relearned" by their children. When some communication barrier separates groups of speakers—be it a physical barrier such as an ocean or a mountain range, or social barriers of a political, racial, class, or religious kind—linguistic changes are not easily spread and dialectal differences are reinforced.

Dialect differences tend to increase proportionately to the degree of communicative isolation between the groups. Communicative isolation refers to a situation such as existed among America, Australia, and England in the eighteenth century. There was some contact through commerce and emigration, but an Australian was less likely to talk to an Englishman than to another Australian. Today the isolation is less pronounced because of the mass media and travel by jet, but even within one country, regionalisms persist. In fact, there is no evidence to show that any **dialect leveling,** that is, movement toward greater uniformity or decrease in variations, occurs due to the mass media, and recent studies even suggest that dialect variation is increasing, particularly in urban areas.

Changes in the grammar do not take place all at once within the speech community. They take place gradually, often originating in one region and slowly spreading to others, and often taking place throughout the lives of several generations of speakers.

A change that occurs in one region and fails to spread to other regions of the language community gives rise to dialect differences. When enough such differences give the language spoken in a particular region (for example, the city of Boston or the southern area of the United States) its own "flavor," that version of the language is referred to as a **regional dialect.**

Accents

Calvin and Hobbs © Watterson. Dist. by Universal Press Syndicate. Reprinted with permission. All rights reserved.

Regional phonological or phonetic distinctions are often referred to as different **accents.** A person is said to have a Boston accent, a Southern accent, a Brooklyn accent, a Midwestern drawl, and so on. Thus, *accent* refers to the characteristics of speech that convey information about the speaker's dialect, which may reveal in what country or what part of the country the speaker grew up or to which sociolinguistic group the speaker belongs. People in the United States often refer to someone as having a British accent or an Australian accent; in Britain they refer to an American accent.

The term *accent* is also used to refer to the speech of someone who speaks a language nonnatively; for example, a French person speaking English is described as having a French accent. In this sense, *accent* refers to phonological differences or "interference" from a different language spoken elsewhere. Unlike the regional dialectal accents, such foreign accents do not reflect differences in the language of the community where the language was acquired.

DIALECTS OF ENGLISH

The educated Southerner has no use for an r except at the beginning of a word.

Mark Twain, *Life on the Mississippi*

In 1950 a radio comedian remarked that "the Mason-Dixon line is the dividing line between *you-all* and *youse-guys*," pointing to the kinds of varieties of English that exist in the United States. Regional dialects tell us a great deal about how languages change, which is discussed in the next chapter. The origins of many regional dialects of American English can be traced to the people who first settled North America in the seventeenth and eighteenth centuries. The early settlers came from different parts of England, speaking different dialects. Therefore regional dialect differences existed in the first colonies.

By the time of the American Revolution, there were three major dialect areas in the British colonies: the Northern dialect spoken in New England and around the Hudson River; the Midland dialect spoken in Pennsylvania; and the Southern dialect. These dialects differed from each other, and from the English spoken in England, in systematic ways. Some of the changes that occurred in British English spread to the colonies; others did not.

How regional dialects developed is illustrated by changes in the pronunciation of words with an *r*. The British in southern England were already dropping their *r*'s before consonants and at the ends of words as early as the eighteenth century. Words such as *farm, farther,* and *father* were pronounced as [fɑ:m], [fɑ:ðə], and [fɑ:ðə], respectively. By the end of the eighteenth century, this practice was a general rule among the early settlers in New England and the southern Atlantic seaboard. Close commercial ties were maintained between the New England colonies and London, and Southerners sent their children to England to be educated, which reinforced the "*r*-dropping" rule. The "*r*-less" dialect still spoken today in Boston, New York, and Savannah maintained this characteristic. Later settlers, however, came from northern England, where the *r* had been retained; as the frontier moved westward so did the *r*.

Pioneers from all three dialect areas spread westward. The intermingling of their dialects "leveled" or "submerged" many of their dialectal differences, which is why the English used in large sections of the Midwest and the West is similar.

In addition to the English settlers, other waves of immigration brought speakers of other dialects and other languages to different regions. Each group left its imprint on the language of the communities in which they settled. For example, the settlers in various regions developed different dialects—the Germans in the southeastern section, the Welsh west of Philadelphia, the Germans and Scotch-Irish in the section of the state called the Midlands area.

The last half of the twentieth century has brought hundreds of thousands of Spanish-speaking immigrants from Cuba, Puerto Rico, Central America, and Mexico to both the east and west coasts of the United States. It is estimated that a majority of Southern Californians will be native Spanish speakers by the year 2000. In addition, English is being enriched by the languages spoken by the large numbers of new residents coming from the Pacific Rim countries of Japan, China, Korea, Samoa, Malaysia, Vietnam, Thailand, the Philippines, and Indonesia. Large new groups of Russian and Armenian speakers also contribute to the richness of the vocabulary and culture of American cities.

The language of the regions where the new immigrants settle may thus be differentially affected by the native languages of the settlers, further adding to the varieties of American English.

English is the most widely spoken language in the world if one counts all those who use it as a native language or as a second or third language. It is the national language of a number of countries, such as the United States, large parts of Canada, the British Isles, Australia, New Zealand. For many years it was the official language in countries that were once colonies of Britain, including India, Nigeria, Ghana, Kenya and the other "anglophone" countries of Africa. Different dialects of English are spoken in these countries for the reasons discussed above.

Phonological Differences

I have noticed in traveling about the country a good many differences in the pronunciation of common words. . . . Now what I want to know is whether there is any right or wrong about this matter. . . . If one way is right, why don't we all pronounce that way and compel the other fellow to do the same? If there isn't any right or wrong, why do some persons make so much fuss about it?

Letter quoted in "The Standard American," in J. V. Williamson and V. M. Burke, eds., *A Various Language*

A comparison between the "*r*-less" dialect and other dialects illustrates phonological differences between dialects. There are many such differences in the United States, which created difficulties for the authors of this book in writing Chapter 6, where we wished to illustrate the different sounds of English by reference to words in which the sounds occur. As mentioned, some students pronounce *caught* as /kɔt/ with the vowel /ɔ/ and *cot* as /kat/ with /a/, whereas other students will pronounce them identically as /kat/. Some readers pronounce *Mary, marry,* and *merry* identically; others pronounce all three words differently as /meri/, /mæri/, and /mɛri/; and still others pronounce two of them the same. In the southern area of the country, *creek* is pronounced with a tense /i/ as /krik/, and in the north Midlands, it is pronounced with a lax /ɪ/ as /krɪk/. Many speakers of American English pronounce *pin* and *pen* identically, whereas others pronounce the first as /pɪn/ and the second as /pɛn/. If variety is indeed the spice of life, then American English dialects add zest to our existence.

As mentioned in Chapter 6, the pronunciation of British English differs in systematic ways from that spoken in Standard American English. A survey conducted by John Wells of the pronunciations of a number of words in Britain was compared by Yuko Shitara with the pronunciations by American English speakers. The American data were obtained from 395 speakers who replied to a questionnaire on the Linguist List, a computer network of over 6,000 linguists worldwide. The results show consistent differences. For example 48 percent of the Americans pronounced the mid consonants in *luxury* as voiceless [lʌkʃəri] whereas 96 percent of the British pronounced them as voiced [lʌgʒəri]. Sixty-four percent of the Americans pronounced the first vowel in *data* as [e] and 35 percent as [æ] as opposed to 92 percent of the British pronouncing it with an [e] and only 2 percent with [æ]. The most consistent difference occurred in placement of primary stress, with most Americans putting stress on the first syllable and most British on the second or third in multisyllabic words like *cigarette, applicable, formidable, kilometer,* and *submarine.*

Britain also has many regional dialects. The British vowels described in the phonetics chapter are the ones used by speakers of the most prestigious British dialect.[1] In this dialect, /h/ is pronounced at the beginning of both *head* and *herb,* whereas in American English dialects it is not pronounced in the second word. In some English dialects, the /h/ is regularly dropped from most words in which it is pronounced in American, such as *house,* pronounced /aws/, and *hero,* pronounced /iro/.

There are many other phonological differences found in the many dialects of English used around the world.

Lexical Differences

Regional dialects may differ in the words people use for the same object, as well as in phonology. Hans Kurath,[2] an eminent dialectologist, in his paper "What Do You Call It?" asked:

> Do you call it a *pail* or a *bucket?* Do you draw water from a *faucet* or from a *spigot?* Do you pull down the *blinds,* the *shades,* or the *curtains* when it gets dark? Do you *wheel* the baby, or do you *ride* it or *roll* it? In a *baby carriage,* a *buggy,* a *coach,* or a *cab?*

People take a *lift* to the *first floor* (our *second floor*) in England, but an *elevator* in the United States; they get five gallons of *petrol* (not *gas*) in London; in Britain a *public school* is "private" (you have to pay), and if a student showed up there wearing *pants* ("underpants") instead of *trousers* ("pants"), he would be sent home to get dressed.

If you ask for a *tonic* in Boston, you will get a drink called *soda* or *soda-pop* in Los Angeles; and a *freeway* in Los Angeles is a *thruway* in New York, a *parkway* in New Jersey, a *motorway* in England, and an *expressway* or *turnpike* in other dialect areas.

Dialect Atlases

Kurath produced **dialect maps** and **dialect atlases** of a region (an example of which may be seen in Figure 10-1), on which dialect differences are geographically plotted.

The dialectologists who created the map noted the places where speakers use one word or another word for the same item. For example, the area where the term *Dutch cheese* is used is not contiguous; there is a small pocket mostly in West Virginia where speakers use that term for what other speakers call *smearcase.*

In other, similarly drawn maps, areas where the pronunciation of the same word varied, such as [krik] and [krɪk] for *creek,* were differentiated.

---

[1] This dialect is often referred to as RP, standing for "received pronunciation" because it was once considered to be the dialect used in court and "received by" the British king and queen.

[2] Hans Kurath. 1971. "What Do You Call It?" In Juanita V. Williamson and Virginia M. Burke, eds., *A Various Language: Perspective on American Dialects,* New York: Holt, Rinehart and Winston.

FIGURE 10-1 A dialect map from Hans Kurath's *A Word Geography of the Eastern United States,* showing the isoglosses separating the use of different words that refer to the same cheese.

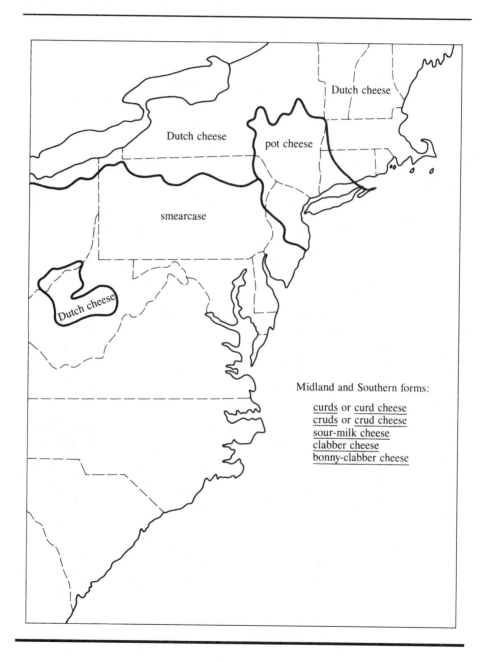

The concentrations defined by different word usage and varying pronunciations, among other linguistic differences, form **dialect areas.**

A line drawn on the map separating the areas is called an **isogloss.** When you "cross" an isogloss, you are passing from one dialect area to another. Sometimes several isoglosses will coincide, often at a political boundary or at a natural boundary such as a river or mountain range. Linguists call these groupings a *bundle* of isoglosses. Such a bundle will define a particular regional dialect.

The first volume of a long-awaited *Dictionary of Regional English* by Frederick G. Cassidy was published in 1985. This work represents years of research and scholarship by Cassidy and other American dialectologists and is a major resource for those interested in American English dialectal differences.

Syntactic Differences

Systematic syntactic differences also distinguish dialects. In most American dialects, sentences may be conjoined as follows:

John will eat and Mary will eat → John and Mary will eat.

In the Ozark dialect the following conjunction is also possible:

John will eat and Mary will eat → John will eat and Mary.

Both shortened conjoined sentences are the result of deletion transformations similar to the ones discussed in Exercise 19 of Chapter 4. It was shown there that the ambiguous sentence *George wants the presidency more than Martha* may be derived from two possible deep structures:

(a) George wants the presidency more than he wants Martha.
(b) George wants the presidency more than Martha wants the presidency.

A deletion transformation either deletes *he wants* from the structure of (a), or *wants the presidency* from the structure of (b). A similar transformation derives *John and Mary will eat* by deleting the first occurrence of the verb phrase *will eat.* Most dialects of English, however, do not have a rule that deletes the *second* verb phrase in conjoined sentences, and in those dialects *John will eat and Mary* is ungrammatical. The Ozark dialect differs in allowing the second verb phrase deletion rule.

Speakers of some American dialects say *Have them come early!* where others would say *Have them to come early!* Some American speakers use *gotten* in a sentence such as *He should have gotten to school on time;* in British English, only the form *got* occurs. In a number of American English dialects, the pronoun *I* occurs when *me* would be used in other dialects. This difference is a syntactically conditioned morphological difference.

Dialect 1	**Dialect 2**
between you and I	between you and me .
Won't he let you and I swim?	Won't he let you and me swim?
*Won't he let I swim?	

The use of *I* in these structures is only permitted in a conjoined NP as the starred ungrammatical sentence shows. *Won't he let me swim?* is used in both dialects. Dialect 1 is growing and these forms are becoming standard English, used by TV announcers, governors of states, and university professors, although language "purists" probably still would disallow this usage.

In British English the pronoun *it* in the sentence *I could have done it* can be deleted to form *I could have done,* which is not permitted in the American English grammar.

Despite such differences, we are still able to understand speakers of another dialect. Although regional dialects differ in pronunciation, vocabulary, and syntactic rules, they are minor differences when compared with the totality of the grammar. The largest part of the vocabulary, the sound-meaning relations of words and the syntactic rules, are shared, which is why dialects of one language are mutually intelligible.

THE "STANDARD"

We don't talk fancy grammar and eat anchovy toast. But to live under the kitchen doesn't say we aren't educated.

Mary Norton, *The Borrowers*

Drawing by Richter; 1989 The New Yorker Magazine, Inc.

> Standard English is the customary use of a community when it is recognized and accepted as the customary use of the community. Beyond this is the larger field of good English, any English that justifies itself by accomplishing its end, by hitting the mark.
>
> George Philip Krapp, *Modern English: Its Growth and Present Use*

Even though every language is a composite of dialects, many people talk and think about a language as if it were a well-defined fixed system with various dialects diverging from this norm. Such was the view of Mario Pei,[3] the author of a number of books on language that were quite popular at one time. He accused the editors of *Webster's Third New International Dictionary,* published in 1961, of confusing "to the point of obliteration the older distinction between standard, substandard, colloquial, vulgar, and slang," attributing to them the view that "good and bad, right and wrong, correct and incorrect no longer exist" (p. 82).

Language Purists

> A woman who utters such depressing and disgusting sounds has no right to be anywhere—no right to live. Remember that you are a human being with a soul and the divine gift of articulate speech: that your native language is the language of Shakespeare and Milton and The Bible; and don't sit there crooning like a bilious pigeon.
>
> George Bernard Shaw, *Pygmalion*

Prescriptive grammarians, or language "purists," usually consider the dialect used by political leaders and the upper socioeconomic classes, the dialect used for literature or printed documents, the dialect taught in the schools, as the correct form of the language.

Otto Jespersen, the great Danish linguist, ridiculed the view that a particular dialect is better than any other when he wrote: "We set up as the best language that which is found in the best writers, and count as the best writers those that best write the language. We are therefore no further advanced than before."[4]

The dominant or prestige dialect is often called the standard dialect. **Standard American English (SAE)** is a dialect of English that many Americans almost speak; divergences from this "norm" are labeled "Philadelphia dialect," "Chicago dialect," "African American English," and so on.

SAE is an idealization. Nobody speaks this dialect; and if somebody did, we would not know it, because SAE is not defined precisely. Several years ago there was an entire conference devoted to one subject: a precise definition of SAE. This meeting did not succeed in satisfying everyone as to what SAE should be. It used to be the case that the language used by national news broadcasters represented SAE, but today many of these people speak a regional dialect, or themselves violate the English preferred by the purists.

---

[3] M. Pei. 1964. "A Loss for Words," *Saturday Review.* Nov. 14: 82–84.

[4] O. Jesperson. 1925 (reprinted 1964). *Mankind, Nation, and Individual,* Bloomington, IA: Indiana University Press.

Deviations from this "standard" that no one can define, let alone use, are seen by many as reflecting a language crisis. Edwin Newman, in his best seller *Strictly Speaking,* asks, "Will Americans be the death of English?" and answers, "My mature, considered opinion is that they will." All this fuss is reminiscent of Mark Twain's cable to the Associated Press, after reading his obituary: "The reports of my death are greatly exaggerated."

The idea that language change equals corruption goes back at least as far as the Greek grammarians at Alexandria, of around 100–200 B.C.E. They were concerned that the Greek spoken in their time was different from the Greek of Homer, and they believed that the earlier forms were purer. They also tried to "correct" the imperfections but failed as miserably as do any modern counterparts. Similarly, the Moslem Arabic grammarians working at Basra in the eighth and ninth centuries C.E. attempted to purify Arabic to restore it to the perfection of Arabic in the Koran.

For many years after the American Revolution, British writers and journalists railed against American English. Thomas Jefferson was an early target in a commentary on his *Notes on the State of Virginia,* which appeared in the *London Review:*

> For shame, Mr. Jefferson! Why, after trampling upon the honour of our country, and representing it as little better than a land of barbarism—why, we say, perpetually trample also upon the very grammar of our language. . . . Freely, good sir, we will forgive all your attacks, impotent as they are illiberal, upon our *national character;* but for the future spare—O spare, we beseech you, our mother-tongue!

The fears of the British journalists in 1787 proved unfounded, and so will the fears of Edwin Newman. One dialect is neither better nor worse than another, nor purer nor more corrupt; it is simply different.

No academy and no guardians of language purity can stem language change, nor should anyone attempt to do so since such change does not mean corruption. The fact that for the great majority of American English speakers *criteria* and *data* are now mass nouns like *information* is no cause for concern. Information can include one fact or many facts, but one would still say "The information is." For some speakers it is equally correct to say "The criteria is" or "The criteria are." Those who say "The data are" would or could say "The datum (singular) is."

A standard dialect (or prestige dialect) of a particular language may have social functions—to bind people together or to provide a common written form for multidialectal speakers. It is, however, neither more expressive, more logical, more complex, nor more regular than any other dialect or language. Any judgments, therefore, as to the superiority or inferiority of a particular dialect or language are social judgments, not linguistic or scientific ones.

Banned Languages

Language purists wish to stem change in language or dialect differentiation because of their false belief that some languages are better than others or that change leads to corruption. Languages and dialects have also been banned as a means of political control.

Russian was the only legal language permitted by the Russian tsars who banned the use of Ukrainian, Lithuanian, Georgian, Armenian, Azerbaijan, and all the other languages spoken by national groups under the rule of Russia.

Cajun English and French were banned in southern Louisiana by practice if not by law until about twenty years ago. Individuals over the age of fifty years report that they were often punished in school if they spoke in French even though many of them had never heard English before attending school.

For many years, American Indian languages were banned in federal and state schools on reservations. Speaking Faroese was formerly forbidden in the Faroe Islands. Japanese movies and songs were once banned in Korea. In a recent discussion among linguists via a computer network called Linguist Net, various degrees of the banning of languages and dialects were reported to exist or to have existed in many countries throughout history.

In France, a notion of the "standard" as the only correct form of the language is propagated by an official academy of "scholars" who determine what usage constitutes the "official French language." A number of years ago, this academy enacted a law forbidding the use of "Franglais" words in advertising (words of English origin like *le parking, le weekend, le hotdog*), but the French continue to use them. Many of the hundreds of local village dialects (called *patois* [patwa] by the academy) are actually separate languages, derived from Latin (as are French, Spanish, and Italian). There were political as well as misguided linguistic motivations behind the efforts to maintain only one official language.

In the past (and to some extent in the present) a Frenchman or Frenchwoman from the provinces who wished to succeed in French society nearly always had to learn Parisian French and be bidialectal. In recent years in France the regional "nationalist" movements made a major demand for the right to use their own languages in their schools and for official business. In the section of France known as l'Occitanie, the popular singers sing in the regional language, Langue d'oc (sometimes referred to simply as Languedoc), both as a protest against the official language policy and as part of the cultural revival movement. Here is the final chorus of a popular song sung in Langue d'oc (shown below with its French and English translations):

Langue d'oc	French	English
Mas perqué, perqué	Mais pourquoi, pourquoi	But why, why
M'an pas dit à l'escóla	Ne m'a-t-on pas dit à l'école	Did they not speak to me at school
La lega de mon pais?	La langue de mon pays?	The language of my country?

In the province of Brittany in France there has also been a strong movement for the use of Breton in the schools, as opposed to the "standard" French. Breton is not even in the same language family as French, which is a Romance language; Breton is a Celtic language in the same family as Irish, Gaelic, and Welsh. (We will discuss such family groupings in Chapter 11.) It is not, however, the structure of the language or the genetic family grouping that has led to the Breton movement. It is rather the pride of a people who speak a language or a dialect not considered as good as the "standard," and their efforts to change this political view of language use.

These efforts have proved successful. In 1982, the newly elected French government decreed that the languages and cultures of Brittany (Breton), the southern Languedoc region, and other areas would be promoted through schooling, exhibitions, and festivals. No longer would schoolchildren who spoke Breton be punished by having to wear a wooden shoe tied around their necks, as had been the custom.

In many places in the world (including the United States), the use of sign languages of the deaf was banned. Children in schools for the deaf where the aim was to teach them to read lips and to communicate through sound were often punished if they used any gestures at all. This view prevented early exposure to language. It was mistakenly thought that children if exposed to sign would not learn to read lips or produce sounds. Individuals who become deaf after learning a spoken language are often able to use their knowledge to learn to read lips and continue to speak. This is, however, very difficult if one has never heard the sounds produced. But even the best lip readers can only comprehend about one-third of the sounds of spoken language. Imagine trying to decide whether *lid* or *led* was said by reading the speaker's lips.

There is no reference to a national language in the Constitution of the United States. John Adams proposed that a national academy be established, similar to the French Academy, to standardize American English, but this view was roundly rejected as not in keeping with the goals of "liberty and justice for all."

In recent years in the United States a movement has arisen in the attempt to establish English as an official language by amending the Constitution. An "Official English" initiative was passed by the electorate in California in 1986; in Colorado, Florida, and Arizona in 1988; and in Alabama in 1990. Such measures have also been adopted by seventeen state legislatures. This kind of linguistic chauvinism is opposed by civil-rights minority-group advocates, who point out that such measures prevent large numbers of non-English speakers from participating in the electoral process if ballots and other educational material are printed only in English. Leading educators also oppose such moves since they could halt programs in bilingual education that are proving to be effective as means both to educate nonnative speakers and to aid their acquisition of English.

The Revival of Languages

The attempts to ban certain languages and dialects is countered by the efforts on the part of certain peoples to preserve their own languages and cultures. This attempt to slow down or reverse the dying out of a language is illustrated by the French in Quebec. But such "antilinguicide" moves should not include the banning of any use of a language.

A dramatic example of the efforts to revive not only a dying but a dead language occurred in Israel. The Academy of the Hebrew Language in Israel was established to accomplish a task never before done in the history of humanity—to revive an ancient written language to serve the daily colloquial needs of the people. Twenty-three lexicologists work with the Bible and the Talmud in order to add new words to the language. While there is some attempt to keep the language "pure," the academy has given way to popular pressure. Thus, a bank check is called a *check* /čɛk/ in the singular and pluralized by adding the Hebrew suffix to form *check-im*, although the Hebrew word *hamcha* was proposed. Similarly, *lipstick* has triumphed over *faton* and *pajama* over *chalifatsheina.*

AFRICAN AMERICAN ENGLISH (AAE)

The language, only the language. . . . It is the thing that black people love so much—the saying of words, holding them on the tongue, experimenting with them, playing with them. It's a love, a passion. Its function is like a preacher's: to make you stand up out of your seat, make you lose yourself and hear yourself. The worst of all possible things that could happen would be to lose that language.

Toni Morrison, interview in *The New Republic*, March 21, 1981

KUDZU by Doug Marlette. By permission of Doug Marlette and Creators Syndicate.

The majority of regional dialects of the United States are, to a great extent, free from stigma. Some regional dialects, like the *r*-less Brooklynese, are unfortunately the victims of so-called humor, and speakers of one dialect may deride the "drawl" of southerners or the "nasal twang" of Texans (even though all speakers of southern dialects do not drawl nor do all Texans twang). There is one dialect of North American English, however, that has been a victim of prejudicial ignorance. This dialect, **African American English (AAE),** [5] is spoken by a large section of African Americans who live in urban areas euphemistically called the *inner city* that were traditionally referred to as *ghettos.* The distinguishing features of this English dialect persist for social, educational, and economic reasons. The historical discrimination against African Americans[6] has created ghetto living and segregated schools. Where social isolation exists, dialect differences are intensified. In addition, particularly in recent years, many blacks no longer consider their dialect to be inferior, and it has become a means of positive identification.

Since the onset of the civil rights movement in the 1960s, African American English has been the focus of national attention. There are critics who attempt to equate the use

---

[5] It is actually a group of closely related dialects also called African American Vernacular English (AAVE), Black English (BE), Inner City English (ICE), and Ebonics.

[6] As used here, "American" refers to the United States.

of African American English with inferior genetic intelligence and cultural deprivation, justifying these incorrect notions by stating that AAE is a "deficient, illogical, and incomplete" language. Such epithets cannot be applied to any language, and they are as unscientific in reference to AAE as to Russian, Chinese, or Standard American English. The cultural-deprivation myth is as false as the idea that some dialects or languages are inferior. A person may be "deprived" of one cultural background but be rich in another.

Some people, white and black, think they can identify someone's race by hearing an unseen person talk, believing that different races inherently speak differently. This assumption is equally false; a black child raised in an upper-class British household will speak that dialect of English. A white child raised in an environment where African American English is spoken will speak African American English. Children construct grammars based on the language they hear.

AAE is discussed here more extensively than other American dialects because it provides an informative illustration of the regularities of a dialect of a standard language and the systematic differences from that standard language. A vast body of research shows that there are the same kinds of linguistic differences between AAE and SAE as occur between many of the world's major dialects.

Phonology of African American English

Some of the differences between AAE and SAE phonology are as follows:

R-Deletion

Like a number of dialects of both British and American English, AAE includes a rule of **r-deletion** that deletes /r/ everywhere except before a vowel. Pairs of words like *guard* and *god, nor* and *gnaw, sore* and *saw, poor* and *pa, fort* and *fought,* and *court* and *caught* are pronounced identically in AAE because of the presence of this phonological rule in the grammar.

L-Deletion

There is also an **l-deletion rule** for some speakers of AAE, creating identically pronounced pairs like *toll* and *toe, all* and *awe, help* and *hep.*

Consonant Cluster Simplification

A **Consonant Cluster Simplification** rule in AAE simplifies consonant clusters, particularly at the ends of words and when one of the two consonants is an alveolar (/t/, /d/, /s/, /z/). The application of this rule may delete the past-tense morpheme so that *meant* and *mend* are both pronounced as *men* and *past* and *passed* (*pass* + *ed*) may both be pronounced like *pass.* When speakers of this dialect say *I pass the test yesterday,* they are not showing an ignorance of past and present, but are pronouncing the past tense according to this rule in their grammar.

The deletion rule is optional; it does not always apply, and studies have shown that it is more likely to apply when the final [t] or [d] does not represent the past-tense morpheme, as in nouns like *paste* [pes] as opposed to verbs like *chased* [čest], where the final past tense [t] will not always be deleted. This has also been observed with final [s] or [z], which will be retained more often by speakers of AAE in words like *seats* /sit + s/, where the /s/ represents "plural," than in words like *Keats* /kit/, where it is more likely to be deleted.

Consonant cluster simplification is not unique to AAE. It exists optionally for many speakers of other dialects including SAE. For example, the medial [d] in *didn't* is often deleted producing [dɪ̃nt]. Furthermore, nasals are commonly deleted before final voiceless stops, to result in [hɪ̃t] versus [hɪ̃nt].

Neutralization of [i] and [ɛ] before Nasals

AAE shares with many regional dialects the lack of any distinction between /ɪ/ and /ɛ/ before nasal consonants, producing identical pronunciations of *pin* and *pen, bin* and *Ben, tin* and *ten,* and so on. The vowel used in these words is roughly between the [ɪ] of *pit* and the [ɛ] of *pet*.

/ɔj/ → /ɔ/

Another change has reduced the diphthong /ɔj/ (particularly before /l/) to the simple vowel [ɔ] without the glide, so that *boil* and *boy* are pronounced [bɔ].

Loss of Interdental Fricatives

A regular feature is the change of a /θ/ to /f/ and /ð/ to /v/ so that *Ruth* is pronounced [ruf] and *brother* is pronounced [brʌver]. This [θ]–[f] correspondence also is true of some dialects of British English, where /θ/ is not even a phoneme in the language. *Think* is regularly [fink] in Cockney English.

Initial /ð/ in such words as *this, that, these,* and *those* are pronounced as [d]. This is again not unique to AAE, but a common characteristic of many nonstandard, nonethnic dialects of English.

All these differences are systematic and "rule-governed" and similar to sound changes that have taken place in languages all over the world, including Standard English.

Syntactic Differences between AAE and SAE

Syntactic differences also exist between dialects. It is the syntactic differences that have often been used to illustrate the "illogic" of AAE, and yet it is just such differences that point up the fact that AAE is as syntactically complex and as "logical" as SAE.

Double Negatives

Following the lead ᵢ f early "prescriptive" grammarians, some "scholars" and teachers conclude that it is illogical to say *he don't know nothing* because two negatives make a positive.

Since such negative constructions occur in AAE, it has been concluded by some "educators" that speakers of AAE are deficient because they use language "illogically." However double negatives are part of many current white dialects in the English-speaking world, and were the standard in an earlier stage of English. Furthermore, multiple negation is the regular rule in many other languages of the world.

Deletion of the Verb "Be"

In most cases, if in Standard English the verb can be contracted, in African American English sentences it is deleted; where it can't be contracted in SAE, it can't be deleted in AAE, as shown in the following sentences:

SAE	AAE
He is nice/He's nice.	He nice.
They are mine/They're mine.	They mine.
I am going to do it/I'm gonna do it.	I gonna do it.[7]
He is/he's as nice as he says he is.	He as nice as he say he is.
*He's as nice as he says he's.	*He as nice as he say he.
How beautiful you are.	How beautiful you are.
*How beautiful you're	*How beautiful you
Here I am.	Here I am.
*Here I'm	*Here I

These examples show that syntactic rules operate in both dialects although they show slight systematic differences.

Habitual "Be"

In SAE, the sentence *John is happy* can be interpreted to mean John is happy at the moment or John is generally happy. One can only make the distinction clear in SAE by lexical means, that is, the addition of words. One would have to say *John is generally happy* or *John is always happy* to disambiguate the meaning from *John is happy right now.*

In AAE, this distinction is made syntactically; an uninflected form of *be* is used if the speaker is referring to *habitual* action.

John be happy.	"John is always happy."
John happy.	"John is happy now."
He be late.	"He is habitually late."
He late.	"He is late this time."
Do you be tired?	"Are you generally tired?"
You tired?	"Are you tired now?"

This syntactic distinction between habitual and nonhabitual aspect occurs in languages other than AAE, but it does not occur in SAE. It has been suggested that the uninflected *be* is the result of a convergence of similar rules in African, Creole, and Irish English sources.[8]

---

[7] Sentences taken from W. Labov, *The Logic of Nonstandard English,* Georgetown University, 20th Annual Round Table, No. 22, 1969.

[8] John Holm. 1988–1989. *Pidgins and Creoles,* Vols. 1 & 2, Cambridge, England: Cambridge University Press.

History of African American English

It is simple to date the beginning of African American English—the first blacks were brought in chains to Virginia in 1619. There are, however, different theories as to the factors that led to the systematic differences between African American English and other American English dialects.

One view suggests that African American English originated when the African slaves learned English from their colonial masters as a second language. Although the basic grammar was learned, many surface differences persisted, which were reflected in the grammars constructed by the children of the slaves, who heard English primarily from their parents. Had the children been exposed to the English spoken by the whites, their grammars would have been more similar if not identical to the general Southern dialect. The dialect differences persisted and grew because blacks in America were isolated by social and racial barriers. The proponents of this theory point to the fact that the grammars of African American English and Standard American English are basically identical except for a few syntactic and phonological rules that produce surface differences.

Another view that is receiving increasing support is that many of the unique features of African American English are traceable to influences of the African languages spoken by the slaves. During the seventeenth and eighteenth centuries, Africans who spoke different languages were purposefully grouped together to discourage communication and to prevent slave revolts. In order to communicate, the slaves were forced to use the one common language all had access to, namely English. They invented a simplified form—called a pidgin (to be discussed below)—that incorporated many features from West African languages. According to this view, the differences between AAE and other dialects are due more to basic syntactic differences than to surface distinctions.

It is apparent that African American English is closer to the Southern dialect of English than to other dialects. The theory that suggests that the Negro slaves learned the English of white Southerners as a second language explains these similarities. They might also be explained by the fact that for many decades a large number of Southern white children were raised by black women and played with black children. It is not unlikely that many of the distinguishing features of Southern dialects were acquired from African American English in this way. A publication of the American Dialect Society in 1908–1909 makes this point clearly:

> For my part, after a somewhat careful study of east Alabama dialect, I am convinced that the speech of the white people, the dialect I have spoken all my life and the one I tried to record here, is more largely colored by the language of the negroes [*sic*] than by any other single influence.[9]

The two-way interchange still goes on. Standard American English is constantly enriched by words, phrases, and usage originating in African American English; and African American English, whatever its origins, is influenced by the changes that go on in the many other dialects of English.

LATINO (HISPANIC) ENGLISH

A major group of American English dialects is spoken by native Spanish speakers or their descendants. The Southwest was once part of Mexico, and for more than a century

---

[9] L. W. Payne. 1909. "A Word-List from East Alabama," *Dialect Notes* 3: 279–328, 343–391.

large numbers of immigrants from Spanish-speaking countries of South and Central America have enriched the country with their language and culture. Among these groups are those who are native speakers of Spanish who have learned or are learning English as a second language. There are also those born in Spanish-speaking homes whose native language is English, some of whom are monolingual, and others who speak Spanish as a second language.

One cannot speak of a homogeneous Latino dialect. In addition to the differences between bilingual and monolingual speakers, the dialects spoken by Puerto Rican, Cuban, Guatemalan, and El Salvadoran immigrants or their children are somewhat different from each other and also from those spoken by Mexican Americans in the Southwest and California, called Chicano English (ChE).

A description of the Latino dialects of English is complicated by historical and social factors. While many Latinos are bilingual speakers, it has been suggested that close to 20 percent of Chicanos are monolingual English speakers.[10] Recent studies also show that the shift to monolingual English is growing rapidly. Furthermore, the bilingual speakers are not a homogeneous group; native Spanish speakers' knowledge of English ranges from passive to full competence. The Spanish influence on both immigrant and native English speakers is reinforced by border contact between the United States and Mexico and the social cohesion of a large segment of this population.

Bilingual Latinos, when speaking English, may insert a Spanish word or phrase within a single sentence or move back and forth between Spanish and English, a process called **code-switching.** This is a universal language-contact phenomenon that reflects the grammars of both languages working simultaneously. Quebecois in Canada switch from French to English and vice versa; the Swiss switch between French and German. Code-switching occurs wherever there are groups of bilinguals who speak the same two languages. Furthermore, code-switching occurs in specific social situations, enriching the repertoire of the speakers.

Because of the ignorance of what code-switching is, there is a common misconception that bilingual Latinos speak a sort of "broken" English, sometimes called Spanglish or Tex-Mex. This is not the case. In fact, the phrases inserted into a sentence are always in keeping with the syntactic rules of that language. For example, in a Spanish noun phrase, the adjective usually follows the noun, as opposed to the English NP in which it precedes, as shown by the following:

> English: My mom fixes **green tamales.**   Adj N
> Spanish: Mi mamá hace **tamales verdes.**   N Adj

A bilingual Spanish-English speaker might, in a code-switching situation, say:

> My mom fixes **tamales verdes**.
> or   Mi mamá hace **green tamales**

---

[10] Otto A. Santa Ana. 1993. "Chicano English and the Nature of the Chicano Language Setting," *Hispanic Journal of Behavioral Sciences,* 15.1.3–35.

but would not produce the sentences

> *My mom fixes **verdes tamales.**
> or *Mi mamá hace **tamales green**

because the Spanish word order was reversed in the inserted Spanish NP and the English word order was reversed in the English NP.

What monolingual speakers of English should realize is that these are individuals who know not one, but two languages.

Chicano English (ChE)

We have seen that there is no one form of Latino English, just as there is no single dialect of SAE or American English. Nor is the Chicano English dialect, spoken by a major group of descendants of Mexican Americans, homogeneous. With this in mind, we can still recognize it as a distinct dialect of American English, one that is acquired as a first language by many children and which is the native language of hundreds of thousands, if not millions of Americans. It is not English with a Spanish accent nor an incorrect version of SAE but, like African American English, a mutually intelligible dialect that differs systematically from SAE. Many of the differences, however, represent variables that may or may not occur in the speech of a speaker of ChE. The use of the nonstandard forms on the part of native speakers of English is often associated with pride of ethnicity.

Phonological Variables of ChE

ChE is, like other dialects, the result of many factors, a major one being the influence of Spanish. Phonological differences between ChE and SAE reveal this influence.

Here are some systematic differences:[11]

1. Chapters 6 and 7 discussed the fact that English has eleven stressed vowel phonemes (not counting the three diphthongs): /i, ɪ, e, ɛ, æ, u, ʊ, o, ɔ, a, ʌ/. Spanish, however, has only five: /i, e, u, o, a/. Chicano speakers whose native language is Spanish may substitute the Spanish vowel system for the English. When this is done, a number of homonyms result that have distinct pronunciations in SAE. Thus *ship* and *sheep* are both pronounced like *sheep* /šip/, *rid* is pronounced like *read* /rid/, and so on. Chicano speakers whose native language is English may make these substitutions but have the full set of American English vowels.
2. Alternation of *ch* /č/ and *sh* /š/; *show* is pronounced as if spelled with a *ch* /čo/ and *check* as if spelled with an *sh* /šɛk/.
3. Devoicing of some consonants, such as /z/ in *easy* /isi/ and *guys* /gajs/.

---

[11] Joyce Penfield and Jacob L. Ornstein-Galicia. 1985. *Chicano English: An Ethnic Contact,* Philadelphia: John Benjamins. Information on ChE was also provided by Otto Santa Ana.

4. The substitution of /t/ for /θ/ and /d/ for /ð/ word initially, as in /tin/ for *thin* and /de/ for *they.*

5. Word-final consonant cluster simplification. *War* and *ward* are both pronounced /war/; *star* and *start* are /star/. This process may also delete past-tense suffixes (*poked* becomes /pok/) and third-person singular agreement (*He loves her* becomes *he love her*), by a process similar to that in AAE. Alveolar-cluster simplification has become widespread among all dialects of English, even among SAE speakers, and although it is a process often singled out for ChE and AAE speakers, this is really no longer dialect specific.

6. Prosodic aspects of speech in ChE, such as stress and intonation, also differ from SAE. Stress, for example, may occur on a different syllable in ChE than in SAE.

7. The Spanish sequential constraint, which does not permit a word to begin with an /s/ cluster, is sometimes carried over to ChE. Thus *scare* may be pronounced as if it were spelled *escare* /ɛsker/, and *school* as if it were spelled *eschool.*

Syntactic Variables in ChE

There are also regular syntactic differences between ChE and SAE. In Spanish, a negative sentence includes a negative morpheme before the verb even if another negative appears; thus negative concord ("double negatives") is a regular rule of ChE syntax:

SAE	ChE
I don't have any money.	I don have no money.
I don't want anything.	I no want nothin.

Another regular difference between ChE and SAE is in the use of the comparative *more* to mean *more often* and the preposition *out from* to mean *away from*, as in the following:

SAE	ChE
I use English more often.	I use English more.
They use Spanish more often.	They use more Spanish.
They hope to get away from their problems.	They hope to get out from their problems.

Lexical differences also occur, such as the use of *borrow* in ChE for *lend* in SAE (*Borrow me a pencil*) as well as many other substitutions.

As noted above, many Chicano speakers (and speakers of AAE) are bidialectal; they can use either ChE (or AAE) or SAE, depending on the social situation.

LINGUA FRANCAS

Language is a steed that carries one into a far country.

Arab proverb

Many areas of the world are populated by people speaking divergent languages. In such areas, where groups desire social or commercial communication, one language is often used by common agreement. Such a language is called a **lingua franca.**

In medieval times, a trade language came into use in the Mediterranean ports, based largely on the medieval languages that became modern Italian and Provencal. This came to be called Lingua Franca, "Frankish language." The term *lingua franca* was generalized to other languages similarly used. Thus, any language can be a lingua franca.

English has been called "the lingua franca of the whole world." French, at one time, was "the lingua franca of diplomacy," and Latin and Greek were the lingua francas of Christianity in the West and East, respectively, for a millennium. Among Jews, Yiddish has long served as a lingua franca.

More frequently, lingua francas serve as "trade languages." East Africa is populated by hundreds of tribes, each speaking its own language, but most Africans of this area learn at least some Swahili as a second language, and this lingua franca is used and understood in nearly every marketplace. A similar situation exists in Nigeria, where Hausa is the lingua franca.

Hindi and Urdu are the lingua francas of India and Pakistan, respectively. The linguistic situation of this area of the world is so complex that there are often regional lingua francas—usually the popular dialects near commercial centers. The same situation existed in Imperial China.

In modern China, the Chinese language as a whole is often referred to as *Zhongwen,* which technically refers to the written language, whereas *Zhongguo hua* refers to the spoken language. Ninety-four percent of the people living in the People's Republic of China are said to speak Han languages, which can be divided into eight major dialects (or language groups) that for the most part are mutually unintelligible. Within each group there are hundreds of dialects. In addition to these Han languages, there are more than fifty "national minority" languages, including the five principal ones: Mongolian, Uighur, Tibetan, Zhuang, and Korean. The situation is clearly complex, and for this reason an extensive language reform policy was inaugurated to spread a standard language, called *Putonghua,* which embodies the pronunciation of the Beijing (Peking) dialect, the grammar of northern Chinese dialects, and the vocabulary of modern colloquial Chinese. The native languages and dialects are not considered inferior; rather, the approach is to spread the "common speech" (the literal meaning of Putonghua) so that all may communicate with each other in this lingua franca.

Certain lingua francas arise naturally; others are developed by government policy and intervention. In many places of the world, however, people still cannot speak with neighbors only a few miles away.

PIDGINS AND CREOLES

Padi dɛm; kɔntri; una ɔl we de na Rom.
Mɛk una ɔl kak una yes. A Kam bɛr siza,
a nɔ kam prez am.

> William Shakespeare, *Julius Caesar,* 3.2,
> translated to Krio by Thomas Decker

Pidgins

Further Studies in Pigeon English

Drawing by J. B. Handlesman © 1990 The New Yorker Magazine, Inc.

A lingua franca is typically a language with a broad base of native speakers, likely to be used and learned by persons whose native language is in the same language family. Often in history, however, traders and missionaries from one part of the world have visited and attempted to communicate with peoples residing in another area. In such cases the contact is too specialized and the cultures too widely separated for the usual kind of lingua franca to arise. Instead, the two (or possibly more) groups use their native languages as a basis for a rudimentary language of few lexical items and less complex grammatical rules. Such a "marginal language" is called a **pidgin.**

There are a number of such languages in the world, including a large number of English-based pidgins. One such pidgin, called *Tok Pisin,* originally was called Melanesian Pidgin English. It is widely used in Papua New Guinea. Like most pidgins, many of its lexical items and much of its structure are based on only one language of the two or more contact languages, in this case English. The variety of Tok Pisin used as a primary language in urban centers is more highly developed and more complex than the Tok Pisin used as a lingua franca in remote areas. Papers in Tok Pisin have been presented at linguistics conferences in Papua New Guinea, and it is commonly used for debates in the parliament of the country.

Although pidgins are in some sense rudimentary, they are not devoid of grammar. The phonological system is rule-governed, as in any human language. The inventory of phonemes is generally small, and each phoneme may have many allophonic pronunciations. In Tok Pisin, for example, [č], [š], and [s] are all possible pronunciations of the phoneme /s/; [masin], [mašin], and [mačin] all mean "machine."

Tok Pisin has its own writing system, its own literature, and its own newspapers and radio programs; it has even been used to address a United Nations meeting.

With their small vocabularies, however, pidgins are not good at expressing fine distinctions of meaning. Many lexical items bear a heavy semantic burden, with context being relied on to remove ambiguity. Much circumlocution and metaphorical extension is necessary. All of these factors combine to give pidgins a unique flavor. What could be a friendlier definition of "friend" than the Australian aborigine's *him brother belong me,* or more poetic than this description of the sun: *lamp belong Jesus*? A policeman is *gubmint catchum-fella,* whiskers are *grass belong face,* and when a man is thirsty *him belly allatime burn.*

Pidgin has come to have negative connotations, perhaps because the best-known pidgins are all associated with European colonial empires. The *Encyclopedia Britannica* once described Pidgin English as "an unruly bastard jargon, filled with nursery imbecilities, vulgarisms and corruptions." It no longer uses such a definition. In recent times there is greater recognition of the fact that pidgins reflect human creative linguistic ability, as is beautifully revealed by the Chinese servant asking whether his master's prize sow had given birth to a litter: *Him cow pig have kittens?* Prince Philip, the husband of Queen Elizabeth of England, on a visit to New Guinea, was referred to as *fella belong Mrs. Queen.*

Some people would like to eradicate pidgins. A pidgin spoken on New Zealand by the Maoris was replaced, through massive education, by Standard English, and the use of Chinese Pidgin English was forbidden by the government of China. Its use had died out by the end of the nineteenth century because the Chinese gained access to learning Standard English, which proved to be more useful in communicating with non-Chinese speakers.

Pidgins have been unjustly maligned; they may serve a useful function.[12] For example, a New Guinean can learn Tok Pisin well enough in six months to begin many kinds of semiprofessional training. To learn English for the same purpose might require ten times as long. In an area with over eight hundred mutually unintelligible languages, Tok Pisin plays a vital role in unifying similar cultures.

During the seventeenth, eighteenth, and nineteenth centuries many pidgins sprang up along the coasts of China, Africa, and the New World to accommodate the Europeans. Chinook Jargon is a pidginized American Indian language used by various tribes of the Pacific Northwest to carry on trade. Some linguists have suggested that Proto-Germanic (the earliest form of the Germanic languages) was originally a pidgin, arguing that ordinary linguistic change cannot account for certain striking differences between the Germanic tongues and other Indo-European languages. They theorized that in the first millennium B.C.E. the primitive Germanic tribes that resided along the Baltic Sea traded with the more sophisticated, seagoing cultures. The two peoples communicated by means of a pidgin, which either grossly affected Proto-Germanic, or

---

[12] Robert A. Hall. 1955. *Hands Off Pidgin English,* New South Wales: Pacific Publications, 1955.

actually became Proto-Germanic. If this is true, English, German, Dutch, and Yiddish had humble beginnings as a pidgin.

Case, tense, mood, and voice are generally absent from pidgins. One cannot, however, speak an English pidgin by merely using English without inflecting verbs or declining pronouns. Pidgins are not "baby talk" or Hollywood's version of American Indians talking English. *Me Tarzan, you Jane* may be understood, but it is not pidgin as it is used in West Africa.

Pidgins are simple, but are rule-governed. In Tok Pisin, most verbs that take a direct object must have the suffix -*m* or -*im,* even if the direct object is absent; here are some examples of the results of the application of this rule of the language:

Tok Pisin:	Mi driman long kilim wanpela snek.
English:	I dream of killing a snake.
Tok Pisin:	Bandarap I bin kukim.
English:	Bandarap cooked (it).

Other rules determine word order, which, as in English, is usually quite strict in pidgins because of the lack of case endings on nouns.

The set of pronouns is often simpler in pidgins. In Cameroonian Pidgin (CP), which is also an English-based pidgin, the pronoun system does not show gender or all the case differences that exist in standard English (SE).[13]

CP			**SE**		
a	mi	ma	I	me	my
yu	yu	yu	you	you	your
i	i/am	i	he	him	his
i	i/am	i	she	her	her
wi	wi	wi	we	us	our
wuna	wuna	wuna	you	you	your
dɛm	dɛm/am	dɛm	they	them	their

Pidgins also may have fewer prepositions than the languages on which they are based. In CP, for example, *fɔ* means "to," "at," "in," "for," and "from," as shown in the following examples:

Gif di buk fɔ mi.	"Give the book to me."
I dei fɔ fam.	"She is at the farm."
Dɛm dei fɔ chɔs.	"They are in the church."
Du dis wan fɔ mi, a bɛg.	"Do this for me, please."
Di mɔni dei fɔ tebul.	"The money is on the table."
You fit muf tɛn frangk fɔ ma kwa.	"You can take ten francs from my bag."

Characteristics of pidgins differ in detail from one pidgin to another, and often vary depending on the native language of the pidgin speaker. Thus the verb generally comes

---

[13] The data from CP are from Loreto Todd. 1984. *Modern Englishes: Pidgins & Creoles,* Oxford, England: Basil Blackwell.

at the end of a sentence for a Japanese speaker ol
poor people all potato eat), whereas a Filipino spe
subject (*Work hard these people*).

Creoles

One distinguishing characteristic of pidgin languag
native speakers. When a pidgin comes to be adopte
tongue, and children learn it as a first language, that lan
gin has become **creolized.**

The term *creole* comes originally from the Portugu   ...iaii of
European descent born and raised in a tropical or semi   ony. . . . The term
was . . . subsequently applied to certain languages spoken . . . in and around the
Caribbean and in West Africa, and then more generally to other similar languages."[14]

Creoles often arose on slave plantations in certain areas where Africans of many different tribes could communicate only via the plantation pidgin. Haitian Creole, based
on French, developed in this way, as did the "English" spoken in parts of Jamaica. Gul-
lah is an English-based creole spoken by the descendants of African slaves on islands
off the coast of Georgia and South Carolina. Louisiana Creole, related to Haitian Creole, is spoken by large numbers of blacks and whites in Louisiana. Krio, the language
spoken by as many as 200,000 Sierra Leoneans, developed, at least in part, from an
English-based pidgin.

Creoles become fully developed languages, having more lexical items and a broader
array of grammatical distinctions than pidgins. In time, they become languages as complete in every way as other languages.

The study of pidgins and creoles has contributed a great deal to our understanding of
the nature of human language and the genetically determined constraints on grammars.

STYLES, SLANG, AND JARGON

Slang is language which takes off its coat, spits on its hands—and goes
to work.

Carl Sandburg

Styles

Most speakers of a language know many dialects. They use one dialect when out with
friends, another when on a job interview or presenting a report in class, and another
when talking to their parents. These "situation dialects" are called **styles** or **registers.**

Nearly everybody has at least an informal and a formal style. In an informal style the
rules of contraction are used more often, the syntactic rules of negation and agreement
may be altered, and many words are used that do not occur in the formal style.

---

[14] Suzanne Romaine. 1988. *Pidgin and Creole Languages,* London/New York: Longman, p. 38.

...al styles, although permitting certain abbreviations and deletions not permit-
... formal speech, are also rule-governed. For example, questions are often short-
...ed with the *you* subject and the auxiliary deleted. One can ask *Running the marathon?*
or *You running the marathon?* instead of the more formal *Are you running the
marathon?* but you cannot shorten the question to **Are running the marathon?* Similarly, *Are you going to take the Linguistics 1 course?* can be abbreviated to *You gonna
take the Ling 1 course?* or simply *Gonna take Ling 1?* but not to **Are gonna take Ling
1?* Everything doesn't go in informal talk, but the rules permit greater deletion than the
rules in the grammar of the formal language.

Many speakers have the ability to use a number of different styles, ranging between
the two extremes of formal and informal. Speakers of minority dialects sometimes display virtuosic ability to slide back and forth along a continuum of styles that range from
the informal patterns learned in a ghetto to formal standard. When William Labov was
studying African American English used by Harlem youths, he encountered difficulties
because the youths (subconsciously) adopted a different style in the presence of white
strangers. It took time and effort to gain their confidence to the point where they would
"forget" that their conversations were being recorded and so use their less formal style.

Many cultures have rules of social behavior that strictly govern style. In some Indo-
European languages there is the distinction between "you (familiar)" and "you
(polite)." German *du* and French *tu* are to be used only with "intimates"; *Sie* and *vous*
are more formal and used with nonintimates. French even has a verb *tutoyer,* which
means "to use the *tu* form," and German uses the verb *duzen* to express the informal or
less honorific style of speaking.

Other languages have a much more elaborate code of style usage. Speakers of Thai
use *kin* "eat" to their intimates, informally, or in more formal situations when talking
about animals or when showing contempt for people such as criminals. *Thaan* "eat" is
used informally with strangers, *rabprathaan* "eat" on formal occasions or when con-
versing with dignitaries or esteemed persons (such as parents), and *chan* "eat" when
referring to Buddhist monks. Japanese and Javanese are also languages with elaborate
styles that must be adhered to in certain social situations.

Slang

> Police are notorious for creating new words by shortening existing ones,
> such as *perp* for *perpetrator, ped* for *pedestrian* and *wit* for *witness.* More
> baffling to court reporters is the gang member who . . . might testify that he
> was in his *hoopty* around *dimday* when some *mud duck* with a *tray-eight*
> tried to take him *out of the box.* Translation: The man was in his car about
> dusk when a woman armed with a .38 caliber gun tried to kill him.
>
> *Los Angeles Times,* August 11, 1986

One mark of an informal style is the frequent occurrence of **slang.** Almost everyone
uses slang on some occasions, but it is not easy to define the word. Slang has been
defined as "one of those things that everybody can recognize and nobody can define."[15]

---

[15] Paul Roberts. 1958. *Understanding English,* New York: Harper & Row, p. 342.

The use of slang, or colloquial language, int...
by recombining old words into new meaning...
off have all gained a degree of acceptance. S...
word, such as *barf, flub,* and *pooped.* Finally,...
new meanings to old words. *Grass* and *pot* wi...
and *fuzz* are derogatory terms for "police offic...
split have all extended their semantic domain.

The words we have cited sound "slangy" beca...
ability. Words such as *dwindle, freshman, glib,* an...
time overcame their "unsavory" origin. It is not al\...
line between slang words and regular words. This c...
around. In 1890, John S. Farmer, coeditor with V...
logues, remarked: "The borderland between slang ɛ ... ...ısn' is an ill-
defined territory, the limits of which have never beer ... ...y mapped out."

One generation's slang is another generation's standard vocabulary. *Fan* (as in
"Dodger fan") was once a slang term, short for *fanatic. Phone,* too, was once a slangy,
clipped version of *telephone,* as *TV* was of *television.* In Shakespeare's time, *fretful* and
dwindle were slang, and more recently *blimp* and *hot dog* were both "hard-core" slang.

The use of slang varies from region to region, so slang in New York and slang in Los
Angeles differ. The word *slang* itself is slang in British English for "scold."

Slang words and phrases are often "invented" in keeping with new ideas and customs. They may represent "in" attitudes better than the more conservative items of the
vocabulary. Their importance is shown by the fact that it was thought necessary to give
the returning Vietnam prisoners of war a glossary of eighty-six new slang words and
phrases, from *acid* to *zonked.* The words on this list—prepared by the Air Force—had
come into use during only five years. Furthermore, by the time this book was published,
many of these terms may have passed out of the language, and many new ones added.

A number of slang words have entered English from the "underworld," such as *crack*
for a special form of cocaine, *payola, C-note, G-man, to hang paper* ("to write 'bum'
checks"), *sawbuck,* and so forth.

The now ordinary French word meaning "head," *tête,* was once a slang word derived
from the Latin *testa,* which meant "earthen pot." Some slang words seem to hang on
and on in the language, though, never changing their status from slang to "respectable."
Shakespeare used the expression *beat it* to mean "scram" (or more politely, "leave!"),
and *beat it* would be considered by most English speakers still to be a slang expression.
Similarly, the use of the word *pig* for "policeman" goes back at least as far as 1785,
when a writer of the time called a Bow Street police officer a "China Street pig."

Jargon and Argot

It is common knowledge that students have a language that is quite peculiar
to them and that is not understood very well outside student society. . . . But
if the code of behaviour somewhere is particularly lively, then the language
of the students is all the richer for it—and vice versa.

Friedrich Ch. Laukhard (1792)

conceivable science, profession, trade, and occupation has its own set
some of which are considered to be "slang" and others "technical," depend-
the status of the people using these "in" words. Such words are sometimes called
jargon or **argot.** Linguistic jargon, some of which is used in this book, consists of terms
such as *phoneme, morpheme, case, lexicon, phrase structure rule,* and so on.

The existence of argots or jargons is illustrated by the story of a seaman witness
being cross-examined at a trial, who was asked if he knew the plaintiff. Indicating that
he did not know what *plaintiff* meant brought a chide from the attorney: "You mean you
came into this court as a witness and don't know what 'plaintiff' means?" Later the
sailor was asked where he was standing when the boat lurched. "Abaft the binnacle,"
was the reply, and to the attorney's questioning stare he responded: "You mean you
came into this court and don't know where abaft the binnacle is?"

Because the jargon terms used by different professional groups are so extensive (and
so obscure in meaning), court reporters in the Los Angeles Criminal Courts Building
have a library that includes books on medical terms, guns, trade names, and computer
jargon, as well as street slang.

The computer age not only ushered in a technological revolution, it also introduced
a huge jargon of "computerese" used by computer "hackers," including the words
modem (a blend of *modulator* and *demodulator*), *bit* (a contraction of *binary digit*), *byte*
(a collection of some number of bits), *floppy* (a noun or adjective referring to a flexible
disk), *ROM* (an acronym for *read-only memory*), *RAM* (an acronym for *random-access
memory*), *morf* (an abbreviation for the question *Male or female?*), and *OOPS* (an
acronym for *object-oriented program systems*).

Many jargon terms pass into the standard language. Jargon, like slang, spreads from
a narrow group until it is used and understood by a large segment of the population. In
fact, it is not always possible to distinguish between what is jargon and what is slang,
as illustrated in the book *Slang U: The Official Dictionary of College Slang,*[16] a collection of slang used on the campus of the University of California, Los Angeles, by
Professor Munro and the students in her UCLA Honors Collegium seminar. One cannot tell from the hundreds of entries in this collection which of the entries are used
solely by UCLA students, which by the definitions above would make it a UCLA student jargon. It is highly probable that the word *fossil,* meaning a "person who has been
a college student for more than four years" is used in this way only at UCLA or on college campuses, but certainly the term *prick,* referring to a "mean, offensive, inconsiderate, rude person (usually, a male)" is used as a general slang term on and off
university campuses.

TABOO OR NOT TABOO?

Sex is a four-letter word.

Bumper sticker slogan

---

[16] Pamela Munro, ed. 1990. *Slang U,* New York: Harmony Books.

"There are some words I will not tolerate in this house—and 'awesome' is one of them."

A recent item in a newspaper included the following paragraph (the names have been deleted to protect the guilty):

> "This is not a Sunday school, but it is a school of law," the judge said in warning the defendants he would not tolerate the "use of expletives during jury selection." "I'm not going to have my fellow citizens and prospective jurors subjected to filthy language," the judge added.

How can language be filthy? In fact, how can it be clean? The filth or beauty of language must be in the ear of the listener, or in the collective ear of society.

There cannot be anything about a particular string of sounds that makes it intrinsically clean or dirty, ugly or beautiful. If you say that you pricked your finger when sewing, no one would raise an eyebrow; but if you refer to your professor as a *prick,* the judge quoted above would undoubtedly censure this "dirty" word.

Words that are not acceptable in America are acceptable in England and vice versa. And the acceptance changes over time. In the 1830s, a British visitor to America, Fanny Trollope, remarked:

> Hardly a day passed in which I did not discover something or other which I had been taught to consider as natural as eating, was held in abhorrence by those around me; many words to which I had never heard an objectionable meaning attached, were totally interdicted, and the strangest paraphrastic phrases substituted.

Some of the words that were taboo at that time in America but not in England were *corset, shirt, leg*, and *woman*. Fanny Trollope remarked:

> The ladies here have an extreme aversion to being called *women*. . . . Their idea is, that that term designates only the lower or less-refined classes of female human-kind. This is a mistake which I wonder they should fall into, for in all countries in the world, queens, duchesses, and countesses, are called women.

Certain words in all societies are considered **taboo**—they are not to be used, or at least, not in "polite company." The word *taboo* was borrowed from Tongan, a Polynesian language, in which it refers to acts that are forbidden or to be avoided. When an act is taboo, reference to this act may also become taboo. That is, first you are forbidden to do something; then you are forbidden to talk about it.

What acts or words are forbidden reflect the particular customs and views of the society. Some words may be used in certain circumstances and not in others; for example, among the Zuni Indians, it is improper to use the word *takka,* meaning "frogs," during a religious ceremony; a complex compound word must be used instead, which literally translated would be "several-are-sitting-in-a-shallow-basin-where-they-are-in-liquid."[17]

In certain societies, words that have religious connotations are considered profane if used outside of formal or religious ceremonies. Christians are forbidden to "take the Lord's name in vain," and this prohibition has been extended to the use of curses, which are believed to have magical powers. Thus *hell* and *damn* are changed to *heck* and *darn,* perhaps with the belief or hope that this change will fool the "powers that be." In England the word *bloody* is a taboo word.

In Shaw's *Pygmalion* the following lines "startled London and indeed, fluttered the whole Empire," according to the British scholar Eric Partridge,[18] when the play was first produced in London in 1910.

---

[17] Peter Farb. 1975. *Word Play,* New York: Bantam.
[18] As quoted in "The History of Some 'Dirty' Words" by Falk Johnson. 1950. In *The American Mercury,* Vol. 71, pp. 538–545.

"Are you walking across the Park, Miss Doolittle?"
"Walk! Not bloody likely. I am going in a taxi."

Partridge adds that "Much of the interest in the play was due to the heroine's utterance of this banned word. It was waited for with trembling, heard shudderingly."

The *Oxford English Dictionary* states that *bloody* has been in general colloquial use from the Restoration and is "now constantly in the mouths of the lowest classes, but by respectable people considered 'a horrid word' on a par with obscene or profane language, and usually printed in the newspapers 'b_____y.' " The origin of the term is not quite certain. One view is that the word is derived from an oath involving the "blood of Christ"; another that it relates to menstruation. The scholars do not agree and the public has no idea. This uncertainty itself gives us a clue about "dirty" words: People who use them often do not know why they are taboo, only that they are, and to some extent, this is why they remain in the language, to give vent to strong emotion.

Words relating to sex, sex organs, and natural bodily functions make up a large part of the set of taboo words of many cultures. Some languages have no native words to mean "sexual intercourse" but do borrow such words from neighboring people. Other languages have many words for this common and universal act, most of which are considered taboo.

Two or more words or expressions can have the same linguistic meaning, with one acceptable and the others the cause of embarrassment or horror. In English, words borrowed from Latin sound "scientific" and therefore appear to be technical and "clean," whereas native Anglo-Saxon counterparts are taboo. This fact reflects the opinion that the vocabulary used by the upper classes was superior to that used by the lower classes, a distinction going back at least to the Norman Conquest in 1066, when "a duchess perspired and expectorated and menstruated—while a kitchen maid sweated and spat and bled."[19] Such pairs of words are illustrated below:

Anglo-Saxon Taboo Words	Latinate Acceptable Words
cunt	vagina
cock	penis
prick	penis
tits	breasts
shit	feces

There is no linguistic reason why the word *vagina* is "clean" whereas *cunt* is "dirty" or why *prick* or *cock* is taboo but *penis* is acknowledged as referring to part of the male anatomy or why everyone *defecates* but only vulgar people *shit*. Many people even avoid words like *breasts, intercourse,* and *testicles* as much as words like *tits, fuck,* and *balls.* There is no linguistic basis for such views, but pointing this fact out does not imply advocating the use or nonuse of any such words.

---

[19] Peter Farb. 1975. *Word Play,* New York: Bantam.

Euphemisms

Reprinted by permission of The Washington Post.

> Banish the use of the four letter words
>   Whose meaning is never obscure.
> The Anglos, the Saxons, those bawdy old birds
>   Were vulgar, obscene, and impure.
> But cherish the use of the weaseling phrase
>   That never quite says what it means;
> You'd better be known for your hypocrite ways
>   Than vulgar, impure, and obscene.
>
> Ogden Nash, "Ode to the Four Letter Words"

The existence of taboo words or taboo ideas stimulates the creation of **euphemisms.** A euphemism is a word or phrase that replaces a taboo word or serves to avoid frightening or unpleasant subjects. In many societies, because death is feared, there are a number of euphemisms related to this subject. People are less apt to *die* and more apt to *pass on* or *pass away.* Those who take care of your loved ones who have passed away are more likely to be *funeral directors* than *morticians* or *undertakers.*

Ogden Nash's poem, quoted above, exhorts against such euphemisms, as another verse demonstrates:

> When in calling, plain speaking is out;
> When the ladies (God bless 'em) are milling about,
> You may wet, make water, or empty the glass;
> You can powder your nose, or the "johnny" will pass.
> It's a drain for the lily, or man about dog
> When everyone's drunk, it's condensing the fog;
> But sure as the devil, that word with a hiss,
> It's only in Shakespeare that characters _____.

There are scholars who are as bemused as Ogden Nash with the attitudes revealed by the use of euphemisms in society. A journal, *Maledicta,* subtitled *The International Journal of Verbal Aggression* and edited by Reinhold Aman, "specializes in uncensored glossaries and studies of all offensive and negatively valued words and expressions, in all languages and from all cultures, past and present." A review of this journal by Bill Katz in the *Library Journal* (November 1977) points out, "The history of the dirty word or phrase is the focus of this substantial . . . journal [whose articles] are written in a scholarly yet entertaining fashion by professors . . . as well as by a few outsiders."

A scholarly study of Australian English euphemisms shows the considerable creativity involved:[20]

urinate:	drain the dragon
	syphon the python
	water the horse
	squeeze the lemon
	drain the spuds
	wring the rattlesnake
	shake hands with the wife's best friend
	point Percy at the porcelain
	train Terence on the terracotta
have intercourse:	shag
	root
	crack a fat
	dip the wick
	play hospital
	hide the ferret
	play cars and garages
	hide the egg roll (sausage, salami)
	boil bangers
	slip a length
	go off like a beltfed motor
	go like a rat up a rhododendron
	go like a rat up a drain pipe
	have a northwest cocktail

These euphemisms, as well as the difference between the accepted Latinate "genteel" terms and the "dirty" Anglo-Saxon terms, show that a word or phrase not only has a linguistic **denotative meaning** but also has a **connotative meaning,** reflecting attitudes, emotions, value judgments, and so on. In learning a language, children learn which words are taboo, and these taboo words differ from one child to another, depending on the value system accepted in the family or group in which the child grows up.

Racial and National Epithets

The use of epithets for people of different religions, nationalities, or race tell us something about the users of these words. The word *boy* is not a taboo word when used

---

[20] Jay Powell. 1972. Paper delivered at the Western Conference of Linguistics, University of Oregon.

generally, but when a twenty-year-old white man calls a forty-year-old African American man "boy," the word takes on an additional meaning; it reflects the racist attitude of the speaker. So also words like *kike* (for Jew), *wop* (for Italian), *nigger* or *coon* (for African American), *slant* (for Asian), *towelhead* (for Middle Eastern Arab), and so forth express racist and chauvinist views of society.

The use of the verbs *to jew* or *to gyp/jip* also reflect the stereotypical views of Jews and Gypsies. Most people do not even realize that *gyp,* which is used meaning *cheat,* comes from the view that Gypsies are duplicitous charlatans. In time these words would either disappear or lose their racist connotations if bigotry and oppression ceased to exist, but since they show no signs of doing so, the use of such words perpetuates stereotypes, separates one people from another, and reflects racism.

LANGUAGE, SEX, AND GENDER

doctor, n. . . . a man of great learning.

The American College Dictionary, 1947

A businessman is aggressive; a businesswoman is pushy. A businessman is good on details; she's picky. . . . He follows through; she doesn't know when to quit. He stands firm; she's hard. . . . His judgments are her prejudices. He is a man of the world; she's been around. He isn't afraid to say what is on his mind; she's mouthy. He exercises authority diligently; she's power mad. He's closemouthed; she's secretive. He climbed the ladder of success; she slept her way to the top.

From "How to Tell a Businessman from a Businesswoman,"
Graduate School of Management, UCLA, *The Balloon* XXII, (6).

The discussion of obscenities, blasphemies, taboo words, and euphemisms showed that words of a language are not intrinsically good or bad but reflect individual or societal values. In addition, one speaker may use a word with positive connotations while another may select a different word with negative connotations to refer to the same person. For example, the same individual may be referred to as a *terrorist* by one group and as a *freedom fighter* by another. A woman may be called a *castrating female* (or *ballsy women's libber*) or may be referred to as a *courageous feminist advocate.* The words we use to refer to certain individuals or groups reflect our individual nonlinguistic attitudes and may also reflect the culture and views of society.

Language reflects sexism in society. Language itself is not sexist, just as it is not obscene; but it can connote sexist attitudes as well as attitudes about social taboos or racism.

Dictionaries often give clues to social attitudes. In the 1969 edition of the *American Heritage Dictionary,* examples used to illustrate the meaning of words include "manly courage" and "masculine charm." Women do not fare as well, as exemplified by "womanish tears" and "feminine wiles." In *Webster's New World Dictionary of the American Language* (1961), *honorarium* is defined as "a payment to a professional man for services on which no fee is set or legally obtainable."

Sections in history textbooks still in use are headed "Pioneers and Their Wives"; children read that "courageous pioneers crossed the country in covered wagons with their wives, children, and cattle." Presumably women are not considered to be as courageous as their husbands.

Until 1972, at Columbia University, the women's faculty toilet doors were labeled "Women," whereas the men's doors were labeled "Officers of Instruction." Yet, linguistically, the word *officer* is not marked semantically for gender. There were apparently few women professors at Columbia at that time, which was reflected in these designations. This is because our interpretation of the meaning of words is influenced by nonlinguistic aspects of society. This is further shown by the way we interpret other neutral (non-gender-specific) terms. At least until recently, most people, hearing *My cousin is a professor* (or a *doctor,* or *the Chancellor of the University,* or *a steel worker*), assume the cousin is a man. This assumption has nothing to do with the English language but a great deal to do with the fact that, historically, women have not been prominent in these positions. This is beginning to change as more women become professors and doctors and chancellors.

Similarly, if you heard someone say *My cousin is a nurse* (or *elementary school teacher,* or *clerk-typist,* or *houseworker*), you would probably conclude that the speaker's cousin is a woman. It is less evident why the sentence *My neighbor is a blonde* is understood as referring to a woman, perhaps because the physical characteristics of women in our society seem to assume greater importance than those of men.

Studies analyzing the language used by men in reference to women, which often has derogatory or sexual connotations, indicate that such terms go far back into history, and sometimes enter the language with no pejorative implications but gradually gain them. Thus, from Old English *huswif* "housewife," the word *hussy* was derived. In their original employment, "a laundress made beds, a needlewoman came to sew, a spinster tended the spinning wheel, and a nurse cared for the sick. But all apparently acquired secondary duties in some households, because all became euphemisms for a mistress or a prostitute at some time during their existence."[21]

Words for women—all with abusive or sexual overtones—abound: *dish, tomato, piece, piece of ass, chick, piece of tail, bunny, pussy, pussycat, bitch, doll, slut, cow,* to name just a few. Far fewer such pejorative terms exist for men.

Marked and Unmarked Forms

> Long afterward, Oedipus, old and blinded, walked the
> roads. He smelled a familiar smell. It was
> the Sphinx. Oedipus said, "I want to ask one question.
> Why didn't I recognize my mother?" "You gave the
> wrong answer," said the Sphinx. "But that was what
> made everything possible," said Oedipus. "No," she said.
> "When I asked, 'What walks on four legs in the morning,

---

[21] Muriel R. Schulz. 1975. "The Semantic Derogation of Woman," in B. Thorne and N. Henley, eds., *Language and Sex,* Rowley, MA: Newbury House Publishers, pp. 66–67.

two at noon, and three in the evening,' you answered,
'Man.' You didn't say anything about woman."
"When you say Man," said Oedipus, "you include women
too. Everyone knows that." She said, "That's what
you think."

Muriel Rukeyser, *Myth*[22]

By permission of Johnny Hart and Creators Syndicate, Inc.

One striking fact about the asymmetry between male and female terms in many languages is that when there are male/female pairs, the male form for the most part is **unmarked** and the female term is created by adding a bound morpheme or by compounding. We have many such examples in English:

Male	Female
prince	princess
author	authoress
count	countess
actor	actress
host	hostess
poet	poetess
heir	heiress
hero	heroine
Paul	Pauline

Since the advent of the feminist movement, many of the marked female forms have now been replaced by the male forms, which are used to refer to either sex. Thus women, as well as men, are authors and actors and poets and heroes and heirs. Women, however, remain countesses, if they are among this small group of female aristocrats in England.

Given these asymmetries, **folk etymologies** arise that misinterpret a number of nonsexist words. Folk etymology is the process, normally unconscious, whereby words or their origins are changed through nonscientific speculations or false analogies with other words. When we borrowed the French word *crevisse*, for example, it became

---

[22] *A Murial Rukeyser Reader.* 1994. Edited by Jan Heller Levi. New York: W. W. Norton & Co., p 252.

crayfish. The English-speaking borrowers did not know that *-isse* was a feminine suffix. *Female* is not the feminine form of *male,* which some people claim, but came into English from the Latin word *femina,* with the same morpheme *fe* that occurs in the Latin *fecundus* meaning "fertile" (originally derived from an Indo-European word meaning "to give suck to"). It entered English through the Old French word *femme* and its diminutive form *femelle,* "little woman."

Other male/female gender pairs have interesting meaning differences. Although a *governor* governs a state, a *governess* takes care of children; a *mistress,* in its most widely used meaning, is not a female master, nor is a *majorette* a woman major. We talk of "unwed mothers" but not "unwed fathers," of "career women" but not "career men," because there has been historically no stigma for a bachelor to father a child, and men are supposed to have careers. It is only recently that the term *househusband* has come into being, again reflecting changes in social customs.

Possibly as a protest against the reference to new and important ideas as being *seminal* (from *semen*), Clare Booth Luce updated Ibsen's drama *A Doll's House* by having Nora tell her husband that she is pregnant "in the way only men are supposed to get pregnant." When he asks, "Men pregnant?" she replies, "With ideas. Pregnancies there (she taps her head) are masculine. And a very superior form of labor. Pregnancies here (she taps her stomach) are feminine—a very inferior form of labor."

Other linguistic asymmetries exist, such as the fact that most women continue to adopt their husbands' names in marriage. This name change can be traced back to early legal practices, some of which are perpetuated currently. Thus we often refer to a woman as Mrs. Jack Fromkin, but seldom refer to a man as Mr. Vicki Fromkin, except in an insulting sense. This convention, however, is not true in other cultures.

We talk of Professor and Mrs. John Smith but seldom, if ever, of Mr. and Dr. Mary Jones. At a UCLA alumni association dinner, place cards designated where "Dr. Fromkin" and "Mrs. Fromkin" were to sit, although both individuals have doctoral degrees.

It is insulting to a woman to be called a *spinster* or an *old maid,* but it is not insulting to a man to be called a *bachelor.* There is nothing inherently pejorative about the word *spinster.* The connotations reflect the different views society has about an unmarried woman as opposed to an unmarried man. It is not the language that is sexist; it is society.

The Generic "He"

The unmarked, or male, nouns also serve as general terms, as do the male pronouns. The *brotherhood of man* includes women, but *sisterhood* does not include men.

When Thomas Jefferson wrote in the Declaration of Independence that "all *men* are created equal" and "governments are instituted among *men* deriving their just powers from the consent of the governed," he was not using *men* as a general term to include women. His use of the word *men* was precise at the time that women could not vote. In the sixteenth and seventeenth centuries, masculine pronouns were not used as the **generic terms;** the various forms of *he* were used when referring to males, and of *she* when referring to females. The pronoun *they* was used to refer to people of either sex even if the referent was a singular noun, as shown by Lord Chesterfield's statement in 1759: "If a person is born of a gloomy temper . . . they cannot help it."

By the eighteenth century, grammarians (males to be sure) created the rule designating the male pronouns as the general term, and it wasn't until the nineteenth century that the rule was applied widely, after an act of Parliament in Britain in 1850 sanctioned its use. But this generic use of *he* was ignored. In 1879, women doctors were barred from membership in the all-male Massachusetts Medical Society on the basis that the bylaws of the organization referred to members by the pronoun *he.*

Changes in English are taking place that reflect the feminist movement and the growing awareness on the part of both men and women that language may reflect attitudes of society and reinforce stereotypes and bias. More and more, the word *people* is replacing *mankind, personnel* is used instead of *manpower, nurturing* instead of *mothering,* and *to operate* instead of *to man. Chair* or *moderator* is used instead of *chairman* (particularly by those who do not like the "clumsiness" of *chairperson*) and terms like *postal worker, firefighter,* and *public safety officer* or *police officer* are replacing *mailman, fireman,* and *policeman.*

Language and Gender

An increasing number of scholars have been conducting research on language and gender, and language and sexism, since 1973 when the first article specifically concerned with women and language was published in a major linguistics journal.[23] Robin Lakoff's study suggested that women's insecurity due to sexism in society resulted in more "proper" use of the rules of SAE grammar than was found in the speech of men. Differences between male and female speech were investigated.

Variations in the dialects of men and women occur in America and in other countries. In Japanese, women may choose to speak a distinct dialect although they are fully aware of the standard dialect used by both men and women. It has been said that "seeing eye" guide dogs in Japan are trained in English, because the sex of the owner is not known in advance and it is easier for a blind person to use English than to train the dog in both language styles.

In the Muskogean language Koasati, spoken in Louisiana, words that end in an /s/ when spoken by men, end in /l/ or /n/ when used by women; for example, the word meaning "lift it" is *lakawhol* for women and *lakawhos* for men. Early explorers reported that the men and women of the Carib Indians used different dialects. In Chiquita, a Bolivian language, the grammar of male language includes a noun-class gender distinction, with names for males and supernatural beings morphologically marked in one way, and nouns referring to females marked in another.

There is nothing inherently wrong in the development of different styles, which may include intonation, phonology, syntax, and lexicon. It is wrong, however, to continue stereotypes regarding female speech, which are more myths than truth. For example, a common stereotype is that women talk a lot, yet controlled studies show just the opposite is true when men and women are together. That is, in mixed groups, the women seem to talk less than the men.

---

[23] Robin Lakoff. 1973. "Language and Woman's Place," *Language in Society* 2:45–80.

One characteristic of female speech is the higher pitch used by women, due, to a great extent, to the shorter vocal tracts of women. But studies conducted by the phonetician Caroline Henton showed that the difference in pitch between male and female voices was, on the average, greater than could be accounted for by physiology alone, suggesting that some social factor must be involved during the acquisition period.

This chapter has stressed the fact that language is neither good nor evil but its use may be one or the other. If one views women or blacks or Hispanics as inferior, then special speech characteristics will be viewed as inferior. Furthermore, when society itself institutionalizes such attitudes, the language reflects this. When everyone in society is truly equal, and treated as such, there will be little concern for the asymmetries that exist in language.

SECRET LANGUAGES AND LANGUAGE GAMES

Throughout the world and throughout history, people have invented secret languages and language games. These special languages are used either as a means of identifying with a special group, for fun, or to prevent others from knowing what is being said. When the aim is secrecy, a number of methods are used; immigrant parents sometimes use their native language when they do not want their children to understand what is being said, or parents may spell out words. American slaves developed an elaborate code that could not be understood by the slave owners. References to "the promised land" or the "flight of the Israelites from Egypt" sung in spirituals were codes for the north and the underground railway.

One special language is called Cockney rhyming slang. No one is completely sure of how it first arose. One view is that it began as a secret language among the criminals of the underworld in London in the mid-nineteenth century to confuse the "snitchers," called "peelers," and the police. Another view is that during the building of the London docks at the beginning of the century, the Irish immigrant workers invented rhyming slang to confuse the non-Irish workers. Still another view is that it was spread by street chanters who went from market to market in England telling tales, reporting the news, reciting ballads. Whatever its origins, it is a tribute to the creativity of human language.

The way to play this language game is to create a rhyme as a substitute for a specific word. Thus, for *table* the rhymed slang may be *Cain and Abel*, and the *missus* is called *cows and kisses*.

Other language games, such as Pig Latin, used for amusement by children and adults, exist in the world's languages. In some, a suffix is added to each word; in others a syllable is inserted after each vowel; there are rhyming games and games in which phonemes are reversed. A game in Brazil substitutes an /i/ for all the vowels; Indian children learn a Bengali language game in which the syllables are reversed, as in pronouncing *bisri* "ugly" as *sribi*.

There is a game used by the Walbiri, natives of central Australia, in which the meanings of words are distorted rather than the phonological forms. In this language, all nouns, verbs, pronouns, and adjectives are replaced by their semantic opposites. Thus, the sentence *Those men are small* means *This woman is big.*

These language games provide evidence for the phonemes, words, morphemes, semantic features, and so on that are posited by linguists for descriptive grammars.

SUMMARY

Every person has their own individual way of speaking, called an **idiolect.** The language used by a group of speakers may also show systematic differences called a **dialect.** The dialects of a language are the mutually intelligible forms of that language that differ in systematic ways from each other. Dialects develop and are reinforced because languages change, and the changes that occur in one group or area may differ from those that occur in another. **Regional dialects** and **social dialects** develop for this reason. Some of the differences in the regional dialects of America may be traced to the different dialects spoken by the colonial settlers from England; those from southern England, who arrived first, spoke one dialect and those from the north spoke another. In addition, the colonists who maintained close contact with England reflected the changes occurring in British English while earlier forms were preserved among Americans who spread westward and broke communication contact with England and the Atlantic coast. The study of regional dialects has produced **dialect atlases** with **dialect maps** showing the areas where specific dialectal characteristics occur in the speech of the region. Each area is delineated by a boundary line called an **isogloss.**

Dialect differences include phonological or pronunciation differences (often called **accents**), vocabulary distinctions, and syntactic rule differences. The grammar differences between dialects are not as great as the similarities that are shared, thus permitting speakers of different dialects to communicate with each other.

In many countries, one dialect or dialect group is viewed as the **standard,** such as **Standard American English (SAE).** While this particular dialect is not linguistically superior, it may be considered by some language purists to be the only correct form of the language. Such a view has led to the idea that some nonstandard dialects are deficient, as is erroneously suggested regarding **African American English** (recently referred to as **Ebonics**), a dialect used by some African Americans. A study of African American English shows it to be as logical, complete, rule-governed, and expressive as any other dialect. This is also true of the dialects spoken by Latino Americans whose native language or those of their parents is Spanish. There are bilingual and monolingual Latino speakers of English. One Latino dialect spoken in the Southwest, referred to as **Chicano English** (ChE), shows interesting systematic phonological and syntactic differences from SAE, some of which stem from the influence of Spanish. Other differences are shared with many nonstandard ethnic and nonethnic dialects. Bilingual Latinos may switch from one language to another, which is called **code-switching.** This is a common universal language-contact phenomenon that reflects the grammars of both languages working simultaneously; it does not represent a form of "broken" English.

Attempts to legislate the use of a particular dialect or language have been made throughout history and exist today, even extending to the banning of the use of languages other than the "accepted" one.

In areas where many languages are spoken, one language may become a **lingua franca** to ease communication among the people. In other cases, where traders or missionaries or travelers need to communicate with people who speak a language unknown to them, a **pidgin** based on one language may develop, which is simplified lexically, phonologically, and syntactically. When a pidgin is widely used, and is learned by children as their first language, it is **creolized.** The grammars of creole languages are similar to those of other languages, and languages of **creole** origin now exist in many parts of the world.

Besides regional and social dialects, speakers may use different **styles** or **registers** depending on the particular context. **Slang** is not often used in formal situations or writing, but is widely used in speech; **argot** and **jargon** refer to the unique vocabulary used by professional or trade groups.

In all societies certain acts or behaviors are frowned on, forbidden, or considered **taboo.** The words or expressions referring to these taboo acts are then also avoided, or considered "dirty." Language itself cannot be obscene or clean; the views toward specific words or linguistic expressions reflect the attitudes of a culture or society toward the behaviors and actions of the language users. At times slang words may be taboo whereas scientific or standard terms with the same meaning are acceptable in "polite society." Taboo words and acts give rise to **euphemisms,** which are words or phrases that replace the expressions to be avoided. Thus, *powder room* is a euphemism for *toilet,* which itself started as a euphemism for *lavatory,* which is now more acceptable than its replacement. The use of euphemisms is not new. It is reported that the Greek historian Plutarch in the first century C.E. wrote that "the ancient Athenians of the sixth century B.C.E. used to cover up the ugliness of things with auspicious and kindly terms, giving them polite and endearing names. Thus they called harlots *companions*, taxes *contributions* and prison a *chamber*."

Just as the use of some words may reflect society's views toward sex or natural bodily functions or religious beliefs, so also some words may reflect racist, chauvinist, and sexist attitudes in society. The language itself is not racist or sexist but reflects these views of various sectors of a society. Such terms, however, may perpetuate and reinforce biased views, and be demeaning and insulting to those addressed. Popular movements and changes in the institutions of society may then be reflected in changes in the language.

The invention or construction of secret languages and language games like Pig Latin attest to the creativity of language use and the unconscious knowledge that speakers have of the phonological, morphological, and semantic rules of their language.

References for Further Reading

Allan, Keith, and Kate Burridge. 1991. *Euphemism and Dysphemism.* New York: Oxford University Press.

Andersson, Lars, and Peter Trudgill. 1990. *Bad Language.* Oxford, England: Basil Blackwell.

Ayto, John. 1993. *Euphemisms: Over 3000 Ways to Avoid Being Rude or Giving Offence.* London: Bloomsbury.

Baugh, John. 1983. *Black Street Speech.* Austin, TX: University of Texas Press.

Bickerton, Derek. 1981. *Roots of Language.* Ann Arbor, MI: Karoma.

Cameron, Deborah. 1992. *Feminism and Linguistic Theory,* 2nd ed. London: Macmillan.

Carver, Craig M. 1987. *American Regional Dialects: A Word Georgraphy.* Ann Arbor, MI: University of Michigan Press.

Cassidy, Frederick G. 1985. *Dictionary of American Regional English.* Cambridge, MA: Belknap Press, Harvard University.

Coates, Jennifer. 1986. *Women, Men and Language: A Sociolinguistic Account of Sex Differences in Language.* London and New York: Longman.

Dillard, J. L. 1972. *African American English: Its History and Usage in the United States.* New York: Random House.

Ferguson, Charles, and Shirley Brice Health, eds. 1981. *Language in the USA.* Cambridge, England: Cambridge University Press.

Folb, Edith. 1980. *Runnin' down Some Lines: The Language and Culture of Black Teenagers.* Cambridge, MA: Harvard University Press.

Frank, Francine, and Frank Ashen. 1983. *Language and the Sexes.* Albany, NY: State University of New York Press.

Holm, John. 1988–1989. *Pidgins and Creoles,* Vols. 1–2. Cambridge, England: Cambridge University Press.

Jay, Timothy. 1992. *Cursing in America.* Philadelphia/Amsterdam: John Benjamins.

King, Ruth. 1991. *Talking Gender: A Guide to Nonsexist Communication.* Toronto: Copp Clark Pitman.

Labov, William. 1969. *The Logic of Nonstandard English.* Georgetown University 20th Annual Round Table, Monograph Series on Languages and Linguistics, No. 22.

Michaels, Leonard, and Christopher Ricks, eds. 1980. *The State of the Language.* Berkeley, CA: University of California Press.

Lakoff, Robin. 1990. *Talking Power: The Politics of Language.* New York: Basic Books.

Miller, Casey, and Kate Swift. 1980. *The Handbook of Nonsexist Writing.* New York: Barnes & Noble.

Mulhausler, Peter. 1986. *Pidgin and Creole Linguistics.* Oxford, England: Basil Blackwell.

Munro, Pamela. 1990. *Slang U: The Official Dictionary of College Slang.* New York: Harmony Books.

Newmeyer, Frederick J., ed. 1988. *Linguistics: The Cambridge Survey, Vol. IV. Language: The Socio-Cultural Context.* Cambridge, England: Cambridge University Press.

Penfield, Joyce, and Jacob L. Ornstein-Galicia. 1985. *Chicano English: An Ethnic Contact Dialect.* Amsterdam/Philadelphia: John Benjamins Publishing Co.

Reed, Carroll E. 1977. *Dialects of American English,* rev. ed. Amherst, MA: University of Massachusetts Press.

Romaine, Suzanne. 1988. *Pidgin and Creole Languages.* London/New York: Longman.

Shopen, Timothy, and Joseph M. Williams, eds. 1981. *Style and Variables in English.* Cambridge, MA: Winthrop Publishers.

Smith, Philip M. 1985. *Language, the Sexes and Society.* Oxford: Basil Blackwell.

Spears, Richard A. 1981. *Slang and Euphemism: A Dictionary of Oaths, Curses, Insults, Sexual Slang and Metaphor, Racial Slurs, Drug Talk, Homosexual Lingo, and Related Matter.* New York: Jonathan David Publishers.

Tannen, Deborah. 1990. *You Just Don't Understand: Women and Men in Conversation.* New York: Ballantine.

Thorne, Barrie, Cheris Kramarae, and Nancy Henley, eds. 1983. *Language, Gender, and Society.* Rowley, MA: Newbury House.

Todd, Loreto. 1984. *Modern Englishes: Pidgins and Creoles.* Oxford, England: Basil Blackwell.

Trudgill, Peter. 1977. *Sociolinguistics.* Middlesex, England: Penguin Books.

Williams, Glyn. 1992. *Sociolinguistics.* London/New York: Routledge.

Williamson, Juanita V., and Virginia M. Burke. 1971. *A Various Language: Perspectives on American Dialects.* New York: Holt, Rinehart and Winston.

EXERCISES

1. Each pair of words is pronounced as shown phonetically in at least one American English dialect. Write in phonetic transcription your pronunciation of each word that you pronounce differently.

a. "horse"	[hɔrs]	_____	"hoarse"	[hors]	_____
b. "morning"	[mɔrnĩŋ]	_____	"mourning"	[mornĩŋ]	_____
c. "for"	[fɔr]	_____	"four"	[for]	_____
d. "ice"	[ʌjs]	_____	"eyes"	[ajz]	_____
e. "knife"	[nʌjf]	_____	"knives"	[najvz]	_____
f. "mute"	[mjut]	_____	"nude"	[njud]	_____
g. "din"	[dĩn]	_____	"den"	[dẽn]	_____
h. "hog"	[hɔg]	_____	"hot"	[hat]	_____
i. "marry"	[mæri]	_____	"Mary"	[meri]	_____
j. "merry"	[mɛri]	_____	"marry"	[mæri]	_____
k. "rot"	[rat]	_____	"wrought"	[rɔt]	_____
l. "lease"	[lis]	_____	"grease" (v.)	[griz]	_____
m. "what"	[ʌat]	_____	"watt"	[wat]	_____
n. "ant"	[ænt]	_____	"aunt"	[ãnt]	_____
o. "creek"	[kʰrɪk]	_____	"creak"	[kʰrik]	_____

2. Below is a passage from *The Gospel According to St. Mark* in Cameroon English Pidgin. See how much you are able to understand before consulting the English translation given below. State some of the similarities and differences between CEP and SAE.

1. Di fos tok fo di gud nuus fo Jesus Christ God yi Pikin.

2. I bi sem as i di tok fo di buk fo Isaiah, God yi nchinda (Prophet), "Lukam, mi a di sen man nchinda fo bifo yoa fes weh yi go fix yoa rud fan."

3. Di vos fo som man di krai fo bush: "Fix di ples weh Papa God di go, mek yi rud tret."

Translation:

1. The beginning of the gospel of Jesus Christ, the Son of God.

2. As it is written in the book of Isaiah the prophet, "Behold, I send my messenger before thy face, which shall prepare thy way before thee."

3. The voice of one crying in the wilderness, "Prepare ye the way of the Lord, make his paths straight."

3. In the period from 1890 to 1904, *Slang and Its Analogues* by J. S. Farmer and W. E. Henley was published in seven volumes. The following entries are included in this dictionary. For each item (1) state whether the word or phrase still exists; (2) if not, state what the modern slang term would be;

(3) if the word remains but its meaning has changed, provide the modern meaning.

all out: completely, as in "All out the best." (The expression goes back to as early as 1300.)

to have apartments to let: be an idiot; one who is empty-headed.

been there: in "Oh, yes, I've been there." Applied to a man who is shrewd and who has had many experiences.

belly-button: the navel.

berkeleys: a woman's breasts.

bitch: most offensive appellation that can be given to a woman, even more provoking than that of whore.

once in a blue moon: extremely seldom.

boss: master; one who directs.

bread: employment. (1785—"out of bread" = "out of work.")

claim: to steal.

cut dirt: to escape.

dog cheap: of little worth. (Used in 1616 by Dekker: "Three things there are dog-cheap, learning, poorman's sweat, and oathes.")

funeral: as in "It's not my funeral." "It's no business of mine."

to get over: to seduce, to fascinate.

groovy: settled in habit; limited in mind.

grub: food.

head: toilet (nautical use only).

hook: to marry.

hump: to spoil.

hush money: money paid for silence; blackmail.

itch: to be sexually excited.

jam: a sweetheart or a mistress.

leg bags: stockings.

to lie low: to keep quiet; to bide one's time.

to lift a leg on: to have sexual intercourse.

looby: a fool.

malady of France: syphilis (used by Shakespeare in 1599).

nix: nothing.

noddle: the head.

old: money. (1900—"Perhaps it's somebody you owe a bit of the old to, Jack.")

to pill: talk platitudes.

pipe layer: a political intriguer; a schemer.

poky: cramped, stuffy, stupid.

pot: a quart; a large sum; a prize; a urinal; to excel.

puny: a freshman.

puss-gentleman: an effeminate.

4. Suppose someone asked you to help compile items for a new dictionary of slang. List ten slang words that you know, and provide a short definition for each.

    1)

    2)

    3)

    4)

    5)

    6)

    7)

    8)

    9)

    10)

5. Below are given some words used in British English for which different words are usually used in American English. See if you can match the British and American equivalents.

British		**American**	
a. clothes peg	k. biscuits	A. candy	K. baby buggy
b. braces	l. queue	B. truck	L. elevator
c. lift	m. torch	C. line	M. can
d. pram	n. underground	D. main street	N. cop
e. waistcoat	o. high street	E. crackers	O. wake up
f. shop assistant	p. crisps	F. suspenders	P. trunk
g. sweets	q. lorry	G. wrench	Q. vest
h. boot (of car)	r. holiday	H. flashlight	R. subway
i. bobby	s. tin	I. potato chips	S. clothes pin
j. spanner	t. knock up	J. vacation	T. clerk

6. Pig Latin is a common language game of English; but even Pig Latin has dialects, forms of the "language game" with different rules.

A. Consider the following data from three dialects of Pig Latin, each with its own rule applied to words beginning with vowels:

	Dialect 1	**Dialect 2**	**Dialect 3**
"eat"	[itme]	[ithe]	[ite]
"arc"	[arkme]	[arkhe]	[arke]

    (1) State the rule that accounts for the Pig Latin forms in each dialect.

        Dialect 1:

        Dialect 2:

        Dialect 3:

(2) How would you say *honest, admire,* and *illegal* in each dialect? Give the phonetic transcription of the Pig Latin forms.

honest	1. _____	2. _____	3. _____
admire	1. _____	2. _____	3. _____
illegal	1. _____	2. _____	3. _____

B. In one dialect of Pig Latin, the word "strike" is pronounced [ajkstre], and in another dialect it is pronounced [trajkse]. In the first dialect "slot" is pronounced [atsle] and in the second dialect, it is pronounced [latse].

   (1) State the rules for each of these dialects that account for these different Pig Latin forms of the same words.

     Dialect 1:

     Dialect 2:

   (2) Give the phonetic transcriptions for the following words in both dialects.

	1	2
spot		
crisis		
scratch		

7. Below are some sentences representing different English language games. Write each sentence in its undistorted form; state the language-game "rule."

   a. /aj-o tʊk-o maj-o dɔg-o awt-o sajd-o/

   b. /hirli ɪzli əli mɔrli kamlɪplɪliketliədli gemli/

   c. Mary-shmary can-shman talk-shmalk in-shmin rhyme-shmyme.

   d. Betpetterper latepate thanpan nevpeverper.

   e. thop-e fop-oot bop-all stop-a dop-i op-um blop-ew dop-own /ðape fapɛt bapɔl stape dapi apem blapu dapawn/

   f. /kʌbæn jʌbu spʌbik ðʌbɪs kʌbajnd ʌbəv ʌbɪnglʌbɪš/ (This sentence is in "Ubby Dubby" from a children's television program popular in the 1970s.)

8. Below are some sentences as might be spoken between two friends chatting informally. For each, state what the nonabbreviated full sentence in SAE would be. In addition, state in your own words (or formally if you wish) the rule or rules that derived the informal sentences from the formal ones.

   a. Where've ya been today?

   b. Watcha gonna do for fun?

   c. Him go to church?

   d. There's four books there.

   e. Who ya wanna go with?

9. Compile a list of argot (or jargon) terms from some profession or trade (for example, lawyer, musician, doctor, longshoreman, and so forth). Give a definition for each term in nonjargon terms.

10. "Translate" the first paragraph of any well-known document or speech—such as the Declaration of Independence, the Gettysburg Address, or the Preamble to the Constitution—into informal, colloquial language.

11. In Column A are Cockney rhyming slang expressions. Match these to the items in Column B to which they refer.

A	B
a. drip dry	(1) balls (testicles)
b. In the mood	(2) bread
c. Insects and ants	(3) ale
d. orchestra stalls	(4) cry
e. Oxford scholar	(5) food
f. strike me dead	(6) dollar
g. ship in full sail	(7) pants

Now construct your own version of Cockney rhyming slang for the following words:

h. chair _____
i. house _____
j. coat _____
k. eggs _____
l. pencil _____

12. Column A lists euphemisms used for words in Column B. Match up each item in A with its appropriate B word.

A	B
a. Montezuma's revenge	(1) condom
b. joy stick	(2) genocide
c. friggin	(3) fire
d. ethnic cleansing	(4) diarrhea
e. French letter (old)	(5) masturbate
f. diddle oneself	(6) kill
g. holy of holies	(7) urinate
h. spend a penny (British)	(8) penis
i. ladies' cloak room	(9) die
j. knock off (from 1919)	(10) waging war
k. vertically challenged	(11) vagina
l. hand in one's dinner pail	(12) women's toilet
m. sanitation engineer	(13) short
n. downsize	(14) fuckin
o. peace keeping	(15) garbage collector

Chapter 11

Language Change: The Syllables of Time

Some method should be thought on for ascertaining and fixing our language forever. . . . I see no absolute necessity why any language should be perpetually changing.

Jonathan Swift (1712)

All living languages change with time, despite Jonathan Swift's lamentation. It is fortunate that they do so rather slowly compared to the human life span. It would be inconvenient to have to relearn our native language every twenty years. Stargazers find a similar situation. Because of the movement of individual stars, the constellations are continuously changing their shape. Fifty thousand years from now we would hardly recognize Orion or the Big Dipper, but from season to season the changes are imperceptible. Linguistic change is also slow, in human—if not astronomical—terms. As years pass we hardly notice any change. Yet if we were to turn on a radio and miraculously receive a broadcast in our "native language" from the year 3000, we would probably think we had tuned in a foreign language station. Many of the changes are revealed when languages have written records. We know a great deal of the history of English because it has been written for about 1,000 years. Old English, spoken in England around the end of the first millennium, is scarcely recognizable as English. (Of course, our linguistic ancestors did not call their language Old English!) A speaker of Modern English would find the language unintelligible. There are college courses in which Old English is studied as a foreign language.

A line from *Beowulf* illustrates why Old English must be translated.[1]

Wolde guman findan þone þe him on sweofote sare geteode.

He wanted to find the man who harmed him while he slept.

Approximately five hundred years after *Beowulf,* Chaucer wrote *The Canterbury Tales* in what is now called Middle English, spoken from around 1100 to 1500. It is more easily understood by present-day readers, as seen by looking at the opening of the *Tales.*

---

[1] The letter þ, called *thorn,* is pronounced [θ], i.e., as the *th* in *think.*

Whan that Aprille with his shoures soote
The droght of March hath perced to the roote . . .
When April with its sweet showers
The drought of March has pierced to the root . . .

Two hundred years after Chaucer, in a language that can be considered an earlier form of Modern English, Shakespeare's Hamlet says:

A man may fish with the worm that hath eat of a king, and eat of the fish that hath fed of that worm.

The division of English into Old English (449–1100 C.E.), Middle English (1100–1500), and Modern English (1500–present) is somewhat arbitrary, being marked by the dates of events in English history, such as the Norman Conquest of 1066, that profoundly influenced the English language. Thus the history of English and the changes that occurred in the language reflect nonlinguistic history to some extent, as suggested by the following dates:

449–1066 Old English	449	Saxons invade Britain
	sixth century	Religious literature
	eighth century	*Beowulf*
	1066	Norman Conquest
1066–1500 Middle English	1387	*Canterbury Tales*
	1476	Caxton's printing press
	1500	Great vowel shift
1500–Modern English	1564	Birth of Shakespeare

Changes in a language are changes in the grammars of the speakers of the language, and are perpetuated when new generations of children learn the language by acquiring the new grammar. This is true of sign languages as well as spoken languages. Like all living languages, American Sign Language continues to change. Only 60 percent of the present ASL vocabulary is of French origin, although it was first brought to this country in 1775 from France by the Abbé de l'Épée and Laurent Clerc. Not only have new signs entered the language, but the forms of the signs have changed in ways similar to the historical changes in spoken languages.

An examination of the changes that have occurred in English during the past 1,500 years shows changes in the lexicon as well as the phonological, morphological, syntactic, and semantic components of the grammar. No part of the grammar remains the same over the course of history. Although most of the examples in this chapter are from English, the histories of all languages show similar changes.

THE REGULARITY OF SOUND CHANGE

That's not a regular rule: you invented it just now.

Lewis Carroll, *Alice's Adventures in Wonderland*

The southern United States represents a major dialect area of American English. For example, words pronounced with the diphthong [aj] in non-Southern English will usually be pronounced with the monophthong [a:] in the South. Local radio and TV announcers at the 1996 Olympics in Atlanta called athletes to the [ha:] "high" jump, and local natives invited visitors to try Georgia's famous pecan [pa:] "pie." The [aj]-[a:] correspondence between these two dialects is an example of a **regular sound correspondence.** When [aj] occurs in a word in non-Southern dialects, [a:] occurs in the Southern dialect, and this is true for all such words.

The different pronunciations of *I, my, high, pie,* etc. did not always exist in English. This chapter will discuss how such dialect differences arose and why the sound differences are usually regular and not confined to just a few words.

Sound Correspondences

In Middle English a mouse [maws] was called a *mūs* [mu:s], and this mūs may have lived in someone's *hūs* [hu:s], the way *house* [haws] was pronounced at that time. In general, where we now pronounce [aw], Middle English speakers pronounced [u:]. This is a regular correspondence like the one between [aj] and [a:]. Thus *out* [awt] was pronounced [u:t], *south* [sawθ] was pronounced [su:θ], and so on. Many such regular correspondences can be found, relating older and newer forms of English.

The regular sound correspondences we observe between older and modern forms of a language are due to phonological changes that affect certain sounds, or classes of sounds, rather than individual words. Centuries ago English underwent a phonological change called a **sound shift** in which [u:] became [aw].

Phonological changes can also account for dialect differences. At an earlier stage of American English a sound shift of [aj] to [a:] took place among certain speakers in the southern region of the country. The change did not spread beyond the South because the region was somewhat isolated. Many dialect differences in pronunciation result from a sound shift whose spread is limited.

Regional dialect differences may also arise when innovative changes occur everywhere but in a particular region. The regional dialect may be conservative relative to other dialects. The pronunciation of *it* as *hit,* found in the Appalachian region of the United States, was standard in older forms of English. The dropping of the [h] was the innovation.

Ancestral Protolanguages

Many of the world's modern languages were at first regional dialects that became widely spoken and highly differentiated, finally becoming separate languages. The Romance languages, French, Spanish, etc., were once dialects of Latin spoken in the Roman Empire. There is nothing degenerate about regional pronunciations. They result from natural sound change that occurs wherever human language is spoken.

In a sense, the Romance languages are offspring of Latin, their metaphorical parent. Because of their common ancestry, the Romance languages are said to be **genetically related.** Early forms of English and German, too, were once dialects of a common ancestor called **Proto-Germanic**. A **protolanguage** is the ancestral language from which related languages have developed. Both Latin and Proto-Germanic were themselves descendants of an older language called **Indo-European.**[2] Thus, Germanic languages such as English and German are genetically related to the Romance languages such as French and Spanish. All these important national languages were once regional dialects.

How do we know that the Germanic and Romance languages have a common ancestor? One clue is the large number of sound correspondences that exist between them. If you have studied a Romance language such as French or Spanish, you may have noticed that where an English word begins with *f,* the corresponding word in a Romance language often begins with *p* as shown in the following examples.

English /f/	**French /p/**	**Spanish /p/**
father	père	padre
fish	poisson	pescado

This **/f/-/p/** correspondence is another example of a regular sound correspondence. There are many between the Germanic and Romance languages. The prevalence of such regular sound correspondences cannot be explained by chance. What then accounts for them? A reasonable guess is that a common ancestor language used a **p** in words for *fish, father,* and so on. A /p/ rather than an /f/ since more languages show a /p/ in these words. At some point speakers of this language separated into two groups, retaining little contact. In one of the groups a sound change of *p → f* took place. This group eventually became the ancestor of the Germanic languages. This ancient sound change left its trace in the *f-p* sound correspondence that we observe today, as illustrated in the diagram.

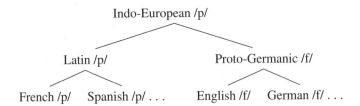

PHONOLOGICAL CHANGE

> Etymologists . . . for whom vowels did not matter and who cared not a jot for consonants.
>
> Voltaire

Regular sound correspondences illustrate changes in the phonological system. In earlier chapters we discussed speakers' knowledge of their phonological system, including knowledge of the phonemes and phonological rules of the language. Any of these aspects of the phonology is subject to change.

---

[2] It may also be called Proto-Indo-European.

The velar fricative /x/ is no longer part of the phonemic inventory of most Modern English dialects as it once was. *Night* used to be pronounced [nɪxt] and *drought* was pronounced [druxt]. In the history of English this sound was lost. This phonological change—the loss of /x/—took place between the times of Chaucer and Shakespeare. All words once pronounced with an /x/ no longer include this sound. In some cases it disappeared altogether, as in *night* and *light*. In other cases the /x/ became a /k/, as in *elk* (Old English *eolh* [ɛɔlx]). In yet other cases it disappeared to be replaced by a vowel, as in *hollow* (Old English *holh* [hɔlx]). Dialects of Modern English spoken in Scotland have retained the /x/ sound in some words, such as *loch* [lɔx] meaning "lake."

These examples show that the inventory of sounds can change by the loss of phonemes. The inventory can also change by the addition of new phonemes. Old English did not have the phoneme /ž/ of *leisure* [ližər]. Through a process of palatalization—the change in place of articulation to the palatal region—certain occurrences of /z/ were pronounced as [ž]. Eventually the [ž] sound became a phoneme in its own right, reinforced by the fact that it occurs in French words familiar to many English speakers such as *azure* [æžər].

An allophone of a phoneme may, through sound change, become phonemic. Old English lacked a phoneme /v/. The phoneme /f/, however had the allophone [v] when it occurred between vowels. Thus *ofer* /ofer/ meaning "over" was pronounced [ɔvɛr] in Old English.

Old English also had a geminate phoneme /f:/ that contrasted with /f/, and was pronounced as a long [f:] between vowels. The name *Offa* /of:a/ was pronounced [ɔf:a]. A sound change occurred in which the pronunciation of /f:/ was simplified to [f]. Once the geminate /f:/ was pronounced as [f] it contrasted with the intervocalic [v] and a reinterpretation occurred, creating a new phoneme /v/.

Similar changes occur in the history of all languages. Neither /č/ nor /š/ were phonemes of Latin, but /č/ is a phoneme of modern Italian and /š/ a phoneme of modern French, both of which evolved from Latin. In American Sign Language many signs that were originally formed at the waist or chest level are now produced at a higher level near the neck or upper chest, a reflection of changes in the "phonology."

Phonemes thus may be lost (/x/) or added (/ž/) or result from a change in the status of allophones (the [v] allophone of /f/ becoming /v/).

Phonological Rules

An interaction of phonological rules may result in changes in the lexicon. The nouns *house* and *bath* were once differentiated from the verbs *house* and *bathe* by the fact that the verbs ended with a short vowel sound. Furthermore, the same rule that realized /f/ as [v] between vowels also realized /s/ and /θ/ as [z] and [ð] between vowels. This·̵ a general rule that voiced intervocalic fricatives. Thus the /s/ in the verb *hou*ᵉ nounced [z], and the /θ/ in the verb *bathe* was pronounced [ð].

Later a rule was added to the grammar of English deletiᵣ̵ at the end of words. Once the unstressed final vowel was deleᵢ̵ voiced and voiceless fricatives resulted, and the new phonemᵤ̵ to the phonemic inventory. Prior to this change they were allopᵣ̵ /s/ and /θ/ between vowels. The verbs *house* and *bathe* were nᵢ̵ mental lexicon with final voiced consonants.

Eventually, both the unstressed vowel deletion rule and the intervocalic-voicing rule were lost from the grammar of English. Thus the set of phonological rules can change both by addition and loss of rules.

Changes in phonological rules can, and often do, result in dialect differences. In the previous chapter we discussed the addition of an "r-dropping" rule in English (/r/ is not pronounced unless followed by a vowel) that did not spread throughout the language. Today, we see the effect of that rule in the "r-less" pronunciation of British English and of American English dialects spoken in the Boston area and the southern United States.

From the standpoint of the language as a whole, phonological changes occur gradually over the course of many generations of speakers, although a given speaker's grammar may or may not reflect the change. The changes are not planned any more than we are presently planning what changes will take place in English by the year 2300. Speakers are aware of the changes only through dialect differences.

The Great Vowel Shift

The sniffles in 14th-century England

© 1995 Denise P. Meyer.

A major change in the history of English that resulted in new phonemic representations of words and morphemes took place approximately between 1400 and 1600. It is known as the **Great Vowel Shift.** The seven long, or tense, vowels of Middle English underwent the following change:

Shift		Example		
Middle English	**Modern English**	**Middle English**	**Modern English**	
[i:] →	[aj]	[mi:s] →	[majs]	*mice*
[u:] →	[aw]	[mu:s] →	[maws]	*mouse*
[e:] →	[i:]	[ge:s] →	[gi:s]	*geese*
[o:] →	[u:]	[go:s] →	[gu:s]	*goose*
[ɛ:] →	[e:]	[brɛ:ken] →	[bre:k]	*break*
[ɔ:] →	[o:]	[brɔ:ken] →	[bro:k]	*broke*
[a:] →	[e:]	[na:mə] →	[ne:m]	*name*

By diagraming the Great Vowel Shift on a vowel chart (Figure 11.1), we can see that the high vowels [i:] and [u:] became the diphthongs [aj] and [aw], while the long vowels underwent an increase in tongue height, as if to fill in the space vacated by the high vowels. In addition, [a] was "fronted."

These changes are among the most dramatic examples of regular sound shift. The phonemic representation of many thousands of words changed. Today, some reflection of this vowel shift is seen in the alternating forms of morphemes in English: *please—pleasant; serene—serenity; sane—sanity; crime—criminal; sign—signal;* and so on. Once, the vowels in each pair were the same. Then the vowels in the second word of each pair were shortened by a rule called the **Early Middle English Vowel Shortening** rule. As a result the Great Vowel Shift, which occurred later, affected only the first word in each pair. The second word, with its short vowel, was unaffected. This is why the vowels in the morphologically related words are pronounced differently today, as shown in Table 11-1.

FIGURE 11-1 The Great Vowel Shift

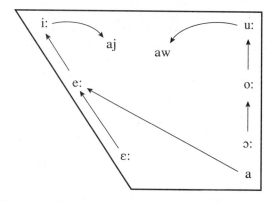

TABLE 11-1   Effect of the Vowel Shift on Modern English

Middle English Vowel	Shifted Vowel	Short Counterpart	Word with Shifted Vowel	Word with Short Vowel
ī	aj	ɪ	divine	divinity
ū	aw	ʊ	profound	profundity
ē	i	ɛ	serene	serenity
ō	u	a	fool	folly
ā	e	æ	sane	sanity

The Great Vowel Shift is a primary source of many of the spelling inconsistencies of English because our spelling system still reflects the way words were pronounced before the Great Vowel Shift took place.

MORPHOLOGICAL CHANGE

Like phonological rules, rules of morphology may be lost, added, or changed. We can observe some of these changes by comparing older and newer forms of the language or by looking at different dialects.

Extensive changes in rules of morphology have occurred in the history of the Indo-European languages. Latin, once had **case endings,** suffixes on the noun based on its grammatical relationship to the verb. These are no longer found in the Romance languages. (See Chapter 5 for a more extensive discussion of grammatical case.) Following are several forms for the Latin noun *lupus* "wolf":

Case	Noun Stem	Case Ending		
nominative	lup +	us	lupus	The *wolf* runs.
genitive	lup +	ī	lupī	A sheep in *wolf's* clothing.
dative	lup +	ō	lupō	Give food to *the wolf.*
accusative	lup +	um	lupum	I love *the wolf.*
vocative	lup +	e	lupe	*Wolf,* come here!

In *Alice's Adventures in Wonderland,* Lewis Carroll has Alice give us a brief lesson in grammatical case. Alice has become very small and is swimming around in a pool of her own tears with a mouse whom she wishes to befriend:

> "Would it be of any use, now," thought Alice, "to speak to this mouse? Everything is so out-of-the-way down here, that I should think very likely it can talk: at any rate, there's no harm in trying." So she began: "O Mouse, do you know the way out of this pool? I am very tired of swimming about here, O Mouse!" (Alice thought this must be the right way of speaking to a mouse: she had never done such a thing before, but she remembered having seen in her brother's Latin Grammar, "A mouse–of a mouse–to a mouse– a mouse–O mouse!")

Alice gives the English corresponding to the nominative, genitive, dative, accusative, and vocative cases.

Ancient Greek and Sanskrit also had extensive case systems expressed morphologically through noun suffixing, as did Old English, as illustrated by the following noun forms:

Case	OE Singular		OE Plural	
nominative	stān	"stone"	stānas	"stones"
genitive	stānes	"stone's"	stāna	"stones' "
dative	stāne	"stone"	stānum	"stones"
accusative	stān	"stone"	stānas	"stones"

Lithuanian and Russian retain much of the early Indo-European case system, but changes have all but obliterated it in most modern Indo-European languages. In English, phonological changes occurring over the centuries resulted in the loss of many case endings.

English still retains the genitive case, which is written with an apostrophe *s,* as in *Robert's dog,* but that's all that remains as far as nouns are concerned. Pronouns retain a few more traces: *he/she* are nominative, *him/her* accusative and dative, and *his/hers* genitive.

English has replaced its depleted case system with an equally expressive system of prepositions. For example the dative case is often indicated by the preposition *to* and the genitive case by the preposition *of.* A noun occurring after a verb with no intervening preposition is often, but not always, in the accusative case.

English and most of the Indo-European languages, then, have undergone extensive morphological changes over the past 1,000 years, many of them induced by changes that took place in the phonological rules of the language.

SYNTACTIC CHANGE

The loss of case endings in English occurred together with changes in the rules of syntax governing word order. In Old English, word order was freer because the case endings on nouns indicated the meaning relations in a sentence.

Additionally, Modern English is an SVO (Subject-Verb-Object) language. Old English was both an SVO and an SOV language.[3] Sentences like *Se man þone kyning sloh,* literally *the man the king slew,* were grammatical. Thus the phrase structure rules that determine the word order of basic sentences changed in the history of English.

The syntactic rules relating to the English negative construction also underwent a number of changes from Old English to the present. In Modern English, negation is expressed by adding *not* or *do not.* We may also express negation by adding words like *never* or *no:*

> I am going → I am not going
> I went → I did not go
> I go to school → I never go to school
> I want food → I don't want any food; I want no food

In Old English the main negation element was *ne.* It usually occurred before a verbal element:[4]

> þæt he *na*   siþþan geboren *ne* wurde
> that he never after born   not would-be
> that he should never be born after that

> ac hie *ne* dorston þær on cuman
> but they not dared   there on come
> but they dared not land there

In the first example, the word order is different from that of Modern English, and there are two negatives: *na* (a contraction of *ne + a,* "not" + "ever" = "never") and *ne.* As shown, a double negative was grammatical in Old English. Although double negatives are ungrammatical in Modern Standard American English, they are grammatical in some English dialects.

In addition to the contraction of *ne + a → na,* other negative contractions occurred in Old English: *ne* could be attached to *habb-* "have," *wes-* "be," *wit-* "know," and *will-* "will" to form *nabb-, nes-, nyt-,* and *nyll-,* respectively.

Modern English also has contraction rules that change *do + not* into *don't, will + not* into *won't,* and so on. In these contractions the phonetic form of the negation element always comes at the *end* of the word because Modern English word order puts the *not* after the auxiliary verb. In Old English, the negative element occurred at the beginning of the contraction because it preceded the auxiliary verb. The rules determining the placement of the negative morpheme have changed. Such syntactic changes may take centuries to be fully completed, and there are often intermediate stages.

Another syntactic change in English affected the rules of comparative and superlative constructions. Today we form the comparative by adding *-er* to the adjective or by inserting *more* before it; the superlative is formed by adding *-est* or by inserting *most.* In Malory's *Tales of King Arthur,* written in 1470, double comparatives and double

---

[3] A later section in this chapter entitled "Types of Languages" explains this in more detail.

[4] From E. C. Traugott. 1972. *The History of English Syntax,* New York: Holt, Rinehart and Winston.

superlatives occur, which today are ungrammatical: *more gladder, more lower, moost royallest, moost shamefullest.*

When we study a language solely from written records, which is necessarily the case with nonmodern languages such as Elizabethan English (sixteenth century), we see only sentences that are grammatical unless ungrammatical sentences are used deliberately. Without native speakers of Elizabethan English to query, we can only infer what was ungrammatical. Such inference leads us to believe that expressions like *the Queen of England's crown* were ungrammatical in former versions of English. The title *The Wife's Tale of Bath* (rather than *The Wife of Bath's Tale*) in *The Canterbury Tales* supports this inference. Modern English, on the other hand, allows some rather complex constructions that involve the possessive marker. An English speaker can use possessive constructions such as

> The girl whose sister I'm dating's roommate is pretty.
> The man from Boston's hat fell off.

Older versions of English had to resort to an *of* construction to express the same thought (*The hat of the man from Boston fell off*). A syntactic change took place that accounts for the extended use of the possessive morpheme *'s.*

LEXICAL CHANGE

All things change except the love of change.

Anonymous, *Madrigal* (1601)

Changes in the lexicon also occur, including the addition of new words, changes in the meanings of words, and the loss of words.

Borrowings

Reprinted with special permission of King Feature Syndicate.

Borrowing words from other languages is another important source of new words. Borrowing occurs when one language adds to its own lexicon a word or morpheme from another language, often altering its pronunciation to fit the phonological rules of the borrowing language. The borrowed word, of course, remains in the source language, so there is no need for it to be returned. Most languages are borrowers, so the lexicon can be divided into native and nonnative words or **loan words.** A native word is one whose history or **etymology** can be traced back to the earliest known stages of the language.

A language may borrow a word directly or indirectly. A direct borrowing means that the borrowed item is a native word in the language from which it is borrowed. *Feast* was borrowed directly from French and can be traced back to Latin *festum*. On the other hand, the word *algebra* was borrowed from Spanish, which in turn had borrowed it from Arabic. Thus *algebra* was indirectly borrowed from Arabic, with Spanish as an intermediary.

Some languages are heavy borrowers. Albanian has borrowed so heavily that few native words are retained. On the other hand, most Native American languages borrowed little from their neighbors.

English has borrowed extensively. Of the 20,000 or so words in common use, about three-fifths are borrowed. Of the 500 most frequently used words, however, only two-sevenths are borrowed, and since these words are used repeatedly in sentences, the actual frequency of appearance of native words is about 80 percent. *And, be, have, it, of, the, to, will, you, on, that,* and *is* are all native to English.

History and Borrowed Words

A morsel of genuine history is a thing so rare as to be always valuable.

Thomas Jefferson

The history of the English-speaking peoples can be followed by studying the kinds of loan words in the language and when they entered. Until the Norman Conquest in 1066, England was inhabited chiefly by the Angles, the Saxons, and the Jutes, peoples of Germanic origin who came to England in the fifth century C.E. and eventually became the English.[5] Originally, they spoke Germanic dialects, from which Old English developed directly. These dialects contained a number of Latin borrowings but few foreign elements beyond that. These Germanic tribes had displaced the earlier Celtic inhabitants, whose influence on Old English was confined to a few Celtic place-names. (The modern languages Welsh, Irish, and Scots Gaelic are descended from the Celtic dialects.)

For three centuries after the Norman Conquest, French was the language used for all affairs of state and for most commercial, social, and cultural matters. The West Saxon literary language was abandoned, but regional varieties of English continued to be used in homes, in the churches, and in the marketplace. During these three centuries, vast numbers of French words entered English, of which the following are representative:

government	crown	prince	estate	parliament
nation	jury	judge	crime	sue
attorney	saint	miracle	charity	court
lechery	virgin	value	pray	mercy
religion	value	royal	money	society

---

[5] The word *England* is derived from Anglaland, "Land of the Angles."

Until the Norman Conquest, when an Englishman slaughtered an ox for food, he ate *ox*. If it was a pig, he ate *pig*. If it was a sheep, he ate *sheep*. However, "ox" served at the Norman tables was *beef (boeuf)*, "pig" was *pork (porc)*, and "sheep" was *mutton (mouton)*. These words were borrowed from French into English, as were the food-preparation words *boil, fry, stew,* and *roast*.

English borrowed many "learned" words from foreign sources during the Renaissance. In 1476 the printing press was introduced in England by William Caxton. By 1640, 55,000 books had been printed in English. The authors of these books used many Greek and Latin words, and as a result, many words of ancient Greek and Latin entered the language.

From Greek came *drama, comedy, tragedy, scene, botany, physics, zoology,* and *atomic*. Latin loan words in English are numerous. They include:

> bonus   scientific   exit   alumnus   quorum   describe

During the ninth and tenth centuries, the Scandinavians, who first raided and then settled in the British Isles, left their traces in the English language. The pronouns *they, their,* and *them* are loan words from the Scandinavian language Old Norse, from which modern Danish, Norwegian, and Swedish have descended. This period is the only time that English ever borrowed pronouns.

Bin, flannel, clan, slogan, and *whisky* are all words of Celtic origin, borrowed at various times from Welsh, Scots Gaelic, or Irish.

Dutch was a source of borrowed words, too, many of which are related to shipping: *buoy, freight, leak, pump, yacht*.

From German came *quartz, cobalt,* and—as we might guess—*sauerkraut*.

From Italian, many musical terms, including words describing opera houses, have been borrowed: *opera, piano, virtuoso, balcony,* and *mezzanine*.

Words having to do with mathematics and chemistry were borrowed indirectly from Arabic, because early Arab scholarship in these fields was quite advanced. *Alcohol, algebra, cipher,* and *zero* are a representative sample.

Spanish has loaned us (directly) *barbecue, cockroach,* and *ranch,* as well as *California,* literally "hot furnace."

In America, the English-speaking colonists borrowed from Native American languages. They provided us with *hickory, chipmunk, opossum,* and *squash,* to mention only a few. Nearly half the names of states of the United States are borrowed from one American Indian language or another.

English has borrowed from Yiddish. Yiddish words are used by many non-Jews as well as by non-Yiddish-speaking Jews in the United States. There was even a bumper sticker proclaiming: "Marcel Proust is a yenta." *Yenta* is a Yiddish word meaning "gossipy woman" or "shrew." *Lox* "smoked salmon" and *bagel* "a hard roll resembling a doughnut," belong to American English, as well as Yiddish expressions like *chutzpah, schmaltz, schlemiel, schmuck, schmo,* and *kibitz*.

English is also a provider of copious numbers of loan words to other languages. Words and expressions such as *jazz, whisky, blue jeans, rock music, supermarket, baseball, picnic,* etc. have been borrowed by languages as diverse as Twi, Hungarian, Russian, and Japanese.

Loan translations are compound words or expressions whose parts are translated directly into the borrowing language. *Marriage of convenience* is a loan-translation borrowed from French *mariage de convenance.* Spanish speakers eat *perros calientes,* a loan translation of *hot dogs* with an adjustment reversing the order of the adjective and noun, as required by the rules of Spanish syntax.

New Words

Calvin and Hobbs © Watterson. Dist. by Universal Press Syndicate. Reprinted by permission. All rights reserved.

In Chapter 3 we discussed ways in which new words can enter the language—for example, by compounding, the recombining of old words to form new ones with new meanings. Thousands of common English words have entered the language by this process, including *afternoon, bigmouth, chickenhearted, egghead, force feed, g-string, icecap, jet set, longshoreman, moreover, nursemaid, offshore, pothole, railroad, sailboat, takeover, undergo, water cooler, X ray,* and *zookeeper.*

We also saw that new words may be formed by derivational processes, as in *uglification, finalize,* and *finalization.* Other methods for enlarging the vocabulary that were discussed include word coinage, deriving words from names, blends, back-formations, acronyms, and abbreviations or clippings.

Loss of Words

Words also can be lost from a language, though an old word's departure is never as striking as a new word's arrival. When a new word comes into vogue, its unusual presence draws attention; but a word is lost through inattention—nobody thinks of it; nobody uses it; and it fades out of the language.

A reading of Shakespeare's work shows that English has lost many words, such as these taken from *Romeo and Juliet: beseem* "to be suitable," *mammet* "a doll or puppet," *wot* "to know," *gyve* "a fetter," *fain* "gladly," and *wherefore* "why."

Semantic Change

> The language of this country being always upon the flux, the Struldbruggs
> of one age do not understand those of another, neither are they able after
> two hundred years to hold any conversation (farther than by a few general
> words) with their neighbors the mortals, and thus they lie under the disad-
> vantage of living like foreigners in their own country.
>
> Jonathan Swift, *Gulliver's Travels*

We have seen that a language may gain or lose lexical items. Additionally, the meaning
or semantic representation of words may change, shifting or becoming broader or nar-
rower.

Broadening

When the meaning of a word becomes broader, that word means everything it used to
mean, and more. The Middle English word *dogge* meant a specific breed of dog, but it
was eventually **broadened** to encompass all members of the species *canis familiaris*.
The word *holiday* originally meant "holy day," a day of religious significance. Today
the word signifies any day on which we do not have to work. *Picture* used to mean
"painted representation," but today you can take a picture with a camera. *Quarantine*
once had the restricted meaning of "forty days' isolation."

Narrowing

In the King James Version of the Bible (1611), God says of the herbs and trees, "to you
they shall be for meat" (Genesis 1:29). To a speaker of seventeenth-century English,
meat meant "food," and *flesh* meant "meat." Since that time, semantic change has **narrowed** the meaning of meat to what it is in Modern English. The word *deer* once meant
"beast" or "animal," as its German cognate *Tier* still does. The meaning of *deer* has
been narrowed to a particular kind of animal. Similarly, the word *hound* used to be the
general term for "dog," like the German *Hund*. Today *hound* means a special kind of
dog, one used for hunting.

Meaning Shifts

The third kind of semantic change that a lexical item may undergo is a shift in meaning.
The word *knight* once meant "youth" but shifted to "mounted man-at-arms." *Lust* used
to mean simply "pleasure," with no negative or sexual overtones. *Lewd* was merely
"ignorant," and *immoral* meant "not customary." *Silly* used to mean "happy" in Old
English. By the Middle English period it had come to mean "naive," and only in Modern English does it mean "foolish." The overworked Modern English word *nice* meant
"ignorant" a thousand years ago. When Juliet tells Romeo, "I am too *fond,*" she is not
claiming she likes Romeo too much. She means "I am too *foolish.*"

RECONSTRUCTING "DEAD" LANGUAGES

The branch of linguistics that deals with how languages change, what kinds of changes occur, and why they occurred is called **historical and comparative linguistics.** It is "historical" because it deals with the history of particular languages; it is "comparative" because it deals with relations between languages.

The Nineteenth-Century Comparativists

> When agreement is found in words in two languages, and so frequently that rules may be drawn up for the shift in letters from one to the other, then there is a fundamental relationship between the two languages.
>
> Rasmus Rask

The nineteenth-century historical and comparative linguists based their theories on the observations that there are regular sound correspondences among certain languages, and that languages displaying systematic similarities and differences must have descended from a common source language—that is, were genetically related.

The chief goal of these linguists was to develop and elucidate the genetic relationships that exist among the world's languages. They aimed to establish the major language families of the world and to define principles for the classification of languages. Their work grew out of earlier research.

As a child, Sir William Jones had an astounding propensity for learning languages, including so-called "dead" ones such as Ancient Greek and Latin. As an adult he found it best to reside in India because of his sympathy for the rebellious American colonists. There he distinguished himself both as a jurist, holding a position on the Bengal Supreme Court, and as an "Orientalist," as certain linguists were then called.

While in Calcutta he took up the study of Sanskrit, just for fun, mind you, and in 1786 delivered a paper in which he observed that Sanskrit bore to Greek and Latin "a stronger affinity . . . than could possibly have been produced by accident." Jones suggested that these three languages had "sprung from a common source" and that probably Germanic and Celtic had the same origin.

About thirty years after Jones delivered his important paper, the German linguist Franz Bopp pointed out the relationships among Sanskrit, Latin, Greek, Persian, and Germanic. At the same time, a young Danish scholar named Rasmus Rask corroborated

FIGURE 11-2   Grimm's Law (an early Germanic sound shift)

Grimm's Law can be expressed in terms of natural classes of speech sounds: Voiced aspirates become unaspirated; voiced stops become voiceless; voiceless stops become fricatives.

Earlier stage:[6]	bh	dh	gh	b	d	g	p	t	k
	↓	↓	↓	↓	↓	↓	↓	↓	↓
Later stage:	b	d	g	p	t	k	f	θ	x (or h)

these results, and brought Lithuanian and Armenian into the relationship as well. Rask was the first scholar to describe formally the regularity of certain phonological differences between related languages.

Rask's investigation of these regularities was followed up by the German linguist Jakob Grimm (of fairy-tale fame), who published a four-volume treatise (1819–1822) that specified the regular sound correspondences among Sanskrit, Greek, Latin, and the Germanic languages. It was not only the similarities that intrigued Grimm and the other linguists, but the systematic nature of the differences. Where Latin has a [p], English often has an [f]; where Latin has a [t], English often has a [θ]; where Latin has a [k], English often has an [h].

Grimm pointed out that certain phonological changes that did not take place in Sanskrit, Greek, or Latin must have occurred early in the history of the Germanic languages. Because the changes were so strikingly regular, they became known as **Grimm's Law,** which is illustrated in Figure 11-2.

Cognates

"Shouldn't a unicorn be
called a uniHORN?"

Reprinted with special permission of King Feature Syndicate.

---

[6] This "earlier stage" is the original parent of Sanskrit, Greek, the Romance and Germanic languages, and other languages—namely, Indo-European. The symbols *bh, dh,* and *gh* are breathy voiced stop phonemes, often called "voiced aspirates."

FIGURE 11-3 Cognates of Indo-European *p.

Indo-European	Sanskrit	Latin	English
*p	p	p	f
	pitar-	pater	father
	pad-	ped-	foot
	No cognate	piscis	fish
	paśu[7]	pecu	fee

Cognates are words in related languages that developed from the same ancestral root, such as English *horn* and Latin *cornū*. Cognates often, but not always, have the same meaning in the different languages. From cognates we can observe sound correspondences and from them deduce sound changes. Thus, from the cognates of Sanskrit, Latin, and English (representing Germanic) shown in Figure 11-3, the regular correspondence *p–p–f* indicates that the languages are genetically related. Indo-European *p is posited as the origin of the *p–p–f* correspondence.[8]

A more complete chart of correspondences is given in Figure 11-4, where a single representative example of each regular correspondence is presented. In most cases many cognate sets exhibit the same correspondence, which leads to the reconstruction of the Indo-European sound shown in the first column.

Sanskrit underwent the fewest consonant changes, while Latin underwent somewhat more, and Germanic (under Grimm's Law) underwent almost a complete restructuring. Still, the fact that it was the phonemes and phonological rules that changed, and not individual words, has resulted in the remarkably regular correspondences that allow us to reconstruct much of the sound system of Indo-European.

Exceptions can be found to these regular correspondences, as Grimm was aware. He stated: "The sound shift is a general tendency; it is not followed in every case." Karl Verner explained some of the exceptions to Grimm's Law in 1875. He formulated **Verner's Law** to show why Indo-European *p, t,* and *k* failed to correspond to *f,* θ, and *x* in certain cases:

> Verner's Law: *When the preceding vowel was unstressed,* **f, θ,** *and* **x** *underwent a further change to* **b, d,** *and* **g.**

---

[7] *ś* is a sibilant different from *s*.

[8] The asterisk before a letter indicates a reconstructed sound. It does not mean an unacceptable form. This use of the asterisk occurs only in this chapter.

FIGURE 11-4   Some Indo-European sound correspondences.

Indo-European	Sanskrit		Latin		English	
*p	p	pitar-	p	pater	f	father
*t	t	trayas	t	trēs	θ	three
*k	ś	śun	k	canis	h	hound
*b	b	No cognate	b	labium	p	lip
*d	d	dva-	d	duo	t	two
*g	j	ajras	g	ager	k	acre
*bh	bh	bhrātar-	f	frāter	b	brother
*dh	dh	dhā	f	fē-ci	d	do
*gh	h	vah-	h	veh-ō	g	wagon

A group of young linguists known as the **Neo-Grammarians** went beyond the idea that such sound shifts represented only a tendency, and claimed that sound laws have no exception. They viewed linguistics as a natural science and therefore believed that laws of sound change were unexceptionable natural laws. The "laws" they put forth often had exceptions, however, which could not always be explained as dramatically as Verner's Law explained the exceptions to Grimm's Law. Still, the work of these linguists provided important data and insights into language change and why such changes occur.

The linguistic work of the early nineteenth century had some influence on Charles Darwin, and in turn, Darwin's theory of evolution had a profound influence on linguistics and on all science. Some linguists thought that languages had a "life cycle" and developed according to evolutionary laws. In addition, it was believed that each language can be traced to a common ancestor. This theory of biological naturalism has an element of truth to it, but it is a vast oversimplification of the way languages change and evolve into other languages.

Comparative Reconstruction

> . . . Philologists who chase
> A panting syllable through time and space
> Start it at home, and hunt it in the dark,
> To Gaul, to Greece, and into Noah's Ark.
>
> Cowper, "Retirement"

When languages resemble one another in ways not attributable to chance or borrowing, we may conclude they are related. That is, they evolved via linguistic change from a single ancestral protolanguage.

The similarity of the basic vocabulary of languages such as English, German, Danish, Dutch, Norwegian, and Swedish is too pervasive for chance or borrowing. We therefore conclude that these languages have a common parent, Proto-Germanic. There are no written records of Proto-Germanic, and certainly no native speakers alive today. Proto-Germanic is a hypothetical language whose properties have been deduced based on its descendants.

In addition to similar vocabulary, the Germanic languages share grammatical properties such as irregularity in the verb *to be,* and similar irregular past tense forms of verbs, further supporting their relatedness.

Once we know or suspect that several languages are related, their protolanguage may be partially determined by **comparative reconstruction.** One proceeds by applying the **comparative method,** which we illustrate with a brief example:

Restricting ourselves to English, German, and Swedish we find the word for "man" is *man, Mann,* and *man,* respectively. This is one of many word sets in which we can observe the regular sound correspondence [m]–[m]–[m] and [n]–[n]–[n] in the three languages. Based on this evidence the comparative method has us reconstruct **mVn* as the word for "man" in Proto-Germanic. The *V* indicates a vowel whose quality we are unsure of since, despite the similar spelling, the vowel is phonetically different in the various Germanic languages, and it is unclear how to reconstruct it without further evidence.

Although we are confident that we can reconstruct much of Proto-Germanic with accuracy, we may never know for sure, and many details remain obscured. To give us confidence in the comparative method, we can apply it to Romance languages such as French, Italian, Spanish, and Portuguese. Their protolanguage is the well-known Latin, so we can verify the method. Consider the following data, focusing on the initial consonant of each word. In these data, *ch* in French is [š] and *c* in the other languages is [k].[9]

French	Italian	Spanish	Portuguese	
cher	caro	caro	caro	"dear"
champ	campo	campo	campo	"field"
chandelle	candela	candela	candeia	"candle"

In French, [š] corresponds to [k] in the three other languages. This regular sound correspondence, [š]–[k]–[k]–[k], supports the view that French, Italian, Spanish, and Portuguese descended from a common language. The comparative method leads to the reconstruction of [k] in "dear," "field," and "candle" of the parent language, and shows that [k] underwent a change to [š] in French, but not in Italian, Spanish, or Portuguese, which retained the original [k] of the parent language, Latin.

To use the comparative method, analysts identify regular sound correspondences in the cognates of potentially related languages. For each correspondence, they deduce what the most likely one sound must have been in the parent language. In this way much of the sound system of the parent may be reconstructed. The various phonological changes that occurred in the development of each daughter language as it descended and changed from the parent are then identified. Sometimes the sound that analysts choose in their reconstruction of the parent language will be the sound that appears most frequently in the correspondence. This approach was illustrated above with the four Romance languages.

---

[9] Data from Winfred P. Lehmann. 1973. *Historical Linguistics,* 2nd ed, New York: Holt, Rinehart and Winston.

Other considerations may outweigh the "majority rules" principle. The likelihood or unlikelihood of certain phonological changes may persuade the analyst to reconstruct a less frequently occurring sound, or even a sound that does not occur at all in the correspondence. Consider the data in these four hypothetical languages:

Language A	Language B	Language C	Language D
hono	hono	fono	vono
hari	hari	fari	veli
rahima	rahima	rafima	levima
hor	hor	for	vol

Wherever Languages A and B have an *h,* Language C has an *f* and Language D has a *v.* Therefore we have the sound correspondence *h–h–f–v.* Using the comparative method, we might first consider reconstructing the sound *h* in the parent language; but from other data on historical change, and from phonetic research, we know that *h* seldom becomes *f* or *v.* The reverse, /f/ and /v/ becoming [h], occurs both historically and as a phonological rule and has an acoustic explanation. Therefore linguists reconstruct an **f* in the parent, and posit the sound change "*f* becomes *h*" in Languages A and B, and "*f* becomes *v*" in Language D. One obviously needs experience and knowledge to conclude this.

The other correspondences are not problematic insofar as these data are concerned. They are:

o–o–o–o   n–n–n–n   a–a–a–e   r–r–r–l   m–m–m–m

They lead to the reconstructed forms **o, *n, *a, *r, *m* for the parent language, and the sound changes "*a* becomes *e*" and "*r* becomes *l*" in Language D. These are natural sound changes often found in the world's languages.

It is now possible to reconstruct the words of the protolanguage. They are *fono, fari, rafima, for.* Language D, in this example, is the most innovative of the three languages, as it has undergone three sound changes. Language C is the most conservative, being identical to the protolanguage insofar as these data are concerned.

The sound changes seen in the previous illustrations are examples of **unconditioned sound change.** The changes occurred irrespective of phonetic context. Below is an example of **conditioned sound change,** taken from three dialects of Italian:

Standard	Northern	Lombard	
fisso	fiso	fis	"fixed"
kassa	kasa	kasə	"cabinet"

The correspondence sets are:

f–f–f   i–i–i   o–o–<>[10]   k–k–k   a–a–a   a–a–ə   s:–s–s

---

[10] The empty angled brackets indicate a loss of the sound.

It is straightforward to reconstruct *f, *i, and *k. Knowing that a geminate like *s:* commonly becomes *s* (recall Old English *f:* became *f*), we reconstruct *s: for the s:–s–s correspondence. A shortening change took place in the Northern and Lombard dialects.

There is evidence in these (very limited) data for a weakening of word-final vowels, again a change we discussed earlier for English. We reconstruct *o and *a for o–o–<> and a–a–ə. In Lombard, conditioned sound changes took place. The sound *o* was deleted in word-final position, but remained *o* elsewhere. The sound *a* became ə in word-final position and remained *a* elsewhere. The conditioning factor is word-final position as far as we can tell from the data presented.

We reconstruct the protodialect as having had the words **fisso* meaning "fixed" and **kassa* meaning "cabinet."

It is by means of the comparative method that nineteenth-century linguists were able to initiate the reconstruction of the long-lost ancestral language so aptly conceived by Jones, Bopp, Rask, and Grimm, a language that flourished about 6,000 years ago, the language that we have been calling Indo-European.

Historical Evidence

> You know my method. It is founded upon the observance of trifles.
>
> Sir Arthur Conan Doyle, "The Boscombe Valley Mystery,"
> *The Memoirs of Sherlock Holmes*

How do we discover phonological changes? How do we know how Shakespeare or Chaucer or the author of *Beowulf* pronounced their versions of English? We have no phonograph records or tape recordings that give us direct knowledge.

For many languages, historical records go back more than a thousand years. These records are studied to find out how languages were once pronounced. The spelling in early manuscripts tells us a great deal about the sound systems of older forms of modern languages. Two words spelled differently were probably pronounced differently. Once a number of orthographic contrasts are identified, good guesses can be made as to actual pronunciation. These guesses are supplemented by common words that show up in all stages of the language, allowing their pronunciation to be traced from the present, step by step, into the past.

Another clue to earlier pronunciation is provided by non-English words used in the manuscripts of English. Suppose a French word known to contain the vowel [o:] is borrowed into English. The way the borrowed word is spelled reveals a particular letter-sound correspondence.

Other documents can be examined for evidence. Private letters are an excellent source of data. Linguists prefer letters written by naive spellers, who will misspell words according to the way they pronounce them. For instance, at one point in English history all words spelled with *er* in their stems were pronounced as if they were spelled with *ar*, just as in modern British English *clerk* and *derby* are pronounced "clark" and "darby." Some poor speller kept writing *parfet* for *perfect*, which helped linguists to discover the older pronunciation.

Clues are also provided by the writings of the prescriptive grammarians of the period. Between 1550 and 1750 a group of prescriptivists in England known as **orthoepists** attempted to preserve the "purity" of English. In prescribing how people should speak, they told us how people actually spoke. An orthoepist alive in the United States today might write in a manual: "It is incorrect to pronounce *Cuba* with a final *r.*" Future scholars would know that there were speakers of English who pronounced it that way.

Some of the best clues to earlier pronunciation are provided by puns and rhymes in literature. Two words rhyme if the vowels and final consonants are the same. When a poet rhymes the verb *found* with the noun *wound,* it strongly suggests that the vowels of these two words were identical:

BENVOLIO: . . . 'tis in vain to seek him here that means not to be found.
ROMEO: He jests at scars that never felt a wound.

Shakespeare's rhymes are helpful in reconstructing the sound system of Elizabethan English. The rhyming of *convert* with *depart* in Sonnet XI strengthens the conclusion that *er* was pronounced as *ar.*

Dialect differences may provide clues as to what earlier stages of a language were like. There are many dialects of English spoken throughout the world. By comparing the pronunciation of various words in several dialects, we can draw conclusions about earlier forms and see what changes took place in the inventory of sounds and in the phonological rules.

For example, since some speakers of English pronounce *Mary, merry,* and *marry* with three different vowels (that is, [meri], [mɛri], and [mæri]), we may conclude that at one time all speakers of English did so. (The different spellings are also a clue.) For some dialects, however, only one of these sounds can occur before /r/, namely the sound [ɛ]. Those dialects underwent a sound shift in which both /e/ and /æ/ shifted to /ɛ/ when followed immediately by /r/. This is another instance of a conditioned sound shift.

This same change can also be inferred from this drinking song of the University of California:

> They had to carry Harry to the ferry
> And the ferry carried Harry to the shore
> And the reason that they had to carry Harry to the ferry
> Was that Harry couldn't carry any more.

This song was likely written by someone who rhymed *carry, Harry,* and *ferry.* It does not sound quite as good to those who do not rhyme the three words.

The historical-comparativists working with languages with written records have a difficult job, but not nearly as difficult as scholars who are attempting to discover genetic relationships among languages with no written history.

Linguists must first transcribe large amounts of language data from all the languages, analyze them phonologically, morphologically, and syntactically, and establish a basis for relatedness such as similarities in basic vocabulary, and regular sound correspondences that could not possibly be due to chance or borrowing. Only then can the comparative method be applied to reconstructing the extinct protolanguage.

The enormousness of this task can be appreciated when you realize the vast amount of readily available texts for nearly all the Indo-European languages dating back thousands of years. Even so, Indo-European is far from being completely reconstructed or completely understood.

Linguists proceeding in this manner have discovered many relationships among Native American languages and have successfully reconstructed Amerindian protolanguages. Similar achievements have been made with the numerous languages spoken in Africa. Joseph Greenberg of Stanford was able to group the large number of languages of Africa into four families: Afroasiatic, Nilo-Saharan, Niger-Kordofanian, and Khoisan.

EXTINCT AND ENDANGERED LANGUAGES

Any language is the supreme achievement of a uniquely human collective genius, as divine and unfathomable a mystery as a living organism.

Michael Krauss

A language dies, becomes extinct, when no children learn it. This situation may come about in two ways: either all the speakers of the language are annihilated by some cataclysm, or, more commonly, the speakers of the language are absorbed by another culture that speaks a different language. Sometimes this absorption is due to political suppression of the language of an oppressed people. The children, at first bilingual, grow up using the language of the dominant culture. Their children, or their children's children, fail to learn the old language and so it passes into oblivion.

This fate has befallen, and is befalling, many Native American languages. According to the linguist Michael Krauss, only 20 percent of the remaining native languages in the United States are being learned by children. Already, hundreds have been lost. Once widely spoken American Indian languages such as Comanche, Apache, and Cherokee have less and less native speakers every generation.

Doomed languages have existed throughout time. The Indo-European languages Hittite and Tocharian no longer exist, Hittite having passed away 3,500 years ago, and both dialects of Tocharian giving up the ghost in the first millennium of this century. Cornish, a Celtic language akin to Breton, expired in England in the late eighteenth century.

Linguists have placed many languages on an endangered language list. They attempt to preserve these languages by studying and documenting their grammars—the phonetics, phonology, and so on—and by recording for posterity the speech of the last few speakers. Through its grammar, each language provides new evidence on the nature of human cognition. And in its literature, poetry, ritual speech, and word structure, each language stores the collective intellectual achievements of a culture, offering unique perspectives on fundamental problems of the human condition. The disappearance of a language is tragic, for not only are these insights and perspectives lost, but the major medium through which a culture maintains and renews itself is gone as well.

Dialects, too, may become extinct. Many dialects spoken in the United States are considered endangered by linguists. For example, the dialect spoken on Ocracoke Island off the coast of North Carolina is being studied extensively by the dialectologist Walt Wolfram. One reason for the study is to preserve the dialect, which is in danger of extinction because so many young Ocracokers leave the island and raise their children elsewhere. The dialect-speaking population is also becoming diluted by vacationers and retirees, attracted to the island by its unique character, including, ironically, the quaint speech of the islanders.

Linguists are not alone in their preservation efforts. Under the sponsorship of language clubs, and occasionally even governments, many endangered languages such as Irish are learned by adults and children as a symbol of the culture. In the state of Hawaii a movement is underway to preserve and teach Hawaiian, the native language of the island.

The United Nations, too, is concerned. In 1991, UNESCO (United Nations Educational, Scientific, and Cultural Organization) passed a resolution that states:

> As the disappearance of any one language constitutes an irretrievable loss to mankind, it is for UNESCO a task of great urgency to respond to this situation by promoting . . . the description—in the form of grammars, dictionaries, and texts—of endangered and dying languages.

Occasionally a language is resurrected from written records. For centuries classical Hebrew was used only in religious ceremonies, but today, with some modernization, and through a great desire among Jews to speak the language of their forefathers, it has become the national language of Israel..

The preservation of both dying languages and dialects is essential to the study of Universal Grammar, an attempt to define linguistic properties shared by all languages. This in turn will help linguists develop a comprehensive theory of language that will include a specific description of the innate human capacity for language.

THE GENETIC CLASSIFICATION OF LANGUAGES

> The Sanskrit language, whatever be its antiquity, is of a wonderful structure, more perfect than the Greek, more copious than the Latin, and more exquisitely refined than either, yet bearing to both of them a stronger affinity, both in the roots of verbs and in the forms of grammar, than could possibly have been produced by accident; so strong, indeed, that no philologer could examine all three, without believing that they have sprung from some common source, which, perhaps, no longer exists. . . .
>
> Sir William Jones (1786)

We have discussed how different languages evolve from one language and how historical and comparative linguists classify languages into families such as Germanic or Romance and reconstruct earlier forms of the ancestral language. When we examine the languages of the world, we perceive similarities and differences among them that provide evidence for relatedness or suggest very distant or nonrelatedness.

Counting to five in English, German, and Vietnamese shows similarities between English and German not shared by Vietnamese.

English	German	Vietnamese[11]
one	eins	mot
two	zwei	hai
three	drei	ba
four	vier	bon
five	fünf	nam

The similarity between English and German is pervasive. Sometimes it is extremely obvious (*man/Mann*), at other times a little less obvious (*child/Kind*). No regular similarities or differences apart from those due to chance are found between them and Vietnamese.

Pursuing the metaphor of human genealogy, we say that English, German, Norwegian, Danish, Swedish, Icelandic, and so on are sisters in that they descended from one parent and are more closely related to one another than any of them are to non-Germanic languages such as French or Russian.

The Romance languages are also sister languages whose parent is Latin. If we carry the family metaphor to an extreme, we might describe the Germanic languages and the Romance languages as cousins, since their respective parents, Proto-Germanic and early forms of Latin, were siblings.

As anyone from a large family knows, there are cousins, and then there are "distant" cousins, encompassing nearly anyone with a claim to family bloodlines. This is true of the Indo-European family of languages. If the Germanic and Romance languages are truly cousins, then languages such as Greek, Armenian, Albanian, and even the extinct Hittite and Tocharian are distant cousins. So are Irish, Scots Gaelic, Welsh, and Breton, whose protolanguage, Celtic, was once widespread throughout Europe and the British Isles. Breton is spoken by the people living in the northwest coastal regions of France, called Brittany. It was brought there by Celts fleeing from Britain in the seventh century and has been preserved as the language of some Celtic descendants in Brittany ever since.

Russian is also a distant cousin, as are its sisters, Bulgarian, Serbo-Croatian, Polish, Czech, and Slovak. The Baltic language Lithuanian is related to English, as is its sister language, Latvian. A neighboring language, Estonian, however, is not a relative. Sanskrit, as pointed out by Sir William Jones, though far removed geographically and temporally, is nonetheless a relative. Its offspring, Hindi and Bengali, spoken primarily in South Asia, are distantly related to English. Even the Persian spoken in modern Iran is a distant cousin of English.

All the languages mentioned in the last paragraph, except for Estonian, are related, more or less distantly, to one another because they all descended from Indo-European.

Figure 11-5 is an abbreviated family tree of the Indo-European languages that gives a genealogical and historical classification of the languages shown. This diagram is somewhat simplified. For example, it appears that all the Slavic languages are sisters. This suggests the comical situation of speakers of Proto-Slavic dividing themselves into nine clans one fine morning, with each going its separate way. In fact the nine languages shown can be organized hierarchically, showing some more closely related than

---

[11] Tones are omitted for simplicity.

FIGURE 11-5 The Indo-European family of languages.

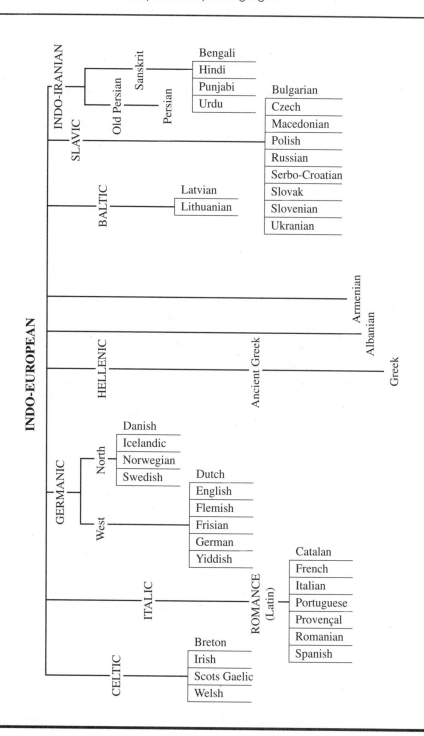

others. In other words the various separations that resulted in the nine languages we see today occurred several times over a long stretch of time. Similar remarks apply to the other families.

Another simplification is that the "dead ends"—languages that evolved and died leaving no offspring—are not included. We have already mentioned Hittite and Tocharian as two such Indo-European languages.

The family tree also fails to show a number of intermediate stages that must have existed in the evolution of modern languages. Languages do not evolve abruptly, which is why comparisons with the genealogical trees of biology have limited usefulness.

Finally, the diagram fails to show a number of Indo-European languages because of lack of space.

Languages of the World

And the whole earth was of one language, and of one speech.

Genesis 11:1

Let us go down, and there confound their language, that they may not understand one another's speech.

Genesis 11:7

There are no primitive languages. The great and abstract ideas of Christianity can be discussed even by the wretched Greenlanders.

Johann Peter Suessmilch, 1756, in a paper delivered before the Prussian Academy

Most of the world's languages do not belong to the Indo-European family. Linguists have also attempted to classify the non-Indo-European languages according to their genetic relationships. The task is to identify the languages that constitute a family and the relationships that exist among them.

The two most common questions asked of linguists are: "How many languages do you speak?" and "How many languages are there in the world?" Both are difficult to answer precisely. Most linguists have varying degrees of familiarity with a lot of languages. Some linguists speak only one, their native language. Individuals who speak many languages are **polyglots,** not linguists, despite the common misconception.

As to the second question, it's hard to ascertain the number of languages in the world because of disagreement as to what comprises a language as opposed to a dialect.

A difficulty with both these questions is that the answers rely on a sliding scale. Familiarity with a language is not an all-or-nothing affair, so how much of a language do you have to know before you can be said to "speak" that language? And how different must two dialects be before they become separate languages? One criterion is that of mutual intelligibility. As long as two dialects remain mutually intelligible, it is generally believed that they cannot be considered separate languages. But mutual intelligibility itself lies on a sliding scale, as all of us know who have conversed with persons speaking dialects of our native language that we do not understand completely.

The Indo-Iranian languages Hindi and Urdu are listed as separate languages in Figure 11-5, yet they are mutually intelligible in their spoken form and are arguably dialects of one language. However each uses a different writing system and each is spoken in communities of differing religious beliefs and nationalities. (Hindi, for the most part, is spoken in India by Hindus. Urdu is spoken in Pakistan by Muslims.) So what constitutes a separate language is not always determined by linguistic factors alone.

On the other hand, mutually unintelligible languages spoken in China, because they share the same writing system and culture, and are spoken within a single political boundary, are often thought of as dialects.

Estimates vary widely. The minimum has been set at 4,000 and the maximum at 8,000 languages spoken in the world today. In the city of Los Angeles, alone, more than 80 languages are spoken. Students at Hollywood High School go home to hear their parents speak Amharic, Armenian, Arabic, Marshallese, Urdu, Sinhalese, Ibo, Gujarati, Hmong, Afrikaans, Khmer, Ukrainian, Cambodian, Spanish, Tagalog, Russian, and more.

It is often surprising to discover what languages are genetically related and which ones aren't. Within the Indo-European family we find faraway Punjabi is an Indo-European language, whereas Hungarian, surrounded on all sides by Indo-European languages, is not.

It is not possible in an introductory text to give an exhaustive table of families, subfamilies, and individual languages. Besides, a number of genetic relationships have not yet been firmly established. For example, linguists are divided as to whether Japanese and Turkish are related or not. We'll simply mention several language families with a few of their member languages. These language families are not thought to be related to one another or to Indo-European. This, however, may be an artifact of being unable to delve into the past far enough to see commonalities that time has since erased. We can never entirely eliminate the possibility that all the world's languages sprang ultimately from a single source, an "ur-language" lost forever in the depths of the past.

Uralic is the other major family of languages, besides Indo-European, spoken on the European continent. Hungarian, Finnish, and Estonia are the major representatives of this group.

Afro-Asiatic languages are a large family spoken in northern Africa and the Middle East. They include the modern **Semitic** languages of Hebrew and Arabic, as well as languages spoken in biblical times such as Aramaic, Babylonian, Canaanite, and Moabite.

The **Sino-Tibetan** family includes Mandarin, the most populous language in the world, spoken by around one billion Chinese. It also includes all of the Chinese "dialects," plus Burmese and Tibetan.

Most of the languages of Africa belong to the **Niger-Kordofanian** family. These include over nine hundred languages grouped into a number of subfamilies like Bantu, Kwa, and individual languages like Swahili, Kikuyu, and Zulu.

Equally numerous, the **Austronesian** family contains about nine hundred languages, spoken over a wide expanse of the globe, from Madagascar, off the coast of Africa, to Hawaii. Hawaiian itself, of course, is an Austronesian language, as are Maori, spoken in New Zealand; Tagalog, spoken in the Philippine Islands; and Malay, spoken in Malaysia and Singapore, to mention just a few.

Dozens of families and hundreds of languages are, or were, spoken in North and South America. Knowledge of the genetic relationships among these families of languages is often tenuous, and because so many of the languages are approaching extinction, there may be little hope for as complete an understanding of the Amerindian Language families as linguists have achieved for Indo-European.

TYPES OF LANGUAGES

All the Oriental nations jam tongue and words together in the throat, like the Hebrews and Syrians. All the Mediterranean peoples push their enunciation forward to the palate, like the Greeks and the Asians. All the Occidentals break their words on the teeth, like the Italians and Spaniards. . . .

Isidore of Seville, seventh century C.E.

"We get a lot of foreign visitors."

Herman Copyright 1991 Jim Unger. Reprinted with permission of Universal Syndicate. All rights reserved.

There are many ways to classify languages. One way discussed in this chapter is according to the language "family." This method would be like classifying people according to whether they were Smiths, Johnsons, Fromkins, or Rodmans. Another way of classifying languages is by certain linguistic traits, regardless of family. With people, this method would be like classifying them according to height and weight, or hair and eye color.

Every language has sentences that include a subject (S),[12] an object (O), and a verb (V), although some sentences do not have all three elements. Languages have been classified according to the basic or most common order in which these occur in the language.

There are six possible orders—SOV (subject, object, verb), SVO, VSO, VOS, OVS, OSV—permitting six possible language types. Here are examples of some of the languages in these classes.[13]

---

[12] In this section *only,* S will abbreviate subject rather than sentence.

[13] The examples of VOS, OVS, and OSV languages are from G. K. Pullum. 1981. "Languages with Object before Subject: A Comment and a Catalogue," *Linguistics* 19: 147–155.

SVO: English, French, Swahili, Hausa, Thai
VSO: Tagalog, Irish, (Classical) Arabic, (Biblical) Hebrew
SOV: Turkish, Japanese, Persian, Georgian, Eskimo
OVS: Apalai (Brazil), Barasano (Colombia), Panare (Venezuela)
OSV: Apurina and Xavante (Brazil)
VOS: Cakchiquel (Guatemala), Huave (Mexico), Coeur d'Alene (Idaho)

The most frequent word orders found in languages of the world are SVO, VSO, and SOV. The basic VSO and SOV sentences may be illustrated as follows:

VSO (Tagalog): Sumagot siya sa propesor
answered he the professor
"He answered the professor."

SOV (Turkish): Romalilar barbarlari yendiler
Romans barbarians defeated
"The Romans defeated the Barbarians."

Languages with OVS, OSV, and VOS basic word order are much rarer.

The order of other sentence components in a language is most frequently correlated with the language type. If a language is of a type in which the verb precedes the object—a VO language, which includes SVO, VSO, or VOS—then the auxiliary verb tends to precede the verb; adverbs tend to follow the verb; and the language utilizes **prepositions,** which precede the noun, among other such ordering relationships. English exhibits all these tendencies.

In OV languages, most of which are SOV, the opposite tendency occurs: Auxiliary verbs tend to follow the verb; adverbs tend to precede the verb; and there are postpositions, which function similarly to prepositions but follow the noun. Japanese, an SOV language, has postpositions, as we saw in a previous section. Also in Japanese, the auxiliary verb follows the verb, as illustrated by the following sentence:

Akiko	wa	sakana	o	tabete	iru
Akiko	*topic marker*	fish	*object marker*	eating	is

"Akiko is eating fish."

It must be emphasized that the correlations between language type and the word order of syntactic categories in sentences are "tendencies," not inviolable rules, and different languages follow them to a greater or lesser degree.

The knowledge that speakers of the various languages have about word order is revealed in the particular phrase structure rules of the language. In English, an SVO language, the V precedes its NP Object: VP → V NP. In Turkish or Japanese, SOV languages, the NP Object precedes the Verb in the corresponding phrase structure rule of that language. Similarly, the rule PP → P NP occurs in SVO languages, whereas the rule PP → NP P is the correlate occurring in SOV languages.

If a language is, say, SVO, this does not mean that SVO is the only possible word order. Yoda, the Jedi Master from the motion picture *Return of the Jedi,* speaks a strange but perfectly understandable style of English that achieves its eccentricity by being OSV. Some of Yoda's utterances are:

Sick I've become.
Strong with the Force you are.
Your father he is.
When nine hundred years you reach, look as good you will not.

For linguists, the many languages and language families provide essential data for the study of universal grammar. Although these languages are diverse in many ways, they are also remarkably similar in many ways. We find that the languages of the "wretched Greenlanders," the Maoris of New Zealand, the Zulus of Africa, and the native peoples of North and South America all have similar sounds, similar phonological and syntactic rules, and similar semantic systems.

WHY DO LANGUAGES CHANGE?

Stability in language is synonymous with rigor mortis.

Ernest Weekley

No one knows exactly how or why languages change. As we have shown, linguistic changes do not happen suddenly. Speakers of English did not wake up one morning and decide to use the word *beef* for "ox meat," nor do all the children of one particular generation grow up to adopt a new word. Changes are more gradual, particularly changes in the phonological and syntactic system.

Of course, certain changes may occur instantaneously for any one speaker. When a new word is acquired by a speaker, it is not gradually acquired, although full appreciation for all of its possible uses may come slowly. When a new rule is incorporated into a speaker's grammar, it is either in or not in the grammar. It may at first be an optional rule, so that sometimes it is used and sometimes it is not, possibly determined by social context or other external factors, but the rule is either there and available for use or not. What is gradual about language change is the spread of certain changes over an entire speech community.

A basic cause of change is the way children acquire the language. No one teaches a child the rules of the grammar. Each child constructs a personal grammar alone, generalizing rules from the linguistic input received. As discussed in Chapter 8, the child's language develops in stages until it approximates the adult grammar. The child's grammar is never exactly like that of the adult community, because children receive diverse linguistic input. Certain rules may be simplified or overgeneralized, and vocabularies may show small differences that accumulate over several generations.

The older generation may be using certain rules optionally. For example, at certain times they may say "It's I" and at other times "It's me." The less formal style is usually used with children, who as the next generation may use only the "me" form of the pronoun in this construction. In such cases the grammar will have changed.

The reasons for some changes are relatively easy to understand. Before television there was no such word as *television*. It soon became a common lexical item. Borrowed words, too, generally serve a useful purpose, and their entry into the language is not mysterious. Other changes are more difficult to explain, such as the Great Vowel Shift in English.

One plausible source of change is **assimilation,** a kind of **ease of articulation** process in which one sound influences the pronunciation of another adjacent or nearby sound. Due to assimilation, vowels are frequently nasalized before nasal consonants because it is easiest to lower the velum to produce nasality in advance of the actual consonant articulation. This results in the preceding vowel being nasalized. Once the vowel is nasalized, the contrast that the nasal consonant provided can be equally well provided by the nasalized vowel alone, and the redundant consonant may be deleted. The contrast between oral and nasal vowels that exists in many languages of the world today results from just such a historical sound change.

In French at one time, *bol* "basin," *botte* "high boot," *bog* "a card game," *bock* "Bock beer," and *bon* "good" were pronounced [bɔl], [bɔt], [bɔg], [bɔk], and [bɔ̃n], respectively. The nasalized vowel in *bon* was due to the final nasal consonant. Owing to a conditioned sound change that deleted nasal consonants in word-final position, *bon* is pronounced [bɔ̃] in modern French. The nasal vowel alone maintains the contrast with the other words.

Another example from English illustrates how such assimilative processes can change a language. In Old English, word initial *[kʲ]* (like the initial sound of *cute*), when followed by /i/, was further palatalized to become our modern palatal affricate /č/, as illustrated by the following words:

Old English (c = [kʲ])	Modern English (ch = [č])
ciese	cheese
cinn	chin
cild	child

The process of palatalization is found in the history of many languages. In Twi, the word meaning "to hate" was once pronounced [ki]. The [k] became first [kʲ] and then finally [č], so that today "to hate" is [či].

Ease of articulation processes, which make sounds more alike, are countered by the need to maintain contrast. Thus sound change also occurs when two sounds are acoustically similar, with risk of confusion. We saw a sound change of /f/ to /h/ in an earlier example that can be explained by the acoustic similarity of [f] to other sounds.

Another kind of change that can be thought of as "economy of memory" results in a reduction of the number of exceptional or irregular morphemes. This is called **analogic change.** It may be by analogy to *foe/foes* and *dog/dogs* that speakers started saying *cows* as the plural of *cow* instead of the earlier plural *kine*. By analogy to *reap/reaped, seem/seemed,* and *ignite/ignited,* children and adults are presently saying *I sweeped the floor* (instead of *swept*), *I dreamed last night* (instead of *dreamt*), and *She lighted the bonfire* (instead of *lit*).

The same kind of analogic change is exemplified by our regularization of exceptional plural forms, which is a kind of morphological change. We have borrowed words like *datum/data, agendum/agenda, curriculum/curricula, bandit/banditi, memorandum/memoranda, medium/media, criterion/criteria,* and *virtuoso/virtuosi,* to name just a few. The irregular plurals of these nouns have been replaced by regular plurals among many speakers: *agendas, curriculums, memorandums, criterias, virtuosos.* In some cases the borrowed original plural forms were considered to be the singular (as in *agenda* and *criteria*) and the new plural is therefore a "plural-plural." Also, many speakers now regard *data* and *media* as nouns that do not have plural forms, like *information.* All these changes lessen the number of irregular forms that must be remembered.

Assimilation and analogic change account for some linguistic changes, but they cannot account for others. Simplification and regularization of grammars occur, but so does elaboration or complication. Old English rules of syntax became more complex, imposing a stricter word order on the language, at the same time that case endings were being simplified. A tendency toward simplification is counteracted by the need to limit potential ambiguity. Much of language change is a balance between the two.

Many factors contribute to linguistic change: simplification of grammars, elaboration to maintain intelligibility, borrowing, and so on. Changes are actualized by children learning the language, who incorporate them into their grammar. The exact reasons for linguistic change are still elusive, though it is clear that the imperfect learning of the adult dialects by children is a contributing factor. Perhaps language changes for the same reason all things change: that it is the nature of things to change. As Heraclitus pointed out thousands of years ago, "All is flux, nothing stays still. Nothing endures but change."

SUMMARY

Languages change. Linguistic change such as **sound shift** is found in the history of all languages, as evidenced by the **regular sound correspondences** that exist between different stages of the same language, different dialects of the same language, and different languages. Languages that evolve from a common source are **genetically related.** Genetically related languages were once dialects of the same language. For example, earlier forms of Germanic languages, such as English, German, Swedish, etc. were dialects of **Proto-Germanic,** while earlier forms of Romance languages, such as Spanish, French, Italian, and so on were dialects of Latin. Going back even farther in time, earlier forms of Proto-Germanic, Latin, and other languages were dialects of **Indo-European.**

All components of the grammar may change. Phonological, morphological, syntactic, lexical, and semantic changes occur. Words, morphemes, phonemes, and rules of all types may be added, lost, or altered. The meaning of words and morphemes may **broaden, narrow,** or shift. The lexicon may expand by **borrowing,** which results in **loan words** in the vocabulary. It also grows through word **coinage, blends, acronyms,** and other processes of new word formation. On the other hand, the lexicon may shrink as certain words become obsolete and no longer used.

No one knows all the causes of linguistic change. Basically, change comes about through the restructuring of the grammar by children learning the language. Grammars may appear to change in the direction of simplicity and regularity, as in the loss of the Indo-European case morphology, but such simplifications may be compensated for by other complexities, such as stricter word order. Always there must be a balance between simplicity—languages must be learnable—and complexity: languages must be expressive and relatively unambiguous.

Some sound changes result from **assimilation,** a fundamentally physiological process of **ease of articulation.** Others, like the **Great Vowel Shift,** are more difficult to explain. Some grammatical changes are **analogic changes,** generalizations that lead to more regularity, such as *sweeped* instead of *swept,*

The study of linguistic change is called **historical and comparative linguistics.** Linguists use the **comparative method** to identify regular sound correspondences among the **cognates** of related languages and systematically reconstruct an earlier **protolanguage.** This **comparative reconstruction** allows linguists to peer backward in time and determine the linguistic history of a language family, which may then be represented in a tree diagram similar to Figure 11-5.

Linguists estimate that there are four thousand to eight thousand languages spoken in the world today (1997). These languages are grouped into families, subfamilies, and so on based on their genetic relationships. A vast number of these languages are dying out because in each generation less and less children learn them. However, attempts are being made to preserve dying languages and dialects for the knowledge they bring to the study of Universal Grammar and the culture in which they are spoken.

References for Further Reading

Aitchison, Jean. 1985. *Language Change: Progress or Decay.* New York: Universe Books.

Anttila, Raimo. 1989. *Historical and Comparative Linguistics.* New York: John Benjamins.

Baugh, A. C. 1978. *A History of the English Language,* 3rd ed. Englewood Cliffs, NJ: Prentice-Hall.

Cassidy, Frederic G., ed. 1986. *Dictionary of American Regional English.* Cambridge, MA: The Belknap Press of Harvard University Press.

Comrie, Bernard, ed. 1990. *The World's Major Languages.* New York: Oxford University Press.

Hock, Hans Henrich. 1986. *Principles of Historical Linguistics.* New York: Mouton de Gruyter.

Jeffers, Robert J., and Ilse Lehiste. 1979. *Principles and Methods for Historical Linguistics.* Cambridge, MA: MIT Press.

Lehmann, W. P. 1973. *Historical Linguistics: An Introduction,* 2d ed. New York: Holt, Rinehart and Winston.

Pyles, Thomas. 1993. *The Origins and Development of the English Language,* 4th ed. New York: Harcourt Brace.

Renfrew, C. 1989. "The Origins of the Indo-European Languages." *Scientific American* 261.4: 106–114.

Traugott, E. C. 1972. *A History of English Syntax.* New York: Holt, Rinehart and Winston.

Voegelin, C. F., and F. M. Voegelin. 1977. *Classification and Index of the World's Languages.* New York: Elsevier.

EXERCISES

1. Many changes in the phonological system have occurred in English since 449 C.E. Below are some Old English words (given in their spelling and phonetic forms), and the same words as we pronounce them today. They are typical of regular sound changes that took place in English. What sound changes have occurred in each case?

   Example: OE hlud [xlu:d] → Mod. Eng. loud

           Changes: (1) The [x] was lost.

                     (2) The long vowel [u:] became [aw].

	OE	**Mod E**

a. crabba [kraba] → crab

Changes:

b. fisc [fɪsk] → fish

Changes:

c. fūl [fu:l] → foul

Changes:

d. gāt [ga:t] → goat

Changes:

e. lǣfan [læ:van] → leave

Changes:

f. tēþ [te:θ] → teeth

Changes:

2. The Great Vowel Shift left its traces in Modern English in such meaning-related pairs as:

a. serene/serenity [i]/[ɛ]

b. divine/divinity [aj]/[ɪ]

c. sane/sanity [e]/[æ]

List five such meaning-related pairs that relate [i] and [ɛ] as in example *a*, [aj] and [ɪ] as in *b*, and [e] and [æ] as in *c*.

	[i]/[ɛ]	**[aj]/[ɪ]**	**[e]/[æ]**
(1)			
(2)			
(3)			
(4)			
(5)			

3. Below are given some sentences taken from Old English, Middle English, and early Modern English texts, illustrating some changes that have occurred in the syntactic rules of English grammar. (Note: In the sentences, the earlier spelling forms and words have been changed to conform to Modern English. That is, the OE sentence *His suna twegen mon brohte to þæm cynige* would be written as *His sons two one brought to that king,* which in Modern English would be *His two sons were brought to the king.*) Underline the parts of each sentence that differ from Modern English. Rewrite the sentence in Modern English. State, if you can, what changes must have occurred.

Example: It *not* belongs to you. (Shakespeare, *Henry IV*)

Mod. Eng.: *It does not belong to you.*

Change: At one time, a negative sentence simply had a *not* before the verb. Today, the word *do,* in its proper morphological form, must appear before the *not.*

a. It nothing pleased his master.

   Mod. Eng.:

   Change:

b. He hath said that we would lift them whom that him please.

   Mod. Eng.:

   Change:

c. I have a brother is condemned to die.

   Mod. Eng.:

   Change:

d. I bade them take away you.

   Mod. Eng.:

   Change:

e. I wish you was still more a Tartar.

   Mod. Eng.:

   Change:

f. Christ slept and his apostles.

   Mod. Eng.:

   Change:

g. Me was told.

   Mod. Eng.:

   Change:

4. It is not unusual to find a yearbook or almanac publishing a new word list. In the 1980s and 1990s several new words entered the English language, such as *Teflon* and *liposuction.* From the computer field, we have new words such as *byte* and *laptop.* Other words have been expanded in meaning, such as *memory* to refer to the storage part of a computer and *crack* meaning a form of cocaine. Sports-related new words include *noseguard* and *skybox,* as well as other compounds such as *air ball* and *contact hitter.*

   A. Think of five other words or compound words that have entered the language in the last ten years. Describe briefly the source of the word.

      (1)

      (2)

      (3)

      (4)

      (5)

B. Think of three words that might be on the way out.(Hint: Consider *flapper, groovy,* and *slay/slew.* Dictionary entries that say "archaic" are a good source.)

      (1)

      (2)

      (3)

5. Here is a table showing, in phonemic form, the Latin ancestors of ten words in modern French:

Latin	French	
kor	kø[14]	"heart"
kantāre	šãte	"to sing"
klārus	kler	"clear"
kervus	sɛrf	"hart" (deer)
karbō	šarbɔ̃	"coal"
kwandō	kã	"when"
kentum	sã	"hundred"
kawsa	šoz	"thing"
kinis	sãdrə	"ashes"
kawda koda	kø	"tail"

Are the following statements true or false?

	True	False
a. The modern French word for "thing" shows that a [k], which occurred before the vowel [o] in Latin, became an [š] in French.	_____	_____
b. The French word for "tail" probably derived from the Latin word [koda] rather than from [kawda].	_____	_____
c. One historical change illustrated by these data is that [s] became an allophone of the phoneme /k/ in French.	_____	_____
d. If there was a Latin word *kertus,* the modern French word would probably be *sert.* (Consider only the initial consonant.)	_____	_____

---

[14] ø is a mid front rounded vowel.

6. Here is how to count to five in a dozen languages, using standard Roman alphabet transcriptions. Six of these languages are Indo-European and six are not. Which are the Indo-European ones?

	L1	L2	L3	L4	L5	L6
1	en	jedyn	i	eka	ichi	echad
2	twene	dwaj	liang	dvau	ni	shnayim
3	thria	tři	san	trayas	san	shlosha
4	fiuwar	štyri	ssu	catur	shi	arbaʔa
5	fif	pjeć	wu	pañca	go	chamishsha

	L7	L8	L9	L10	L11	L12
1	mot	ün	hana	yaw	uno	nigen
2	hai	duos	tul	daw	dos	khoyar
3	ba	trais	set	dree	tres	ghorban
4	bon	quatter	net	tsaloor	cuatro	durben
5	nam	tschinch	tasŏt	pindze	cinco	tabon

7. Recommend three ways in which society can act to preserve linguistic diversity. Be realistic and concrete. For example, "encourage children of endangered languages to learn the language" is *not* a good answer, being neither sufficiently realistic (why should they want to?), nor sufficiently concrete (what is meant by "encourage"?).

8. The vocabulary of English consists of native words as well as thousands of loan words. Look up the following words in a dictionary that provides the etymologies (histories) of words. Speculate how each word came to be borrowed from the particular language.

Example: *Skunk* was a Native American term for an animal unfamiliar to the European colonists, so they borrowed that word into their vocabulary so they could refer to the creature.

a. size	h. robot	o. skunk	v. pagoda
b. royal	i. check	p. catfish	w. khaki
c. aquatic	j. banana	q. hoodlum	x. shampoo
d. heavenly	k. keel	r. filibuster	y. kangaroo
e. skill	l. fact	s. astronaut	z. bulldoze
f. ranch	m. potato	t. emerald	
g. blouse	n. muskrat	u. sugar	

9. Analogic change refers to a tendency to generalize the rules of language, a major cause of language change. We mentioned two instances, the generalization of the plural rule (*cow/kine* becoming *cow/cows*) and the generalization of the past tense formation rule (*light/lit* becoming *light/lighted*). Think

of at least three other instances of nonstandard usage that are analogic; they are indicators of possible future changes in the language. (Hint: Consider fairly general rules and see if you know of dialects or styles that overgeneralize them, for example, comparative formation by adding *-er*.)

10. Below is a passage from Shakespeare's *Hamlet,* Act IV, Scene iii:

HAMLET: A man may fish with the worm that hath eat of a king, and eat of the fish that hath fed of that worm.

KING: What dost thou mean by this?

HAMLET: Nothing but to show you how a king may go a progress through the guts of a beggar.

KING: Where is Polonius?

HAMLET: In heaven. Send thither to see. If your messenger find him not there, seek him i' the other place yourself. But indeed, if you find him not within this month, you shall nose him as you go up the stairs into the lobby.

Study these lines and identify every difference in expression between Elizabethan and current Modern English that is evident. (For example, in line 3, *thou* is now *you*.)

11. Here are some data from four Polynesian languages.

Maori	**Hawaiian**	**Samoan**	**Fijian**	**Gloss**	**Proto-Polynesian (See Part C)**
pou	pou	pou	bou	"post"	
tapu	kapu	tapu	tabu	"forbidden"	
taŋi	kani	taŋi	taŋi	"cry"	
takere	kaʔele	taʔele	takele	"keel"	
hono	hono	fono	vono	"stay, sit"	
marama	malama	malama	malama	"light, moon"	
kaho	ʔaho	ʔaso	kaso	"thatch"	

A. Find the correspondence sets. (Hint: There are 14 of them. For example o–o–o–o, p–p–p–b.)

B. For each correspondence set, reconstruct a proto-sound. Mention any sound changes that you observe. For example:

o–o–o–o   *o

p–p–p–b   *p   p → b in Fijian.

C. Complete the table by filling in the reconstructed words in Proto-Polynesian.

12. Consider these data from two American Indian languages:

Yerington Paviotso = YP	Northfork Monachi = NM	Gloss
mupi	mupi	"nose"
tama	tawa	"tooth"
piwɨ	piwɨ	"heart"
sawaʔpono	sawaʔpono	"a feminine name"
nɨmi	nɨwɨ	"liver"
tamano	tawano	"springtime"
pahwa	pahwa	"aunt"
kuma	kuwa	"husband"
wowaʔa	wowaʔa	"Indians living to the west"
mɨhɨ	mɨhɨ	"porcupine"
noto	noto	"throat"
tapa	tape	"sun"
ʔatapɨ	ʔatapɨ	"jaw"
papiʔi	papiʔi	"older brother"
patɨ	petɨ	"daughter"
nana	nana	"man"
ʔatɨ	ʔetɨ	"bow," "gun"

A. Identify each sound correspondence. (Hint: There are ten different correspondence sets of consonants and six different correspondence sets of vowels: for example, *p–p, m–w, a–a,* and *a–e.*)

B. (1) For each correspondence you identified in A not containing an *m* or *w,* reconstruct a proto-sound. (For example, for *h–h,* *h; o–o, *o.*)

   (2) If the proto-sound underwent a change, indicate what the change is and in which language it took place.

C. (1) Whenever a *w* appears in YP, what appears in the corresponding position in NM?

   (2) Whenever an *m* occurs in YP, what two sounds may correspond to it in NM?

   (3) On the basis of the position of *m* in YP words, can you predict which sound it will correspond to in NM words? How?

D. (1) For the three correspondences you discovered in A involving *m* and *w,* should you reconstruct two or three proto-sounds?

   (2) If you chose three proto-sounds, what are they and what did they become in the two daughter languages, YP and NM?

   (3) If you chose two proto-sounds, what are they and what did they become in the daughter languages? What further statement do you need to make about the sound changes? (Hint: One proto-sound will become two different pairs, depending on its phonetic environment. It is an example of a conditioned sound change.)

E. Based on the above, reconstruct all the words given in the common ancestor from which both YP and NM descended. (For example, "porcupine" is reconstructed as *mɨhɨ.)

Chapter 12

Writing: The ABCs of Language

The Moving Finger writes; and, having writ,
Moves on: nor all thy Piety nor Wit
Shall lure it back to cancel half a Line,
Nor all thy Tears wash out a Word of it.

Omar Khayyám, Rubáiyát

The palest ink is better than the sharpest memory.

Chinese proverb

PEANUTS reprinted by permission of UFS, Inc.

Throughout this book we have emphasized the spoken form of language. The grammar, which represents one's linguistic knowledge, was viewed as the system for relating the sounds and meanings of one's language. The ability to acquire and use language represents a dramatic evolutionary development. No individual or people discovered or created language. The human language faculty appears to be biologically and genetically determined.

This is not true of the written form of human languages. Children learn to speak naturally through exposure to language, without formal teaching. To become literate, to learn to read and write, one must make a conscious effort and receive instruction.

Before the invention of writing, useful knowledge had to be memorized. Messengers carried information in their heads. Crucial lore passed from the older to the newer generation through speaking. Even in today's world many spoken languages lack a writing system, and oral literature still abounds. However, human memory is short-lived, and the brain's storage capacity is limited.

Writing overcomes such problems and allows communication across space and through time. Writing permits a society to permanently record its literature, its history and science, and its technology. The creation and development of writing systems is therefore one of the greatest of human achievements.

By writing we mean any of the many visual (nongestural) systems for representing language, including handwriting, printing, and electronic displays of these written forms. It might be argued that today we have electronic means of recording sound and cameras to produce films and television, so writing is becoming obsolete. If writing became extinct, however, there would be no knowledge of electronics for TV technicians to study; there would be, in fact, little technology in years to come. There would be no film or TV scripts, no literature, no books, no mail, no newspapers. There would be some advantages—no bad novels, junk mail, poison-pen letters, or "fine print"; but the losses would far outweigh the gains.

THE HISTORY OF WRITING

An Egyptian legend relates that when the god Thoth revealed his discovery of the art of writing to King Thamos, the good King denounced it as an enemy of civilization. "Children and young people," protested the monarch, "who had hitherto been forced to apply themselves diligently to learn and retain whatever was taught them, would cease to apply themselves, and would neglect to exercise their memories."

Will Durant, *The Story of Civilization 1*

There are many legends and stories about the invention of writing. Greek legend has it that Cadmus, Prince of Phoenicia and founder of the city of Thebes, invented the alphabet and brought it with him to Greece. (He later was banished to Illyria and changed into a snake.) In one Chinese fable, the four-eyed dragon-god Cang Jie invented writing, but in another, writing first appeared to humans in the form of markings on a turtle shell. In other myths, the Babylonian god Nebo and the Egyptian god Thoth gave humans writing as well as speech. The Talmudic scholar Rabbi Akiba believed that the alphabet existed before humans were created; and according to Islamic teaching, the alphabet was created by Allah himself, who presented it to humans but not to the angels.

Although these are delightful stories, it is evident that before a single word was written, uncountable billions were spoken. The invention of writing comes relatively late in human history, and its development was gradual. It is highly unlikely that a particularly gifted ancestor awoke one morning and decided, "Today I'll invent a writing system."

Pictograms and Ideograms

By permission of Johnny Hart and Creators Syndicate, Inc.

The seeds out of which writing developed were probably the early drawings made by ancient humans. Cave drawings, called **petroglyphs,** such as those found in the Altamira cave in northern Spain, drawn by humans living over twenty thousand years ago, can be "read" today. They are literal portrayals of life at that time. We don't know why they were produced; they may be aesthetic expressions rather than pictorial communications. Later drawings, however, are clearly "picture writings," or **pictograms.** Unlike modern writing systems, each picture or pictogram is a direct image of the object it represents.

There is a nonarbitrary relationship between the form and meaning of the symbol. Comic strips minus captions are pictographic—literal representations of the ideas to be communicated. This early form of "writing" did not have any direct relation to the language spoken, because the pictures represented objects in the world rather than the linguistic names given to these objects; they did not represent the sounds of spoken language.

Pictographic "writing" has been found throughout the world, ancient and modern: among Africans, Native Americans, including the Inuits of Alaska and Canada, the Incas of Peru, the Yukagirians of Siberia, and the people of Oceania. Pictograms are used today in international road signs where the native language of the region might not be adequate. Such symbols can be understood by anyone because they do not depend on the words of any language. To understand the signs used by the National Park Service, for example, a visitor does not need to know English.

Once a pictogram was accepted as the representation of an object, its meaning was extended to attributes of that object, or concepts associated with it. Thus, a picture of the sun could represent "warmth," "heat," "light," "daytime," and so on. Pictograms thus began to represent ideas rather than objects. Such generalized, abstract pictograms are called **ideograms** ("idea pictures" or "idea writing").

The difference between pictograms and ideograms is not always clear. Ideograms tend to be a less direct representation, and one may have to learn what a particular ideogram means. Pictograms tend to be literal. For example, the "no parking" symbol consisting of a black circle with a slanting red line through it is an ideogram: It represents the idea of no parking abstractly. A "no parking" symbol showing an automobile being towed away is more literal, more like a pictogram.

Inevitably, pictograms and ideograms became stylized, possibly because of the ambiguities that could result from "poor artists" or creative "abstractionists" of the time. The simplifying conventions that developed so distorted the literal representations that it was no longer easy to interpret symbols without learning the system. The ideograms became linguistic symbols as they came to also stand for the sounds that

FIGURE 12-1   Six of seventy-seven symbols developed by the National Park Service for use as signs indicating activities and facilities in parks and recreation areas. These symbols denote, from left to right: environmental study area, grocery store, men's restroom, women's restroom, fishing, amphitheater. Certain symbols are available with a *prohibiting slash*—a diagonal red bar across the symbol that means that the activity is forbidden. (National Park Service, U.S. Department of the Interior)

represented the ideas—that is, for the words of the language. This stage represented a revolutionary step in the development of writing systems.

Cuneiform Writing

One picture is worth a thousand words.

Chinese Proverb

Much of our information on the development of writing stems from the records left by the Sumerians, an ancient people of unknown origin who built a civilization in southern Mesopotamia (modern Iraq) over six thousand years ago. They left innumerable clay tablets containing business documents, epics, prayers, poems, proverbs, and so on. So copious are these written records that scholars studying the Sumerians are publishing a seventeen-volume dictionary of their written language. The first of these volumes appeared in 1984.

The writing system of the Sumerians is the oldest one known. They were a commercially oriented people, and as their business deals became increasingly complex, the need for permanent records arose. An elaborate pictography was developed, along with a system of "tallies." Some examples are shown here:

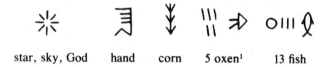

star, sky, God   hand   corn   5 oxen[1]   13 fish

Over the centuries their pictography was simplified and conventionalized. The characters or symbols were produced by using a wedge-shaped stylus that was pressed into soft clay tablets. This form of writing is called **cuneiform**—literally, "wedge-shaped" (from Latin *cuneus* "wedge"). Here is an illustration of how Sumerian pictograms evolved to cuneiform:

※	became	⚹	became	⊢⊤	star

became | hand

became | fish

---

[1] The pictograph for "ox" evolved, much later, into our letter A.

The cuneiform symbols in the right-most column do little to remind us (or the Sumerians) of the meaning represented. As cuneiform evolved, its users began to think of the symbols more in terms of the name of the thing represented than of the actual thing itself. Eventually cuneiform script came to represent words of the language. Such a system is called **logographic,** or **word writing.** In this oldest type of writing system the symbol stands for both the word and the concept, which it may still resemble, however abstractly. Thus **logograms,** the symbols of a word-writing system, are ideograms that represent in addition to the concept, the word or morpheme in the language for that concept.

The cuneiform writing system spread throughout the Middle East and Asia Minor. It was borrowed by the Babylonians, Assyrians, and Persians. In adopting cuneiform characters the borrowers often used them to represent the sounds of the syllables in their own languages. In this way cuneiform evolved into a **syllabic writing** system.

In a syllabic writing system, each syllable in the language is represented by its own symbol, and words are written syllable by syllable. Cuneiform writing was never purely syllabic; there was always a large residue of symbols that stood for whole words. The Assyrians retained a large number of word symbols, even though every word in their language could be written out syllabically if it were desired. Thus they could write *mātu* "country" as:

ma	+	a	+	tu

The Persians (ca. 600–400 B.C.E.) devised a greatly simplified syllabic alphabet for their language, which made little use of word symbols. By the reign of Darius I (522–468 B.C.E.) this writing system was in wide use. It is illustrated by the following characters:

da

di

fa

ma

tu

The Rebus Principle

By permission of Johnny Hart and Creators Syndicate, Inc.

When a graphic sign no longer has any visual relationship to the word it represents, it becomes a **phonographic** symbol, standing for the sounds that represent the word. A single sign can then be used to represent all words with the same sounds—the homophones of the language. If, for example, the symbol ☉ stood for *sun* in English, it could then be used in a sentence like *My* ☉ *is a doctor.* This sentence is an example of the **rebus principle.**

A rebus is a representation of words by pictures of objects whose names sound like the word. Thus 👁 might represent *eye* or the pronoun *I.* The sounds of the two words are identical, even though the meanings are not. Similarly, 🐝🍃 could represent *belief (be + lief = bee + leaf =* /bi/ + /lif/), and 🐝🍃🍃 could be *believes.*

Proper names can also be written in such a way. If the symbol ❘ is used to represent *rod* and the symbol 大 represents *man,* then ❘ 大 could represent *Rodman,* although nowadays the name is unrelated to either rods or men. Such combinations often become stylized or shortened so as to be more easily written. *Rodman,* for example, might be written in such a system as ❘大 or even 人.

Jokes, riddles and advertising make use of the rebus principle. A well-known ice-cream company advertises "31derful flavors."

This system is not an efficient one because in many languages words cannot be subdivided into sequences of sounds that have meaning by themselves. It would be difficult, for example, to represent the word *English* (/iŋ/ + /glıš/) in English according to the rebus principle. *Eng* by itself does not mean anything, nor does *glish.*

From Hieroglyphs to the Alphabet

At the time that Sumerian pictography was flourishing (around 4000 B.C.E.), a similar system was being used by the Egyptians, which the Greeks later called **hieroglyphics** (*hiero* "sacred" + *glyphikos* "carvings"). That the early "sacred carvings" were originally pictography is shown by the following hieroglyphics:

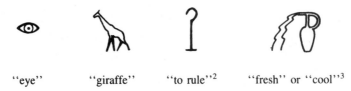

"eye"   "giraffe"   "to rule"[2]   "fresh" or "cool"[3]

Like the Sumerian pictograms, the hieroglyphs came to represent both the concept and the word for the concept. Once this happened, hieroglyphics became a bona fide logographic writing system. Through the rebus principle hieroglyphics also became a syllabic writing system.

The Phoenicians, a Semitic people who lived in what is today Lebanon, were aware of hieroglyphics as well as the offshoots of Sumerian writing. By 1500 B.C.E. they had developed a writing system of twenty-two characters, the West Semitic Syllabary. Mostly, the characters stood for consonants alone. The reader provided the vowels, and hence the rest of the syllable, through knowledge of the language. (Cn y rd ths?). Thus the West Semitic Syllabary was both a **syllabary** and a **consonantal alphabet.**

The ancient Greeks tried to borrow the Phoenician writing system, but it was unsatisfactory as a syllabary because Greek has too complex a syllable structure. In Greek, unlike Phoenician, vowels cannot be determined by grammatical context, so a writing system for Greek required that vowels have their own independent representation. Fortuitously, Phoenician had more consonants than Greek, so when the Greeks borrowed the system they used the left over symbols to represent vowel sounds. The result was **alphabetic writing,** a system where both consonants and vowels are symbolized. (The word *alphabet* is derived from *alpha* and *beta,* the first two letters of the Greek alphabet.)

A majority of alphabetic systems in use today derive from the Greek system. This alphabet became known to the Etruscans and, through them, to the Romans, who used it for Latin. Thus the alphabet spread with Western civilization, and eventually most nations of the world were exposed to, and had the option of using, alphabetic writing.

According to one view, the alphabet was not invented, it was discovered. If language did not include discrete individual sounds, no one could have invented alphabetic letters to represent such sounds. When humans started to use one symbol for one phoneme, they merely brought their intuitive knowledge of the language sound system to consciousness: They discovered what they already "knew." Furthermore, children (and adults) can learn an alphabetic system only if each separate sound has some psychological reality.

---

[2] The symbol portrays the Pharaoh's staff.

[3] Water trickling out of a vase.

MODERN WRITING SYSTEMS

> . . . but their manner of writing is very peculiar, being neither from the left to the right, like the Europeans; nor from the right to the left, like the Arabians; nor from up to down, like the Chinese; nor from down to up, like the Cascagians, but aslant from one corner of the paper to the other, like ladies in England.
>
> Jonathan Swift, *Gulliver's Travels*

We have already mentioned the various types of writing systems used in the world: word or logographic writing, syllabic writing, consonantal alphabet writing, and alphabetic writing. Most of the world's written languages use alphabetic writing. Even Chinese and Japanese, whose native writing systems are not alphabetic, have adopted alphabetic transcription systems for special purposes such as communicating with foreigners.

Word Writing

PEANUTS reprinted by permission of UFS, Inc.

In a word-writing or logographic writing system, the written character represents both the meaning and pronunciation of a word or morpheme. The awkwardness of such a system is obvious. For example, the editors of *Webster's Third New International Dictionary* claim more than 450,000 entries. All these words are written using only twenty-six alphabetic symbols, a dot, a hyphen, an apostrophe, and a space. It is understandable why, historically, word writing gave way to alphabetic systems in most places in the world.

The major exceptions are the writing systems used in China and Japan. The Chinese system has an uninterrupted history that goes back more than thirty-five hundred years. For the most part it is a word-writing system, each character representing an individual word or morpheme. Longer words may be formed by combining two words or morphemes, as shown by the word meaning "business," *mǎ imai,* which is formed by combining the words meaning "buy" and "sell." This system, which could create serious problems if used for English and other Indo-European languages, works for Chinese because spoken Chinese has little affixation of bound morphemes (such as the *un-* in *unhappy* or the *-fy* in *beautify).*

Chinese writing is a logographic system of characters, each of which represents a morpheme or word. Chinese dictionaries contain tens of thousands of characters, but a person needs to know "only" about five thousand to read a newspaper. To promote literacy, the Chinese government has proposed to simplify the characters. This process was first tried in 213 B.C.E., when Li Si published an official list of over three thousand characters whose written form was simplified by omitting unneeded strokes. This would be analogous to dictionary writers simplifying *amoeba* to *ameba*, eliminating the superfluous *o*.

Since that time successive generations of Chinese scholars have added new characters and modified old ones, creating redundancy, ambiguity, and complexity. The character-simplification efforts that have been underway in the last thirty years are therefore of major importance.

The Chinese government has adopted a spelling system using the Roman alphabet, called **Pinyin,** which is now used for certain purposes along with the regular system of characters. Many city street signs are printed in both systems, which is helpful to foreign visitors. It is not the government's intent to replace the traditional writing, which is viewed as an integral part of Chinese culture. To the Chinese, writing is an art—calligraphy—and thousands of years of poetry, literature, and history are preserved in the old system.

An additional reason for keeping the traditional system is that it permits all literate Chinese to communicate even though their spoken languages are mutually unintelligible. Thus writing has served as a unifying factor throughout Chinese history, in an area where hundreds of languages and different dialects coexist. A Chinese proverb states that "people separated by a blade of grass cannot understand each other." The unified writing system is a scythe that cuts across linguistic differences and allows the people to communicate.

This use of written Chinese characters is similar to the use of Arabic numerals, which mean the same in many different countries. The "character" 5, for example, stands for a different sequence of sounds in English, French, and Finnish. In English it is *five* /fajv/, in French it is *cinq* /sæk/, and in Finnish *viisi* /vi:si/, but in all these languages, 5, whatever its phonological form, means "five." Similarly, the spoken word for "rice" is different in the various Chinese languages, but the written character is the same. If the writing system in China were to become alphabetic, each language would be as different in writing as in speaking, and written communication would no longer be possible among the various language communities.

Syllabic Writing

Syllabic writing systems are more efficient than word-writing systems, and they are certainly less taxing on the memory. However, languages with a rich structure of syllables containing many consonant clusters (such as *tr* or *spl*) cannot be efficiently written with a syllabary. To see this difficulty, consider the syllable structures of English.

I	/aj/	V	*an*	/æn/	VC
key	/ki/	CV	*ant*	/ænt/	VCC
ski	/ski/	CCV	*ants*	/ænts/	VCCC
spree	/spri/	CCCV	*pant*	/pænt/	CVCC
seek	/sik/	CVC	*pants*	/pænts/	CVCCC
speak	/spik/	CCVC	*splints*	/splɪnts/	CCCVCCC
scram	/skræm/	CCCVC	*stamp*	/stæmp/	CCVCC
striped	/strajpt/	CCCVCC			

With more than thirty consonants and over twelve vowels, the number of different possible syllables is immense, which is why English, and Indo-European languages in general, are unsuitable for syllabic writing systems.

The Japanese language, on the other hand, is more suited for syllabic writing, because all words in Japanese can be phonologically represented by about one hundred syllables, mostly of the consonant-vowel (CV) type, and there are no underlying consonant clusters. To write these syllables the Japanese have two syllabaries, each containing forty-six characters, called **kana.** The entire Japanese language can be written using kana. One syllabary, **katakana,** is used for loan words and for special effects similar to italics in European writing. The other syllabary, **hiragana,** is used for native words and may occur with Chinese characters, which the Japanese call **kanji.** Thus Japanese writing is part word writing, part syllable writing.

During the first millennium, the Japanese tried to use Chinese characters to write their language. However, spoken Japanese is totally unlike spoken Chinese (they are genetically unrelated languages). A word-writing system alone was not suitable for Japanese, which is a highly inflected language where verbs may occur in thirty or more different forms. Using modified Chinese characters, the syllabaries were devised to represent the inflectional endings and other grammatical morphemes. Thus, in Japanese writing, Chinese characters will commonly be used for the verb roots, and hiragana symbols for the inflectional markings.

For example, 行 is the character meaning "go," pronounced [i]. The word for "went" in formal speech is *ikimashita,* written as 行きました, where the hiragana symbols きました represent the syllables *ki, ma, shi, ta.* Nouns, on the other hand, are not inflected in Japanese, and they can generally be written using Chinese characters alone.

In theory all of Japanese could be written in hiragana. There are many homophones in Japanese, however, and the use of word characters disambiguates a word that would be ambiguous if written syllabically. Also, like Chinese, Japanese kanji writing is an integral part of Japanese culture, and it is unlikely to be abandoned.

In 1821, Sequoyah, often called the "Cherokee Cadmus," invented a syllabic writing system for his native language, Cherokee. Sequoyah's script, which survives today essentially unchanged, proved useful to the Cherokee people and is justifiably a point of great pride for them. The syllabary contains eighty-five symbols, many of them derived from Latin characters, which efficiently transcribe spoken Cherokee. A few symbols are shown here:

J	gu
∩	hu
ℓℓ	we
W	ta
H	mi

An alphabetic character can be used to represent a syllable in some languages. In a word such as *bar-b-q,* the single letters represent syllables (*b* for [bi] or [bə], *q* for [kju]).

Consonantal Alphabet Writing

Semitic languages, such as Hebrew and Arabic, are written with alphabets than consist only of consonants. Such an alphabet works for these languages because consonants form the root of most words. For example, the consonants *ktb* in Arabic form the root of words associated with "write." Thus *katab* means "to write," *aktib* means "I write," *kitab* means "a book," and so on. Inflectional and derivational processes can be expressed by different vowels inserted into the triconsonantal roots.

Because of this structure, vowels can be figured out by a person knowing the spoken language, jst lk y cn rd ths phrs, prvdng y knw nglsh. English, however, is unrelated to the Semitic languages, and its structure is such that vowels are crucial for reading and writing much of the time. The English phrase *I like to eat out* would be incomprehensible without vowels, viz. *lk t t t.*

Semitic alphabets, primarily to preserve the true pronunciations of religious writings, and secondarily out of deference to children and foreigners learning to read and write, provide a way to express vowels. These come in the form of supplementary marks. In Hebrew dots or other small figures are placed under, above, or even in the center of the consonantal letter to indicate the accompanying vowel. For example ל represents an l-sound in Hebrew writing. Unadorned, the vowel that follows would be determined by context. However, לֶ indicates that the vowel that follows is [ɛ], so in effect לֶ represents the syllable [lɛ].

These systems are called consonantal alphabets because only the consonants are fully developed symbols. Sometimes they are considered syllabaries because once the vowel is perceived by the reader or writer, the consonantal letter appears to stand for a syllable. With a true syllabary, however, a person need only know the phonetic value of each symbol to pronounce it correctly and unambiguously. Once you learn a Japanese syllabary, you can read Japanese in a phonetically correct way without any idea of what you are saying. This would be impossible for Arabic or Hebrew.

Alphabetic Writing

Alphabetic writing systems are easy to learn, convenient to use, and maximally efficient for transcribing any human language.

The term **sound writing** is sometimes used in place of alphabetic writing, but it does not truly represent the principle involved in the use of alphabets. One-sound–one-letter is inefficient, because we do not need to represent the [pʰ] in *pit* and the [p] in *spit* by two different letters. It would also be confusing, because the nonphonemic differences between sounds are seldom perceptible to speakers. Except for the phonetic alphabets, whose function is to record the sounds of all languages for descriptive purposes, most, if not all, alphabets have been devised on the **phonemic principle.**

In the twelfth century, an Icelandic scholar developed an orthography derived from the Latin alphabet for the writing of the Icelandic language of his day. Other scholars in this period were also interested in orthographic reform, but the Icelander, who came to be known as "the First Grammarian" (because his anonymous paper was the first entry in a collection of grammatical essays), was the only one of the time who left a record of his principles. The orthography he developed was clearly based on the phonemic principle. He used minimal pairs to show the distinctive contrasts; he did not suggest different symbols for voiced and unvoiced [θ] and [ð], nor for [f] or [v], nor for velar [k] and palatal [č], because these pairs, according to him, represented allophones of the phonemes /θ/, /f/, and /k/, respectively. He did not use these modern technical terms, but the letters of this alphabet represent the distinctive phonemes of Icelandic of that century.

King Seijong of Korea (1418–1450) realized that the same principles held true for Korean when, with the assistance of scholars, he designed a phonemic alphabet. The king was an avid reader and realized that the over thirty thousand Chinese characters used to write Korean discouraged literacy. The fruit of the King's labor was the Korean alphabet called **Hangul,** which had seventeen consonants and eleven vowels.

The Hangul alphabet was designed on the phonemic principle. Although Korean has the sounds [l] and [r], Seijong represented them by a single letter because they are allophonic variants of the same phoneme. The same is true for the sounds [s] and [š], and [ts] and [tš].

Seijong showed further ingenuity in the design of the characters themselves. The consonants are drawn so as to depict the place and manner of articulation. Thus the letter for /g/ is ㄱ to suggest the raising of the back of the tongue to the velum; /m/ is the closed figure ㅁ to suggest the closing of the lips. Vowels in Hangul are easily distinguishable from consonants, being drawn as long vertical or horizontal lines, sometimes with smaller marks attached to them. Thus | represents /i/, — represents /u/, |_ represents /a/.

In Korean writing, the Hangul characters are grouped into squarish blocks, each corresponding to a syllable. The syllabic blocks, though they consist of alphabetic characters, make Korean look as if it were written in a syllabary. If English were written that way "Now is the winter of our discontent" would have this appearance:

```
No i th wi te o ou di co te
 w  se n r f r  s  nt
```

The space between letters is less than the space between syllables, which is less than the space between words. An example of Korean writing can be found in exercise 9, item 10 at the end of the chapter.

These characteristics make Korean writing unique in the world, unlike that of the Europeans, the Arabians, the Chinese, the Cascagians, or even "ladies in England."

Many languages have their own alphabet, and each has developed certain conventions for converting strings of alphabetic characters into sequences of sound (reading), and converting sequences of sounds into strings of alphabetic characters (writing). As we have illustrated with English, Icelandic, and Korean, the rules governing the sound system of the language play an important role in the relation between sound and character.

Most European alphabets use Latin (Roman) letters, making minor adjustments to accommodate individual characteristics of a particular language. For example, Spanish uses /ñ/ to represent the palatalized nasal phoneme of *señor*, and German has added an "umlaut" for certain of its vowel sounds that did not exist in Latin (for example, in *über*). Such extra marks are called **diacritics.** The forty-six kana of the Japanese syllabaries are supplemented by diacritics to represent the one hundred–plus syllables of the language. Diacritic marks are also used in writing systems of tone languages such as Thai to indicate the tone of a syllable.

Some languages use two letters together—called a **digraph**—to represent a single sound. English has many digraphs, such as *sh* /š/ as in *she, ch* /č/ as in *chop, ng* as in *sing* (/siŋ/) and *oa* as in *loaf* /lof/.

Besides the European languages, languages such as Turkish, Indonesian, Swahili, and Vietnamese have adopted the Latin alphabet. Other languages that have more recently developed a writing system use some of the IPA phonetic symbols in their alphabet. Twi, for example, uses ɔ, ɛ, and ŋ.

The Cyrillic alphabet, named for St. Cyril, is used by many Slavic languages, including Russian. It is derived directly from the Greek alphabet without Latin mediation.

FIGURE 12-2   Time line of the development of the Roman alphabet.

15000 B.C.E. — Cave drawings as pictograms

.

.

.

4000 B.C.E. — Sumerian cuneiform

3000 B.C.E. — Hieroglyphics

1500 B.C.E. — West Semitic Syllabary of the Phoenicians

1000 B.C.E. — Ancient Greeks borrow the Phoenician consonantal alphabet
750 B.C.E.   — Etruscans borrow the Greek alphabet
500 B.C.E.   — Romans adapt the Etruscan/Greco alphabet to Latin

The contemporary Semitic alphabets, those used for Persian (Iranian), Urdu (spoken in Pakistan), and many languages of the Indian subcontinent including Hindi, are ultimately derived from the ancient Semitic syllabaries.

Figure 12-2 shows a coarse time line of the development of the Roman alphabet.

READING, WRITING, AND SPEECH

> . . . Ther is so great diversite
> In English, and in wryting of oure tonge,
> So prey I god that non myswrite thee . . .
>
> Geoffrey Chaucer, *Troilus and Cressida*

The development of writing freed us from the limitations of time and geography, but spoken language still has primacy. Writing systems, however, are of interest for their own sake.

The written language reflects, to a certain extent, the elements and rules that together constitute the grammar of the language. The system of phonemes is represented by the letters of the alphabet, although not necessarily in a direct way. The independence of words is revealed by the spaces in the written string; but in languages where words are composed of more than one morpheme, the writing usually does not show the individual morphemes, even though speakers know what they are. In fact, many languages, such as Japanese or Thai, do not space between words, although speakers and writers are aware of the individual words. The sentences of some languages are indicated in the written form by capitals at the beginning and periods at the end. Other punctuation—such as question marks, italics, commas, and exclamation marks—is used to reveal syntactic structure, and to some extent intonation, stress, and contrast; but the written forms of many languages do not use such punctuation.

Consider the difference in meaning between (1) and (2):

(1) The Greeks, who were philosophers, loved to talk a lot.
(2) The Greeks who were philosophers loved to talk a lot.

The relative clause in (1), set off by commas, is nonrestrictive because it means that all the Greeks were philosophers. It may be paraphrased as (1′):

(1′) The Greeks were philosophers, and they loved to talk a lot.

The meaning of the second sentence, without the commas, can be paraphrased as:

(2′) Among the Greeks it was the philosophers who loved to talk a lot.

Similarly, by using an exclamation point or a question mark, the intention of the writer can be made clearer.

(3) The children are going to bed at eight o'clock. (*simple statement*)
(4) The children are going to bed at eight o'clock! (*an order*)
(5) The children are going to bed at eight o'clock? (*a question*)

These punctuation marks reflect the pauses and the intonations that would be used in the spoken language.

In sentence (6) *he* can refer to either John or someone else, but in sentence (7) the pronoun must refer to someone other than John:

(6) John said he's going.
(7) John said, "He's going."

The apostrophe used in contractions and possessives also provides syntactic information not always available in the spoken utterance.

(8) My cousin's friends (*one cousin*)
(9) My cousins' friends (*two or more cousins*)

Writing, then, somewhat reflects the spoken language, and punctuation may even distinguish between two meanings not revealed in the spoken forms, as shown in sentences (8) and (9).

In the normal written version of sentence (10),

(10) John whispered the message to Bill and then he whispered it to Mary

he can refer to either John or Bill. In the spoken sentence, if *he* receives extra stress (called **contrastive stress**), it must refer to Bill; if *he* receives normal stress, it refers to John.

A speaker can usually emphasize any word in a sentence by using contrastive stress. Writers sometimes attempt to show emphasis by using all capital letters, italics, or underlining the emphasized word:

(11) *John* kissed Bill's wife. (Bill didn't)
(12) John *kissed* Bill's wife. (rather than hugging her)
(13) John kissed *Bill's* wife. (not Dick's or his own)
(14) John kissed Bill's *wife*. (not Bill's mother)

Although such visual devices can help in English, it is not clear that they can be used in a language such as Chinese. In Japanese, however, this kind of emphasis can be achieved by writing a word in katakana.

The use of italics has many functions in written language. One use is to indicate reference to the italicized word itself, as in "*the* is an article." A children's riddle, which is sung aloud, plays on this distinction:

Railroad crossing, watch out for cars
How do you spell it without any r's?

The answer is "i-t." The joke is that the second line, were it written, would be:

How do you spell *it* without any r's?

Written language is more conservative than spoken language. When we write we are more apt to obey the prescriptive rules taught in school than when we speak. We may write "it is I" but we say "it's me." Such informalities abound in spoken language, but may be "corrected" by copy editors, diligent English teachers, and careful writers. A linguist wishing to describe the language that people regularly use therefore cannot depend on written records alone.

Reading

Children learn to speak instinctively without being taught. Learning to read and write is not like learning to speak. Recently, however, the Whole Language approach to reading has suggested that children can learn to read just as they learn to talk, through "constant interaction with family and friends, teachers and classmates." This view is given in a National Council of Teachers of English brochure that appears on the World Wide Web. It opposes the view that children be taught to segment speech into individual sounds and relate these sounds to the letters of the alphabet. The view that they oppose is sometimes referred to as phonics.

As we have seen in this chapter, most written languages are based on oral language. The Whole Language advocates do not understand the way in which children acquire language. They deny the fact that the ability to learn language is an innate, biologically determined aspect of the human brain, whereas reading and writing are not. If they were, one would not find so many people who speak so many languages that have no written form.

Many studies have shown that deaf children who have fully acquired a sign language have difficulty learning to read. This is understandable since the alphabetic principle in a system like English requires an understanding of sound-symbol regularities. Hearing children should therefore not be deprived of the advantage they have if their unconscious knowledge of phonemes is made conscious.

While understanding the relationship between speech, reading, and writing is important in developing teaching methods, there may be a number of methodologies that will improve our teaching of reading in the schools. Whatever one is adopted, it should include helping the child relate sounds to letters.

Spelling

Bizarro © by Don Piraro. Reprinted with permission of
Universal Press Syndicate. All rights reserved.

> "Do you spell it with a 'v' or a 'w'?" inquired the judge.
> "That depends upon the taste and fancy of the speller, my Lord,"
> replied Sam.
>
> Charles Dickens, *The Pickwick Papers*

If writing represented the spoken language perfectly, spelling reforms would never have arisen. In Chapter 6 we discussed some of the problems in the English orthographic (spelling) system. These problems prompted George Bernard Shaw to write:

> . . . It was as a reading and writing animal that Man achieved his human eminence above those who are called beasts. Well, it is I and my like who have to do the writing. I have done it professionally for the last sixty years as well as it can be done with a hopelessly inadequate alphabet devised centuries before the English language existed to record another and very different language. Even this alphabet is reduced to absurdity by a foolish orthography based on the notion that the business of spelling is to represent the origin and history of a word instead of its sound and meaning. Thus an intelligent child who is bidden to spell *debt,* and very properly spells it *d-e-t,* is caned for not spelling it with a *b* because Julius Caesar spelt the Latin word for it with a *b*.[4]

The irregularities between **graphemes** (letters) and phonemes have been cited as one reason "why Johnny can't read." Homographs such as *lead* /lid/ and *lead* /lɛd/ have fueled the flames of spelling reform movements. Different spellings for the same sound, silent letters, and missing letters also are cited as reasons why English needs a new orthographic system. The examples below illustrate the discrepancies between spelling and sounds in English:

Same Sound, Different Spelling	Different Sound, Same Spelling		Silent Letters	Missing Letters
/aj/	**th**ought	/θ/	**l**isten	use/**j**uz/
	though	/ð/	de**b**t	fuse/f**j**uz/
aye	**Th**omas	/t/	**g**nome	
b**uy**			**k**now	
b**y**	ate	/e/	**p**sychology	
d**ie**	at	/æ/	ri**gh**t	
h**i**	father	/a/	**m**nemonic	
Th**ai**	many	/ɛ/	s**c**ience	
he**igh**t			tal**k**	
gu**i**de			**h**onest	
			s**w**ord	
			bom**b**	
			cl**u**e	
			Wed**n**esday	

---

4 George Bernard Shaw. 1948. Preface to R. A. Wilson, *The Miraculous Birth of Language,* New York: Philosophical Library.

The spelling of most English words today is based on English spoken in the fourteenth, fifteenth, and sixteenth centuries. Spellers in those times saw no need to spell the same word consistently. Shakespeare spelled his own name in several different ways. The first person singular pronoun is spelled in Shakespeare's plays as "I", "ay," and "aye."

When the printing press was introduced in the fifteenth century, archaic and idiosyncratic spellings became widespread and more permanent. Words in print were frequently misspelled outright because many of the early printers were not native speakers of English.

Spelling reformers saw the need for consistent spelling that correctly reflected the pronunciation of words. To that extent, spelling reform was necessary. But many scholars became overzealous. Because of their reverence for Classical Greek and Latin these scholars changed the spelling of English words to conform to their etymologies. Where Latin had a *b,* they added a *b* even if it was not pronounced; and where the original spelling had a *c* or *p* or *h,* these letters were added, as is shown by these few examples:

Middle English Spelling		"Reformed" Spelling
indite	→	indi**c**t
dette	→	de**b**t
receit	→	recei**p**t
oure	→	**h**our

Such spelling habits inspired Robert N. Feinstein to compose the following poem, entitled "Gnormal Pspelling":[5]

> Gnus and gnomes and gnats and such—
> Gnouns with just one G too much.
> Pseudonym and psychedelic—
> P becomes a psurplus relic. Knit and knack and knife and knocked—
> Kneedless Ks are overstocked.
> Rhubarb, rhetoric and rhyme
> Should lose an H from thyme to time.

Even today spelling reform is an issue. Advertisers often spell *though* as *tho, through* as *thru,* and *night* as *nite.* For a period of time the *Chicago Tribune* used such spellings, but it gave up the practice in 1975. Spelling habits are hard to change, and revised spelling is regarded as substandard by many.

The current English spelling system is based primarily on the earlier pronunciations of words. The many changes that have occurred in the sound system of English since then are not reflected in the current spelling, which was frozen due to widespread printed material and scholastic conservatism.

For these reasons, modern English orthography does not always represent what we know about the phonology of the language. The disadvantage is partially offset by the fact that the writing system allows us to read and understand what people wrote hundreds of years ago without the need for translations. If there were a one-to-one

---

[5] Reprinted with permission from *National Forum: The Phi Kappa Phi Journal,* Summer 1986.

correspondence between our spelling and the sounds of our language, we would have difficulty reading the Constitution or the Declaration of Independence, let alone Shakespeare.

Languages change. It is not possible to maintain a perfect correspondence between pronunciation and spelling, nor is it 100 percent desirable. For instance, in the case of homophones, it is helpful at times to have different spellings for the same sounds, as in the following pair:

The book was red.   The book was read.

Lewis Carroll makes the point with humor:

"And how many hours a day did you do lessons?" said Alice.
"Ten hours the first day," said the Mock Turtle, "nine the next, and so on."
"What a curious plan!" exclaimed Alice.
"That's the reason they're called *lessons*," the Gryphon remarked, "because they *lessen* from day to day."

There are also reasons for using the same spelling for different pronunciations. A morpheme may be pronounced differently when it occurs in different contexts. The identical spelling reflects the fact that the different pronunciations represent the same morpheme. This is the case with the plural morpheme. It is always spelled with an *s* despite being pronounced [s] in *cats* and [z] in *dogs*. The sound of the morpheme is determined by rules, in this case as in other cases.

Similarly, the phonetic realizations of the vowels in the following forms follow a regular pattern:

aj/ɪ	**i/ɛ**	**e/æ**
divine/divinity	*serene/serenity*	*sane/sanity*
sublime/sublimate	*obscene/obscenity*	*profane/profanity*
sign/signature	*hygiene/hygienic*	*humane/humanity*

These considerations have led some scholars to suggest that English orthography is a **morphophonemic orthography** in addition to being phonemic. To read English with correct pronunciations, morphophonemic knowledge is required. This contrasts with a language such as Spanish, whose orthography is almost purely phonemic.

Other examples provide further motivation for spelling irregularities. The *b* in *"debt"* may remind us of the related word *debit*, in which the *b* is pronounced. The same principle is true of pairs such as *sign/signal, bomb/bombardier,* and *gnosis/ prognosis/ agnostic.*

There are also different spellings that represent the different pronunciations of a morpheme when confusion would arise from using the same spelling. For example, there is a rule in English phonology that changes a /t/ to an /s/ in certain cases:

democrat → democracy

The different spellings are due in part to the fact that this rule does not apply to all morphemes, so that *art + y* is *arty,* not **arcy.* Regular phoneme-to-grapheme rules determine in many cases when a morpheme is to be spelled identically and when it is to be changed.

Other subregularities are apparent. A *c* always represents the /s/ sound when it is followed by a *y, i,* or *e,* as in *cynic, citizen,* and *censure.* Because it is always pronounced [k] when it is the final letter in a word or when it is followed by any other vowel (*coat, cat, cut,* and so on), no confusion results. The *th* spelling is usually pronounced voiced as [ð] between vowels (the result of an historical intervocalic voicing rule).

There is another important reason why spelling should not always be tied to the phonetic pronunciation of words. Different dialects of English have divergent pronunciations. Cockneys drop their "(h)aitches" and Bostonians and southerners drop their "*r*'s"; *neither* is pronounced [niðər], [najðər], and [niðə] by Americans, [najðə] by the British, and [neðər] by the Irish; some Scots pronounce *night* as [nɪxt]; people say "Chicago" and "Chicawgo," "hog" and "hawg," "bird" and "boyd"; *four* is pronounced [fɔ:] by the British, [for] in the Midwest, and [foə] in the South; *orange* is pronounced in at least two ways in the United States: [arənĵ] and [ɔrənĵ].

While dialectal pronunciations differ, the common spellings indicate the intended word. It is necessary for the written language to transcend local dialects. With a uniform spelling system, a native of Atlanta and a native of Glasgow can communicate through writing. If each dialect were spelled according to its own pronunciation, written communication among the English-speaking peoples of the world would suffer.

Spelling Pronunciations

> For pronunciation, the best general rule is to consider those as the most elegant speakers who deviate least from written words.
>
> Samuel Johnson (1755)

Despite the primacy of the spoken over the written language, the written word is often regarded with excessive reverence. The stability, permanency, and graphic nature of writing cause some people to favor it over ephemeral and elusive speech. Humpty Dumpty expressed a rather typical attitude: "I'd rather see that done on paper."

Writing has affected speech only marginally, however, most notably in the phenomenon of **spelling pronunciation.** Since the sixteenth century, we find that spelling has to some extent influenced standard pronunciation. The most important of such changes stem from the eighteenth century under the influence and decrees of the dictionary-makers and the schoolteachers. The struggle between those who demanded that words be pronounced according to the spelling and those who demanded that words be spelled according to their pronunciation generated great heat in that century. The preferred pronunciations were given in the many dictionaries printed in the eighteenth century, and the "supreme authority" of the dictionaries influenced pronunciation in this way.

Spelling also has influenced pronunciation in words that are infrequently used in normal daily speech. Many words that were spelled with an initial *h* were not pronounced with any /h/ sound as late as the eighteenth century. Thus, at that time no /h/ was pronounced in *honest, hour, habit, heretic, hotel, hospital, herb.* Frequently used words like *honest* and *hour* continued to be pronounced without the /h/, despite the spelling; but all those other words were given a "spelling pronunciation." Because people did not hear them often, when they saw them written they concluded that they must begin with an /h/. *Herb* is currently undergoing this change; in British English the *h* is pronounced, whereas in American English it is not.

Similarly, many words now spelled with a *th* were once pronounced /t/ as in Thomas; later most of these words underwent a change in pronunciation from /t/ to /θ/, as in *anthem, author, theater.* "Nicknames" often reflect the earlier pronunciations: "Ka*t*e" for "Ca*t*herine," "Be*tt*y" for "Elizabe*th*," "Ar*t*" for "Ar*t*hur." The words *often* and *soften,* which are usually pronounced without a /t/ sound, are pronounced with the /t/ by some people because of the spelling.

The clear influence of spelling on pronunciation is observable in the way place-names are pronounced. *Berkeley* is pronounced [bʊrkli] in California, although it stems from the British [ba:kli]; *Worcester* [wʊstər] or [wʊstə] in Massachusetts is often pronounced [wʊrčɛstər] in other parts of the country. *Salmon* is pronounced [sæmən] in most parts of the United States, but many southern speakers pronounce the [l] and say [sælmən].

Although the written language has some influence on the spoken, it does not change the basic system—the grammar—of the language. The writing system, conversely, reflects, in a more or less direct way, the grammar that every speaker knows.

SUMMARY

Writing is a basic tool of civilization. Without it, the world as we know it could not exist.

The precursor of writing was "picture writing," which used **pictograms** to represent objects directly and literally. Pictograms are called **ideograms** when the drawing becomes less literal, and the meaning extends to concepts associated with the object originally pictured. When ideograms become associated with the words for the concepts they signify, they are called **logograms.** Logographic systems are true writing systems in the sense that the symbols stand for words of a language.

The Sumerians first developed a pictographic writing system to keep track of commercial transactions. It was later expanded for other uses and eventually evolved into the highly stylized (and stylus-ized) **cuneiform writing.** Cuneiform was generalized to other writing systems by application of the **rebus principle,** which uses the symbol of one word or syllable to represent another word or syllable pronounced the same.

The Egyptians also developed a pictographic system known as **hieroglyphics.** This system influenced many peoples, including the Phoenicians, who developed the West Semitic Syllabary. The Greeks borrowed the Phoenician system, and in adapting it to their own language they used the symbols to represent both consonant and vowel sound segments, thus inventing the first alphabet.

There are four types of writing systems: **logographic** (word writing), where every symbol or character represents a word or morpheme (as in Chinese); **syllabic,** where each symbol represents a syllable (as in Japanese); **consonantal alphabetic,** where each symbol represents a consonant and vowels may be represented by diacritical marks as in Hebrew; and **alphabetic,** where each symbol represents (for the most part) a vowel or consonant (as in English).

The writing system may have some small effect on the spoken language. Languages change in time, but writing systems tend to be more conservative. Thus spelling no longer accurately reflects pronunciation. Also, when the spoken and written forms of the language become divergent, some words may be pronounced as they are spelled, sometimes due to the efforts of pronunciation reformers.

There are advantages to a conservative spelling system. A common spelling permits speakers whose dialects have diverged to communicate through writing, as is best exemplified in China, where the "dialects" are mutually unintelligible. We are also able to read and understand the language as it was written centuries ago. In addition, despite a certain lack of correspondences between sound and spelling, the spelling often reflects speakers' morphological and phonological knowledge.

References for Further Reading

Biber, Douglas. 1988. *Variation across Speech and Writing.* Cambridge, England: Cambridge University Press.

Coulmas, Florian. 1989. *The Writing Systems of the World.* Cambridge, MA: Blackwell.

Cummings, D. W. 1988. *American English Spelling.* Baltimore, MD: The Johns Hopkins University Press.

Daniels, P. T., and W. Bright, eds. 1996. *The World's Writing Systems.* New York: Oxford University Press.

DeFrancis, John. 1989. *Visible Speech: The Diverse Oneness of Writing Systems.* Honolulu, HI: University of Hawaii Press.

Gaur, Albertine. 1984. *A History of Writing.* London, England: The British Library.

Sampson, Geoffrey. 1985. *Writing Systems: A Linguistic Introduction.* Stanford, CA: Stanford University Press.

EXERCISES

1. A. "Write" the following words and phrases, using pictograms that you invent:

    a. eye

    b. a boy

    c. two boys

    d. library

    e. tree

    f. forest

    g. war

    h. honesty

    i. ugly

    j. run

    k. Scotch tape

    l. smoke

B. Which words are most difficult to symbolize in this way? Why?

C. How does the following sentence reveal the problems in pictographic writing? "A grammar represents the unconscious, internalized linguistic competence of a native speaker."

2. A *rebus* is a written representation of words or syllables using pictures of objects whose names resemble the sounds of the intended words or syllables. For example, might be the symbol for "eye" or "I" or the first syllable in "idea."

A. Using the rebus principle, "write" the following words:

   a. tearing

   b. icicle

   c. bareback

   d. cookies

B. Why would such a system be a difficult system in which to represent all words in English? Illustrate with an example.

3. A. Construct non-Roman alphabetic letters to replace the letters used to represent the following sounds in English:

   t   r   s   k   w   č   i   æ   f   n

B. Use these symbols plus the regular alphabet symbols for the other sounds to write the following words in your "new orthography."

   a. character

   b. guest

   c. cough

   d. photo

   e. cheat

   f. rang

   g. psychotic

   h. tree

4. Suppose the English writing system were a *syllabic* system instead of an *alphabetic* system. Use capital letters to symbolize the necessary syllabic units for the words below, and list your "syllabary." Example: Given the words *mate, inmate, intake,* and *elfin,* you might use: A = mate, B = in, C = take, and D = elf. In addition, write the words using your syllabary. Example: *inmate*—BA; *elfin*—DB; *intake*—BC; *mate*—A. (Do not use any more syllable symbols than you absolutely need.)

   a. childishness

   b. childlike

   c. Jesuit

   d. lifelessness

   e. likely

   f. zoo

   g. witness

    h. lethal

    i. jealous

    j. witless

    k. lesson

5. In the following pairs of English words the bold-faced portions are pronounced the same but spelled differently. Can you think of any reason why the spelling should remain distinct? (Hint: *reel* and *real* are pronounced the same, but *reality* shows the presence of a phonemic /æ/ in *real*.)

	A	**B**	**Reason**
a.	I **am**	i**amb**	
b.	goo**se**	produ**ce**	
c.	fa**sh**ion	compli**c**ation	
d.	New**ton**	or**gan**	
e.	**no**	**kn**ow	
f.	hy**mn**	**him**	

6. In the following pairs of words the bold-faced portions are spelled the same but pronounced differently. Try to state some reasons why the spelling of the words in column B should not be changed.

	A	**B**	**Reason**
a.	min**g**le	lon**g**	The *g* is pronounced in *longer.*
b.	li**n**e	childre**n**	
c.	**s**onar	re**s**ound	
d.	**c**ent	mysti**c**	
e.	**c**rumble	bom**b**	
f.	cat**s**	dog**s**	
g.	sta**gn**ant	desi**gn**	
h.	se**r**ene	obs**c**enity	

7. Each of the following sentences is ambiguous in the written form. How can these sentences be made unambiguous when they are spoken?

    Example: John hugged Bill and then he kissed him.
    For the meaning "John hugged and kissed Bill," use normal stress (*kissed* receives stress). For the meaning "Bill kissed John," contrastive stress is needed on both *he* and *him*.

    a. What are we having for dinner, Mother?

    b. She's a German language teacher.

    c. They formed a student grievance committee.

    d. Charles kissed his wife and George kissed his wife too.

8. In the written form, the following sentences are not ambiguous, but they would be if spoken. State the devices used in writing that make the meanings explicit.

    a. They're my brothers' keepers.

    b. He said, "He will take the garbage out."

    c. The red book was read.

    d. The flower was on the table.

9. Below are ten samples of writing from the ten languages listed. Match the writing to the language. There are enough hints in this chapter to get most of them. (The source of these examples, and many others, is *Languages of the World* by Kenneth Katzner, 1975, New York: Funk & Wagnalls.)

    a. _____Cherokee
    b. _____Chinese
    c. _____German (Gothic style)
    d. _____Greek
    e. _____Hebrew
    f. _____Icelandic
    g. _____Japanese
    h. _____Korean
    i. _____Russian
    j. _____Twi

    1. 仮に勝手に変えるようなことをすれば.

    2. Κι ὁ νοῦς του ἀγκάλιασε πονετικὰ τὴν Κρήτη.

    3. «Что это? я падаю? у меня ноги подкашиваются»,

    4. וְהָיָה ׀ בְּאַחֲרִית הַיָּמִים נָכוֹן יִהְיֶה הַר

    5. Saá sáre yi bèɲ atɛkyé bí â mpɔ̀torɔ áhyɛ́

    6. 既然必须和新的群众的时代相结合.

    7. ᎢᎦ ᏲᎾ ᎠᏯ ᏗᏯᎤᏎ ᏣᏍᏲ ᏉᎵᏙ.

    8. Þótt þú langförull legðir sérhvert land undir fót,

    9. Pharao's Anblick war wunderbar.

    10. 스위스는 특특한 체제

10. The following appeared on the safety card of a Spanish airline. Identify each of the thirteen languages. (You will probably have to spend some time in the library and/or visit various departments of foreign languages.)

    1. **Para su seguridad** _____
    2. **For your safety** _____
    3. **Pour votre sécurité** _____
    4. **Für ihre Sicherheit** _____
    5. **Per la Vostra sicurezza** _____
    6. **Para sua segurança** _____
    7. **あなたの安全のために** _____
    8. **Для Вашей безогіасности** _____
    9. **Dla bezpieczeństwa pasażerów** _____
    10. **Za vašu sigurnost** _____
    11. **Γιά τήν ἀσφάλειά σας** _____
    12. **Kendi emniyetiniz için** _____
    13. **من أجل سلامتك** _____

11. Diderot and D'Alembert, the French "Encyclopedists," wrote:

> "The Chinese have no alphabet; their very language is incompatible with one, since it is made up of an extremely limited number of sounds. It would be impossible to convey the sound of Chinese through our alphabet or any other alphabet."

Comment on this.

Glossary

Abbreviation   Shortened form of a word (e.g., *prof* from *professor*). Cf. **clipping.**

Accent   (1) Prominence. Cf. **stressed syllable;** (2) the phonology or pronunciation of a specific regional dialect (e.g., southern accent); (3) the pronunciation of a language by a nonnative speaker (e.g., French accent).

Accidental gaps   Phonological or morphological forms that constitute possible but non-occurring lexical items; e.g., *blick, unsad.*

Acoustic   Pertaining to physical aspects of sound.

Acoustic phonetics   The study of the physical characteristics of speech sounds.

Acoustic signal   The sound waves produced by any sound source, including speech.

Acquired dyslexia   Loss of ability to read correctly by persons who were previously literate following brain damage.

Acronym   Word composed of the initials of several words (e.g., *PET* scan from *positron emission tomography* scan).

Active sentence   A sentence in which the noun phrase subject in deep structure is also the noun phrase subject in surface structure. Cf. **passive sentence.**

Adjective (Adj)   The syntactic category, also lexical category, of words that may precede a noun in a noun phrase and have the semantic effect of qualifying the noun.

Adverb (Adv)   The syntactic category, also lexical category, of words that may occur last within a verb phrase in deep structure, and qualify the verb in that verb phrase. A transformation that moves adverbs allows them to occur in many positions in surface structure (e.g., *John wept silently. John silently wept. Silently John wept).*

Affix   Bound morpheme attached to a stem or root morpheme. Cf. **prefix, suffix, infix, circumfix.**

Affricates   Sounds produced by a stop closure followed immediately by a slow release, characteristic of a fricative; phonetically a sequence of stop + fricative.

African American English (AAE)   A dialect of English spoken by some African Americans.

Agent   The thematic role of the noun phrase whose referent deliberately performs the action described by the verb (e.g., *George* in *George hugged Martha*).

Agrammatism   Language disorder usually resulting from damage to Broca's region in which the patient has difficulty with syntax. Cf. **Broca's area.**

Agreement   Subject-verb agreement.

Airstream mechanisms   The ways in which air from the lungs or mouth is moved to produce speech sounds.

Allomorphs   Alternate phonetic forms of a morpheme; e.g., the /-s/, /-z/, and /-əz/ forms of the plural morpheme in *cats, dogs,* and *kisses.*

Allophone   A predictable phonetic realization of a phoneme (e.g., [p] and [pʰ] are allophones of the phoneme /p/ in English).

Alphabetic writing   A writing system in which each symbol typically represents one sound segment.

Alveolar ridge   The part of the hard palate directly behind the front teeth.

Alveolars   Sounds produced by raising the tongue to the *alveolar ridge* (the bony tooth ridge).

Alveopalatals   Sounds whose place of articulation is the hard palate immediately behind the alveolar ridge.

Ambiguous, ambiguity   The term used to describe a word, phrase, or sentence with multiple meanings.

American Sign Language (ASL; AMES-LAN) The sign language used by the deaf community in the United States. Cf. **sign languages.**

Analogic change A language change in which a rule spreads to previously unaffected forms (e.g., the plural of *cow* changed from the earlier *kine* to *cows* by the generalization of the plural formation rule). Also called **internal borrowing.**

Analogy The use of one form as a sample by which other forms can be similarly constructed. One theory of language acquisition suggests that children learn how to put words together to form phrases and sentences by analogy.

Analytic Describes a sentence that is true by virtue of its meaning alone, irrespective of situational context (e.g., *Kings are monarchs*). Cf. **contradictory.**

Anaphor A pronominal or similar expression such as a reflexive pronoun whose reference is determined by an antecedent in the same sentence or discourse (e.g., *herself* is an anaphor coreferential with its antecedent *Sue* in the sentence *Sue bit herself*).

Anaphora The process of replacing a longer expression with a shorter one, especially with a pronoun, that is coreferential with the longer expression.

Anomalous Semantically ill-formed, e.g., *Colorless green ideas sleep furiously.*

Anomaly A violation of semantic rules resulting in expressions that give the impression of being nonsense, e.g., *The verb crumpled the milk.*

Anomia A form of aphasia in which patients have word-finding difficulties.

Antecedent The expression with which an anaphor is coreferential; e.g. (*Sue* is the antecedent of the anaphor *herself* in the sentence *Sue bit herself*).

Anterior A phonetic feature of consonants whose place of articulation is in front of the palato-alveolar area, including labials, interdentals, and alveolars.

Antonyms Words that are opposite in meaning. Cf. **gradable pairs, complementary pairs, relational opposites.**

Aphasia Language loss or disorders following damage to the left cerebral hemisphere of the brain.

Arbitrary The property of language, including sign language, whereby there is no natural or intrinsic relationship between the way a word is pronounced (or signed) and its meaning.

Arc Part of the graphical depiction of a transition network represented as an arrow labeled with a syntactic category and connecting two nodes. Cf. **node, transition network.**

Argot The set of words used by a particular occupational group, such as scientists, artists, musicians, bricklayers, etc. Also called **jargon.**

Article (Art) One of several subclasses of determiners (e.g., *the, a*).

Articulators The tongue and lips, which change the shape of the vocal tract to produce different speech sounds.

Articulatory phonetics The study of how the vocal tract produces speech sounds; the physiological characteristics of speech sounds.

Aspirated Voiceless consonants produced with the vocal cords open for a brief period after the release of the constriction resulting in a puff of air (e.g., the [pʰ] in *pit*). Cf. **unaspirated.**

Assimilation The change or spread of phonetic feature values that makes segments more similar.

Assimilation rules Phonological rules that change feature values of segments to make them more similar.

Asterisk The symbol [*] used to indicate ungrammatical or anomalous examples (e.g., *cried the baby, *sincerity dances). Also used in historical and comparative linguistics to represent a reconstructed form.

Audio-lingual A language teaching method based on the assumption that language is acquired mainly through imitation, repetition, and reinforcement.

Auditory phonetics The study of the perception of speech sounds.

Augmented transition network   A transition network in which the arcs carry information necessary to parsing over and above their syntactic category label. Cf. **transition network, arc, node.**

Automatic machine translation   The use of computers to translate from one language to another. Cf. **source language, target language.**

Auxiliary verb (Aux)   Verbal elements, traditionally called "helping verbs," that co-occur with, and qualify, the main verb in a verb phrase with regard to tense, aspect, modality, etc. (e.g., *have, be, will, may, must*).

Babbling   Sounds produced in the first few months after birth that include sounds that do and do not occur in the language of the household. Deaf children babble with hand gestures similar to the vocal babbling of hearing children.

Baby talk   A term used to label the word forms that many adults use when speaking to children.

Back-formation   A new word created by removing what is mistakenly considered to be an affix (e.g., *edit* from *editor*).

Bilabials   Sounds articulated by bringing both lips together.

Bird calls   One or more short notes that convey messages associated with the immediate environment, such as danger, feeding, nesting, flocking, and so on.

Birdsongs   Complex patterns of notes with no internal structure used to mark territory and to attract mates.

Blend   A word composed of the parts of more than one word (e.g., *smog* from *smoke + fog*).

Bootstrapping   Children's use of their knowledge of syntax to learn the meaning of words. Experiments have shown that knowing that a word is a verb or a noun informs them that it has a meaning referring to an action or to an object of some kind, respectively.

Borrowing   The incorporating of a loan word from one language into another (e.g., English borrowed *buoy* from Dutch). Cf. **loan words.**

Bound   Describes a pronoun that is coreferential with a noun phrase under at least one interpretation of the sentence or discourse (e.g., *she* in *Jane believes she loves Tarzan*). Cf. **free.**

Bound morphemes   Morphemes that can only occur in words attached to other morphemes; prefixes, suffixes, infixes, circumfixes, and some roots such as *cran* in *cranberry*. Cf. **free morphemes.**

Broadening   A semantic change in which the meaning of a word changes in time to become more encompassing (e.g., *dog* once meant a particular breed of dog).

Broca's aphasia   Language disorder following damage to Broca's area in which speech is nonfluent, lacking in grammatical morphemes, and agrammatic. Comprehension is fairly good except for difficulties in comprehending sentences that depend on syntactic structures.

Broca's area   A front part of the left hemisphere of the brain, damage to which causes Broca's aphasia.

Broca, Paul   A French neurologist who in 1861 suggested that the left side of the brain was the language hemisphere.

Case   The morphological form of nouns and pronouns, and in some languages articles and adjectives as well, indicating the grammatical relationship to the verb (e.g., *I* is in the *nominative* case of the first person singular pronoun in English and functions as a subject; *me* is in the *accusative* case and can only function as an object).

Case endings   Suffixes on the noun based on its grammatical relationship to the verb.

Case theory   The study of thematic roles and grammatical case in languages of the world.

Cause   The thematic role of the noun phrase whose referent is a natural force that causes a change (e.g., *the wind* in *The wind damaged the roof*).

Cerebral hemispheres   The two parts of the brain, the left hemisphere controlling the movements of the right side of the body, the right hemisphere those of the left side.

Characters (Chinese)   The units of Chinese writing, each of which represents a morpheme or word. Cf. **ideogram, ideograph, logogram.**

Chicano English (ChE)   A dialect of English spoken by some bilingual Mexican Americans in the Southwest and California.

Circumfix   Bound morpheme, parts of which occur in a word both before and after the root (e.g., *ge - - - t* in German *geliebt*, "loved" from the root *lieb*).

Click   A speech sound, found in certain African languages, that is produced by a **velaric airstream mechanism**.

Clipping   The deletion of some part of a longer word to give a shorter word with the same meaning (e.g., *phone* from *telephone*). Sometimes called **abbreviation**.

Closed class   The class of function words; a category of words which rarely if ever has new words added to it (e.g., prepositions, pronouns, conjunctions).

Coarticulation   The spreading of phonetic features either in anticipation of sounds or the perseveration of articulatory processes.

Coda   One or more phonological segments that follow the nucleus of a syllable (e.g., the /st/ in /prist/ *priest*).

Code-switching   The insertion of a word or phrase of a language other than that being spoken into a single sentence, or the movement back and forth between two languages or dialects.

Cognates   Words in related languages that developed from the same ancestral root, such as English *horn* and Latin *cornū*.

Coinage   The construction and addition of new words to the lexicon.

Communicative competence   Knowledge of the appropriate social use of language such as greetings, taboo words, polite forms of address, various styles that are suitable to different situations, and so forth.

Comparative linguistics   The branch of historical and comparative linguistics that explores language change by comparing related languages.

Comparative method   The technique used by linguists to deduce forms in an earlier stage of a language by examining corresponding forms in several of its daughter languages.

Comparative reconstruction   The deducing of an earlier form of genetically related languages by application of the comparative method.

Competence, linguistic   The knowledge of a language represented by the mental grammar that accounts for speakers' linguistic creativity. For the most part, linguistic competence is unconscious knowledge.

Complementary distribution   Phones that never occur in the same phonetic environment (e.g., [p] and [pʰ] in English). Cf. **allophones.**

Complementary pairs   Two antonyms related in such a way that the negation of one is the meaning of the other (e.g., *alive* means not *dead*). Cf. **gradable pairs, relational opposites.**

Compound   A word composed of two words (e.g., *washcloth*).

Computational linguistics   A subfield of linguistics and computer science that is concerned with computer processing of human language.

Concordance   An alphabetical index of all the words of a text that gives the frequency of every word and the location of each occurrence in the text.

Conditioned sound change   Phonological change that occurs in specific phonetic contexts only.

Connotative meaning/connotation   The evocative or affective meaning associated with a word. Two words may have the same referential, denotative meaning but different connotations.

Consonant   A speech sound produced with some constriction of the airstream.

Consonant harmony   Consonant articulation agreement within a word. This often occurs in children's first words. For example, *doggy* may be pronounced as *goggy* or *doddy*.

Consonantal alphabet   The symbols of a consonantal writing system.

Consonantal Phonetic feature distinguishing the class of obstruents, liquids, and nasals that are [+ consonantal], from other sounds which are [– consonantal].

Consonantal writing A writing system in which only symbols representing consonants are used; vowels are inferred from context , e.g., Arabic.

Constituent A syntactic unit in a phrase structure tree (e.g., *the girl* is a noun phrase constituent in the sentence *the boy loves the girl*).

Constituent structure The hierarchically arranged syntactic units such as noun phrase and verb phrase that underlie every sentence.

Constituent structure tree Phrase structure tree.

Content words The nouns, verbs, adjectives, and adverbs constituting the major part of the vocabulary. Cf. **open class.**

Continuants Speech sounds in which the airstream continues without complete interruption through the mouth.

Contour tones Tones in which the pitch glides from one level to another (e.g., from low to high as in a rising tone).

Contradiction Negative entailment: the truth of one sentence necessarily implies the falseness of another sentence (e.g., *He opened the door* and *The door is closed*). Cf. **entailment.**

Contradictory Describes a sentence that is false by virtue of its meaning alone (e.g., *My aunt is a man*).

Contralateral The control of one side of the body by the cerebral hemisphere on the opposite side.

Contrast The difference between two speech sounds that can result in a difference in meaning. Contrasting sounds are allophones, i.e., represent distinct phonemes.

Contrastive stress Additional stress placed on a word to highlight it or to clarify the referent of a pronoun (e.g., in *Joe hired Bill and* he *hired Sam,* with contrastive stress on *he,* it is usually understood that Bill rather than Joe hired Sam).

Convention; conventional The agreed-on arbitrary relationship between the form and meaning of words.

Cooperative Principle A broad principle within whose scope fall the various **maxims of conversation.** It states that in order to communicate effectively, speakers should agree to be informative and relevant.

Coordinate structure A syntactic structure in which two or more constituents of the same syntactic category are joined together with a conjunction such as *and* or *or.* E.g., *bread and butter, the big dog or the small cat, huffing and puffing.*

Coordinate Structure Constraint A constraint on all languages that prohibits the movement of constituents out of a coordinate structure.

Coreference The relation between two noun phrases that refer to the same entity.

Coreferential Describes noun phrases (including pronouns) that refer to the same entity.

Coronals The class of sounds including labials, alveolars, and palatals.

Corpus A collection of utterances, gathered from spoken or written sources, used for linguistic research and analysis.

Corpus callosum The nerve fibers connecting the right and left cerebral hemispheres.

Cortex The approximately ten billion neurons forming the outside surface of the brain; also referred to as *gray matter.*

Count nouns Nouns that can be enumerated, e.g., *one potato, two potatoes.* Cf. **mass nouns.**

Cover symbol A symbol that represents a class of sounds (e.g., C for consonants; V for vowels).

Creativity of language; creative aspect of linguistic knowledge Speakers' ability to combine the finite number of linguistic units of their language to produce and understand an infinite range of novel sentences never produced or heard previously.

Creole A language, which started as a pidgin, adopted by a community as its native tongue and learned by children as their first language.

Critical age   The period between early childhood and puberty during which a child can acquire language without instruction. During this period, language learning proceeds easily, swiftly, and without external intervention. After this period, the acquisition of the grammar is difficult and, for some individuals, never fully achieved.

Cuneiform   A form of writing in which the characters are produced using a wedge-shaped stylus. It was developed by the Sumerians in the fourth millennium B.C.E. and was borrowed by several civilizations, including the Assyrians and Babylonians. It was in use as late as the fifth century B.C.E.

Deep structure   Any phrase structure tree generated by the phrase structure rules of a transformational grammar. The basic syntactic structures of the grammar.

Definite   Describes a noun phrase that refers to a unique object insofar as the speaker and listeners are concerned.

Deictic   Describes words or expressions whose reference relies entirely on context (e.g., *I, now, here, this cat*).

Deixis   The aspect of pragmatics in which deictic terms are used to refer. Cf. **deictic.**

Demonstrative articles, demonstratives   Words such as *this, that, those, these* that function syntactically as articles but are semantically deictic because context is needed to determine the referent of the noun phrase in which they occur. Cf. **deictic, person deixis, place deixis, time deixis.**

Denotative meaning   The referential meaning of a word.

Derivation   The steps in the application of phonological rules to a phonemic representation ending with a phonetic representation.

Derivational morphemes   Morphemes added to stem morphemes to form new stems or words that may or may not change the syntactic category of a word.

Derived structure   Any structure resulting from the application of transformational rules, i.e., any underlying structure except deep structure.

Descriptive grammar   A linguist's description or model of the mental grammar, including the units, structures, and rules. The attempt to state what speakers unconsciously know about their language.

Determiner (Det)   The syntactic category, also lexical category, of words and expressions which when combined with a noun form a noun phrase; a category of expressions that can directly qualify the noun in a noun phrase. Includes the articles *the* and *a,* the demonstratives such as *this* and *that,* quantifiers such as *each* and *every*, expressions such as *William Jefferson Clinton's,* etc.

Diacritics   Additional markings on written symbols to specify various phonetic properties such as length, tone, stress, nasalization; extra marks added to a written character that change its usual value (e.g., the tilde [~] drawn over the letter *n* in Spanish represents a palatalized nasal rather than an alveolar nasal).

Dialect   A language variety used by a particular group of speakers. Cf. **regional dialect, social dialect.** Dialects are the mutually intelligible forms of a language that differ in systematic ways from each other.

Dialect area   A section of the country defined by distinct word usage and pronunciations bounded by isoglosses.

Dialect atlas   A book of **dialect maps** showing the areas where specific dialectal characteristics occur in the speech of the region.

Dialect leveling   Movement toward greater uniformity or decrease in variations among dialects.

Dialect map   A map showing the areas where specific dialectal characteristics occur in the speech of the region.

Dichotic listening   Experimental method for testing brain lateralization in which subjects hear different auditory signals in the left and right ears.

Digraph   Two letters used to represent a single sound (e.g., *gh* represents [f] in *enough*).

Diphthong   Vowel + glide, e.g., [aj, aw, ɔj] as in *bite, bout, boy*.

Direct method   Second-language teaching without any reference to the native language, and without use of translation or grammar instructions. It is an attempt to simulate learning a foreign language in the way children learn their native language.

Direct object   The grammatical relation of a noun phrase when it appears immediately below the verb phrase (VP) in deep structure.

Discontinuous dependency   A situation in which two syntactic elements that occur adjacent in deep structure, and function together to give a certain meaning, are separated in surface structure by a transformation (e.g., *they ran a big bill up*. The deep structure is *they ran up a big bill. Ran* and *up* depend on each other for the meaning of "ran up").

Discontinuous morpheme   A morpheme with multiple parts which occur in more than one place in a word or sentence. Cf. **circumfix.**

Discourse   Linguistic units composed of several sentences.

Discourse analysis   The study of discourse.

Dissimilation rules   Phonological rules that change feature values of segments to make them less similar.

Distinctive   Describes linguistic elements that contrast.

Distinctive features   Phonetic properties of phonemes that account for their ability to contrast meanings of words, e.g., *voice, nasal, labial*.

Ditransitive verb   A verb that appears to take two noun-phrase objects, e.g., *give* in *he gave Sally the gift*. Ditransitive verb phrases often have an alternate form with a prepositional phrase in place of the first noun phrase, as in *he gave the gift to Sally*.

Dominate   In a phrase structure tree, when a continuous downward path can be traced from a node labeled **A** to a node labeled **B,** then **A dominates B.**

Downdrift   The lowering of pitch (and tones) of a phrase or utterance.

Early Middle English Vowel Shortening   A sound change that shortened vowels such as the first *i* in *criminal. As a result criminal* was unaffected by the Great Vowel Shift, leading to word pairs such as *crime/criminal*. Other similar alternations occur in modern English for the same reason.

Ease of articulation   Expression referring to the tendency when we speak to make it easier to move the articulators.

Ebonics   An alternative term for the various dialects of African American English, first used in 1997.

Egressive airstream mechanism   Method by which lung air is pushed out of the mouth.

Egressive sounds   Produced by air moving out of the mouth.

Ejective   A speech sound produced with a glottalic airstream mechanism.

Embedded sentence   A sentence occurring within a sentence in a phrase structure tree (e.g., *You know that* sheepdogs cannot swim).

Entailment   The relationship between two sentences where the truth of one infers the truth of the other (e.g., such a relationship holds between *Corday assassinated Marat* and *Marat is dead* since if the first is true, the second must be true).

Entails   One sentence entails another if the truth of the first necessarily implies the truth of the second (e.g., *The sun melted the ice* entails *The ice melted* since if the first is true, the second must be true).

Epenthesis   The insertion of consonants or vowels in a word.

Eponym   A word taken from a proper name, such as *john* for "toilet."

Etymology   The history of words; the study of the history of words.

Euphemism   A word or phrase that replaces a taboo word or is used to avoid reference to certain acts or subjects (e.g., *powder room* for *toilet*).

Event-related brain potentials; ERP   The electrical signals emitted from different areas of the brain in response to different kinds of stimuli.

Experiencer The thematic role of the noun phrase whose referent perceives something (e.g., *Helen* in *Helen heard Robert playing the piano*).

Extension The reference of an expression.

Feature Matrix A representation of phonological segments in which the columns represent segments and the rows represent features, each cell being marked with a + or – to designate the value of the feature for that segment.

Feature-changing rules; Feature-spreading rules Phonological rules that change feature values of segments to make them more similar (Cf. **assimilation rules**) or less similar (Cf. **dissimilation rules**).

Finger spelling The use of hand gestures symbolizing the letters of the alphabet used to spell a word when there is no sign for the word in the sign language.

Folk etymology The process whereby words or their origins are changed through nonscientific speculations or false analogies with other words.

Form Phonological or gestural representation of a morpheme or word.

Free Describes a pronoun that refers to some object not explicitly mentioned in the sentence or discourse (e.g., *it* in *Everyone saw it*).

Free morphemes Single morphemes that constitute words.

Free variation Alternative pronunciations of a word in which one sound is substituted for another without changing the word's meaning (e.g., pronunciation of *bottle* with a glottal stop as the medial consonant).

Fricatives Sounds produced in which a constriction in the vocal tract is narrow, creating a hiss or friction; sometimes called **spirants.**

Front vowels Vowel sounds in which the tongue is positioned forward in the mouth.

Function words Grammatical words including conjunctions, prepositions, articles, etc. Cf. **closed class.**

Fundamental frequency In speech, the rate at which the vocal cords vibrate, symbolized as F_o, called *F-zero,* perceived by the listener as pitch.

Gapping The syntactic process of deletion in which subsequent occurrences of a verb are omitted in similar contexts, e.g., *Bill washed the grapes and Mary, the cherries.*

Geminates A sequence of two identical sounds; an alternative way of representing long or doubled segments.

Generic term A general term that applies to a whole class; the use of a word that ordinarily has the semantic feature [+ male] to refer to both sexes (e.g., *mankind* meaning "the human race"; the use of the [+ male] pronoun as the neutral form, as in *Everyone should do his duty*).

Genetically related Describes two or more languages that developed from a common, earlier language (e.g., French, Italian, and Spanish all developed from Latin).

Glides Sounds produced with little or no obstruction of the airstream that are always preceded or followed by a vowel (e.g., /w/ and /j/ in *we, you*).

Gloss A word in one language given to express the meaning of a word in another language (e.g., "house" is the gloss for the French word *maison*); a brief definition of a difficult word or expression.

Glottalic airstream mechanism Air in the pharynx moved through action of the glottis. It is the articulatory method for the production of implosive and ejective sounds.

Glottals/glottal stop Sounds produced with constriction at the glottis; when the air is stopped completely at the glottis by tightly closed vocal cords, a glottal stop is produced.

Glottis The opening between the vocal cords.

Goal The thematic role of the noun phrase toward whose referent the action of the verb is directed (e.g., *the theater* in *The kids went to the theater*).

Gradable pairs   Two antonyms related in such a way that more of one is less of the other (e.g., *warm* and *cool,* more warm is less cool and vice versa). Cf. **complementary pairs, relational opposites.**

Grammar   The mental representation of a speaker's linguistic competence; what a speaker knows about a language, including its phonology, morphology, syntax, semantics, and lexicon. A linguistic description of a speaker's mental grammar.

Grammar-translation   The method for teaching a second language (L2) by which the student memorizes words, inflected words, and syntactic rules and uses them to translate from English to L2 and vice versa.

Grammatical   Describes a well-formed sequence of words, one conforming to rules of syntax.

Grammatical case   See **case.**

Grammatical categories   Traditionally called "parts of speech"; expressions that can substitute for one another without loss of grammaticality (e.g., Noun Phrases).

Grammatical morpheme/word   Free function word or bound morpheme required by the syntactic rules (e.g., *to* and *s* in *he wants **to** go*). Cf. **inflectional morpheme.**

Grammatical relation   Anyone of several structural positions that a noun phrase may assume in a sentence. Cf. **subject, direct object.**

Grammaticality   Conformation to the rules of syntax.

Graphemes   The symbols of an alphabetic writing system; the letters of an alphabet.

Great Vowel Shift   A sound change that took place in English sometime between 1400 and 1600 C.E. in which seven long vowel phonemes were changed.

Grimm's Law   The description of a phonological change in the sound system of an early ancestor of the Germanic languages formulated by Jakob Grimm.

Hangul   An alphabet for writing the Korean language designed in the fifteenth century around the phonemic principle.

Hemidecorticates   Individuals with one brain hemisphere removed.

Hemiplegics   Individuals (including children) with acquired unilateral lesions of the brain who retain both hemispheres (one normal and one diseased).

Heteronyms   Different words spelled the same (i.e., homographs) but pronounced differently, (e.g. *bass,* meaning either "low tone" or "a kind of fish").

Hierarchical structure   The groupings, subgroupings, etc., of words in a phrase or sentence.

Hieroglyphics   A pictographic writing system used by the Egyptians around 4000 B.C.E.

Hiragana   A Japanese syllabary used to write native words of the language; may co-occur with ideographic characters.

Historical and comparative linguistics   The branch of linguistics that deals with how languages change, what kinds of changes occur, and why they occurred

Historical linguistics   See **historical and comparative linguistics.**

Holophrastic   The stage of child language acquisition in which one word = one sentence.

Homographs   Different words spelled identically, and possibly pronounced the same (e.g., *lead* the metal and *lead,* what leaders do).

Homonyms   Different words pronounced, and possibly spelled, the same (e.g., *to, too, two;* or *bat* the animal, *bat* the stick, and *bat* as in *bat the eyelashes*).

Homorganic consonants   Two sounds produced at the same place of articulation.

Hyponyms   A set of related words whose meanings are specific instances of a more general word (e.g., *red, white, blue,* etc., are hyponyms of the word *color*).

Hyponymy   The relationship between a general term such as *polygon* and specific instances of it, such as the word *triangle.*

Iconic; iconicity   A nonarbitrary relationship between form and meaning, such as the male and female symbols on toilet doors.

Ideogram, ideograph   A character of a word-writing system, often highly stylized, that represents a concept, or the pronunciation of the word representing that concept.

Idiolect   An individual's way of speaking, reflecting that person's grammar.

Idiom   An expression whose meaning may be unrelated to the meaning of its parts (e.g., *kick the bucket* meaning "to die").

Ill-formed   Describes an ungrammatical or anomalous sequence of words.

Illocutionary force   The effect of a speech act, such as a warning, a promise, a threat, a bet, etc. (e.g., the illocutionary force of *I resign!* is the act of resignation).

Imitation theory   A theory of child language acquisition that claims that children learn their language by imitating adult speech.

Immediately dominate   If a node labeled **A** is the first node above a node labeled **B** in a phrase structure tree, then **A** immediately dominates **B.**

Implosive   Sounds produced with a glottalic ingressive airstream.

Impoverished data   Refers to the incomplete, noisy, and unstructured utterances that children hear, including slips of the tongue, false starts, ungrammatical and incomplete sentences; and lack of negative evidence (which utterances are well formed and which are not). Also referred to as **poverty of the stimulus**.

Indo-European   The descriptive name given to the ancestor language of many modern language families, including Germanic, Slavic, Romance, etc.

Infix   A bound morpheme that is inserted in the middle of a word or stem.

Inflectional morphemes   Bound grammatical morphemes that are added to complete words according to rules of syntax, (e.g. third person singular verbal suffix -*s*).

Ingressive airstream mechanism   Method of producing speech sounds in which air is sucked into the vocal tract through the mouth during part of the articulation.

Innateness hypothesis   Scientific hypothesis that posits that the human species is genetically equipped to acquire universal grammar, which is the basis for all human languages. Cf. **universal grammar (UG).**

Instrument   The thematic role of the noun phrase whose referent is the means by which an action is performed (e.g., *a paper clip* in *Houdini picked the lock with a paper clip.*)

Intension   The nonreferential part of the meaning of an expression. Cf. **sense, extension.**

Interdentals   Sounds produced by inserting the tip of the tongue between the upper and lower teeth.

Internal borrowing   Cf. **analogic change.**

International Phonetic Alphabet (IPA)   The phonetic alphabet designed by the International Phonetic Association to be used to represent the sounds found in all human languages.

International Phonetic Association   The organization founded in 1888 to further phonetic research and develop the IPA.

Intonation   Pitch contour of phrase or sentence.

Intransitive verb   A verb that may not be followed by a noun phrase direct object in deep structure, e.g., *sleep.*

IPA   International Phonetic Association.

Ipsilateral   Refers to the processing of auditory signals by the same side of the brain in which the signal is received. Cf. **contralateral.**

Isogloss   The boundary separating one regional dialect or dialectal characteristic from another.

Jargon   Special words peculiar to the members of a profession or group. Cf. **argot.**

Jargon aphasia   Form of aphasia in which phonemes are substituted, often producing nonsense words. Such jargon is often produced by Wernicke's aphasics.

Kana   The characters of either of the two Japanese syllabaries, **Katakana** and **Hiragana.**

Kanji   The Japanese term for the Chinese characters used in Japanese writing.

Katakana   A Japanese syllabary generally used for writing loan words and to achieve the effect of italics.

Labials   Sounds articulated at the lips.

Labiodentals Sounds produced by touching the bottom lip to the upper teeth.

Language generation A computer process in which grammatical sentences and discourses are constructed as part of a human-computer interaction.

Larynx The structure of muscles and cartilage in the throat that contains the vocal cords; often called the "voice box."

Lateralization Term used to refer to any cognitive functions localized to one or the other side of the brain.

Laterals Sounds produced with air flowing past one or both sides of the tongue.

Lax vowels Short vowels produced with little tension in the vocal cords.

Length A prosodic feature referring to duration of segment. Two sounds may contrast in length (e.g., [+ long] long vs. [– long] short).

Level tones Relatively stable (nongliding) pitch on syllables of tone languages. Also called **register tones.**

Lexical ambiguity Ambiguity—multiple meanings—due to an ambiguous word (e.g., *He was lying on a stack of Bibles*).

Lexical category A syntactic category whose members are words (e.g., Noun, Verb, Article); those categories occurring only on the right side of phrase structure rules; those categories occurring just above the words in a phrase structure tree.

Lexical content morphemes Morphemes that constitute the major word classes—nouns, verbs, adjectives, adverbs. Cf. **open class.**

Lexical decision Task of subjects in psycholinguistic experiments who on presentation of a spoken or printed stimulus must decide whether it is a word or not.

Lexical gap Possible but nonoccurring words; forms that obey the phonological rules of a language yet have no meaning (e.g., *blick* in English).

Lexical insertion The collection of principles governing the position of words and morphemes in deep structure phrase structure trees.

Lexical paraphrases Paraphrases based on synonyms (e.g., *She lost her purse* and *She lost her handbag*).

Lexical semantics The subfield of semantics concerned with the meanings of words and the meaning relationships among words.

Lexicographer One who edits or works on a dictionary.

Lexicography The editing or making of a dictionary.

Lexicon The component of the grammar containing speakers' knowledge about morphemes and words; a speaker's mental dictionary.

Lingua franca The major language used in an area where speakers of more than one language live that permits communication and commerce among them.

Linguistic theory The principles that characterize all human languages; the linguist's goal is to discover the "laws of human language."

Liquids Sounds like /r/ and /l/ in which there is obstruction of the air, but not sufficient to cause friction.

Loan translations Compound words or expressions whose parts are translated directly into the borrowing language. Marriage of convenience is a loan translation borrowed from French *mariage de convenance.*

Loan words Words in one language whose origins are in another language (in Japanese *besiboru* ["baseball"] is a loan word from English). Cf. **borrowing.**

Localization The term used to refer to the fact that different areas of the brain appear to be responsible for representation and processing of distinct cognitive systems.

Location The thematic role of the noun phrase whose referent is the place where the action of the verb takes place (e.g., *Oslo* in *It snows in Oslo*).

Logical problem of language acquisition Refers to the question posed by Chomsky when he asked: "What accounts for the ease, rapidity and uniformity of language acquisition in the face of impoverished data?"

Logical representation Method of representing semantic information that utilizes notations from symbolic logic.

Logograms The symbols of a word-writing or logographic-writing system.

Logographic writing Word writing.

Lookahead parser A parser capable of scanning forward in a sequence of words to avoid mistaken assumptions.

Magnetic Resonance Imaging (MRI) A technique used to investigate the sites of brain lesions.

Main verb The nonauxiliary verb in the verb phrase in the deep structure of a sentence.

Manner of articulation The way the airstream is obstructed as it travels through the vocal tract. Stop, nasal, affricate, fricative are some manners of articulation. Cf. **place of articulation.**

Marked The term used to refer to that member of a gradable pair of antonyms that is not used in questions of degree (e.g., *low* is the marked member of the pair *high/low* because we ordinarily ask *How high is the mountain?* not **How low is the mountain?*); in a male/female pair of words, the word that contains a derivational morpheme, usually the female word (e.g. *princess* is marked, whereas *prince* is unmarked). Cf. **unmarked.**

Mass nouns Nouns that cannot ordinarily be enumerated, e.g., *milk, water; *two milks* is grammatical only when it means "two kinds of milk," or "two containers of milk," etc.

Maxim of manner A conversational convention that states that a speaker's discourse should be brief and orderly, and should avoid ambiguity and obscurity.

Maxim of quality A conversational convention that states that a speaker should not lie or make unsupported claims.

Maxim of quantity A conversational convention that states that a speaker's contribution to the discourse should be as informative as is required—neither more nor less.

Maxim of relevance A conversational convention that states that a speaker's

contribution to a discourse should always have a bearing on, and a connection with, the matter under discussion.

Maxims of conversation Conversational conventions such as the maxim of quantity that people appear to obey so as to give coherence to discourse.

Mean length of utterances (MLU) A measure used by child-language researchers to refer to the number of words or morphemes in a child's utterance; a more accurate measure of the acquisition stage than chronological age of a child.

Meaning Refers to the conceptual or semantic aspect of a word or sentence that permits us to comprehend the message being conveyed. The linguistic sign has both a form (its pronunciation) and a meaning.

Metaphor Nonliteral meaning (e.g., *The night has a thousand eyes,* meaning "One may be unknowingly observed at night").

Metathesis The phonological process that reorders segments, often by transposing two sequential sounds.

Metonym A word used in place of another word or expression to convey the same meaning (e.g., the use of *brass* to refer to military officers).

Metonymy The use of a word or expression in place of another word or expression that conveys the same meaning (e.g., *Washington* to mean *the government of the United States of America*).

Mimetic Similar to imitating, acting out, or miming.

Minimal pair (or set) A pair (or set) of words that are identical except for one phoneme, occurring in the same place in the string (e.g., *pain* /pen/, *bane* /ben/, *main* /men/).

Modularity The organization of the brain and mind into distinct, independent, and autonomous parts that interact with each other.

Monogenetic theory of language origin The belief that all languages originated from a single source.

Monomorphemic word   A word that consists of one morpheme.

Monophthong   Simple vowel. Cf. **diphthong.**

Monosyllabic   Having one syllable, e.g., words like *boy, through.*

Morpheme   Smallest unit of linguistic meaning or function.

Morphological parser   A parser that uses rules of word formation to decompose words into their component morphemes.

Morphological rules   Rules for the combination of morphemes to form stems and words.

Morphology   The study of the structure of words; the component of the grammar that includes the rules of word formation.

Morphophonemic orthography   A writing system, usually alphabetic, in which knowledge of how different forms of a word are pronounced is needed to read 100 percent correctly. For example, one needs to know English to know that the 'ea' in *please* represents a high front tense vowel, whereas in *pleasant* 'ea' represents a mid front lax vowel.

Morphophonemic rules   Rules that specify the pronunciation of morphemes; a morpheme may have more than one pronunciation determined by such rules (e.g., the plural morpheme in English is regularly pronounced /s/, /z/, or /əz/).

Narrowing   A semantic change in which the meaning of a word changes in time to become less encompassing (e.g., *deer* once meant "animal").

Nasal (nasalized) sounds   [+ Nasal] speech sounds produced with an open nasal passage permitting air to go through the nose as well as the mouth (e.g., /m, n, ŋ /). Cf. **oral sounds.**

Nasal cavity   The passageways between the throat and the nose through which air passes if the velum is open.

Natural class   A class of sounds characterized by a phonetic property or feature pertaining to all members of the set (e.g., class of stops).

Neo-Grammarians   A group of nineteenth-century linguists who claimed that sound shifts (i.e., changes in phonological systems) took place without any exceptions.

Neurolinguistics   The branch of linguistics concerned with the brain mechanisms underlying the acquisition and use of human language; the study of the neurobiology of language.

Neutralization rules   Phonological rules that obliterate the contrast between two phonemes in certain environments (e.g., in some dialects of English, /t/ and /d/ are both pronounced as voiced flaps intervocalically as in *writer, rider*).

Node   A labeled branch point in a phrase structure tree; part of the graphical depiction of a transition network represented as a circle, pairs of which are connected by arcs. Cf. **arc, phrase structure tree, transition network.**

Noncontinuants   Sounds in which air is totally constricted as it passes through the vocal tract. Cf. **stops, affricates.**

Nondistinctive features   Phonetics features of phonemes that are predictable by rule, e.g., aspiration in English.

Nonsense word   Permissible phonological forms without meanings, e.g., *slithy.*

Noun (N)   The syntactic category, also lexical category, of words that can comprise the core of a noun phrase such as *book, Jean, sincerity.* In many languages nouns have grammatical alternations for number, case, and gender, and are modified by determiners.

Noun Phrase (NP)   The syntactic category of expressions containing some form of a noun or pronoun and capable of functioning as the subject or as various objects in a sentence.

Nucleus   That part of the syllable that has the greatest acoustic energy; the vowel portion of a syllable, e.g., /i/ in /prist/ *priest.*

Obligatory transformation   A transformation that must apply in order for the derived sentence to be grammatical (e.g., the transformation which, in some grammatical theories, enforces subject-verb agreement).

Obstruents The class of sounds consisting of nonnasal stops, fricatives, and affricates. Cf. **sonorants.**

Onomatopoeia; onomatopoeic Describes words whose pronunciations suggest their meaning (e.g., *meow, buzz*).

Onset One or more phonemes that precede the syllable nucleus (e.g., /pr/ in /prist/ *priest*).

Open class The class of lexical content words; a category of words that commonly adds new words (e.g., nouns, verbs).

Optional transformation A transformation whose application is immaterial insofar as the grammaticality of the derived sentence is concerned, e.g., the transformation that moves adverbs.

Oral cavity The mouth area through which air passes during the production of speech.

Oral sounds Nonnasal speech sounds produced by raising the velum to close the nasal passage so that air can only escape through the mouth. Cf. **nasal sounds.**

Orthoepists Prescriptivist grammarians in the sixteenth to eighteenth centuries who were concerned with the pronunciation of words and the spelling/pronunciation relationship.

Orthography The written form of a language; spelling.

Overgeneralization Children's treatment of irregular verbs and nouns as if they were regular (e.g., *bringed, goed, foots, mouses,* for *brought, went, feet, mice,* respectively). This shows that the child has acquired the regular rules but has not yet learned that there are exceptions. Overgeneralization also refers to the process used by children to extend the meaning of a word (e.g., *papa* to refer to all men). Cf. **undergeneralization.**

Palatals Sounds produced by raising the front part of the tongue to the palate.

Palate The bony section of the roof of the mouth behind the alveolar ridge.

Paradigm A set of forms derived from a single root morpheme (e.g. *give, gives,*

given, gave, giving; or *woman, women, woman's women's*).

Parallel processing The ability of a computer to carry out several tasks simultaneously due to the presence of multiple central processors.

Paraphrases Sentences with the same meaning, except possibly for minor differences in emphasis (e.g., *He ran up a big bill* and *He ran a big bill up*).

Parse The act of determining the grammaticality of sequences of words according to certain rules of grammar and assigning a linguistic structure to the grammatical ones.

Parser A computer program that determines the grammaticality of sequences of words according to whatever rules of grammar are stored in the computer's memory, and assigns a linguistic structure to the grammatical ones.

Participle The form of a verb that occurs after the auxiliary verb *have* (e.g., *kissed* in *John has kissed many girls,* or *seen* in *I have seen trouble*).

Passive sentence A sentence in which the verbal complex contains a form of *to be* followed by a verb in its participle form (e.g., *The girl was kissed by the boy; The robbers must not have been seen*). In a passive sentence, the direct object of a transitive verb in deep structure functions as the subject in surface structure. Cf. **active sentence.**

Performance, linguistic The use of linguistic competence in the production and comprehension of language; behavior as distinguished from linguistic knowledge.

Performative sentence A sentence containing a performative verb used to accomplish some act. Performative sentences are affirmative and declarative, and are in first person, present tense (e.g., *I now pronounce you husband and wife,* when spoken by a justice of the peace in the appropriate situation, is an act of marrying).

Performative verb A verb, certain usages of which comprise a speech act (e.g., *resign* when the sentence *I resign!* is interpreted as an act of resignation).

Person deixis   The use of terms to refer to persons whose reference relies entirely on context (e.g., pronouns such as *I, he, you* and expressions such as *this child*). Cf. **deictic, time deixis, place deixis, demonstrative articles.**

Petroglyph   A drawing on rock made by prehistoric people.

Pharynx   The tube or cavity in the vocal tract through which the air passes during speech production.

Phone   A phonetic realization of a Phoneme.

Phoneme   A contrastive phonological segment whose phonetic realizations are predictable by rule (e.g., /p/ as in *pit* and /b/ in *bit*).

Phonemic principle   The principle underlying alphabetic writing systems in which one symbol typically represents one phoneme.

Phonemic representation   The phonological representation of words and sentences prior to the application of phonological rules.

Phonetic alphabet   Alphabetic symbols used to represent the phonetic segments of speech, in which there is a one-to-one relationship between sound and symbol.

Phonetic Features   Phonetic properties of segments (e.g., *voice, nasal, labial*) that distinguish one segment from another

Phonetic representation   The representation of words and sentences after the application of phonological rules; symbolic transcription of the pronunciation of words and sentences.

Phonetic similarity   Refers to sounds that share most of the same phonetic features.

Phonetics   The study of linguistic speech sounds, how they are produced (articulatory phonetics), how they are perceived (auditory or perceptual phonetics), and their physical aspects (acoustic phonetics).

Phonographic symbol   A symbol in a writing system that stands for the sounds of a word.

Phonological rules   Rules that state what speakers know about the predictable

aspects—the phonological regularities—of the speech sounds in their language; rules in the phonological component of a grammar that apply to phonemic representations to derive phonetic representations or pronunciation.

Phonology   The sound system of a language; the component of a grammar that includes the inventory of sounds (phonetic and phonemic units) and rules for their combination and pronunciation; the study of the sound systems of all languages.

Phonotactics   Sequential constraints; rules stating permissible strings of phonemes.

Phrasal category   A syntactic category composed of other syntactic categories; those categories occurring on the left side of phrase structure rules, e.g., noun phrase. Cf. **lexical category**

Phrasal semantics   See **sentential semantics.**

Phrasal verb   A verbal complex consisting of a lexical verb and a verbal particle, e.g., *look up.* The phrasal verb may be discontinuous, as in *look the number up.*

Phrase structure rules   Principles of grammar that specify the constituency of syntactic categories (e.g., NP → (Art) (Adj) N (PP)).

Phrase structure tree   A tree diagram with syntactic categories at each node that reveals both the linear and hierarchical structure of phrases and sentences.

Phrenology   A pseudoscience developed by Spurzheim on the basis of some of Gall's views in the nineteenth century; the practice of determining personality traits and intellectual ability by examination of the bumps on the skull.

Pictogram   A form of writing in which the symbols resemble the objects represented; a nonarbitrary form of writing.

Pidgin   A simple but rule-governed language developed for communication among speakers of mutually unintelligible languages, often based on one of those languages.

Pinyin   An alphabetic writing system for Mandarin Chinese using a western-style alphabet to represent individual sounds.

Pitch   The fundamental frequency as perceived by the listener.

Pitch contour   Intonation of a sentence.

Place deixis   The use of terms to refer to places whose reference relies entirely on context, e.g., *here, there, next door.* Cf. **deictic, time deixis, person deixis, demonstrative articles**.

Place of articulation   The part of the vocal tract at which constriction occurs during the production of speech sounds. Cf. **manner of articulation.**

Plosives   Oral or nonnasal stop consonants, so called because the air that is stopped explodes with the release of the closure.

Polyglot   A person who speaks many languages.

Polymorphemic word   Word consisting of more than one morpheme.

Polysemous   Describes a single word with several closely related but slightly different meanings (e.g., *face,* as in *the face of a person, a building, or a clock*).

Positron Emission Tomography (PET)   Method to detect changes in brain activities and relate these changes to focal brain damage and cognitive tasks.

Possessor   The thematic role of the noun phrase to whose referent something belongs (e.g., *the dog* in *The tail of the dog got caught in the door*).

Poverty of the stimulus   See **impoverished data.**

Pragmatics   The study of how context and situation affect meaning.

Predictable feature   A nondistinctive, noncontrastive, redundant phonetic feature of a phone (e.g., aspiration is a predictable feature of English voiceless stops that occur initially in stressed syllables).

Prefix   Bound morpheme that occurs before a root or stem of a word; affix that is attached to the beginning of a morpheme or word.

Preposition (P)   The syntactic category, also lexical category, of words that occur first in a prepositional phrase.

Prepositional object   The grammatical relation of the noun phrase that occurs immediately below a prepositional phrase (PP) in deep structure.

Prepositional phrase (PP)   The syntactic category occurring within both noun phrases and verb phrases consisting of a preposition followed by a noun phrase in deep structure.

Prescriptive grammar   Rules of grammar brought about by grammarians' attempts to legislate what speakers' grammatical rules should be, rather than what they are.

Prestige dialect   That dialect that is usually spoken by those in positions of power and the one deemed to be correct by prescriptive grammarians.

Presupposition   Implicit assumptions about the world required to make an utterance meaningful or appropriate (e.g., *Take some more tea!* presupposes that you already had some tea).

Primes   The basic formal units of sign languages corresponding to phonological elements of spoken language.

Priming   The effect on response time of words previously read or heard on the accessing of subsequent words.

Productive   Refers to morphological rules that can be used freely to form new words.

Proper names   Words that refer to persons, places, and other entities with unique reference insofar as the speaker and listener are concerned. Usually capitalized in writing.

Prosodic feature   Duration (length), pitch, or loudness of vowel sounds.

Proto-Germanic   The name given by linguists to the language that was an ancestor of English, German, and other Germanic languages.

Protolanguage   The first identifiable language from which genetically related languages developed.

Psycholinguistics   The branch of linguistics concerned with linguistic performance, language acquisition, and speech production and comprehension.

Pulmonic egressive   Speech sounds produced by movement of lung air flowing through the vocal tract and out the mouth or nose. Cf. **glottalic airstream mechanism, ingressive airstream mechanism velaric airstream mechanism.**

Rebus principle   Using a pictogram for its phonetic value (e.g., printing a picture of a bee to represent the verb *be* or the sound [b]).

Reduced vowels   Unstressed vowels. In English all unstressed nonfinal vowels are reduced to [ə] schwa.

Redundant   A nondistinctive, nonphonemic feature of a phone; the value (+ or −) of a phonetic feature that is predictable either from its context or from other feature values of the segment (e.g., [+ voicing] is redundant for any nasal phoneme in English since all nasals are voiced).

Reduplication   A morphological process that repeats or copies all or part of a word to change its meaning, i.e., to derive a new word.

Reference   That part of the meaning of a noun phrase that associates it with some entity. That part of the meaning of a declarative sentence that associates it with a truth value, either *true* or *false.* Also called **extension.** Cf. **referent, sense.**

Referent   The entity designated by a noun phrase (e.g., the referent of *John* in *John knows Sue* is the actual person under discussion named John).

Reflexive pronoun   A pronoun ending with -self that requires a noun-phrase antecedent within the same S (e.g., *A gnome bit himself).*

Register   A stylistic variant of a language appropriate to a particular social setting. Also called **style.**

Register tones   Level tones; high, mid, or low tones.

Regular sound correspondence   The occurrence of different sounds in the same position of the same word in two different languages or dialects, with this parallel holding for a significant number of words (e.g., [aj] in non-Southern American English corresponds to [a:] in Southern American English). Also found between newer and older forms of the same language.

Reinforcement theory   A theory of child-language acquisition that claims that children are conditioned into speaking correctly by being negatively reinforced for "errors" and positively reinforced for "correct" usage.

Relational opposites   Pairs of antonyms in which one describes a relationship between two objects and the other describes the same relationship when the two objects are reversed (e.g., *parent* and *child; John is the parent of Susie* describes the same relationship between John and Susie as *Susie is the child of John).* Cf. **gradable pairs, complementary pairs.**

Retroflex sounds   Sounds produced by curling the tip of the tongue back behind the alveolar ridge.

Retronym   An expression that would have once been redundant, but which changes in society or technology have made nonredundant (e.g., *silent movie,* which was redundant before the advent of the "talkies").

Rhyme   The nucleus + coda of a syllable (e.g., the /en/ of /ren/ *rain).*

Root   Nonaffix lexical-content morpheme, which cannot be analyzed into smaller parts, e.g., *system, boy,* or *cran).*

Rounded vowels   Vowel sounds produced with pursed lips (e.g., [o, u]).

Rules of syntax   Principles of grammar that account for (1) the grammaticality of sentences; (2) word order; (3) structural ambiguity; and much more.

Savants   Individuals who show special abilities in one cognitive area while being deficient in others. Linguistic savants are fluent in language and deficient in general intelligence.

Segment   (1) An individual sound that occurs in a language. (2) The act of dividing utterances into individuals sounds, morphemes, words, and phrases.

Semantic features   A notational device for expressing the presence or absence of semantic properties by pluses and minuses (e.g., baby is [+ young], [− abstract]).

Semantic network   A network of arcs and nodes used to represent semantic information about sentences.

Semantic properties The components of meaning of a word (e.g., "young" is a semantic property of *baby, colt, puppy*).

Semantics The study of the linguistic meaning of morphemes, words, phrases, and sentences.

Sense That part of the meaning of an expression which, together with context, determines its referent. Also called **intension.** For example, knowing the sense or intension of a noun phrase such as *the president of the United States in 1962* allows one to determine that John F. Kennedy is the referent. Cf. **reference.**

Sentence (S) A syntactic category of expressions consisting minimally of a noun phrase followed by a verb phrase in deep structure.

Sentential semantics The subfield of semantics concerned with the meaning of syntactic units larger than the word.

Sibilants The class of sounds that includes affricates, and alveolar and palatal fricatives, characterized acoustically by a hissing sound.

Siglish The name used for Signed English, consisting of the replacement of each spoken English word (and morpheme) by a sign.

Sign (1) Term used in traditional linguistics to refer to a form arbitrarily related to a meaning, that is, a morpheme or word. (2) A single gesture (possibly with complex meaning) in the sign languages used by the deaf that is equivalent to the term "word" in spoken languages.

Sign languages The languages used by the deaf in which hand and body gestures are the forms of morphemes and words.

Situational context Knowledge of who is speaking, who is listening, what objects are being discussed, and general facts about the world we live in, used to interpret meaning.

Slang Words and phrases used in casual speech often invented and spread by close-knit social or age groups.

Slip of the tongue; Speech error An involuntary deviation of an intended utterance. Cf. **spoonerism.**

Sluicing The syntactic process in which material following a *wh-* word is deleted when it is identical to previous material (e.g., *John is talking with* is deleted from the second clause in *John is talking with someone but nobody knows who _____*).

Sonorants The class of sounds that includes vowels, glides, liquids, and nasals; nonobstruents. Cf. **obstruents.**

Sound shift Historical phonological change.

Sound symbolism Certain sound combinations that occur in semantically similar words, such as *gl* in *gleam, glisten, glitter,* which all relate to sight.

Sound writing A term sometimes used to mean a writing system in which one sound is represented by one letter. Sound-writing systems do not employ the phonemic principle and are similar to phonetic transcriptions.

Source The thematic role of the noun phrase whose referent is the place from which an action originates (e.g., *Mars* in *They just arrived from Mars*).

Source language In automatic machine translation, the language being translated. Cf. **target language, automatic machine translation.**

Specific Language Impairment (SLI) Difficulty faced by certain children with no other cognitive deficits in acquiring language; they are much slower than the average child but only their linguistic ability is affected.

Speech act The nonlinguistic accomplishments of an utterance, such as a warning or a promise, as determined in part by context (e.g., *There is a bear behind you* is a warning in certain contexts).

Speech recognition Computer processing for transcribing speech.

Speech synthesis An electronic process in which speech is reproduced.

Speech understanding Computer processing for interpreting speech.

Spelling pronunciation Pronouncing a word as it is spelled, irrespective of its actual pronunciation by native speakers (e.g., pronouncing *Wednesday* as "wed-ness-day").

Spirants   Another term for **fricatives.**

Split brain   The result of an operation for epilepsy in which the corpus callosum is cut, thus separating the brain into its two halves; split-brain patients are studied to determine the role of each hemisphere in cognitive and language processing.

Spoonerism   A speech error in which phonemic segments are reversed or exchanged as in *tip of the slongue* for the intended *slip of the tongue*, named after the nineteenth-century Oxford don Reverend Spooner.

Standard   The dialect (regional or social) considered to be the norm.

Standard American English (SAE)   An idealized dialect of English that is considered by some prescriptive grammarians to be the proper form of English.

Stem   A root morpheme combined with affix morphemes; other affixes can be added to a stem to form a more complex stem.

Stops   [– Continuant] sounds in which the airflow is briefly but completely stopped in the oral cavity (e.g., /p, n, g/).

Stress, Stressed syllable   A syllable with relatively greater length, loudness, and/or higher pitch. Includes primary and secondary stress in a word or phrase. Also called **accent.**

Structural ambiguity   The phenomenon where the same sequence of words has two or more meanings based on different phrase structure analyses (e.g., *He saw a boy with a telescope*).

Structure dependent   (1) Describes the fact that the application of transformational rules is determined by phrase structure properties, as opposed to structureless sequences of words or specific sentences. (2) Describes how children construct rules using their knowledge of syntactic structure irrespective of the specific words in the structure or their meaning.

Styles   Situation dialects (e.g., formal speech, casual speech); also called **register.**

Subcategorization   Restrictions on a verb specifying which syntactic categories can and cannot occur with it (e.g., specification that the verb *sleep* may not be followed by a noun phrase, but the verb *find* must be followed by a noun phrase).

Subject-Verb agreement   The addition of an inflectional morpheme to the main verb required by some property of the noun phrase subject, such as number or gender. In English it is the requirement that whenever the subject of a sentence is third-person singular, the main verb must have an "s" or "es" added to it (orthographically)—e.g., *The boys I know think* but *The boy I know thinks.*

Subject   The grammatical relation of a noun phrase when it appears immediately below the S in a phrase structure.

Suffix   Bound morpheme that occurs after the root or stem of a word; affix that is attached to the end of a morpheme or word.

Suppletive forms   A term used to refer to inflected morphemes in which the regular rules do not apply (e.g., *went* as the past tense of *go*).

Suprasegmentals   Prosodic features (e.g., length, tone).

Surface structure   The final transformationally derived structure, which is the end result of applying transformational rules to a deep structure and all but the last derived structure. It is syntactically closest to actual utterances.

Syllabary   The symbols of a syllabic writing system.

Syllabic   A phonetic feature present in sounds that constitute the nucleus of syllables; all vowels are syllabic, and liquids and nasals may be syllabic in such words as *towel, button, bottom.*

Syllabic writing   A writing system in which each syllable in the language is represented by its own symbol.

Synonyms   Different words with the same or nearly the same meaning (e.g., *purse* and *handbag*).

Syntactic category   Units of phrase structure that can substitute for one another without loss of grammaticality (e.g., noun phrase). Traditionally called "part of speech."

Syntactic classes/categories   Same as **grammatical categories.**

Syntactic label   A term used for indicating the syntactic categories in a phrase structure tree.

Syntax   The rules of sentence formation; the component of the mental grammar that represents speakers' knowledge of the structure of phrases and sentences.

Taboo   A term used in reference to words (or acts) that are not to be used (or performed) in "polite society."

Tap   Sound in which the tongue touches the alveolar ridge, as in some British pronunciations of /r/. Also called **flap.**

Target language   In automatic machine translation, the language into which the source language is translated. Cf. **source language, automatic machine translation.**

Teaching grammars   A set of language rules written to help speakers learn a foreign language or a different dialect of their language.

Telegraphic speech   Utterances of children after the two-word stage when many grammatical morphemes are omitted.

Tense/Lax   Features that divide vowels into two classes. Tense vowels are often slightly longer in duration and higher in tongue position and pitch than the corresponding lax vowels. In English [+ tense] vowels include: [i, e, u, o] and their [– tense] lax counterparts [ɪ, ɛ, ʊ, ɔ].

Thematic role   The semantic relationship between the verb and the noun phrases of a sentence, such as **agent, theme, location, instrument, goal, source.**

Theme   The thematic role of the noun phrase whose referent undergoes the action of the verb (e.g., *Martha* in *George hugged Martha*).

Theta-criterion   A proposed universal principle stating that a particular thematic role may only occur once in a sentence.

Time deixis   The use of terms to refer to time whose reference relies entirely on

context (e.g., *now, then, tomorrow, next month*). Cf. **deictic, deixis, demonstrative articles, person deixis, place deixis.**

Tip of the Tongue; TOT   The difficulty encountered from time to time in finding a particular word. Anomic aphasics suffer from an extreme form of this problem.

Tone   Contrastive pitch of syllables in languages where two words may be identical except for such differences in pitch. Cf. **register tones, contour tones.**

Topicalization   A transformation that moves a syntactic element to the front of a sentence, deriving, for example, *dogs I love* from *I love dogs.*

Transcription, phonemic   The phonemic representation of speech sounds using phonetic symbols, ignoring phonetic details that are predictable by rule, usually given between slashes (e.g., /pat/ /spat/ for *pot, spot*).

Transcription, phonetic   The representation of speech sounds using phonetic symbols between square brackets. They may reflect nondistinctive predictable features (e.g., [pʰat], [spat] for *pot, spot*).

Transformational rule, Transformation   A structurally based formal statement relating two phrase structure trees, one of which is basic—nearer to deep structure—and the other of which is derived—nearer to surface structure. (E.g., the passive transformation relates the basic structure underlying *Fido bit Lee* to the derived structure of *Lee was bitten by Fido.*)

Transformationally induced ambiguity   An ambiguity that results when two different deep structures with two different meanings are transformed into a single surface structure (e.g., *George wants the presidency more than Martha*).

Transition network   A method for representing rules of grammar that can be graphically depicted by means of nodes connected by arcs. Cf. **node, arc, augmented transition network.**

Transitive verb   A verb that must be followed by a noun-phrase direct object in deep structure.

Tree diagram   A graphical representation of the hierarchical structure of a phrase or sentence.

Trills   Sounds in which the tip of the tongue vibrates against the roof of the mouth.

Truth conditions   The circumstances that must be known to determine whether a sentence is true, and therefore part of the meaning of declarative sentences.

Unaspirated   Voiceless sounds in which the vocal cords start vibrating immediately upon release of constriction (e.g., [p] in *spit*). Cf. **aspirated.**

Unbound   Cf. **free.**

Unconditioned sound change Phonological change that occurs in all phonetic contexts.

Undergeneralization   Children's use of a general term such as *dog* to refer only to a single instance (e.g., *Fido* or the family pet).

Underlying representation   Phonemic representation.

Underlying structure   (1) The phrase structure tree manifestation of a grammatical sequence of words. (2) Deep structure and any structure resulting from the application of transformational rules except surface structure.

Underspecification   The omission of the values of predictable features in a phonemic matrix, revealing the redundancy of such features.

Ungrammatical   Describes an ill-formed sequence of words, one not conforming to rules of syntax. Cf. **ill-formed.**

Uninterpretable   A condition whereby a sentence cannot be interpreted because of nonsense words, e.g., *All mimsy were the borogoves.*

Universal Grammar (UG)   The principles or properties that pertain to the grammars of all human languages; the initial state of the language faculty. Cf. **language faculty.** The principles of Universal Grammar that determine the class of human languages that can be acquired unconsciously, without instruction, in the early years of life.

Unmarked   The term used to refer to that member of a gradable pair of antonyms used in questions of degree (e.g., *high* is the unmarked member of *high/low*). In a male/female pair of words, the word that does not contain a derivational morpheme, usually the male word (e.g., *prince* is unmarked, whereas *princess* is marked). Cf. **marked.**

Uvula   The fleshy appendage hanging down from the end of the velum or soft palate.

Uvular   A sound produced by raising the back of the tongue to the uvula.

Velaric airstream mechanism   Method by which clicks are produced in which there is a slight inflow of air into the mouth.

Velars   Sounds produced by raising the back of the tongue to the soft palate or velum.

Velum   The soft palate; the part of the roof of the mouth behind the hard palate.

Verb (V)   The syntactic category, also lexical category, of words that can occur as the first syntactic unit in a verb phrase in deep structure.

Verb Phrase (VP)   The syntactic category of expressions containing a verb and possibly other syntactic units such as noun phrases and prepositional phrases, e.g., *gave the book to the child.*

Verbal particle   A word that resembles a preposition in form, and co-occurs with a particular verb to give a phrasal verb that has a meaning different than the meaning of the verb without the particle (e.g., *ran up* in *they ran up a big bill*). Unlike true prepositions, verbal particles may occur after a direct object, as in *they ran a big bill up.* Cf. **they ran a big hill up.* Cf. **phrasal verb.**

Verner's Law   The description of a phonological change in the sound system of certain Indo-European languages. It was formulated by Karl Verner as an explanation to some of the exceptions to Grimm's Law. Cf. **Grimm's Law.**

Voiced sounds   Speech sounds produced with closed and vibrating vocal cords.

Voiceless sounds Speech sounds produced with open and nonvibrating vocal cords.

Vowel A sound produced without significant constriction of the air flowing through the mouth.

Well-formed Describes a grammatical sequence of words, one conforming to rules of syntax. Cf. **grammatical.**

Wernicke's aphasia The type of aphasia resulting from damage to Wernicke's area.

Wernicke's area The back (posterior) part of the left brain that if damaged causes a specific type of aphasia.

Wernicke, Carl Neurologist who showed that damage to specific parts of the left cerebral hemisphere cause differential language disorders.

Word writing A system of writing in which each character represents a word or morpheme of the language (e.g., Chinese). Sometimes called ideographic or logographic writing.

Zero form A term used by Hindu grammarians to refer to the absence of any phonological form of a unit of meaning (e.g., the plural "morpheme" of *sheep* in *sheep are beautiful*).

Index

A (article), 194–195
AAE. *See* African American English (AAE)
Abbreviations, 88
Abstract unit, 265–266
Accented vowels or syllables, 240
Accents, 277
  as pronunciation differences, 401
Accidental gaps, 79, 271, 307
Acoustic components, of speech, 378–379
Acoustic phonetics, 216, 364
Acoustic signal. *See* Speech production
Acoustic terms, 364
Acquired dyslexia, 44, 47
Acquisition of language, 317–357
  ASL, 345–346
  biological foundations of, 339–346
  by children, 328–338
  by chimpanzees, 350–355
  critical-age hypothesis, 342–344
  first sounds, 319–320
  first words, 321–324
  innateness hypothesis, 339–342
  logical problem of, 340
  second language, 346–349
  stages in, 318–328
  telegraphic speech, 325–328
  two-word stage, 324–325
Acronyms, 86–87. *See also* Change, language
Active sentence, 145–147
Addition rules
  feature, 284–285
  segment, 285–286
Adjective (Adj), 67, 84, 114
  proper names and, 171
  suffixes and, 77–78
Adverb (Adv), 67, 114
  moving of, 139, 142
Aesop's fables, 22
Affixes, stem morphemes and, 75
Affricates, 231, 239
African American English (AAE), 16, 412–417
  history of, 416–417
  phonology of, 413–414
  syntactic differences with SAE, 414–415
African American Vernacular English (AAVE), 16n, 412n

African languages, 216, 223, 267, 284, 312, 421, 472, 494
Afro-Asiatic languages, 472, 477
Age. *See also* Acquisition of language; Children's acquisition of language
  second language acquisition and, 347
Agent (doer), 175
Agrammatic aphasics, 45–46
Agreement, 143
  marker, 91
  modifier-noun, 337
  rules, 337
  subject-verb, 143, 337
Airstream mechanisms, 223
Akan (Twi), 68, 241, 242, 264–265, 266, 274, 283–284, 288, 461
Albanian, 460, 474
Alice's Adventures in Wonderland (Carroll), 457
Allomorphs, 295
Allophones, 260–261, 266, 288
Alphabet
  consonantal, 498
  cuneiform writing and, 496
  Latin (Roman), 504
  phonetic, 218–221
  Roman, 220
  Shaw and, 219
  sign language and, 21
Alphabetic spelling, 217
Alphabetic writing, 498
  consonantal, 502
Alsted (German philosopher), 19, 27
Alveolar fricatives, 230
Alveolar ridge, 224
Alveolars, 224, 234, 239, 240
Alveolar stop, 230, 290
Alveopalatals, 224
Amala, 342
Aman, Reinhold, 432
Ambiguous, ambiguity, 109, 117, 163–164
  of sounds, 214
  structural, 110
  transformationally induced, 156
American Anthropological Association, 51
American Dialect Society, on AAE, 417

American Dictionary of the English Language, An (Webster), 66

American English. *See also* British English; English; English language
and African American English (AAE), 412–417
and Chicano English (ChE), 419–420
corpus of, 375–376
dialects of, 402
feature specifications for consonants and vowels, 273–274
impact of immigrants' languages on, 402–403
and Latino (Hispanic) English, 417–420
phonemic features of consonants, 275
phonetic symbols for consonants, 233
pronunciation of, 403–404
spoken, 376
Standard American English (SAE) and, 408–409
stress patterns in, 277
syntactic differences in, 406–407
vowel classification for, 237

American Heritage Dictionary, 434

American Indian languages, 223, 241, 410, 460, 471, 472, 488–489, 494
Navajo, 162

American Sign Language (ASL), 7, 8
acquisition of, 345–346
babbling and, 321
change in, 450
DECIDE sign in, 21, 22
and language acquisition, 344–345
minimal pairs in, 258–259
morphology of, 81–82
syntax in, 147

Amerindian protolanguages, 472

AMESLAN. *See* American Sign Language

Analogic change, 481

Analogy, 88
language acquisition and, 330

Analytic, 208

Anaphora, 192–193

Ancestral protolanguages, 451–452

Androcles and the Lion (Shaw), 219

Animal languages, 22–26
communication by, 24–26

Animals
bird songs and, 344–345
language acquisition by chimpanzees, 350–355

Anomalous, 184–185

Anomaly, 184–187

Anomia, 48

Anterior sounds, 240

Antonyms, 79, 166–168

Aphasia, 44–48
agrammatic, 45–46
Broca's, 37, 39
jargon, 46
Wernicke's, 37, 39, 46–47

Apostrophe, 506

Appropriate styles, 318

Arabic, 231, 267, 409, 461, 502

Arabic numerals, 500

Arabs, grammars and, 15

Arawaken language, 71

Arbitrary meaning, 5–6, 7, 8

Arcs, 385

Argot, 427–428

Armenian, 410

Art(s), in sign language, 21

Article (Art), 67, 170, 337
demonstrative, 200
Determiners as, 115
proper name and, 170
The and *A,* 194–195

Articulation
ease of, 280, 481
vocal tract and, 222

Articulators, 223

Articulatory phonetics, 216, 221–242
affricates, 231
airstream mechanisms, 223
consonants and, 223–233, 234
diacritics, 242–243
fricatives, 230–231
glides, 232–233
liquids, 232
major sound classes in, 239–240
manners of articulation, 225–227
nasal and oral sounds, 228–229
place of articulation of English consonants, 225
places of articulation, 223–225
prosodic suprasegmental features and, 240–242
stops, 229–230
tone and intonation, 240–242
vocal tract and, 222
vowels and, 234–238

Artificial language, chimpanzees and, 351, 352

Asia Minor, cuneiform writing in, 496

Asian languages, 241

Ask, 197

ASL. *See* American Sign Language (ASL)

Aspirated sounds, 226–227

Aspiration, 263, 265, 266, 284–285, 295
Assimilation, 481
Assimilation rules, 280–283. *See also*
    Dissimilation rules
    feature changing rules and, 283–284
Assyrians, 496
Asymmetry of abilities, 49–51
Atlases, dialect, 404–406
ATN. *See* Augmented transition networks
    (ATN)
Audio-lingual method, 349
Auditory phonetics, 216
Augmented transition networks (ATN), 386
Augustine, 319
Australian English, euphemisms in, 433
Austronesian family, 477
Automatic machine translation, 374–375
Autonomy of language, 49–51
    asymmetry of abilities and, 49–51
    genetic evidence for, 51
Auxiliary Verbs (Aux), 114, 139, 140
    placement of, 479
Azerbaijan, 410

Babbling, 320–321
Babies. *See* Children's acquisition of language
Babylonians, 496
Back-formations, 87–88
Back vowel, 236
Bacon, Roger, 346
Baltic languages, 474
Banned languages, 409–411
Bantu languages, 223, 307, 313
Bar-Hillel, Yeshua, 374
"Be"
    deletion in AAE, 415
    habitual in AAE, 415
Becanus, J. G., 54
Behavior, language styles and, 426
Beijing (Peking) dialect, 421
Bellugi, Ursula, 21n, 45, 82n, 258n, 345
Bengali, 439, 474
Beowulf, 449
Berko-Gleason, Jean. *See* Gleason, Jean Berko
Berwick, Robert, 389
Bever, Thomas, 353n
Bierce, Ambrose, 65
Bilabials, 223, 234, 239, 240
    stops, 230
Bilingual speakers, 347
    Latino dialects and, 418–419
    Quebecois as, 418

Biological foundations of language acquisition,
    339–342
Biology, language, species development, and,
    55–56
Bird calls, 24
Bird songs, 24, 344–345
Black English (BE), 16n, 412n. *See also*
    African American English (AAE)
Blends, 89, 372
Bloody, use of word, 431
Bloom, L. M., 324–325
Bloomfield, Leonard, 317
Blumstein, S., 46n
Bobrow, Daniel, 383
Bontoc language, 72
Boothe, A. D., 374n
Bootstrapping, 338
Bopp, Franz, 464
Borrowed words, 460–462
Borrowings, from other languages, 459–462
Bottom-up processing, 367
Bound morphemes, 71, 73, 95
    derivational morphemes and, 76
    inflectional morphemes as, 91
Bourdillon, Frances William, 187
Bow-wow theory, 54
Brain
    aphasia and, 44–48
    computer reconstruction of, 44
    conceptual knowledge and, 48
    description of, 34–35
    historical beliefs about, 33
    images of, 34
    and language, 33–58
    language autonomy and, 49–51
    lesions in, 38–40
    modularity of, 35–48
    MRI and PET studies of, 37–38
    neurolinguistics and, 33, 43–44
    specialization for language vs. sound, 42
    split, 40–42
Brainvox computer program, 44
    MRI data, 34
Bremond, J., 25n
Breton language, 410–411, 474
British English, 232, 403–404, 407. *See also*
    American English; English language
    infixes in, 72–73
    stress in, 277
British RP (Received Pronunciation), 238, 404
Brittany. *See* Breton language
Broadening, 463
Broca, Paul, 36

Broca's aphasia, 37, 39
Broca's area, 36–37, 38, 45
Brown, Roger, 327, 329, 358–359
Bulgarian, 474
Burke, Virginia M., 403, 404n
Burmese, 241
Burton, Robert, 279
Bushmen, languages of, 223
Busnel, R. G., 25n
Butler, Samuel, 184

Cajun English, 410
Cajun French, 410
Cameroonian language, 236
Cameroonian Pidgin (CP), 424
Campbell, L., 91n
Canterbury Tales, The (Chaucer), 449–450
Cantonese, 232, 400
Capital letters, 505
Carlyle, Thomas, 253
Carroll, Lewis, 12, 75, 89, 90, 93, 108, 158,
    169, 185, 363, 371, 450, 457, 510
Case, 177–178
Case endings, 456–457
Case theory, 177
Cassidy, Frederick G., 406
Categories, repetition of, 119
Caucasus languages, 223
Causative force, 176
Cave drawings, 493
Caxton, William, 461
Cazden, Courtney, 328
Celtic, 410, 460, 461, 474
Cerebral hemispheres, 35
Cervantes, Miguel de, 187
Change, language, 449–483
    analogic, 481
    assimilative process, 481
    borrowings and, 459–462
    ease of articulation, 481
    extinct and endangered languages, 472–473
    genetic classification of languages, 473–477
    Great Vowel Shift and, 454–456
    lexical change, 459–463
    loss of words, 462
    morphological change, 456–457
    new words, 462
    phonological change, 452–456
    purists and, 16–17, 470–471
    reasons for, 480–482
    reconstructing "dead" languages, 464–472
    sound change, 450–452

syntactic change, 457–459
    types of languages, 478–480
Characters (Chinese). *See* Ideograms
Chaucer, Geoffrey, 449–450, 505
ChE. *See* Chicano English
Cherokee language, 501
Chicano English (ChE), 419–420
Children, with brain lesions, 38–40
Children's acquisition of language, 318,
    328–338
    analogy and, 330
    construction of rules and grammar in,
        331–332
    critical-age hypothesis and, 342–344
    first sounds, 319–320
    formal instruction and, 331–333
    imitation and, 328–329
    innateness hypothesis of, 341–342
    meaning of words and, 337–338
    morphology and, 334–336
    phonology and, 333–334
    reinforcement and, 329–330
    structure-dependent rules and, 340–341
    syntax and, 336–337
Chimpanzees, language acquisition by,
    350–355
Chinese, 232, 236, 241, 274, 337, 400, 421,
    499–500, 501
Chinese Sign Language (CSL), 7, 8
Chomsky, Carol, 348
Chomsky, Noam, 3, 9, 14, 19, 55, 61, 141n,
    185n, 318n, 340, 353, 389
Church, Russell M., 354
Churchill, Winston, 15
Circumfixes, 73
Civil Tongue, A (Newman), 16
Clarke, Arthur C., 377
Classes, grammars and, 16
Classification of languages, 478–480
Clauses, 505
Clerc, Laurent, 450
Clever Hans, 354
Clicks, as speech sounds, 216, 223
Clipping, 88
Closed class words, 67, 68
Coarticulation, 281
Cockney language, 439
Coda, 269
Code-switching, 418
Cognates, 465–467
Cognitive module, language as, 36
Coinage, 82–89. *See also* Change, language
Colloquial language, 427

Colloquial speech, nasal consonants in, 237n
Commas, 505
Communication. *See also* Language; Society
  by animals, 24–26
  barriers to, 400–401
Communicative competence, 318
Comparative linguistics, 464–467. *See also*
  Comparative reconstruction
Comparative method, 468
Comparative reconstruction, 464–470
Competence, linguistic, 12
Complementary distribution, 261–262
Complementary pairs, 166
Complements, 261
Compounds
  forming, 83–86
  meaning of, 85–86
  pronunciation of, 85–86
  universality of, 86
Comprehension, 361, 363–369
    models and experimental studies,
    367–369
Computational linguistics, 374
  computers that talk and listen, 376–377
  machines for understanding speech,
    381–388
  machine translation and, 374–375
  speech synthesis and, 377–381
  text processing and, 375–376
Computers
  grammar transition networks of, 385
  language processing by, 388–389
  models of grammars, 388–389
  parallel processing by, 389
  pragmatic processing by, 387–388
  semantic processing by, 386–387
  speech processing by, 83
  speech recognition by, 382–383
  speech synthesis by, 377–381
  speech understanding by, 377, 380–388
Concept, 7
Conceptual knowledge
  categories of, 48
  about language, 65
Concordance, 376
Conditioned sound change, 469–470
Conjunctions, 67
Connotative meaning, 433
Conscious knowledge, 13
Consonant, 223–233, 234, 239
  anterior, 240
  coronals, 239
  in English words, 234

feature specifications for American English,
  273–274
homorganic, 272
labial, 239
manners of articulation, 225–233
nasal, 264–265, 272
nasalization of, 280
phonemic features in American English, 275
phonetic symbols for American English
  consonants, 233
places of articulation, 223–225
sibilants, 240
word-final, 285–286
Consonantal alphabet, 498
Consonantal alphabet writing, 502
Consonant Cluster Simplification rule, in AAE,
  413
Consonant harmony, 333
Constituents, 112
Constituent structures, 112
Constituent structure tree, 115
Constraints
  coordinate structure, 341
  sequential, 269–271, 297–300
Construction, language changes and, 458
Content words, 67, 159
Context, 280, 281
  deixis and, 199–201
  linguistic, 191–195
  morphemes in, 74
  situational, 195–199
Continuants, 229, 239
Continuity view, 55
Contour tones, 241, 242
Contraction rules, 458
Contractions, 506
Contradiction, 180
Contradictory, 208
Contralateral brain function, 35
Contrastive stress, 506
Contrast words, 254
Convention, 122–124
Conventional signs, 7
Conversation, maxims of, 195–196
Cooperative Principle, 196
Coordinate structure, 341
Coordinate structure constraint, 341
Coreferential, 174
Coreferentiality, pronouns and, 183–184
Coronals, 239
Corpus, 375
Corpus callosum, 35
Cortex, 34

Count nouns, 161
Courtroom, presuppositions and, 199
Cover symbols, 243, 263
Cowper, William, 467
CP. *See* Cameroonian Pidgin
Cratylus (Plato), 54
Creativity, linguistic, 9–10
Creole languages, 425
Creolized language, 425
Cresti, E., 327n
Cries of nature theory of language, 54
Critic, The (Sheridan), in sign language, 21
Critical age, 342–344
CSL. *See* Chinese Sign Language (CSL)
Culture. *See* Society
Cuneiform, 495–496
Curtiss, Susan, 343
Cyrillic alphabet, 504
Czech, 231, 474

Dahl, H., 376n
Damasio, Antonio, 33, 39n, 44, 48n
Damasio, Hanna, 33, 37, 39n, 44, 48n
Danish, 267, 400, 474
Darwin, Charles, 51, 467. *See also* Evolution
    language evolution and, 56
"Dead" languages, 464–472
Deaf. *See also* American Sign Language
        (ASL); Sign language
    American Sign Language and, 20
sign language and, 4, 20
Deaf children
    ASL acquisition by, 345–346
    hearing parents and, 346
Decker, Thomas, 421
Declarative sentences, 139
Deep structures, 138, 142
Definite, 170
Definitions, 66
Deictic terms, 199–201
Deixis, 199–201
Deletion of verb "be," in AAE, 415
Deletion rules, segment, 285–286
Demonstrative articles, 200
Denotative meaning, 433
Derivation, 291
Derivational morphemes, 76–81, 289
    inflectional morphemes and, 91–92
Derivational morphology, 90
Derived representation, 280
Descartes, René, 20, 25n, 137, 372
Descriptive grammar, 14–15

Determiner (Det), 67, 114, 115, 124. *See also*
    Phrase structure rules
Devoiced vowels, 282
Devoicing rules, 282–283
Diacritics, 237, 242–243, 504
Diagrams. *See* Tree diagrams
Dialect, 14, 16, 400. *See also* Change,
        language; Dialects of English; R-dropping
        rule; Sound change
    accent and, 401
    African American English as, 412–417
    Black English (BE), 16n
    in China, 421
    extinction of, 472–473
    French, 410–411
    gender and, 438
    language change and, 471
    Latino (Hispanic) English, 417–420
    metathesis in, 287
    prestige, 16
    regional, 400–401
    standard, 17, 407–411
    styles and, 425
    velar fricatives and, 230
    vowel differences among, 238
Dialect areas, 406
Dialect atlas, 404–406
Dialect leveling, 401
Dialect map, 404–406
Dialects of English, 402–407. *See also*
        Dialects
    atlases of, 404–406
    lexical differences in, 404
    phonological differences in, 403–404
    syntactic differences in, 406–407
Dichotic listening, 42
Dickens, Charles, 508
Dickinson, Emily, 63
Dictionary, 8–9, 63, 65–66
    lexicon and, 18, 158
    sexism in, 434
Dictionary of Regional English (Cassidy), 406
Dictionary of the English Language (Johnson),
    66
Digraph, 504
Dionysius Thrax, 14
Diphthongs, 236–237, 280
Direct method, 349
Direct object, 110, 116
"Dirty" words. *See* Taboo words
Discontinuity view, 55
Discontinuous dependency, 153
Discontinuous morpheme, 73

Discourse, 191–195
Discourse analysis, 191
Dissimilation rules, 284
Distinctive features, 262–269
   feature values, 262–264
   predictability of redundant (nondistinctive)
      features, 264–266
   redundancies and, 267
   unpredictability of phonemic features,
      266–267
Distinctive sounds, 254
Distribution, complementary, 261–262
Ditransitive verbs, 153
Divine origin of language, theories of, 53
Dominate, 116
Doolittle, Doctor (fictional character), 22
Double negatives, 16, 414, 458
Downdrift, 242
Doyle, Arthur Conan, 198, 470
Drawing. *See* Petroglyphs
"Drawl," 412
Dryden, John, 114
Du Marsais (universalist philosopher), 18, 27
Durant, Will, 492
Dutch, 461
Dyslexia, 44
Dyslexics, acquired, 47

Ear, 55
Early Middle English Vowel Shortening rule,
   455
Ease of articulation, 280, 481
Ebonics, 16n, 412n. *See also* African American
   English (AAE)
Egressive sounds, 223
Egypt, story of language development in, 54
Eigen, Manfred, 388
Ejectives, 223
Elizabethan English, 459
ELIZA program, 380
Elkins, Joseph, 54
Ellis, Havelock, 177
Embedded sentence, 130–131
Emerson, Ralph Waldo, 399
-en, as suffix, 80
Endings, 47n, 96. *See also* Suffixes
England. *See also* English language
   British RP (Received Pronunciation) in, 238
   derivation of word, 460n
   grammars and, 15
English language, 5, 6, 8–9, 16, 111, 112, 232,
   265, 299, 300, 402–407. *See also* American English; British English; Change,
   language; Dialects of English; Sounds
and African American English (AAE),
   412–417
airstream mechanisms in, 223
anaphora in, 193
antonym formation in, 168
aspiration in, 266, 284–285, 295, 298
assimilation in, 481
Australian, 433
borrowing by, 460
Cajun, 410
classification of morphemes in, 94
Cockney and, 439
consonants in, 234
content words of, 67
counting in, 473–474
dialect atlases of, 404–406
dialects of, 308, 402–407
digraphs in, 504
dissimilation in, 284
ditransitive verbs in, 153–154
division into periods, 450
epenthesis in, 287
first dictionary in, 66
flaps in, 291
future meaning in, 94
glides in, 232–233
idiolects of, 399
incorrect word sequences in, 126–128
infixing in, 72–73
inflections in, 91
language acquisition and, 327, 348
Latino (Hispanic) English and, 417–420
lexical differences in, 404
as lingua franca, 421
morphemes in, 71, 293
Mother Goose in, 64
nasalization in, 280, 281–282
palatal fricative in, 230
passive construction in, 46
past-tense rule in, 296–297
phonemes in, 300
phonetic alphabet for, 220
phonetic symbols for consonants, 233
phonetic symbol/spelling correspondences,
   244–245
phonological differences in, 403–404
phrase structure rules in, 120–133
pidgins and, 422
pitch in, 240–241
places of articulation of consonants,
   223–225

English language *(Continued)*
Quebecois and, 418
redundant features in, 264, 265
rounded vowels in, 236
signed, 21
sounds and spellings in, 508–510
speech sounds and, 214
Standard, 67–68, 407–411
suffixes in, 80
as SVO language, 374
syllabic writing and, 500–501
syntactic differences in, 406–407
thematic roles and, 177
word derivation in, 288–289
word sequences in, 107
worldwide use of, 403
Entailment, 180
Environment, phonemic, 280, 281
Épée, Abbé de l', 450
Epenthesis, 286–287
Epenthesis rule, plurals and, 294
Epithets, racial and national, 433–434
Eponyms, 88
ERPs. *See* Event related brain potentials
(ERPs)
Errors, spontaneous, 372
Espy, W. R., 88
Essay towards an English Grammar (Fell), 19
Estonian, 474
Ethnicity, Chicano English and, 419
Etruscans, 498
Etymology, 66, 460
Euphemisms, 432–433
European languages, 504. *See also* specific
languages
Event related brain potentials (ERPs), 43
Evolution
development of language in species, 55–56
of language, 51–56
language changes and, 467
of languages, 473–477
Exclamation marks, 505
Experiencer, of action, 176
Extension, 174
Extinct and endangered language, 472–473

Falsehood, 179
Families, language. *See* Genetic classification
of languages
Family tree, of Indo-European languages, 475
Farb, Peter, 430n, 431
Farmer, John S., 427

Feature addition rules, 284–285
Feature-changing (feature-spreading) rules,
283
nasal homorganic rule as, 298
Features
phonemic, of American English consonants,
275
specifications for American English
consonants and vowels, 273–274
unpredictability of, 266–267
Feature values, 262–264
Fe?Fe? language, 236
Feinstein, Robert N., 509
Fell, John, 19
Female. *See* Gender; Sexism; Women
Female forms. *See* Gender; Sexism; Women
Feminist movement, 438
Feral children, 342
Fijian, 488
Filled pauses, 9
Finger spelling, 21
Finnish language, 177, 267, 301
inflected nouns in, 91
First person pronouns, 199
First sounds, 319–320
First words, 321–324
Flap, 232
Flap rule, 290, 291
Folk etymologies, 430–437
Form, and meaning, 5
Formal instruction, 331
Formants, 365
Forms of address, 318
Forster, Kenneth, 368–369
f-p sound correspondence, 452
Fragments, of lexicon, 135
France. *See also* French language
standard dialect in, 410–411
Francis, W. N., 376n
Franglais, 410
Frank, R., 44n
Frederick II (Hohenstaufen), 54
Free morphemes, 71
Free variation, 257, 282
Frege, Gottlob, 173
French language, 5, 6, 9, 18, 155, 236, 238,
264, 266, 285, 286, 346, 348
borrowings from, 460
Cajun, 410
future tense inflections in, 94
Mother Goose in, 64
in Quebec, 411, 418
uvular fricative in, 231

Frequency, 368
  fundamental, 240
Fricatives, 230–231
Friction, 230
Friedman, Joyce, 389
Fromkin, V. A., 96
Functional MRI, 42
Function words, 47, 67–68, 93, 159
  for future tense, 94
Fundamental frequency, 240, 364
Future meaning, 94

Gaelic, 410, 460, 474
Gage, Phineas, 43
Galaburda, A. M., 44n
Gall, Franz Joseph, 35
Gallaudet, Thomas Hopkins, 21
Gaps. *See* Accidental gaps
Gardner, Allen and Beatrice, 351
Gazzaniga, Michael, 41
Geminates, 248, 267
Gender
  "he" as generic term, 437–438
  language and, 434–439
  male/female word pairs and, 436–437
  pronouns for, 214n
Generating tree diagrams, 122–124
Generic term, 67
  "he" as, 437–438
Genetic classification of languages, 451–452,
    473–477
Genetic disorders, autonomy of language and,
    51
Genie (child), 343
Georgian, 410
Germanic languages, 460, 464, 474
  pidgins and, 423–424
German language, 5, 54, 73, 177, 231, 291,
    461, 473–474
  syntax in, 128–129
Geschwind, Norman, 1
Gesner, Johanne, 44
Gestures, meaning and, 23, 24
Ghana, 68
Ghanaian languages, 264
Gleason, Jean Berko, 315, 335, 362n
Gleitman, Lila R., 330, 337n, 338
Glides, 232–233
Gloss, 18, 488
Glottalic airstream mechanism, 223
Glottals/glottal stop, 224–225, 234
Glottis, 222

"Gnormal Pspelling" (Feinstein), 509
Goal, 175
Goldwyn, Samuel, 69
Goodglass, Harold, 46n
Gould, Stephen Jay, 36n, 55–56
Grabowski, T. J., 44n, 48n
Gradable pairs, 166
Grammars. *See also* Function words;
    Grammaticality; Morphemes;
    Morphology; Parts of speech; Syntax
  of ASL, 21
  computer models of, 388–389
  defined, 14
  derivational morphemes and, 77–78
  descriptive, 14–15
  language acquisition and, 338
  lexicon and, 133–136
  mental, 14
  morphemes and, 70
  prescriptive, 15–17
  teaching, 17–18
  theory of, 61
  universal, 19
Grammar transition networks, 385
Grammar-translation method, 349
Grammatical case, 177–178
Grammatical category, 65
Grammaticality, 106–109
  basis of, 107–109
  syntax and, 106–109
Grammatical morphemes, 89–95, 327
Grammatical relations, 110
Grammatical sentence, 14
Grammatical sequence, 106
Grammatical words, 67
Graphemes, 508
Great Vowel Shift, 454–456
Greek language, 74, 170, 301, 421, 457, 464,
    498
  grammar and, 15
  language corruption and, 409
Greenberg, Joseph, 472
Greene, Amsel, 81, 253n
Greenfield, Patricia Marks, 355
Grice, H. Paul, 196n
Grimm, Jakob, 465
Grimm's Law, 465, 466

Habitual "Be," in AAE, 415
Haldane, E. S., 25n
Halle, M., 14
Hangul, 503

Han languages, 421
Harlowe, John, 43–44
Hausa, 421
Hawaiian, 488
Hayes, Keith and Cathy, 351
"He," as generic term, 437–438
Head, of phrases, 173
Hearing. *See also* entries under Deaf; Hearing
    deficiency
  language development and, 55
Hearing deficiency. *See also* Sign language
  sign language and, 20, 21
Hebrew language, 287, 311, 337, 411, 502
Hemidecorticates, 40
Hemiplegics, 40
Hemispheres of brain, 35
  lateral, 38
  left, 45
Henley, W. E., 427
Henry, O., 136, 162
Henton, Caroline, 439
Herodotus, 53
Heteronym, 164
Hichwa, R. D., 48n
Hierarchical structure, 111, 269
  of words, 77
Hieroglyphics, 498
Hindi, 400, 421, 474, 476–477, 505
Hipp, R., 377n
Hippocratic physicians, 37
Hippocratic Treatise on the Sacred Disease, 33
Hiragana, 501
Hispanic English. *See* Latino (Hispanic)
    English
Historical and comparative linguistics,
    464–472
History. *See also* Change, language
  of African American English (AAE),
    416–417
  and borrowed words, 460–462
  evidence for language change, 470–472
  of writing, 492–498
Hittite, 474
Holm, John, 415n
Holophrastic stage, 322, 324
Homographs, 164, 508
Homonyms, 64, 163–164
Homophones, 64
Homorganic consonants, 272
Hopi, 346
Human brain. *See* Brain
Human language, compared with animal
    language. *See* Animal language

Humans, language processing by, 361–374
Hungarian, 170, 477
Hyams, Nina, 327, 333n, 336, 337
Hyphenation, in compounds, 84
Hyponyms, 168
Hyponymy, 168

Icelandic, 474, 503
Iconic signs, 7
Ideograms, 494–495
Idiolect, 399
Idioms, 188–190
Ill formed sequence, 106
Illocutionary force, of speech act, 198
Imagery, semantic rules and, 189–190
Imitation, by animals, 23–24
Imitation theory, language acquisition and,
    328–329
Immediately dominate, 116
Immigration, impact on American English,
    402–403
Implication, 199
Implosives, 223
Impoverished data, 340
India, 400
Indian languages, 223
Indo-European languages, 423, 452, 466, 467,
    474, 501
  family tree of, 475
Indo-Iranian languages, 476
Indonesian, 504
Infants. *See* Children's acquisition of language
Infinitive marker, 90
Infixes, 72–73
Inflected language, 91–92
Inflectional forms, 93
Inflectional morphemes, 90–93
Inflectional rules, 372
Informal language
  argot and, 427–428
  jargon and, 427–428
  slang and, 426–427
  style and, 425–426
Ingressive sounds, 223
Innateness hypothesis, 339–342
Inner City English (ICE), 412n
Instruction, children's language acquisition
    and, 331–333
Instrument, of action, 176
Intelligence, brain and, 36n
Intension (sense), 174
Intensity, 364

Interdental fricatives, 230
  in AAE, 414
Interdentals, 224, 234
Internal borrowing. *See* Analogic change
International Phonetic Alphabet (IPA), 220
International Phonetic Association, 220, 221
Interrogative sentences, 140
Intonation, 240–242, 274–276
Intonation languages, 242
Intransitive verb, 134
Involuntary cries, 9
Iowa, University of, 48
IPA. *See* International Phonetic Association
  (IPA)
Ipsilateral stimuli, 42
Iranian. *See* Persian
Irish, 410, 460, 474
Irregular forms, 92–93
Isidore of Seville, 478
Isogloss, 406
Italian, 327, 336, 337, 461
Italics, 505, 506
-ity, as suffix, 80

Jakobson, Roman, 157, 324
James IV (Scotland), 54
Japanese, 155, 200, 236, 282–283, 309, 314,
  326, 337, 374, 438, 499, 501, 505
  syntax in, 128
Jargon, 37, 427–428
  dictionaries of, 66
Jargon aphasia, 44, 46
Jefferson, Thomas, 409, 460
Jespersen, Otto, 52, 55, 408
Jews and Judaism. *See* Hebrew language;
  Yiddish
Johnson, Falk, 430n
Johnson, Mark, 389
Johnson, Samuel, 66, 511
Jones, William, 464, 473, 474
Judaeo-Christian beliefs, language origins and,
  53

Kamala, 342
Kana, 501, 504
Kanji, 501
Karuk language, 71, 72
Katakana, 501
Katz, Bill, 433
Keller, Helen, 337
Kellogg, Winthrop and Luella, 351

Kelvin, Lord (William Thomson), 388
Khoikhoi, 216, 223
Khoisan, 472
Kikuyu, 284
Kilmer, Joyce, 122
Kilwardby, Robert, 19
King James Version, of Bible, 463
Klima, Edward S., 8n, 21n, 45n, 82n, 258n,
  345
Knowledge. *See also* Language
  categories of conceptual, 48
  language processing and, 361
Koasati, 438
Kongo, 307
Korean, 155, 267, 307, 421, 503
Krapp, George Philip, 408
Krashen, Stephen, 349
Kratzenstein, Christian Gottlieb, 378
Krauss, Michael, 472
Kucera, H., 376n
Kurath, Hans, 404, 405

L2. *See* Second language
Labeo-velar glide, 232
Labial sounds, 239
Labiodentals, 224, 234, 240
  fricatives, 230
Labov, William, 415n, 426
Ladefoged, Peter, 213n, 364
Lakoff, Robin, 438
Language. *See also* Acquisition of language;
  Aphasia; Brain; Change, language;
  Historical and comparative linguistics;
  Linguistic knowledge; Phonology; Sign
  language; specific languages
  African American English (AAE), 412–417
  American Indian, 410
  animal, 22–26
  aphasia and, 44–48
  autonomy of, 49–51
  banned, 409–411
  bow-wow theory of, 54
  brain and, 33–58
  code-switching in, 418–419
  computer, 377
  conceptual knowledge about, 65
  Creole, 425
  cries of nature theory of, 54
  "dead," 464–472
  defined, 3
  dialects and, 14, 400
  elements in, 11

Language *(Continued)*
  etymology and, 460
  evolution of, 51–56
  extinct and endangered, 472–473
  French, 410–411
  gender and, 438–439
  genetic classification of, 473–477
  historical efforts to explain, 53–55
  as human distinguishing characteristic, 3
  human evolution and, 55–56
  idiolects of, 399
  infinitude of, 118–120
  informal, 425–428
  knowledge of, 216
  Latino (Hispanic) English, 417–420
  lingua franca and, 420–421
  linguistic knowledge and, 4–11, 26–27
  location in brain, 35–38
  meanings of, 157–203
  monogenetic theory of, 54
  morphology of Paku, 96
  natural, 53–54
  number spoken, 483
  origin of, 51–55
  pidgins and, 421–425
  protolanguages, 451–452
  purists and, 16–17
  relationships among, 472
  repetition of categories within categories in,
    119
  revival of, 411
  secret, 439–440
  sex, gender, and, 434–439
  sign language as, 4
  in society, 397, 399–441
  source, 374
  species-specific nature of, 55–56
  "standard" versions of, 407–411
  study of nature of, 19
  syntactic categories in, 113
  taboo words and, 430–431
  target, 374
  theories of divine origin of, 53
  types of, 478–480
  of world, 476–477
  written, 491–512
Language families. *See* Genetic classification
  of languages
Language games, 439–440
Language generation, 377, 380
Language processing, 361–391
  bottom-up, 367
  comprehension, 363–369

  computer, 375–389
  human, 361–374
  by machines, 374–375
  speech production, 370–374
  syntactic, 369–370
  town-down, 367
Language purists, 408–409
Language universals, 18–22, 26–27
  American Sign Language (ASL) and, 21–22
  sign languages and, 20
Langue d'oc, 410
Larynx, 222
Lash, J. P., 337n
Lasknik, Howard, 108
Lateralization, 37
Lateral liquid, 232
Laterals, 224
Latin, 284, 421, 456, 460, 464, 466, 468, 503
Latin alphabet, 504
Latin-English dictionary, 66
Latin grammar, 16
Latino (Hispanic) English, 417–420
Laukhard, Friedrich Ch., 427n
Lax vowels, 238
L-deletion rule, in AAE, 413
Lear, Edward, 165
Learning. *See also* Acquisition of language
  humanizing through, 3
Learn Zulu (Nyembezi), 18
Left-handers, lateralization and, 45n
Left hemisphere, 45
Legends, about invention of writing, 492
Lehmann, Winfred P., 468
Length, of vowels, 238
Lenneberg, Eric, 342n
Lesions, 48
  brain and, 38–40
  in Broca's area, 45
  language and, 37
Letters, 508. *See also* Alphabet
  Roman, 220
  sounds of, 219
Level tones, 241
Levi, Jan Heller, 436n
Lexical access, 366
  and word recognition, 367–369
Lexical ambiguity. *See* Ambiguous, ambiguity
Lexical categories, 116, 124. *See also* Parts of
  speech
Lexical change, 459–463
  borrowings, 459–462
  loss of words, 462
  semantic change, 463

Lexical content morphemes, 75
Lexical decision experiments, 368
Lexical differences, in English dialects, 404
Lexical gaps, 76, 271
Lexical insertion, 134
Lexical paraphrase, 166
Lexical semantics, 158–171, 366
  defined, 158
  -nyms and, 162–168
  proper names and, 168–169
  semantic properties, 160–161
Lexicon, 18, 63, 133–136, 158
  differences in, 135–136
  semantic properties and, 161
  subcategorization of, 134–135
Lingua franca, 420–421
Linguistic breakdowns, 44–45. *See also*
  Aphasia
Linguistic context, 190, 191–195
  articles *The* and *A,* 194–195
  pronouns and, 191–194
Linguistic Data Consortium (LDC), 376
Linguistic knowledge, 4–11. *See also*
  Grammar; Language
  creative aspect of, 9–10
  morphology and, 69–70
  and performance, 12–13
  sound system and, 4–5
  speech sounds and, 216
Linguistic language acquisition, 319
Linguistics. *See also* Neurolinguistics
  computational, 374
  historical and comparative, 464–472
  language knowledge and, 26–27
  psycholinguistics and, 315, 361
  taboo words and, 431
Linguistic Society of Paris, 52
Linguistic theory, 19
Linguist List, 72
Linguists, nature of language and, 19
Linnaeus, Carl, 44, 342
Lip rounding, 236
Liquids, 232, 240
Li Si, 499
Listening. *See also* Speech understanding
  auditory phonetics and, 216
  dichotic, 42
Lithuanian, 474
Loan translations, 462
Loan words, 459
Localization, in brain, 35
Location, of action, 176
Locke, W. N., 374n

Lofting, Hugh, 22
Logical problem of language acquisition, 340
Logical representations, 391
Logograms, 496
Logographic writing, 496, 499–500
Long and short vowels, 267
Look-ahead parser, 384
Lord, Carol, 332
Loss of words, 462
Loudness, of vowels, 235
Louisiana Creole. *See* Creole languages
Lounsbury, Thomas R., 16
Lowth, Robert, 16
Luganda, 267, 313
Luria, S. E., 1

Machines. *See* Computers
Machine translation, 374–375
MacKay, Donald, 67
Magnetic Resonance Imaging (MRI), 37–38, 42
Main stress, 277
Main verb. *See* Verb (V)
Male. *See* Gender
Maledicta (journal), 432–433
Male forms. *See* Gender; Men
Malory, Thomas, 458
Mandarin Chinese, 236, 400
Maninka, 312
Manner, in conversation, 196
Manner of articulation, 225–233
Maoris, 480, 488
Maps, dialect, 404–406
Marantette, P. F., 321n
Marked and unmarked forms, gender
  designations and, 435–437
Marked antonyms, 166–167
Markers, 90–91
Marshall, J., 47n
Mass nouns, 161
Maxim of manner, 196
Maxim of quality, 196
Maxim of quantity, 196
Maxim of relevance, 196
Maxims of conversation, 196
Maximus, Valerius, 44
Mayle, Peter, 195
Mead, Margaret, 21
Meanings, 157–203. *See also* Acquisition of
  language; Semantics
  anomaly and, 184–187
  of compounds, 85–86
  connotative, 433

Meanings *(Continued)*
 denotative, 433
 human vs. animal language and, 23–24
 idioms and, 188–190
 language acquisition and, 338
 lexical semantics and, 158–171
 metaphor and, 187–188
 morphemes and, 68–75
 phrasal, 172–178
 pragmatics and, 190–201
 semantics, syntax, and, 181–184
 sentential, 178–181
 shifts in, 463
 and truth conditions of sentences, 179
 of words, 5–9
Mean length of utterances (MLU), 325
Melanesian Pidgin English, 422
Memorization, of sentences, 10
Men. *See also* Gender; Sexism
 language, gender, and, 434–439
Mental lexicons. *See* Dictionary; Lexicon
Mesopotamia, 495
 analysis of spoken language in, 26
Message, speech chain and, 362
Metaphor, 187–188
Metathesis rules, 287–288
Metonyms, 168
Metonymy, 168
Mexican Americans, Chicano English and,
  418, 419
Michaelis, 120
Middle East, cuneiform writing in, 496
Middle English, 449, 450, 451
Mill, John Stuart, 116
Milne, A. A., 34, 363n
Mimetic signs, 7
Mind. *See* Brain
Minimal pairs, 255
 in ASL, 258–259
Minimal set, 255, 256
Missing parts, 193–194
MLU. *See* Mean length of utterances (MLU)
Modern English, 450. *See also* American
  English; English language
Modifier-noun agreement, 337. *See also*
  Agreement
Modularity, of language faculty, 35–48
Molière, J. B., 105
Moneglia, M., 327n
Mongolian, 421
Monogenetic theory of language origin, 54
Monomorphemic words, 75
Monophthongs, 237

Monosyllabic words, 256
Morphemes, 63, 68–75, 288
 bound and free, 71
 circumfixes as, 73
 classification of English, 94
 context and, 74
 defined, 69
 derivational, 76–81
 grammatical, 89–95, 327
 identifying, 95
 infixes, 72–73
 inflectional, 90–93
 morphophonemics, 295–297
 -nym words, 162–168
 plurals and, 294–295
 prefixes, 71
 pronunciation of, 293–300
 root, 73, 75
 sequential constraints, 297–300
 single, 75
 stem, 73, 75
 suffixes, 71–72
Morphological change, 456–457
Morphological parsers, 385
Morphological rules, 76
 productive, 79
Morphology, 18, 63–98. *See also* Words
 acquisition of, 334–336
 identifying morphemes, 95–96
 of sign language, 81–82
 and syntax, 93–95
Morphophonemic orthography, 510
Morphophonemic rules, 295, 372
Morphophonemics, 295–297
Mother Goose Rhymes, 64
Movement (metathesis) rules, 287–288
MRI. *See* Magnetic Resonance Imaging (MRI)
Muller, M., 51
Multilingual speakers, 347
Munro, Allen, 323n
Munro, Pamela, 323n, 428
Music, 42
Muskogean language, 438
My Fair Lady (musical), 220

Names
 proper, 168–171
 words from, 88–89
Naming task, 368
Narrowing, 463
Narrow phonetic transcription, 233, 249
Nasal cavity, 222

Nasal homorganic rule, 298
Nasalization, 264–265
Nasal sounds, 228–229, 240, 261
    consonants, 272
    vowels, 237, 259, 260, 272
Nash, Ogden, 217, 432
National Council of Teachers of English, 16
National epithets, 433–434
National minority languages, in China, 421
National Park Service, symbols of, 494
National Theatre of the Deaf (NTD), 21
Native Americans. *See also* American Indian
        languages
    animal language and, 22
    Karuk language of, 71, 72
Native language, 18
Natural classes of sounds, 271–274
Natural language, 53–54
Navajo language, 162
Negative meanings, 69, 77
Negatives
    double, 414
    rules about, 458
Neo-Grammarians, 467
Networks
    augmented transition, 386
    semantic, 387
    transition, 385
Neurolinguistics, 33, 43
Neutralization, 290
    of vowels in AAE, 414
Neutralized contrast, 290
Newcombe, F., 47n
New England, dialect of, 402
Newman, Edwin, 16, 409
Newport, Elissa, 344
New words, 462
New York Academy of Sciences, 51
Nigeria, 421
Niger-Kordofanian languages, 472, 477
Nilo-Saharan languages, 472
Nodes, 116, 385–386
Noncontinuants, 239
Nondistinctive features. *See* Redundant
        (nondistinctive) features
Nonlinguistic influences, 373–374
Nonphonemic feature, 265
Nonredundant features, 264
Nonsense, 184–187
Nonsense strings, 366
Nonsense words, 37, 53, 108–109, 271
Nonsentences, 11
Norman Conquest, 460–461

Northfork Monachi, 489
Norton, Mary, 407
Norwegian, 400, 474
Nose, 222
Noun (N), 67, 84, 114, 124. *See also* Proper
        names
    count, 161
    mass, 161–162
    singular and plural, 92
    suffixes and, 78
Noun-centered meaning, 172–174
    sense and reference, 173–174
Noun Phrase (NP), 113, 115, 116, 119, 141,
        170. *See also* Phrase structure rules
    proper name and, 170
Nucleus, of syllable, 269
Nupe, 241
Nyembezi, Sibusiso, 18
-nym words, 162–168
    antonyms, 166–168
    homonyms, 163–164
    hyponyms, 168
    metonyms, 168
    retronyms, 168
    synonyms, 165–166

Object
    direct, 110, 116
    prepositional, 116
Object subject verb (OSV) word order,
        478–480
Object verb subject (OVS) word order,
        478–480
Obligatory transformation, 153
Obstruents, 239
Occam's Razor, 298
Oceania, writing in, 494
Ocracoke Island, 472–473
OED. See Oxford English Dictionary (OED)
Official language. *See* Standard dialects;
        Standard language
Old English, 449, 450
Old Norse, 461
O'Neill, Eugene, 81
One to many and many to one, 288–291
Onomatopoeic words, 8
Onset, syllable, 269
Open class words, 67, 68
Opposites, relational, 167
Optional transformations, 153
Oral cavity, 222, 223
Oral sounds, 228–229, 261

Oral vowels, 237, 259, 260
Order, 197
Ordering, of sentences, 137–143
Origin of language, 51–55
Ornstein-Galicia, Jacob L., 419n
Orthoepists, 218, 470–471
Orthography, 65, 217. *See also* Spelling
  for Icelandic language, 503
  morphophonemic, 510
Osborn, Robert, 83n
OSV. *See* Object subject verb (OSV) word
  order
Overgeneralization, 334–335
OVS. *See* Object verb subject (OVS) word
  order
Oxford English Dictionary (OED), 66, 431

Pairs of words, 255–257
  in ASL, 258–259
Pakistan, 421
Pakistani languages, 223, 400
Paku, 96, 310
Palatal glide, 232
Palatalization, 481
Palatals, 224, 234, 239, 240, 302
Palate, 228
Panini, 53
Papua New Guinea, 422
Parallel processing, 389
Paraphrases, 166, 179–180
Pareto, Vilfredo, 333
Parse, 366
Parsers
  look-ahead, 384
  morphological, 385
Parsing, computer, 383–386
Participle, 145, 146
Partridge, Eric, 430–431
Parts of speech, 66, 124. *See also* Function
  words
Passive construction, in English, 46
Passives, 182–183
Passive sentence, 145–147
Passive voice marker, 90
Past-tense rule, 296–297
Patterson, Francine "Penny," 352
Pauses, in speech, 9, 64. *See also* Spacing
Payne, L. W., 417n
Pei, Mario, 408
Penfield, Joyce, 419n
People's Republic of China, 421
Pepperberg, Irene M., 24

Pepys, Samuel, 350
Perception, of speech, 365–366
Performance, 12
  linguistic knowledge and, 12–13
Performative sentences, 197
Performative verbs, 197
Periods, 505
Persian, 464, 474, 504
Persians, 496
Person deixis, 200
PET. *See* Positron Emission Photography
  (PET)
Petitto, Laura, 321, 353n
Petroglyphs, 493
PET word-retrieval experiment, 48
Pharyngeal fricatives, 231
Pharynx, 222
Phoenicians, 498
Phon (word part), 69
Phone, 259–261, 266
  phonemes and, 288–291
Phonemes, 254–262, 300–302, 372
  as abstract unit, 265–266
  complementary distribution of, 261–262
  graphemes and, 508
  minimal pairs, 255–257
  and phones, 288–291
  phones, allophones, and, 259–261
  phonological analysis and, 300–302
  in pidgin languages, 423
  sequential constraints and, 269–271,
    297–300
  sounds that contrast, 254–259
  unpredictability of features, 266–267
Phonemic environment, 280, 281
Phonemic features, of consonants in American
  English, 275
Phonemic principle, 502–503
Phonemic representation, 304, 313
Phonemics, morphophonemics and, 295–297
Phonemic transcriptions, 260
Phonetically similar phones, 262
Phonetic alphabet, 218–221
Phonetic change, 280
Phonetic features, 229
Phonetic representation, 304, 313
Phonetics, 213–248, 296. *See also* Sounds
  acoustic, 216, 364
  allomorphs and, 295, 297
  allophones and, 260
  articulatory, 216, 221–242
  auditory, 216
  defined, 214

diacritics and, 242–243
distinctive features and, 262–269
examples of consonants in English words, 234
identity of speech sounds, 215–216
oral and nasal vowels and, 259
phonology and, 253
and sign-language primes, 246
sound segments, 214–215
spelling and speech, 216–221
Phonetic symbols, 220–221. *See also* Pronunciation
for American English consonants, 233
for aspirated sounds, 227
diacritics and, 242–243
schwa as, 220
and spelling correspondences, 243–245
used in place of IPA symbols, 221
Phonetic transcription, 221, 233, 289
Phonographic symbol, 497
Phonological change, 452–456
Phonological rules, 271–273, 453–454
Phonology, 18, 21n, 253–305
acquisition of, 333–334
of African American English, 413–414
assimilation rules, 280–283
in ChE, 419–420
dissimilation rules, 284
distinctive features and, 262–269
of English dialects, 403–404
feature addition rules, 284–285
feature changing rules, 283–284
function of rules, 291–292
language changes and, 467–468
movement (metathesis) rules, 287–288
natural classes, 271–274
nondistinctive features, 264–266
one to many and many to one, 288–291
phonemes and, 254–262, 300–302
predictability of redundant features, 264–266
prosodic, 274–279
and redundancy, 267–269
rules of, 279–293
segment deletion and addition rules, 285–287
sequential constraints, 269–271
and slips of the tongue, 292–293
surface structures and, 138
unpredictability of phonemic features, 266–267
Phonotactics, 270
Phrasal categories, 124

Phrasal meaning, 171–178
noun-centered, 172–174
verb-centered, 175–178
Phrasal semantics, 158
Phrases
stress in, 278–279
words and, 181–182
Phrase structure rules, 120–133
Phrase structure trees, 114–118
limitless aspect of language and, 119
and phrase structure rules, 122–125
Phrenology, 35–36
Physiology, of speech, 222–223
Pictograms, 493–495
Pidgin languages, 422–425
Pig Latin, 439
Pinker, Stephen, 56
Pinyin, 500
Piro language, 71
Pitch, 240, 274, 364
of vowels, 235
Pitch contour, 276
Pitt, William, 184
Place deixis, 200
Places of articulation, 223–225
Plato, 54
Pliny, 44
Plosives, 230
Plural, 92
Pluralization, proper names and, 171
Plural rule, 294–295
morphophonemics and, 295–297
Poetry, computer studies of, 376
Poincaré, Henri, 333
Poizner, Howard, 8n, 45n, 82n
Polish, 238, 474
Polyglots, 476
Polymorphemic words, 97
Polynesian languages, 488
Polysemous, 164
Polysemy, 163–164
Portuguese, 238
Positron Emission Tomography (PET), 38
Possessives, 506
Possessor, 176
Postpositions, 128
Poverty of the stimulus, 340
Powell, Jay, 433n
Pragmatic processing, 387–388
Pragmatics, 158, 190–201
deixis and, 199–201
linguistic context and, 191–195
situational context and, 195–199

Predictable feature, 265
Predictable phonetic variant, 260
Prefixes, 71
  antonyms and, 168
  un-, 68–69
Prefixing, 69
Prelinguistic language acquisition, 319
Premack, David, 351, 354, 355
Preposition (P), 67, 114, 116, 124, 479
Prepositional object, 116
Prepositional Phrase (PP), 114, 116, 170. *See also* Phrase structure rules
  moving of, 139
  proper name and, 170
Prescriptive grammar, 408
Prestige dialect, 16. *See also* Standard dialect
Presupposition(s), 198–199
Primary stress, 277
Primates. *See* Chimpanzees
Primes, 246
Priming technique, 368
Printing press, 461
Processing. *See* Language processing
Productive morphological rules, 79
Pro-forms, 193
Progressive marker, 90
Pronoun (Pro), 67, 114, 191–194
  anaphora, 192–193
  and coreferentiality, 183–184
  deixis and, 199–201
  for gender, 214n
  missing parts, 193–194
  reflexive, 136
Pronunciation, 66
  articulation and, 221–223
  of British and American English, 403–404
  of compounds, 85–86
  historical evidence for changes, 470–472
  of morphemes, 293–300
  and phonetic alphabet, 218–221
  rule-governed, 279
  spelling, 511–512
Proper names, 168–171
  words from, 88–89
Prose, computer studies of, 376
Prosodic feature, 274–279
Prosodic suprasegmental features, 240
Proto-Germanic, 423–424, 451, 468
Proto-Indo-European language. *See* Indo-European language
Protolanguages, 54, 451–452
  Amerindian, 472
Proto-Slavic languages, 474

Psammetichus, 53
Psycholinguistics, 315, 361
Psychology
  neurolinguistics and, 33
  split brain studies and, 41
Psychology of language. *See* Language; Psycholinguistics
Pullet Surprises, 80–81
Pullum, G. K., 478n
Pulmonic egressive, 223
Pulmonic sounds, 223
Punctuation, 505–506
Punjabi, 477
Purists, 16–17
  language change and, 470–471
  "standard" languages and, 408–409
Putonghua, 421
Pygmalion (Shaw), 220, 430

Quality, of conversation, 196
Quantity, of conversation, 196
Quebec, 411
Question, transformations and, 142
Question marks, 505

Racial epithets, 433–434
Rask, Rasmus, 464–465
Ratner, Nan Bernstein, 315, 362n
R-dropping rule, 402, 403
  in AAE, 413
  and language change, 454
Reaction time measurements, 368
Reading, 505–506, 507. *See also* Dyslexia
Rebus principle, 497
Received Pronunciation (RP). *See* British RP (Received Pronunciation)
Reciprocal suffix, 71
Reconstruction, of languages, 467–470
Recurring forms, 95
Reduced vowel, 289
Redundant (nondistinctive) features, predictability of, 264–266, 267
Reduplication, 102–103
Reference, 173
  deixis and, 199–201
  pronouns and coreferentiality, 183–184
  truth and, 179
Referent, 173
Reflexive pronoun, 136
  syntax, semantics, and, 183

Regional dialects, 400–401, 404
   lexical differences and, 404
   maps and atlases of, 404–406
   standard languages and, 408–409
Registers, 425
Register tones, 241
Regular sound correspondence, 451
Reinforcement. *See also* Acquisition of
     language
   language acquisition and, 329–330
Relational opposites, 167
Relationships. *See also* Genetic classification
     of languages
   sentences and, 136–145
   structure-dependent, 145–147
Relevance, of conversation, 196
Religion, language use in, 53
Response time (RT) measurements, 368
Retroflex sounds, 224
Retronyms, 168
Rhymes, 118, 269
Roberts, Paul, 426n
Robinson, Robert, 220
Roles, thematic, 110
Romaine, Suzanne, 425n
Roman alphabet, 220, 504
Romance languages, 474
Root morphemes, 75, 95
Rosenblueth, Arturo, 367
Ross, G. R., 25n
Rounded vowels, 236
Rousseau, Jean Jacques, 54
RP. *See* British RP (Received Pronunciation)
RT. *See* Response time (RT) measurements
Rukeyser, Muriel, 436n
Rule-governed, 260
Rule-governed pronunciation, 279
Rules, 16. *See also* Grammar; Grammaticality
   application and misapplication of, 372–373
   assimilation, 280–283
   breaking of, 184–190
   children's formation of, 331–332
   dissimilation, 284
   feature addition, 284–285
   feature changing, 283–284
   function of phonological, 291–292
   in grammar, 14
   movement (metathesis), 287–288
   of noun phrase semantics, 173
   one to many and many to one, 288–291
   phonological, 271–273, 279–293, 453–454
   phonology of AAE, 413–414
   phrase structure, 120–133

   plural, 294–295
   segment deletion and addition, 285–287
   for sentence formation, 11
   slips of the tongue and, 292–293
   structure-dependent, 340–341
   of syntax, 120–133
   transformational, 137–142
Rumbaugh, Duane and Sue, 352, 354, 355
Russell, Bertrand, 22, 339
Russian language, 5, 6, 8, 72, 291, 337, 410, 474

SAE. *See* Standard American English (SAE)
St. Augustine, 319
Salmon, V., 19n
Samoan, 488
Sandburg, Carl, 425
Sanders, Richard, 353n
San Juan, Huarte de, 145
Sanskrit, 53, 457, 464, 466, 473
Santa Ana, Otto A., 418n
Savage-Rumbaugh, E. Sue, 355n. *See also*
     Rumbaugh, Duane and Sue
Savants, 49–51
Scandinavian languages, 461
Scandinavians, 461
Schane, Sanford, 285–286
Schulz, Muriel R., 435n
Schwa symbol, 220, 235, 289
Scots Gaelic, 460, 474
SE. *See* Standard English
Searchinger, Gene, 330n
Search model, 368–369
Second language
   acquisition of, 346–349
   sign language as, 21
   teaching methods and, 349
Second person pronouns, 199
Secret language, 439–440
Segments, 214–215, 280
   deletion and addition rules, 285–287
Seijong (Korea), 503
-self, as word ending, 136
Semantic change, 463
   broadening, 463
   meaning shifts, 463
   narrowing, 463
Semantic features, 161
Semantic networks, 387
Semantic processing, 386–387
Semantic properties, 159–160
   evidence for, 160–161
   and lexicon, 161–162

Semantic rules, breaking of, 184–190
Semantics, 18, 185
  defined, 158
  lexical, 158–171, 366
  and syntax, 181–184
Semitic alphabet, 505
Semitic languages, 477, 502
Sense, 173–174
  anomaly and, 184–187
Sentence-formation rules, 90
Sentences (S), 113, 170. *See also* Pragmatics;
    Sentential meaning; Tree diagrams
  active, 145–147
  agreement and, 143
  creative formation of, 9, 10
  embedded, 130–131
  grammaticality of, 14, 107–109
  knowledge of, 11
  linguistic knowledge and, 12–13
  passive, 145–147
  performative, 197
  proper name and, 170
  relatedness of, 136–145
  stress in, 278–279
  syntax and, 18
  transformational rules, 137–143
  "Wh-" sentences and, 144–145
Sentence structure, 111–120
  in German, 128
  relationships dependent on, 145–147
Sentential meaning, 178–180
  contradiction and, 180
  entailment and, 180
  paraphrase and, 179–180
Sentential semantics, 158
Sequences of words, 106. *See also* Grammar;
    Sentences (S); Syntax
  syntactically incorrect, 126–128
Sequential constraints, 269–271, 297–300
Sequoyah, 501
Serbo-Croatian, 474
Sets, minimal, 355
Seuss, Dr., 85
Sex. *See also* Gender
  language and, 434–439
Sexism, 434–435. *See also* Gender
Shadowing, 369
Shakespeare, William, 187, 191, 195, 279, 421
Shaw, George Bernard, 15, 218, 219, 220, 234,
    400, 408, 430, 508
Sheridan, R. B., 21, 374
Shifts, in meaning, 463

*Short Introduction to English Grammar with
    Critical Notes* (Lowth), 16
Sibilants, 240
Siglish. *See* Signed English
Signaling, by animals, 24–26
Signals. *See* Speech signal
Signed English, 21
Signing, 21
Sign language, 4, 20. *See also* American Sign
    Language (ASL)
  acquisition of, 345–346
  American Sign Language (ASL), 7, 8, 21
  as banned language, 411
  Chinese Sign Language (CSL), 7, 8
  morphology of, 81–82
  primes in, 246
  syntax of, 147
Signs. *See also* Chimpanzees; Symbols
  linguistic, 7
Simmons, Eva K., 379
Single feature, 262–263
Single morphemes, 75
Singular nouns, 92
Sino-Tibetan family, 477
Situational context, 191, 195–199
  maxims of conversation, 195–196
  presuppositions and, 198–199
  speech acts, 197–198
Slang, 426–427
  dictionaries of, 66
Slang and Its Analogues (Farmer and Henley),
    427
*Slang U: The Official Dictionary of College
    Slang* (Munro), 428
Slavery. *See* African American English
Slavic languages, Cyrillic alphabet and,
    504
SLI. *See* Specific Language Impairment (SLI)
Slips of the tongue, 13, 68, 292–293
Slobin, Dan, 317
Slovak, 474
Smith, Neil, 43, 50n
Smith, R., 377n
Social dialects, 440
Society
  African-American English and, 412–417
  English dialects and, 402–407
  language in, 397, 399–441
  Latino (Hispanic) English and, 417–420
  lingua francas and, 420–421
  pidgins, creoles, and, 421–425
  standard languages and, 407–411

styles, slang, jargon, and, 425–428
taboo words and, 428–434
Soft palate, 228
Song, language derivation from, 55
Song-learning, by birds, 344–345
Sonorants, 239
Sotho, 216
Sound change, 451–452
Sounds, 7. *See also* Acquisition of language;
    Phonetics; Phonology; Sound segments;
    Speech sounds
  acoustic phonetics and, 216
  acoustics and, 364
  affricates, 231
  alveolar, 224
  anterior, 240
  aspirated and unaspirated, 226–227
  bilabial, 224
  brain specialization and, 42
  changes across languages, 468–470
  clicks, 216, 223
  concordance of, 376
  contrasting, 254–259
  coronals, 239
  correspondence of, 451
  diacritics, 242–243
  egressive, 223
  ejectives, 223
  fricatives, 230–231
  fundamental frequency of, 240, 364
  glides, 232–233
  glottal, 224–225
  implosives, 223
  ingressive, 223
  intensity of, 364
  interdental, 224
  labials, 239
  labiodental, 224
  lateral, 224
  of letters, 219
  liquids, 232
  major classes of, 239–240
  nasal, 228–229, 237–238, 261
  natural classes of, 271–274
  oral, 228–229, 237–238, 261
  palatal, 224
  phonology as, 18
  pitch of, 240, 364
  prosodic suprasegmental features of, 240
  pulmonic egressive, 223
  regularity of changes in, 450–452
  retroflex, 224

sibilants, 240
spectrograms of, 364–365
spellings and, 508–510
stops and continuants, 229–230
stressed or accented, 240
syllabic, 240
tense and lax vowels, 238
tone and intonation of, 240–242
uvular, 224
velar, 224
voiced and voiceless, 225–227
of vowels, 220, 234–238
Sound segments, 214–215
Sound shift, 451
Sound symbolism, 8
Sound system. *See also* Phonetics
  of language, 4–5
Sound writing, 502
Source, of action, 176
Source language, 374
South, Robert, 379
South African languages, 216
Southern English, 451
  AAE and, 417
  "drawl" and, 412
Southern Kongo, 307
SOV language. *See* Subject Object Verb (SOV)
  word order
Spacing. *See also* Pauses
  in compounds, 84
  between words, 505
Spanish language, 5, 232, 287, 461
  impact on American English, 402
  transformational rules in, 141
Speakers, 12–13
Speaking, 361. *See also* Speech
Specialization. *See* Brain; Language
Species-specific nature of language, 55–56
Specific Language Impairment (SLI), 49
Spectrograms, 364–365
Speech. *See also* Sounds
  acoustic description of, 364–365
  articulatory phonetics and, 216
  computer recognition of, 382–383
  computer understanding of, 383
  contrastive stress and, 506
  language and, 23, 24
  male vs. female, 438–439
  parsing of, 383–386
  pauses in, 64
  perception and comprehension, 365–366
  phonetics and, 213

Speech *(Continued)*
  places of articulation of consonants,
    223–225
  reading, writing, and, 505–512
  spelling and, 216–221
  telegraphic, 325–328
  thought organization as, 13
Speech acts, 197–198
Speech chain, 361–362
Speech production, 370–374
  application and misapplication of rules,
    372–373
  lexical selection, 371–372
  nonlinguistic influences and, 373–374
  planning units, 370–371
Speech recognition, 377
Speech signal, 363–365
Speech sounds. *See also* Sounds
  clicks as, 216
  four classes of, 229
  identity of, 215–216
  phonetic features of, 229
Speech synthesis, 377–381
Speech understanding, 377
  by computers, 381–388
Spelling, 66, 507–512. *See also* Orthography
  of compounds, 84
  phonetic, 218–221
  phonetic symbols and, 243–245
  reform of, 219–220
  sign language and, 21, 246
  and speech, 216–221
Spelling pronunciation, 511–512
Spirants, 230
Split brains, 40–42
Spoken American English, 376
Spoken language, knowledge of, 26
Spontaneous errors, 372
Spooner, William Archibald, 292
Spoonerisms, 292
Spurzheim, Johann, 35
Stabler, Ed, 389
Standard American English (SAE), 408–409.
    See also American English; English
    language
Standard British English, 67–68
Standard dialects, 17, 407–411
  banned languages and, 409–411
  language purists and, 408–409
  revivals of languages and, 411
Standard English (SE), 407–408, 424
  banned language and, 410, 411
  language purists and, 408–409

Standard language, French and,
    410–411
State, 197
Stein, Gertrude, 111
Stem morphemes, 73, 75
Stimuli, ipsilateral, 42
Stopped completely (sounds), 229
Stops, 229–230, 301
  in aspirated and unaspirated sounds,
    226–227
  glottal, 224–225
  timing of articulators for, 227
Stress
  in sentences and phrases, 278–279
  in vowels or syllables, 240
  word, 276–278
Strictly Speaking (Newman), 16
Structural ambiguity, 110
Structure, 106. *See also* Syntax
  constituent, 112
  deep, 138
  hierarchical, 269
  of phrases, 173
  phrase structure rules, 120–133
  surface, 138
  of syllables, 269
  underlying, 141
Structure dependent, 139
  relationships, 145–147
Structure-dependent rules, 340–341
Structure trees, phrase, 115
Styles, 425–426
  appropriate, 318
Subcategorization, 134–135
Subconscious knowledge, 13
Subject, 110, 116
Subject-Object-Verb (SOV) word order, 326,
    374, 478–480
Subject-verb agreement, 143, 337
Subject-Verb-Object (SVO) word order, 374,
    458, 478–480
Substitutions, in aphasia, 46, 47
Suessmilch, Johann Peter, 476
Suffixes, 71, 80, 289. *See also* Endings
  -en, 80
  inflectional, 93
  -ity, 80
Suffixing, 69
Sumerians, 495, 498
Suppletive forms, 92–93
Supraglottal cavity, 225, 247
Suprasegmental features, 304
Surface structures, 138

SVO language. *See* Subject-Verb-Object
(SVO) word order
Swahili, 155, 421, 504
Swedish, 236, 400, 474
  syntax in, 128
Sweet, Henry, 220
Swift, Jonathan, 83, 118, 133, 172, 375, 449,
  463, 499
Syllabary, 498
Syllabic sounds, 240
Syllabic writing, 496, 500–502
Syllables
  nasal vowels and consonants in, 260n
  oral and nasal vowel sounds in, 261
  structure of, 269
Symbolism, sound, 8
Symbols. *See also* Phonetic symbols; Writing
  cover, 263
Symmetry, relational opposites and, 167
Synonyms, 165–166
Syntactic analysis, 366
Syntactic category, 67, 113–114
Syntactic change, 457–459
Syntactic class, 65
Syntactic labels, 114
Syntactic processing, 369–370
Syntax, 18, 105–148
  acquisition of, 336–337
  African American English and Standard
    American English compared, 414–415
  categories of, 112–114
  in Chicano English, 420
  defined, 106
  in English dialects, 406–407
  grammaticality and, 106–109
  knowledge of, 109–111
  lexicon and, 133–136
  morphology and, 93
  in other languages, 128–129
  phrase structure rules, 120–133
  phrase structure trees, 122–128
  semantics and, 181–184
  sentence relatedness and, 136–145
  sentence structure and, 111–120, 136–145
  of sign language, 147
  transformational rules and, 137–142
Synthesized speech. *See* Speech synthesis

Taboo words, 318, 428–434
  euphemisms and, 432–433
  racial and national epithets, 433–434
Tagalog, 156

Tales of King Arthur (Malory), 458–459
Talking machines. *See* Speech synthesis
Tap, 232
Target language, 18, 374
Teaching grammar, 17–18
Teaching methods, for second-language
  acquisition, 349
Technology, brain imaging and, 37–38
Telegraphic speech, 325–328
Tense (lax) vowels, 238, 267
Terrace, H. S., 353, 354
Textbooks, sexist language in, 435
Text processing, 375–376
Thai language, 147, 154, 241, 242, 266, 274,
  505
That, transformations and, 139
The, 194–195
Thematic roles, 110
  in other languages, 177–178
  of verb, 175–178
Theme, 176
Theta-criterion, 178
Third person pronouns, 200
Thomas, Dylan, 186
Thompson, Claudia R., 354
Thompson, Sandra, 79–80
Thorn (letter), 449n
Thoughts, organizing, 13
Through the Looking-Glass (Carroll), 898
Tibetan, 421
Time deixis, 200
Tip-of-the-tongue (TOT) phenomenon, 48
Tocharian, 474
Todd, Loreto, 424n
Tok Pisin, 422, 423
Tone, 240–242, 274–275
Tone languages, 241
Tongan, 430
Tongue. *See also* Articulatory phonetics;
  Consonants; Phonetics; Slips of the
  tongue; Sounds; Speech
  in vowel sounds, 235, 236, 237
Top-down processing, 367
Topicalization, 147
TOT phenomenon. *See* Tip-of-the-tongue
  (TOT) phenomenon
Trade languages, lingua franca and, 421
Tranel, D., 48n
Transcriptions, 221, 233
  narrow, 249
  phonemic, 260
  phonetic, 233
Transformationally induced ambiguity, 156

Transformational rules, 137–142
Transformations
  obligatory, 153
  optional, 153
Transition networks, 385
Transitive verb, 134
Translation, machine, 374–375
Traugott, E. C., 458
Tree diagrams, 111
  conventions on generating, 122–124
  improper syntax and, 126–128
  and phrase structures, 120–133
  phrase structure trees and, 114–118
Trills, 224, 232
Trollope, Fanny, 430
Truffaut, François, 342
Truth conditions, 179
Tsimpli, Ianthi-Maria, 43, 50n
Turkish, 72, 504
  morphemes in, 71
Turn-taking, in conversation, 196n
Twain, Mark, 5, 6, 24, 128, 186, 367, 402, 409
Twi, 86, 241, 242, 264–265, 461
Two-word stage, 324–325

UG. *See* Universal Grammar (UG)
Uighur, 421
Ukrainian, 410
Un- (prefix), 68–69, 77
Unaspirated sounds, 226–227
Unbound. *See* Free morephemes
Unconditioned sound change, 469
Underlying phonemic vowels, 293
Underlying representation. *See* Phonemic
  representation
Underlying structure, 141, 142
Underspecification, 279–280
Understanding. *See* Speech understanding
UNESCO, language extinction and, 473
Ungrammatical sentence, 14
Ungrammatical sequence, 106
Unicorn Society of Lake Superior State
    College, 17
Uninterpretable, 185
United States
  dialect development in, 402
  national language in, 411
Universal Grammar (UG), 19, 341–342, 473
University of Iowa, 48
Unmarked antonyms, 166–167
Unmarked forms, 436
Uralic, 477

Urdu, 400, 421, 476–477, 505
Uvula, 228
Uvular, 224
Uvular fricative, 231
Uvular stops, 230

Van Rooten, Luis d'Antin, 64n
Vedics, 53
Velar fricatives, 230–231
Velaric airstream mechanism, 223
Velars, 224, 234, 302
Velar stops, 230
Velum, 228
Verb (V), 67, 84, 114, 124. *See also* Auxiliary
    Verbs (Aux)
  future meaning of, 94
  intransitive, 134
  performative, 197
  position of, 128
  suffixes and, 77–78
  transitive, 134
Verbal particle, 152–153
Verb-centered meaning, 175–178
  thematic roles, 175–178
Verb object subject (VOS) word order,
    478–480
Verb Phrase (VP), 113–114, 115, 116. *See also*
    Phrase structure rules
  position of, 128
Verb subject object (VSO) word order, 478–480
Verner, Karl, 466
Verner's Law, 466
Vietnamese, 473–474, 504
Visual devices, in writing, 506
Vocabulary, similarities among languages,
    467–468
Vocal tract, 55, 222
Voice box. *See* Larynx
Voiced flap, 290
Voiced sounds, 225–227
Voiceless sounds, 225–227
Voiceless stops, 266
Voiceless vowels, 282
Voice marker, passive, 90
Voiceprints, 365
Voicing, single feature, 262–263
Voltaire, 452
Von Frisch, K., 25n
Von Goens, Ryklof Michel, 44–45
Von Kempelen, Wolfgang, 378
VOS. *See* Verb object subject (VOS) word
    order

Vowels, 234–238, 239, 280
American English, 237
devoiced (voiceless), 282
dialects and, 238
diphthongs and, 236–237
do not contrast, 259
feature specifications for American English, 273–274
formants of, 365
language change and, 454–456
long and short, 267
nasal, 264–265, 272
nasalization of, 237–238, 280
oral and nasal, 259, 260
pronunciation of, 220
reduced, 289
rounded, 236
tense, 267
tense and lax, 238
VP. *See* Verb Phrase (VP)
VSO. *See* Verb subject object (VSO) word order

Walbiri, 439–440
Walker, John, 222
Wanner, Eric, 338
Webster, Noah, 54, 66
Webster's New World Dictionary of the American Language, 434
Webster's Third New Dictionary of the English Language: Unabridged, 66
Webster's Third New International Dictionary, 8, 63, 408, 499
Weekley, Ernest, 480
Weinberg, Amy, 389
Well formed sequence, 106
Welsh, 410, 460, 474
Wengler, Eve, 83n
Wernicke, Carl, 37
Wernicke's aphasia, 37, 39, 46–47
Wernicke's area, 37, 38
West Semitic Syllabary, 498
Whitman, Walt, 397
"Wh-" sentences, 144–145
Wild Child, The (Truffaut), 342
Wild children, 342
Williamson, Juanita V., 403, 404n
Wilson, R. A., 508n
Winter, Jack, 73
Wolfram, Walt, 472
Women. *See also* Gender; Sex; Sexism
language, gender, and, 434–439

Word coinage, 82–89
abbreviations and, 88
acronyms, 86–87
back-formations and, 87–88
compounds and, 83–86
from names, 88–89
Word endings, 47n
Word-final consonants, 285–286
Word formation. *See also* Words
derivational morphology and, 76–81
lexical gaps and, 76
rules of, 75–81
Word Geography of the Eastern United States, A (Kurath), 405
Word order, 478–480. *See also* specific types of word order
Word recognition, 366
lexical access and, 367–369
Words. *See also* Acquisition of language; Morphology; Spelling; Syntax; Vocabulary; Word formation
as blends, 89
classes of, 67–68
first, 321–324
form of, 5–9
function, 47
gender and, 434–439
hierarchical structure of, 77
lexical semantics and, 158–171
loan, 459
loss of, 462
meanings of, 5–9, 158–171
monosyllabic, 256
morphology and, 18
from names, 88–89
new, 462
nonsense, 37
orthography and, 217
pairs of, 255–257, 258
and phrases, 181–182
processing of classes, 48
semantics and, 18
structure of, 69
syntactic behavior and, 135–136
taboo, 428–434
Word stress, 276–278
Word writing, 496, 499–500
Writing, 491–513
alphabetic, 498, 502–505
consonantal alphabet, 502
cuneiform, 495–496
history of, 492–498
logographic (word), 496

Writing *(Continued)*
  modern systems of, 499–505
  pictograms and ideograms, 493–495
  punctuation and, 505–506
  reading, speech, and, 505–506
  rebus principle, 497
  spelling and, 507–511
  spelling pronunciations and,
    511–512
  syllabic, 500–502
  word, 499–500

Xhosa, 216, 223

Yamada, Jeni E., 49
Yerington Paviotso, 489
Yerkes Regional Primate Research Center, 352
Yiddish, 421, 461
Yoo, Dal, 103n

Zacharias (New Testament), 44
Zero-form, 93
Zhongguo hua, 421
Zhongwen, 421
Zhuang, 421
Zulu, 216, 223, 480
Zuni, 430